The Collected Supernatural and Weird Fiction of Wilkie Collins Volume 3

The Collected Supernatural and Weird Fiction of Wilkie Collins Volume 3

Contains one novel 'Dead Secret,'
two novelettes 'Mrs Zant and the Ghost' and
'The Nun's Story of Gabriel's Marriage'
and five short stories to chill the blood

Wilkie Collins

LEONAUR

*The Collected
Supernatural and Weird
Fiction of Wilkie Collins
Volume 3
Contains one novel 'Dead Secret,'
two novelettes 'Mrs Zant and the Ghost' and
'The Nun's Story of Gabriel's Marriage'
and five short stories to chill the blood*

by Wilkie Collins

FIRST EDITION

Leonaur is an imprint
of Oakpast Ltd

Copyright in this form © 2009 Oakpast Ltd

ISBN: 978-1-84677-826-1 (hardcover)
ISBN: 978-1-84677-825-4 (softcover)

http://www.leonaur.com

Publisher's Notes

In the interests of authenticity, the spellings, grammar and place names used have been retained from the original editions.

The opinions of the authors represent a view of events in which he was a participant related from his own perspective, as such the text is relevant as an historical document.

The views expressed in this book are not necessarily those of the publisher.

Contents

The Dead Secret

Book 1

Chapter 1

The Twenty-Third of August, 1829

"Will she last out the night, I wonder?"

"Look at the clock, Mathew."

"Ten minutes past twelve! She has lasted the night out. She has lived, Robert, to see ten minutes of the new day."

These words were spoken in the kitchen of a large country-house situated on the west coast of Cornwall, The speakers were two of the men-servants composing the establishment of Captain Treverton, an officer in the navy, and the eldest male representative of an old Cornish family. Both the servants communicated with each other restrainedly, in whispers—sitting close together, and looking round expectantly toward the door whenever the talk flagged between them.

"It's an awful thing," said the elder of the men, "for us two to be alone here, at this dark time, counting out the minutes that our mistress has left to live!"

"Robert," said the other, "you have been in the service here since you were a boy—did you ever hear that our mistress was a play-actress when our master married her?"

"How came you to know that?" inquired the elder servant, sharply.

"Hush!" cried the other, rising quickly from his chair.

A bell rang in the passage outside.

"Is that for one of us?" asked Mathew.

"Can't you tell, by the sound, which is which of those bells yet?" exclaimed Robert, contemptuously. "That bell is for Sarah Leeson. Go out into the passage and look."

The younger servant took a candle and obeyed. "When he opened the kitchen-door, a long row of bells met his eye on the wall opposite. Above each of them was painted, in neat black letters, the distinguishing title of the servant whom it was specially intended to summon. The row of letters began with Housekeeper and Butler, and ended with Kitchen-maid and Footman's Boy.

Looking along the bells, Mathew easily discovered that one of them was still in motion. Above it were the words Lady's Maid. Observing this, he passed quickly along the passage, and knocked at an old-fashioned oak door at the end of it. No answer being given, he opened the door and looked into the room. It was dark and empty.

"Sarah is not in the housekeeper's room," said Mathew, returning to his fellow-servant in the kitchen.

"She is gone to her own room, then," rejoined the other. "Go up and tell her that she is wanted by her mistress."

The bell rang again as Mathew went out.

"Quick!—Quick!" cried Robert. "Tell her she is wanted directly. Wanted," he continued to himself in lower tones, "perhaps for the last time!"

Mathew ascended three flights of stairs—passed half-way down a long arched gallery—and knocked at another old-fashioned oak door. This time the signal was answered. A low, clear, sweet voice, inside the room, inquired who was waiting without. In a few hasty words Mathew told his errand. Before he had done speaking the door was quietly and quickly opened, and Sarah Leeson confronted him on the threshold, with her candle in her hand.

Not tall, not handsome, not in her first youth—shy and irres-

8

olute in manner—simple in dress to the utmost limits of plainness—the lady's-maid, in spite of all these disadvantages, was a woman whom it was impossible to look at without a feeling of curiosity, if not of interest. Few men, at first sight of her, could have resisted the desire to find out who she was; few would have been satisfied with receiving for answer.

She is Mrs. Treverton's maid; few would have refrained from the attempt to extract some secret information for themselves from her face and manner; and none, not even the most patient and practiced of observers, could have succeeded in discovering more than that she must have passed through the ordeal of some great suffering at some former period of her life. Much in her manner, and more in her face, said plainly and sadly: I am the wreck of something that you might once have liked to see; a wreck that can never be repaired—that must drift on through life unnoticed, unguided, unpitied—drift till the fatal shore is touched, and the waves of time have swallowed up these broken relics of me forever. This was the story that was told in Sarah Leeson's face—this, and no more.

No two men interpreting that story for themselves, would probably have agreed on the nature of the suffering which this woman had undergone. It was hard to say, at the outset, whether the past pain that had set its ineffaceable mark on her had been pain of the body or pain of the mind. But whatever the nature of the affliction she had suffered, the traces it had left were deeply and strikingly visible in every part of her face.

Her cheeks had lost their roundness and their natural colour; her lips, singularly flexible in movement and delicate in form, had faded to an unhealthy paleness; her eyes, large and black and overshadowed by unusually thick lashes, had contracted an anxious startled look, which never left them, and which piteously expressed the painful acuteness of her sensibility, the inherent timidity of her disposition. So far, the marks which sorrow or sickness had set on her were the marks common to most victims of mental or physical suffering. The one extraordinary personal deterioration which she had undergone consisted in the unnatural change that had passed over the colour of her hair. It was as thick and soft, it grew as gracefully, as the hair of a young girl; but it was as gray as the hair of an old woman.

It seemed to contradict, in the most startling manner, every personal assertion of youth that still existed in her face. With all its haggardness and paleness, no one could have looked at it and supposed for a moment that it was the face of an elderly woman. Wan as they might be, there was not a wrinkle in her cheeks. Her eyes, viewed apart from their prevailing expression of un-easiness and timidity, still preserved that bright, clear moisture which is never seen in the eyes of the old. The skin about her temples was as delicately smooth as the skin of a child.

These and other physical signs which never mislead, showed that she was still, as to years, in the very prime of her life. Sickly and sorrow-stricken as she was, she looked, from the eyes down-ward, a woman who had barely reached thirty years of age. From the eyes upward, the effect of her abundant gray hair, seen in connection with her face, was not simply incongruous—it was absolutely startling; so startling as to make it no paradox to say that she would have looked most natural, most like herself, if her hair had been dyed. In her case, Art would have seemed to be the truth, because Nature looked like falsehood.

What shock had stricken her hair, in the very maturity of its luxuriance, with the hue of an unnatural old age? Was it a serious illness, or a dreadful grief, that had turned her gray in the prime of her womanhood? That question had often been agitated among her fellow-servants, who were all struck by the peculiarities of her personal appearance, and rendered a little suspicious of her, as well, by an inveterate habit that she had of talking to herself.

Inquire as they might, however, their curiosity was always baffled. Nothing more could be discovered than that Sarah Lee-son was, in the common phrase, touchy on the subject of her gray hair and her habit of talking to herself, and that Sarah Lee-son's mistress had long since forbidden everyone, from her hus-band downward, to ruffle her maid's tranquillity by inquisitive questions.

She stood for an instant speechless, on that momentous morning of the twenty-third of August, before the servant who summoned her to her mistress's deathbed—the light of the candle flaring brightly over her large, startled, black eyes, and the luxuriant, unnatural gray hair above them. She stood a moment silent—her hand trembling while she held the candlestick, so that the extinguisher lying loose in it rattled incessantly—then thanked the servant for calling her.

The trouble and fear in her voice, as she spoke, seemed to add to its sweetness; the agitation of her manner took nothing away from its habitual gentleness, its delicate, winning, feminine restraint. Mathew, who, like the other servants, secretly distrusted and disliked her for differing from the ordinary pattern of professed lady's-maids, was, on this particular occasion, so subdued by her manner and her tone as she thanked him, that he offered to carry her candle for her to the door of her mistress's bed-chamber. She shook her head, and thanked him again, then passed before him quickly on her way out of the gallery.

The room in which Mrs. Treverton lay dying was on the floor beneath. Sarah hesitated twice before she knocked at the door. It was opened by Captain Treverton.

The instant she saw her master she started back from him. If she had dreaded a blow she could hardly have drawn away more suddenly, or with an expression of greater alarm. There was nothing in Captain Treverton's face to warrant the suspicion of ill-treatment, or even of harsh words. His countenance was kind, hearty, and open; and the tears were still trickling down it which he had shed by his wife's bedside.

"Go in," he said, turning away his face. "She does not wish the nurse to attend; she only wishes for you. Call me if the doctor—" His voice faltered, and he hurried away without attempting to finish the sentence.

Sarah Leeson, instead of entering her mistress's room, stood looking after her master attentively, with her pale cheeks turned to a deathly whiteness—with an eager, doubting, questioning terror in her eyes. When he had disappeared round the corner of the gallery, she listened for a moment outside the door of the sick-room—whispered affrightedly to herself, "Can she have told him?"—then opened the door, with a visible effort to recover her self-control; and, after lingering suspiciously on the threshold for a moment, went in.

Mrs. Treverton's bed-chamber was a large, lofty room, situated in the western front of the house, and consequently overlooking the sea-view. The night-light burning by the bedside displayed rather than dispelled the darkness in the corners of the room. The bed was of the old-fashioned pattern, with heavy hangings and thick curtains drawn all round it. Of the other objects in the chamber, only those of the largest and most solid kind were prominent enough to be tolerably visible in the dim light. The cabinets, the wardrobe, the full-length looking-glass, the high-backed arm-chair, these, with the great shapeless bulk of the bed itself, towered up heavily and gloomily into view.

Other objects were all merged together in the general obscurity. Through the open window, opened to admit the fresh air of the new morning after the sultriness of the August night, there poured monotonously into the room the dull, still, distant roaring of the surf on the sandy coast. All outer noises were hushed at that first dark hour of the new day. Inside the room the one audible sound was the slow, toilsome breathing of the dying woman, raising itself in its mortal frailness, awfully and distinctly, even through the far thunder-breathing from the bosom of the everlasting sea.

"Mistress," said Sarah Leeson, standing close to the curtains, but not withdrawing them, "my master has left the room, and has sent me here in his place."

"Light!—give me more light."

The feebleness of mortal sickness was in the voice; but the accent of the speaker sounded resolute even yet doubly resolute by contrast with the hesitation of the tones in which Sarah had spoken. The strong nature of the mistress and the weak nature of the maid came out, even in that short interchange of words spoken through the curtain of a deathbed.

Sarah lit two candles with a wavering hand—placed them hesitatingly on a table by the bedside—waited for a moment, looking all round her with suspicious timidity—then undrew the curtains.

The disease of which Mrs. Treverton was dying was one of the most terrible of all the maladies that afflict humanity, one to which women are especially subject, and one which under-mines life without, in most cases, showing any remarkable traces of its corroding progress in the face. No uninstructed person, looking at Mrs. Treverton when her attendant undrew the bed-curtain, could possibly have imagined that she was past all help that mortal skill could offer to her.

The slight marks of illness in her face, the inevitable changes in the grace and roundness of its outline, were rendered hardly noticeable by the marvellous preservation of her complexion in all the light and delicacy of its first girlish beauty. There lay her face on the pillow—tenderly framed in by the rich lace of her cap, softly crowned by her shining brown hair—to all outward appearance, the face of a beautiful woman recovering from a slight illness, or reposing after unusual fatigue. Even Sarah Lee-son, who had watched her all through her malady, could hardly believe, as she looked at her mistress, that the Gates of Life had closed behind her, and that the beckoning hand of Death was signing to her already from the Gates of the Grave.

Some dog's-eared books in paper covers lay on the coun-terpane of the bed. As soon as the curtain was drawn aside Mrs. Treverton ordered her attendant by a gesture to remove them. They were plays, underscored in certain places by ink lines, and marked with marginal annotations referring to entrances, exits, and places on the stage. The servants, talking downstairs of their mistress's occupation before her marriage, had not been misled by false reports.

Their master, after he had passed the prime of life, had, in very truth, taken his wife from the obscure stage of a country theatre, when little more than two years had elapsed since her first appearance in public. The dog's-eared old plays had been once her treasured dramatic library; she had always retained a fondness for them from old associations; and, during the latter part of her illness, they had remained on her bed for days and days together.

Having put away the plays, Sarah went back to her mistress; and, with more of dread and bewilderment in her face than grief, opened her lips to speak. Mrs. Treverton held up her hand, as a sign that she had another order to give.

"Bolt the door," she said, in the same enfeebled voice, but with the same accent of resolution which had so strikingly marked her first request to have more light in the room. "Bolt the door. Let no one in, till I give you leave."

"No one?" repeated Sarah, faintly. "Not the doctor? Not even my master?"

"Not the doctor—not even your master," said Mrs. Treverton, and pointed to the door. The hand was weak; but even in that momentary action of it there was no mistaking the gesture of command.

Sarah bolted the door, returned irresolutely to the bedside, fixed her large, eager, startled eyes inquiringly on her mistress's face, and, suddenly bending over her, said in a whisper:

"Have you told my master?"

"No," was the answer. "I sent for him, to tell him—I tried hard to speak the words it—shook me to my very soul, only to think how I should best break it to him I am so fond of him! I love him so dearly! But I should have spoken in spite of that, if he had not talked of the child. Sarah! He did nothing but talk of the child—and that silenced me."

Sarah, with a forgetfulness of her station which might have appeared extraordinary even in the eyes of the most lenient of mistresses, flung herself back in a chair when the first word of Mrs. Treverton's reply was uttered, clasped her trembling hands over her face, and groaned to herself, "Oh, what will happen! What will happen now!"

Mrs. Treverton's eyes had softened and moistened when she

spoke of her love for her husband. She lay silent for a few minutes; the working of some strong emotion in her being expressed by her quick, hard, laboured breathing, and by the painful contraction of her eyebrows. Ere long, she turned her head uneasily toward the chair in which her attendant was sitting, and spoke again—this time in a voice which had sunk to a whisper.

"Look for my medicine," said she; "I want it."

Sarah started up, and with the quick instinct of obedience brushed away the tears that were rolling fast over her cheeks.

"The doctor," she said. "Let me call the doctor."

"No! The medicine—look for the medicine."

"Which bottle? The opiate—"

"No. Not the opiate. The other."

Sarah took a bottle from the table, and looking attentively at the written direction on the label, said that it was not yet time to take that medicine again.

"Give me the bottle."

"Oh, pray don't ask me. Pray wait. The doctor said it was as bad as dram-drinking, if you took too much."

Mrs. Treverton's clear gray eyes began to flash; the rosy flush deepened on her cheeks; the commanding hand was raised again, by an effort, from the counterpane on which it lay.

"Take the cork out of the bottle," she said, "and give it to me. I want strength. No matter whether I die in an hour's time or a week's. Give me the bottle."

"No, no—not the bottle!" said Sarah, giving it up, nevertheless, under the influence of her mistress's look. "There are two doses left. Wait, pray wait till I get a glass."

She turned again toward the table. At the same instant Mrs. Treverton raised the bottle to her lips, drained it of its contents, and flung it from her on the bed.

"She has killed herself!" cried Sarah, running in terror to the door.

"Stop!" said the voice from the bed, more resolute than ever, already. "Stop! Comeback and prop me up higher on the pillows."

Sarah put her hand on the bolt.

"Come back!" reiterated Mrs. Treverton. "While there is life in me, I will be obeyed. Come back!" The colour began to deepen perceptibly all over her face, and the light to grow brighter in her widely opened eyes.

Sarah came back; and with shaking hands added one more to the many pillows which supported the dying woman's head and shoulders. While this was being done the bedclothes became a little discomposed. Mrs. Treverton shuddered, and drew them up to their former position, close round her neck.

"Did you unbolt the door?" she asked.

"No."

"I forbid you to go near it again. Get my writing-case, and the pen and ink, from the cabinet near the window."

Sarah went to the cabinet and opened it; then stopped, as if some sudden suspicion had crossed her mind, and asked what the writing materials were wanted for.

"Bring them, and you will see."

The writing-case, with a sheet of notepaper on it, was placed upon Mrs. Treverton's knees; the pen was dipped into the ink, and given to her; she paused, closed her eyes for a minute, and sighed heavily; then began to write, saying to her waiting-maid, as the pen touched the paper—"Look."

Sarah peered anxiously over her shoulder, and saw the pen slowly and feebly form these three words: To my Husband.

"Oh, no! No! For God's sake, don't write it!" she cried, catching at her mistress's hand but suddenly letting it go again the moment Mrs. Treverton looked at her.

The pen went on; and more slowly, more feebly, formed words enough to fill a line—then stopped. The letters of the last syllable were all blotted together.

"Don't!" reiterated Sarah, dropping on her knees at the bedside. "Don't write it to him if you can't tell it to him. Let me go on bearing what I have borne so long already. Let the Secret die with you and die with me, and be never known in this world- never, never, never!"

The Secret must be told," answered Mrs Treverton. "My husband ought to know it, and must know it. I tried to tell him, and my courage failed me. I cannot trust you to tell him, after I am gone. It must be written. Take you the pen; my sight is failing, my touch is dull. Take the pen, and write what I tell you."

Sarah, instead of obeying, hid her face in the bedcover, and wept bitterly.

"You have been with me ever since my marriage," Mrs. Treverton went on. "You have been my friend more than my servant. Do you refuse my last request? You do! Fool! Look up and listen to me. On your peril, refuse to take the pen. Write, or I shall not rest in my grave. Write, or, as true as there is a heaven above us, I will come to you from the other world!"

Sarah started to her feet with a faint scream.

"You make my flesh creep!" she whispered, fixing her eyes on her mistress's face with a stare of superstitious horror.

At the same instant, the overdose of the stimulating medicine began to affect Mrs. Treverton's brain. She rolled her head restlessly from side to side of the pillow—repeated vacantly a few lines from one of the old play-books which had been removed from her bed—and suddenly held out the pen to the servant, with a theatrical wave of the hand, and a glance upward at an imaginary gallery of spectators.

"Write!" she cried, with an awful mimicry of her old stage voice. "Write!" And the weak hand was waved again with a forlorn, feeble imitation of the old stage gesture.

Closing her fingers mechanically on the pen that was thrust between them, Sarah, with her eyes still expressing the superstitious terror which her mistress's words had aroused, waited for the next command. Some minutes elapsed before Mrs. Treverton spoke again. She still retained her senses sufficiently to be vaguely conscious of the effect which the medicine was producing on her, and to be desirous of combating its further progress before it succeeded in utterly confusing her ideas. She asked first for the smelling-bottle, next for some Eau de Cologne.

This last, poured on to her handkerchief and applied to her

forehead, seemed to prove successful in partially clearing her faculties. Her eyes recovered their steady look of intelligence; and, when she again addressed her maid, reiterating the word "Write," she was able to enforce the direction by beginning immediately to dictate in quiet, deliberate, determined tones. Sarah's tears fell fast; her lips murmured fragments of sentences in which entreaties, expressions of penitence and exclamations of fear were all strangely mingled together; but she wrote on submissively, in wavering lines, until she had nearly filled the first two sides of the notepaper.

Then Mrs. Treverton paused, looked the writing over, and, taking the pen, signed her name at the end of it. With this effort, her powers of resistance to the exciting effect of the medicine seemed to fail her again. The deep flush began to tinge her cheeks once more, and she spoke hurriedly and unsteadily when she handed the pen back to her maid.

"Sign!" she cried, beating her hand feebly on the bed-clothes. "Sign 'Sarah Leeson, witness.' No!—write 'Accomplice.' Take your share of it; I won't have it shifted on me. Sign, I insist on it! Sign as I tell you."

Sarah obeyed; and Mrs. Treverton, taking the paper from her, pointed to it solemnly, with a return of the stage gesture which had escaped her a little while back.

"You will give this to your master," she said, "when I am dead; and you will answer any questions he puts to you as truly as if you were before the judgment-seat."

Clasping her hands fast together, Sarah regarded her mistress, for the first time, with steady eyes, and spoke to her for the first time in steady tones.

"If I only knew that I was fit to die," she said, "oh, how gladly I would change places with you!"

"Promise me that you will give the paper to your master," repeated Mrs. Treverton. "Promise—no! I won't trust your promise—I'll have your oath. Get the Bible—the Bible the clergyman used when he was here this morning. Get it, or I shall not rest in my grave. Get it, or I will come to you from the other world."

The mistress laughed as she reiterated that threat. The maid shuddered, as she obeyed the command which it was designed to impress on her.

"Yes, yes—the Bible the clergyman used," continued Mrs. Treverton, vacantly, after the book had been produced. "The clergyman—a poor weak man—I frightened him, Sarah. He said: 'Are you at peace with all the world?' and I said: 'All but one.' You know who."

"The Captain's brother? Oh, don't die at enmity with anybody. Don't die at enmity even with him," pleaded Sarah.

"The clergyman said so too," murmured Mr. Treverton, her eyes beginning to wander childishly round the room, her tones growing suddenly lower and more confused. "'You must forgive him,' the clergyman said. And I said: 'No, I forgive all the world, but not my husband's brother.' The clergyman got up from the bedside, frightened, Sarah. He talked about praying for me and coming back. Will he come back?"

"Yes, yes," answered Sarah. "He is a good man—he will come back—and oh, tell him that you forgive the Captain's brother! Those vile words he spoke of you when you were married will come home to him some day. Forgive him—forgive him before you die!"

Saying those words, she attempted to remove the Bible softly out of her mistress's sight. The action attracted Mrs. Treverton's attention, and roused her sinking faculties into observation of present things.

"Stop!" she cried, with a gleam of the old resolution flashing once more over the dying dimness of her eyes. She caught at Sarah's hand with a great effort, placed it on the Bible, and held it there. Her other hand wandered a little over the bedclothes, until it encountered the written paper addressed to her husband. Her fingers closed on it, and a sigh of relief escaped her lips.

"Ah!" she said, "I know what I wanted the Bible for. I'm dying with all my senses about me, Sarah; you can't deceive me even yet."

She stopped again, smiled a little, whispered to herself rapidly, "Wait, wait, wait!" then added aloud, with the old stage voice and the old stage gesture: "No! I won't trust you on your promise. I'll have your oath. Kneel down. These are my last words in this world—disobey them if you dare!"

Sarah dropped on her knees by the bed. The breeze outside, strengthening just then with the slow advance of the morning, parted the window-curtains a little, and wafted a breath of its sweet fragrance joyously into the sick-room. The heavy beating hum of the distant surf came in at the same time, and poured out its unresting music in louder strains. Then the window-curtains fell again heavily, the wavering flame of the candle grew steady once more, and the awful silence in the room sank deeper than ever.

"Swear!" said Mrs. Treverton. Her voice failed her when she had pronounced that one word. She struggled a little, recovered the power of utterance, and went on: "Swear that you will not destroy this paper after I am dead."

Even while she pronounced these solemn words, even at that last struggle for life and strength, the ineradicable theatrical instinct showed, with a fearful inappropriateness, how firmly it kept its place in her mind. Sarah felt the cold hand that was still laid on hers lifted for a moment—saw it waving gracefully toward her—felt it descend again, and clasp her own hand with a trembling, impatient pressure. At that final appeal, she answered, faintly:

"I swear it."

"Swear that you will not take this paper away with you, if you leave the house, after I am dead."

Again Sarah paused before she answered—again the trembling pressure made itself felt on her hand, but more weakly this time—and again the words dropped affrightedly from her lips:

"I swear it."

"Swear!" Mrs. Treverton began for the third time. Her voice failed her once more; and she struggled vainly to regain the command over it.

Sarah looked up, and saw signs of convulsion beginning to disfigure the white face—saw the fingers of the white, delicate hand getting crooked as they reached over toward the table on which the medicine-bottles were placed.

"You drank it all," she cried, starting to her feet, as she comprehended the meaning of that gesture. "Mistress, dear mistress, you drank it all—there is nothing but the opiate left. Let me go—let me go and call—"

A look from Mrs. Treverton stopped her before she could utter another word. The lips of the dying woman were moving rapidly. Sarah put her ear close to them. At first she heard nothing but panting, quick-drawn breaths—then a few broken words mingled confusedly with them:

"I haven't done—you must swear—close, close, come close—a third thing your master swear to give it—"

The last words died away very softly. The lips that had been forming them so laboriously parted on a sudden and closed again no more. Sarah sprang to the door, opened it, and called into the passage for help; then ran back to the bedside, caught up the sheet of notepaper on which she had written from her mistress's dictation, and hid it in her bosom.

The last look of Mrs. Treverton's eyes fastened sternly and reproachfully on her as she did this, and kept their expression unchanged, through the momentary distortion of the rest of the features, for one breathless moment. That moment passed, and, with the next, the shadow which goes before the presence of death stole up and shut out the light of life in one quiet instant from all the face.

The doctor, followed by the nurse and by one of the servants, entered the room; and, hurrying to the bedside, saw at a glance that the time for his attendance there had passed away forever. He spoke first to the servant who had followed him.

"Go to your master," he said, "and beg him to wait in his own room until I can come and speak to him."

Sarah still stood—without moving or speaking, or noticing anyone—by the bedside.

The nurse, approaching to draw the curtains together, started at the sight of her face, and turned to the doctor.

"I think this person had better leave the room, sir?" said the nurse, with some appearance of contempt in her tones and looks. "She seems unreasonably shocked and terrified by what has happened."

"Quite right," said the doctor. "It is best that she should withdraw.—Let me recommend you to leave us for a little while," he added, touching Sarah on the arm.

She shrank back suspiciously, raised one of her hands to the place where the letter lay hidden in her bosom, and pressed it there firmly while she held out the other hand for a candle.

"You had better rest for a little in your own room," said the doctor, giving her a candle. "Stop, though," he continued, after a moment's reflection. "I am going to break the sad news to your master, and I may find that he is anxious to hear any last words that Mrs. Treverton may have spoken in your presence. Perhaps you had better come with me, and wait while I go into Captain Treverton's room."

"No! No!—oh, not now—not now, for God's sake!" Speaking those words in low, quick, pleading tones, and drawing back affrightedly to the door, Sarah disappeared without waiting a moment to be spoken to again.

"A strange woman!" said the doctor, addressing the nurse. "Follow her, and see where she goes to, in case she is wanted and we are obliged to send for her. I will wait here until you come back."

When the nurse returned she had nothing to report but that she had followed Sarah Leeson to her own bedroom, had seen her enter it, had listened outside, and had heard her lock the door.

"A strange woman!" repeated the doctor. "One of the silent, secret sort."

"One of the wrong sort," said the nurse. "She is always talking to herself, and that is a bad sign, in my opinion. I distrusted her, sir, the very first day I entered the house."

CHAPTER 2
THE CHILD

The instant Sarah Leeson had turned the key of her bedroom door, she took the sheet of notepaper from its place of conceal-ment in her bosom—shuddering, when she drew it out, as if the mere contact of it hurt her—placed it open on her little dressing-table, and fixed her eyes eagerly on the lines which the note contained. At first they swam and mingled together before her. She pressed her hands over her eyes, for a few minutes, and then looked at the writing again.

The characters were clear now—vividly clear, and, as she fan-cied, unnaturally large and near to view. There was 'the address: "To my Husband"; there the first blotted line beneath, in her dead mistress's handwriting; there the lines that followed, traced by her own pen, with the signature at the end—Mrs. Treverton's first, and then her own. The whole amounted to but very few sentences, written on one perishable fragment of paper, which the flame of a candle would have consumed in a moment. Yet there she sat, reading, reading, reading, over and over again; never touching the note, except when it was absolutely necessary to turn over the first page; never moving, never speaking, never raising her eyes from the paper. As a condemned prisoner might read his death-warrant, so did Sarah Leeson now read the few lines which she and her mistress had written together not half an hour since.

The secret of the paralyzing effect of that writing on her mind lay, not only in itself, but in the circumstances which had attended the act of its production.

The oath which had been proposed by Mrs. Treverton under no more serious influence than the last caprice of her disordered faculties, stimulated by confused remembrances of stage words and stage situations, had been accepted by Sarah Leeson as the most sacred and inviolable engagement to which she could bind herself. The threat of enforcing obedience to her last commands from beyond the grave, which the mistress had uttered in mock-ing experiment on the superstitious fears of the maid, now hung darkly over the weak mind of Sarah, as a judgment which might descend on her, visibly and inexorably, at any moment of her future life. When she roused herself at last, and pushed away the paper and rose to her feet, she stood quite still for an instant, before she ventured to look behind her. When she did look, it was with an effort and a start, with a searching distrust of the empty dimness in the remoter corners of the room.

Her old habit of talking to herself began to resume its influence, as she now walked rapidly backward and forward, sometimes along the room and sometimes across it. She repeated incessantly such broken phrases as these:

"How can I give him the letter?—Such a good master; so kind to us all.—Why did she die, and leave it all to me?—I can't bear it alone; it's too much for me."

While reiterating these sentences, she vacantly occupied herself in putting things about the room in order, which were set in perfect order already. All her looks, all her actions, betrayed the vain struggle of a weak mind to sustain itself under the weight of a heavy responsibility. She arranged and re-arranged the cheap china ornaments on her chimney-piece a dozen times over—put her pincushion first on the looking-glass, then on the table in front of it—changed the position of the little porcelain dish and tray on her wash-hand-stand, now to one side of the basin and now to the other.

Throughout all these trifling actions the natural grace, delicacy, and prim neat-handedness of the woman still waited mechanically on the most useless and aimless of her occupations of the moment. She knocked nothing down, she put nothing awry; her footsteps at the fastest made no sound—the very skirts of her dress were kept as properly and prudishly composed as if it was broad daylight and the eyes of all her neighbours were looking at her.

From time to time the sense of the words she was murmuring confusedly to herself changed. Sometimes they disjointedly expressed bolder and more self-reliant thoughts. Once they seemed to urge her again to the dressing-table and the open letter on it, against her own will. She read aloud the address, "To my Husband," and caught the letter up sharply, and spoke in firmer tones. "Why give it to him at all? Why not let the secret die with her and die with me, as it ought? Why should he know it? He shall not know it!"

Saying those last words, she desperately held the letter within an inch of the flame of the candle. At the same moment the white curtain over the window before her stirred a little, as the freshening air found its way through the old-fashioned, ill-fitting sashes. Her eye caught sight of it, as it waved gently backward and forward. She clasped the letter suddenly to her breast with both hands, and shrank back against the wall of the room, her eyes still fastened on the curtain with the same blank look of horror which they had exhibited when Mrs. Treverton had threatened to claim her servant's obedience from the other world.

"Something moves," she gasped to herself, in a breathless whisper. "Something moves in the room."

The curtain waved slowly to and fro for the second time. Still fixedly looking at it over her shoulder, she crept along the wall to the door.

"Do you come to me already?" she said, her eyes riveted on the curtain while her hand groped over the lock for the key. "Before your grave is dug? Before your coffin is made? Before your body is cold?"

She opened the door and glided into the passage; stopped there for a moment, and looked back into the room.

"Rest!" she said. "Rest, mistress—he shall have the letter."

The staircase-lamp guided her out of the passage. Descending hurriedly, as if she feared to give herself time to think, she reached Captain Treverton's study, on the ground-floor, in a minute or two. The door was wide open and the room was empty.

After reflecting a little, she lighted one of the chamber-candles standing on the hall-table, at the lamp in the study, and ascended the stairs again to her master's bedroom. After repeatedly knocking at the door and obtaining no answer, she ventured to go in. The bed had not been disturbed, the candles had not been lit—to all appearance the room had not even been entered during the night.

There was but one other place to seek him—the chamber in which his wife lay dead. Could she summon the courage to give him the letter there? She hesitated a little—then whispered: "I must! I must!"

The direction she now compelled herself to take led her a little way down the stairs again, descended very slowly this time, holding cautiously by the banisters, and pausing to take breath almost at every step. The door of what had been Mrs. Treverton's bedroom, was opened, when she ventured to knock at it, by the nurse, who inquired, roughly and suspiciously, what she wanted there.

"I want to speak to my master."

"Look for him somewhere else. He was here half an hour ago. He is gone now."

"Do you know where he has gone?"

"No. I don't pry into other people's goings and comings. I mind my own business."

With that discourteous answer the nurse closed the door again. Just as Sarah turned away from it she looked toward the inner end of the passage. The door of the nursery was situated there. It was ajar, and a dim gleam of candle-light was flickering through it.

She went in immediately, and saw that the candle-light came from, the inner room, usually occupied, as she well knew, by the nursery-maid and by the only child of the house of Treverton—a little girl named Rosamond, aged, at that time, nearly five years.

"Can he be there?—in that room, of all the rooms in the house!"

Quickly as the thought arose in her mind, Sarah raised the letter (which she had hitherto carried in her hand) to the bosom of her dress, and hid it for the second time, exactly as she had hidden it on leaving her mistress's bedside.

She then stole across the nursery on tiptoe toward the inner room. The entrance to it, to please some caprice of the child's, had been arched, and framed with trelliswork, gaily coloured, so as to resemble the entrance to a summer-house. Two pretty chintz curtains, hanging inside the trelliswork, formed the only barrier between the day-room and the bedroom. One of these was looped up, and toward the opening thus made Sarah now advanced, after cautiously leaving her candle in the passage outside.

The first object that attracted her attention in the child's bedroom was the figure of the nurse- maid, leaning back, fast asleep, in an easy-chair by the window. Venturing, after this discovery, to look more boldly into the room, she next saw her master sitting with his back toward her, by the side of the child's crib. Little Rosamond was awake, and was standing up in bed with her arms round her father's neck. One of her hands held over his shoulder the doll that she had taken to bed with her, the other was twined gently in his hair. The child had been crying bitterly, and had now exhausted herself, so that she was only moaning a little from time to time, with her head laid wearily on her father's bosom.

The tears stood thick in Sarah's eyes as they looked on her master and on the little hands that lay round his neck. She lingered by the raised curtain, heedless of the risk she ran, from moment to moment, of being discovered and questioned lingered—until she heard Captain Treverton say soothingly to the child:

"Hush, Rosie, dear! Hush, my own love! Don't cry any more for poor mamma. Think of poor papa, and try to comfort him."

Simple as the words were, quietly and tenderly as they were spoken, they seemed instantly to deprive Sarah Leeson of all power of self-control. Reckless whether she was heard or not, she turned and ran into the passage as if she had been flying for her life. Passing the candle she had left there, without so much as a look at it, she made for the stairs, and descended them with headlong rapidity to the kitchen-floor. There one of the servants who had been sitting up met her, and, with a face of astonishment and alarm, asked what was the matter.

"I'm ill—I'm faint—I want air," she answered, speaking thickly and confusedly. "Open the garden door and let me out."

The man obeyed, but doubtfully, as if he thought her unfit to be trusted by herself.

"She gets stranger than ever in her ways," he said, when he rejoined his fellow-servant, after Sarah had hurried past him into the open air. "Now our mistress is dead, she will have to find another place, I suppose. I, for one, shan't break my heart when she's gone. Shall you?"

CHAPTER 3
THE HIDING OF THE SECRET

The cool, sweet air in the garden, blowing freshly over Sarah's face, seemed to calm the violence of her agitation. She turned down a side walk, which led to a terrace and overlooked the church of the neighbouring village.

The daylight out of doors was clear already. The misty auburn light that goes before sunrise was flowing up, peaceful and lovely, behind a line of black-brown moorland, overall the eastern sky. The old church, with the hedge of myrtle and fuchsia growing round the little cemetery in all the luxuriance which is only seen in Cornwall, was clearing and brightening to view, almost as fast as the morning firmament itself.

Sarah leaned her arms heavily on the back of a garden-seat, and turned her face toward the church. Her eyes wandered from the building itself to the cemetery by its side, rested there, and watched the light growing warmer and warmer over the lonesome refuge where the dead lay at rest.

"Oh, my heart! My heart!" she said. "What must it be made of not to break?"

She remained for some time leaning on the seat, looking sadly toward the churchyard, and pondering over the words which she had heard Captain Treverton say to the child. They seemed to connect themselves, as everything else now appeared to connect itself in her mind, with the letter that had been written on Mrs. Treverton's deathbed. She drew it from her bosom once more, and crushed it up angrily in her fingers.

"Still in my hands! Still not seen by any eyes but mine!" she said, looking down at the crumpled pages. "Is it all my fault? If she was alive now—if she had seen what I saw, if she had heard what I heard in the nursery—could she expect me to give him the letter?"

Her mind was apparently steadied by the reflection which her last words expressed. She moved away thoughtfully from the garden-seat, crossed the terrace, descended some wooden steps, and followed a shrubbery path which led round by a winding track from the east to the north side of the house.

This part of the building had been uninhabited and neglected for more than half a century past. In the time of Captain Treverton's father the whole range of the north rooms had been stripped of their finest pictures and their most valuable furniture, to assist in redecorating the west rooms, which now formed the only inhabited part of the house, and which were amply sufficient for the accommodation of the family and of any visitors who came to stay with them. The mansion had been originally built in the form of a square, and had been strongly fortified.

Of the many defences of the place, but one now remained—a heavy, low tower (from which and from the village near, the house derived its name of Porthgenna Tower), standing at the southern extremity of the west front. The south side itself consisted of stables and outhouses, with a ruinous wall in front of them, which, running back eastward at right angles, joined the north side, and so completed, the square which the whole outline of the building represented.

The outside view of the range of north rooms, from the weedy, deserted garden below, showed plainly enough that many years had passed since any human creature had inhabited them. The window-panes were broken in some places, and covered thickly with dirt and dust in others. Here, the shutters were closed—there, they were only half opened. The untrained ivy, the rank vegetation growing in fissures of the stone-work, the festoons of spiders' webs, the rubbish of wood, bricks, plaster, broken glass, rags, and strips of soiled cloth, which lay beneath the windows, all told the same tale of neglect.

Shadowed by its position, this ruinous side of the house had a dark, cold, wintry aspect, even on the sunny August morning when Sarah Leeson strayed into the deserted northern garden. Lost in the labyrinth of her own thoughts, she moved slowly past flower-beds, long since rooted up, and along gravel walks overgrown by weeds; her eyes wandering mechanically over the prospect, her feet mechanically carrying her on wherever there was a trace of a footpath, lead where it might.

The shock which the words spoken by her master in the nursery had communicated to her mind, had set her whole nature, so to speak, at bay, and had roused in her, at last, the moral courage to arm herself with a final and desperate resolution. Wandering more and more slowly along the pathways of the forsaken garden, as the course of her ideas withdrew her more and more completely from all outward things, she stopped insensibly on an open patch of ground, which had once been a well-kept lawn, and which still commanded a full view of the long range of uninhabited north rooms.

"What binds me to give the letter to my master at all?" she thought to herself, smoothing out the crumpled paper dreamily in the palm of her hand. "My mistress died without making me swear to do that. Can she visit it on me from the other world, if I keep the promises I swore to observe, and do no more? May I not risk the worst that can happen, so long as I hold religiously to all that I undertook to do on my oath?"

She paused here in reasoning with herself—her superstitious fears still influencing her out of doors, in the daylight, as they had influenced her in her own room, in the time of darkness. She paused—then fell to smoothing the letter again, and began to recall the terms of the solemn engagement which Mrs. Treverton had forced her to contract.

What had she actually bound herself to do? Not to destroy

the letter, and not to take it away with her if she left the house. Beyond that, Mrs. Treverton's desire had been that the letter should be given to her husband. Was that last wish binding on the person to whom it had been confided? Yes. As binding as an oath? No.

As she arrived at that conclusion, she looked up.

At first her eyes rested vacantly on the lonely, deserted north front of the house; gradually they became attracted by one particular window exactly in the middle, on the floor above the ground—the largest and the gloomiest of all the row; suddenly they brightened with an expression of intelligence. She started; a faint flush of colour flew into her cheeks, and she hastily advanced closer to the wall of the house.

The panes of the large window were yellow with dust and dirt, and festooned about fantastically with cobwebs. Below it was a heap of rubbish, scattered over the dry mould of what might once have been a bed of flowers or shrubs. The form of the bed was still marked out by an oblong boundary of weeds and rank grass. She followed it irresolutely all round, looking up at the window at every step then stopped close under it, glanced at the letter in her hand, and said to herself abruptly—

"I'll risk it!"

As the words fell from her lips, she hastened back to the inhabited part of the house, followed the passage on the kitchen-floor which led to the housekeeper's room, entered it, and took down from a nail in the wall a bunch of keys, having a large ivory label attached to the ring that connected them, on which was inscribed, *Keys of the North Rooms*.

She placed the keys on a writing-table near her, took up a pen, and rapidly added these lines on the blank side of the letter which she had written under her mistress's dictation—

If this paper should ever be found (which I pray with my whole heart it never may be), I wish to say that I have come to the resolution of hiding it, because I dare not show the writing that it contains to my master, to whom it is addressed. In doing what I now propose to do, though I am

31

acting against my mistress's last wishes, I am not breaking the solemn engagement which she obliged me to make before her on her death-bed. That engagement forbids me to destroy this letter, or to take it away with me if I leave the house. I shall do neither my purpose is to conceal it in the place, of all others, where I think there is least chance of its ever being found again. Any hardship or misfortune which may follow as a consequence of this deceitful proceeding on my part, will fall on myself. Others, I believe in my conscience, will be the happier for the hiding of the dreadful Secret which this letter contains.

She signed those lines with her name—pressed them hurriedly over the blotting-pad that lay with the rest of the writing materials on the table—took the note in her hand, after first folding it up—and then, snatching at the bunch of keys, with a look all round her as if she dreaded being secretly observed, left the room. All her actions since she had entered it had been hasty and sudden; she was evidently afraid of allowing herself one leisure moment to reflect.

On quitting the housekeeper's room, she turned to the left, ascended a back staircase, and unlocked a door at the top of it. A cloud of dust flew all about her as she softly opened the door; a mouldy coolness made her shiver as she crossed a large stone hall, with some black old family portraits hanging on the walls, the canvasses of which were bulging out of the frames. Ascending more stairs, she came upon a row of doors, all leading into rooms on the first floor of the north side of the house.

She knelt down, putting the letter on the boards beside her, opposite the key-hole of the fourth door she came to after reaching the top of the stairs, peered in distrustfully for an instant, then began to try the different keys till she found one that fitted the lock. She had great difficulty in accomplishing this, from the violence of her agitation, which made her hands tremble to such a degree that she was hardly able to keep the keys separate one from the other. At length she succeeded in opening the door. Thicker clouds of dust than she had yet met with flew out the moment the interior of the room was visible; a dry, air-less, suffocating atmosphere almost choked her as she stooped to pick up the letter from the floor. She recoiled from it at first, and took a few steps back toward the staircase. But she recovered her resolution immediately.

"I can't go back now!" she said, desperately, and entered the room.

She did not remain in it more than two or three minutes. When she came out again her face was white with fear, and the hand which had held the letter when she went into the room held nothing now but a small rusty key.

After locking the door again, she examined the large bunch of keys which she had taken from the housekeeper's room, with closer attention than she had yet bestowed on them.

Besides the ivory label attached to the ring that connected them, there were smaller labels, of parchment, tied to the handles of some of the keys, to indicate the rooms to which they gave admission. The particular key which she had used had one of these labels hanging to it. She held the little strip of parchment close to the light, and read on it, in written characters faded by time—

The Myrtle Room.

The room in which the letter was hidden had a name, then! A prettily sounding name that would attract most people, and keep pleasantly in their memories. A name to be distrusted by her, after what she had done, on that very account.

She took her housewife from its usual place in the pocket of her apron, and, with the scissors which it contained, cut the label from the key. Was it enough to destroy that one only? She lost herself in a maze of useless conjecture; and ended by cutting off the other labels, from no other motive than instinctive suspicion of them.

Carefully gathering up the strips of parchment from the floor, she put them, along with the little rusty key which she had brought out of the Myrtle Room, in the empty pocket of her apron. Then, carrying the large bunch of keys in her hand, and carefully locking the doors that she had opened on her way to the north side of Porthgenna Tower, she retraced her steps to the housekeeper's room, entered it without seeing anybody, and hung up the bunch of keys again on the nail in the wall.

Fearful, as the morning hours wore on, of meeting with some of the female servants, she next hastened back to her bedroom. The candle she had left there was still burning feebly in the fresh daylight. When she drew aside the window-curtain, after extinguishing the candle, a shadow of her former fear passed over her face, even in the broad daylight that now flowed in upon it. She opened the window, and leaned out eagerly into the cool air.

Whether for good or for evil, the fatal Secret was hidden now—the act was done. There was something calming in the first consciousness of that one fact. She could think more composedly, after that, of herself, and of the uncertain future that lay before her.

Under no circumstances could she have expected to remain in her situation, now that the connection between herself and her mistress had been severed by death. She knew that Mrs. Treverton, in the last days of her illness, had earnestly recommended her maid to Captain Treverton's kindness and protection, and she felt assured that the wife's last entreaties, in this as in all other instances, would be viewed as the most sacred of obligations by the husband.

But could she accept protection and kindness at the hand of the master whom she had been accessory to deceiving, and whom she had now committed herself to deceiving still? The bare idea of such baseness was so revolting that she accepted, almost with a sense of relief, the one sad alternative that remained—the alternative of leaving the house immediately.

And how was she to leave it? By giving formal warning, and so exposing herself to questions which would be sure to confuse and terrify her? Could she venture to face her master again, after what she had done—to face him, when his first inquiries would refer to her mistress, when he would be certain to ask her for the last mournful details, for the slightest word that had been spoken during the death-scene that she alone had witnessed? She started to her feet, as the certain consequences of submitting herself to that unendurable trial all crowded together warningly on her mind, took her cloak from its place on the wall, and listened at her door in sudden suspicion and fear. Had she heard footsteps? Was her master sending for her already?

No; all was silent outside. A few tears rolled over her cheeks as she put on her bonnet, and felt that she was facing, by the performance of that simple action, the last, and perhaps the hardest to meet, of the cruel necessities in which the hiding of the Secret had involved her. There was no help for it. She must run the risk of betraying everything, or brave the double trial of leaving Porthgenna Tower, and leaving it secretly.

Secretly—as a thief might go? Without a word to her master? Without so much as one line of writing to thank him for his kindness and to ask his pardon? She had unlocked her desk, and had taken from it her purse, one or two letters, and a little book of Wesley's Hymns, before these considerations occurred to her. They made her pause in the act of shutting up the desk, "Shall I write?" she asked herself, "and leave the letter here, to be found when I am gone?"

A little more reflection decided her in the affirmative. As rapidly as her pen could form the letters she wrote a few lines addressed to Captain Treverton, in which she confessed to having kept a secret from his knowledge which had been left in her charge to divulge; adding, that she honestly believed no harm could come to him, or to any one in whom he was interested, by her failing to perform the duty intrusted to her; and ended by asking his pardon for leaving the house secretly, and by begging, as a last favour, that no search might ever be made for her.

Having sealed this short note, and left it on the table, with her master's name written outside, she listened again at the door; and, after satisfying herself that no one was yet stirring, began to descend the stairs at Porthgenna Tower for the last time.

At the entrance of the passage leading to the nursery she

stopped. The tears which she had restrained since leaving her room began to flow again. Urgent as her reasons now were for effecting her departure without a moment's loss of time, she advanced, with the strangest inconsistency, a few steps toward the nursery door. Before she had gone far, a slight noise in the lower part of the house caught her ear and instantly checked her further progress.

While she stood doubtful, the grief at her heart—a greater grief than any she had yet betrayed—rose irresistibly to her lips, and burst from them in one deep gasping sob. The sound of it seemed to terrify her into a sense of the danger of her position, if she delayed a moment longer. She ran out again to the stairs, reached the kitchen-floor in safety, and made her escape by the garden door which the servant had opened for her at the dawn of the morning.

On getting clear of the premises at Porthgenna Tower, instead of taking the nearest path over the moor that led to the high-road, she diverged to the church; but stopped before she came to it, at the public well of the neighbourhood, which had been sunk near the cottages of the Porthgenna fishermen. Cautiously looking round her, she dropped into the well the little rusty key which she had brought out of the Myrtle Room; then hurried on, and entered the churchyard. She directed her course straight to one of the graves, situated a little apart from the rest. On the headstone were inscribed these words:

Sacred to the Memory
of
Hugh Polwheal,
Aged 26 years.
He Met With His Death
Through the Fall of a Rock
in
Porthgenna Mine, December 17th, 1823.

Gathering a few leaves of grass from the grave, Sarah opened the little book of Wesley's Hymns which she had brought with her from the bedroom of Porthgenna Tower, and placed the leaves delicately and carefully between the pages. As she did this, the wind blew open the title-page of the Hymns, and displayed this inscription on it, written in large, clumsy characters—*Sarah Leeson, her book. The gift of Hugh Polwheal.*

Having secured the blades of grass between the pages of the book, she retraced her way toward the path leading to the high-road. Arrived on the moor, she took out of her apron pocket the parchment labels that had been cut from the keys, and scattered them under the furze-bushes.

"Gone," she said, "as I am gone! God help and forgive me—it is all done and over now!"

With those words she turned her back on the old house and the sea-view below it, and followed the moorland path on her way to the high-road.

Four hours afterward Captain Treverton desired one of the servants at Porthgenna Tower to inform Sarah Leeson that he wished to hear all she had to tell him of the dying moments of her mistress. The messenger returned with looks and words of amazement, and with the letter that Sarah had addressed to her master in his hand.

The moment Captain Treverton had read the letter, he ordered an immediate search to be made after the missing woman. She was so easy to describe and to recognize, by the premature grayness of her hair, by the odd, scared look in her eyes, and by her habit of constantly talking to herself, that she was traced with certainty as far as Truro. In that large town the track of her was lost, and never recovered again.

Rewards were offered; the magistrates of the district were interested in the case; all that wealth and power could do to discover her was done—and done in vain. No clew was found to suggest a suspicion of her whereabouts, or to help in the slightest degree toward explaining the nature of the secret at which she had hinted in her letter. Her master never saw her again, never heard of her again, after the morning of the twenty-third of August, eighteen hundred and twenty-nine.

BOOK 2

CHAPTER 1
FIFTEEN YEARS AFTER

The church of Long Beckley (a large agricultural village in one of the midland counties of England), although a building in no way remarkable either tor its size, its architecture, or its antiquity, possesses, nevertheless, one advantage which mercantile London has barbarously denied to the noble cathedral church of St. Paul. It has plenty of room to stand in, and it can consequently be seen with perfect convenience from every point of view, all around the compass.

The large open space around the church can be approached in three different directions. There is a road from the village, leading straight to the principal door. There is a broad gravel walk, which begins at the vicarage gates, crosses the churchyard, and stops, as in duty bound, at the vestry entrance. There is a footpath over the fields, by which the lord of the manor, and the gentry in general who live in his august neighbourhood, can reach the side door of the building, whenever their natural humility may incline them to encourage Sabbath observance in the stables by going to church, like the lower sort of worshipers, on their own legs.

At half-past seven o'clock on a certain fine summer morning, in the year eighteen hundred and forty-four, if any observant stranger had happened to be standing in some unnoticed corner of the churchyard, and to be looking about him with sharp eyes, he would probably have been the witness of proceedings which might have led him to believe that there was a conspiracy going on in Long Beckley, of which the church was the rallying-point, and some of the most respectable inhabitants the principal leaders. Supposing him to have been looking forward toward the vicarage as the clock chimed the half-hour, he would have seen the vicar of Long Beckley, the Reverend Doctor Chennery, leaving his house suspiciously, by the back way, glancing behind him guiltily as he approached the gravel walk that led to the vestry, stopping mysteriously just outside the door, and gazing anxiously down the road that led from the village.

Assuming that our observant stranger would, upon this, keep out of sight, and look down the road, like the vicar, he would next have seen the clerk of the church—an austere, yellow-faced man—a Protestant Loyola in appearance, and a working shoe-maker by trade—approaching with a look of unutterable mystery in his face, and a bunch of big keys in his hands. He would have seen the vicar nod in an abstracted manner to the clerk, and say: "Fine morning, Thomas. Have you had your breakfast yet?"

He would have heard Thomas reply, with a suspicious regard for minute particulars: "I have had a cup of tea and a crust, sir." And he would then have seen these two local conspirators, after looking up with one accord at the church clock, draw off together to the side door which commanded a view of the foot-path across the fields.

Following them—as our inquisitive stranger could not fail to do—he would have detected three more conspirators advancing along the footpath. The leader of this treasonable party was an elderly gentleman, with a weather-beaten face and a bluff, hearty manner. His two followers were a young gentleman and a young lady, walking arm-in-arm, and talking together in whispers. They were dressed in the plainest morning costume. The faces of both were rather pale, and the manner of the lady was a little flurried.

Otherwise there was nothing remarkable to observe in them, until they came to the wicket-gate leading into the churchyard; and there the conduct of the young gentleman seemed, at first sight, rather inexplicable. Instead of holding the gate open for the lady to pass through, he hung back, allowed her to open it for herself, waited till she had got to the churchyard side, and then, stretching out his hand over the gate, allowed her to lead him through the entrance, as if he had suddenly changed from a grown man to a helpless little child.

Noting this, and remarking also that, when the party from the fields had arrived within greeting distance of the vicar, and when the clerk had used his bunch of keys to open the church-door, the young lady's companion was led into the building (this time by Doctor Chennery's hand), as he had been previously led through the wicket-gate, our observant stranger must have arrived at one inevitable conclusion—that the person requiring such assistance as this was suffering under the affliction of blindness.

Startled a little by that discovery, he would have been still further amazed, if he had looked into the church, by seeing the blind man and the young lady standing together before the altar rails, with the elderly gentleman in parental attendance. Any suspicions he might now entertain that the bond which united the conspirators at that early hour of the morning was of the hymeneal sort, and that the object of their plot was to celebrate a wedding with the strictest secrecy, would have been confirmed in five minutes by the appearance of Doctor Chennery from the vestry in full canonicals, and by the reading of the marriage service in the reverend gentleman's most harmonious officiating tones.

The ceremony concluded, the attendant stranger must have been more perplexed than ever by observing that the persons concerned in it all separated, the moment the signing, the kissing and congratulating duties proper to the occasion had been performed, and quickly retired in the various directions by which they had approached the church.

Leaving the clerk to return by the village road, the bride, bridegroom and elderly gentleman to turn back by the footpath over the fields, and the visionary stranger of these pages to vanish out of them in any direction that he pleases—let us follow Doctor Chennery to the vicarage breakfast-table, and hear what he has to say about his professional exertions of the morning in the familiar atmosphere of his own family circle.

The persons assembled at the breakfast were, first, Mr. Phippen, a guest; secondly, Miss Sturch, a governess; thirdly, fourthly and fifthly, Miss Louisa Chennery (aged eleven years), Miss Amelia Chennery (aged nine years), and Master Robert Chennery (aged eight years). There was no mother's face present to make the household picture complete. Doctor Chennery had been a widower since the birth of his youngest child.

The guest was an old college acquaintance of the vicar's, and he was supposed to be now staying at Long Beckley for the benefit of his health. Most men of any character at all contrive to get a reputation of some sort which individualizes them in the social circle amid which they move. Mr. Phippen was a man of some little character, and he lived with great distinction in the estimation of his friends on the reputation of being A Martyr to Dyspepsia.

Wherever Mr. Phippen went, the woes of Mr. Phippen's stomach went with him. He dieted himself publicly, and physicked himself publicly. He was so intensely occupied with himself and his maladies, that he would let a chance acquaintance into the secret of the condition of his tongue at five minutes' notice; being just as perpetually ready to discuss the state of his digestion as people in general are to discuss the state of the weather.

On this favourite subject, as on all others, he spoke with a wheedling gentleness of manner, sometimes in softly mournful, sometimes in languidly sentimental tones. His politeness was of the oppressively affectionate sort, and he used the word "dear" continually in addressing himself to others.

Personally, he could not be called a handsome man. His eyes were watery, large, and light gray; they were always rolling from side to side in a state of moist admiration of something or somebody. His nose was long, drooping, profoundly melancholy—if such an expression may be permitted in reference to that particular feature. For the rest, his lips had a lachrymose twist; his stature was small; his head large, bald, and loosely set on his shoulders; his manner of dressing himself eccentric, on the side of smartness; his age about five-and-forty; his condition that of a single man. Such was Mr. Phippen, the Martyr to Dyspepsia, and the guest of the vicar of Long Beckley.

Miss Sturch, the governess, may be briefly and accurately described as a young lady who had never been troubled with an idea or a sensation since the day when she was born. She was a little, plump, quiet, white-skinned, smiling, neatly-dressed girl, wound up accurately to the performance of certain duties at certain times; and possessed of an inexhaustible vocabulary of commonplace talk, which dribbled placidly out of her lips whenever it was called for, always in the same quantity, and always of the same quality, at every hour in the day, and through every change in the seasons.

Miss Sturch never laughed, and never cried, but took the safe middle course of smiling perpetually. She smiled when she came down on a morning in January, and said it was very cold. She smiled when she came down on a morning in July, and said it was very hot. She smiled when the bishop came once a year to see the vicar; she smiled when the butcher's boy came every morning for orders. Let what might happen at the vicarage, nothing ever jerked Miss Sturch out of the one smooth groove in which she ran perpetually, always at the same pace.

If she had lived in a royalist family, during the civil wars in England, she would have rung for the cook, to order dinner, on the morning of the execution of Charles the First. If Shakespeare had come back to life again, and had called at the vicarage at six o'clock on Saturday evening, to explain to Miss Sturch exactly what his views were in composing the tragedy of Hamlet, she would have smiled and said it was extremely interesting, until the striking of seven o'clock; at which time she would have left him in the middle of a sentence, to superintend the house-maid in the verification of the washing-book.

A very estimable young person, Miss Sturch (as the ladies of Long Beckley were accustomed to say); so judicious with the children, and so attached to her household duties; such a well-regulated mind, and such a crisp touch on the piano; just nice-looking enough, just well-dressed enough, just talkative enough; not quite old enough, perhaps, and a little too much inclined to be embraceably plump about the region of the waist—but, on the whole, a most estimable young person—very much so, indeed.

On the characteristic peculiarities of Miss Sturch's pupils it is not necessary to dwell at very great length. Miss Louisa's habitual weakness was an inveterate tendency to catch cold. Miss Amelia's principal defect was a disposition to gratify her palate by eating supplementary dinners and breakfasts at unauthorized times and seasons. Master Robert's most noticeable failings were caused by alacrity in tearing his clothes and obtuseness in learning the Multiplication Table. The virtues of all three were of much the same nature—they were well grown, they were genuine children, and they were boisterously fond of Miss Sturch.

To complete the gallery of family portraits, an outline, at the least, must be attempted of the vicar himself. Doctor Chennery was, in a physical point of view, a credit to the Establishment to which he was attached. He stood six feet two in his shooting-shoes; he weighed fifteen stone; he was the best bowler in the Long Beckley cricket-club; he was a strictly orthodox man in the matter of wine and mutton; he never started disagreeable theories about people's future destinies in the pulpit, never quarrelled with anybody out of the pulpit, never buttoned up his pockets when the necessities of his poor brethren (Dissenters included) pleaded with him to open them.

His course through the world was a steady march along the high and dry middle of a safe turnpike road. The serpentine side-paths of controversy might open as alluringly as they pleased on his right hand and on his left, but he kept on his way sturdily, and never regarded them. Innovating young recruits in the Church army might entrappingly open the *Thirty-nine Articles* under his very nose, but the veteran's wary eye never looked a hair-breadth further than his own signature at the bottom of them.

He knew as little as possible of theology, he had never given the Privy Council a minute's trouble, in the whole course of his life, he was innocent of all meddling with the reading or writing of pamphlets, and he was quite incapable of finding his way to the platform of Exeter Hall. In short, he was the most unclerical of clergymen—but, for all that, he had such a figure for a surplice as is seldom seen. Fifteen stone weight of upright muscular flesh, without an angry spot or sore place in any part of it, has the merit of suggesting stability, at any rate—an excellent virtue in pillars of all kinds, but an especially precious quality, at the present time, in a pillar o the church.

As soon as the vicar entered the breakfast-parlour the children assailed him with a chorus of shouts. He was a severe disciplinarian in the observance of punctuality at mealtimes; and he now stood convicted by the clock of being too late for breakfast by a quarter of an hour.

"Sorry to have kept you waiting, Miss Sturch," said the vicar; "but I have a good excuse for being late this morning."

"Pray don't mention it, sir," said Miss Sturch, blandly rubbing her plump little hands one over the other. "A beautiful morning. I fear we shall have another warm day.—Robert, my love, your elbow is on the table.—A beautiful morning, indeed!"

"Stomach still out of order—eh, Phippen?" asked the vicar, beginning to carve the ham.

Mr. Phippen shook his large head dolefully, placed his yellow forefinger, ornamented with a large turquoise ring, on the centre check of his light-green summer waistcoat—looked piteously at Doctor Chennery, and sighed removed the finger, and produced from the breast pocket of his wrapper a little mahogany case—took out of it a neat pair of apothecary's scales, with the accompanying weights, a morsel of ginger, and a highly polished silver nutmeg-grater. "Dear Miss Sturch will pardon an invalid?" said Mr. Phippen, beginning to grate the ginger feebly into the nearest tea-cup.

"Guess what has made me a quarter of an hour late this morning," said the vicar, looking mysteriously all round the table.

"Lying in bed, papa," cried the three children, clapping their hands in triumph.

"What do you say, Miss Sturch?" asked Doctor Chennery.

Miss Sturch smiled as usual, rubbed her hands as usual, cleared her throat softly as usual, looked at the tea-urn, and begged, with the most graceful politeness, to be excused if she said nothing.

"Your turn now, Phippen," said the vicar. "Come, guess what has kept me late this morning."

"My dear friend," said Mr. Phippen, giving the doctor a brotherly squeeze of the hand, "don't ask me to guess—I know! I saw what you eat at dinner yesterday I saw what you drank after dinner. No digestion could stand it—not even yours. Guess what has made you late this morning? Pooh! pooh! I know. You dear, good soul, you have been taking physic!"

"Haven't touched a drop, thank God, for the last ten years!" said Doctor Chennery, with a look of devout gratitude. "No, no; you're all wrong. The fact is, I have been to church; and what do you think I have been doing there? Listen, Miss Sturch—listen, girls, with all your ears. Poor blind young Frankland is a happy man at last—I have married him to our dear Rosamond Treverton this very morning!"

"Without telling us, papa!" cried the two girls together in their shrillest tones of vexation and surprise. "Without telling us, when you know how we should have liked to see it!"

"That was the very reason why I did not tell you, my dears," answered the vicar. "Young Frankland has not got so used to his affliction yet, poor fellow, as to bear being publicly pitied and stared at in the character of a blind bridegroom. He had such a nervous horror of being an object of curiosity on his wedding-day, and Rosamond, like a kind-hearted girl as she is, was so anxious that his slightest caprices should be humoured, that we settled to have the wedding at an hour in the morning when no idlers were likely to be lounging about the neighbourhood of the church.

"I was bound over to the strictest secrecy about the day, and so was my clerk Thomas. Excepting us two, and the bride and bridegroom, and the bride's father, Captain Treverton, nobody knew—"

"Treverton!" exclaimed Mr. Phippen, holding his tea-cup, with the grated ginger in the bottom of it, to be filled by Miss

Sturch. "Treverton! (No more tea, dear Miss Sturch.) How very remarkable! I know the name. (Fill up with water, if you please.) Tell me, my dear doctor (many, many thanks; no sugar—it turns acid on the stomach), is this Miss Treverton whom you have been marrying (many thanks again; no milk, either) one of the Cornish Trevertons?"

"To be sure she is!" rejoined the vicar. "Her father, Captain Treverton, is the head of the family. Not that there's much family to speak of now. The Captain, and Rosamond, and that whimsical old brute of an uncle of hers, Andrew Treverton, are the last left now of the old stock-a rich family, and a fine family, in former times—good friends to Church and State, you know, and all that—"

"Do you approve, sir, of Amelia having a second helping of bread and marmalade?" asked Miss Sturch, appealing to Doctor Chennery, with the most perfect unconsciousness of interrupting him. Having no spare room in her mind for putting things away in until the appropriate time came for bringing them out, Miss Sturch always asked questions and made remarks the moment they occurred to her, without waiting for the beginning, middle, or end of any conversations that might be proceeding in her presence. She invariably looked the part of a listener to perfection, but she never acted it except in the case of talk that was aimed point-blank at her own ears.

"Oh, give her a second helping, by all means I" said the vicar, carelessly; "if she must over-eat herself, she may as well do it on bread and marmalade as on anything else."

"My dear, good soul," exclaimed Mr. Phippen, "look what a wreck I am, and don't talk in that shockingly thoughtless way of letting our sweet Amelia over-eat herself. Load the stomach in youth, and what becomes of the digestion in age? The thing which vulgar people call the inside I appeal to Miss Sturch's interest in her charming pupil as an excuse for going into physiological particulars—is, in point of fact, an Apparatus. Digestively considered, Miss Sturch, even the fairest and youngest of us is an Apparatus. Oil our wheels, if you like; but clog them at your peril.

"Farinaceous puddings and mutton-chops; mutton-chops and farinaceous puddings—those should be the parents' watch-words, if I had my way, from one end of England to the other. Look here, my sweet child—look at me. There is no fun, dear, about these little scales, but dreadful earnest. See! I put in the balance on one side dry bread (stale, dry bread, Amelia!), and on the other some ounce weights. 'Mr. Phippen, eat by weight. Mr. Phippen! eat the same quantity, day by day, to a hair-breadth. Mr. Phippen! exceed your allowance (though it is only stale, dry bread) if you dare!'

"Amelia, love, this is not fun this is what the doctors tell me—the doctors, my child, who have been searching my Apparatus through and through for thirty years past with little pills, and have not found out where my wheels are clogged yet. Think of that, Amelia—think of Mr. Phippen's clogged Apparatus—and say 'No, thank you,' next time. Miss Sturch, I beg a thousand pardons for intruding on your province; but my interest in that sweet child—Chennery, you dear, good soul, what were we talking about? Ah! the bride—the interesting bride! And so she is one of the Cornish Trevertons? I knew something of Andrew years ago. He was a bachelor, like myself, Miss Sturch. His Apparatus was out of order, like mine, dear Amelia. Not at all like his brother, the Captain, I should suppose? And so she is married? A charming girl, I have no doubt. A charming girl!"

"No better, truer, prettier girl in the world," said the vicar.

"A very lively, energetic person," remarked Miss Sturch.

"How I shall miss her!" cried Miss Louisa. "Nobody else amused me as Rosamond did, when I was laid up with that last bad cold of mine."

"She used to give us such nice little early supper-parties, " said Miss Amelia.

"She was the only girl I ever saw who was fit to play with boys," said Master Robert. "She could catch a ball, Mr. Phippen, sir, with one hand, and go down a slide with both her legs together."

47

"Bless me!" said Mr. Phippen. "What an extraordinary wife for a blind man! You said he was blind from his birth, my dear doctor, did you not? Let me see, what was his name? You will not bear too hardly on my loss of memory, Miss Sturch? "When indigestion has done with the body, it begins to prey on the mind. Mr. Frank Something, was it not?"

"No, no—Frankland," answered the vicar, "Leonard Frankland. And not blind from his birth by any means. It is not much more than a year ago since he could see almost as well as any of us."

"An accident, I suppose!" said Mr. Phippen. "You will excuse me if I take the armchair?—a partially reclining posture is of great assistance to me after meals. So an accident happened to his eyes? Ah, what a delightfully easy chair to sit in!"

"Scarcely an accident," said Doctor Chennery. "Leonard Frankland was a difficult child to bring up: great constitutional weakness, you know, at first. He seemed to get over that with time, and grew into a quiet, sedate, orderly sort of boy—as unlike my son there as possible—very amiable, and what you call easy to deal with. Well, he had a turn for mechanics (I am telling you all this to make you understand about his blindness), and, after veering from one occupation of that sort to another, he took at last to watch-making.

"Curious amusement for a boy; but anything that required delicacy of touch, and plenty of patience and perseverance, was just the thing to amuse and occupy Leonard. I always said to his father and mother, 'Get him off that stool, break his magnifying-glasses, send him to me, and I'll give him a back at leap-frog, and teach him the use of a bat.' But it was no use. His parents knew best, I suppose, and they said he must be humoured.

"Well, things went on smoothly enough for some time, till he got another long illness—as I believe, from not taking exercise enough. As soon as he began to get round, back he went to his old watch-making occupations again. But the bad end of it all was coming.

"About the last work he did, poor fellow, was the repairing of

48

my watch—here it is; goes as regular as a steam-engine. I hadn't got it back into my fob very long before I heard that he was getting a bad pain at the back of his head, and that he saw all sorts of moving spots before his eyes. 'String him up with lots of port wine, and give him three hours a day on the back of a quiet pony'—that was my advice.

"Instead of taking it, they sent for doctors from London, and blistered him behind the ears and between the shoulders, and drenched the lad with mercury, and moped him up in a dark room. No use. The sight got worse and worse, flickered and flickered, and went out at last like the flame of a candle, His mother died—luckily for her, poor soul—before that happened. His father was half out of his mind; took him to oculists in London and oculists in Paris.

"All they did was to call the blindness by a long Latin name, and to say that it was hopeless and useless to try an operation. Some of them said it was the result of the long weaknesses from which he had twice suffered after illness. Some said it was an apoplectic effusion in his brain. All of them shook their heads when they heard of the watch-making. So they brought him back home, blind; blind he is now; and blind he will remain, poor dear fellow, for the rest of his life."

"You shock me; my dear Chennery, you shock me dreadfully," said Mr. Phippen. "Especially when you state that theory about long weakness after illness. Good heavens! Why, I have had long weaknesses—I have got them now. Spots did he see before his eyes? I see spots, black spots, dancing black spots, dancing black bilious spots. Upon my word of honour, Chennery, this comes home to me—my sympathies are painfully acute—I feel this blind story in every nerve of my body; I do, indeed!"

"You would hardly know that Leonard was blind, to look at him," said Miss Louisa, striking into the conversation with a view to restoring Mr. Phippen's equanimity. "Except that his eyes look quieter than other people's, there seems no difference in them now. Who was that famous character you told us about, Miss Sturch, who was blind, and didn't show it any more than

Leonard Frankland?"

"Milton, my love. I begged you to remember that he was the most famous of British epic poets," answered Miss Sturch with suavity. "He poetically describes his blindness as being caused by 'so thick a drop serene.' You shall read about it, Louisa. After we have had a little French, we will have a little Milton, this morning. Hush, love, your papa is speaking."

"Poor young Frankland!" said the vicar, warmly. "That good, tender, noble creature I married him to this morning seems sent as a consolation to him in his affliction. If any human being can make him happy for the rest of his life, Rosamond Treverton is the girl to do it."

"She has made a sacrifice," said Mr. Phippen; "but I like her for that, having made a sacrifice myself in remaining single. It seems indispensable, indeed, on the score of humanity, that I should do so. How could I conscientiously inflict such a digestion as mine on a member of the fairer portion of creation? No; I am a sacrifice in my own proper person, and I have a fellow-feeling for others who are like me. Did she cry much, Chennery, when you were marrying her?"

"Cry!" exclaimed the vicar, contemptuously.

"Rosamond Treverton is not one of the puling, sentimental sort, I can tell you. A fine buxom, warm-hearted, quick-tempered girl, who looks what she means when she tolls a man she is going to marry him. And, mind you, she has been tried. If she hadn't loved him with all her heart and soul, she might have been free months ago to marry anybody she pleased.

"They were engaged long before this cruel affliction befell young Frankland—the fathers, on both sides, having lived as near neighbours in these parts for years. Well, when the blindness came, Leonard at once offered to release Rosamond from her engagement. You should have read the letter she wrote to him, Phippen, upon that.

"I don't mind confessing that I blubbered like a baby over it when they showed it to me. I should have married them at once the instant I read it, but old Frankland was a fidgety, punctilious kind of man, and he insisted on a six months' probation, so that she might be certain of knowing her own mind. He died before the term was out, and that caused the marriage to be put off again.

"But no delays could alter Rosamond—six years, instead of six months, would not have changed her. There she was this morning as fond of that poor, patient blind fellow as she was the first day they were engaged. 'You shall never know a sad moment, Lenny, if I can help it, as long as you live'—these were the first words she said to him when we all came out of church. 'I hear you, Rosamond,' said I.

"'And you shall judge me, too, Doctor,' says she, quick as lightning. 'We will come back to Long Beckley, and you shall ask Lenny if I have not kept my word.' With that she gave me a kiss that you might have heard down here at the vicarage, bless her heart! We'll drink her health after dinner, Miss Sturch—we'll drink both their healths, Phippen, in a bottle of the best wine I have in my cellar."

"In a glass of toast and water, so far as I am concerned, if you will allow me," said Mr. Phippen, mournfully. "But, my dear Chennery, when you were talking of the fathers of these two interesting young people, you spoke of their living as near neighbours here, at Long Beckley. My memory is impaired, as I am painfully aware; but I thought Captain Treverton was the eldest of the two brothers, and that he always lived, when he was on shore, at the family place in Cornwall?"

"So he did," returned the vicar, "in his wife's lifetime. But since her death, which happened as long ago as the year 'twenty-nine—let me see, we are now in the year 'forty-four—and that makes—"

The vicar stopped for an instant to calculate, and looked at Miss Sturch.

"Fifteen years ago, sir," said Miss Sturch, offering the accommodation of a little simple subtraction to the vicar, with her blandest smile.

"Of course," continued Doctor Chennery. "Well, since Mrs.

Treverton died, fifteen years ago, Captain Treverton has never been near Porthgenna Tower. And, what is more, Phippen, at the first opportunity he could get, he sold the place—sold it, out and out, mine, fisheries, and all—for forty thousand pounds."

"You don't say so!" exclaimed Mr. Phippen. "Did he find the air unhealthy? I should think the local produce, in the way of food, must be coarse now, in those barbarous regions? Who bought the place?"

"Leonard Frankland's father," said the vicar. "It is rather a long story, that sale of Porthgenna Tower, with some curious circumstances involved in it. Suppose we take a turn in the garden, Phippen? I'll tell you all about it over my morning cigar. Miss Sturch, if you want me, I shall be on the lawn somewhere. Girls! mind you know your lessons. Bob! remember that I've got a cane in the hall, and a birch-rod in my dressing-room. Come, Phippen, rouse up out of that arm-chair. You won't say No to a turn in the garden?"

"My dear fellow, I will say Yes—if you will kindly lend me an umbrella, and allow me to carry my camp-stool in my hand," said Mr. Phippen. "I am too weak to encounter the sun, and I can't go far without sitting down.—The moment I feel fatigued, Miss Sturch, I open my camp-stool, and sit down anywhere, without the slightest regard for appearances.—I am ready, Chennery, whenever you are—equally ready, my good friend, for the garden and the story about the sale of Porthgenna Tower. You said it was a curious story, did you not?"

"I said there was some curious circumstances connected with it," replied the vicar. "And when you hear about them, I think you will say so too, Come along! you will find your camp- stool, and a choice of all the umbrellas in the house, in the hall."

With those words, Doctor Chennery opened his cigar-case and led the way out of the breakfast- parlour.

CHAPTER 2
THE SALE OF PORTHGENNA TOWER

"How charming! how pastoral! how exquisitely soothing!"

said Mr. Phippen, sentimentally surveying the lawn at the back of the vicarage-house, under the shadow of the lightest umbrella he could pick out of the hall. "Three years have passed, Chennery, since I last stood on this lawn. There is the window of your old study, where I had my attack of heart-burn last time—in the strawberry season; don't you remember? Ah! and there is the schoolroom!

"Shall I ever forget dear Miss Sturch coming to me out of that room—a ministering angel with soda and ginger—so comforting, so sweetly anxious about stirring it up, so unaffectedly grieved that there was no *sal-volatile* in the house! I do so enjoy these pleasant recollections, Chennery; they are as great a, luxury to me as your cigar is to you. Could you walk on the other side, my dear fellow? I like the smell, but the smoke is a little too much for me. Thank you. And now about the story? What was the name of the old place—I am so interested in it—it began with a P, surely?"

"Porthgenna Tower," said the vicar.

"Exactly," rejoined Mr. Phippen, shifting the umbrella tenderly from one shoulder to the other. "And what in the world made Captain Treverton sell Porthgenna Tower?"

"I believe the reason was that he could not endure the place after the death of his wife," answered Doctor Chennery. "The estate, you know, has never been entailed; so the Captain had no difficulty in parting with it, except, of course, the difficulty of finding a purchaser."

"Why not his brother?" asked Mr. Phippen. "Why not our eccentric friend, Andrew Treverton?"

"Don't call him my friend," said the vicar. "A mean, grovelling, cynical, selfish old wretch! It's no use shaking your head, Phippen, and trying to look shocked. I know Andrew Treverton's early history as well as you do. I know that he was treated with the basest ingratitude by a college friend, who took all he had to give, and swindled him at last in the grossest manner. I know all about that.

"But one instance of ingratitude does not justify a man in

shutting himself up from society, and railing against all mankind as a disgrace to the earth they walk on. I myself have heard the old brute say that the greatest benefactor to our generation would be a second Herod, who could prevent another generation from succeeding it. Ought a man who can talk in that way to be the friend of any human being with the slightest respect for his species or himself?"

"My friend!" said Mr. Phippen, catching the vicar by the arm, and mysteriously lowering his voice—"My dear and reverend friend! I admire your honest indignation against the utterer of that exceedingly misanthropical sentiment; but—I confide this to you, Chennery, in the strictest secrecy there are moments morning moments generally—when my digestion is in such a state that I have actually agreed with that annihilating person, Andrew Treverton! I have woke up with my tongue like a cinder—I have crawled to the glass and looked at it—and I have said to myself: 'Let there be an end of the human race rather than a continuance of this!'"

"Pooh! pooh!" cried the vicar, receiving Mr. Phippen 's confession with a burst of irreverent laughter. "Take a glass of cool small beer next time your tongue is in that state, and you will pray for a continuance of the brewing part of the human race, at any rate. But let us go back to Porthgenna Tower, or I shall never get on with my story.

"When Captain Treverton had once made up his mind to sell the place, I have no doubt that, under ordinary circumstances, he would have thought of offering it to his brother, with a view, of course, to keeping the estate in the family. Andrew was rich enough to have bought it; for, though he got nothing at his father's death but the old gentleman's rare collection of books, he inherited his mother's fortune, as the second son.

"However, as things were at that time (and are still, I am sorry to say), the Captain could make no personal offers of any kind to Andrew; for the two were not then, and are not now, on speaking, or even on writing terms. It is a shocking thing to say, but the worst quarrel of the kind I ever heard of is the quarrel between those two brothers."

"Pardon me, my dear friend," said Mr. Phippen, opening his camp-stool, which had hitherto dangled by its silken tassel from the hooked handle of the umbrella. "May I sit down before you go any further? I am getting a little excited about this part of the story, and I dare not fatigue myself. Pray go on. I don't think the legs of my camp-stool will make holes in the lawn. I am so light a mere skeleton, in fact. Do go on!"

"You must have heard," pursued the vicar, "that Captain Treverton, when he was advanced in life, married an actress—rather a violent temper, I believe; but a person of spotless character, and as fond of her husband as a woman could be; therefore, according to my view of it, a very good wife for him to marry.

"However, the Captain's friends, of course, made the usual senseless outcry, and the Captain's brother, as the only near relation, took it on himself to attempt breaking off the marriage in the most offensively indelicate way. Failing in that, and hating the poor woman like poison, he left this brother's house, saying, among many other savage speeches, one infamous thing about the bride, which—which, upon my honour, Phippen, I am ashamed to repeat.

"Whatever the words were, they were unluckily carried to Mrs. Treverton's ears, and they were of the kind that no woman—let alone a quick-tempered woman like the Captain's wife—ever forgives. An interview followed between the two brothers—and it led, as you may easily imagine, to very unhappy results. They parted in the most deplorable manner.

"The Captain declared, in the heat of his passion, that Andrew had never had one generous impulse in his heart since he was born, and that he would die without one kind feeling toward any living soul in the world. Andrew replied that, if he had no heart, he had a memory, and that he should remember those farewell words as long as he lived. So they separated.

"Twice afterward the Captain made overtures of reconciliation. The first time when his daughter Rosamond was born; the second time when Mrs. Treverton died. On each occasion the elder brother wrote to say that, if the younger would retract the atrocious words he had spoken against his sister-in-law, every atonement should be offered to him for the harsh language which the Captain had used, in the hastiness of anger, when they last met.

"No answer was received from Andrew to either letter; and the estrangement between the two brothers has continued to the present time. You understand now why Captain Treverton could not privately consult Andrew's inclinations before he publicly announced his intention of parting with Porthgenna Tower."

Although Mr. Phippen declared, in answer to this appeal, that he understood perfectly, and although he begged with the utmost politeness that the vicar would go on, his attention seemed, for the moment, to be entirely absorbed in inspecting the legs of his camp-stool, and in ascertaining what impression they made on the vicarage lawn. Doctor Chennery's own interest, however, in the circumstances that he was relating, seemed sufficiently strong to make up for any transient lapse of attention on the part of his guest. After a few vigorous puffs at his cigar (which had been several times in imminent danger of going out while he was speaking), he went on with his narrative in these words:

"Well, the house, the estate, the mine, and the fisheries of Porthgenna were all publicly put up for sale a few months after Mrs. Treverton's death; but no offers were made for the property which it was possible to accept. The ruinous state of the house, the bad cultivation of the land, legal difficulties in connection with the mine, and quarter-day difficulties in the collection of the rents, all contributed to make Porthgenna what the auctioneers would call a bad lot to dispose of.

"Failing to sell the place, Captain Treverton could not be prevailed on to change his mind and live there again. The death of his wife almost broke his heart—for he was, by all accounts, just as fond of her as she had been of him—and the very sight of the place that was associated with the greatest affliction of his life became hateful to him. He removed, with his little girl and a relative of Mrs. Treverton, who was her governess, to our neighbourhood, and rented a pretty little cottage across the church fields.

"The house nearest to it was inhabited at that time by Leonard Frankland's father and mother. The new neighbours soon became intimate; and thus it happened that the couple whom I have been marrying this morning were brought up together as children, and fell in love with each other almost before they were out of their pinafores."

"Chennery, my dear fellow, I don't look as if I was sitting all on one side, do I?" cried Mr. Phippen, suddenly breaking into the vicar's narrative, with a look of alarm. "I am shocked to interrupt you; but surely your grass is amazingly soft in this part of the country. One of my camp-stool legs is getting shorter and shorter every moment. I'm drilling a hole! I'm toppling over! Gracious heavens! 1 feel myself going—I shall be down, Chennery; upon my life, I shall be down!"

"Stuff!" cried the vicar, pulling up first Mr. Phippen, and then Mr. Phippen's camp-stool, which had rooted itself in the grass, all on one side. "Here, come on to the gravel walk; you can't drill holes in that. What's the matter now?"

"Palpitations," said Mr. Phippen, dropping his umbrella, and placing his hand over his heart, "and bile. I see those black spots again—those infernal, lively black spots dancing before my eyes. Chennery, suppose you consult some agricultural friend about the quality of your grass. Take my word for it, your lawn is softer than it ought to be.—Lawn!" repeated Mr. Phippen to himself, contemptuously, as he turned round to pick up his umbrella. "It isn't a lawn—it is a bog!"

"There, sit down," said the vicar, "and don't pay the palpitations and the black spots the compliment of bestowing the smallest attention on them. Do you want anything to drink? Shall it be physic, or beer, or what?"

"No, no! I am so unwilling to give trouble," answered Mr. Phippen. "I would rather suffer—rather, a great deal. I think if you would go on with your story, Chennery, it would compose me. I have not the faintest idea of what led to it, but I think you were saying something interesting on the subject of pinafores!"

"Nonsense!" said Doctor Chennery. "I was only telling you of the fondness between the two children who have now grown up to be man and wife. And I was going on to tell you that Captain Treverton, shortly after he settled in our neighbourhood, took to the active practice of his profession again. Nothing else seemed to fill up the gap that the loss of Mrs. Treverton had made in his life.

"Having good interest with the Admiralty, he can always get a ship when he applies for one; and up to the present time, with intervals on shore, he has resolutely stuck to the sea—though he is getting, as his daughter and his friends think, rather too old for it now. Don't look puzzled, Phippen; I am not going so wide of the mark as you think. These are some of the necessary particulars that must be stated first. And now they are comfortably disposed of, I can get round at last to the main part of my story—the sale of Porthgenna Tower. What is it now? Do you want to get up again?"

Yes, Mr. Phippen did want to get up again, for the purpose of composing the palpitations and dispersing the black spots, by trying the experiment of a little gentle exercise. He was most unwilling to occasion any trouble, but would his worthy friend Chennery give him an arm, and carry the camp-stool, and walk slowly in the direction of the school-room window, so as to keep Miss Sturch within easy hailing distance, in case it became necessary to try the last resource of taking a composing draught?

The vicar, whose inexhaustible good nature was proof against every trial that Mr. Phippen's dyspeptic infirmities could inflict on it, complied with all these requests, and went on with his story, unconsciously adopting the tone and manner of a good-humoured parent who was doing his best to soothe the temper of a fretful child.

"I told you," he said, "that the elder Mr. Frankland and Captain Treverton were near neighbours here. They had not been long acquainted before the one found out from the other that Porthgenna Tower was for sale. On first hearing this, old Frankland asked a few questions about the place, but said not a word on the subject of purchasing it.

"Soon after that the Captain got a ship and went to sea. During his absence old Frankland privately set off for Cornwall to look at the estate, and to find out all he could about its advantages and defects from the persons left in charge of the house and lands. He said nothing when he came back, until Captain Treverton returned from his first cruise; and then the old gentleman spoke out one morning, in his quiet, decided way.

"'Treverton,' said he, 'if you will sell Porthgenna Tower at the price at which you bought it in, when you tried to dispose of it by auction, write to your lawyer, and tell him to take the title-deeds to mine, and ask for the purchase-money.'

"Captain Treverton was naturally a little astonished at the readiness of this offer; but people like myself, who knew old Frankland's history, were not so surprised. His fortune had been made by trade, and he was foolish enough to be always a little ashamed of acknowledging that one simple and creditable fact. The truth was, that his ancestors had been landed gentry of importance' before the time of the Civil War, and the old gentleman's great ambition was to sink the merchant in the landed grandee, and to leave his son to succeed him in the character of a squire of large estate and great county influence.

"He was willing to devote half his fortune to accomplish this scheme; but half his fortune would not buy him such an estate as he wanted, in an important agricultural county like ours. Rents are high, and land is made the most of with us. An estate as extensive as the estate at Porthgenna would fetch more than double the money which Captain Treverton could venture to ask for it, if it were situated in these parts.

"Old Frankland was well aware of that fact, and attached all possible importance to it. Besides, there was something in the feudal look of Porthgenna Tower, and in the right over the mine and fisheries, which the purchase of the estate included, that flattered his notions of restoring the family greatness.

"Here he and his son after him could lord it, as he thought, on a large scale, and direct at their sovereign will and pleasure the industry of hundreds of poor people, scattered along the coast, or huddled together in the little villages inland. This was a tempting prospect, and it could be secured for forty thousand pounds—which was just ten thousand pounds less than he had made up his mind to give, when he first determined to metamorphose himself from a plain merchant into a magnificent landed gentleman.

"People who knew these facts were, as I have said, not much surprised at Mr. Frankland's readiness to purchase Porthgenna Tower; and Captain Treverton, it is hardly necessary to say, was not long in clinching the bargain on his side. The estate changed hands; and away went old Frankland, with a tail of wiseacres from London at his heels, to work the mine and the fisheries on new scientific principles, and to beautify the old house from top to bottom with brand-new mediaeval decorations under the direction of a gentleman who was said to be an architect, but who looked, to my mind, the very image of a Popish priest in disguise. "Wonderful plans and projects were they not? And how do you think they succeeded?"

"Do tell me, my dear fellow!" was the answer that fell from Mr. Phippen's lips.—"I wonder whether Miss Sturch keeps a bottle of camphor julep in the family medicine-chest?" was the thought that passed through Mr. Phippen's mind.

"Tell you!" exclaimed the vicar. "Why, of course, every one of his plans turned out a complete failure. His Cornish tenantry received him as an interloper. The antiquity of his family made no impression upon them. It might be an old family, but it was not a Cornish family, and, therefore, it was of no importance in their eyes. They would have gone to the world's end for the Trevertons; but not a man would move a step out of his way for the Franklands. As for the mine, it seemed to be inspired with the same mutinous spirit that possessed the tenantry.

" The wiseacres from London blasted in all directions on the profoundest scientific principles, and brought about sixpenny-worth of ore to the surface for every five pounds spent in getting it up. The fisheries turned out little better. A new plan for curing pilchards, which was a marvel of economy in theory, proved to be a perfect phenomenon of extravagance in practice.

" The only item of luck in old Frankland's large sum of misfortunes was produced by his quarrelling in good time with the mediaeval architect, who was like a Popish priest in disguise. This fortunate event saved the new owner of Porthgenna all the money he might otherwise have spent in restoring and redecorating the whole suite of rooms on the north side of the house, which had been left to go to rack and ruin for more than fifty years past, and which remain in their old neglected condition to this day.

"To make a long story short, after uselessly spending more thousands of pounds at Porthgenna than I should like to reckon up, old Frankland gave in at last, left the place in disgust to the care of his steward, who was charged never to lay out another farthing on it, and returned to this neighbourhood. Being in high dudgeon, and happening to catch Captain Treverton on shore when he got back, the first thing he did was to abuse Porthgenna and all the people about it a little too vehemently in the Captain's presence.

"This led to a coolness between the two neighbours, which might have ended in the breaking off of all intercourse, but for the children on either side, who would see each other just as often as ever, and who ended, by dint of wilful persistency, in putting an end to the estrangement between the fathers by making it look simply ridiculous. Here, in my opinion, lies the most curious part of the story.

"Important family interests depended on those two young people falling in love with each other; and wonderful to relate, that (as you know, after my confession at breakfast-time) was exactly what they did. Here is a case of the most romantic love-match, which is also the marriage, of all others, that the parents on both sides had the strongest worldly interest in promoting. Shakespeare may say what he pleases, the course of true love does run smooth sometimes.

"Never was the marriage service performed to better pur-pose than when I read it this morning. The estate being entailed on Leonard, Captain Treverton's daughter now goes back, in the capacity of mistress, to the house and lands which her father said. Rosamond being an only child, the purchase-money of Porth-genna, which old Frankland once lamented as money thrown away, will now, when the Captain dies, be the marriage-portion of young Frankland's wife. I don't know what you think of the beginning and middle of my story, Phippen, but the end ought to satisfy you, at any rate. Did you ever hear of a bride and bride-groom who started with fairer prospects in life than our bride and bridegroom of today?"

Before Mr. Phippen could make any reply, Miss Sturch put her head out of the schoolroom window; and seeing the two gentlemen approaching, beamed on them with her invariable smile. Then addressing the vicar, said in her softest tones:

"I regret extremely to trouble you, sir, but I find Robert very intractable this morning with his Multiplication table."

"Where does he stick now?" asked Doctor Chennery.

"At seven times eight, sir," replied Miss Sturch.

"Bob!' shouted the vicar through the window. "Seven times eight?"

"Forty-three," answered the whimpering voice of the invis-ible Bob.

"You shall have one more chance before I get my cane," said Doctor Chennery. "Now, then, look out! Seven times—"

"My dear, good friend," interposed Mr, Phippen, "if you cane that very unhappy boy he will scream. My nerves have been tried once this morning by the camp-stool. I shall be totally shattered if 1 hear screams. Give me time to get out of the way, and allow me also to spare dear Miss Sturch the sad spectacle of correction (so shocking to sensibilities like hers) by asking her for a little camphor julep, and so giving her an excuse for getting out of the way like me. I think 1 could have done without the camphor julep under any other circumstances; but I ask for it unhesitatingly now, as much for Miss Sturch's sake as for the sake of my own poor nerves.—Have you got camphor julep, Miss Sturch? Say yes, I beg and entreat, and give me an opportunity of escorting you out of the way of the screams."

While Miss Sturch—whose well-trained sensibilities were proof against the longest paternal caning and the loudest filial acknowledgment of it in the way of screams—tripped upstairs to fetch the camphor julep, as smiling and self-possessed as ever, Master Bob, finding himself left alone with his sisters in the school-room, sidled up to the youngest of the two, produced from the pocket of his trousers three frowsy acidulated drops looking very much the worse for wear, and, attacking Miss Amelia on the weak, or greedy side of her character, artfully offered the drops in exchange for information on the subject of seven times eight. "You like 'em?" whispered Bob.

"Oh, don't I!" answered Amelia.

"Seven times eight?" asked Bob.

"Fifty-six," answered Amelia.

"Sure?" said Bob.

"Certain," said Amelia.

The drops changed hands, and the catastrophe of the domestic drama changed with them. Just as Miss Sturch appeared with the camphor julep at the garden door, in the character of medical Hebe to Mr. Phippen, her intractable pupil showed himself to his father at the school-room window, in the character, arithmetically speaking, of a reformed son. The cane reposed for the day; and Mr. Phippen drank his glass of camphor julep with a mind at ease on the twin subjects of Miss Sturch's sensibilities and Master Bob's screams.

"Most gratifying in every way," said the Martyr to Dyspepsia, smacking his lips with great relish, as he drained the last drops out of the glass. "My nerves are spared, Miss Sturch's feelings are spared, and the dear boy's back is spared. You have no idea how relieved I feel, Chennery. Whereabouts were we in that delightful story of yours when this little domestic interruption occurred?"

"At the end of it, to be sure," said the vicar.

"The bride and bridegroom are some miles on their way by this time to spend the honeymoon at St. Swithin's-on-Sea. Captain Treverton is only left behind for a day. He received his sailing orders on Monday, and he will be off to Portsmouth tomorrow morning to take command of his ship. Though he won't admit it in plain words, I happen to know that Rosamond has persuaded him to make this his last cruise. She has a plan for getting him back to Porthgenna, to live there with her husband, which I hope and believe will succeed.

"The west rooms at the old house, in one of which Mrs. Treverton died, are not to be used at all by the young married couple. They have engaged a builder—a sensible, practical man, this time—to survey the neglected north rooms, with a view to their redecoration and thorough repair in every way. This part of the house cannot possibly be associated with any melancholy recollections in Captain Treverton's mind, for neither he nor anyone else ever entered it during the period of his residence at Porthgenna.

"Considering the change in the look of the place which this project of repairing the north rooms is sure to produce, and taking into account also the softening effect of time on all painful recollections, I should say there was a fair prospect of Captain Treverton's returning to pass the end of his days among his old tenantry.

"It will be a great chance for Leonard Frankland if he does, for he would be sure to dispose the people at Porthgenna kindly toward their new master. Introduced among his Cornish tenants under Captain Treverton's wing, Leonard is sure to get on well with them, provided he abstains from showing too much of the family pride which he has inherited from his father.

"He is a little given to overrate the advantages of birth and the importance of rank—but that is really the only noticeable defect in his character. In all other respects I can honestly say of him that he deserves what he has got—the best wife in the world. What a life of happiness, Phippen, seems to be awaiting these lucky young people! It is a bold thing to say of any mortal creatures; but, look as far as I may, not a cloud can I see anywhere on their future prospects."

"You excellent creature!" exclaimed Mr. Phippen, affectionately squeezing the vicar's hand. "How I enjoy hearing you! how I luxuriate in your bright view of life!"

"And is it not the true view especially in the case of young Frankland and his wife?" inquired the vicar.

"If you ask me," said Mr. Phippen, with a mournful smile, and a philosophic calmness of manner, "I can only answer that the direction of a man's speculative views depends—not to mince the matter—on the state of his secretions. Your biliary secretions, dear friend, are all right, and you take bright views. My biliary secretions are all wrong, and I take dark views. You look at the future prospects of this young married couple, and say there is no cloud over them.

"I don't dispute the assertion, not having the pleasure of knowing either bride or bridegroom. But I look up at the sky over our heads—I remember that there was not a cloud on it when we first entered the garden—I now see, just over those two trees growing so close together, a cloud that has appeared unexpectedly from nobody knows where—and I draw my own conclusions. Such," said Mr. Phippen, ascending the garden steps on his way into the house, "is my philosophy. It may be tinged with bile, but it is philosophy for all that."

"All the philosophy in the world," said the vicar, following his guest up the steps, "will not shake my conviction that Leonard Frankland and his wife have a happy future before them."

Mr. Phippen laughed, and, waiting on the steps till his host joined him, took Doctor Chennery's arm in the friendliest manner.

"You have told a charming story, Chennery," he said, "and you have ended it with a charming sentiment. But, my dear friend, though your healthy mind (influenced by an enviably easy digestion) despises my bilious philosophy, don't quite forget the cloud over the two trees. Look up at it now—it is getting darker and bigger already."

CHAPTER 3
THE BRIDE AND BRIDEGROOM

Under the roof of a widowed mother, Miss Mowlem lived humbly at St. Swithin's-on-Sea.

In the spring of the year eighteen hundred and forty-four, the heart of Miss Mowlem's widowed mother was gladdened by a small legacy. Turning over in her mind the various uses to which the money might be put, the discreet old lady finally decided on investing it in furniture, on fitting up the first floor and the second floor of her house in the best taste, and on hanging a card in the parlour window to inform the public that she had furnished apartments to let.

By the summer the apartments were ready, and the card was put up. It had hardly been exhibited a week before a dignified personage in black applied to look at the rooms, expressed himself as satisfied with their appearance, and engaged them for a month certain, for a newly married lady and gentleman, who might be expected to take possession in a few days. The dignified personage in black was Captain Treverton's servant, and the lady and gentleman, who arrived in due time to take possession, were Mr. and Mrs. Frankland.

The natural interest which Mrs. Mowlem felt in her youthful first lodgers was necessarily vivid in its nature; but it was apathy itself compared to the sentimental interest which her daughter took in observing the manners and customs of the lady and gentleman in their capacity of bride and bridegroom.

From the moment when Mr. and Mrs. Frankland entered the house Miss Mowlem began to study them with all the ardour of an industrious scholar who attacks a new branch of knowledge. At every spare moment of the day, this industrious young lady occupied herself in stealing upstairs to collect observations and in running downstairs to communicate them to her mother.

By the time the married couple had been in the house a week, Miss Mowlem had made such good use of her eyes, ears and opportunities that she could have written a seven days' diary of the lives of Mr. and Mrs. Frankland with the truth and minuteness of Mr. Samuel Pepys himself.

But, learn as much as we may, the longer we live the more information there is to acquire. Seven days' patient accumulation of facts in connection with the honeymoon had not placed Miss Mowlem beyond the reach of further discoveries.

On the morning of the eighth day, after bringing down the breakfast tray, this observant spinster stole upstairs again, according to custom, to drink at the spring of knowledge through the keyhole channel of the drawing-room door. After an absence of five minutes she descended to the kitchen, breathless with excitement, to announce a fresh discovery in connection with Mr. and Mrs. Frankland to her venerable mother.

"Whatever do you think she's doing now," cried Miss Mowlem, with widely opened eyes and highly elevated hands.

"Nothing that's useful," answered Mrs. Mowlem, with sarcastic readiness.

"She's actually sitting on his knee! Mother, did you ever sit on father's knee when you were married?"

"Certainly not, my dear. When me and your poor father married, we were neither of us flighty young people, and we knew better."

"She's got her bead on his shoulder," proceeded Miss Mowlem, more and more agitatedly, "and her arms round his neck both her arms, mother, as tight as can be."

"I won't believe it," exclaimed Mrs. Mowlem, indignantly. "A ladylike her, with riches, and accomplishments, and all that, demean herself like a housemaid with a sweetheart. Don't tell me, I won't believe it!"

It was true enough, for all that. There were plenty of chairs in Mrs. Mowlem's drawing-room; there were three beautifully bound books on Mrs. Mowlem's Pembroke table (the *Antiquities of St. Swithin's, Smallridge's Sermons'* and Klopstock's *Messiah* in English prose)—Mrs. Frankland might have sat on purple morocco leather, stuffed with the best horse-hair, might have informed and soothed her mind with archaeological diversions, with orthodox native theology, and with devotional poetry of foreign origin—and yet, so frivolous is the nature of woman, she was perverse enough to prefer doing nothing, and perching herself uncomfortably on her husband's knee!

She sat for some time in the undignified position which Miss Mowlem had described with such graphic correctness to her mother—then drew back a little, raised her head, and looked earnestly into the quiet, meditative face of the blind man.

"Lenny, you are very silent this morning," she said. "What are you thinking about? If you will tell me all your thoughts, I will tell you all mine."

"Would you really care to hear all my thoughts?" asked Leonard.

"Yes; all. I shall be jealous of any thoughts that you keep to yourself. Tell me what you were thinking of just now! Me?"

"Not exactly of you."

"More shame for you. Are you tired of me in eight days? I have not thought of anybody but you ever since we have been here. Ah! you laugh. Oh, Lenny, I do love you so; how can I think of anybody but you? No! I shan't kiss you. I want to know what you were thinking about first."

"Of a dream, Rosamond, that I had last night. Ever since the first days of my blindness—Why, I thought you were not going to kiss me again till I had told you what I was thinking about?"

"I can't help kissing you, Lenny, when you talk of the loss of your sight. Tell me, my poor love, do I help to make up for that loss? Are you happier than you used to be? and have I some share in making that happiness, though it is ever so little?"

She turned her head away as she spoke, but Leonard was too quick for her. His inquiring fingers touched her cheek. "Rosamond, you are crying," he said.

"I crying!" she answered, with a sudden assumption of gayety. "No," she continued, after a moment's pause. "I will never deceive you, love, even in the veriest trifle. My eyes serve for both of us now, don't they? you depend on me for all that your touch fails to tell you, and I must never be unworthy of my trust—must I? I did cry, Lenny—but only a very little. I don't know how it was, but I never, in all my life, seemed to pity you and feel for you as I did just at that moment. Never mind, I've done now. Go on—do go on with what you were going to say."

"I was going to say, Rosamond, that I have observed one curious thing about myself since I lost my sight. I dream a great deal, but I never dream of myself as a blind man. I often visit in my dreams places that I saw and people whom I knew when I had my sight, and though I feel as much myself, at those visionary times, as I am now when I am wide-awake, I never by any chance feel blind.

"I wander about all sorts of old walks in my sleep, and never grope my way. I talk to all sorts of old friends in my sleep, and see the expression in their faces which, waking, I shall never see again. I have lost my sight more than a year now, and yet it was like the shock of a new discovery to me to wake up last night from my dream, and remember suddenly that I was blind."

"What dream was it, Lenny?"

"Only a dream of the place where I first met you when we were both children. I saw the glen, as it was years ago, with the great twisted roots of the trees, and the blackberry bushes twining about them in a still shadowed light that came through thick leaves from the rainy sky. I saw the mud on the walk in the middle of the glen, with the marks of the cows' hoofs in some places, and the sharp circles in others where some countrywoman had been lately trudging by on pattens.

"I saw the muddy water running down on either side of the path after the shower; and I saw you, Rosamond, a naughty girl, all covered with clay and wet—just as you were in the reality— sailing your bright blue pelisse and your pretty little chubby hands by making a dam to stop the running water, and laughing at the indignation of your nurse-maid when she tried to pull you away and take you home. I saw all that exactly as it really was in the by-gone time; but, strangely enough, I did not see myself as the boy I then was.

"You were a little girl, and the glen was in its old neglected state, and yet, though I was all in the past so far, I was in the present as regarded myself. Throughout the whole dream I was uneasily conscious of being a grown man—of being, in short, exactly what I am now, excepting always that I was not blind."

"What a memory you must have, love, to be able to recall all those little circumstances after the years that have passed since that wet day in the glen! How well you recollect what I was as a child! Do you remember in the same vivid way what I looked like a year ago when you saw me—Oh, Lenny, it almost breaks my heart to think of it!—when you saw me for the last time?"

"Do I remember, Rosamond! My last look at your face has painted your portrait in my memory in colours that can never change. I have many pictures in my mind, but your picture is the clearest and brightest of all."

"And it is the picture of me at my best—painted in my youth, dear, when my face was always confessing how I loved you, though my lips said nothing. There is some consolation in that thought. When years have passed over us both, Lenny, and when time begins to set his mark on me, you will not say to yourself, 'My Rosamond is beginning to fade; she grows less and less like what she was when I married her.' I shall never grow old, love, for you! The bright young picture in your mind will still be my picture when my cheeks are wrinkled and my hair is gray!"

"Still your picture—always the same, grow as old as I may."

"But are you sure it is clear in every part? Are there no doubtful lines, no unfinished corners anywhere? I have not altered yet since you saw me—I am just what I was a year ago. Suppose I ask you what I am like now, could you tell me without making a mistake?"

"Try me."

"May I? You shall be put through a complete catechism! I don't tire you sitting on your knee, do I? Well, in the first place, how tall am I when we both stand up side by side?"

"You just reach to my ear."

"Quite right, to begin with. Now for the next question. What does my hair look like in your portrait?"

"It is dark brown—there is a great deal of it—and it grows

rather too low on your forehead for the taste of some people—"

"Never mind about 'some people'; does it grow too low for your taste?"

"Certainly not. I like it to grow low; I like all those little natural waves that it makes against your forehead; I like it taken back, as you wear it, in plain bands, which leave your ears and your cheeks visible; and above all things, I like that big glossy knot that it makes where it is all gathered up together at the back of your head."

"Oh, Lenny, how well you remember me, so far! Now go a little lower."

"A little lower is down to your eyebrows. They are very nicely shaped eyebrows in my picture—"

"Yes, but they have a fault. Come! tell me what the fault is."

"They are not quite so strongly marked as they might be."

"Right again! And my eyes?"

"Brown eyes, large eyes, wakeful eyes, that are always looking about them. Eyes that can be very soft at one time, and very bright at another. Eyes tender and clear, just at the present moment, but capable, on very slight provocation, of opening rather too widely, and looking rather too brilliantly resolute."

"Mind you don't make them look so now! What is there below the eyes?"

"A nose that is not quite big enough to be in proper proportion with them. A nose that has a slight tendency to be—"

"Don't say the horrid English word! Spare my feelings by putting it in French. Say *retroussé*, and skip over my nose as fast as possible."

"I must stop at the mouth, then, and own that it is as near perfection as possible. The lips are lovely in shape, fresh in colour, and irresistible in expression. They smile in my portrait, and I am sure they are smiling at me now."

"How could they do otherwise when they are getting so much praise? My vanity whispers to me that I had better stop the catechism here. If I talk about my complexion, I shall only hear that it is of the dusky sort; and that there is never red enough in it except when I am walking, or confused, or angry. If I ask a question about my figure, I shall receive the dreadful answer, 'You are dangerously inclined to be fat.' If I say, How do I dress? I shall be told, Not soberly enough; you are as fond as a child of gay colours—No! I will venture no more questions.

"But, vanity apart, Lenny, I am so glad, so proud, so happy to find that you can keep the image of me clearly in your mind. I shall do my best now to look and dress like your last remembrance of me. My love of loves! I will do you credit—I will try if I can't make you envied for your wife. You deserve a hundred thousand kisses for saying your catechism so well—and there they are!"

While Mrs. Frankland was conferring the reward of merit on her husband, the sound of a faint, small, courteously significant cough made itself timidly audible in a corner of the room. Turning round instantly, with the quickness that characterized all her actions, Mrs. Frankland, to her horror and indignation, confronted Miss Mowlem standing just inside the door, with a letter in her hand and a blush of sentimental agitation on her simpering face.

"You wretch! how dare you come in without knocking at the door?" cried Rosamond, starting to her feet with a stamp, and passing in an instant from the height of fondness to the height of indignation.

Miss Mowlem shook guiltily before the bright, angry eyes that looked through and through her, turned very pale, held out the letter apologetically, and said in her meekest tones that she was very sorry.

"Sorry!" exclaimed Rosamond, getting even more irritated by the apology than she had been by the intrusion, and showing it by another stamp of the foot; "who cares whether you are sorry? I don't want your sorrow—I won't have it. I never was so insulted in my life—never, you mean, prying, inquisitive creature!"

"Rosamond! Rosamond! pray don't forget yourself!" interposed the quiet voice of Mr. Frankland.

"Lenny, dear, I can't help it! That creature would drive a saint mad. She has been prying after us ever since we have been here—you have, you ill-bred, indelicate woman!—I suspected it before—I am certain of it now! Must we lock our doors to keep you out?—we won't lock our doors! Fetch the bill! We give you warning. Mr. Frankland gives you warning—don't you, Lenny?

"I'll pack up all your things, dear: she shan't touch one of them, Go downstairs and make out your bill, and give your mother warning. Mr. Frankland says he won't have his rooms burst into, and his doors listened at by inquisitive women—and I say so, too. Put that letter down on the table—unless you want to open it and read it—put it down, you audacious woman, and fetch the bill, and tell your mother we are going to leave the house directly!"

At this dreadful threat, Miss Mowlem, who was soft and timid, as well as curious, by nature, wrung her hands in despair, and overflowed meekly in a shower of tears.

"Oh! good gracious heavens above!" cried Miss Mowlem, addressing herself distractedly to the ceiling, "what will mother say! whatever will become of me now! Oh, ma'am! I thought I knocked—I did, indeed! Oh, ma'am! I humbly beg pardon, and I'll never intrude again. Oh, ma'am! mother's a widow, and this is the first time we have let the lodgings, and the furniture's swallowed up all our money, and oh, ma'am! ma'am! how I shall catch it if you go!" Here words failed Miss Mowlem, and hysterical sobs pathetically supplied their place.

"Rosamond!" said Mr. Frankland. There was an accent of sorrow in his voice this time, as well as an accent of remonstrance. Rosamond's quick ear caught the alteration in his tone. As she looked round at him her colour changed, her head drooped a little, and her whole expression altered on the instant. She stole gently to her husband's side with softened, saddened eyes, and put her lips caressingly close to his ear.

"Lenny," she whispered, "have I made you angry with me?"

"I can't be angry with you, Rosamond," was the quiet answer. "I only wish, love, that you could have controlled yourself a little sooner."

"I am so sorry—so very, very sorry!" The fresh, soft lips came closer still to his ear as they whispered these penitent words; and the cunning little hand crept up tremblingly round his neck and began to play with his hair. "So sorry, and so ashamed of myself! But it was enough to make almost anybody angry, just at first—wasn't it, dear? And you will forgive me—won't you, Lenny?—if I promise never to behave so badly again?

"Never mind that wretched whimpering fool at the door," said Rosamond, undergoing a slight relapse as she looked round at Miss Mowlem, standing immovably repentant against the wall, with her face buried in a dingy-white pocket-handkerchief. "I'll make it up with her; I'll stop her crying; I'll take her out of the room; I'll do anything in the world that's kind to her, if you will only forgive me."

"A polite word or two is all that is wanted—nothing more than a polite word or two," said Mr. Frankland, rather coldly and constrainedly.

"Don't cry anymore, for goodness' sake!" said Rosamond, walking straight up to Miss Mowlem, and pulling the dingy-white pocket-handkerchief away from her face without the least ceremony. "There! leave off, will you? I am very sorry I was in a passion—though you had no business to come in without knocking—I never meant to distress you, and I'll never say a hard word to you again, if you will only knock at the door for the future, and leave off crying now.

"Do leave off crying, you tiresome creature! We are not going away. We don't want your mother, or the bill, or anything. Here! here's a present for you, if you'll leave off crying. Here's my neck-ribbon—I saw you trying it on yesterday afternoon, when I was lying down on the bedroom sofa and you thought I was asleep. Never mind; I'm not angry about that. Take the ribbon—take it as a peace-offering, if you won't as a present. You shall take it!—No, I don't mean that—I mean, please take it! There, I've pinned it on. And now, shake hands and be friends, and go upstairs and see how it looks in the glass."

With these words, Mrs. Frankland opened the door, administered, under the pretence of a pat on the shoulder, a good-humoured shove to the amazed and embarrassed Miss Mowlem, closed the door again, and resumed her place in a moment on her husband's knee.

"I've made it up with her, dear. I've sent her away with my bright green ribbon, and it makes her look as yellow as a guinea, and as ugly as—" Rosamond stopped, and looked anxiously into Mr. Frankland's face. "Lenny !" she said, sadly, putting her cheek against his, "are you angry with me still?"

"My love, I was never angry with you. I never can be."

"I will always keep my temper down for the future, Lenny!"

"I am sure you will, Rosamond. But never mind that. I am not thinking of your temper now."

"Of what, then?"

"Of the apology you made to Miss Mowlem."

"Did I not say enough? I'll call her back if you like—I'll make another penitent speech I'll do anything but kiss her. I really can't do that—I can't kiss anybody now but you."

"My dear, dear love, how very much like a child you are still in some of your ways! You said more than enough to Miss Mowlem—far more. And if you will pardon me for making the remark, I think in your generosity and good-nature you a little forgot yourself with the young woman. I don't so much allude to your giving her the ribbon—though, perhaps, that might have been done a little less familiarly—but, from what I heard you say, I infer that you actually went the length of shaking hands with her."

"Was that wrong? I thought it was the kindest way of making it up."

"My dear, it is an excellent way of making it up between equals. But consider the difference between your station in society and Miss Mowlem's"

"I will try and consider it, if you wish me, love. But I think I take after my father, who never troubles his head (dear old man!)

about differences of station. I can't help liking people who are kind to me, without thinking whether they are above my rank or below it; and when I got cool, I must confess I felt just as vexed with myself for frightening and distressing that unlucky Miss Mowlem as if her station had been equal to mine. I will try to think as you do, Lenny; but I am very much afraid that I have got, without knowing exactly how, to be what the newspapers call a Radical."

"My dear Rosamond! don't talk of yourself in that way, even in joke. You ought to be the last person in the world to confuse those distinctions in rank on which the whole well-being of society depends."

"Does it really? And yet, dear, we don't seem to have been created with such very wide distinctions between us. We have all got the same number of arms and legs; we are all hungry and thirsty, and hot in the summer and cold in the winter; we all laugh when we are pleased, and cry when we are distressed; and, surely, we have all got very much the same feelings, whether we are high or whether we are low. I could not have loved you better, Lenny, than I do now if I had been a duchess, or less than I do now if I had been a servant-girl."

"My love, you are not a servant-girl. And, as to what you say about being a duchess, let me remind you that you are not so much below a duchess as you seem to think. Many a lady of high title cannot look back oil such a line of ancestors as yours. Your father's family, Rosamond, is one of the oldest in England: even my father's family hardly dates back so far; and we were landed gentry when many a name in the peerage was not heard of. It is really almost laughably absurd to hear you talking of yourself as a Radical."

"I won't talk of myself so again, Lenny—only don't look so serious. I will be a Tory, dear, if you will give me a kiss, and let me sit on your knee a little longer."

Mr. Frankland's gravity was not proof against his wife's change of political principles, and the conditions which she annexed to it. His face cleared up, and he laughed almost as gaily as Rosamond herself.

"By-the-by," he said, after an interval of silence had given him time to collect his thoughts, "did I not hear you tell Miss Mowlem to put a letter down on the table? Is it a letter for you or for me?"

"Ah! I forgot all about the letter," said Rosamond, running to the table. "It is for you, Lenny—and, goodness me! here's the Porthgenna postmark on it."

"It must be from the builder whom I sent down to the old house about the repairs. Lend me your eyes, love, and let us hear what he says."

Rosamond opened the letter, drew a stool to her husband's feet, and, sitting down with her arms on his knees, read as follows:

To Leonard Frankland, Esq.:

Sir—Agreeably to the instructions with which you favoured me, I have proceeded to survey Porthgenna Tower, with a view to ascertaining what repairs the house in general, and the north side of it in particular, may stand in need of.

As regards the outside, a little cleaning and new pointing is all that the building wants. The walls and foundations seem made to last forever. Such strong, solid work I never set eyes on before.

Inside the house, I cannot report so favourably. The rooms in the west front, having been inhabited during the period of Captain Treverton's occupation, and having been well looked after since, are in tolerably sound condition. I should say two hundred pounds would cover the expense of all repairs in my line which these rooms need. This sum would not include the restoration of the western staircase, which has given a little in some places, and the banisters of which are decidedly insecure from the first to the second landing. From twenty-five to thirty pounds would suffice to set this all right.

In the rooms on the north front, the state of dilapidation,

from top to bottom, is as bad as can be. From all that I could ascertain, nobody ever went near these rooms in Captain Treverton's time, or has ever entered them since. The people who now keep the house have a superstitious dread of opening any of the north doors, in consequence of the time that has elapsed since any living being has passed through them.

Nobody would volunteer to accompany me in my survey, and nobody could tell me which keys fitted which room doors in any part of the north side. I could find no plan containing the names or numbers of the rooms; nor, to my surprise, were there any labels attached separately to the keys. They were given to me, all hanging together on a large ring, with an ivory label on it, which was only marked—Keys of the North Rooms.

I take the liberty of mentioning these particulars in order to account for my having, as you might think, delayed my stay at Porthgenna Tower longer than is needful. I lost nearly a whole day in taking the keys off the ring, and fitting them at hazard to the right doors. And I occupied some hours of another day in marking each door with a number on the outside, and putting a corresponding label to each key, before I replaced it on the ring, in order to prevent the possibility of future errors and delays.

As I hope to furnish you, in a few days, with a detailed estimate of the repairs needed in the north part of the house, from basement to roof, I need only say here that they will occupy some time, and will be of the most extensive nature. The beams of the staircase and the flooring of the first story have got the dry rot. The damp in some rooms, and the rats in others, have almost destroyed the wainscotings.

Four of the mantelpieces have given out from the walls, and all the ceilings are either stained, cracked, or peeled away in large patches. The flooring is, in general, in a better condition than I had anticipated; but the shutters and window-sashes are so warped as to be useless. It is only fair to acknowledge that the expense of setting all these things to rights—that is to say, of making the rooms safe and habitable, and of putting them in proper condition for the upholsterer—will be considerable.

I would respectfully suggest, in the event of your feeling any surprise or dissatisfaction at the amount of my esti-mate, that you should name a friend in whom you place confidence, to go over the north rooms with me, keeping my estimate in his hand. I will undertake to prove, if need-ful, the necessity of each separate repair, and the justice of each separate charge for the same, to the satisfaction of any competent and impartial person whom you may please to select.

Trusting to send you the estimate in a few days, I remain, sir,

Your humble servant,

Thomas Horlock."

"A very honest straightforward letter," said Mr. Frankland.

"I wish he had sent the estimate with it," said Rosamond. "Why could not the provoking man tell us at once in round numbers what the repairs will really cost?"

"I suspect, my dear, he was afraid of shocking us, if he men-tioned the amount in round numbers."

"That horrid money! It is always getting in one's way, and upsetting one's plans. If we haven't got enough, let us go and borrow of somebody who has. Do you mean to dispatch a friend to Porthgenna to go over the house with Mr. Horlock? If you do I know who I wish you would send."

"Who?"

"Me, if you please—under your escort, of course. Don't laugh, Lenny; I would be very sharp with Mr. Horlock; I would object to every one of his charges, and beat him down without mercy. I once saw a surveyor go over a house, and I know ex-actly what to do. You stamp on the floor, and knock at the walls, and scrape at the brick-work, and look up all the chimneys, and out of all the windows—sometimes you make notes in a little book, sometimes you measure with a foot-rule, sometimes you sit down all of a sudden, and think profoundly and the end of it is that you say the house will do very well indeed, if the tenant will pull out his purse and put it in proper repair."

"Well done, Rosamond! You have one more accomplishment than I knew of; and I suppose I have no choice now but to give you an opportunity of displaying it. If you don't object, my dear, to being associated with a professional assistant in the important business of checking Mr. Horlock's estimate, I don't object to paying a short visit to Porthgenna whenever you please especially—now I know that the west rooms are still habitable."

"Oh, how kind of you! how pleased I shall be! how I shall enjoy seeing the old place again before it is altered! I was only five years old, Lenny, when we left Porthgenna, and I am so anxious to see what I can remember of it, after such a long, long absence as mine. Do you know, I never saw anything of that ruinous north side of the house?—and I do so dote on old rooms!

"We will go all through them, Lenny. You shall have hold of my hand, and look with my eyes, and make as many discoveries as I do. I prophesy that we shall see ghosts, and find treasures, and hear mysterious noises—and, oh heavens! what clouds of dust we shall have to go through. Pouf! the very anticipation of them chokes me already!"

"Now we are on the subject of Porthgenna, Rosamond, let us be serious for one moment. It is clear to me that these repairs of the north rooms will cost a large sum of money. Now, my love, I consider no sum of money misspent, however large it may be, if it procures you pleasure. I am with you heart and soul—"

He paused. His wife's caressing arms were twining round his neck again, and her cheek was laid gently against his. "Go on, Lenny," she said, with such an accent of tenderness in the utterance of those three simple words that his speech failed him for the moment, and all his sensations seemed absorbed in the one luxury of listening.

"Rosamond," he whispered, "there is no music in the world

that touches me as your voice touches me now! I feel it all through me, as I used sometimes to feel the sky at night, in the time when I could see."

As he spoke, the caressing arms tightened round his neck, and the fervent lips softly took the place which the cheek had occupied. "Go on, Lenny," they repeated, happily as well as tenderly now, "you said you were with me, heart and soul. With me in. what?"

"In your project, love, for inducing your father to retire from his profession after this last cruise, and in your hope of prevailing on him to pass the evening of his days happily with us at Porthgenna. If the money spent in restoring the north rooms, so that we may all live in them for the future, does indeed so alter the look of the place to his eyes as to dissipate his old sorrowful associations with it, and to make his living there again a pleasure instead of a pain to him, I shall regard it as money well laid out. But, Rosamond, are you sure of the success of your plan before we undertake it? Have you dropped any hint of the Porthgenna project to your father?"

"I told him, Lenny, that I should never be quite comfortable unless he left the sea and came to live with us—and he said that he would. I did not mention a word about Porthgenna—nor did he—but he knows that we shall live there when we are settled, and he made no conditions when he promised that our home should be his home."

"Is the loss of your mother the only sad association he has with the place?"

"Not quite. There is another association, which has never been mentioned, but which I may tell you, because there are no secrets between us. My mother had a favourite maid who lived with her from the time of her marriage, and who was, accidentally, the only person present in her room when she died. I remember hearing, of this woman as being odd in her look and manner, and no great favourite with anybody but her mistress.

"Well, on the morning of my mother's death, she disappeared from the house in the strangest way, leaving behind her a most singular and mysterious letter to my father, asserting that in my mother's dying moments a secret had been confided to her which she was charged to divulge to her master when her mistress was no more; and adding that she was afraid to mention this secret, and that, to avoid being questioned about it, she had resolved on leaving the house forever.

"She had been gone some hours when the letter was opened—and she has never been seen or heard of since that time. This circumstance seemed to make almost as strong an impression on my father's mind as the shock of my mother's death. Our neighbours and servants all thought (as I think) that the woman was mad; but he never agreed with them, and I know that he has neither destroyed nor forgotten the letter from that time to this."

"A strange event, Rosamond—a very strange event. I don't wonder that it has made a lasting impression on him."

"Depend upon it, Lenny, the servants and the neighbours were right—the woman was mad. Anyway, however, it was certainly a singular event in our family. All old houses have their romance—and that is the romance of our house. But years and years have passed since then; and, what with time, and what with the changes we are going to make, I have no fear that my dear, good father will spoil our plans.

"Give him a new north garden at Porthgenna, where he can walk the decks, as I call it—give him new north rooms to live in—and I will answer for the result. But all this is in the future; let us get back to the present time. When shall we pay our flying visit to Porthgenna, Lenny, and plunge into the important business of checking Mr. Horlock's estimate for the repairs."

"We have three weeks more to stay here, Rosamond."

"Yes; and then we must go back to Long Beckley. I promised that best and biggest of men, the vicar, that we would pay our first visit to him. He is sure not to let us off under three weeks or a month."

"In that case, then, we had better say two months hence for the visit to Porthgenna. Is your writing-case in the room, Rosamond?"

"Yes; close by us, on the table."

"Write to Mr. Horlock then, love—and appoint a meeting in two months' time at the old house. Tell him also, as we must not trust ourselves on unsafe stairs—especially considering how dependent I am on banisters—to have the west staircase repaired immediately. And, while you have the pen in your hand, perhaps it may save trouble if you write a second note to the house-keeper at Porthgenna, to tell her when she may expect us."

Rosamond sat down gaily at the table, and dipped her pen in the ink with a little flourish of triumph.

"In two months," she exclaimed, joyfully, "I shall see the dear old place again! In two months, Lenny, our profane feet will be raising the dust in the solitudes of the North Rooms."

Book 3

Chapter 1
Timon of London

Timon of Athens retreated from an ungrateful world to a cavern by the sea-shore, vented his misanthropy in magnificent poetry, and enjoyed the honour of being called "My Lord." Timon of London took refuge from his species in a detached house at Bayswater—expressed his sentiments in shabby prose—and was only addressed as "Mr. Treverton." The one point of resemblance which it is possible to set against these points of contrast between the two Timons consisted in this: that their misanthropy was, at least, genuine. Both were incorrigible haters of mankind.

There is probably no better proof of the accuracy of that definition of man which describes him as an imitative animal, than is to be found in the fact that the verdict of humanity is always against any individual member of the species who presumes to differ from the rest. A man is one of a flock, and his wool must be of the general colour. He must drink when the rest drink, and graze where the rest graze.

Let him walk at noonday with perfect composure of countenance and decency of gait, with not the slightest appearance of vacancy in his eyes or wildness in his manner, from one end of Oxford Street to the other without his hat, and let every one of the thousands of hat-wearing people whom he passes be asked separately what they think of him, how many will abstain from deciding instantly that he is mad, on no other evidence than the evidence of his bare head?

Nay, more; let him politely stop each one of those passengers, and let him explain in the plainest form of words, and in the most intelligible manner, that his head feels more easy and comfortable without a hat than with one, how many of his fellow-mortals who decided that he was mad on first meeting him, will change their opinion when they part from him after hearing his explanation? In the vast majority of cases, the very explanation itself would be accepted as an excellent additional proof that the intellect of the hatless man was indisputably deranged.

Starting at the beginning of the march of life out of step with the rest of the mortal regiment, Andrew Treverton paid the penalty of his irregularity from his earliest days. He was a phenomenon in the nursery, a butt at school, and a victim at college. The ignorant nursemaid reported him as a queer child; the learned schoolmaster genteelly varied the phrase, and described him as an eccentric boy; the college tutor, harping on the same string, facetiously likened his head to a roof, and said there was a slate loose in it.

When a slate is loose, if nobody fixes it in time, it ends by falling off. In the roof of a house we view that consequence as a necessary result of neglect; in the roof of a man's head we are generally very much shocked and surprised by it.

Overlooked in some directions and misdirected in others, Andrew's uncouth capacities for good tried helplessly to shape themselves. The better side of his eccentricity took the form of friendship. He became violently and unintelligibly fond of one among his school-fellows—a boy who treated him with no especial consideration in the playground, and who gave him no particular help in the class.

Nobody could discover the smallest reason for it, but it was nevertheless a notorious fact that Andrew's pocket-money was always at this boy's service, that Andrew ran about after him like a dog, and that Andrew over and over again took the blame and punishment on his own shoulders which ought to have fallen on the shoulders of his friend.

When, a few years afterward, that friend went to college, the lad petitioned to be sent to college, too, and attached himself there more closely than ever to the strangely chosen comrade of his schoolboy days. Such devotion as this must have touched any man possessed of ordinary generosity of disposition.

It made no impression whatever on the inherently base nature of Andrew's friend. After three years of intercourse at college—intercourse which was all selfishness on one side and all self-sacrifice on the other—the end came, and the light was let in cruelly on Andrew's eyes. When his purse grew light in his friend's hand, and when his acceptances were most numerous on his friend's bills, the brother of his honest affection, the hero of his simple admiration, abandoned him to embarrassment, to ridicule, and to solitude, without the faintest affectation of penitence—without so much even as a word of farewell.

He returned to his father's house, a soured man at the outset of life—returned to be upbraided for the debts that he had contracted to serve the man who had heartlessly outraged and shamelessly cheated him. He left home in disgrace to travel on a small allowance. The travels were protracted, and they ended, as such travels often do, in settled expatriation.

The life he led, the company he kept, during his long residence abroad, did him permanent and fatal harm. When he at last returned to England, he presented himself in the most hopeless of all characters—the character of a man who believes in nothing. At this period of his life, his one chance for the future lay in the good results which his brother's influence over him might have produced.

The two had hardly resumed their intercourse of early days, when the quarrel occasioned by Captain Treverton's marriage broke it off forever. From that time, for all social interests and purposes, Andrew was a lost man. From that time he met the last remonstrances that were made to him by the last friends who took any interest in his fortunes always with the same bitter and hopeless form of reply:

"My dearest friend forsook and cheated me," he would say. "My only brother has quarrelled with me for the sake of a play-actress. What am I to expect of the rest of mankind after that? I have suffered twice for my belief in others—I will never suffer a third time. The wise man is the man who does not disturb his heart at its natural occupation of pumping blood through his body. I have gathered my experience abroad and at home, and have learned enough to see through the delusions of life which look like realities to other men's eyes. My business in this world is to eat, drink, sleep, and die. Everything else is superfluity—and I have done with it."

The few people who ever cared to inquire about him again, after being repulsed by such an avowal as this, heard of him three or four years after his brother's marriage in the neighbourhood of Bayswater. Local report described him as having bought the first cottage he could find which was cut off from other houses by a wall all around it.

It was further rumoured that he was living like a miser; that he had got an old man-servant, named Shrowl, who was even a greater enemy to mankind than himself; that he allowed no living soul, not even an occasional charwoman, to enter the house; that he was letting his beard grow, and that he had ordered his servant Shrowl to follow his example. In the year eighteen hundred and forty-four, the fact of a man's not shaving was regarded by the enlightened majority of the English nation as a proof of unsoundness of intellect.

At the present time Mr. Treverton's beard would only have interfered with his reputation for respectability. Seventeen years ago it was accepted as so much additional evidence in support of the old theory that his intellects were deranged. He was at that very time, as his stockbroker could have testified, one of the sharpest men of business in London; he could argue on the wrong side of any question with an acuteness of sophistry and sarcasm that Dr. Johnson himself might have envied; he kept his household accounts right to a farthing—but what did these advantages avail him, in the estimation of his neighbours, when he presumed to live on another plan than theirs, and when he wore a hairy certificate of lunacy on the lower part of his face?

We have advanced a little in the matter of partial toleration of beards since that time; but we have still a good deal of ground to get over. In the present year of progress, eighteen hundred and sixty-one, would the most trustworthy banker's clerk in the whole metropolis have the slightest chance of keeping his situation if he left off shaving his chin?

Common report, which calumniated Mr. Treverton as mad, had another error to answer for in describing him as a miser. He saved more than two-thirds of the income derived from his comfortable fortune, not because he liked hoarding up money, but because he had no enjoyment of the comforts and luxuries which money is spent in procuring.

To do him justice, his contempt for his own wealth was quite as hearty as his contempt for the wealth of his neighbours. Thus characteristically wrong in endeavouring to delineate his character, report was, nevertheless, for once in a way, inconsistently right in describing his manner of life. It was true that he had bought the first cottage he could find that was secluded within its own walls—true that nobody was allowed, on any pretence whatever, to enter his doors—and true that he had met with a servant, who was even bitterer against all mankind than himself, in the person of Mr. Shrowl.

The life these two led approached as nearly to the existence of the primitive man (or savage) as the surrounding conditions of civilization would allow. Admitting the necessity of eating and drinking, the first object of Mr. Treverton's ambition was to sustain life with the least possible dependence on the race of men who professed to supply their neighbours' bodily wants, and who, as he conceived, cheated them infamously on the strength of their profession.

Having a garden at the back of the house, Timon of London dispensed with the greengrocer altogether by cultivating his own vegetables. There was no room for growing wheat, or he would have turned farmer also on his own account; but he could outwit the miller and the baker, at any rate, by buying a sack of corn, grinding it in his own hand-mill, arid giving the flour to Shrowl to make into bread.

On the same principle, the meat for the house was bought wholesale of the City salesmen—the master and servant eating as much of it in the fresh state as they could, salting the rest, and setting butchers at defiance. As for drink, neither brewer nor publican ever had the chance of extorting a farthing from Mr. Treverton's pocket. He and Shrowl were satisfied with beer—and they brewed for themselves. With bread, vegetables, meat and malt liquor, these two hermits of modern days achieved the great double purpose of keeping life in and keeping tradesmen out.

Eating like primitive men, they lived in all other respects like primitive men also. They had pots, pans and pipkins, two deal tables, two chairs, two old sofas, two short pipes, and two long cloaks. They had no stated meal-times, no carpets and bedsteads, no cabinets, bookcases, or ornamental knickknacks of any kind, no laundress, and no charwoman.

When either of the two wanted to eat and drink, he cut off his crust of bread, cooked his bit of meat, drew his drop of beer, without the slightest reference to the other. When either of the two thought he wanted a clean shirt, which was very seldom, he went and washed one for himself. When either of the two discovered that any part of the house was getting very dirty indeed, he took a bucket of water and a birch-broom, and washed the place out like a dog-kennel.

And, lastly, when either of the two wanted to go to sleep, he wrapped himself up in his cloak, lay down on one of the sofas, and took what repose he required, early in the evening or late in the morning, just as he pleased.

When there was no baking, brewing, gardening or cleaning to be done, the two sat down opposite each other and smoked for hours, generally without uttering a word. Whenever they did speak they quarrelled. Their ordinary dialogue was a species of conversational prize-fight, beginning with a sarcastic affectation of goodwill on either side, and ending in hearty exchanges of violent abuse—just as the boxers go through the feeble formality of shaking hands before they enter on the serious practical business of beating each other's faces out of all likeness to the image of man.

Not having so many disadvantages of early refinement and education to contend against as his master, Shrowl generally won the victory in these engagements of the tongue. Indeed, though nominally the servant, he was really the ruling spirit of the house—acquiring unbounded influence over his master by dint of outmarching Mr. Treverton in every direction on his own ground. Shrowl's was the harshest voice; Shrowl's were the bitterest sayings; and Shrowl's was the longest beard.

The surest of all retributions is the retribution that lies in wait for a man who boasts. Mr. Treverton was rashly given to boasting of his independence, and when retribution overtook him it assumed a personal form, and bore the name of Shrowl.

On a certain morning, about three weeks after Mrs. Frankland had written to the housekeeper at Porthgenna Tower to mention the period at which her husband and herself might be expected there, Mr. Treverton descended, with his sourest face and his surliest manner, from the upper regions of the cottage to one of the rooms on the ground-floor, which civilized tenants would probably have called the parlour. Like his elder brother, he was a tall, well-built man; but his bony, haggard, sallow face bore not the slightest resemblance to the handsome, open, sun-burned face of the Captain.

No one seeing them together could possibly have guessed

that they were brothers—so completely did they differ in expression as well as in feature. The heartaches that he had suffered in youth; the reckless, wandering, dissipated life that he had led in manhood; the petulance, the disappointment and the physical exhaustion of his latter days had so wasted and worn him away that he looked his brother's elder by almost twenty years.

With unbrushed hair and unwashed face, with a tangled gray beard, and an old, patched, dirty flannel dressing-gown that hung about him like a sack, this descendant of a wealthy and ancient family looked as if his birthplace had been the workhouse, and his vocation in life the selling of castoff clothes.

It was breakfast-time with Mr. Treverton—that is to say, it was the time at which he felt hungry enough to think about eating something. In the same position over the mantel-piece in which a looking-glass would have been placed in a household of ordinary refinement, there hung in the cottage of Timon of London a side of bacon.

On the deal table by the fire stood half a loaf of heavy-looking brown-bread; in a corner of the room was a barrel of beer, with two battered pewter pots hitched onto nails in the wall above it; and under the grate lay a smoky old grid- iron, left just as it had been thrown down when last used and done with. Mr. Treverton took a greasy clasp-knife out of the pocket of his dressing-gown, cut off a rasher of bacon, jerked the gridiron onto the fire, and began to cook his breakfast. He had just turned the rasher, when the door opened, and Shrowl entered the room, with his pipe in his mouth, bent on the same eating errand as his master.

In personal appearance, Shrowl was short, fat, flabby, and perfectly bald, except at the back of his head, where a ring of bristly iron-gray hair projected like a collar that had got hitched out of its place. To make amends for the scantiness of his hair, the beard which he had cultivated by his master's desire grew far over his cheeks, and drooped down on his chest in two thick jagged peaks.

He wore a very old long-tailed dress-coat, which he had picked up at a bargain in Petticoat Lane—a faded yellow shirt, with a large torn frill velveteen trousers, turned up at the ankles—and Blucher boots that had never been blacked since the day when they last left the cobbler's stall. His colour was unhealthily florid, his thick lips curled upward with a malicious grin, and his eyes were the nearest approach, in form and expression, to the eyes of a bull terrier which those features are capable of achieving when they are placed in the countenance of a man.

Any painter wanting to express strength, insolence, ugliness, coarseness, and cunning in the face and figure of one and the same individual, could have discovered no better model for the purpose, all the world over, than he might have found in the person of Mr. Shrowl.

Neither master nor servant exchanged a word or took the smallest notice of each other on first meeting. Shrowl stood stolidly contemplative, with his hands in his pockets, waiting for his turn at the gridiron. Mr. Treverton finished his cooking, took his bacon to the table, and, cutting a crust of bread, began to eat his breakfast. When he had disposed of the first mouthful, he condescended to look up at Shrowl, who was at that moment opening his clasp-knife and approaching the side of bacon with slouching steps and sleepily greedy eyes.

"What do you mean by that?" asked Mr. Treverton, pointing with indignant surprise at Shrowl's breast. "You ugly brute, you've got a clean shirt on!"

"Thankee, sir, for noticing it," said Shrowl, with a sarcastic affectation of humility. "This is a joyful occasion, this is. I couldn't do no less than put a clean shirt on, when it's my master's birthday. Many happy returns, sir. Perhaps you thought I should forget that today was your birthday? Lord bless your sweet face, I wouldn't have forgot it on any account.

How old are you today? It's a long time ago, sir, since you was a plump, smiling little boy, with a frill round your neck, and marbles in your pocket, and trousers and waistcoat all in one, and kisses and presents from Pa and Ma, and uncle and aunt, on your birthday. Don't you be afraid of me wearing out this shirt by too much washing. I mean to put it away in lavender against your next birthday; or against your funeral, which is just as likely at your time of life—isn't it, sir?"

"Don't waste a clean shirt on my funeral," retorted Mr. Treverton. "I haven't left you any money in my will, Shrowl. You'll be on your way to the workhouse when I'm on my way to the grave."

"Have you really made your will at last, sir?" inquired Shrowl, pausing, with an appearance of the greatest interest, in the act of cutting off his slice of bacon. "I humbly beg pardon, but I always thought you was afraid to do it."

The servant had evidently touched intentionally on one of the master's sore points. Mr. Treverton thumped his crust of bread on the table and looked up angrily at Shrowl.

"Afraid of making my will, you fool!" said he. "I don't make it, and I won't make it, on principle."

Shrowl slowly sawed off his slice of bacon, and began to whistle a tune.

"On principle," repeated Mr. Treverton. "Rich men who leave money behind them are the farmers who raise the crop of human wickedness. When a man has any spark of generosity in his nature, if you want to put it out, leave him a legacy. When a man is bad, if you want to make him worse, leave him a legacy. If you want to collect a number of men together for the purpose of perpetuating corruption and oppression on a large scale, leave them a legacy under the form of endowing a public charity.

"If you want to give a woman the best chance in the world of getting a bad husband, leave her a legacy. Make my will! I have a pretty strong dislike of my species, Shrowl, but I don't quite hate mankind enough yet to do such mischief among them as that!" Ending his diatribe in those words, Mr. Treverton took down one of the battered pewter pots, and refreshed himself with a pint of beer.

Shrowl shifted the gridiron to a clear place in the fire, and chuckled sarcastically.

"Who the devil would you have me leave my money to?" cried Mr. Treverton, overhearing him. "To my brother, who thinks me a brute now; who would think me a fool then; and who would encourage swindling, anyhow, by spending all my money among doxies and strolling players? To the child of that player-woman, whom I have never set eyes on, who has been brought up to hate me, and who would turn hypocrite directly by pretending, for decency's sake, to be sorry for my death?

"To you, you human baboon!—you, who would set up a usury office directly, and prey upon the widow, the fatherless, and the unfortunate generally, all over the world? Your good health, Mr. Shrowl! I can laugh as well as you—especially when I know I'm not going to leave you sixpence."

Shrowl, in his turn, began to get a little irritated now. The jeering civility which he had chosen to assume on first entering the room gave place to his habitual surliness of manner and his natural growling intonation of voice.

"You just let me alone—will you?" he said, sitting down sulkily to his breakfast. "I've done joking for today; suppose you finish too. What's the use of talking nonsense about your money. You must leave it to somebody."

"Yes, I will," said Mr. Treverton. "I will leave it, as I have told you over and over again, to the first Somebody I can find who honestly despises money, and who can't be made the worse, therefore, by having it."

"That means nobody," grunted Shrowl.

"I know it does!" retorted his master.

Before Shrowl could utter a word of rejoinder, there was a ring at the gate-bell of the cottage.

"Go out," said Mr. Treverton, "and see what that is. If it's a woman visitor, show her what a scarecrow you are, and frighten her away. If it's a man visitor—"

"If it's a man visitor," interposed Shrowl, "I'll punch his head for interrupting me at my breakfast,"

Mr. Treverton filled and lighted his pipe during his servant's absence. Before the tobacco was well alight, Shrowl returned, and reported a man visitor.

"Did you punch his head" asked Mr. Treverton.

"No," said Shrowl. "I picked up his letter. He poked it under the gate and went away. Here it is."

The letter was written on foolscap paper, superscribed in a round legal hand. As Mr. Treverton opened it, two slips cut from newspapers dropped out. One fell on the table before which he was sitting; the other fluttered to the floor. This last slip Shrowl picked up and looked over its contents, without troubling himself to go through the ceremony of first asking leave.

After slowly drawing in and slowly puffing out again one mouthful of tobacco-smoke, Mr. Treverton began to read the letter. As his eye fell on the first lines, his lips began to work round the mouthpiece of the pipe in a manner that was very unusual with him.

The letter was not long enough to require him to turn over the first leaf of it—it ended at the bottom of the opening sheet. He read it down to the signature—then looked up to the address, and went through it again from the beginning. His lips still continued to work round the mouth-piece of the pipe, but he smoked no more. When he had finished the second reading, he set the letter down very gently on the table, looked at his servant with an unaccustomed vacancy in the expression of his eyes, and took the pipe out of his mouth with a hand that trembled a little.

"Shrowl," he said, very quietly, "my brother, the Captain, is drowned."

"I know he is," answered Shrowl, without looking up from the newspaper-slip. "I'm reading about it here."

"The last words my brother said to me when we quarrelled about the player-woman," continued Mr. Treverton, speaking as much to himself as to his servant, "were that I should die without one kind feeling in my heart toward any living creature."

"So you will," muttered Shrowl, turning the slip over to see if there was anything worth reading at the back of it.

"I wonder what he thought about me when he was dying?" said Mr. Treverton, abstractedly, taking up the letter again from the table.

"He didn't waste a thought on you or anybody else," remarked Shrowl. "If bethought at all, he thought about how he could save his life. When he had done thinking about that, he had done living too." With this expression of opinion Mr. Shrowl went to the beer-barrel, and drew his morning draught.

"Damn that player-woman!" muttered Mr. Treverton. As he said the words his face darkened and his lips closed firmly. He smoothed the letter out on the table. There seemed to be some doubt in his mind whether he had mastered all its contents yet—some idea that there ought to be more in it than he had yet discovered. In going over it for the third time, he read it to himself aloud and very slowly, as if he was determined to fix every separate word firmly in his memory. This was the letter:

Sir—As the old legal adviser and faithful friend of your family, I am desired by Mrs. Frankland, formerly Miss Treverton to acquaint you with the sad news of your brother's death. This deplorable event occurred on board the ship of which he was captain, during a gale in which the vessel was lost on a reef of rocks off the island of Antigua. I inclose a detailed account of the shipwreck, extracted from *The Times*, by which you will see that your brother died nobly in the performance of his duty toward the officers and men whom he commanded. I also send a slip from the local Cornish paper, containing a memoir of the deceased gentleman.

Before closing this communication, I must add that no will has been found, after the most rigorous search, among the papers of the late Captain Treverton. Having disposed, as you know, of Porthgenna, the only property of which he was possessed at the time of his death was personal property, derived from the sale of this estate; and this, in consequence of his dying intestate, will go in due course of law to his daughter, as his nearest of kin.

I am, sir, your obedient servant,
Alexander Nixon.

The newspaper-slip, which had fallen on the table, contained the paragraph from *The Times*. The slip from the Cornish paper, which had dropped to the floor, Shrowl poked under his master's eyes, in a fit of temporary civility, as soon as he had done reading it. Mr. Treverton took not the slightest notice either of the one paragraph or the other. He still sat looking at the letter, even after he had read it for the third time.

"Why don't you give the strip of print a turn, as well as the sheet of writing?" asked Shrowl. "Why don't you read about what a great man your brother was, and what a good life he led, and what a wonderful handsome daughter he's left behind him, and what a capital marriage she's made along with the man that's owner of your old family estate?

"She don't want your money now, at any rate! The ill wind that blowed her father's ship on the rocks has blowed forty thousand pounds of good into her lap. Why don't you read about it? She and her husband have got a better house in Cornwall than you have got here. Ain't you glad of that? They were going to have repaired the place from top to bottom for your brother to go and live along with 'em in clover when he came back from sea. Who will ever repair a place for you? I wonder whether your niece would knock the old house about for your sake, now, if you was to clean yourself up and go and ask her?"

At the last question, Shrowl paused in the work of aggravation—not for want of more words, but for want of encouragement to utter them. For the first time since they had kept house together, he had tried to provoke his master and had failed. Mr. Treverton listened, or appeared to listen, without moving a muscle—without the faintest change to anger in his face. The only words he said when Shrowl had done were these two—

"Go out!"

Shrowl was not an easy man to move, but he absolutely changed colour when he heard himself suddenly ordered to leave the room.

"Go out!" reiterated Mr. Treverton. "And hold your tongue henceforth and forever about my brother and my brother's daughter. I never have set eyes upon the player-woman's child, and I never will. Hold your tongue—leave me alone—go out!"

"I'll be even with him for this," thought Shrowl as he slowly withdrew from the room.

"When he had closed the door, he listened outside of it, and heard Mr. Treverton push aside his chair, and walk up and down, talking to himself. Judging by the confused words that escaped him, Shrowl concluded that his thoughts were still running on the "player-woman" who had set his brother and himself at variance. He seemed to feel a barbarous sense of relief in venting his dissatisfaction with himself, after the news of Captain Treverton's death, on the memory of the woman whom he hated so bitterly, and on the child whom she had left behind her.

After a while the low rumbling tones of his voice ceased altogether. Shrowl peeped through the key-hole, and saw that he was reading the newspaper-slips which contained the account of the shipwreck and the *Memoir* of his brother. The latter adverted to some of those family particulars which the vicar of Long Beckley had mentioned to his guest; and the writer of the *Memoir* concluded by expressing a hope that the bereavement which Mr. and Mrs. Frankland had suffered would not interfere with their project for repairing Porthgenna Tower, after they had gone the length already of sending a builder to survey the place.

Something in the wording of that paragraph seemed to take Mr. Treverton's memory back to his youth-time when the old family house had been his home. He whispered a few words to himself which gloomily referred to the days that were gone, rose from his chair impatiently, threw both the newspaper-slips into the fire, watched them while they were burning, and sighed when the black gossamer ashes floated upward on the draught, and were lost in the chimney.

The sound of that sigh startled Shrowl as the sound of a pistol-shot might have startled another man. His bull-terrier eyes opened wide in astonishment, and he shook his head ominously as he walked away from the door.

Chapter 2
Will They Come?

The housekeeper at Porthgenna Tower had just completed the necessary preparations for the reception of her master and mistress, at the time mentioned in Mrs. Frankland's letter from St. Swithin's-on-Sea, when she was startled by receiving a note sealed with black wax, and surrounded by a thick mourning border. The note briefly communicated the news of Captain Treverton's death, and informed her that the visit of Mr. and Mrs. Frankland to Porthgenna was deferred for an indefinite period.

By the same post the builder, who was superintending the renovation of the west staircase, also received a letter, requesting him to send in his account as soon as the repairs on which he was then engaged were completed; and telling him that Mr. Frankland was unable, for the present, to give any further attention to the project for making the north rooms habitable. On the receipt of this communication, the builder withdrew himself and his men as soon as the west stairs and banisters had been made secure; and Porthgenna Tower was again left to the care of the housekeeper and her servant, without master or mistress, friends or strangers, to thread its solitary passages or enliven its empty rooms.

From this time eight months passed away, and the housekeeper heard nothing of her master and mistress, except through the medium of paragraphs in the local newspaper, which dubiously referred to the probability of their occupying the old house, and interesting themselves in the affairs of their tenantry, at no very distant period. Occasionally, too, when business took him to the post-town, the steward collected reports about his employers among the old friends and dependents of the Treverton family.

From these sources of information, the housekeeper was led to conclude that Mr. and Mrs. Frankland had returned to Long Beckley, after receiving the news of Captain Treverton's death, and had lived there for some months in strict retirement. When they left that place, they moved (if the newspaper report was to be credited) to the neighbourhood of London, and occupied the house of some friends who were travelling on the Continent.

Here they must have remained for some time, for the new year came and brought no rumours of any change in their place of abode. January and February passed without any news of them. Early in March the steward had occasion to go to the pest-town. When he returned to Porthgenna, he came back with a new report relating to Mr. and Mrs. Frankland, which excited the housekeeper's interest in an extraordinary degree.

In two different quarters, each highly respectable, the steward had heard it facetiously announced that the domestic responsibilities of his master and mistress were likely to be increased by their having a nurse to engage and a crib to buy at the end of the spring or the beginning of the summer. In plain English, among the many babies who might be expected to make their appearance in the world in the course of the next three months, there was one who would inherit the name of Frankland, and who (if the infant luckily turned out to be a boy) would cause a sensation throughout West Cornwall as heir to the Porthgenna estate.

In the next month, the month of April, before the housekeeper and the steward had done discussing their last and most important fragment of news, the postman made his welcome appearance at Porthgenna Tower, and brought another note from Mrs. Frankland. The housekeeper's face brightened with unaccustomed pleasure and surprise as she read the first line.

The letter announced that the long-deferred visit of her master and mistress to the old house would take place early in May, and that they might be expected to arrive any day from the first to the tenth of the mouth.

The reasons which had led the owners of Porthgenna to fix a period, at last, for visiting their country seat, were connected with certain particulars into which Mrs. Frankland had not thought it advisable to enter in her letter. The plain facts of the case were, that a little discussion had arisen between the husband and wife in relation to the next place of residence which they should select, after the return from the Continent of the friends whose house they were occupying.

Mr. Frankland had very reasonably suggested returning again to Long Beckley—not only because all their oldest friends lived in the neighbourhood, but also (and circumstances made this an important consideration) because the place had the advantage of possessing an excellent resident medical man. Unfortunately this latter advantage, so far from carrying any weight with it in Mrs. Frankland's estimation, actually prejudiced her mind against the project of going to Long Beckley.

She had always, she acknowledged, felt an unreasonable antipathy to the doctor there. He might be a very skilful, an extremely polite, and an undeniably respectable man; but she never had liked him, and never should, and she was resolved to oppose the plan for living at Long Beckley, because the execution of it would oblige her to commit herself to his care.

Two other places of residence were next suggested; but Mrs. Frankland had the same objection to oppose to both—in each case the resident doctor would be a stranger to her, and she did not like the notion of being attended by a stranger. Finally, as she had all along anticipated, the choice of the future abode was left entirely to her own inclinations; and then, to the amazement of her husband and her friends, she immediately decided on going to Porthgenna.

She had formed this strange project, and was now resolved on executing it, partly because she was more curious than ever to see the place again; partly because the doctor who had been with her mother in Mrs. Treverton's last illness, and who had attended her through all her own little maladies when she was a child, was still living and practicing in the Porthgenna neighbourhood. Her father and the doctor had been old cronies, and had met for years at the same chessboard every Saturday night.

They had kept up their friendship, when circumstances separated them, by exchanges of Christmas presents every year; and when the sad news of the Captain's death had reached Cornwall, the doctor had written a letter of sympathy and condolence to

Rosamond, speaking in such terms of his former friend and patron as she could never forget.

He must be a nice, fatherly old man now, the man of all others who was fittest, on every account, to attend her. In short, Mrs. Frankland was just as strongly prejudiced in favour of employing the Porthgenna doctor as she was prejudiced against employing the Long Beckley doctor; and she ended, as all young married women with affectionate husbands may, and do end, whenever they please—by carrying her own point, and having her own way.

On the first of May the west rooms were all ready for the reception of the master and mistress of the house. The beds were aired, the carpets cleaned, the sofas and chairs uncovered. The housekeeper put on her satin gown and her garnet brooch; the maid followed suit, at a respectful distance, in brown merino and a pink ribbon; and the steward, determining not to be outdone by the women, arrayed himself in a black brocaded waistcoat, which almost rivalled the gloom and grandeur of the housekeeper's satin gown. The day wore on, evening closed in, bedtime came, and there were no signs yet of Mr. and Mrs. Frankland.

But the first was an early day on which to expect them. The steward thought so, and the housekeeper added that it would be foolish to feel disappointed, even if they did not arrive until the fifth. The fifth came, and still nothing happened. The sixth, seventh, eighth, and ninth followed, and no sound of the expected carriage-wheels came near the lonely house.

On the tenth, and last day, the housekeeper, the steward, and the maid, all three rose earlier than usual; all three opened and shut doors, and went up and down stairs oftener than was needful; all three looked out perpetually toward the moor and the high-road, and thought the view flatter and duller and emptier than ever it had appeared to them before.

The day waned, the sunset came; darkness changed the perpetual looking-out of the housekeeper, the steward, and the maid into perpetual listening; ten o'clock struck, and still there was nothing to be heard when they went to the open window but the wearisome beating of the surf on the sandy shore.

The housekeeper began to calculate the time that would be consumed on the railway journey from London to Exeter, and on the posting journey afterward through Cornwall to Porthgenna. When had Mr. and Mrs. Frankland left Exeter?—that was the first question. And what delays might they have encountered afterward in getting horses?—that was the second.

The housekeeper and the steward differed in debating these points; but both agreed that it was necessary to sit up until midnight, on the chance of the master and mistress arriving late. The maid, hearing her sentence of banishment from bed for the next two hours pronounced by the superior authorities, yawned and sighed mournfully was reproved by the steward—and was furnished by the housekeeper with a book of hymns to read to keep up her spirits.

Twelve o'clock struck, and still the monotonous beating of the surf, varied occasionally by those loud, mysterious, cracking noises which make themselves heard at night in an old house, were the only audible sounds.

The steward was dozing; the maid was fast asleep under the soothing influence of the hymns; the housekeeper was wide awake, with her eyes fixed on the window, and her head shaking forebodingly from time to time. At the last stroke of the clock she left her chair, listened attentively, and still hearing nothing, shook the maid irritably by the shoulder, and stamped on the floor to arouse the steward.

"We may go to bed," she said. "They are not coming. This is the second time they have disappointed us. The first time the Captain's death stood in the way. What stops them now? Another death? I shouldn't wonder if it was."

"Now I think of it, no more should I," said the steward, ominously knitting his brows.

"Another death!" repeated the housekeeper, superstitiously. "If it is another death, I should take it, in their place, as a warning to keep away from the house."

CHAPTER 3
MRS. JAZEPH

If, instead of hazarding the guess that a second death stood in the way of Mr. and Mrs. Frankland's arrival at Porthgenna, the housekeeper had, by way of variety, surmised this time that a birth was the obstacle which delayed them, she might have established her character as a wise woman, by hitting at random on the actual truth. Her master and mistress had started from London on the ninth of May, and had got through the greater part of their railway journey, when they were suddenly obliged to stop, on Mrs. Frankland's account, at the station of a small town in Somersetshire.

The little visitor, who was destined to increase the domestic responsibilities of the young married couple, had chosen to enter on the scene, in the character of a robust boy-baby, a month earlier than he had been expected, and had modestly preferred to make his first appearance in a small Somersetshire inn, rather than wait to be ceremoniously welcomed to life in the great house of Porthgenna, which he was one day to inherit.

Very few events had ever produced a greater sensation in the town of West Winston than the one small event of the unexpected stoppage of Mr. and Mrs. Frankland's journey at that place. Never since the last election had the landlord and landlady of the Tiger's Head Hotel bustled about their house in such a fever of excitement as possessed them when Mr. Frankland's servant and Mrs. Frankland's maid drew up at the door in a fly from the station, to announce that their master and mistress were behind, and that the largest and quietest rooms in the hotel were wanted immediately, under the most unexpected circumstances.

Never since he had triumphantly passed his examination had young Mr. Orridge, the new doctor, who had started in life by purchasing the West Winston practice, felt such a thrill of pleasurable agitation pervade him from top to toe as when he heard that the wife of a blind gentleman of great fortune had been taken ill on the railway journey from London to Devonshire, and required all that his skill and attention could do for her without a moment's delay.

Never since the last archery meeting and fancy fair had the ladies of the town been favoured with such an all-absorbing subject for conversation as was now afforded to them by Mrs. Frankland's mishap. Fabulous accounts of the wife's beauty and the husband's fortune poured from the original source of the Tiger's Head, and trickled through the highways and byways of the little town.

There were a dozen different reports, one more elaborately false than the other, about Mr. Frankland's blindness, and the cause of it; about the lamentable condition in which his wife had arrived at the hotel; and about the painful sense of responsibility which had unnerved the inexperienced Mr. Orridge from the first moment when he set eyes on his patient.

It was not till eight o'clock in the evening that the public mind was relieved at last from all suspense by an announcement that the child was born, and screaming lustily; that the mother was wonderfully well, considering all things; and that Mr. Orridge had covered himself with distinction by the skill, tenderness, and attention with which he had performed his duties.

On the next day, and the next, and for a week after that, the accounts wore still favourable. But on the tenth day a catastrophe was reported. The nurse who was in attendance on Mrs. Frankland had been suddenly taken ill, and was rendered quite incapable of performing any further service for at least a week to come, and perhaps for a much longer period.

In a large town this misfortune might have been readily remedied, but in a place like West Winston it was not so easy to supply the loss of an experienced nurse at a few hours' notice. When Mr. Orridge was consulted in the new emergency, he candidly acknowledged that he required a little time for consideration before he could undertake to find another professed nurse of sufficient character and experience to wait on a lady like Mrs. Frankland.

Mr. Frankland suggested telegraphing to a medical friend in London for a nurse, but the doctor was unwilling for many reasons to adopt that plan, except as a last resource. It would take some time to find the right person, and to send her to West Winston; and, moreover, he would infinitely prefer employing a woman with whose character and capacity he was himself acquainted.

He therefore proposed that Mrs. Frankland should be trusted for a few hours to the care of her maid, under supervision of the landlady of the Tiger's Head, while he made inquiries in the neighbourhood. If the inquiries produced no satisfactory result, he should be ready, when he called in the evening, to adopt Mr. Frankland's idea of telegraphing to London for a nurse.

On proceeding to make the investigation that he had proposed, Mr. Orridge, although he spared no trouble, met with no success. He found plenty of volunteers for the office of nurse, but they were all loud-voiced, clumsy-handed, heavy-footed countrywomen, kind and willing enough, but sadly awkward, blundering attendants to place at the bedside of such a lady as Mrs. Frankland. The morning hours passed away, and the afternoon came, and still Mr. Orridge had found no substitute for the invalided nurse whom he could venture to engage.

At two o'clock he had half an hour's drive before him to a country-house where he had a child-patient to see. "Perhaps I may remember somebody who may do, on the way out or on the way back again," thought Mr. Orridge, as he got into his gig. "I have some hours at my disposal still before the time comes for my evening visit at the inn."

Puzzling his brains, with the best intention in the world, all along the road to the country-house, Mr. Orridge reached his destination without having arrived at any other conclusion than that he might just as well state his difficulty to Mrs. Norbury, the lady whose child he was about to prescribe for. He had called on her when he bought the West Winston practice, and had found her one of those frank, good-humoured, middle-aged women who are generally designated by the epithet "motherly."

Her husband was a country squire, famous for his old politics, his old stories, and his old wine. He had seconded his wife's hearty reception of the new doctor, with all the usual jokes about never giving him any employment, and never letting any bottles into the house except the bottles that went down into the cellar. Mr. Orridge had been amused by the husband and pleased with the wife; and he thought it might be at least worthwhile, before he gave up all hope of finding a fit nurse, to ask Mrs. Norbury, as an old resident in the West Winston neighbourhood, for a word of advice.

Accordingly, after seeing the child, and pronouncing that there were no symptoms about the little patient which need cause the slightest alarm to anybody, Mr. Orridge paved the way for a statement of the difficulty that beset him by asking Mrs. Norbury if she had heard of the "interesting event" that had happened at the Tiger's Head.

"You mean," answered Mrs. Norbury, who was a downright woman, and a resolute speaker of the plainest possible English-"You mean, have I heard about that poor unfortunate lady who was taken ill on her journey, and who had a child born at the inn? We have heard so much, and no more—living as we do (thank Heaven!) out of reach of the West Winston gossip. How is the lady? Who is she? Is the child well? Is she tolerably comfortable? poor thing! Can I send her anything, or do any- thing for her?"

"You would do a great thing for her, and render a great assistance to me," said Mr. Orridge, "if you could tell me of any respectable woman in this neighbourhood who would be a proper nurse for her."

"You don't mean to say that the poor creature has not got a nurse!" exclaimed Mrs. Norbury.

"She has had the best nurse in West Winston," replied Mr. Orridge. "But, most unfortunately, the woman was taken ill this morning, and was obliged to go home. I am now at my wit's end for somebody to supply her place. Mrs. Frankland has been used to the luxury of being well waited on; and where I am to find an attendant who is likely to satisfy her, is more than I can tell."

"Frankland, did you say her name was?" inquired Mrs. Norbury.

"Yes. She is, I understand, a daughter of that Captain Treverton who was lost with his ship a year ago in the West Indies. Perhaps you may remember the account of the disaster in the newspapers?"

"Of course I do! and I remember the Captain too. I was acquainted with him when he was a young man, at Portsmouth. His daughter and I ought not to be strangers, especially under such circumstances as the poor thing is placed in now. I will call at the inn, Mr. Orridge, as soon as you will allow me to introduce myself to her. But, in the meantime, what is to be done in this difficulty about the nurse? Who is with Mrs. Frankland now?"

"Her maid; but she is a very young woman, and doesn't understand nursing duties. The landlady of the inn is ready to help when she can; but then she has constant demands on her time and attention. I suppose we shall have to telegraph to London and get somebody sent here by railway."

"And that will take time, of course. And the new nurse may turn out to be a drunkard or a thief, or both—when you have got her here," said the outspoken Mrs. Norbury. "Dear, dear me! can't we do something better than that? I am ready, I am sure, to take any trouble, or make any sacrifice, if I can be of use. to Mrs. Frankland. Do you know, Mr. Orridge, I think it would be a good plan if we consulted my housekeeper, Mrs. Jazeph.

"She is an odd woman, with an odd name, you will say; but she has lived with me in this house more than five years, and she may know of somebody in our neighbourhood who might suit you, though I don't." With those words, Mrs. Norbury rang the bell, and ordered the servant who answered it to tell Mrs. Jazeph that she was wanted upstairs immediately.

After the lapse of a minute or so a soft knock was heard at the door, and the housekeeper entered the room.

Mr. Orridge looked at her, the moment she appeared, with an interest and curiosity for which he was hardly able to account. He judged her, at a rough guess, to be a woman of about fifty years of age. At the first glance, his medical eye detected that some of the intricate machinery of the nervous system had gone wrong with Mrs. Jazeph.

He noted the painful working of the muscles of her face, and the hectic flush that flew into her cheeks when she entered the room and found a visitor there. He observed a strangely scared look in her eyes, and remarked that it did not leave them when the rest of her face became gradually composed. "That woman has had some dreadful fright, some great grief, or some wasting complaint," he thought to himself. "I wonder which it is?"

"This is Mr. Orridge, the medical gentleman who has lately settled at West Winston," said Mrs. Norbury, addressing the housekeeper. "He is in attendance on a lady who was obliged to stop, on her journey westward, at our station, and who is now staying at the Tiger's Head. You have heard something about it, have you not, Mrs. Jazeph?"

Mrs. Jazeph, standing just inside the door, looked respectfully toward the doctor, and answered in the affirmative. Although she only said the two common words, "Yes, ma'am," in a quiet, uninterested way, Mr. Orridge was struck by the sweetness and tenderness of her voice. If he had not been looking at her, he would have supposed it to be the voice of a young woman. His eyes remained fixed on her after she had spoken, though he felt that they ought to have been looking toward her mistress.

He, the most unobservant of men in such things, found himself noticing her dress, so that he remembered, long afterward, the form of the spotless muslin cap that primly covered her smooth gray hair, and the quiet brown colour of the silk dress that fitted so neatly and hung around her in such spare and disciplined folds.

The little confusion which she evidently felt at finding herself the object of the doctor's attention did not betray her into the slightest awkwardness of gesture or manner. If there can be such a thing, physically speaking, as the grace of restraint, that was the grace which seemed to govern Mrs. Jazeph's slightest movements; which led her feet smoothly over the carpet, as she advanced when her mistress next spoke to her; which governed the action of her wan right hand as it rested lightly on a table by her side, while she stopped to hear the next question that was addressed to her.

"Well," continued Mrs. Norbury, "this poor lady was just getting on comfortably, when the nurse who was looking after her fell ill this morning; and there she is now, in a strange place, with a first child, and no proper attendance—no woman of age and experience to help her as she ought to be helped. We want somebody fit to wait on a delicate woman who has seen nothing of the rough side of humanity.

"Mr. Orridge can find nobody at a day's notice, and I can tell him of nobody. Can you help us, Mrs. Jazeph? Are there any women down in the village, or among Mr. Norbury's tenants, who understand nursing, and have some tact and tenderness to recommend them into the bargain?"

Mrs. Jazeph reflected for a little while, and then said, very respectfully, but very briefly also, and still without any appearance of interest in her manner, that she knew of no one whom she could recommend.

"Don't make too sure of that till you have thought a little longer," said Mrs. Norbury. "I have a particular interest in serving this lady, for Mr. Orridge told me just before you came in that she is the daughter of Captain Treverton, whose shipwreck—"

The instant those words were spoken, Mrs. Jazeph turned round with a start, and looked at the doctor. Apparently forgetting that her right band was on the table, she moved it so suddenly that it struck against a bronze statuette of a dog placed on some writing materials. The statuette fell to the ground, and Mrs. Jazeph stooped to pick it up with a cry of alarm which seemed strangely exaggerated by comparison with the trifling nature of the accident.

"Bless the woman! what is she frightened about?" exclaimed Mrs. Norbury. "The dog is not hurt—put it back again! This is the first time. Mrs. Jazeph, that I ever knew you do an awkward thing. You may take that as a compliment, I think. Well, as I was saying, this lady is the daughter of Captain Treverton, whose dreadful shipwreck we all read about in the papers. I knew her father in my early days, and on that account I am doubly anxious to be of service to her now. Do think again. Is there nobody within reach who can be trusted to nurse her?"

The doctor, still watching Mrs. Jazeph with that secret medical interest of his in her case, had seen her turn so deadly pale when she started and looked toward him that he would not have been surprised if she had fainted on the spot. He now observed that she changed colour again when her mistress left off speaking. The hectic red tinged her cheeks once more with two bright spots. Her timid eyes wandered uneasily about the room; and her fingers, as she clasped her hands together, interlaced themselves mechanically. "That would be an interesting case to treat," thought the doctor, following every nervous movement of the housekeeper's hands with watchful eyes.

"Do think again," repeated Mrs. Norbury. "I am so anxious to help this poor lady through her difficulty, if I can."

"I am very sorry," said Mrs. Jazeph, in faint, trembling tones, but still always with the same sweetness in her voice—"very sorry that I can think of no one who is fit; but—"

She stopped. No shy child on its first introduction to the society of strangers could have looked more disconcerted than she looked now. Her eyes were on the ground; her colour was deepening; the fingers of her clasped hands were working together faster and faster every moment.

"But what?" asked Mrs. Norbury.

"I was about to say, ma'am," answered Mrs. Jazeph, speaking with the greatest difficulty and uneasiness, and never raising her eyes to her mistress's face, "that, rather than this lady should want for a mine, I would—considering the interest, ma'am, which you take in her I would, if you thought you could spare me—"

"What, nurse her yourself!" exclaimed Mrs. Norbury. "Upon my word, although you have got to it in rather a roundabout way, you have come to the point at last, in a manner which does infinite credit to your kindness of heart and your readiness to make yourself useful. As to sparing you, of course I am not so selfish, under the circumstances, as to think twice of the inconvenience of losing my housekeeper. But the question is, are you competent as well as willing? Have you ever had any practice in nursing?"

"Yes, ma'am," answered Mrs. Jazeph, still without raising her eyes from the ground. "Shortly after my marriage" (the flush disappeared and her face turned pale again as she said those words), "I had some practice in nursing, and continued it at in tervals until the time of my husband's death. I only presume to offer myself, sir," she went on, turning toward the doctor, and becoming more earnest and self-possessed in her manner as she did so—"I only presume to offer myself, with my mistress's permission, as a substitute for a nurse until some better qualified person can be found."

"What do you say, Mr. Orridge?" asked Mrs. Norbury.

It had been the doctor's turn to start when he first heard Mrs. Jazeph propose herself for the office of nurse. He hesitated before he answered Mrs. Norbury's question, then said:

"I can have but one doubt about the propriety of thankfully accepting Mrs. Jazeph's offer."

Mrs. Jazeph's timid eyes looked anxiously and perplexedly at him as he spoke. Mrs. Norbury, in her downright, abrupt way, asked immediately what the doubt was.

"I feel some uncertainty," replied Mr. Orridge, "as to whether Mrs. Jazeph—she will pardon me, as a medical man, for mentioning it—as to whether Mrs. Jazeph is strong enough, and has her nerves sufficiently under control, to perform the duties which she is so kindly ready to undertake."

In spite of the politeness of the explanation, Mrs. Jazeph was evidently disconcerted and distressed by it. A certain quiet, uncomplaining sadness, which it was very touching to see, overspread her face as she turned away, without another word, and walked slowly to the door.

"Don't go yet!" cried Mrs. Norbury, kindly, "or, at least, if you do go. come back again in five minutes. I am quite certain we shall have something more to say to you then."

Mrs. Jazeph's eyes expressed her thanks in one grateful glance. They looked so much brighter than usual while they rested on her mistress's face that Mrs. Norbury half doubted whether the tears were not just rising in them at that moment. Before she could look again, Mrs. Jazeph had curtsied to the doctor and had noiselessly left the room.

"Now we are alone, Mr. Orridge," said Mrs. Norbury, "I may tell you, with all submission to your medical judgment, that you are a little exaggerating Mrs. Jazeph's nervous infirmities. She looks poorly enough, I own; but, after five years' experience of her, I can tell you that she is stronger than she looks, and I honestly think you will be doing good service to Mrs. Frankland if you try our volunteer nurse, at least for a day or two.

"She is the gentlest, tenderest creature I ever met with, and conscientious to a fault in the performance of any duty that she undertakes. Don't be under any delicacy about taking her away. I gave a dinner-party last week, and shall not give another for some time to come. I never could have spared my housekeeper more easily than I can spare her now."

"I am sure I may offer Mrs. Frankland's thanks to you as well as my own," said Mr. Orridge. "After what you have said, it would be ungracious and ungrateful in me not to follow your advice. But will you excuse me if I ask one question? Did you ever hear that Mrs. Jazeph was subject to fits of any kind?"

"Never."

"Not even to hysterical affections, now and then?"

"Never, since she has been in this house."

"You surprise me, there is something in her look and manner—"

"Yes, yes; everybody remarks that at first; but it simply means that she is in delicate health, and that she has not led a very happy life (as I suspect) in her younger days. The lady from whom I had her (with an excellent character) told me that she had married unhappily, when she was in a sadly poor, unprotected state. She never says anything about her married troubles herself; but

I believe her husband ill-used her.

"However, it does not seem to me that this is our business. I can only tell you again that she has been an excellent servant here for the last five years, and that, in your place, poorly as she may look, I should consider her as the best nurse that Mrs. Frankland could possibly wish for, under the circumstances. There is no need for me to say any more. Take Mrs. Jazeph, or telegraph to London for a stranger—the decision of course rests with you."

Mr. Orridge thought he detected a slight tone of irritability in Mrs. Norbury's last sentence. He was a prudent man; and he suppressed any doubts he might still feel in reference to Mrs. Jazeph's physical capacities for nursing, rather than risk offending the most important lady in the neighbourhood at the outset of his practice in West Winston as a medical man.

"I cannot hesitate a moment after what you have been good enough to tell me," he said. "Pray believe that I gratefully accept your kindness and your housekeeper's offer."

Mrs. Norbury rang the bell. It was answered on the instant by the housekeeper herself.

The doctor wondered whether she had been listening outside the door, and thought it rather strange, if she had, that she should be so anxious to learn his decision.

"Mr. Orridge accepts your offer with thanks," said Mrs. Norbury, beckoning to Mrs. Jazeph to advance into the room. "I have persuaded him that you are not quite so weak and ill as you look."

A gleam of joyful surprise broke over the housekeeper's face. It looked suddenly younger by years and years, as she smiled and expressed her grateful sense of the trust that was about to be reposed in her. For the first time, also, since the doctor had seen her, she ventured on speaking before she was spoken to.

"When will my attendance be required, sir?" she asked.

"As soon as possible," replied Mr. Orridge. How quickly and brightly her dim eyes seemed to clear as she heard that answer! How much more hasty than her usual movements was the movement with which she now turned round and looked appealingly at her mistress!

"Go whenever Mr. Orridge wants you," said Mrs. Norbury. "I know your accounts are always in order, and your keys always in their proper places. You never make confusion, and you never leave confusion. Go, by all means, as soon as the doctor wants you."

"I suppose you have some preparations to make?" said Mr. Orridge.

"None, sir, that need delay me more than half an hour," answered Mrs. Jazeph.

"This evening will be early enough," said the doctor, taking his hat, and bowing to Mrs. Norbury. "Come to the Tiger's Head and ask for me. I shall be there between seven and eight. Many thanks again, Mrs. Norbury."

"My best wishes and compliments to your patient, doctor."

"At the Tiger's Head, between seven and eight this evening," reiterated. Mr. Orridge, as the housekeeper opened the door for him.

"Between seven and eight, sir," repeated the soft, sweet voice, sounding younger than ever, now that there was an under-note of pleasure running through its tones.

CHAPTER 4
THE NEW NURSE

As the clock struck seven, Mr. Orridge put on his hat to go to the Tiger's Head. He had just opened his own door, when he was met on the step by a messenger, who summoned him immediately to a case of sudden illness in the poor quarter of the town. The inquiries he made satisfied him that the appeal was really of an urgent nature, and that there was no help for it but to delay his attendance for a little while at the inn.

On reaching the bedside of the patient, he discovered symptoms in the case which rendered an immediate operation necessary. The performance of this professional duty occupied some time. It was a quarter to eight before he left. his house, for the second time, on his way to the Tiger's Head.

On entering the inn door, he was informed that the new nurse had arrived as early as seven o'clock, and had been waiting for him in a room by herself ever since. Having received no orders from Mr. Orridge, the landlady had thought it safest not to introduce the stranger to Mrs. Frankland before the doctor came.

"Did she ask to go up into Mrs. Frankland's room?" inquired Mr. Orridge.

"Yes, sir," replied the landlady. "And I thought she seemed rather put out when I said that I must beg her to wait till you got here. Will you step this way, and see her at once, sir? She is in my parlour."

Mr. Orridge followed the landlady into a little room at the back of the house, and found Mrs. Jazeph sitting alone in the corner furthest from the window. He was rather surprised to see that she drew her veil down the moment the door was opened.

"I am sorry you should have been kept waiting," he said; "but I was called away to a patient. Besides, I told you between seven and eight, if you remember; and it is not eight o'clock yet."

"I was very anxious to be in good time, sir," said Mrs. Jazeph.

There was an accent of restraint in the quiet tones in which she spoke which struck Mr. Orridge's ear, and a little perplexed him. She was, apparently, not only afraid that her face might betray something, but apprehensive also that her voice might tell him more than her words expressed. What feeling was she anxious to conceal? Was it irritation at having been kept waiting so long by herself in the landlady's room?

"If you will follow me," said Mr. Orridge, "I will take you to Mrs. Frankland immediately."

Mrs. Jazeph rose slowly, and, when she was on her feet, rested her hand for an instant on a table near her. That action, momentary as it was, helped to confirm the doctor in his conviction of her physical unfitness for the position which she had volunteered to occupy.

"You seem tired," he said, as he led the way out of the door. "Surely, you did not walk all the way here?"

"No, sir. My mistress was so kind as to let one of the servants drive me in the pony-chaise." There was the same restraint in her voice as she made that answer; and still she never attempted to lift her veil. While ascending the inn stairs Mr. Orridge mentally resolved to watch her first proceedings in Mrs. Frankland's room closely, and to send, after all, for the London nurse unless Mrs. Jazeph showed remarkable aptitude in the performance of her new duties.

The room which Mrs. Frankland occupied was situated at the back of the house, having been chosen in that position with the object of removing her as much as possible from the bustle and noise about the inn door. It was lighted by one window overlooking a few cottages, beyond which spread the rich grazing grounds of West Somersetshire, bounded by a long monotonous line of thickly wooded hills.

The bed was of the old-fashioned kind, with the customary four posts and the inevitable damask curtains. It projected from the wall into the middle of the room, in such a situation as to keep the door on the right hand of the person occupying it, the window on the left, and the fireplace opposite the foot of the bed.

On the side of the bed nearest the window the curtains were open, while at the foot, and on the side near the door, they were closely drawn. By this arrangement the interior of the bed was necessarily concealed from the view of any person on first entering the room.

"How do you find yourself tonight, Mrs. Frankland?" asked Mr. Orridge, reaching out his hand to undraw the curtains. "Do you think you will be any the worse for a little freer circulation of air?"

"On the contrary, doctor, I shall be all the better," was the answer. "But I am afraid—in case you have ever been disposed to consider me a sensible woman—that my character will suffer a little in your estimation when you see how I have been occupying myself for the last hour."

Mr. Orridge smiled as he undrew the curtains, and laughed outright when he looked at the mother and child.

Mrs. Frankland had been amusing herself, and gratifying her taste for bright colours, by dressing out her baby with blue ribbons as he lay asleep. He had a necklace, shoulder-knots, and bracelets, all of blue ribbon; and, to complete the quaint finery of his costume, his mother's smart little lace cap had been hitched comically on one side of his head. Rosamond herself, as if determined to vie with the baby in gayety of dress, wore a light pink jacket, ornamented down the bosom and over the sleeves with bows of white satin ribbon.

Laburnum blossoms, gathered that morning, lay scattered about over the white counterpane, intermixed with some flowers of the lily of the valley, tied up into two nosegays with strips of cherry-coloured ribbon. Over this varied assemblage of colours, over the baby's smoothly rounded cheeks and arms, over his mother's happy, youthful face, the tender light of the May evening poured tranquil and warm.

Thoroughly appreciating the charm of the picture which he had disclosed on undrawing the curtains, the doctor stood looking at it for a few moments, quite forgetful of the errand that had brought him into the room. He was only recalled to a remembrance of the new nurse by a chance question which Mrs. Frankland addressed to him.

"I can't help it, doctor," said Rosamond, with a look of apology. " I really can't help treating my baby, now I am a grown woman, just as I used to treat my doll when I was a little girl. Did anybody come into the room with you? Lenny, are you there? Have you done dinner, darling, and did you drink my health when you were left at dessert all by yourself?"

"Mr. Frankland is still at dinner," said the doctor. "Bat I certainly brought someone into the room with me. Where, in the name of wonder, has she gone to?—Mrs. Jazeph!"

The housekeeper had slipped round to the part of the room between the foot of the bed and the fireplace, where she was hidden by the curtains that still remained drawn. When Mr. Orridge called to her, instead of joining him where he stood, opposite the window, she appeared at the other side of the bed, where the window was behind her. Her shadow stole darkly over the bright picture which the doctor had been admiring. It stretched obliquely across the counter-pane, and its dusky edges touched the figures of the mother and child.

"Gracious goodness! who are you?" exclaimed Rosamond. "A woman or a ghost?"

Mrs. Jazeph's veil was up at last. Although her face was necessarily in shadow in the position which she had chosen to occupy, the doctor saw a change pass over it when Mrs. Frankland spoke. The lips dropped and quivered a little; the marks of care and age about the mouth deepened; and the eyebrows contracted suddenly.

The eyes Mr. Orridge could not see; they were cast down on the counterpane at the first word that Rosamond uttered. Judging by the light of his medical experience, the doctor concluded that she was suffering pain, and trying to suppress any outward manifestation of it. "An affection of the heart, most likely," he thought to himself. "She has concealed it from her mistress, but she can't hide it from me."

"Who are you?" repeated Rosamond. "And what in the world do you stand there for—between us and the sunlight?"

Mrs. Jazeph neither answered nor raised her eyes. She only moved back timidly to the furthest corner of the window.

"Did you not get a message from me this afternoon?" asked the doctor, appealing to Mrs. Frankland.

"To be sure I did," replied Rosamond. "A very kind, flattering message about a new nurse."

"There she is," said Mr. Orridge, pointing across the bed to Mrs. Jazeph.

"You don't say so!" exclaimed Rosamond. "But of course it must be. Who else could have come in with you? I ought to have known that. Pray come here—(what is her name, doctor? Joseph, did you say?—No?—Jazeph?)—pray come nearer, Mrs.

Jazeph, and let me apologize for speaking so abruptly to you. I am more obliged than I can say for your kindness in coming here, and for your mistress's good-nature in resigning you to me. I hope I shall not give you much trouble, and I am sure you will find the baby easy to manage.

"He is a perfect angel, and sleeps like a dormouse. Dear me! now I look at you a little closer, I am afraid you are in very delicate health yourself. Doctor, if Mrs. Jazeph would not be offended with me, I should almost feel inclined to say that she looks in want of nursing herself."

Mrs. Jazeph bent down over the laburnum blossoms on the bed, and began hurriedly and confusedly to gather them to-gether.

"I thought as you do, Mrs. Frankland," said Mr. Orridge. "But I have been assured that Mrs. Jazeph's looks belie her, and that her capabilities as a nurse quite equal her zeal."

"Are you going to make all that laburnum into a nosegay?" asked Mrs. Frankland, noticing how the new nurse was occupy-ing herself. "How thoughtful of you! and how magnificent it will be! I am afraid you will find the room very untidy. I will ring for my maid to set it to rights."

"If you will allow me to put it in order, ma'am, I shall be very glad to begin being of use to you in that way," said Mrs. Jazeph. When she made the offer she looked up, and her eyes and Mrs. Frankland's met. Rosamond instantly drew back on the pillow, and her colour altered a little.

"How strangely you look at me!" she said.

Mrs. Jazeph started at the words, as if something had struck her, and moved away suddenly to the window.

"You are not offended with me, I hope?" said Rosamond, noticing the action. "I have a sad habit of saying anything that comes uppermost. And I really thought you looked just now as if you saw something about me that frightened or grieved you. Pray put the room in order, if you are kindly willing to undertake the trouble. And never mind what I say; you will soon get used to my ways—and we shall be as comfortable and friendly—"

Just as Mrs. Frankland said the words "comfortable and friendly," the new nurse left the window, and went back to the part of the room where she was hidden from view, between the fireplace and the closed curtains at the foot of the bed. Rosamond looked round to express her surprise to the doctor, but he turned away at the same moment so as to occupy a position which might enable him to observe what Mrs. Jazeph was doing on the other side of the bed-curtains.

When he first caught sight of her, her hands were both raised to her face. Before he could decide whether he had surprised her in the act of clasping them over her eyes or not, they changed their position, and were occupied in removing her bonnet. After she had placed this part of her wearing apparel, and her shawl and gloves, on a chair in a corner of the room, she went to the dressing-table, and began to arrange the various useful and ornamental objects scattered about it.

She set them in order with remarkable dexterity and neatness, showing a taste for arrangement, and a capacity for discriminating between things that were likely to be wanted and things that were not, which impressed Mr. Orridge very favourably. He particularly noticed the carefulness with which she handled some bottles of physic, reading the labels on each, and arranging the medicine that might be required at night on one side of the table, and the medicine that might be required in the daytime on the other.

When she left the dressing-table, and occupied herself in setting the furniture straight, and in folding up articles of clothing that had been thrown on one side, not the slightest movement of her thin, wasted hands seemed ever to be made at hazard or in vain. Noiselessly, modestly, observantly, she moved from side to side of the room, and neatness and order followed her steps wherever she went. When Mr. Orridge resumed his place at Mrs. Frankland's bedside, his mind was at ease on one point at least—it was perfectly evident that the new nurse could be depended on to make no mistakes.

"What an odd woman she is," whispered Rosamond.

"Odd, indeed," returned Mr. Orridge, "and desperately broken in health, though she may not confess to it. However, she is wonderfully neat-handed and careful, and there can be no harm in trying her for one night—that is to say, unless you feel any objection."

"On the contrary," said Rosamond, "she rather interests me. There is something in her face and manner—I can't say what—that makes me feel curious to know more of her. I must get her to talk, and try if I can't bring out all her peculiarities. Don't be afraid of my exciting myself, and don't stop here in this dull room on my account. I would much rather you went downstairs, and kept my husband company over his wine.

"Do go and talk to him, and amuse him a little—he must be so dull, poor fellow, while I am up here; and he likes you, Mr. Orridge—he does, very much. Stop one moment, and just look at the baby again. He doesn't take a dangerous quantity of sleep, does he? And, Mr. Orridge, one word more: When you have done your wine, you will promise to lend my husband the use of your eyes, and bring him upstairs to wish me goodnight, won't you?"

Willingly engaging to pay attention to Mrs. Frankland's request, Mr. Orridge left the bedside.

As he opened the room door, he stopped to tell Mrs. Jazeph that he should be downstairs if she wanted him, and that he would give her any instructions of which she might stand in need later in the evening, before he left the inn for the night.

The new nurse, when he passed by her, was kneeling over one of Mrs. Frankland's open trunks, arranging some articles of clothing which had been rather carelessly folded up. Just before he spoke to her, he observed that she had a chemisette in her hand, the frill of which was laced through with ribbon.

One end of this ribbon she appeared to him to be on the point of drawing out, when the sound of his footsteps disturbed her. The moment she became aware of his approach she dropped the chemisette suddenly in the trunk, and covered it over with some handkerchiefs.

Although this proceeding on Mrs. Jazeph's part rather surprised the doctor, he abstained from showing that he had noticed it. Her mistress had vouched for her character, after five years' experience of it, and the bit of ribbon was intrinsically worthless. On both accounts, it was impossible to suspect her of attempting to steal it; and yet, as Mr. Orridge could not help feeling when he had left the room, her conduct, when he surprised her over the trunk, was exactly the conduct of a person who is about to commit a theft.

"Pray don't trouble yourself about my luggage," said Rosamond, remarking Mrs. Jazeph's occupation as soon as the doctor had gone. "That is my idle maid's business, and you will only make her more careless than ever if you do it for her. I am sure the room is beautifully set in order. Come here and sit down and rest yourself. You must be a very unselfish, kind-hearted woman to give yourself all this trouble to serve a stranger."

"The doctor's message this afternoon told me that your mistress was a friend of my poor, dear father's. I suppose she must have known him before my time. Anyway, I feel doubly grateful to her for taking an interest in me for my father's sake. But you can have no such feeling; you must have come here from pure good-nature and anxiety to help others. Don't go away, there, to the window. Come and sit down by me."

Mrs. Jazeph had risen from the trunk, and was approaching the bedside—when she suddenly turned away in the direction of the fireplace, just as Mrs. Frankland began to speak of her father.

"Come and sit here," reiterated Rosamond, getting impatient at receiving no answer. "What in the world are you doing there at the foot of the bed?"

The figure of the new nurse again interposed between the bed and the fading evening light that glimmered through the window before there was any reply.

"The evening is closing in," said Mrs. Jazeph, "and the window is not quite shut. I was thinking of making it fast, and of drawing down the blind—if you had no objection, ma'am?"

"Oh, not yet! not yet! Shut the window, if you please, in case the baby should catch cold, but don't draw down the blind. Let me get my peep at the view as long as there is any light left to see it by. That long flat stretch of grazing-ground out there is just beginning, at this dim time, to look a little like my childish recollections of a Cornish moor. Do you know anything about Cornwall, Mrs. Jazeph?"

"I have heard—" At those first three words of reply the nurse stopped. She was just then engaged in shutting the window, and she seemed to find some difficulty in closing the lock.

"What have you heard?" asked Rosamond.

"I have heard that Cornwall is a wild, dreary country," said Mrs. Jazeph, still busying herself with the lock of the window, and, by consequence, still keeping her back turned to Mrs. Frankland.

"Can't you shut the window, yet?" said Rosamond. "My maid always does it quite easily. Leave it till she comes up—I am going to ring for her directly. I want her to brush my hair and cool my face with a little Eau de Cologne and water."

"I have shut it, ma'am," said Mrs. Jazeph, suddenly succeeding in closing the lock. "And if you will allow me, I should be very glad to make you comfortable for the night, and save you the trouble of ringing for the maid."

Thinking the new nurse the oddest woman she had ever met with, Mrs. Frankland accepted the offer. By the time Mrs. Jazeph had prepared the Eau de Cologne and water, the twilight was falling softly over the landscape outside, and the room was beginning to grow dark.

"Had you not better light a candle?" suggested Rosamond.

"I think not, ma'am," said Mrs. Jazeph, rather hastily. "I can see quite well without."

She began to brush Mrs. Frankland's hair as she spoke; and, at the same time, asked a question which referred to the few words that had passed between them on the subject of Cornwall. Pleased to find that the new nurse had grown familiar enough at last to speak before she was spoken to, Rosamond desired nothing better than to talk about her recollections of her native country.

But, from some inexplicable reason, Mrs. Jazeph's touch, light and tender as it was, had such a strangely disconcerting effect on her, that she could not succeed, for the moment, in collecting her thoughts so as to reply, except in the briefest manner. The careful hands of the nurse lingered with a stealthy gentleness among the locks of her hair; the pale, wasted face of the new nurse approached, every now and then, more closely to her own than appeared at all needful.

A vague sensation of uneasiness, which she could not trace to any particular part of her—which she could hardly say that she really felt, in a bodily sense, at all—seemed to be floating about her, to be hanging around and over her, like the air she breathed. She could not move, though she wanted to move in the bed; she could not turn her head so as to humour the action of the brush; she could not look round; she could not break the embarrassing silence which had been caused by her own short, discouraging answer.

At last the sense of oppression—whether fancied or real—irritated her into snatching the brush out of Mrs. Jazeph's hand. The instant she had done so, she felt ashamed of the discourteous abruptness of the action, and confused at the alarm and surprise which the manner of the nurse exhibited. With the strongest sense of the absurdity of her own conduct, and yet without the least power of controlling herself, she burst out laughing, and tossed the brush away to the foot of the bed.

"Pray don't look surprised, Mrs. Jazeph," she said, still laughing without knowing why, and without feeling in the slightest degree amused.

"I'm very rude and odd, I know. You have brushed my hair delightfully; but—I can't tell how—it seemed, all the time, as if you were brushing the strangest fancies into my head. I can't help laughing at them—I can't indeed! Do you know, once or twice, I absolutely fancied, when your face was closest to mine, that you wanted to kiss me! Did you ever hear of anything so ridiculous? I declare I am more of a baby, in some things, than the little darling here by my side!"

Mrs. Jazeph made no answer. She left the bed while Rosamond was speaking, and came back, after an unaccountably long delay, with the Eau de Cologne and water. As she held the basin while Mrs. Frankland bathed her face, she kept away at arms' length, and came no nearer when it was time to offer the towel.

Rosamond began to be afraid that she had seriously offended Mrs. Jazeph, and tried to soothe and propitiate her by asking questions about the management of the baby. There was a slight trembling in the sweet voice of the new nurse, but not the faintest tone of sullenness or anger, as she simply and quietly answered the inquiries addressed to her. By dint of keeping the conversation still on the subject of the child, Mrs. Frankland succeeded, little by little, in luring her back to the bedside—in tempting her to bend down admiringly over the infant in emboldening her, at last, to kiss him tenderly on the cheek. One kiss was all that she gave; and she turned away from the bed, after it, and sighed heavily.

The sound of that sigh fell very sadly on Rosamond's heart. Up to this time the baby's little span of life had always been associated with smiling faces and pleasant words. It made her uneasy to think that anyone could caress him and sigh after it.

"I am sure you must be fond of children," she said, hesitating a little from natural delicacy of feeling. "But will you excuse me for noticing that it seems rather a mournful fondness? Pray-pray don't answer my question if it gives you any pain—if you have any loss to deplore; but—but I do so want to ask if you have ever had a child of your own?"

Mrs. Jazeph was standing near a chair when that question was put. She caught fast hold of the back of it, grasping it so firmly, or perhaps leaning on it so heavily, that the woodwork cracked. Her head dropped low on her bosom. She did not utter, or even attempt to utter, a single word.

Fearing that she must have lost a child of her own, and dreading to distress her unnecessarily by venturing to ask any more questions, Rosamond said nothing, as she stooped over the baby to kiss him in her turn. Her lips rested on his cheek a little above where Mrs. Jazeph's lips had rested the moment before, and they touched a spot of wet on his smooth warm skin.

Fearing that some of the water in which she had been bathing her face might have dropped on him, she passed her fingers lightly over his head, neck, and bosom, and felt no other spots of wet anywhere. The one drop that had fallen on him was the drop that wetted the cheek which the new nurse had kissed.

The twilight faded over the landscape, the room grew darker and darker; and still, though she was now sitting close to the table on which the candles and matches were placed, Mrs. Jazeph made no attempt to strike a light. Rosamond did not feel quite comfortable at the idea of lying awake in the darkness, with nobody in the room but a person who was as yet almost a total stranger; and she resolved to have the candles lighted immediately.

"Mrs. Jazeph," she said, looking toward the gathering obscurity outside the window, "I shall be much obliged to you, if you will light the candles and pull down the blind. I can trace no more resemblances out there, now, to a Cornish prospect; the view has gone altogether."

"Are you very fond of Cornwall, ma'am?" asked Mrs. Jazeph, rising, in rather a dilatory manner, to light the candles.

"Indeed I am," said Rosamond. "I was born there; and my husband and I were on our way to Cornwall when we were obliged to stop, on my account, at this place. You are a long time getting the candles lighted. Can't you find the matchbox?"

Mrs. Jazeph, with an awkwardness which was rather surprising in a person who had shown so much neat-handedness in setting the room to rights, broke the first match in attempting to light it, and let the second go out the instant after the flame was kindled. At the third attempt she was more successful; but she only lit one candle, and that one she carried away from the table which Mrs. Frankland could see, to the dressing-table, which

126

was hidden from her by the curtains at the foot of the bed.

"Why do you move the candle?" asked Rosamond.

"I thought it was best for your eyes, ma'am, not to have the light too near them," replied Mrs. Jazeph; and then added hastily, as if she was unwilling to give Mrs. Frankland time to make any objections—"And so you were going to Cornwall, ma'am, when you stopped at this place? To travel about there a little, I suppose?" After saying these words, she took up the second candle, and passed out of sight as she carried it to the dressing-table.

Rosamond thought that the nurse, in spite of her gentle looks and manners, was a remarkably obstinate woman. But she was too good-natured to care about asserting her right to have the candles placed where she pleased; and when she answered Mrs. Jazeph's question, she still spoke to her as cheerfully and familiarly as ever.

"Oh, dear no! Not to travel about," she said, "but to go straight to the old country-house where I was born. It belongs to my husband now, Mrs. Jazeph. I have not been near it since I was a little girl of five years of age. Such a ruinous, rambling old place! You, who talk of the dreariness and wildness of Cornwall, would be quite horrified at the very idea of living in Porthgenna Tower."

The faintly rustling sound of Mrs. Jazeph's silk dress, as she moved about the dressing-table, had been audible all the while Rosamond was speaking. It ceased instantaneously when she said the words "Porthgenna Tower"; and for one moment there was a dead silence in the room.

"You, who have been living all your life, I suppose, in nicely repaired houses, cannot imagine what a place it is that we are going to, when I am well enough to travel again," pursued .Rosamond. "What do you think, Mrs. Jazeph, of a house with one whole side of it that has never been inhabited for sixty or seventy years past? You may get some notion of the size of Porthgenna Tower from that. There is a west side that we are to live in when we get there, and a north side, where the empty old rooms are, which I hope we shall be able to repair.

"Only think of the hosts of odd, old-fashioned things that we may find in those uninhabited rooms! I mean to put on the cook's apron and the gardener's gloves, and rummage all over them from top to bottom. How I shall astonish the housekeeper, when I get to Porthgenna, and ask her for the keys of the ghostly north rooms!"

A low cry, and a sound as if something had struck against the dressing-table, followed Mrs. Frankland's last words. She started in the bed and asked eagerly what was the matter.

"Nothing," answered Mrs. Jazeph, speaking so constrainedly that her voice dropped to a whisper. "Nothing, ma'am—nothing, I assure you. I struck my side, by accident, against the table—pray don't be alarmed!—it's not worth noticing."

"But you speak as if you were in pain," said Rosamond.

"No, no—not in pain. Not hurt—not hurt, indeed."

"While Mrs. Jazeph was declaring that she was not hurt, the door of the room was opened, and the doctor entered, leading in Mr. Frankland.

"We come early, Mrs. Frankland, but we are going to give you plenty of time to compose yourself for the night," said Mr. Orridge. He paused, and noticed that Rosamond's colour was heightened. "I am afraid you have been talking and exciting yourself a little too much," he went on. "If you will excuse me for venturing on the suggestion, Mr. Frankland, I think the sooner goodnight is said the better. Where is the nurse?"

Mrs. Jazeph sat down with her back to the lighted candle when she heard herself asked for. Just before that, she had been looking at Mr. Frankland with an eager, undisguised curiosity, which, if anyone had noticed it, must have appeared surprisingly out of character with her usual modesty and refinement of manner.

"I am afraid the nurse has accidentally hurt her side more than she is willing to confess," said Rosamond to the doctor, pointing with one hand to the place in which Mrs. Jazeph was sitting, and raising the other to her husband's neck as he stooped over her pillow.

Mr. Orridge, on inquiring what had happened, could not prevail on the new nurse to acknowledge that the accident was of the slightest consequence. He suspected, nevertheless, that she was suffering, or, at least, that something had happened to discompose her; for he found the greatest difficulty in fixing her attention, while he gave her a few needful directions in case her services were required during the night.

All the time he was speaking, her eyes wandered away from him to the part of the room where Mr. and Mrs. Frankland were talking together. Mrs. Jazeph looked like the last person in the world who would be guilty of an act of impertinent curiosity; and yet she openly betrayed all the characteristics of an inquisitive woman while Mr. Frankland was standing by his wife's pillow. The doctor was obliged to assume his most peremptory manner before he could get her to attend to him at all.

"And now, Mrs. Frankland," said Mr. Orridge, turning away from the nurse, "as I have given Mrs. Jazeph all the directions she wants, I shall set the example of leaving you in quiet by saying goodnight."

Understanding the hint conveyed in these words, Mr. Frankland attempted to say goodnight too, but his wife kept tight hold of both his hands, and declared that it was unreasonable to expect her to let him go for another half-hour at least. Mr. Orridge shook his head, and began to expatiate on the evils of over-excitement, and the blessings of composure and sleep.

His remonstrances, however, would have produced very little effect, even if Rosamond had allowed him to continue them, but for the interposition of the baby, who happened to wake up at that moment, and who proved himself a powerful auxiliary on the doctor's side, by absorbing all his mother's attention immediately. Seizing his opportunity at the right moment, Mr. Orridge quietly led Mr. Frankland out of the room, just as Rosamond was taking the child up in her arms. He stopped before closing the door to whisper one last word to Mrs. Jazeph.

"If Mrs. Frankland wants to talk, you must not encourage

her," he said. "As soon as she has quieted the baby, she ought to go to sleep. There is a chair-bedstead in that corner, which you can open for yourself when you want to lie down. Keep the candle where it is now, behind the curtain. The less light Mrs. Frankland sees, the sooner she will compose herself to sleep."

Mrs. Jazeph made no answer; she only looked at the doctor and curtsied. That strangely scared expression in her eyes, which he had noticed on first seeing her, was more painfully apparent than ever when he left her alone for the night with the mother and child. "She will never do," thought Mr. Orridge, as he led Mr. Frankland down the inn stairs. "We shall have to send to London for a nurse, after all."

Feeling a little irritated by the summary manner in which her husband had been taken away from her, Rosamond fretfully rejected the offers of assistance which were made to her by Mrs. Jazeph as soon as the doctor had left the room. The nurse said nothing when her services were declined; and yet, judging by her conduct, she seemed anxious to speak.

Twice she advanced toward the bedside—opened her lips—stopped—and retired confusedly, before she settled herself finally in her former place by the dressing-table. Here she remained, silent and out of sight, until the child had been quieted, and had fallen asleep in his mother's arms, with one little pink, half-closed hand resting on her bosom. Rosamond could not resist raising the hand to her lips, though she risked waking him again by doing so. As she kissed it, the sound of the kiss was followed by a faint, suppressed sob, proceeding from the other side of the curtains at the lower end of the bed.

"What is that?" she exclaimed.

"Nothing, ma'am," said Mrs Jazeph, in the same constrained, whispering tones in which she had answered Mrs. Frankland's former question. "I think I was just falling asleep in the armchair here; and I ought to have told you perhaps that, having had my troubles, and being afflicted with a heart complaint, I have a habit of sighing in my sleep. It means nothing, ma'am, and I hope you will be good enough to excuse it,"

Rosamond's generous instincts were aroused in a moment.

"Excuse it!" she said. "I hope I may do better than that, Mrs. Jazeph, and be the means of relieving it. When Mr. Orridge comes tomorrow you shall consult him, and I will take care that you want for nothing that he may order. No! no! Don't thank me until I have been the means of making you well—and keep where you are, if the armchair is comfortable. The baby is asleep again; and I should like to have half an hour's quiet before I change to the night side of the bed, Stop where you are for the present: I will call as soon as I want you."

So far from exercising a soothing effect on Mrs. Jazeph, these kindly meant words produced the precisely opposite result of making her restless. She began to walk about the room, and confusedly attempted to account for the change in her conduct by saying that she wished to satisfy herself that all her arrangements were properly made for the night. In a few minutes more she began, in defiance of the doctor's prohibition, to tempt Mrs. Frankland into talking again, by asking questions about Porthgenna Tower, and by referring to the chances for and against its being chosen as a permanent residence by the young married couple.

"Perhaps, ma'am," she said, speaking on a sudden, with an eagerness in her voice which was curiously at variance with the apparent indifference of her manner—"Perhaps when you see Porthgenna Tower you may not like it so well as you think you will now. Who can tell that you may not get tired and leave the place again after a few days—especially if you go into the empty rooms? I should have thought—if you will excuse my saying so, ma'am—I should have thought that a lady like you would have liked to get as far away as possible from dirt and dust, and disagreeable smells."

"I can face worse inconveniences than those, where my curiosity is concerned," said Rosamond. "And I am more curious to see the uninhabited rooms at Porthgenna than to see the Seven Wonders of the World. Even if we don't settle altogether at the old house, I feel certain that we shall stay there for some time."

At that answer, Mrs. Jazeph abruptly turned away and asked no more questions. She retired to a corner of the room near the door, where the chair-bedstead stood which the doctor had pointed out to her—occupied herself for a few minutes in making it ready for the night—then left it as suddenly as she had approached it, and began to walk up and down once more.

This unaccountable restlessness, which had already surprised Rosamond, now made her feel rather uneasy—especially when she once or twice overheard Mrs. Jazeph talking to herself. Judging by words and fragments of sentences that were audible now and then, her mind was still running, with the most inexplicable persistency, on the subject of Porthgenna Tower.

As the minutes wore on, and she continued to walk up and down, and still went on talking, Rosamond's uneasiness began to strengthen into something like alarm. She resolved to awaken Mrs. Jazeph, in the least offensive manner, to a sense of the strangeness of her own conduct, by noticing that she was talking, but by not appearing to understand that she was talking to herself.

"What did you say?" asked Rosamond, putting the question at a moment when the nurse's voice was most distinctly betraying her in the act of thinking aloud.

Mrs. Jazeph stopped, and raised her head vacantly, as if she had been awakened out of a heavy sleep.

"I thought you were saying something more about our old house," continued Rosamond. "I thought I heard you say that I ought not to go to Porthgenna, or that you would not go there in my place, or something of that sort."

Mrs. Jazeph blushed like a young girl. "I think you must have been mistaken, ma'am," she said, and stooped over the chair-bedstead again.

Watching her anxiously, Rosamond saw that, while she was affecting to arrange the bedstead, she was doing nothing whatever to prepare it for being slept in. What did that mean? What did her whole conduct mean for the last half-hour? As Mrs. Frankland asked herself those questions, the thrill of a terrible suspicion turned her cold to the very roots of her hair. It had never occurred to her before, but it suddenly struck her now, with the force of positive conviction, that the new nurse was not in her right senses.

All that was unaccountable in her behaviour—her odd disappearances behind the curtains at the foot of the bed; her lingering, stealthy, over-familiar way of using the hair-brush; her silence at one time, her talkativeness at another; her restlessness, her whispering to herself, her affectation of being deeply engaged in doing something which she was not doing at all—every one of her strange actions (otherwise incomprehensible) became intelligible in a moment on that one dreadful supposition that she was mad.

Terrified as she was, Rosamond kept her presence of mind. One of her arms stole instinctively round the child; and she had half raised the other to catch at the bell-rope hanging above her pillow, when she saw Mrs. Jazeph turn and look at her.

A woman possessed only of ordinary nerve would, probably, at that instant have pulled at the bell-rope in the unreasoning desperation of sheer fright. Rosamond had courage enough to calculate consequences, and to remember that Mrs. Jazeph would have time to lock the door, before assistance could arrive, if she betrayed her suspicions by ringing without first assigning some plausible reason for doing so.

She slowly closed her eyes as the nurse looked at her, partly to convey the notion that she was composing herself to sleep—partly to gain time to think of some safe excuse for summoning her maid. The flurry of her spirits, however, interfered with the exercise of her ingenuity. Minute after minute dragged on heavily, and still she could think of no assignable reason for ringing the bell.

She was just doubting whether it would not be safest to send Mrs. Jazeph out of the room, on some message to her husband, to lock the door the moment she was alone, and then to ring—she was just doubting whether she would boldly adopt this course of proceeding or not, when she heard the rustle of the nurse's silk dress approaching the bedside.

Her first impulse was to snatch at the bell-rope; but fear had paralysed her hand; she could not raise it from the pillow.

The rustling of the silk dress ceased. She half unclosed her eyes, and saw that the nurse was stopping midway between the part of the room from which she had advanced and the bedside. There was nothing wild or angry in her look. The agitation which her face expressed was the agitation of perplexity and alarm. She stood rapidly clasping and unclasping her hands, the image of bewilderment and distress—stood so for nearly a minute—then came forward a few steps more, and said inquiringly, in a whisper:

"Not asleep? not quite asleep yet?"

Rosamond tried to speak in answer, but the quick beating of her heart seemed to rise up to her very lips, and to stifle the words on them.

The nurse came on, still with the same perplexity and distress in her face, to within a foot of the bedside—knelt down by the pillow, and looked earnestly at Rosamond—shuddered a little, and glanced all round her, as if to make sure that the room was empty—bent forward—hesitated—bent nearer, and whispered into her ear these words:

"When you go to Porthgenna, keep out of the Myrtle Room!"

The hot breath of the woman, as she spoke, beat on Rosamond's cheek, and seemed to fly in one fever-throb through every vein of her body. The nervous shock of that unutterable sensation burst the bonds of the terror that had hitherto held her motionless and speechless. She started up in bed with a scream, caught hold of the bell-rope, and pulled it violently.

"Oh, hush! hush!" cried Mrs. Jazeph, sinking back on her knees, and beating her hands together despairingly with the helpless gesticulation of a child.

Rosamond rang again and again. Hurrying footsteps and eager voices were heard outside on the stairs. It was not ten o'clock yet—nobody had retired for the night—and the violent ringing had already alarmed the house.

The nurse rose to her feet, staggered back from the bed-side, and supported herself against the wall of the room, as the footsteps and the voices reached the door. She said not another word. The hands that she had been beating together so violently but an instant before hung down nerveless at her side. The blank of a great agony spread over all her face, and stilled it awfully.

The first person who entered the room was Mrs. Frankland's maid, and the landlady followed her.

"Fetch Mr. Frankland," said Rosamond, faintly, addressing the landlady. "I want to speak to him directly.—You," she continued, beckoning to the maid, "sit by me here till your master comes. I have been dreadfully frightened. Don't ask me questions; but stop here."

The maid stared at her mistress in amazement; then looked round with a disparaging frown at the nurse. When the landlady left the room to fetch Mr. Frankland, she had moved a little away from the wall, so as to command a full view of the bed. Her eyes were fixed with a look of breathless suspense, of devouring anxi-ety, on Rosamond's face. From all her other features the expres-sion seemed to be gone. She said nothing, she noticed nothing. She did not start, she did not move aside an inch, when the landlady returned, and led Mr. Frankland to his wife.

"Lenny! don't let the new nurse stop here tonight—pray, pray don't!" whispered Rosamond, eagerly catching her husband by the arm.

"Warned by the trembling of her hand, Mr. Frankland laid his fingers lightly on her temples and on her heart.

"Good heavens, Rosamond! what has happened? I left you quiet and comfortable, and now—"

"I've been frightened, dear—dreadfully frightened, by the new nurse. Don't be hard on her, poor creature; she is not in her right senses—I am certain she is not. Only get her away quietly—only send her back at once to where she came from. I shall die of the fright, if she steps here. She has been behav-ing so strangely—she has spoken such words to me—Lenny!

Lenny! don't let go of my hand. She came stealing up to me so horribly, just where you are now; she knelt down at my ear, and whispered—oh, such words!"

"Hush, hush, love!" said Mr. Frankland, getting seriously alarmed by the violence of Rosamond's agitation. "Never mind repeating the words now; wait till you are calmer—I beg and entreat of you, wait till you are calmer. I will do everything you wish, if you will only lie down and be quiet, and try to compose yourself before you say another word. It is quite enough for me to know that this woman has frightened you, and that you wish her to be sent away with as little harshness as possible. We will put off all further explanations till tomorrow morning. I deeply regret now that I did not persist in carrying out my own idea of sending for a proper nurse from London. Where is the landlady?"

The landlady placed herself by Mr. Frankland's side.

"Is it late?" asked Leonard.

"Oh no, sir; not ten o'clock yet."

"Order a fly to be brought to the door, then, as soon as possible, if you please. Where is the nurse?"

"Standing behind you, sir, near 'the wall," said the maid.

As Mr. Frankland turned in that direction, Rosamond whispered to him: "Don't be hard on her, Lenny."

The maid, looking with contemptuous curiosity at Mrs. Jazeph, saw the whole expression of her countenance alter, as those words were spoken. The tears rose thick in her eyes, and flowed down her cheeks. The deathly spell of stillness that had lain on her face was broken in an instant. She drew back again, close to the wall, and leaned against it as before.

"Don't be hard on her!" the maid heard her repeat to herself, in a low sobbing voice. "Don't be hard on her! Oh, my God! she said that kindly—she said that kindly, at least!"

"I have no desire to speak to you, or to use you unkindly," said Mr. Frankland, imperfectly hearing what she said. "I know nothing of what has happened, and I make no accusations. I find Mrs. Frankland violently agitated and frightened; I hear her connect that agitation with you—not angrily, but compassionately—and, instead of speaking harshly, I prefer leaving it to your own sense of what is right, to decide whether your attendance here ought not to cease at once. I have provided the proper means for your conveyance from this place; and I would suggest that you should make our apologies to your mistress, and say nothing more than that circumstances have happened which oblige us to dispense with your services."

"You have been considerate toward me, sir," said Mrs. Jazeph, speaking quietly, and with a certain gentle dignity in her manner, "and I will not prove myself unworthy of your forbearance by saying what I might say in my own defence." She advanced into the middle of the room, and stopped where she could see Rosamond plainly. Twice she attempted to speak, and twice her voice failed her. At the third effort she succeeded in controlling herself.

"Before I go, ma'am," she said, "I hope you will believe that I have no bitter feeling against you for sending me away. I am not angry—pray remember always that I was not angry, and that I never complained."

There was such a forlornness in her face, such a sweet, sorrowful resignation in every tone of her voice during the utterance of these few words, that Rosamond's heart smote her.

"Why did you frighten me?" she asked, half relenting.

"Frighten you? How could I frighten you? Oh, me! of all the people in the world, how could I frighten you?"

Mournfully saying those words, the nurse went to the chair on which she had placed her bonnet and shawl, and put them on. The landlady and the maid, watching her with curious eyes, detected that she was again weeping bitterly, and noticed with astonishment, at the same time, how neatly she put on her bonnet and shawl. The wasted hands were moving mechanically, and were trembling while they moved—and yet, slight thing though it was, the inexorable instinct of propriety guided their most trifling actions still.

On her way to the door, she stopped again at passing the bedside, looked through her tears at Rosamond and the child, struggled a little with herself, and then spoke her farewell words—

"God bless you, and keep you and your child happy and prosperous," she said. "I am not angry at being sent away. If you ever think of me again, after tonight, please to remember that I was not angry, and that I never complained." She stood for a moment longer, still weeping, and still looking through her tears at the mother and child then turned away and walked to the door. Something in the last tones of her voice caused a silence in the room. Of the four persons in it not one could utter a word, as the nurse closed the door gently, and went out from them alone.

CHAPTER 5
A COUNCIL OF THREE

On the morning after the departure of Mrs. Jazeph, the news that she had been sent away from the Tiger's Head by Mr. Frankland's directions, reached the doctor's residence from the inn just as he was sitting down to breakfast. Finding that the report of the nurse's dismissal was not accompanied by any satisfactory explanation of the cause of it, Mr. Orridge refused to believe that her attendance on Mrs. Frankland had really ceased. However, although he declined to credit the news, he was so far disturbed by it that he finished his breakfast in a hurry, and went to pay his morning visit at the Tiger's Head nearly two hours before the time at which he usually attended on his patient.

On his way to the inn, he was met and stopped by the one waiter attached to the establishment. "I was just bringing you a message from Mr. Frankland, sir," said the man. "He wants to see you as soon as possible."

"Is it true that Mrs. Frankland's nurse was sent away last night by Mr. Frankland's order?" asked Mr. Orridge.

"Quite true, sir," answered the waiter.

The doctor coloured, and looked seriously discomposed. One of the most precious things we have about us—especially if we happen to belong to the medical profession—is our dignity. It struck Mr. Orridge that he ought to have been consulted before a nurse of his recommending was dismissed from her situation at a moment's notice. Was Mr. Frankland presuming upon his position as a gentleman of fortune?

The power of wealth may do much with impunity, but it is not privileged to offer any practical contradictions to a man's good opinion of himself. Never had the doctor thought more disrespectfully of rank and riches; never had he been conscious of reflecting on republican principles with such absolute impartiality, as when he now followed the waiter in sullen silence to Mr. Frankland's room.

"Who is that?" asked Leonard, when he heard the door open.

"Mr. Orridge, sir," said the waiter.

"Good-morning," said Mr. Orridge, with self, asserting abruptness and familiarity.

Mr. Frankland was sitting in an armchair, with his legs crossed. Mr. Orridge carefully selected another armchair, and crossed his legs on the model of Mr. Frankland's the moment he sat down. Mr. Frankland's hands were in the pockets of his dressing-gown. Mr. Orridge had no pockets, except in his coat-tails, which he could not conveniently get at; but he put his thumbs into the armholes of his waistcoat, and asserted himself against the easy insolence of wealth in that way.

It made no difference to him—so curiously narrow is the range of a man's perceptions when he is insisting on his own importance—that Mr. Frankland was blind, and consequently incapable of being impressed by the independence of his bearing. Mr. Orridge's own dignity was vindicated in Mr. Orridge's own presence, and that was enough.

"I am glad you have come so early, doctor," said Mr. Frankland. "A very unpleasant thing happened here last night. I was obliged to send the new nurse away at a moment's notice."

"Were you, indeed?" said Mr. Orridge, defensively matching Mr. Frankland's composure by an assumption of the completest indifference. "Aha! were you, indeed?"

"If there had been time to send and consult you, of course I should have been only too glad to have done so," continued Leonard; "but it was impossible to hesitate. We were all alarmed by a loud ringing of my wife's bell; I was taken up to her room, and found her in a condition of the most violent agitation and alarm. She told me she had been dreadfully frightened by the new nurse; declared her conviction that the woman was not in her right senses; and entreated that I would get her out of the house with as little delay and as little harshness as possible.

"Under these circumstances, what could I do? I may seem to have been wanting in consideration toward you, in proceeding on my own sole responsibility; but Mrs. Frankland was in such a state of excitement that I could not tell what might be the consequence of opposing her, or of venturing on any delays; and after the difficulty had been got over, she would not hear of. your being disturbed by a summons to the inn. I am sure you will understand this explanation, doctor, in the spirit in which I offer it."

Mr. Orridge began to look a little confused. His solid sub-structure of independence was softening and sinking from under him. He suddenly found himself thinking of the cultivated manners of the wealthy classes; his thumbs slipped mechanically out of the armholes of his waistcoat; and, before he well knew what he was about, he was stammering his way through all the choicest intricacies of a complimentary and respectful reply.

"You will naturally be anxious to know what the new nurse said or did to frighten my wife so," pursued Mr. Frankland. "I can tell you nothing in detail; for Mrs. Frankland was in such a state of nervous dread last night that I was really afraid of asking for any explanations; and I have purposely waited to make inquiries this morning until you could come here and accompany me upstairs.

"You kindly took so much trouble to secure this unlucky woman's attendance, that you have a right to hear all that can be alleged against her, now she has been sent away. Considering all things, Mrs. Frankland is not so ill this morning as I was afraid she would be. She expects to see you with me; and, if you will kindly give me your arm, we will go up to her immediately."

On entering Mrs. Frankland's room, the doctor saw at a glance that she had been altered for the worse by the events of the past evening. He remarked that the smile with which she greeted her husband was the faintest and saddest he had seen on her face. Her eyes looked dim and weary, her skin was dry, her pulse was irregular. It was plain that she had passed a wakeful night, and that her mind was not at ease. She dismissed the inquiries of her medical attendant as briefly as possible, and led the conversation immediately, of her own accord, to the subject of Mrs. Jazeph.

"I suppose you have heard what has happened," she said, addressing Mr. Orridge. "I can't tell you how grieved I am about it. My conduct must look in your eyes, as well as in the eyes of the poor unfortunate nurse, the conduct of a capricious, unfeeling woman. I am ready to cry with sorrow and vexation when I remember how thoughtless I was, and how little courage I showed. Oh, Lenny, it is dreadful to hurt the feelings of anybody, but to have pained that unhappy, helpless woman as we pained her, to have made her cry so bitterly, to have caused her such humiliation and wretchedness—"

"My dear Rosamond," interposed Mr. Frankland, "you are lamenting effects, and forgetting causes altogether. Remember what a state of terror I found you in—there must have been some reason for that. Remember, too, how strong your conviction was that the nurse was out of her senses. Surely you have not altered your opinion on that point already?"

"It is that very opinion, love, that has been perplexing and worrying me all night. I can't alter it; I feel more certain than ever that there must be something wrong with the poor creature's intellect—and yet, when I remember how good-naturedly she came here to help me, and how anxious she seemed to make herself useful, I can't help feeling ashamed of my suspicions; I can't help reproaching myself for having been the cause of her dismissal last night. Mr. Orridge, did you notice anything in Mrs.

Jazeph's face or manner which might lead you to doubt whether her intellects were quite as sound as they ought to be?"

"Certainly not, Mrs. Frankland, or I should never have brought her here. I should not have been astonished to hear that she was suddenly taken ill, or that she had been seized with a fit, or that some slight accident, which would have frightened nobody else, had seriously frightened her; but to be told that there is anything approaching to derangement in her faculties, does, I own, fairly surprise me."

"Can I have been mistaken !" exclaimed Rosamond, looking confusedly and self-distrustfully from Mr. Orridge to her husband. "Lenny! Lenny! if I have been mistaken, I shall never forgive myself."

"Suppose you tell us, my dear, what led you to suspect that she was mad?" suggested Mr. Frankland.

Rosamond hesitated. "Things that are great in one's own mind," she said, "seem to get so little when they are put into words. I almost despair of making you understand what good reason I had to be frightened—and then, I am afraid, in trying to do justice to myself, that I may not do justice to the nurse."

"Tell your own story, my love, in your own way, and you will be sure to tell it properly," said Mr. Frankland.

"And pray remember," added Mr. Orridge, "that I attach no real importance to my opinion of Mrs. Jazeph. I have not had time enough to form it. Your opportunities of observing her have been far more numerous than mine."

Thus encouraged, Rosamond plainly and simply related all that had happened in her room on the previous evening, up to the time when she had closed her eyes and had heard the nurse approaching her bedside. Before repeating the extraordinary words that Mrs. Jazeph had whispered in her ear, she made a pause, and looked earnestly in her husband's face.

"Why do you stop?" asked Mr. Frankland.

"I feel nervous and flurried still, Lenny, when I think of the words the nurse said to me, just before I rang the bell."

"What did she say? Was it something you would rather not

142

repeat?"

"No! no! I am most anxious to repeat it, and to hear what you think it means. As I have just told you, Lenny, we had been talking of Porthgenna, and of my project of exploring the north rooms as soon as I got there; and she had been asking many questions about the old house; appearing, I must say, to be unaccountably interested in it, considering she was a stranger."

"Yes?"

"Well, when she came to the bedside, she knelt down close at my ear, and whispered all on a sudden—'When you go to Porthgenna, keep out of the Myrtle Room!'"

Mr. Frankland started. "Is there such a room at Porthgenna?" he asked, eagerly.

"I never heard of it," said Rosamond.

"Are you sure of that?" inquired Mr. Orridge. Up to this moment the doctor had privately suspected that Mrs. Frankland must have fallen asleep soon after he left her the evening before; and that the narrative which she was now relating, with the sincerest conviction of its reality, was actually derived from nothing but a series of vivid impressions produced by a dream.

"I am certain I never heard of such a room," said Rosamond. "I left Porthgenna at five years old; and I had never heard of it then. My father often talked of the house in after years; but I am certain that he never spoke of any of the rooms by any particular names; and I can say the same of your father, Lenny, whenever I was in his company after he had bought the place.

"Besides, don't you remember, when the builder we sent down to survey the house wrote you that letter, he complained that there were no names of the rooms on the different keys to guide him in opening the doors, and that he could get no information from anybody at Porthgenna on the subject? How could I ever have heard of the Myrtle Room? Who was there to tell me?"

Mr. Orridge began to look perplexed; it seemed by no means so certain that Mrs. Frankland had been dreaming, after all.

"I have thought of nothing else," said Rosamond to her husband, in low, whispering tones. "I can't get those mysterious words off my mind. Feel my heart, Lenny—it is beating quicker than usual only with saying them over to you. They are such very strange, startling words. What do you think they mean?"

"Who is the woman who spoke them?—that is the most important question," said Mr. Frankland.

"But why did she say the words to me? That is what I want to know—that is what I must know, if I am ever to feel easy in my mind again!"

"Gently, Mrs. Frankland, gently!" said Mr. Orridge. "For your child's sake, as well as for your own, pray try to be calm, and to look at this very mysterious event as composedly as you can. If any exertions of mine can throw light upon this strange woman and her still stranger conduct, I will not spare them. I am going today to her mistress's house to see one of the children; and, depend upon it, I will manage in some way to make Mrs. Jazeph explain herself. Her mistress shall hear every word that you have told me; and I can assure you she is just the sort of downright, resolute woman who will insist on having the whole mystery instantly cleared up."

Rosamond's weary eyes brightened at the doctor's proposal. "Oh, go at once, Mr. Orridge!" she exclaimed—"go at once!"

"I have a great deal of medical work to do in the town first," said the doctor, smiling at Mrs Frankland's impatience.

"Begin it, then, without losing another instant," said Rosamond. "The baby is quite well, and I am quite well—we need not detain you a moment. And, Mr. Orridge, pray be as gentle and considerate as possible with the poor woman; and tell her that I never should have thought of sending her away if I had not been too frightened to know what I was about. And say how sorry I am this morning, and say—"

"My dear, if Mrs. Jazeph is really not in her right senses, what would be the use of overwhelming her with all these excuses?" interposed Mr. Frankland. "It will be more to the purpose if Mr. Orridge will kindly explain and apologize for us to her mistress."

"Go! Don't stop to talk—pray go at once!" cried Rosamond, as the doctor attempted to reply to Mr. Frankland.

"Don't be afraid; no time shall be lost," said Mr. Orridge, opening the door. "But remember, Mrs. Frankland, I shall expect you to reward your ambassador, when he returns from his mission, by showing him that you are a little more quiet and composed than I find you this morning. With that parting hint, the doctor took his leave.

"'When you go to Porthgenna, keep out of the Myrtle Room,'" repeated Mr. Frankland, thoughtfully. "Those are very strange words, Rosamond. Who can this woman really be? She is a perfect stranger to both of us; we are brought into contact with her by the merest accident; and we find that she knows something about our own house of which we were both perfectly ignorant until she chose to speak."

"But the warning, Lenny—the warning, so pointedly and mysteriously addressed to me? Oh, if I could only go to sleep at once, and not wake again till the doctor comes back!"

"My love, try not to count too certainly on our being enlightened, even then. The woman may refuse to explain herself to anybody."

"Don't even hint at such a disappointment as that, Lenny—or I shall be wanting to get up, and go and question her myself!"

"Even if you could get up and question her, Rosamond, you might find it impossible to make her answer. She may be afraid of certain consequences which we cannot foresee; and, in that case, I can only repeat that it is more than probable she will explain nothing—or, perhaps, still more likely that she will coolly deny her own words altogether."

"Then, Lenny, we will put them to the proof for ourselves."

"And how can we do that?"

"By continuing our journey to Porthgenna the moment I am allowed to travel, and by leaving no stone unturned when we get there until we have discovered whether there is or is not any room in the old house that ever was known, at any time of its existence, by the name of the Myrtle Room."

"And suppose it should turn out that there is such a room?" asked Mr. Frankland, beginning to feel the influence of his wife's enthusiasm.

"If it does turn out so," said Rosamond, her voice rising, and her face lighting up with its accustomed vivacity, "how can you doubt what will happen next? Am I not a woman? And have I not been forbidden to enter the Myrtle Room? Lenny! Lenny! Do you know so little of my half of humanity as to doubt what I should do the moment the room was discovered? My darling, as a matter of course, I should walk into it immediately."

CHAPTER 6
ANOTHER SURPRISE

With all the haste he could make, it was one o'clock in the afternoon before Mr. Orridge's professional avocations allowed him to set forth in his gig for Mrs. Norbury's house. He drove there with such goodwill that he accomplished the half-hour's journey in twenty minutes. The footman having heard the rapid approach of the gig, opened the hall door the instant the horse was pulled up before it, and confronted the doctor with a smile of malicious satisfaction.

"Well," said Mr. Orridge, bustling into the hall, "you were all rather surprised last night when the housekeeper came back, I suppose?"

"Yes, sir, we certainly were surprised when she came back last night," answered the footman; "but we were still more surprised when she went away again this morning."

"Went away! You don't mean to say she is gone?"

"Yes, I do, sir—she has lost her place, and gone for good." The footman smiled again, as he made that reply; and the house-maid, who happened to be on her way downstairs while he was speaking, and to hear what he said, smiled too. Mrs. Jazeph had evidently been no favourite in the servants' hall.

Amazement prevented Mr. Orridge from uttering another word. Hearing no more questions asked, the footman threw open the door of the breakfast-parlour and the doctor followed him into the room. Mrs. Norbury was sitting near the window in a rigidly upright attitude, inflexibly watching the proceedings of her invalid child over a basin of beef-tea.

"I know what you are going to talk about before you open your lips," said the outspoken lady. "But just look to the child first, and say what you have to say on that subject, if you please, before you enter on any other.' '

The child was examined, was pronounced to be improving rapidly, and was carried away by the nurse to lie down and rest a little. As soon as the door of the room had closed, Mrs. Norbury abruptly addressed the doctor, interrupting him, for the second time, just as he was about to speak.

"Now, Mr. Orridge," she said, "I want to tell you something at the outset. I am a remarkably just woman, and I have no quarrel with you. You are the cause of my having been treated with the most audacious insolence by three people—but you are the innocent cause, and, therefore, I don't blame you."

"I am really at a loss," Mr. Orridge began—"quite at a loss, I assure you—"

"To know what I mean?" said Mrs. Norbury, "I will soon tell you. Were you not the original cause of my sending my house-keeper to nurse Mrs. Frankland?"

"Yes." Mr. Orridge could not hesitate to acknowledge that.

"Well," pursued Mrs. Norbury, "and the consequence of my sending her is, as I said before, that I am treated with unparalleled insolence by no less than three people. Mrs. Frankland takes an insolent whim into her head, and affects to be frightened by my housekeeper. Mr. Frankland shows an insolent readiness to humour that whim, and hands me back my housekeeper as if she was a bad shilling; and last, and worst of all, my housekeeper herself insults me to my face as soon as she comes back insults me,—Mr. Orridge, to that degree that I give her twelve hours' notice to leave the place.

"Don't begin to defend yourself! I know all about it; I know you had nothing to do with sending her back; I never said you had. All the mischief you have done is innocent mischief. I don't blame you, remember that—whatever you do, Mr. Orridge, remember that!"

"I had no idea of defending myself," said the doctor, "for I have no reason to do so. But you surprise me beyond all power of expression when you tell me that Mrs. Jazeph treated you with incivility."

"Incivility!" exclaimed Mrs. Norbury. "Don't talk about incivility—it's not the word. Impudence is the word—brazen impudence. The only charitable thing to say of Mrs. Jazeph is that she is not right in her head. I never noticed anything odd about her myself; but the servants used to laugh at her for being as timid in the dark as a child, and for often running away to her candle in her own room when they declined to light the lamps before the night had fairly set in. I never troubled my head about this before; but I thought of it last night, I can tell you, when I found her looking me fiercely in the face, and contradicting me flatly the moment I spoke to her."

"I should have thought she was the very last woman in the world to misbehave herself in that way," answered the doctor.

"Very well. Now hear what happened when she came back last night," said Mrs. Norbury. "She got here just as we were going upstairs to bed. Of course, I was astonished; and, of course, I called her into the drawing-room for an explanation. There was nothing very unnatural in that course of proceeding, I suppose.

"Well, I noticed that her eyes were swollen and red, and that her looks were remarkably wild and queer; but I said nothing, and waited for the explanation. All that she had to tell me was that something she had unintentionally said or done had frightened Mrs. Frankland, and that Mrs. Frankland's husband had sent her away on the spot. I disbelieved this at first—and very naturally, I think—but she persisted in the story, and answered all my questions by declaring that she could tell me nothing more. 'So then,' I said, 'I am to believe that, after I have inconvenienced myself by sparing you, and after you have inconvenienced yourself by undertaking the business of nurse, I am to be insulted, and you are to be insulted, by your being sent away from Mrs.

Frankland on the very day when you get to her, because she chooses to take a whim into her head?'

"'I never accused Mrs. Frankland of taking a whim into her head,' said Mrs. Jazeph, and stares me straight in the face, with such a look as I never saw in her eyes before, after all my five years' experience of her. 'What do you mean?' I asked, giving her back her look, I can promise you. 'Are you base enough to take the treatment you have received in the light of a favour?' 'I am just enough,' said Mrs. Jazeph, as sharp as lightning, and still with that same stare straight at me—'I am just enough not to blame Mrs. Frankland.'

"'Oh, you are, are you?' I said. 'Then all I can tell you is, that I feel this insult, if you don't; and that I consider Mrs. Frankland's conduct to be the conduct of an ill-bred, impudent, capricious, unfeeling woman.' Mrs. Jazeph takes a step up to me—takes a step, I give you my word of honour—and says distinctly, in so many words: 'Mrs. Frankland is neither ill-bred, impudent, capricious, nor unfeeling.'

"'Do you mean to contradict me, Mrs. Jazeph?' I asked. 'I mean to defend Mrs. Frankland from unjust imputations,' says she. Those were her words, Mr. Orridge—on my honour, as a gentlewoman, those were exactly her words.'"

The doctor's face expressed the blankest astonishment. Mrs. Norbury went on:

"I was in a towering passion I don't mind confessing that, Mr. Orridge—but I kept it down. 'Mrs. Jazeph,' I said, 'this is language that I am not accustomed to, and that I certainly never expected to hear from your lips. Why you should take it on yourself to defend Mrs. Frankland for treating us both with contempt, and to contradict me for resenting it, I neither know nor care to know. But I must tell you, in plain words, that I will be spoken to by every person in my employment, from my housekeeper to my scullery-maid, with respect. I would have given warning on the spot to any other servant in this house who had behaved to me as you have behaved.'

"She tried to interrupt me there, but I would not allow her.

'No,' I said, 'you are not to speak to me just yet; you are to hear me out. Any other servant, I tell you again, should have left this place tomorrow morning; but I will be more than just to you. I will give you the benefit of your five years' good conduct in my service. I will leave you the rest of the night to get cool, and to reflect on what has passed between us; and I will not expect you to make the proper apologies to me until the morning.' You see, Mr. Orridge, I was determined to act justly and kindly; I was ready to make allowances—and what do you think she said in return?

"'I am willing to make any apologies, ma'am, for offending you,' she said, without the delay of a single minute; but, whether it is tonight, or whether it is tomorrow morning, I cannot stand by silent when I hear Mrs. Frankland charged with acting unkindly, uncivilly, or improperly toward me or toward any one.' 'Do you tell me that deliberately, Mrs. Jazeph?' I asked. 'I tell it you sincerely, ma'am,' she answered; 'and I am very sorry to be obliged to do so.'

"'Pray don't trouble yourself to be sorry,' I said, 'for you may consider yourself no longer in my service. I will order the steward to pay you the usual month's wages instead of the month's warning the first thing tomorrow; and I beg that you will leave the house as soon as you conveniently can afterward.'

"'I will leave tomorrow, ma'am,' says she, 'but without troubling the steward. I beg respectfully, and with many thanks for your past kindness, to decline taking a month's money which I have not earned by a month's service.'

"And thereupon she courtesies and goes out. That is, word for word, what passed between us, Mr. Orridge. Explain the woman's conduct in your own way, if you can. I say that it is utterly incomprehensible, unless you agree with me that she was not in her right senses when she came back to this house last night."

The doctor began to think, after what he had just heard, that Mrs. Frankland's suspicions in relation to the new nurse were not quite so unfounded as he had been at first disposed to consider them. He wisely refrained, however, from complicating matters by giving utterance to what bethought; and, after answering Mrs. Norbury in a few vaguely polite words, endeavoured to soothe her irritation against Mr, and Mrs. Frankland by assuring her that he came as the bearer of apologies from both husband and wife, for the apparent want of courtesy and consideration in their conduct which circumstances had made inevitable. The offended lady, however, absolutely refused to be propitiated. She rose up and waved her hand with an air of great dignity.

"I cannot hear a word more from you, Mr. Orridge," she said; "I cannot receive any apologies which are made indirectly. If Mr. Frankland chooses to call and if Mrs Frankland condescends to write to me, I am willing to think no more of the matter. Under any other circumstances, I must be allowed to keep my present opinions both of the lady and the gentleman.

"Don't say another word, and be so kind as to excuse me if I leave you, and go up to the nursery to see how the child is getting on. I am delighted to hear that you think her so much better. Pray call again tomorrow or next day, if you conveniently can. Good-morning!"

Half amused at Mrs. Norbury, half displeased at the curt tone she adopted toward him, Mr. Orridge remained for a minute or two alone in the breakfast-parlour, feeling rather undecided about what he should do next.

He was, by this time, almost as much interested in solving the mystery of Mrs. Jazeph's extraordinary conduct as Mrs. Frankland herself; and he felt unwilling, on all accounts, to go back to the Tiger's Head, and merely repeat what Mrs. Norbury had told him, without being able to complete the narrative by informing Mr. and Mrs. Frankland of the direction that the housekeeper had taken on leaving her situation.

After some pondering, he determined to question the footman, under the pretence of desiring to know if his gig was at the door. The man having answered the bell, and having reported the gig to be ready, Mr. Orridge, while crossing the hall, asked him carelessly if he knew at what time in the morning Mrs.

Jazeph had left the place.

"About ten o'clock, sir," answered the foot-man. "When the carrier came by from the village, on his way to the station for the eleven o'clock train."

"Oh! I suppose he took her boxes?" said Mr. Orridge.

"And he took her, too, sir," said the man, with a grin. "She had to ride, for once in her life, at any rate, in a carrier's cart."

On getting back to West Winston, the doctor stopped at the station to collect further particulars, before he returned to the Tiger's Head. No trains, either up or down, happened to be due just at that time. The station-master was reading the newspaper, and the porter was gardening on the slope of the embankment.

"Is the train at eleven in the morning an up-train or a down-train?" asked Mr. Orridge, addressing the porter.

"A down-train."

"Did many people go by it?"

The porter repeated the names of some of the inhabitants of West Winston.

"Were there no passengers but passengers from the town?" inquired the doctor.

"Yes, sir. I think there was one stranger—a lady."

"Did the station-master issue the tickets for that train?"

"Yes, sir."

Mr. Orridge went on to the station-master.

"Do you remember giving a ticket this morning, by the eleven o'clock down-train, to a lady travelling alone?"

The station-master pondered. "I have issued tickets, up and down, to half-a-dozen ladies today," he answered, doubtfully.

"Yes, but I am speaking only of the eleven o'clock train," said Mr. Orridge. "Try if you can't remember?"

"Remember? Stop! I do remember; I know who you mean. A lady who seemed rather flurried, and who put a question to me that I am not often asked at this station. She had her veil down, I recollect, and she got here for the eleven o'clock train. Crouch, the carrier, brought her trunk into the office."

"That is the woman. Where did she take her ticket for?"

"For Exeter."

"You said she asked you a question?"

"Yes: a question about what coaches met the rail at Exeter to take travellers into Cornwall. I told her we were rather too far off here to have the correct timetable, and recommended her to apply for information to the Devonshire people when she got to the end of her journey. She seemed a timid, helpless kind of woman to travel alone. Anything wrong in connection with, her, sir?"

"Oh, no! nothing," said Mr. Orridge, leaving the station-master and hastening back to his gig again.

When he drew up, a few minutes afterward, at the door of the Tiger's Head, he jumped out of his vehicle with the confident air of a man who has done all that could be expected of him. It was easy to face Mrs. Frankland with the unsatisfactory news of Mrs. Jazeph's departure, now that he could add, on the best authority, the important supplementary information that she had gone to Cornwall.

BOOK 4

CHAPTER 1
A PLOT AGAINST THE SECRET

Toward the close of the evening, on the day after Mr. Orridge's interview with Mrs. Norbury, the Druid fast coach, running through Cornwall as far as Truro, set down three inside passengers at the door of the booking-office on arriving at its destination. Two of these passengers were an old gentleman and his daughter; the third was Mrs. Jazeph.

The father and daughter collected their luggage and entered the hotel; the outside passengers branched off in different directions with as little delay as possible; Mrs. Jazeph alone stood irresolute on the pavement, and seemed uncertain what she should do next.

When the coachman good-naturedly endeavoured to assist her in arriving at a decision of some kind, by asking whether he could do anything to help her, she started, and looked at him suspiciously; then, appearing to recollect herself, thanked him for his kindness, and inquired, with a confusion of words and a hesitation of manner which appeared very extraordinary in the coachman's eyes, whether she might be allowed to leave her trunk at the booking-office for a little while, until she could return and call for it again.

Receiving permission to leave her trunk as long as she pleased, she crossed over the principal street of the town, ascended the pavement on the opposite side, and walked down the first turning she came to. On entering the by-street to which the turning led, she glanced back, satisfied herself that nobody was following or watching her, hastened on a few yards, and stopped again at a small shop devoted to the sale of bookcases, cabinets, work-boxes, and writing-desks.

After first looking up at the letters painted over the door—Buschmann, Cabinet-Maker, &c.—she peered in at the shop window. A middle-aged man, with a cheerful face, sat behind the counter, polishing a rosewood bracket, and nodding briskly at regular intervals, as if he were humming a tune and keeping time to it with his head, Seeing no customers in the shop, Mrs. Jazeph opened the door and walked in.

As soon as she was inside, she became aware that the cheerful man behind the counter was keeping time, not to a tune of his own humming, but to a tune played by a musical box. The clear ringing notes came from a parlour behind the shop, and the air the box was playing was the lovely "*Batti, Batti*," of Mozart.

"Is Mr. Buschmann at home?" asked Mrs. Jazeph.

"Yes, ma'am," said the cheerful man, pointing with a smile toward the door that led into the parlour. "The music answers for him. Whenever Mr Buschmann's box is playing, Mr. Buschmann himself is not far off from it. Did you wish to see him, ma'am?"

"If there is nobody with him."

"Oh, no, he is quite alone. Shall I give any name?"

154

Mrs. Jazeph opened her lips to answer, hesitated, and said nothing. The shopman, with a quicker delicacy of perception than might have been expected from him, judging by outward appearances, did not repeat the question, but opened the door at once and admitted the visitor to the presence of Mr, Buschmann.

The shop parlour was a very small room, with an old three-cornered look about it, with a bright green paper on the walls, with a large dried fish in a glass case over the fireplace, with two *meerschaum* pipes hanging together on the wall opposite, and a neat round table placed as accurately as possible in the middle of the floor.

On the table were tea-things, bread, butter, a pot of jam, and a musical box in a quaint, old-fashioned case; and by the side of the table sat a little, rosy-faced, white-haired, simple-looking old man, who started up, when the door was opened, with an appearance of extreme confusion, and touched the top of the musical box so that it might cease playing when it came to the end of the air.

"A lady to speak with you, sir," said the cheerful shopman. "That is Mr. Buschmann, ma'am," he added, in a lower tone, seeing Mrs. Jazeph stop in apparent uncertainty on entering the parlour.

"Will you please to take a seat, ma'am?" said Mr. Buschmann, when the shopman had closed the door and gone back to his counter. "Excuse the music; it will stop directly." He spoke these words in a foreign accent, but with perfect fluency.

Mrs. Jazeph looked at him earnestly while he was addressing her, and advanced a step or two before she said anything. "Am I so changed?" she asked softly. "So sadly, sadly changed, Uncle Joseph?"

"*Gott im Himmel!* it's her voice—it's Sarah Leeson!" cried the old man, running up to his visitor as nimbly as if he was a boy again, taking both her hands, and kissing her with an odd, brisk tenderness on the cheek. Although his niece was not at all above the average height of women, Uncle Joseph was so short that he had to raise himself on tiptoe to perform the ceremony of embracing her.

"To think of Sarah coming at last!" he said, pressing her into a chair. "After all these years and years, to think of Sarah Leeson coming to see Uncle Joseph again!"

"Sarah still, but not Sarah Leeson," said Mrs. Jazeph, pressing her thin, trembling hands firmly together, and looking down on the floor while she spoke.

"Ah! married?" said Mr. Buschmann, gaily. "Married, of course. Tell me all about your husband, Sarah."

"He is dead. Dead and forgiven." She murmured the last three words in a whisper to herself.

"Ah! I am so sorry for you! I spoke too suddenly, did I not, my child?" said the old man. "Never mind! No, no; I don't mean that—I mean let us talk of something else. You will have a bit of bread and jam, won't you, Sarah?—ravishing raspberry jam that melts in your mouth. Some tea, then? So, so, she will have some tea, to be sure.

"And we won't talk of our troubles at least, not just yet. You look very pale, Sarah—very much older than you ought to look no, I don't mean that either; I don't mean to be rude. It was your voice I knew you by, my child—your voice that your poor Uncle Max always said would have made your fortune if you would only have learned to sing. Here's his pretty music box going still. Don't look so downhearted don't, pray. Do listen a little to the music: you remember the box?—my brother Max's box?

"Why, how you look! Have you forgotten the box that the divine Mozart gave to my brother with his own hand, when Max was a boy in the music school at Vienna? Listen! I have set it going again. It's a song they call '*Batti, Batti*'; it's a song in an opera of Mozart's. Ah! beautiful! beautiful! Your Uncle Max said that all music was comprehended in that one song. I know nothing about music, but I have my heart and my ears, and they tell me that Max was right."

Speaking those words with abundant gesticulation and amazing volubility, Mr. Buschmann poured out a cup of tea for his niece, stirred it carefully, and, patting her on the shoulder, begged that she would make him happy by drinking it all up directly. As he came close to her to press this request, he discovered that the tears were in her eyes, and that she was trying to take her handkerchief from her pocket without being observed.

"Don't mind me," she said, seeing the old man's face sadden as he looked at her; "and don't think me forgetful or ungrateful, Uncle Joseph. I remember the box—I remember everything that you used to take an interest in when I was younger and happier than I am now.

"When I last saw you, I came to you in trouble; and I come to you in trouble once more. It seems neglectful in me never to have written to you for so many years past; but my life has been a very sad one, and I thought I had no right to lay the burden of my sorrow on other shoulders than my own."

Uncle Joseph shook his head at these last words, and touched the stop of the musical box. "Mozart shall wait a little," he said, gravely "till I have told you something. Sarah, hear what I say, and drink your tea, and own to me whether I speak the truth or not. What did I, Joseph Buschmann, tell you, when you first came to me in trouble, fourteen, fifteen, ah more! sixteen years ago, in this town, and in this same house? I said then, what I say again now: 'Sarah's sorrow is my sorrow, and Sarah's joy is my joy;' and if any man asks me reasons for that, I have three to give him."

He stopped to stir up his niece's tea for the second time, and to draw her attention to it by tapping with the spoon on the edge of the cup.

"Three reasons," he resumed. "First, you are my sister's child—some of her flesh and blood, and some of mine, therefore, also. Second, my sister, my brother, and lastly me myself, we owe to your good English father—all. A little word that means much, and may be said again and again—all.

"Your father's friends cry, Fie! Agatha Buschmann is poor! Agatha Buschmann is foreign! But your father loves the poor German girl, and he marries her in spite of their Fie, Fie, Your father's friends cry Fie! again; Agatha Buschmann has a musician brother, who gabbles to us about Mozart, and who cannot make to his porridge salt.

"Your father says, Good! I like his gabble; I like his playing; I shall get him people to teach; and while I have pinches of salt in my kitchen, he to his porridge shall have pinches of salt too. Your father's friends cry Fie! for the third time. Agatha Buschmann has another brother, a little Stupid-Head, who to the other's gabble can only listen and say Amen. Send him trotting; for the love of Heaven, shut up all the doors and send Stupid-Head trotting, at least.

"Your father says, No! Stupid-Head has his wits in his hands; he can cut and carve and polish; help him a little at the starting, and after he shall help himself. They are all gone now but me. Your father, your mother, and Uncle Max—they are all gone. Stupid-Head alone remains to remember and to be grateful—to take Sarah's sorrow for his sorrow, and Sarah's joy for his joy." He stopped again to blow a speck of dust off the musical box. His niece endeavoured to speak, but he held up his hand, and shook his forefinger at her warningly.

"No," he said. "It is yet my business to talk, and your business to drink tea. Have I not my third reason still? Ah! you look away from me; you know my third reason before I say a word. When I, in my turn, marry, and my wife dies, and leaves me alone with little Joseph, and when the boy falls sick, who comes then, so quiet, so pretty, so neat, with the bright young eyes, and the hands so tender and light?

"Who helps me with little Joseph by night and by day? Who makes a pillow for him on her arm when his head is weary? Who holds this box patiently at his ear?—yes! this box, that the hand of Mozart has touched—who holds it closer, closer always, when little Joseph's sense grows dull, and he moans for the friendly music that he has known from a baby, the friendly music that he can now so hardly, hardly hear?

"Who kneels down by Uncle Joseph when his heart is breaking, and says, 'Oh! hush! hush! The boy is gone where the better music plays, where the sickness shall never waste or the sorrow touch him more'? Who? Ah, Sarah! you cannot forget those days; you cannot forget the Long Ago! When the trouble is bitter, and the burden is heavy, it is cruelty to Uncle Joseph to keep away; it is kindness to him to come here."

The recollections that the old man had called up found their way tenderly to Sarah's heart. She could not answer him; she could only hold out her hand. Uncle Joseph bent down, with a quaint, affectionate gallantry, and kissed it; then stepped back again to his place by the musical box. "Come!" he said, patting it cheerfully, "we will say no more for a while. Mozart's box, Max's box, little Joseph's box, you shall talk to us again!"

Having put the tiny machinery in motion, he sat down by the table, and remained silent until the air had been played over twice. Then observing that his niece seemed calmer, he spoke to her once more.

"You are in trouble, Sarah," he said, quietly. "You tell me that, and I see it is true in your face. Are you grieving for your husband?"

"I grieve that I ever met him," she answered. "I grieve that I ever married him. Now that he is dead, I cannot grieve—I can only forgive him."

"Forgive him? How you look, Sarah, when you say that! Tell me—"

"Uncle Joseph! I have told you that my husband is dead, and that I have forgiven him."

"You have forgiven him? He was hard and cruel with you, then? I see; I see. That is the end, Sarah—but the beginning? Is the beginning that you loved him?"

Her pale cheeks flushed; and she turned her head aside. "It is hard and humbling to confess it," she murmured, without raising her eyes; "but you force the truth from me, uncle. I had no love to give to my husband—no love to give to any man."

"And yet you married him! Wait! it is not for me to blame. It is for me to find out, not the bad, but the good. Yes, yes; I shall say to myself, she married him when she was poor and helpless;

159

she married him when she should have come to Uncle Joseph instead. I shall say that to myself, and I shall pity, but I shall ask no more."

Sarah half reached her hand out to the old man again—then suddenly pushed her chair back, and changed the position in which she was sitting. "It is true that I was poor," she said, looking about her in confusion, and speaking with difficulty. "But you are so kind and so good, I cannot accept the excuse that your forbearance makes for me. I did not marry him because I was poor, but—" She stopped, clasped her hands together, and pushed her chair back still further from the table.

"So! so!" said the old man, noticing her confusion. "We will talk about it no more."

"I had no excuse of love; I had no excuse of poverty," she said, with a sudden burst of bitterness and despair. "Uncle Joseph, I married him because I was too weak to persist in saying No! The curse of weakness and fear has followed me all the days of my life! I said No to him once. I said No to him twice. Oh, uncle, if I could only have said it for the third time! But he followed me, he frightened me, he took away from me all the little will of my own that I had. He made me speak as he wished me to speak, and go where he wished me to go.

"No, no, no—don't come to me, uncle; don't say anything. He is gone; he is dead—I have got my release; I have given my pardon! Oh, if I could only go away and hide somewhere! All people's eyes seem to look through me; all people's words seem to threaten me. My heart has been weary ever since I was a young woman; and all these long, long years it has never got any rest. Hush! the man in the shop—I forgot the man in the shop. He will hear us; let us talk in a whisper.

"What made me break out so? I'm always wrong. Oh me! I'm wrong when I speak; I'm wrong when I say nothing; wherever I go and whatever I do, I'm not like other people. I seem never to have grown up in my mind since I was a little child. Hark! the man in the shop is moving—has he heard me? Oh, Uncle Joseph! do you think he has heard me?"

Looking hardly less startled than his niece, Uncle Joseph assured her that the door was solid, that the man's place in the shop was at some distance from it, and that it was impossible, even if he heard voices in the parlour, that he could also distinguish any words that were spoken in it.

"You are sure of that?" she whispered, hurriedly. "Yes, yes, you are sure of that, or you would not have told me so, would you? "We may go on talking now. Not about my married life; that is buried and past. Say that I had some years of sorrow and suffering, which I deserved—say that I had other years of quiet, when I was living in service with masters and mistresses who were often kind to me when my fellow-servants were not—say just that much about my life, and it is saying enough.

"The trouble that I am in now, the trouble that brings me to you, goes back further than the years we have been talking about—goes back, back, back, Uncle Joseph, to the distant day when we last met."

"Goes back all through the sixteen years!" exclaimed the old man, incredulously. "Goes back, Sarah, even to the Long Ago!"

"Even to that time. Uncle, you remember where I was living, and what had happened to me, when—"

"When you came here in secret? When you asked me to hide you? That was the same week, Sarah, when your mistress died; your mistress who lived away west in the old house. You were frightened, then—pale and frightened as I see you now."

"As everyone sees me! People are always staring at me; always thinking that I am nervous, always pitying me for being ill."

Saying these words with a sudden fretfulness, she lifted the tea-cup by her side to her lips, drained it of its contents at a draught, and pushed it across the table to be filled again. "I have come all over thirsty and hot," she whispered. "More tea, Uncle Joseph—more tea."

"It is cold," said the old man. "Wait till I ask for hot water."

"No!" she exclaimed, stopping him as he was about to rise. "Give it me cold; I like it cold. Let nobody else come in—I can't speak if anybody else comes in." She drew her chair close to her uncle's, and went on: "You have not forgotten how frightened I was in that bygone time—do you remember why I was frightened?"

"You were afraid of being followed—that was it, Sarah. I grow old, but my memory keeps young. You were afraid of your master, afraid of his sending servants after you. You had run away; you had spoken no word to anybody; and you spoke little—ah, very, very little—even to Uncle Joseph—even to me."

"I told you," said Sarah, dropping her voice to so faint a whisper that the old man could barely hear her—"I told you that my mistress had left me a Secret on her deathbed—a Secret in a letter, which I was to give to my master. I told you I had hidden the letter, because I could not bring myself to deliver it, because I would rather die a thousand times over than be questioned about what I knew of it. I told you so much, I know. Did I tell you no more? Did I not say that my mistress made me take an oath on the Bible?—Uncle! are there candles in the room? Are there candles we can light without disturbing anybody, without calling anybody in here?"

"There are candles and a matchbox in my cupboard," answered Uncle Joseph. "But look out of window, Sarah. It is only twilight—it is not dark yet."

"Not outside; but it is dark here."

"Where?"

"In that corner. Let us have candles. I don't like the darkness when it gathers in corners and creeps along walls,"

Uncle Joseph looked all round the room inquiringly; and smiled to himself as he took two candles from the cupboard and lighted them. "You are like the children," he said, playfully, while he pulled down the window-blind. "You are afraid of the dark."

Sarah did not appear to hear him. Her eyes were fixed on the corner of the room which she had pointed out the moment before. When he resumed his place by her side, she never looked round, but laid her hand on his arm, and said to him suddenly—

"Uncle! Do you believe that the dead can come back to this world, and follow the living everywhere, and see what they do in it?"

The old man started. "Sarah!" he said, "why do you talk so? Why do you ask me such a question?"

"Are there lonely hours," she went on, still never looking away from the corner, still not seeming to hear him, "when you are sometimes frightened without knowing why—frightened all over in an instant, from head to foot? Tell me, uncle, have you ever felt the cold steal round and round the roots of your hair, and crawl bit by bit down your back?

"I have felt that even in the summer. I have been out of doors, alone on a wide heath, in the heat and brightness of noon, and have felt as if chilly fingers were touching me—chilly, damp, softly creeping fingers. It says in the New Testament that the dead came once out of their graves, and went into the holy city. The dead! Have they rested, rested always, rested forever, since that time?"

Uncle Joseph's simple nature recoiled in bewilderment from the dark and daring speculations to which his niece's questions led. Without saying a word, he tried to draw away the arm which she still held; but the only result of the effort was to make her tighten her grasp, and bend forward in her chair so as to look closer still into the corner of the room.

"My mistress was dying," she said—"my mistress was very near her grave, when she made me take my oath on the Bible. She made me swear never to destroy the letter; and I did not destroy it. She made me swear not to take it away with me, if I left the house; and I did not take it away. She would have made me swear, for the third time, to give it to my master, but death was too quick for her—death stopped her from fastening that third oath on my conscience. But she threatened me, uncle, with the dead dampness on her forehead, and the dead whiteness on her cheeks—she threatened to come to me from the other world if I thwarted her—and I have thwarted her!"

She stopped, suddenly removed her hand from the old man's

arm, and made a strange gesture with it toward the part of the room on which her eyes remained fixed. "Rest, mistress, rest," she whispered under her breath. "Is my master alive now? Rest, till the drowned rise. Tell him the Secret when the sea gives up her dead."

"Sarah! Sarah! you are changed—you are ill—you frighten me!" cried Uncle Joseph, starting to his feet.

She turned round slowly, and looked at him with eyes void of all expression, with eyes that seemed to be staring through him vacantly at something beyond.

"*Gott im Himmel*! what does she see?" He looked round as the exclamation escaped him. "Sarah! what is it? Are you faint? Are you ill? Are you dreaming with your eyes open?"

He took her by both arms and shook her. At the instant when she felt the touch of his hands, she started violently and trembled all over. Their natural expression flew back into her eyes with the rapidity of a flash of light. "Without saying a word, she hastily resumed her seat and began stirring the cold tea round and round in her cup, round and round so fast that the liquid overflowed into the saucer.

"Come! she gets more like herself," said Uncle Joseph, watching her.

"More like myself?" she repeated, vacantly.

"So! so!" said the old man, trying to soothe her. "You are ill—what the English call out of sort. They are good doctors here. Wait till tomorrow, you shall have the best. ' '

"I want no doctors. Don't speak of doctors. I can't bear them; they look at me with such curious eyes; they are always prying into me, as if they wanted to find out something. What have we been stopping for? I had so much to say; and we seem to have been stopping just when we ought to have been going on. I am in grief and terror, Uncle Joseph; in grief and terror again about the Secret—"

"No more of that!" pleaded the old man. "No more tonight at least!"

"Why not?"

"Because you will be ill again with talking about it. You will be looking into that corner and dreaming with your eyes open. You are too ill—yes, yes, Sarah; you are too ill."

"I'm not ill! Oh, why does everybody keep telling me that I am ill? Let me talk about it, uncle. I have come to talk about it; I can't rest till I have told you."

She spoke with a changing colour and an embarrassed manner, now apparently conscious for the first time that she had allowed words and actions to escape her which it would have been more prudent to have restrained.

"Don't notice me again," she said, with her soft voice, and her gentle, pleading manner. "Don't notice me if I talk or look as I ought not. I lose myself sometimes, without knowing it; and I suppose I lost myself just now. It means nothing, Uncle Joseph—nothing, indeed."

Endeavouring thus to reassure the old man, she again altered the position of her chair, so as to place her back toward the part of the room to which her face had been hitherto turned.

"Well, well, it is good to hear that," said Uncle Joseph; "but speak no more about the past time, for fear you should lose yourself again. Let us hear about what is now. Yes, yes, give me my way. Leave the Long Ago to me, and take you the present time. I can go back through the sixteen years as well as you. Ah! you doubt it?

"I Iear me tell you what happened when we last met—hear me prove myself in three words: You leave your place at the old house—you run away here—you stop in hiding with me, while your master and his servants are hunting after you—you start off, when your road is clear, to work for your living, as far away from Cornwall as you can get—I beg and pray you to stop with me, but you are afraid of your master, and away you go. There! that is the whole story of your trouble the last time you came to this house. Leave it so; and tell me what is the cause of your trouble now."

"The past cause of my trouble, Uncle Joseph, and the present cause of my trouble are the same. The Secret—"

"What! you will go back to that!"

"I must go back to it."

"And why?"

"Because the Secret is written in a letter—"

"Yes; and what of that?"

"And the letter is in danger of being discovered. It is, uncle-
it is! Sixteen years, it has lain hidden—and now, after all that
long time, the dreadful chance of its being dragged to light has
come like a judgment. The one person in all the world who
ought never to set eyes on that letter is the very person who is
most likely to find it!"

"So! so! Are you very certain, Sarah? How do you know it?"

"I know it from her own lips. Chance brought us together—"

"Us? us? What do you mean by us?"

"I mean—uncle, you remember that Captain Treverton was
my master when I lived at Porthgenna Tower?"

"I had forgotten his name. But no matter—go on."

"When I left my place, Miss Treverton was a little girl of five
years old. She is a married woman now—so beautiful, so clever,
such a sweet, youthful, happy face! And she has a child as lovely
as herself. Oh, uncle, if you could see her! I would give so much
if you could only see her!"

Uncle Joseph kissed his hand and shrugged his shoulders; expressing by the first action homage to the lady's beauty, and by
the second resignation under the misfortune of not being able
to see her. "Well, well," he said, philosophically, "put this shining
woman by, and let us go on."

"Her name is Frankland now," said Sarah. "A prettier name
than Treverton—a much prettier name, I think. Her husband is
fond of her—I am sure he is. How can he have any heart at all,
and not be fond of her?"

"So! so!" exclaimed Uncle Joseph, looking very much perplexed. "Good, if he is fond of her—very good. But what labyrinth are we getting into now? "Wherefore all this about a
husband and a wife? My word of honour, Sarah, but your expla-

nation explains nothing—it only softens my brains."

"I must speak of her and of Mr. Frankland, uncle. Porthgenna Tower belongs to her husband now, and they are both going to live there."

"Ah! we are getting back into the straight road at last."

"They are going to live in the very house that holds the Secret; they are going to repair that very part of it where the letter is hidden. She will go into the old rooms—I heard her say so; she will search about in them to amuse her curiosity; workman will clear them out, and she will stand by in her idle hours, looking on."

"But she suspects nothing of the Secret?"

"God forbid she ever should!"

"And there are many rooms in the house? And the letter in which the Secret is written is hidden in one of the many? Why should she hit on that one?"

"Because I always say the wrong thing! because I always get frightened and lose myself at the wrong time! The letter is hidden in a room called the Myrtle Room, and I was foolish enough, weak enough, crazed enough, to warn her against going into it."

"Ah, Sarah! Sarah! that was a mistake, indeed."

"I can't tell what possessed me—I seemed to lose my senses when I heard her talking so innocently of amusing herself by searching through the old rooms, and when I thought of what she might find there. It was getting on toward night, too; the horrible twilight was gathering in the corners and creeping along the walls. I longed to light the candles, and yet I did not dare, for fear she should see the truth in my face. And when I did light them it was worse. Oh, I don't know how I did it! I don't know why I did it! I could have torn my tongue out for saying the words, and still I said them.

"Other people can think for the best; other people can act for the best; other people have had a heavy weight laid on their minds, and have not dropped under it as I have. Help me, uncle, for the sake of old times when we were happy—help me with a word of advice."

"I will help you; I live to help you, Sarah! No, no, no—you must not look so forlorn; you must not look at me with those crying eyes. Come! I will advise this minute—but say in what; only say in what."

"Have I not told you?"

"No; you have not told me a word yet."

"I will tell you now."

She paused, looked away distrustfully toward the door leading into the shop, listened a little, and resumed "I am not at the end of my journey yet, Uncle Joseph—I am here on my way to Porthgenna Tower—on my way to the Myrtle Room—on my way, step by step, to the place where the letter lies hid. I dare not destroy it; I dare not remove it; but run what risk I may, I must take it out of the Myrtle Room."

Uncle Joseph said nothing, but he shook his head despondingly.

"I must," she repeated; "before Mrs. Frankland gets to Porthgenna, I must take that letter out of the Myrtle Room. There are places in the old house where I may hide it again—places that she would never think of—places that she would never notice. Only let me get it out of the one room that she is sure to search in, and I know where to hide it from her and from every one forever."

Uncle Joseph reflected, and shook his head again—then said: "One word, Sarah; does Mrs. Frankland know which is the Myrtle Room?"

"I did my best to destroy all trace of that name when I hid the letter; I hope and believe she does not. But she may find out—remember the words I was crazed enough to speak; they will set her seeking for the Myrtle Room; they are sure to do that."

"And if she finds it? And if she finds the letter?"

"It will cause misery to innocent people; it will bring death to me. Don't push your chair from me, uncle! It is not shameful death I speak of. The worst injury I have done is injury to myself; the worst death I have to fear is the death that releases a worn-out spirit and cures a broken heart."

"Enough—enough so," said the old man. "I ask for no secret, Sarah, that is not yours to give. It is all dark to me—very dark, very confused. I look away from it; I look only toward you. Not with doubt, my child, but with pity, and with sorrow, too—sorrow that ever you went near that house of Porthgenna—sorrow that you are now going to it again."

"I have no choice, uncle, but to go. If every step on the road to Porthgenna took me nearer and nearer to my death, I must still tread it. Knowing what I know, I can't rest, I can't sleep—my very breath won't come freely—till I have got that letter out of the Myrtle Room. How to do it—oh, Uncle Joseph, how to do it, without being suspected, without being discovered by any-body—that is what I would almost give my life to know! You are a man; you are older and wiser than I am; no living creature ever asked you for help in vain—help me now! my only friend in all the world, help me a little with a word of advice!"

Uncle Joseph rose from his chair, and folded his arms resolutely, and looked his niece full in the face.

"You will go?" he said. "Cost what it may, you will go? Say, for the last time, Sarah, is it yes or no?"

"Yes! For the last time, I say Yes."

"Good. And you will go soon?"

"I must go tomorrow. I dare not waste a single day; hours even may be precious for anything I can tell."

"You promise me, my child, that the hiding of this Secret does good, and that the finding of it will do harm?"

"If it was the last word I had to speak in this world, I would say Yes!"

"You promise me, also, that you want nothing but to take the letter out of the Myrtle Boom, and put it away somewhere else?"

"Nothing but that."

"And it is yours to take and yours to put? No person has a better right to touch it than you?"

"Now that my master is dead, no person."

"Good. You have given me my resolution. I have done. Sit you there, Sarah; and wonder, if you like, but say nothing." With these words, Uncle Joseph stepped lightly to the door leading into the shop, opened it, and called to the man behind the counter.

"Samuel, my friend," he said. "Tomorrow I go a little ways into the country with my niece, who is this lady here. You keep shop and take orders, and be just as careful as you always are, till I get back. If anybody comes and asks for Mr. Buschmann, say he has gone a little ways into the country, and will be back in a few days. That is all. Shut up the shop, Samuel, my friend, for the night; and go to your supper. I wish you good appetite, nice victuals, and sound sleep."

Before Samuel could thank his master the door was shut again. Before Sarah could say a word, Uncle Joseph's hand was on her lips, and Uncle Joseph's handkerchief was wiping away the tears that were now falling fast from her eyes.

"I will have no more talking, and no more crying," said the old man. "I am a German, and I glory in the obstinacy of six Englishmen, all rolled into one. Tonight you sleep here, tomorrow we talk again of all this. You want me to help you with a word of advice. I will help you with myself, which is better than advice, and I say no more till I fetch my pipe down from the wall there, and ask him to make me think. I smoke and think tonight—I talk and do tomorrow.

"And you, you go up to bed; you take Uncle Max's music-box in your hand, and you let Mozart sing the cradle song before you go to sleep. Yes, yes, my child, there is always comfort in Mozart—better comfort than in crying. "What, is there to cry about, or to thank about? Is it so great a wonder that I will not let my sister's child go alone to make a venture in the dark? I said Sarah's sorrow was my sorrow, and Sarah's joy my joy; and now, if there is no way of escape—if it must indeed be done—I also say: Sarah's risk tomorrow is Uncle Joseph's risk tomorrow, too! Goodnight, my child—goodnight."

CHAPTER 2
OUTSIDE THE HOUSE

The next morning wrought no change in the resolution at which Uncle Joseph had arrived overnight. Out of the amazement and confusion produced in his mind by his niece's avowal of the object that had brought her to Cornwall, he had contrived to extract one clear and definite conclusion—that she was obstinately bent on placing herself in a situation of uncertainty, if not of absolute peril. Once persuaded of this, his kindly instincts all sprang into action, his natural firmness on the side of self-sacrifice asserted itself, and his determination not to let Sarah proceed on her journey alone, followed as a matter of course.

Strong in the self-denying generosity of his purpose—though strong in nothing else—when he and his niece met in the morning, and when Sarah spoke self-reproachfully of the sacrifice that he was making, of the serious hazards to which he was exposing himself for her sake, he refused to listen to her just as obstinately as he had refused the previous night.

There was no need, he said, to speak another word on that subject. If she had abandoned her intention of going to Porthgenna, she had only to say so. If she had not, it was mere waste of breath to talk any more, for he was deaf in both ears to everything in the shape of a remonstrance that she could possibly address to him. Having expressed himself in these uncompromising terms, Uncle Joseph abruptly dismissed the subject, and tried to turn the conversation to a cheerful everyday topic by asking his niece how she had passed the night.

"I was too anxious to sleep," she answered. "I can't fight with my fears and misgivings as some people can. All night long they keep me waking and thinking as if it was day."

"Thinking about what?" asked Uncle Joseph. "About the letter that is hidden? about the house of Porthgenna? about the Myrtle Room?"

"About how to get into the Myrtle Room," she said. "The more I try to plan and ponder, and settle beforehand what I shall do, the more confused and helpless I seem to be. All last night, uncle, I was trying to think of some excuse for getting inside the doors of Porthgenna Tower—and yet, if I was standing on the house-step at this moment, I should not know what to say when the servant and I first came face to face. How are we to persuade them to let us in? How am I to slip out of sight, even if we do get in?

"Can't you tell me?—you will try, Uncle Joseph—I am sure you will try. Only help me so far, and I think I can answer for the rest. If they keep the keys where they used to keep them in my time, ten minutes to myself is all I should want ten minutes, only ten short minutes, to make the end of my life easier to me than the beginning has been; to help me to grow old quietly and resignedly, if it is God's will that I should live out my years.

"Oh, how happy people must be who have all the courage they want; who are quick and clever, and have their wits about them! You are readier than I am, uncle; you said last night that you would think about how to advise me for the best—what did your thoughts end in? You will make me so much easier if you will only tell me that."

Uncle Joseph nodded assentingly, assumed a look of the profoundest gravity, and slowly laid his forefinger along the side of his nose.

"What did I promise you last night?" he said. "Was it not to take my pipe, and ask him to make me think? Good, I smoke three pipes, and think three thoughts. My first thought is—Wait! My second thought is, again—Wait! My third thought is yet once more Wait! You say you will be easy, Sarah, if I tell you the end of all my thoughts. Good, I have told you. There is the end—you are easy—it, is all right."

"Wait?" repeated Sarah, with a look of bewilderment which suggested anything rather than a mind at ease. "I am afraid, uncle, I don't quite understand. Wait for what? Wait till when?"

"Wait till we arrive at the house, to be sure! Wait till we are got outside the door; then is time enough to think how we are to get in," said Uncle Joseph, with an air of conviction. "You understand now?"

"Yes—at least I understand better than I did. But there is still another difficulty left, Uncle! I must tell you more than I intended ever to tell anybody—I must tell you that the letter is locked up."

"Locked up in a room?"

"Worse than that—locked up in something inside the room. The key that opens the door—even if I get it—the key that opens the door of the room is not all I want. There is another key besides that, a little key—" She stopped, with a confused, startled look.

"A little key that you have lost?" asked Uncle Joseph.

"I threw it down the well in the village on the morning when I made my escape from Porthgenna. Oh, if I had only kept it about me! If it had only crossed my mind that I might want it again!"

"Well, well; there is no help for that now. Tell me, Sarah, what the something is which the letter is hidden in."

"I am afraid of the very walls hearing me."

"What nonsense! Come! whisper it to me."

She looked all round her distrustfully, and then whispered into the old man's ear. He listened eagerly, and laughed when she was silent again. "Bah!" he cried. "If that is all, make yourself happy. As you wicked English people say, it is as easy as lying. Why, my child, you can burst him open for yourself."

"Burst it open? How?"

Uncle Joseph went to the window-seat, which was made on the old-fashioned plan, to serve the purpose of a chest as well as a seat. He opened the lid, searched among some tools which lay in the receptacle beneath, and took out a chisel.

"See," he said, demonstrating on the top of the window-seat the use to which the tool was to be put. "You push him in so—crick! Then you pull him up so—crack! It is the business of one little moment—crick! crack!—and the lock is done for. Take the chisel yourself, wrap him up in a bit of that stout paper there, and put him in your pocket. What are you waiting for? Do you want me to show you again, or do you think you can do it now for yourself?"

"I should like you to show me again, Uncle Joseph, but not now—not till we have got to the end of our journey."

"Good. Then I may finish my packing up, and go ask about the coach. First and foremost, Mozart must put on his great coat, and travel with us." He took up the musical box, and placed it carefully in a leather case, which he slung by a strap over one shoulder.

"Next, there is my pipe, the tobacco to feed him with, and the matches to set him alight. Last, here is my old German knap-sack, which I pack last night. See! here is shirt, nightcap, comb, pocket-handkerchief, sock. Say I am an emperor, and what do I want more than that? Good. I have Mozart, I have the pipe, I have the knapsack. I have—stop! stop! there is the old leather purse; he must not be forgotten.

"Look! here he is. Listen! Ting, ting, ting! He jingles; he has in his inside money. Aha, my friend, my good Leather, you shall be lighter and leaner before you come home again. So, so—it is all complete; we are ready for the march now, from our tops to our toes. Goodbye, Sarah, my child, for a little half-hour; you shall wait here and amuse yourself while I go ask for the coach."

When Uncle Joseph came back, he brought his niece in-formation that a coach would pass through Truro in an hour's time, which would set them down at a stage not more than five or six miles distant from the regular post-town of Porthgenna. The only direct conveyance to the post-town was a night-coach which carried the letter-bags, and which stopped to change horses at Truro at the very inconvenient hour of two o'clock in the morning.

Being of opinion that to travel at bedtime was to make a toil of a pleasure, Uncle Joseph recommended taking places in the day-coach, and hiring any conveyance that could be afterward obtained to carry his niece and himself on to the post-town. By this arrangement they would not only secure their own com-fort, but gain the additional advantage of losing as little time as possible at Truro before proceeding on their journey to Porthgenna.

The plan thus proposed was the plan followed, the coach stopped to change horses, Uncle Joseph and his niece were waiting to take their places by it. They found all the inside seats but one disengaged, were set down two hours afterward at the stage that was nearest to the destination for which they were bound, hired a pony-chaise there, and reached the post-town between one and two o'clock in the afternoon.

Dismissing their conveyance at the inn, from motives of caution which were urged by Sarah, they set forth to walk across the moor to Porthgenna. On their way out of the town they met the postman returning from his morning's delivery of letters in the surrounding district. His bag had been much heavier and his walk much longer that morning than usual. Among the extra letters that had taken him out of his ordinary course was one addressed to the housekeeper at Porthgenna Tower, which he had delivered early in the morning, when he first started on his rounds.

Throughout the whole journey, Uncle Joseph had not made a single reference to the object for which it had been undertaken. Possessing a child's simplicity of nature, he was also endowed with a child's elasticity of disposition. The doubts and forebodings which troubled his niece's spirit, and kept her silent and thoughtful and sad, cast no darkening shadow over the natural sunshine of his mind.

If he had really been travelling for pleasure alone, he could not have enjoyed more thoroughly than he did the different sights and events of the journey. All the happiness which the passing minute had to give him he took as readily and gratefully as if there was no uncertainty in the future, no doubt, difficulty, or danger lying in wait for him at the journey's end.

Before he had been half an hour in the coach he had begun to tell the third inside passenger—a rigid old lady, who stared at him in speechless amazement—the whole history of the musical box, ending the narrative by setting it playing, in defiance of all the noise that the rolling wheels could make.

When they left the coach, he was just as sociable afterward with the driver of the chaise, vaunting the superiority of German beer over Cornish cider, and making his remarks upon the objects which they passed on the road with the pleasantest familiarity and the heartiest enjoyment of his own jokes. It was not till he and Sarah were well out of the little town, and away by themselves on the great moor which stretched beyond it, that his manner altered, and his talk ceased altogether. After walking on in silence for some little time, with his niece's arm in his, he suddenly stopped, looked her earnestly and kindly in the face, and laid his hand on hers.

"There is yet one thing more I want to ask you, my child," he said. "The journey has put it out of my head, but it has been in my heart all the time. When we leave this place of Porthgenna, and get back to my house, you will not go away? you will not leave Uncle Joseph again? Are you in service still, Sarah. Are you not your own master yet?"

"I was in service a few days since," she answered; "but I am free now. I have lost my place."

"Aha! You have lost your place; and why?"

"Because I would not hear an innocent person unjustly blamed. Because—"

She checked herself. But the few words she had said were spoken with such a suddenly heightened colour, and with such an extraordinary emphasis and resolution of tone, that the old man opened his eyes as widely as possible, and looked at his niece in undisguised astonishment.

"So! so! so!" he exclaimed. "What! You have had a quarrel, Sarah!"

"Hush! Don't ask me any more questions now!" she pleaded, earnestly. "I am too anxious and too frightened to answer. Uncle! this is Porthgenna Moor—this is the road I passed over, sixteen years ago, when I ran away to you. Oh! let us get on, pray let us get on! I can't think of anything now but the house we are so near, and the risk we are going to run."

They went on quickly, in silence. Half an hour's rapid walking brought them to the highest elevation on the moor, and gave the whole western prospect grandly to their view.

There, below them, was the dark, lonesome, spacious structure of Porthgenna Tower, with the sunlight already stealing round toward the windows of the west front! There was the path winding away to it gracefully over the brown moor, in curves of dazzling white! There, lower down, was the solitary old church, with the peaceful burial-ground nestling by its side! There, lower still, were the little scattered roofs of the fishermen's cottages! And there, beyond all, was the changeless glory of the sea, with its old seething lines of white foam, with the old winding margin of its yellow shores!

Sixteen long years—such years of sorrow, such years of suffering, such years of change, counted by the pulses of the living heart!—had passed over the dead tranquillity of Porthgenna, and had altered it as little as if they had all been contained within the lapse of a single day!

The moments when the spirit within us is most deeply stirred are almost invariably the moments also when its outward manifestations are hardest to detect. Our own thoughts rise above us; our own feelings lie deeper than we can reach. How seldom words can help us, when their help is most wanted! How often our tears are dried up when we most long for them to relieve us!

Was there ever a strong emotion in this world that could adequately express its own strength? What third person, brought face to face with the old man and his niece, as they now stood together on the moor, would have suspected, to look at them, that the one was contemplating the landscape with nothing more than a stranger's curiosity, and that the other was viewing it through the recollections of half a lifetime?

The eyes of both were dry, the tongues of both were silent, the faces of both were set with equal attention toward the prospect. Even between themselves there was no real sympathy, no intelligible appeal from one spirit to the other. The old man's quiet admiration of the view was not more briefly and readily expressed, when they moved forward and spoke to each other, than the customary phrases of assent by which his niece replied to the little that he said. How many moments there are in this mortal life, when, with all our boasted powers of speech, the words of our vocabulary treacherously fade out, and the page presents nothing to us but the sight of a perfect blank!

Slowly descending the slope of the moor, the uncle and niece drew nearer and nearer to Porthgenna Tower. They were within a quarter of an hour's walk of the house when Sarah stopped at a place where a second path intersected the main foot-track which they had hitherto been following. On the left hand, as they now stood, the cross-path ran on until it was lost to the eye in the expanse of the moor. On the right hand it led straight to the church.

"What do we stop for now?" asked Uncle Joseph, looking first in one direction and then in the other.

"Would you mind waiting for me here a little while, uncle? I can't pass the church path—" (she paused, in some trouble how to express herself)—"without wishing (as I don't know what may happen after we get to the house), without wishing to see—to look at something—" She stopped again, and turned her face wistfully toward the church. The tears, which had never wetted her eyes at the first view of Porthgenna, were beginning to rise in them now.

Uncle Joseph's natural delicacy warned him that it would be best to abstain from asking her for any explanations.

"Go you where you like, to see what you like," he said, patting her on the shoulder. "I shall stop here to make myself happy with my pipe; and Mozart shall come out of his cage, and sing a little in this fine fresh air." He unslung the leather case from his shoulder while he spoke, took out the musical box, and set it ringing its tiny peal to the second of the two airs which it was constructed to play—the minuet in Don Giovanni.

Sarah left him looking about carefully, not for a seat for himself, but for a smooth bit of rock to place the box upon. When he had found this, he lit his pipe, and sat down to his music and his smoking, like an epicure to a good dinner. "Aha!" he exclaimed to himself, looking round as composedly at the wild prospect on all sides of him as if he was still in his own little parlour at Truro—"Aha! Here is a fine big music-room, my friend Mozart, for you to sing in! Ouf! there is wind enough in this place to blow your pretty dance-tune out to sea, and give the sailor-people a taste of it as they roll about in their ships."

Meanwhile Sarah walked on rapidly toward the church, and entered the inclosure of the little burial-ground. Toward that same part of it to which she had directed her steps on the morning of her mistress's death, she now turned her face again, after a lapse of sixteen years. Here, at least, the march of time had left its palpable track—its footprints whose marks were graves. How many a little spot of ground, empty when she last saw it, had its mound and its headstone now!

The one grave that she had come to see—the grave which had stood apart in the bygone days, had companion graves on the right hand and on the left. She could not have singled it out but for the weather stains on the headstone, which told of storm and rain over it, that had not passed over the rest. The mound was still kept in shape; but the grass grew long, and waved a dreary welcome to her as the wind swept through it. She knelt down by the stone and tried to read the inscription.

The black paint which had once made the carved words distinct was all flayed off from them now. To any other eyes but hers the very name of the dead man would have been hard to trace. She sighed heavily as she followed the letters of the inscription mechanically, one by one, with her finger:

Sacred to the Memory
of
Hugh Polwheal,
Aged 26 Years.
He Met With His Death
Through the Fall of a Rock
in
Porthgenna Mine, December 17th, 1823.

Her hand lingered over the letters after it had followed them to the last line, and she bent forward and pressed her lips on the stone.

"Better so!" she said to herself, as she rose from her knees and looked down at the inscription for the last time. "Better it should fade out so! Fewer strangers' eyes will see it; fewer strangers' feet will follow where mine have been—he will lie all the quieter in the place of his rest!"

She brushed the tears from her eyes and gathered a few blades of grass from the grave—then left the churchyard. Outside the hedge that surrounded the inclosure she stopped for a moment, and drew from the bosom of her dress the little book of Wesley's Hymns which she had taken with her from the desk in her bedroom on the morning of her flight from Porthgenna.

The withered remains of the grass that she had plucked from the grave sixteen years ago lay between the pages still. She added to them the fresh fragments that she had just gathered, replaced the book in the bosom of her dress, and hastened back over the moor to the spot where the old man was waiting for her.

She found him packing up the musical box again in its leather case. "A good wind," he said, holding up the palm of his hand to the fresh breeze that was sweeping over the moor—"A very good wind, indeed, if you take him by himself—but a bitter bad wind if you take him with Mozart. He blows off the tune as if it was the hat on my head. You come back, my child, just at the nick of time—just when my pipe is done, and Mozart is ready to travel along the road once more. Ah, have you got the crying look in your eyes again, Sarah? What have you met with to make you cry? So! so! I see—the fewer questions I ask just now, the better you will like me. Good. I have done. No! I have a last question yet. What are we standing here for? why do we not go on?"

"Yes, yes; you are right, Uncle Joseph; let us go on at once. I shall lose all the little courage I have if we stay here much longer looking at the house."

They proceeded down the path without another moment of

delay. When they had reached the end of it, they stood opposite the eastern boundary wall of Porthgenna Tower. The principal entrance to the house, which had been very rarely used of late years, was in the west front, and was approached by a terrace road that overlooked the sea.

The smaller entrance, which was generally used, was situated on the south side of the building, and led through the servants' offices to the great hall and the west staircase. Sarah's old experience of Porthgenna guided her instinctively toward this part of the house. She led her companion on until they gained the southern angle of the east wall—then stopped and looked about her. Since they had passed the postman and had entered on the moor, they had not set eyes on a living creature; and still, though they were now under the very walls of Porthgenna, neither man, woman, nor child—not even a domestic animal appeared in view.

"It is very lonely here," said Sarah, looking round her distrustfully; "much lonelier than it used to be."

"Is it only to tell me what I can see for myself that you are stopping now?" asked Uncle Joseph, whose inveterate cheerfulness would have been proof against the solitude of Sahara itself.

"No, no!" she answered, in a quick, anxious whisper. "But the bell we must ring at is so close—only round there—I should like to know what we are to say when we come face to face with the servant. You told me it was time enough to think about that when we were at the door. Uncle! we are all but at the door now. What shall we do?"

"The first thing to do," said Uncle Joseph, shrugging his shoulders, "is surely to ring."

"Yes—but when the servant comes, what are we to say?"

"Say?" repeated Uncle Joseph, knitting his eyebrows quite fiercely with the effort of thinking, and rapping his forehead with his forefinger just under his hat—"Say? Stop, stop, stop, stop! Ah, I have got it! I know! Make yourself quite easy, Sarah. The moment the door is opened, all the speaking to the servant shall be done by me."

"Oh, how you relieve me! "What shall you say?"

"Say? This—'How do you do? We have come to see the house.'"

When he had disclosed that remarkable expedient for effecting an entrance into Porthgenna Tower, he spread out both his hands interrogatively, drew back several paces from his niece, and looked at her with the serenely self-satisfied air of a man who has leaped, at one mental bound, from a doubt to a discovery. Sarah gazed at him in astonishment. The expression of absolute conviction on his face staggered her. The poorest of all the poor excuses for gaining admission into the house which she herself had thought of, and had rejected, during the previous night, seemed like the very perfection of artifice by comparison with such a childishly simple expedient as that suggested by Uncle Joseph.

And yet there he stood, apparently quite convinced that he had hit on the means of smoothing away all obstacles at once. Not knowing what to say, not believing sufficiently in the validity of her own doubts to venture on openly expressing an opinion either one way or the other, she took the last refuge that was now left open to her—she endeavoured to gain time.

"It is very, very good of you, uncle, to take all the difficulty of speaking to the servant on your own shoulders," she said; the hidden despondency at her heart expressing itself, in spite of her, in the faintness of her voice and the forlorn perplexity of her eyes. "But would you mind waiting a little before we ring at the door, and walking up and down for a few minutes by the side of this wall, where nobody is likely to see us? I want to get a little more time to prepare myself for the trial that I have to go through; and—and in case the servant makes any difficulties about letting us in—I mean difficulties that we cannot just now anticipate—would it not be as well to think of something else to say at the door? Perhaps, if you were to consider again—"

"There is not the least need," interposed Uncle Joseph. "I have only to speak to the servant, and—crick! crack!—you will see that we shall get in. But I will walk up and down as long as you please. There is no reason, because I have done all my thinking in one moment, that you should have done all your thinking in one moment too. No, no, no—no reason at all."

Saying those words with a patronizing air and a self-satisfied smile, which would have been irresistibly comical under any less critical circumstances, the old man again offered his arm to his niece, and led her back over the broken ground that lay under the eastern wall of Porthgonna Tower.

While Sarah was waiting in doubt outside the walls, it happened, by a curious coincidence, that another person, vested with the highest domestic authority, was also waiting in doubt inside the walls. This person was no other than the housekeeper of Porthgenna Tower; and the cause of her perplexity was nothing less than the letter which had been delivered by the postman that very morning.

It was a letter from Mrs. Frankland, which had been written after she had held a long conversation with her husband and Mr. Orridge, on receiving the last fragments of information which the doctor was able to communicate in reference to Mrs. Jazeph.

The housekeeper had read the letter through over and over again, and was more puzzled and astonished by it at every fresh reading. She was now waiting for the return of the steward, Mr. Munder, from his occupations out of doors, with the intention of taking his opinion on the singular communication which she had received from her mistress.

While Sarah and her uncle were still walking up and down outside the eastern wall, Mr. Munder entered the housekeeper's room. He was one of those tall, grave, benevolent-looking men, with a conical head, a deep voice, a slow step, and a heavy manner, who passively contrive to get a great reputation for wisdom without the trouble of saying or doing anything to deserve it. All round the Porthgenna neighbourhood the steward was popularly spoken of as a remarkably sound, sensible man; and the housekeeper, although a sharp woman in other matters, in this one respect shared to a large extent in the general delusion.

" Good-morning, Mrs. Pentreath," said Mr. Munder. "Any news today?" What a weight and importance his deep voice and his impressively slow method of using it, gave to those two insignificant sentences!

"News, Mr. Munder, that will astonish you," replied the housekeeper. "I have received a letter this morning from Mrs. Frankland, which is, without any exception, the most mystifying thing of the sort I ever met with. I am told to communicate the letter to you; and I have been waiting the whole morning to hear your opinion of it. Pray sit down, and give me all your attention—for I do positively assure you that the letter requires it."

Mr. Munder sat down, and became the picture of attention immediately—not of ordinary attention, which can be wearied, but of judicial attention, which knows no fatigue, and is superior alike to the power of dullness and the power of time. The housekeeper, without wasting the precious minutes—Mr. Munder's minutes, which ranked next on the scale of importance to a prime minister's!—opened her mistress's letter, and, resisting the natural temptation to make a few more prefatory remarks on it, immediately favoured the steward with the first paragraph, in the following terms:

Mrs. Pentreath You must be tired of receiving letters from me, fixing a day for the arrival of Mr. Frankland and myself. On this, the third occasion of my writing to you about our plans, it will be best, I think, to make no third appointment, but merely to say that we shall leave West Winston for Porthgenna the moment I can get the doctor's permission to travel.

"So far," remarked Mrs. Pentreath, placing the letter on her lap, and smoothing it out rather irritably while she spoke—"so far, there is nothing of much consequence. The letter certainly seems to me (between ourselves) to be written in rather poor language—too much like common talking to come up to my idea of what a lady's style of composition ought to be—but that is a matter of opinion. I can't say, and I should be the last person to wish to say, that the beginning of Mrs. Frankland's letter is not, upon the whole, perfectly clear. It is the middle and the end that I wish to consult you about, Mr. Munder."

"Just so," said Mr. Munder. Only two words, but more meaning in them than two hundred in the mouth of an ordinary man! The housekeeper cleared her throat with extraordinary loudness and elaboration, and read on thus:

My principal object in writing these lines is to request, by Mr. Frankland's desire, that you and Mr. Munder will endeavour to ascertain, as privately as possible, whether a person now travelling in Cornwall—in whom we happen to be much interested—has been yet seen in the neighbourhood of Porthgenna.

The person in question is known to us by the name of Mrs. Jazeph. She is an elderly woman, of quiet, ladylike manners, looking nervous and in delicate health. She dresses, according to our experience of her, with extreme propriety and neatness, and in dark colours. Her eyes have a singular expression of timidity, her voice is particularly soft and low, and her manner is frequently marked by extreme hesitation. I am thus particular in describing her, in case she should not be travelling under the name by which we know her.

For reasons which it is not necessary to state, both my husband and myself think it probable that, at some former period of her life, Mrs. Jazeph may have been connected with the Porthgenna neighbourhood. Whether this be the fact or no, it is indisputably certain that she is familiar with the interior of Porthgenna Tower, and that she has an interest of some kind, quite incomprehensible to us, in the house.

Coupling these facts with the knowledge we have of her being now in Cornwall, we think it just within the range of possibility that you or Mr. Munder, or some other person in our employment, may meet with her; and we are particularly anxious, if she should by any chance ask to see the house, not only that you should show her over it with perfect readiness and civility, but also that you should take private and particular notice of her conduct from the time when she enters the building to the time when she leaves it.

Do not let her out of your sight for a moment; and, if possible, pray get some trustworthy person to follow her unperceived, and ascertain where she goes to after she has quitted the house. It is of the most vital importance that these instructions (strange as they may seem to you) should be implicitly obeyed to the very letter.

I have only room and time to add that we know nothing to the discredit of this person, and that we particularly desire you will manage matters with sufficient discretion (in case you meet with her) to prevent her from having any suspicion that you are acting under orders, or that you have any especial interest in watching her movements. You will be good enough to communicate this letter to the steward, and you are at liberty to repeat the instructions in it to any other trustworthy person, if necessary.

Yours truly, Rosamond Frankland.

P.S.—I have left my room, and the baby is getting on charmingly."

"There!" said the housekeeper. "Who is to make head or tail of that, I should like to know! Did you ever, in all your experience, Mr. Munder, meet with such a letter before? Here is a very heavy responsibility laid on our shoulders, without one word of explanation. I have been puzzling my brains about what their interest in this mysterious woman can be the whole morning; and the more I think, the less comes of it. What is your opinion, Mr. Munder? We ought to do something immediately. Is there any course in particular which you feel disposed to point out?"

Mr. Munder coughed dubiously, crossed his right leg over his left, put his head critically on one side, coughed for the second time, and looked at the housekeeper. If it had belonged to any other man in the world, Mrs. Pentreath would have considered that the face which now confronted hers expressed nothing but the most profound and vacant bewilderment. But it was Mr. Munder's face, and it was only to be looked at with sentiments of respectful expectation.

"I rather think—" began Mr. Munder.

"Yes?" said the housekeeper, eagerly.

Before another word could be spoken, the maidservant entered the room to lay the cloth for Mrs. Pentreath's dinner.

"There, there! never mind now, Betsey," said the housekeeper, impatiently. "Don't lay the cloth till I ring for you. Mr. Munder and I have something very important to talk about, and we can't be interrupted just yet."

She had hardly said the word, before an interruption of the most unexpected kind happened. The doorbell rang. This was a very unusual occurrence at Porthgenna Tower. The few persons who had any occasion to come to the house on domestic business always entered by a small side gate, which was left on the latch in the daytime.

"Who in the world can that be!" exclaimed Mrs. Pentreath, hastening to the window, which commanded a side view of the lower doorsteps.

The first object that met her eye when she looked out was a lady standing on the lowest step—a lady dressed very neatly in quiet, dark colours,

"Good Heavens, Mr. Munder!" cried the housekeeper, hurrying back to the table, and snatching up Mrs. Frankland's letter, which she had left on it. "There is a stranger waiting at the door at this very moment! a lady! or, at least, a woman—and dressed neatly, dressed in dark colours! You might knock me down, Mr. Munder, with a feather! Stop, Betsey—stop where you are!"

"I was only going, ma'am, to answer the door," said Betsey, in amazement.

"Stop where you are," reiterated Mrs. Pentreath, composing herself by a great effort, happen to have certain reasons, on this particular occasion, for descending out of my own place and putting myself into yours. Stand out of the way, you staring fool! I am going upstairs to answer that ring at the door myself."

CHAPTER 3

INSIDE THE HOUSE

Mrs. Pentreath's surprise at seeing a lady through the window, was doubled by her amazement at seeing a gentleman when she opened the door. Waiting close to the bell-handle, after he had rung, instead of rejoining his niece on the step, Uncle Joseph stood near enough to the house to be out of the range of view from Mrs. Pentreath's window. To the housekeeper's excited imagination, he appeared on the threshold with the suddenness of an apparition—the apparition of a little rosy-faced old gentleman, smiling, bowing, and taking off his hat with a superb flourish of politeness, which had something quite superhuman in the sweep and the dexterity of it.

"How do you do? We have come to see the house," said Uncle Joseph, trying his infallible expedient for gaining admission the instant the door was open.

Mrs. Pentreath was struck speechless. Who was this familiar old gentleman with the foreign accent and the fantastic bow? and what did he mean by talking to her as if she was his intimate friend? Mrs. Frankland's letter said not so much, from beginning to end, as one word about him.

"How do you do? We have come to see the house," repeated Uncle Joseph, giving his irresistible form of salutation the benefit of a second trial.

"So you said just now, sir," remarked Mrs. Pentreath, recovering self-possession enough to use her tongue in her own defence. "Does the lady," she continued, looking down over the old man's shoulder at the step on which his niece was standing—"does the lady wish to see the house, too?"

Sarah's gently spoken reply in the affirmative, short as it was, convinced the housekeeper that the woman described in Mrs. Frankland's letter really and truly stood before her. Besides the neat, quiet dress, there was now the softly toned voice, and, when she looked up for a moment, there were the timid eyes also to identify her by!

In relation to this one of the two strangers, Mrs. Pentreath, however agitated and surprised she might be, could no longer feel any uncertainty about the course she ought to adopt. But in relation to the other visitor, the incomprehensible old foreigner, she was beset by the most bewildering doubts. Would it be safest to hold to the letter of Mrs. Frankland's instructions, and ask him to wait outside while the lady was being shown over the house? or would it be best to act on her own responsibility, and to risk giving him admission as well as his companion? This was a difficult point to decide, and therefore one which it was necessary to submit to the superior sagacity of Mr. Munder.

"Will you step in for a moment, and wait here while I speak to the steward?" said Mrs. Pentreath, pointedly neglecting to notice the familiar old foreigner, and addressing herself straight through him to the lady on the steps below.

"Thank you very much," said Uncle Joseph, smiling and bowing, impervious to rebuke. "What did I tell you?" he whispered triumphantly to his niece, as she passed him on her way into the house.

Mrs. Pentreath's first impulse was to go downstairs at once, and speak to Mr. Munder. But a timely recollection of that part of Mrs. Frankland's letter which enjoined her not to lose sight of the lady in the quiet dress, brought her to a standstill the next moment. She was the more easily recalled to a remembrance of this particular injunction by a curious alteration in the conduct of the lady herself, who seemed to lose all her diffidence, and to become surprisingly impatient to lead the way into the interior of the house, the moment she had stepped across the threshold.

"Betsey!" cried Mrs. Pentreath, cautiously calling to the servant after she had only retired a few paces from the visitors- "Betsey! ask Mr. Munder to be so kind as to step this way."

Mr. Munder presented himself with great deliberation, and with a certain lowering dignity in his face. He had been accustomed to be treated with deference, and he was not pleased with the housekeeper for unceremoniously leaving him the moment she heard the ring at the bell, without giving him time to pronounce an opinion on Mrs. Frankland's letter.

Accordingly when Mrs. Pentreath, in a high state of excitement, drew him aside out of hearing, and confided to him, in a whisper, the astounding intelligence that the lady in whom Mr. and Mrs. Frankland were so mysteriously interested was, at that moment, actually standing before him in the house, he received her communication with an air of the most provoking indifference.

It was worse still when she proceeded to state her difficulties—warily keeping her eye on the two strangers all the while. Appeal as respectfully as she might to Mr. Munder's superior wisdom for guidance, he persisted in listening with a disparaging frown, and ended by irritably contradicting her when she ventured to add, in conclusion, that her own ideas inclined her to assume no responsibility, and to beg the foreign gentleman to wait outside while the lady, in conformity with Mrs. Frankland's instructions, was being shown over the house.

"Such may be your opinion, ma'am," said Mr. Munder, severely. "It is not mine."

The housekeeper looked aghast. "Perhaps," she suggested, deferentially, "you think that the foreign old gentleman would be likely to insist on going over the house with the lady?"

"Of course I think so," said Mr. Munder. (He had thought nothing of the sort; his only idea just then being the idea of asserting his own supremacy by setting himself steadily in opposition to any preconceived arrangements of Mrs. Pentreath.) "Then you would take the responsibility of showing them both over the house, seeing that they have both come to the door together?" asked the housekeeper.

"Of course I would," answered the steward, with the promptitude of resolution which distinguishes all superior men.

"Well, Mr. Munder, I am always glad to be guided by your opinion, and I will be guided by it now," said Mrs. Pentreath.

"But, as there will be two people to look after—for I would not trust the foreigner out of my sight on any consideration whatever—I must really beg you to share the trouble of showing them over the house along with me.

"I am so excited and nervous that I don't feel as if I had all my wits about me—I never was placed in such a position as this before—I am in the midst of mysteries that I don't understand—and, in short, if I can't count on your assistance, I won't answer for it that I shall not make some mistake. I should be very sorry to make a mistake, not only on my own account, but—" Here the housekeeper stopped, and looked hard at Mr. Munder.

"Go on, ma'am," said Mr. Munder, with cruel composure.

"Not only on my own account," resumed Mrs. Pentreath, demurely, "but on yours; for Mrs. Frankland's letter certainly casts the responsibility of conducting this delicate business on your shoulders as well as on mine."

Mr. Munder recoiled a few steps, turned red, opened his lips indignantly, hesitated, and closed them again. He was fairly caught in a trap of his own setting. He could not retreat from the responsibility of directing the housekeeper's conduct, the moment after he had voluntarily assumed it; and he could not deny that Mrs. Frankland's letter positively and repeatedly referred to him by name.

There was only one way of getting out of the difficulty with dignity, and Mr, Munder unblushingly took that way the moment he had recovered self-possession enough to collect himself for the effort.

"I am perfectly amazed, Mrs, Pentreath," he began, with the gravest dignity. "Yes, I repeat, I am perfectly amazed that you should think me capable of leaving you to go over the house alone, under such remarkable circumstances as those we are now placed in. No, ma'am! whatever my other faults may be, shrinking from my share of responsibility is not one of them. I don't require to be reminded of Mrs. Frankland's letter; and—no!—I don't require any apologies. I am quite ready, ma'am—quite ready to show the way upstairs whenever you are."

"The sooner the better, Mr. Munder—for there is that audacious old foreigner actually chattering to Betsey now, as if he had known her all his life!"

The assertion was quite true. Uncle Joseph was exercising his gift of familiarity on the maidservant (who had lingered to stare at the strangers, instead of going back to the kitchen), just as he had already exercised it on the old lady passenger in the stagecoach, and on the driver of the pony-chaise which took his niece and himself to the post-town of Porthgenna.

While the housekeeper and the steward were holding their private conference, he was keeping Betsey in ecstasies of suppressed giggling by the odd questions that he asked about the house, and about how she got on with her work in it. His inquiries had naturally led from the south side of the building, by which he and his companion had entered, to the west side, which they were shortly to explore; and thence round to the north side, which was forbidden ground to everybody in the house. When Mrs. Pentreath came forward with the steward, she overheard this exchange of question and answer passing between the foreigner and the maid:

"But tell me, Betzee, my dear," said Uncle Joseph. "Why does nobody ever go into these mouldy old rooms?"

"Because there's a ghost in them," answered Betsey, with a burst of laughter, as if a series of haunted rooms and a series of excellent jokes meant precisely the same thing.

"Hold your tongue directly, and go back to the kitchen," cried Mrs. Pentreath, indignantly. "The ignorant people about here," she continued, still pointedly overlooking Uncle Joseph, and addressing herself only to Sarah, "tell absurd stories about some old rooms on the unrepaired side of the house, which have not been inhabited for more than half a century past—absurd stories about a ghost; and my servant is foolish enough to believe them."

"No, I'm not," said Betsey, retiring, under protest, to the lower regions. "I don't believe a word about the ghost—at least not in the daytime." Adding that important saving clause in a whisper,

Betsey unwillingly withdrew from the scene.

Mrs. Pentreath observed, with some surprise, that the mysterious lady in the quiet dress turned very pale at the mention of the ghost story, and made no remark on it whatever. While she was still wondering what this meant, Mr. Munder emerged into dignified prominence, and loftily addressed himself, not to Uncle Joseph, and not to Sarah, but to the empty air between them.

"If you wish to see the house," he said, "you will have the goodness to follow me."

With those words, Mr. Munder turned solemnly into the passage that led to the foot of the west staircase, walking with that peculiar, slow strut in which all serious-minded English people indulge when they go out to take a little exercise on Sunday. The housekeeper, adapting her pace with feminine pliancy to the pace of the steward, walked the national Sabbatarian Polonaise by his side, as if she was out with him for a mouthful of fresh air between the services.

"As I am a living sinner, this going over the house is like going to a funeral!" whispered Uncle Joseph to his niece. He drew her arm into his, and felt, as he did so, that she was trembling.

"What is the matter?" he asked, under his breath.

"Uncle! there is something unnatural about the readiness of these people to show us over the house," was the faintly whispered answer. "What were they talking about just now, out of our hearing? Why did that woman keep her eyes fixed so constantly on me?"

Before the old man could answer, the housekeeper looked round, and begged, with the severest emphasis, that they would be good enough to follow. In less than another minute they were all standing at the foot of the west staircase.

"Aha!" cried Uncle Joseph, as easy and talkative as ever, even in presence of Mr. Munder himself. "A fine big house, and a very good staircase."

"We are not accustomed to hear either the house or the staircase spoken of in these terms, sir," said Mr. Munder, resolving to nip the foreigner's familiarity in the bud. "*The Guide to West Cornwall*, which you would have done well to make yourself acquainted with before you came here, describes Porthgenna Tower as a Mansion, and uses the word Spacious in speaking of the west staircase. I regret to find, sir, that you have not consulted the *Guide-book to West Cornwall.*"

"And why?" rejoined the unabashed German. "What do I want with a book, when I have got you for my guide? Ah, dear sir, but you are not just to yourself! Is not a living guide like you, who talks and walks about, better for me than dead leaves of print and paper? Ah, no, no! I shall not hear another word—I shall not hear you do any more injustice to yourself." Here Uncle Joseph made another fantastic bow, looked up smiling into the steward's face, and shook his head several times with an air of friendly reproach.

Mr. Munder felt paralysed. He could not have been treated with more ease and indifferent familiarity if this obscure foreign stranger had been an English duke. He had often heard of 'the climax of audacity; and here it was visibly embodied in one small, elderly individual, who did not rise quite five feet from the ground he stood on!

While the steward was swelling with a sense of injury too large for utterance, the housekeeper, followed by Sarah, was slowly ascending the stairs. Uncle Joseph, seeing them go up, hastened to join his niece, and Mr Munder, after waiting a little while on the mat to recover himself, followed the audacious foreigner with the intention of watching his conduct narrowly, and chastising his insolence at the first opportunity with stinging words of rebuke.

The procession up the stairs thus formed was not, however, closed by the steward; it was further adorned and completed by Betsey, the servant-maid, who stole out of the kitchen to follow the strange visitors over the house, as closely as she could without attracting the notice of Mrs. Pentreath. Betsey had her share of natural human curiosity and love of change. No such event as the arrival of strangers had ever before enlivened the dreary monotony of Porthgenna Tower within her experience; and she was resolved not to stay alone in the kitchen while there was a chance of hearing a stray word of the conversation, or catching a chance glimpse of the proceedings among the company upstairs.

In the meantime, the housekeeper had led the way as far as the first-floor landing, on either side of which the principal rooms in the west front were situated. Sharpened by fear and suspicion, Sarah's eyes immediately detected the repairs which had been effected in the banisters and stairs of the second flight.

"You have had workmen in the house?" she said quickly to Mrs. Pentreath.

"You mean on the stairs?" returned the housekeeper. "Yes, we have had workmen there."

"And nowhere else?"

"No. But they are wanted in other places badly enough. Even here, on the best side of the house, half the bedrooms upstairs are hardly fit to sleep in. They were anything but comfortable, as I have heard, even in the late Mrs. Treverton's time; and since she died—"

The housekeeper stopped with a frown and a look of surprise. The lady in the quiet dress, instead of sustaining the reputation for good manners which had been conferred on her in Mrs. Frankland's letter, was guilty of the unpardonable discourtesy of turning away from Mrs. Pentreath before she had done speaking. Determined not to allow herself to-be impertinently silenced in that way, she coldly and distinctly repeated her last words:

"And since Mrs. Treverton died—"

She was interrupted for the second time. The strange lady, turning quickly round again, confronted her with a very pale face and a very eager look, and asked, in the most abrupt manner, an utterly irrelevant question:

"Tell me about that ghost story," she said. "Do they say it is the ghost of a man or of a woman?"

"I was speaking of the late Mrs. Treverton," said the housekeeper, in her severest tones of reproof, "and not of the ghost story about the north rooms. You would have known that, if you had done me the favour to listen to what I said."

"I beg your pardon; I beg your pardon a thousand times for seeming inattentive! It struck me just then—or, at least, I wanted to know—"

"If you care to know about anything so absurd," said Mrs. Pentreath, mollified by the evident sincerity of the apology that had been offered to her, "the ghost, according to the story, is the ghost of a woman."

The strange lady's face grew whiter than ever; and she turned away once more to the open window on the landing.

"How hot it is!" she said, putting her head out into the air.

"Hot, with a northeast wind!" exclaimed Mrs. Pentreath, in amazement.

Here Uncle Joseph came forward with a polite request to know when they were going to look over the rooms. For the last few minutes he had been asking all sorts of questions of Mr. Munder; and, having received no answers which were not of the shortest and most ungracious kind, had given up talking to the steward in despair.

Mrs. Pentreath prepared to lead the way into the breakfast-room, library, and drawing-room. All three communicated with each other, and each room had a second door opening on a long passage, the entrance to which was on the right-hand side of the first-floor landing. Before leading the way into these rooms, the housekeeper touched Sarah on the shoulder to intimate that it was time to be moving on.

"As for the ghost story," resumed Mrs. Pentreath, while she opened the breakfast-room door, "you must apply to the ignorant people who believe in it, if you want to hear it all told. Whether the ghost is an old ghost or a new ghost, and why she is supposed to walk, is more than I can tell you." In spite of the housekeeper's affectation of indifference toward the popular superstition, she had heard enough of the ghost-story to frighten her, though she would not confess it. Inside the house, or outside the house, nobody much less willing to venture into the north rooms alone could in real truth have been found than Mrs. Pentreath herself.

While the housekeeper was drawing up the blinds in the breakfast-parlour, and while Mr. Munder was opening the door that led out of it into the library, Uncle Joseph stole to his niece's side and spoke a few words of encouragement to her in his quaint, kindly way.

"Courage!" he whispered. "Keep your wits about you, Sarah, and catch your little opportunity whenever you can."

"My thoughts! My thoughts!" she answered in the same low key. "This house rouses them all against me. Oh, why did I ever venture into it again!"

"You had better look at the view from the window now," said Mrs. Pentreath, after she had drawn up the blind. "It is very much admired."

While affairs were in this stage of progress on the first floor of the house, Betsey, who had been hitherto stealing up by a stair at a time from the hall, and listening with all her ears in the intervals of the ascent, finding that no sound of voices now reached her, bethought herself of returning to the kitchen again, and of looking after the housekeeper's dinner, which was being kept warm by the fire. She descended to the lower regions, wondering what part of the house the strangers would want to see next, and puzzling her brains to find out some excuse for attaching herself to the exploring party.

After the view from the breakfast-room window had been duly contemplated, the library was next entered. In this room, Mrs. Pentreath, having some leisure to look about her, and employing that leisure in observing the conduct of the steward, arrived at the unpleasant conviction that Mr. Munder was by no means to be depended on to assist her in the important business of watching the proceedings of the two strangers.

Doubly stimulated to assert his own dignity by the disrespectfully easy manner in which he had been treated by Uncle Joseph, the sole object of Mr. Munder's ambition seemed to be to divest himself as completely as possible of the character of guide, which the unscrupulous foreigner sought to confer on him. He sauntered heavily about the rooms, with the air of a casual visitor, staring out of window, peeping into books on tables, frowning at himself in the chimney-glasses—looking, in short, anywhere but where he ought to look. The housekeeper, exasperated by this affectation of indifference, whispered to him irritably to keep his eye on the foreigner, as it was quite as much as she could do to look after the lady in the quiet dress.

"Very good; very good," said Mr. Munder, with sulky carelessness. "And where are you going to next, ma'am, after we have been into the drawing-room? Back again, through the library, into the breakfast-room? or out at once into the passage? Be good enough to settle which, as you seem to be in the way of settling everything."

"Into the passage, to be sure," answered Mrs. Pentreath, "to show the next three rooms beyond these."

Mr. Munder sauntered out of the library, through the doorway of communication, into the drawing-room, unlocked the door leading into the passage—then, to the great disgust of the housekeeper, strolled to the fireplace and looked at himself in the glass over it, just as attentively as he had looked at himself in the library mirror hardly a minute before.

"This is the west drawing-room," said Mrs. Pentreath, calling to the visitors. "The carving of the stone chimney-piece," she added, with the mischievous intention of bringing them into the closest proximity to the steward, "is considered the finest thing in the whole apartment."

Driven from the looking-glass by this manoeuvre, Mr. Munder provokingly sauntered to the window and looked out. Sarah, still pale and silent—but with a certain unwonted resolution just gathering, as it were, in the lines about her lips stopped thoughtfully by the chimney-piece when the housekeeper pointed it out to her.

Uncle Joseph, looking all round the room in his discursive manner, spied, in the furthest corner of it from the door that led into the passage, a beautiful maple-wood table and cabinet of a very peculiar pattern. His workmanlike enthusiasm was instantly aroused, and he darted across the room to examine the make of the cabinet closely. The table beneath projected a little way in front of it, and, of all the objects in the world, what should he see reposing on the flat space of the projection but a magnificent musical box at least three times the size of his own!

"*Aïe! Aïe!! Aïe!!!*" cried Uncle Joseph, in an ascending scale of admiration, which ended at the very top of his voice. "Open him! set him going! let me hear what he plays!" He stopped for want of words to express his impatience, and drummed with both hands on the lid of the musical box in a burst of uncontrollable enthusiasm.

"Mr. Munder!" exclaimed the housekeeper, hurrying across the room in great indignation. "Why don't you look? why don't you stop him? He's breaking open the musical box. Be quiet, sir! How dare you touch me?"

"Set him going! set him going!" reiterated Uncle Joseph, dropping Mrs. Pentreath's arm, which he had seized in his agitation. "Look here! this by my side is a music box, too! Set him going! Does he play Mozart? He is three times bigger than ever I saw! See! see! this box of mine—this tiny bit of box that looks nothing by the side of yours—it was given to my own brother by the king of all music-composers that ever lived, by the divine Mozart himself. Set the big box going, and you shall hear the little baby-box pipe after! Ah, dear and good madam, if you love me—"

"Sir!!!" exclaimed the housekeeper, reddening with virtuous indignation to the very roots of her hair.

"What do you mean, sir, by addressing such outrageous language as that to a respectable female?" inquired Mr. Munder, approaching to the rescue. "Do you think we want your foreign noises, and your foreign morals, and your foreign profanity here? Yes, sir! profanity. Any man who calls any human individual, whether musical or otherwise, 'divine,' is a profane man. Who are you, you extremely audacious person? Are you an infidel?"

Before Uncle Joseph could say a word in vindication of his

principles, before Mr. Munder could relieve himself of any more indignation, they were both startled into momentary silence by an exclamation of alarm from the housekeeper.

"Where is she?" cried Mrs. Pentreath, standing in the middle of the drawing-room, and looking with bewildered eyes all around her.

The lady in the quiet dress had vanished.

She was not in the library, not in the breakfast-room, not in the passage outside. After searching in those three places, the housekeeper came back to Mr. Munder with a look of downright terror in her face, and stood staring at him for a moment perfectly helpless and perfectly silent. As soon as she recovered herself she turned fiercely on Uncle Joseph.

"Where is she? I insist on knowing what has become of her! You cunning, wicked, impudent old man! where is she?" cried Mrs. Pentreath, with no colour in her cheeks and no mercy in her eyes.

"I suppose she is looking about the house by herself," said Uncle Joseph. "We shall find her surely as we take our walks through the other rooms." Simple as he was, the old man had, nevertheless, acuteness enough to perceive that be had accidentally rendered the very service to his niece of which she stood in need.

If he had been the most artful of mankind, he could have devised no better means of diverting Mrs. Pentreath's attention from Sarah to himself than the very means which he had just used in perfect innocence, at the very moment when his thoughts were furthest away from the real object with which he and his niece had entered the house. "So! so!" thought Uncle Joseph to himself, "while these two angry people were scolding me for nothing, Sarah has slipped away to the room where the letter is. Good! I have only to wait till she comes back, and to let the two angry people go on scalding me as long as they please."

"What are we to do? Mr. Munder! what on earth are we to do?" asked the housekeeper. "We can't waste the precious minutes staring at each other here. This woman must be found. Stop! she asked questions about the stairs—she looked up at the second floor the moment we got on the landing. Mr. Munder! wait here, and don't let that foreigner out of your sight for a moment. "Wait here while I run up and look into the second-floor passage. All the bedroom doors are locked—I defy her to hide herself if she has gone up there." With those words, the housekeeper ran out of the drawing-room, and breathlessly ascended the second flight of stairs.

While Mrs. Pentreath was searching on the west side of the house Sarah was hurrying, at the top of her speed, along the lonely passages that led to the north rooms.

Terrified into decisive action by the desperate nature of the situation, she had slipped out of the drawing-room into the passage the instant she saw Mrs. Pentreath's back turned on her. Without stopping to think, without attempting to compose herself, she ran down the stairs of the first floor, and made straight for the housekeeper's room. She had no excuses ready, if she had found anybody there, or if she had met anybody on the way.

She had formed no plan where to seek for them next, if the keys of the north rooms were not hanging in the place where she still expected to find them. Her mind was lost in confusion, her temples throbbed as if they would burst with the heat at her brain. The one blind, wild, headlong purpose of getting into the Myrtle Room drove her on, gave unnatural swiftness to her trembling feet, unnatural strength to her shaking hands, unnatural courage to her sinking heart.

She ran into the housekeeper's room, without even the ordinary caution of waiting for a moment to listen outside the door. No one was there. One glance at the well-remembered nail in the wall showed her the keys still hanging to it in a bunch, as they had hung in the long-past time.

She had them in her possession in a moment; and was away again, along the solitary passages that led to the north rooms, threading their turnings and windings as if she had left them but the day before; never pausing to listen or to look behind her, never slackening her speed till she was at the top of the back staircase, and had her hand on the locked door that led into the north hall.

As she turned over the bunch to find the first key that was required, she discovered—what her hurry had hitherto prevented her from noticing—the numbered labels which the builder had methodically attached to all the keys when he had been sent to Porthgenna by Mr. Frankland to survey the house. At the first sight of them, her searching hands paused in their work instantaneously, and she shivered all over, as if a sudden chill had struck her.

If she had been less violently agitated, the discovery of the new labels and the suspicions to which the sight of them instantly gave rise would, in all probability, have checked her further progress. But the confusion of her mind was now too great to allow her to piece together even the veriest fragments of thoughts. Vaguely conscious of a new terror, of a sharpened distrust that doubled and trebled the headlong impatience which had driven heron thus far, she desperately resumed her search through the bunch of keys.

One of them had no label; it was larger than the rest—it was the key that fitted the door of communication before which she stood. She turned it in the rusty lock with a strength which, at any other time, she would have been utterly incapable of exerting; she opened the door with a blow of her hand, which burst it away at one stroke from the jambs to which it stuck. Panting for breath, she flew across the forsaken north hall, without stopping for one second to push the door to behind her.

The creeping creatures, the noisome house-reptiles that possessed the place, crawled away, shadow-like, on either side of her toward the walls. She never noticed them, never turned away for them. Across the hall, and up the stairs at the end of it, she ran, till she gained the open landing at the top—and there she suddenly checked herself in front of the first door.

The first door of the long range of rooms that opened on the landing; the door that fronted the topmost of the flight of stairs. She stopped; she looked at it—it was not the door she had come to open; and yet she could not tear herself away from it. Scrawled on the panel in white chalk was the figure—"1" And when she looked down at the bunch of keys in her hands, there was the figure "1" on a label, answering to it.

She tried to think, to follow out any one of all the thronging suspicions that beset her to the conclusion at which it might point. The effort was useless; her mind was gone; her bodily senses of seeing and hearing—senses which had now become painfully and incomprehensibly sharpened—seemed to be the sole relics of intelligence that she had left to guide her. She put her hand over her eyes, and waited a little so, and then went on slowly along the landing, looking at the doors.

No. "2," No. "3," No. "4," " traced on the panels in the same white chalk, and answering to the numbered labels on the keys, the figures on which were written in ink. No. "4" the middle room of the first floor range of eight. She stopped there again, trembling from head to foot. It was the door of the Myrtle Room.

Did the chalked numbers stop there? She looked on down the landing. No. The four doors remaining were regularly numbered on to "8"

She came back again to the door of the Myrtle Room, sought out the key labelled with the figure "4"—hesitated—and looked back distrustfully over the deserted hall.

The canvases of the old family pictures, which she had seen bulging out of their frames in the past time when she hid the letter, had, for the most part, rotted away from them now, and lay in great black ragged strips on the floor of the hall. Islands and continents of damp spread like the map of some strange region over the lofty vaulted ceiling.

Cobwebs, heavy with dust, hung down in festoons from broken cornices. Dirt stains lay on the stone pavement, like gross reflections of the damp stains on the ceiling. The broad flight of stairs leading up to the open landing before the rooms of the first floor had sunk down bodily toward one side. The banisters which protected the outer edge of the landing were broken away into ragged gaps. The light of day was stained, the air of heaven was stilled, the sounds of earth were silenced in the north hall.

Silenced? Were all sounds silenced? Or was there something stirring that just touched the sense of hearing, that just deepened the dismal stillness, and no more?

Sarah listened, keeping her face still set toward the hall—listened, and heard a faint sound behind her. Was it outside the door on which her back was turned? Or was it inside—in the Myrtle Room.

Inside. With the first conviction of that, all thought, all sensation left her. She forgot the suspicious numbering of the doors; she became insensible to the lapse of time, unconscious of the risk of discovery. All exercise of her other faculties was now merged in the exercise of the one faculty of listening.

It was a still, faint, stealthily rustling sound; and it moved to and fro at intervals, to and fro softly, now at one end, now at the other of the Myrtle Room. There were moments when it grew suddenly distinct—other moments when it died away in gradations too light to follow. Sometimes it seemed to sweep over the floor at a bound—sometimes it crept with slow, continuous rustlings that just wavered on the verge of absolute silence.

Her feet still rooted to the spot on which she stood, Sarah turned her head slowly, inch by inch, toward the door of the Myrtle Room. A moment before, while she was as yet unconscious of the faint sound moving to and fro within it, she had been drawing her breath heavily and quickly. She might have been dead now, her bosom was so still, her breathing so noiseless. The same mysterious change came over her face which had altered it when the darkness began to gather in the little parlour at Truro. The same fearful look of inquiry which she had then fixed on the vacant corner of the room was in her eyes now, as they slowly turned on the door.

"Mistress!" she whispered. "Am I too late? Are you there before me?"

The stealthily rustling sound inside paused—renewed itself-died away again faintly; away at the lower end of the room.

Her eyes still remained fixed on the Myrtle Room, strained, and opened wider and wider—opened as if they would, look through the very door itself—opened as if they were watching for the opaque wood to turn transparent and show what was behind it.

"Over the lonesome floor, over the lonesome floor—how light it moves!" she whispered again. "Mistress! does the black dress I made for you rustle no louder than that?"

The sound stopped again—then suddenly advanced at one stealthy sweep close to the inside of the door.

If she could have moved at that moment; if she could have looked down to the line of open space between the bottom of the door and the flooring below, when the faintly rustling sound came nearest to her, she might have seen the insignificant cause that produced it lying self-betrayed under the door, partly outside, partly inside, in the shape of a fragment of faded red paper from the wall of the Myrtle Room.

Time and damp had loosened the paper all round the apartment. Two or three yards of it had been torn off by the builder while he was examining the walls—sometimes in large pieces, sometimes in small pieces, just as it happened to come away—and had been thrown down by him on the bare, boarded floor, to become the sport of the wind, whenever it happened to blow through the broken panes of glass in the window. If she had only moved! If she had only looked down for one little second of time!

She was past moving and past looking: the paroxysm of superstitious horror that possessed her held her still in every limb and every feature. She never started, she uttered no cry, when the rustling noise came nearest. The one outward sign which showed how the terror of its approach shook her to the very soul expressed itself only in the changed action of her right hand, in which she still held the keys.

At the instant when the wind wafted the fragment of paper closest to the door, her fingers lost their power of contraction, and became as nerveless and helpless as if she had fainted. The heavy bunch of keys slipped from her suddenly loosened grasp, dropped at her side on the outer edge of the landing, rolled off through a gap in the broken banister, and fell on the stone pavement below, with a crash which made the sleeping echoes shriek again, as if they were sentient beings writhing under the torture of sound.

The crash of the falling keys, ringing and ringing again through the stillness, woke her, as it were, to instant consciousness of present events and present perils. She started, staggered backward, and raised both her hands wildly to her head paused so for a few seconds—then made for the top of the stairs with the purpose of descending into the hall to recover the keys.

Before she had advanced three paces the shrill sound of a woman's scream came from the door of communication at the opposite end of the hall.

The scream was twice repeated at a greater distance off, and was followed by a confused noise of rapidly advancing voices and footsteps.

She staggered desperately a few paces further, and reached the first of the row of doors that opened on the landing. There nature sank exhausted; her knees gave way under her—her breath, her sight, her hearing all seemed to fail her together at the same instant—and she dropped down senseless on the floor at the head of the stairs.

Chapter 4
Mr. Munder on the Seat of Judgment

The murmuring voices and the hurrying footsteps came nearer and nearer, then stopped altogether. After an interval of silence, one voice called out loudly, "Sarah! Sarah! where are you?" and the next instant Uncle Joseph appeared alone in the doorway that led into the north hall, looking eagerly all round him.

At first the prostrate figure on the landing at the head of the stairs escaped his view. But the second time he looked in that direction the dark dress, and the arm that lay just over the edge of the top stair, caught his eye. With a loud cry of terror and recognition, he flew across the hall and ascended the stairs. Just as he was kneeling by Sarah's side, and raising her head on his arm, the steward, the housekeeper, and the maid, all three crowded together after him into the doorway.

"Water!" shouted the old man, gesticulating at them wildly with his disengaged hand. "She is here—she has fallen down—she is in a faint! Water! water!"

Mr. Munder looked at Mrs. Pentreath, Mrs. Pentreath looked at Betsey, Betsey looked at the ground. All three stood stock-still; all three seemed equally incapable of walking across the hall. If the science of physiognomy be not an entire delusion, the cause of this amazing unanimity was legibly written in their faces; in other words, they all three looked equally afraid of the ghost.

"Water, I say! Water!" reiterated Uncle Joseph, shaking his fist at them, "She is in a faint! Are you three at the door there, and not one heart of mercy among you? Water! water! water! Must I scream myself into fits before I can make you hear?"

"I'll get the water, ma'am," said Betsey, "if you or Mr. Munder will please to take it from here to the top of the stairs."

She ran to the kitchen, and came back with a glass of water, which she offered, with a respectful courtesy, first to the housekeeper, and then to the steward.

"How dare you ask us to carry things for you?" said Mrs. Pentreath, backing out of the doorway.

"Yes! how dare you ask us?" added Mr. Munder, backing after Mrs. Pentreath.

"Water!" shouted the old man for the third time. He drew his niece backward a little, so that she could be supported against the wall behind her. "Water! or I trample down this dungeon of a place about your ears!" he shouted, stamping with impatience and rage.

"If you please, sir, are you sure it's really the lady who is up there?" asked Betsey, advancing a few paces tremulously with the glass of water.

"Am I sure?" exclaimed Uncle Joseph, descending the stairs

to meet her. "What fool's question is this? Who should it be?"

"The ghost, sir," said Betsey, advancing more and more slowly. "The ghost of the north rooms."

Uncle Joseph met her a few yards in advance of the foot of the stairs, took the glass of water from her with a gesture of contempt, and hastened back to his niece. As Betsey turned to effect her retreat, the bunch of keys lying on the pavement below the landing caught her eye. After a little hesitation she mustered courage enough to pick them, up, and then ran with them out of the hall as fast as her feet could carry her.

Meanwhile Uncle Joseph was moistening his niece's lips with the water, and sprinkling it over her forehead. After a while her breath began to come and go slowly, in faint sighs, the muscles of her face moved a little, and she feebly opened her eyes. They fixed affrightedly on the old man, without any expression of recognition. He made her drink a little water, and spoke to her gently, and so brought her back at last to herself. Her first words were, "Don't leave me." Her first action, when she was able to move, was the action of crouching closer to him.

"No fear, my child," he said, soothingly; "I will keep by you. Tell me, Sarah, what has made you faint? What has frightened you so?"

"Oh, don't ask me! For God's sake, don't ask me!"

"There, there! I shall say nothing, then. Another mouthful of water? A little" mouthful more?"

"Help me up, uncle; help me to try if I can stand."

"Not yet—not quite yet; patience for a little longer."

"Oh, help me! help me! I want to get away from the sight of those doors. If I can only go as far as the bottom of the stairs I shall be better."

"So, so," said Uncle Joseph, assisting her to rise. "Wait now, and feel your feet on the ground. Lean on me, lean hard, lean heavy. Though I am only a light and a little man, I am solid as a rock. Have you been into the room?" he added, in a whisper. "Have you got the letter?"

She sighed bitterly, and laid her head on his shoulder with a weary despair.

"Why, Sarah! Sarah!" he exclaimed. "Have you been all this time away and not got into the room yet?"

She raised her head as suddenly as she had laid it down, shuddered, and tried feebly to draw him toward the stairs. "I shall never see the Myrtle Room again—never, never, never more!" she said. "Let us go; I can walk; I am strong now. Uncle Joseph, if you love me, take me away from this house; away anywhere, so long as we are in the free air and the daylight again; anywhere, so long as we are out of sight of Porthgenna Tower."

Elevating his eyebrows in astonishment, but considerately refraining from asking any more questions, Uncle Joseph assisted his niece to descend the stairs. She was still so weak that she was obliged to pause on gaining the bottom of them to recover her strength. Seeing this, and feeling, as he led her afterward across the hall, that she leaned more and more heavily on his arm at every fresh step, the old man, on arriving within speaking distance of Mr. Munder and Mrs. Pentreath, asked the housekeeper if she possessed any restorative drops which she would allow him to administer to his niece.

Mrs. Pentreath's reply in the affirmative, though not very graciously spoken, was accompanied by an alacrity of action which showed that she was heartily rejoiced to take the first fair excuse for returning to the inhabited quarter of the house. Muttering something about showing the way to the place where the medicine-chest was kept, she immediately retraced her steps along the passage to her own room; while Uncle Joseph, disregarding all Sarah's whispered assurances that she was well enough to depart without another moment of delay, followed her silently, leading his niece.

Mr. Munder, shaking his head, and looking woefully disconcerted, waited behind to lock the door of communication. When he had done this, and had given the keys to Betsey to carry back to their appointed place, he, in his turn, retired from the scene at a pace indecorously approaching to something like a run.

On getting well away from the north hall, however, he regained his self-possession wonderfully. He abruptly slackened his pace, collected his scattered wits, and reflected a little, apparently with perfect satisfaction to himself; for when he entered the housekeeper's room he had quite recovered his usual complacent solemnity of look and manner. Like the vast majority of densely stupid men, he felt intense pleasure in hearing himself talk, and he now discerned such an opportunity of indulging in that luxury, after the events that had just happened in the house, as he seldom enjoyed.

There is only one kind of speaker who is quite certain never to break down under any stress of circumstances—the man whose capability of talking does not include any dangerous underlying capacity for knowing what he means. Among this favoured order of natural orators, Mr. Munder occupied a prominent rank—and he was now vindictively resolved to exercise his abilities on the two strangers, under pretence of asking for an explanation of their conduct, before he could suffer them to quit the house.

On entering the room, he found Uncle Joseph seated with his niece at the lower end of it, engaged in dropping some *sal volatile* into a glass of water. At the upper end stood the housekeeper with an open medicine-chest on the table before her. To this part of the room Mr. Munder slowly advanced, with a portentous countenance; drew an armchair up to the table; sat himself down in it, with extreme deliberation and care in the matter of settling his coat-tails; and immediately became, to all outward appearance, the model of a Lord Chief Justice in plain clothes.

Mrs. Pentreath, conscious from these preparations that something extraordinary was about to happen, seated herself a little behind the steward. Betsey restored the keys to their place on the nail in the wall, and was about to retire modestly to her proper kitchen sphere, when she was stopped by Mr. Munder.

"Wait, if you please," said the steward; "I shall have occasion to call on you presently, young woman, to make a plain statement."

Obedient Betsey waited near the door, terrified by the idea that she must have done something wrong, and that the steward was armed with inscrutable legal power to try, sentence, and punish her for the offense on the spot.

"Now, sir," said Mr. Munder, addressing Uncle Joseph as if he was the Speaker of the House of Commons, "if you have done with that *sal volatile*, and if the person by your side has sufficiently recovered her senses to listen, I should wish to say a word or two to both of you."

At this exordium, Sarah tried affrightedly to rise from her chair; but her uncle caught her by the hand, and pressed her back in it.

"Wait and rest," he whispered. "I shall take all the scolding on my own shoulder, and do all the talking with my own tongue, As soon as you are fit to walk again, I promise you this: whether the big man has said his word or two, or has not said it, we will quietly get up and go our ways out of the house."

"Up to the present moment," said Mr. Munder, "I have refrained from expressing an opinion. The time has now come when, holding a position of trust as I do in this establishment, and being accountable, and indeed responsible, as I am, for what takes place in it, and feeling, as I must, that things cannot be allowed or even permitted to rest as they are—it is my duty to say that I think your conduct is very extraordinary." Directing this forcible conclusion to his sentence straight at Sarah, Mr. Munder leaned back in his chair, quite full of words, and quite empty of meaning, to collect himself comfortably for his next effort.

"My only desire," he resumed, with a plaintive impartiality, "is to act fairly by all parties. I don't wish to frighten anybody, or to startle anybody, or even to terrify anybody. I wish to unravel, or, if you please, to make out, what I may term, with perfect propriety—events. And when I have done that, I should wish to put it to you, ma'am, and to you, sir, whether—I say, I should wish to put it to you both, calmly, and impartially, and politely, and plainly, and smoothly and when I say smoothly,—I mean quietly—whether you are not both of you bound to explain yourselves."

Mr. Munder paused, to let that last irresistible appeal work its way to the consciences of the persons whom he addressed. The housekeeper took advantage of the silence to cough, as congregations cough just before the sermon, apparently on the principle of getting rid of bodily infirmities beforehand, in order to give the mind free play for undisturbed intellectual enjoyment.

Betsey, following Mrs. Pentreath's lead, indulged in a cough on her own account—of the faint, distrustful sort. Uncle Joseph sat perfectly easy and undismayed, still holding his niece's hand in his, and giving it a little squeeze, from time to time, when the steward's oratory became particularly involved and impressive. Sarah never moved, never looked up, never lost the expression of terrified restraint which had taken possession of her face from the first moment when she entered the housekeeper's room.

"Now, what are the facts, and circumstances, and events?" proceeded Mr. Munder, leaning back in his chair, in calm enjoyment of the sound of his own voice. "You, ma'am, and you, sir, ring at the bell of the door of this Mansion" (here he looked bard at Uncle Joseph, as much as to say, "I don't give up that point about the house being a Mansion, you see, even on the judgment-seat")—"you are let in, or, rather, admitted. You, sir, assert that you wish to inspect the Mansion (you say 'see the house,' but, being a foreigner, we are not surprised at your making a little mistake of that sort); you, ma'am, coincide, and even agree, in that request. What follows? You are. shown over the Mansion. It is not usual to show strangers over it, but we happen to have certain reasons—"

Sarah started. "What reasons?" she asked, looking up quickly.

Uncle Joseph felt her hand turn cold, and tremble in his, "Hush! hush!" he said, "leave the talking to me."

At the same moment, Mrs. Pentreath pulled Mr. Munder warily by the coat-tail, and whispered to him to be careful. "Mrs. Frankland's letter," she said in his ear, "tells us particularly not to let it be suspected that we are acting under orders."

"Don't you fancy, Mrs. Pentreath, that I forget what I ought to remember," rejoined Mr. Munder—who had forgotten, nevertheless. "And don't you imagine that I was going to commit myself" (the very thing which he had just been on the point of doing). "Leave this business in my hands, if you will be so good.—What reasons did you say, ma'am?" he added aloud, addressing himself to Sarah. "Never you mind about reasons; we have not got to do with them now; we have got to do with facts, and circumstances, and events. I was observing, or remarking, that you, sir, and you, ma'am, were shown over this Mansion. You were conducted, and indeed led, up the west staircase—the Spacious west staircase, sir!

"You were shown with politeness, and even with courtesy, through the breakfast-room, the library, and the drawing-room. In that drawing-room, you, sir, indulge in outrageous, and, I will add, in violent language. In that drawing-room, you, ma'am, disappear, or, rather, go altogether out of sight. Such conduct as this, so highly unparalleled, so entirely unprecedented, and so very unusual, causes Mrs. Pentreath and myself to feel—" Here Mr. Munder stopped, at a loss for a word for the first time.

"Astonished," suggested Mrs. Pentreath after a long interval of silence.

"No, ma'am!" retorted Mr. Munder. "Nothing of the sort. We were not at all astonished; we were—surprised. And what followed and succeeded that? What did you and I hear, sir, on the first floor?" (looking sternly at Uncle Joseph). "And what did you hear, Mrs. Pentreath, while you were searching for the missing and absent party on the second floor? What?"

Thus personally appealed to, the housekeeper answered briefly—"A scream."

"No! no! no!" said Mr. Munder, fretfully tapping his hand on the table. "A screech, Mrs. Pentreath—a screech. And what is the meaning, purport, and upshot of that screech?—Young woman!" (here Mr. Munder turned suddenly on Betsey) "we have now traced these extraordinary facts and circumstances as far as you. Have the goodness to step forward, and tell us, in the presence of these two parties, how you came to utter, or give, what Mrs. Pentreath calls a scream, but what I call a screech. A plain statement will do, my good girl—quite a plain statement, if you please. And, young woman, one word more—speak up. You understand me? Speak up!"

Covered with confusion by the public and solemn nature of this appeal, Betsey, on starting with her statement, unconsciously followed the oratorical example of no less a person than Mr. Munder himself; that is to say, she spoke on the principle of drowning the smallest possible infusion of ideas in the largest possible dilution of words. Extricated from the mesh of verbal entanglement in which she contrived to involve it, her statement may be not unfairly represented as simply consisting of the following facts:

First, Betsey had to relate that she happened to be just taking the lid off a saucepan, on the kitchen fire, when she heard, in the neighbourhood of the housekeeper's room, a sound of hurried footsteps (vernacularly termed by the witness a "scurrying of somebody's feet").

Secondly, Betsey, on leaving the kitchen to ascertain what the sound meant, heard the footsteps retreating rapidly along the passage which led to the north side of the house, and, stimulated by curiosity, followed the sound of them for a certain distance.

Thirdly, at a sharp turn in the passage, Betsey stopped short, despairing of overtaking the person whose footsteps she heard, and feeling also a sense of dread (termed by the witness, "creeping of the flesh") at the idea of venturing alone, even in broad daylight, into the ghostly quarter of the house.

Fourthly, while still hesitating at the turn in the passage, Betsey heard "the lock of a door go," and, stimulated afresh by curiosity, advanced a few steps further—then stopped again, debating within herself the difficult and dreadful question, whether it is the usual custom of ghosts, when passing from one place to another, to unlock any closed door which may happen to be in their way, or to save trouble by simply passing through it.

Fifthly, after long deliberation, and many false starts—forward toward the north hall and backward toward the kitchen—Betsey decided that it was the immemorial custom of all ghosts to pass through doors, and not unlock them.

Sixthly, fortified by this conviction, Betsey went on boldly close to the door, when she suddenly heard a loud report, as of some heavy body falling (graphically termed by the witness a "banging scrash").

Seventhly, the noise frightened Betsey out of her wits, brought her heart up into her mouth, and took away her breath.

Eighthly, and lastly, on recovering breath enough to scream (or screech), Betsey did, with might and main, scream (or screech), running back toward the kitchen as fast as her legs would carry her, with all her hair "standing up on end," and all her flesh "in a crawl" from the crown of her head to the soles of her feet.

"Just so! just so!" said Mr. Munder, when the statement came to a close—as if the sight of a young woman with all her hair standing on end and all her flesh in a crawl were an ordinary result of his experience of female humanity—"Just so! You may stand back, my good girl—you may stand back.—There is nothing to smile at, sir," he continued, sternly addressing Uncle Joseph, who had been excessively amused by Betsey's manner of delivering her evidence.

"You would be doing better to carry, or rather transport, your mind back to what followed and succeeded the young woman's screech. What did we all do, sir? We rushed to the spot, and we ran to the place. And what did we all see, sir?—We saw you, ma'am, lying horizontally prostrate, on the top of the landing of the first of the flight of the north stairs; and we saw those keys, now hanging up yonder, abstracted and purloined, and, as it were, snatched from their place in this room, and lying horizontally prostrate likewise on the floor of the hall.—There are the facts, the circumstances, and the events, laid, or rather placed, before you. What have you got to say to them? I call upon you both solemnly, and, I will add, seriously! In my own name, in the name of Mrs. Pentreath, in the name of our employers, in the name of decency, in the name of wonder—what do you mean by it?"

With that conclusion, Mr. Munder struck his fist on the table, and waited, with a glare of merciless expectation, for anything in the shape of an answer, an explanation, or a defence which the culprits at the bottom of the room might be disposed to offer.

"Tell him anything," whispered Sarah to the old man. "Anything to keep him quiet; anything to make him let us go! After what I have suffered, these people will drive me mad!"

Never very quick at inventing an excuse, and perfectly ignorant besides of what had really happened to his niece while she was alone in the north hall, Uncle Joseph, with the best will in the world to prove himself equal to the emergency, felt considerable difficulty in deciding what he should say or do.

Determined, however, at all hazards, to spare Sarah any useless suffering, and to remove her from the house as speedily as possible, he rose to take the responsibility of speaking on himself, looking hard, before he opened his lips, at Mr. Munder, who immediately leaned forward on the table with his hand to his ear. Uncle Joseph acknowledged this polite act of attention with one of his fantastic bows; and then replied to the whole of the steward's long harangue in these six unanswerable words:

"I wish you good-day, sir!"

"How dare you wish me anything of the sort!" cried Mr, Munder, jumping out of his chair in violent indignation. "How dare you trifle with a serious subject and a serious question in that way? Wish me good-day, indeed! Do you suppose I am going to let you out of this house without hearing some explanation of the abstracting and purloining and snatching of the keys of the north rooms?"

"Ah! it is that you want to know?" said Uncle Joseph, stimulated to plunge headlong into an excuse by the increasing agitation and terror of his niece. "See, now! I shall explain. What was it, dear and good sir, that we said when we were first let in? This—'We have come to see the house.' Now there is a north side to the house, and a west side to the house. Good! That is two sides; and I and my niece are two people; and we divide ourselves in two, to see the two sides, I am the half that goes

216

west, with you and the dear and good lady behind there.

"My niece here is the other half that goes north, all by herself, and drops the keys, and falls into a faint, because in that old part of the house it is what you call musty-fusty, and there is smells of tombs and spiders—and that is all the explanation, and quite enough, too. I wish you good-day, sir."

"Damme! if ever I met with the like of you before!" roared Mr. Munder, entirely forgetting his dignity, his respectability, and his long words in the exasperation of the moment. "You are going to have it all your own way, are you, Mr. Foreigner? You will walk out of this place when you please, will you, Mr. Foreigner?

"We will see what the justice of the peace for this district has to say to that," cried Mr. Munder, recovering his solemn manner and his lofty phraseology. "Property in this house is confided to my care; and unless I hear some satisfactory explanation of the purloining of those keys hanging up there, sir, on that wall, sir, before your eyes, sirs—I shall consider it my duty to detain you, and the person with you, until I can get legal advice, and lawful advice, and magisterial advice. Do you hear that, sir?"

Uncle Joseph's ruddy cheeks suddenly deepened in colour, and his face assumed an expression which made the housekeeper rather uneasy, and which had an irresistibly cooling effect on the heat of Mr. Munder's anger.

"You will keep us here? You?" said the old man, speaking very quietly, and looking very steadily at the steward. "Now, see. I take this lady (courage, my child, courage! there is nothing to tremble for)s—I take this lady with me; I throw that door open, so! I stand and wait before it; and I say to you, 'Shut that door against us, if you dare.'"

At this defiance, Mr. Munder advanced a few steps, and then stopped. If Uncle Joseph's steady look at him had wavered for an instant, he would have closed the door.

"I say again," repeated the old man, "shut it against us, if you dare. The laws and customs of your country, sir, have made me an Englishman. If you can talk into one ear of a magistrate, I can talk into the other. If he must listen to you, a citizen of this country, he must listen to me, a citizen of this country also. Say the word, if you please. Do you accuse? or do you threaten? or do you shut the door?"

Before Mr. Munder could reply to any one of these three direct questions, the housekeeper begged him to return to his chair and to speak to her. As he resumed his place, she whispered to him in warning tones, "Remember Mrs. Frankland's letter!"

At the same time, Uncle Joseph, considering that he had waited long enough, took a step forward to the door. He was prevented from advancing further by his niece, who caught him suddenly by the arm, and said in his ear, "Look! they are whispering about us again!"

"Well!" said Mr. Munder, replying to the housekeeper. "I do remember Mrs. Frankland's letter, ma'am; and what then?"

"Hush! not so loud," whispered Mrs. Pentreath. "I don't presume, Mr. Munder, to differ in opinion with you; but I want to ask one or two questions. Do you think we have any charge that a magistrate would listen to, to bring against these people?"

Mr. Munder looked puzzled, and seemed, for once in a way, to be at a loss for an answer.

"Does what you remember of Mrs. Frankland's letter," pursued the housekeeper, "incline you to think that she would be pleased at a public exposure of what has happened in the house? She tells us to take private notice of that woman's conduct, and to follow her unperceived when she goes away. I don't venture on the liberty of advising you, Mr. Munder, but, as far as regards myself, I wash my hands of all responsibility, if we do anything but follow Mrs. Frankland's instructions (as she herself tells us) to the letter."

Mr. Munder hesitated. Uncle Joseph, who had paused for a minute when Sarah directed his attention to the whispering at the upper end of the room, now drew her on slowly with him to the door. "Betzee, my dear," he said, addressing the maid, with perfect coolness and composure, "we are strangers here; will you be so kind to us as to show the way out?"

Betsey looked at the housekeeper, who motioned to her to appeal for orders to the steward. Mr. Munder was sorely tempted, for the sake of his own importance, to insist on instantly carrying out the violent measures to which he had threatened to have recourse; but Mrs. Pentreath's objections made him pause in spite of himself.

"Betzee, my dear," repeated Uncle Joseph, "has all this talking been too much for your ears? has it made you deaf?"

"Wait!" cried Mr. Munder, impatiently. "I insist on your waiting, sir!"

"You insist? Well, well, because you are an uncivil man is no reason why I should be an uncivil man too. We will wait a little, sir, if you have anything more to say." Making that concession to the claims of politeness, Uncle Joseph walked gently backward and forward with his niece in the passage outside the door. " Sarah, my child, I have frightened the man of the big words," he whispered. "Try not to tremble so much; we shall soon be out in the fresh air again."

In the meantime, Mr. Munder continued his whispered conversation with the housekeeper, making a desperate effort, in the midst of his perplexities, to maintain his customary air of patronage and his customary assumption of superiority. "There is a great deal of truth, ma'am," he softly begans—"a great deal of truth, certainly, in what you say. But you are talking of the woman, while I am talking of the man. Do you mean to tell me that I am to let him go, after what has happened, without at least insisting on his giving me his name and address?"

"Do you put trust enough in the foreigner to believe that he would give you his right name and address if you asked him?" inquired Mrs. Pentreath. "With submission to your better judgment, I must confess that I don't. But supposing you were to detain him and charge him before the magistrates—and how you are to do that, the magistrate's house being, I suppose, about a couple of hours' walk from here, is more than I can tell—you must surely risk offending Mrs. Frankland by detaining the woman and charging the woman as well; for after all, Mr. Munder, though I believe the foreigner to be capable of anything, it was the woman that took the keys, was it not?"

"Quite so! quite so!" said Mr. Munder, whose sleepy eyes were now opened to this plain and straightforward view of the case for the first time. "I was, oddly enough, putting that point to myself, Mrs. Pentreath, just before you happened to speak of it. Just so! just so!"

"I can't help thinking," continued the housekeeper, in a mysterious whisper, "that the best plan, and the plan most in accordance with our instructions, is to let them both go, as if we did not care to demean ourselves by any more quarrelling or arguing with them, and to have them followed to the next place they stop at.

"The gardener's boy, Jacob, is weeding the broad walk in the west garden this afternoon. These people have not seen him about the premises, and need not see him, if they are let out again by the south door. Jacob is a sharp lad, as you know: and, if he was properly instructed, I really don't sees—"

"It is a most singular circumstance, Mrs. Pentreath," interposed Mr. Munder, with the gravity of consummate assurance; "but when I first sat down to this table, that idea about Jacob occurred to me. What with the effort of speaking, and the heat of argument, I got led away from it in the most unaccountable manners—"

Here Uncle Joseph, whose stock of patience and politeness was getting exhausted, put his head into the room again.

"I shall have one last word to address to you, sir, in a moment," said Mr. Munder, before the old man could speak. "Don't you suppose that your blustering and your bullying has had any effect on me. It may do with foreigners, sir; but it won't do with Englishmen, I can tell you."

Uncle Joseph shrugged his shoulders, smiled, and rejoined his niece in the passage outside. While the housekeeper and the steward had been conferring together, Sarah had been trying hard to persuade her uncle to profit by her knowledge of the passages that led to the south door, and to slip away unperceived.

But the old man steadily refused to be guided by her advice. "I will not go out of a place guiltily," he said, "when I have done no harm. Nothing shall persuade me to put myself, or to put you, in the wrong. I am not a man of much wits; but let my conscience guide me, and so long I shall go right. They let us in here, Sarah, of their own accord; and they shall let us out of their own accord also."

"Mr. Munder! Mr. Munder!" whispered the housekeeper, in terfering to stop a fresh explosion of the steward's indignation, which threatened to break out at the contempt implied by the shrugging of Uncle Joseph's shoulders, "while you are speaking to that audacious man, shall I slip into the garden and give Jacob his instructions?"

Mr. Munder paused before answerings—tried hard to see a more dignified way out of the dilemma in which he had placed himself than the way suggested by the housekeepers—failed entirely to discern anything of the sorts—swallowed his indignation at one heroic gulps—and replied emphatically in two words: "Go, ma'am."

"What does that mean? what has she gone that way for?" said Sarah to her uncle, in a quick, suspicious whisper, as the housekeeper brushed hastily by them on her way to the west garden.

Before there was time to answer the question, it was followed by another, put by Mr. Munder.

"Now, sir!" said the steward, standing in the doorway, with his hands under his coat-tails and his head very high in the air. "Now, sir, and now, ma'am, for my last words. Am I to have a proper explanation of the abstracting and purloining of those keys, or am I not?"

"Certainly, sir, you are to have the explanation," replied Uncle Joseph. "It is, it you please, the same explanation that I had the honour of giving to you a little while ago. Do you wish to hear it again? It is all the explanation we have got about us."

"Oh! it is, is it?" said Mr. Munder. "Then all I have to say to both of you is—leave the house directly! Directly!" he added, in his most coarsely offensive tones, taking refuge in the insolence of authority, from the dim consciousness of the absurdity of his own position, which would force itself en him even while he spoke.

"Yes, sir!" he continued, growing more and more angry at the composure with which Uncle Joseph listened to him—"Yes, sir I you may bow and scrape, and jabber your broken English somewhere else. I won't put up with you here. I have reflected with myself, and reasoned with myself, and asked myself calmly—as Englishmen always do—if it is any use making you of importance, and I have come to a conclusion, and that conclusion is—no, it isn't!

"Don't you go away with a notion that your blusterings and bullyings have had any effect on me. (Show them out, Betsey!) I consider you beneath—aye, and below!—my notice, Language fails, sir, to express my contempt. Leave the house!"

"And I, sir," returned the object of all this withering derision, with the most exasperating politeness, "I shall say, for having your contempt, what I could by no means have said for having your respect, which is, briefly—thank you. I, the small foreigner, take the contempt of you, the big Englishman, as the greatest compliment that can be paid from a man of your composition to a man of mine." With that, Uncle Joseph made a last fantastic bow, took his niece's arm and followed Betsey along the passages that led to the south door, leaving Mr. Munder to compose a fit retort at his leisure.

Ten minutes later the housekeeper returned breathless to her room, and found the steward walking backward and forward in a high state of irritation. "Pray make your mind easy, Mr. Munder," she said. "They are both clear of the house at last, and Jacob has got them well in view on the path over the moor."

CHAPTER 5
MOZART PLAYS FAREWELL

Excepting that he took leave of Betsey, the servant-maid, with great cordiality, Uncle Joseph spoke not another word, after his parting reply to Mr. Munder, until he and his niece were alone again under the east wall of Porthgenna Tower. There he paused, looked up at the house, then at his companion, then back at the house once more, and at last opened his lips to speak.

"I am sorry, my child," he said—"I am sorry from my heart. This has been what you call in England a bad job."

Thinking that he referred to the scene which had just passed in the housekeeper's room, Sarah asked his pardon for having been the innocent means of bringing him into angry collision with such a person as Mr. Munder.

"No! no! no!" he cried. "I was not thinking of the man of the big body and the big words. He made me angry, it is not to be denied; but that is all over and gone now. I put him and his big words away from me, as I kick this stone, here, from the pathway into the road. It is not of your Munders, or your housekeepers, or your Betzees, that I now speak—it is of something that is nearer to you and nearer to me also, because I make of your interest my own interest too.

"I shall tell you what it is while we walk on—for I see in your face, Sarah, that you are restless and in fear so long as we stop in the neighbourhood of this dungeon-house. Come! I am ready for the march. There is the path. Let us go back by it, and pick up our little baggages at the inn where we left them, on the other side of this windy wilderness of a place."

"Yes, yes, uncle! Let us lose no time; let us walk fast. Don't be afraid of tiring me; I am much stronger now."

They turned into the same path by which they had approached Porthgenna Tower in the afternoon. By the time they had walked over a little more than the first hundred yards of their journey, Jacob, the gardener's boy, stole out from behind the ruinous inclosure at the north side of the house with his hoe in his hand.

The sun had just set, but there was a fine light still over the wide, open surface of the moor; and Jacob paused to let the old man and his niece get further away from the building before he followed them. The housekeeper's instructions had directed him just to keep them in sight, and no more; and, if he happened to observe that they stopped and turned round to look behind them, he was to stop, too, and pretend to be digging with his hoe, as if he was at work on the moorland. Stimulated by the promise of a sixpence, if he was careful to do exactly as he had been told, Jacob kept his instructions in his memory, and kept his eye on the two strangers, and promised as fairly to earn the reward in prospect for him as a boy could.

"And now, my child, I shall tell you what it is I am sorry for," resumed Uncle Joseph, as they proceeded along the path. "I am sorry that we have come out upon this journey, and run our little risk, and had our little scolding, and gained nothing. The word you said in my ear, Sarah, when I was getting you out of the faint (and you should have come out of it sooner, if the muddle-headed people of the dungeon-house had been quicker with the water)—the word you said in my ear was not much, but it was enough to tell me that we have taken this journey in vain.

"I may hold my tongue, I may make my best face at it, I may be content to walk blindfolded with a mystery that lets no peep of daylight into my eyes—but it is not the less true that the one thing your heart was most set on doing, when we started on this journey, is the one thing also that you have not done. I know that, if I know nothing else; and I say again, it is a bad job—yes, yes, upon my life and faith, there is no disguise to put upon it; it is, in your plainest English, a very bad job."

As he concluded the expression of his sympathy in these quaint terms, the dread and distrust, the watchful terror, that marred the natural softness of Sarah's eyes, disappeared in an expression of sorrowful tenderness, which seemed to give back to them all their beauty.

"Don't be sorry for me, uncle," she said, stopping, and gently brushing away with her hand some specks of dust that lay on the collar of his coat. "I have suffered so much and suffered so long, that the heaviest disappointments pass lightly over me now."

"I won't hear you say it!" cried Uncle Joseph. "You give me shocks I can't bear when you talk to me in this way. You shall have no more disappointments—no, you shall not! I, Joseph Buschmann, the Obstinate, the Pig-headed, I say it!"

"The day when I shall have no more disappointments, uncle, is not far off now. Let me wait a little longer, and endure a little longer: I have learned to be patient, and to hope for nothing. Fearing and failing,—fearing and failing that has been my life ever since I was a young woman—the life I have become used to by this time.

"If you are surprised, as I know you must be, at my not possessing myself of the letter, when I had the keys of the Myrtle Room in my hand, and when no one was near to stop me, remember the history of my life, and take that as an explanation. Fearing and failing, fearing and failing—if I told you all the truth, I could tell no more than that. Let us walk on, uncle."

The resignation in her voice and manner while she spoke was the resignation of despair. It gave her an unnatural self-possession, which altered her, in the eyes of Uncle Joseph, almost past recognition. He looked at her in undisguised alarm.

"No!" he said, "we will not walk on; we will walk back to the dungeon-house; we will make another plan; we will try to get at this devil's imp of a letter in some other way. I care for no Munders, no housekeepers, no Betzees—I! I care for nothing but the getting you the one thing you want, and the taking you home again as easy in your mind as I am myself. Come! let us go back."

"It is too late to go back."

"How too late? Ah, dismal, dingy, dungeon-house of the devil, how I hate you!" cried Uncle Joseph, looking back over the prospect, and shaking both his fists at Porthgenna Tower.

"It is too late, uncle," she repeated. "Too late, because the opportunity is lost; too late, because if I could bring it back, I dare not go near the Myrtle Room again. My last hope was to change the hiding-place of the letter—and that last hope I have given up. I have only one object in life left now; you may help me in it; but I cannot tell you how unless you come on with me at once—unless you say nothing more about going back to

Porthgenna Tower."

Uncle Joseph began to expostulate. His niece stopped him in the middle of a sentence, by touching him on the shoulder and pointing to a particular spot on the darkening slope of the moor below them.

"Look!" she said, "there is somebody on the path behind us. Is it a boy or a man?"

Uncle Joseph looked through the fading light and saw a figure at some little distance. It seemed like the figure of a boy, and he was apparently engaged in digging on the moor.

"Let us turn round and go on at once," pleaded Sarah, before the old man could answer her. "I can't say what I want to say to you, uncle, until we are safe under shelter at the inn."

They went on until they reached the highest ground on the moor. There they stopped, and looked back again. The rest of their way lay down hill; and the spot on which they stood was the last point from which a view could be obtained of Porthgenna Tower.

"We have lost sight of the boy," said Uncle Joseph, looking over the ground below them.

Sarah's younger and sharper eyes bore witness to the truth of her uncle's words—the view over the moor was lonely now, in every direction, as far as she could see. Before going on again, she moved a little away from the old man, and looked at the tower of the ancient house, rising heavy and black in the dim light, with the dark sea background stretching behind it like a wall. "Never again!" she whispered to herself. "Never, never, never again!"

Her eyes wandered away to the church, and to the cemetery inclosure by its side, barely distinguishable now in the shadows of the coming night. "Wait for me a little longer," she said, looking toward the burial-ground with straining eyes, and pressing her hand on her bosom over the place where the book of Hymns lay hid. "My wanderings are nearly at an end; the day for my coming home again is not far off!"

The tears filled her eyes and shut out the view. She rejoined her uncle, and, taking his arm again, drew him rapidly a few steps along the downward path— then checked herself, as if struck by a sudden suspicion, and walked back a few paces to the highest ridge of the ground. "I am not sure," she said, replying to her companion's look of surprise—"I am not sure whether we have seen the last yet of that boy who was digging on the moor."

As the words passed her lips, a figure stole out from behind one of the large fragments of granite rock which were scattered over the waste on all sides of them. It was once more the figure of the boy, and again he began to dig, without the slightest apparent reason, on the barren ground at his feet.

"Yes, yes, I see," said Uncle Joseph, as his niece eagerly directed his attention to the suspicious figure. "It is the same boy, and he is digging still—and, if you please, what of that?"

Sarah did not attempt to answer. "Let us get on," she said, hurriedly. "Let us get on as fast as we can to the inn."

They turned again, and took the downward path before them. In less than a minute they had lost sight of Porthgenna Tower, of the old church, and of the whole of the western view. Still, though there was now nothing but the blank darkening moorland to look back at, Sarah persisted in stopping at frequent intervals, as long as there was any light left, to glance behind her. She made no remark, she offered no excuse for thus delaying the journey back to the inn. It was only when they arrived within sight of the lights of the post-town that she ceased looking back, and that she spoke to her companion. The few words she addressed to him amounted to nothing more than a request that he would ask for a private sitting-room as soon as they reached their place of sojourn for the night.

They ordered beds at the inn, and were shown into the best parlour to wait for supper. The moment they were alone, Sarah drew a chair close to the old man's side, and whispered these words in his ear:

"Uncle! we have been followed every step of the way from Porthgenna Tower to this place."

"So! so! And how do you know that?" inquired Uncle

Joseph.

"Hush! Somebody may be listening at the door, somebody may be creeping under the window. You noticed that boy who was digging on the moor?—"

"Bah! Why, Sarah! do you frighten yourself, do you try to frighten me about a boy?"

"Oh, not so loud! not so loud! They have laid a trap for us. Uncle! I suspected it when we first entered the doors of Porthgenna Tower; I am sure of it now. What did all that whispering mean between the housekeeper and the steward when we first got into the hall? I watched their faces, and I know they were talking about us. They were not half surprised enough at seeing us, not half surprised enough at hearing what we wanted. Don't laugh at me, uncle! There is real danger: it is no fancy of mine. The keys—come closer—the keys of the north rooms have got new labels on them; the doors have all been numbered.

"Think of that! Think of the whispering when we came in, and the whispering afterward, in the housekeeper's room, when you got up to go away. You noticed the sudden change in that man's behaviour after the housekeeper spoke to him—you must have noticed it? They let us in too easily, and they let us out too easily. No, no! I am not deluding myself. There was some secret motive for letting us into the house, and some secret motive for letting us out again. That boy on the moor betrays it, if nothing else does. I saw him following us all the way here, as plainly as I see you. I am not frightened without reason this time. As surely as we two are together in this room, there is a trap laid for us by the people at Porthgenna Tower!"

"A trap? What trap? And how? and why? and wherefore?" inquired Uncle Joseph, expressing bewilderment by waving both his hands rapidly to and fro close before his eyes.

"They want to make me speak, they want to follow me, they want to find out where I go, they want to ask me questions," she answered, trembling violently, "Uncle! you remember what I told you of those crazed words I said to Mrs. Frankland—I ought to have cut my tongue out rather than have spoken them!

They have done dreadful mischief—I am certain of it—dreadful mischief already. I have made myself suspected! I shall be questioned, if Mrs Frankland finds me out again. She will try to find me out—we shall be inquired after here—we must destroy all trace of where we go to next—we must make sure that the people at this inn can answer no questions—oh, Uncle Joseph! whatever we do, let us make sure of that!"

"Good," said the old man, nodding his head with a perfectly self-satisfied air. "Be quite easy, my child, and leave it to me to make sure. When you are gone to bed, I shall send for the land-lord,' and I shall say: 'Get us a little carriage, if you please, sir, to take us back again tomorrow to the coach for Truro.' "

"No, no, no! we must not hire a carriage here."

"And I say yes, yes, yes! We will hire a carriage here, because I will, first of all, make sure with the landlord. Listen. I shall say to him: 'If there come after us people with inquisitive looks in their eyes and uncomfortable questions in their mouths—if you please, sir, hold your tongue.' Then I shall wink my eye, I shall lay my finger, so, to the side of my nose, I shall give one little laugh that means much—and, crick! crack! I have made sure of the landlord! and there is an end of it!"

"We must not trust the landlord, uncle—we must not trust anybody. When we leave this place tomorrow, we must leave it on foot, and take care no living soul follows us. Look! Here is a map of West Cornwall hanging up on the wall, with roads and cross-roads all marked on it. We may find out beforehand what direction we ought to walk in. A night's rest will give me all the strength I want; and we have no luggage that we cannot carry. You have nothing but your knapsack, and I have nothing but the little carpet-bag you lent me. We can walk six, seven, even ten miles, with resting by the way. Come here and look at the map—pray, pray come and look at the map!"

Protesting against the abandonment of his own project, which he declared, and sincerely believed, to be perfectly adapted to meet the emergency in which they were placed, Uncle Joseph joined his niece in examining the map. A little beyond the post-town, a cross-road was marked, running northward at right angles with the highway that led to Truro, and conducting to another road, which looked large enough to be a coach-road, and which led through a town of sufficient importance to have its name printed in capital letters.

On discovering this, Sarah proposed that they should follow the crossroad (which did not appear on the map to be more than five or six miles long) on foot, abstaining from taking any conveyance until they had arrived at the town marked in capital letters. By pursuing this course they would destroy all trace of their progress after leaving the post-town; unless, indeed, they were followed on foot from this place, as they had been followed, over the moor. In the event of any fresh difficulty of that sort occurring, Sarah had no better remedy to propose than lingering on the road till after nightfall, and leaving it to the darkness to baffle the vigilance of any person who might be watching in the distance to see where they went.

Uncle Joseph shrugged his shoulders resignedly when his niece gave her reasons for wishing to continue the journey on foot. "There is much tramping through dust, and much looking behind us, and much spying and peeping and suspecting and roundabout walking in all this," he said. "It is by no means so easy, my child, as making sure of the landlord, and sitting at our ease on the cushions of the stagecoach. But if you will have it so, so shall it be. What you please, Sarah; what you please—that is all the opinion of my own that I allow myself to have till we are back again at Truro, and are rested for good and all at the end of our journey."

"At the end of your journey, uncle: I dare not say at the end of mine."

Those few words changed the old man's face in an instant. His eyes fixed reproachfully on his niece, his ruddy cheeks lost their colour, his restless hands dropped suddenly to his sides. "Sarah!" he said, in a low, quiet tone, which seemed to have no relation to the voice in which he spoke on ordinary occasions- "Sarah! have you the heart to leave me again?"

"Have I the courage to stay in Cornwall? That is the question to ask me, uncle. If I had only my own heart to consult, oh! how gladly I should live under your roof—live under it, if you would let me, to my dying day! But my lot is not cast for such rest and such happiness as that. The fear that I have of being questioned by Mrs. Frankland drives me away from Porthgenna, away from Cornwall, away from you. Even my dread of the letter being found is hardly so great now as my dread of being traced and questioned. I have said what I ought not to have said already.

"If I find myself in Mrs. Frankland's presence again, there is nothing that she might not draw out of me. Oh, my God! to think of that kind-hearted, lovely young woman, who brings happiness with her wherever she goes, bringing terror to me! Terror when her pitying eyes look at me; terror when her kind voice speaks to me; terror when her tender hand touches mine! Uncle! when Mrs. Frankland comes to Porthgenna, the very children will crowd about her—every creature in that poor village will be drawn toward the light of her beauty and her goodness, as if it was the sunshine of Heaven itself; and I—I, of all living beings—must shun her as if she was a pestilence!

"The day when she comes into Cornwall is the day when I must go out of it—the day when we two must say farewell. Don't, don't add to my wretchedness by asking me if I have the heart to leave you! For my dead mother's sake, Uncle Joseph, believe that I am grateful, believe that it is not my own will that takes me away when I leave you again." She sank down on a sofa near her, laid her head, with one long, deep sigh, wearily on the pillow, and spoke no more.

The tears gathered thick in Uncle Joseph's eyes as he sat down by her side. He took one of her hands, and patted and stroked it as though he were soothing a little child. "I will bear it as well as I can, Sarah," he whispered, faintly, "and I will say no more. You will write to me sometimes, when I am left all alone? You will give a little time to Uncle Joseph, for the poor dead mother's sake?"

She turned toward him suddenly, and threw both her arms

round his neck with a passionate energy that was strangely at variance with her naturally quiet, self-repressed character. "I will write often, dear; I will write always," she whispered, with her head on his bosom. "If I am ever in any trouble or danger, you shall know it." She stopped confusedly, as if the freedom of her own words and actions terrified her, unclasped her arms, and, turning away abruptly from the old man, hid her face in her hands. The tyranny of the restraint that governed her whole life was all expressed—how sadly, how eloquently!—in that one little action.

Uncle Joseph rose from the sofa, and walked gently backward and forward in the room, looking anxiously at his niece, but not speaking to her. After a while the servant came in to prepare the table for supper. It was a welcome interruption, for it obliged Sarah to make an effort to recover her self-possession. After the meal was over, the uncle and niece separated at once for the night, without venturing to exchange another word on the subject of their approaching separation.

When they met the next morning the old man had not recovered his spirits. Although he tried to speak as cheerfully as usual, there was something strangely subdued and quiet about him in voice, look and manner. Sarah's heart smote her as she saw how sadly he was altered by the prospect of their parting. She said a few words of consolation and hope; but he only waved his hand negatively, in his quaint foreign manner, and hastened out of the room to find the landlord and ask for the bill.

Soon after breakfast, to the surprise of the people at the inn, they set forth to continue their journey on foot, Uncle Joseph carrying his knapsack on his back, and his niece's carpet-bag in his hand. When they arrived at the turning that led into the crossroad, they both stopped and looked back. This time they saw nothing to alarm them. There was no living creature visible on the broad highway over which they had been walking for the last quarter of an hour after leaving the inn.

"The way is clear," said Uncle Joseph, as they turned into the crossroad. "Whatever might have happened yesterday, there is nobody following us now."

"Nobody that we can see," answered Sarah. "But I distrust the very stones by the roadside, Let us look back often, uncle, before we allow ourselves to feel secure. The more I think of it, the more I dread the snare that is laid for us by those people at Porthgenna Tower."

"You say us, Sarah. Why should they lay a snare for me?"

"Because they have seen you in my company. You will be safer from them when we are parted; and that is another reason, Uncle Joseph, why we should bear the misfortune of our separation as patiently as we can."

"Are you going far, very far away, Sarah, when you leave me?"

"I dare not stop on my journey till I can feel that I am lost in the great world of London. Don't look at me so sadly! I shall never forget my promise; I shall never forget to write. I have friends—not friends like you, but still friends—to whom I can go. I can feel safe from discovery nowhere but in London. My danger is great—it is, it is, indeed! I know, from what I have seen at Porthgenna, that Mrs. Frankland has an interest already in finding me out; and I am certain that this interest will be increased tenfold when she hears (as she is sure to hear) of what happened yesterday in the house. If they should trace you to Truro, oh, be careful, uncle! be careful how you deal with them; be careful how you answer their questions!"

"I will answer nothing, my child. But tell me—for I want to know all the little chances that there are of your coming back—tell me, if Mrs. Frankland finds the letter, what shall you do then?"

At that question, Sarah's hand, which had been resting languidly on her uncle's arm while they walked together, closed on it suddenly. "Even if Mrs. Frankland gets into the Myrtle Room," she said, stopping and looking affrightedly about her while she replied, "she may not find the letter. It is folded up so small; it is hidden in such an unlikely place."

"But if she does find it?"

"If she does, there will be more reason than ever for my being miles and miles away."

As she gave that answer, she raised both her hands to her heart and pressed them firmly over it. A slight distortion passed rapidly across her features; her eyes closed; her face flushed all over—then turned paler again than ever. She drew out her pocket-handkerchief, and passed it several times over her face, on which the perspiration had gathered thickly.

The old man, who had looked behind him when his niece stopped, under the impression that she had just seen somebody following them, observed this latter action, and asked if she felt too hot. She shook her head, and took his arm again to go on, breathing, as he fancied, with some difficulty. He proposed that they should sit down by the roadside and rest a little; but she only answered, "Not yet." So they went on for another half-hour; then turned to look behind them again, and, still seeing nobody, sat down for a little while to rest on a bank by the way- side.

After stopping twice more at convenient resting-places, they reached the end of the crossroad. On the highway to which it led them they were overtaken by a man driving an empty cart, who offered to give them a lift as far as the next town. They accepted the proposal gratefully; and, arriving at the town, after a drive of half an hour, were set down at the door of the principal inn. Finding on inquiry at this place that they were too late for the coach, they took a private conveyance which brought them to Truro late in the afternoon.

Throughout the whole of the journey, from the time when they left the post-town of Porthgenna to the time when they stopped, by Sarah's desire, at the coach-office in Truro, they had seen nothing to excite the smallest suspicion that their movements were being observed. None of the people whom they saw in the inhabited places, or whom they passed on the road, appeared to take more than the most casual notice of them.

It was five o'clock when they entered the office at Truro to ask about conveyances running in the direction of Exeter. They were informed that a coach would start in an hour's time, and that another coach would pass through Truro at eight o'clock the next morning.

"You will not go tonight?" pleaded Uncle Joseph. "You will wait, my child, and rest with me till tomorrow?"

"I had better go, uncle, while I have some little resolution left," was the sad answer.

"But you are so pale, so tired, so weak."

"I shall never be stronger than I am now. Don't set my own heart against me! It is hard enough to go without that."

Uncle Joseph sighed, and said no more. He led the way across the road and down the by-street to his house. The cheerful man in the shop was polishing a piece of wood behind the counter, sitting in the same position in which Sarah had seen him when she first looked through the window on her arrival at Truro. He had good news for his master of orders received, but Uncle Joseph listened absently to all that his shopman said, and hastened into the little back parlour without the faintest reflection of its customary smile on his face.

"If I had no shop and no orders, I might go away with you, Sarah," he said when he and his niece were alone. "*Aïe! Aïe!* the setting out on this journey has been the only happy part of it. Sit down and rest, my child. 1 must put my best face upon it, and get you some tea."

When the tea-tray had been placed on the table, he left the room, and returned, after an absence of some little time, with a basket in his hand. When the porter came to carry the luggage to the coach-office, he would not allow the basket to be taken away at the same time, but sat down and placed it between his feet while he occupied himself in pouring out a cup of tea for his niece.

The musical box still hung at his side in its travelling case of leather. As soon as he had poured out the cup of tea, he unbuckled the strap, removed the covering from the box, and placed it on the table near him. His eyes wandered hesitatingly toward Sarah, as he did this; he leaned forward, his lips trembling a little, his hand trifling uneasily with the empty leather case that now lay on his knees, and said to her in low, unsteady tones:

"You will hear a little farewell song of Mozart? It may be a long time, Sarah, before he can play to you again. A little farewell song, my child, before you go?"

His hand stole up gently from the leather case to the table, and set the box playing the same air that Sarah had heard on the evening when she entered the parlour, after her journey from Somersetshire and found him sitting alone listening to the music. What depths of sorrow there were now in those few simple notes! What mournful memories of past times gathered and swelled in the heart at the bidding of that one little plaintive melody! Sarah could not summon the courage to lift her eyes to the old man's face they might have betrayed to him that she was thinking of the days when the box that he treasured so dearly played the air they were listening to now by the bedside of his dying child.

The stop had not been set, and the melody, after it had come to an end, began again. But now, after the first few bars, the notes succeeded one another more and more slowly—the air grew less and less recognizable—dropped at last to three notes, following each other at long intervals—then ceased altogether. The chain that governed the action of the machinery had all run out; Mozart's farewell song was silenced on a sudden, like a voice that had broken down.

The old man started, looked earnestly at his niece, and threw the leather case over the box as if he desired to shut out the sight of it. "The music stopped so," he whispered to himself, in his own language, "when little Joseph died! Don't go!" he added, quickly, in English, almost before Sarah had time to feel surprised at the singular change that had taken place in his voice and manner. "Don't go! Think better of it, and stop with me."

"I have no choice, uncle, but to leave you—indeed, indeed I have not! You don't think me ungrateful? Comfort me at the last moment by telling me that!"

He pressed her hand in silence and kissed her on both cheeks.

"My heart is very heavy for you, Sarah," he said. "The fear has come to me that it is not for your own good that you are going away from Uncle Joseph now!"

"I have no choice," she sadly repeated—"no choice but to leave you."

"It is time, then, to get the parting over." The cloud of doubt and fear that had altered his face, from the moment when the music came to its untimely end, seemed to darken, when he had said those words. He took up the basket which he had kept so carefully at his feet, and led the way out in silence.

They were barely in time; the driver was mounting to his seat when they got to the coach-office. "God preserve you, my child, and send you back to me soon, safe and well. Take the basket on your lap; there are some little things in it for your journey." His voice faltered at the last word, and Sarah felt his lips pressed on her hand. The next instant the door was closed, and she saw him dimly through her tears standing among the idlers on the pavement, who were waiting to see the coach drive off.

By the time they were a little way out of the town she was able to dry her eyes and look into the basket. It contained a pot of jam and a horn spoon, a small inlaid work-box from the stock in the shop, a piece of foreign-looking cheese, a French roll, and a little paper packet of money, with the words "Don't be angry" written on it, in Uncle Joseph's hand.

Sarah closed the cover of the basket again, and drew down her veil. She had not felt the sorrow of the parting in all its bitterness until that moment. Oh, how hard it was to be banished from the sheltering home which was offered to her by the one friend she had left in the world!

"While that thought was in her mind, the old man was just closing the door of his lonely parlour. His eyes wandered to the tea-tray on the table and to Sarah's empty cup, and he whispered to himself in his own language again—

"The music stopped so when little Joseph died!"

BOOK 5

CHAPTER 1
AN OLD FRIEND AND A NEW SCHEME

In declaring, positively, that the boy whom she had seen digging on the moor had followed her uncle and herself to the post-town of Porthgenna, Sarah had asserted the literal truth. Jacob had tracked them to the inn, had waited a little while about the door, to ascertain if there was any likelihood of their continuing their journey that evening, and had then returned to Porthgenna Tower to make his report, and to claim his promised reward.

The same night, the housekeeper and the steward devoted themselves to the joint production of a letter to Mrs. Frankland, informing her of all that had taken place, from the time when the visitors first made their appearance, to the time when the gardener's boy had followed them to the door of the inn. The composition was plentifully garnished throughout with the flowers of Mr. Munder's rhetoric, and was, by a necessary consequence, inordinately long as a narrative, and hopelessly confused as a statement of facts.

It is unnecessary to say that the letter, with all its faults and absurdities, was read by Mrs. Frankland with the deepest interest. Her husband and Mr. Orridge, to both of whom she communicated its contents, were as much amazed and perplexed by it as she was herself. Although the discovery of Mrs. Jazeph's departure for Cornwall had led them to consider it within the range of possibility that she might appear at Porthgenna, and although the housekeeper had been written to by Rosamond under the influence of that idea, neither she nor her husband were quite prepared for such a speedy confirmation of their suspicions as they had now received.

Their astonishment, however, on first ascertaining the general purport of the letter, was as nothing compared with their astonishment when they came to those particular passages in it which referred to Uncle Joseph. The fresh element of complication imparted to the thickening mystery of Mrs. Jazeph and the Myrtle Room, by the entrance of the foreign stranger on the scene, and by his intimate connection with the extraordinary proceedings that had taken place in the house, fairly baffled them all.

The letter was read again and again; was critically dissected paragraph by paragraph; was carefully annotated by the doctor, for the purpose of extricating all the facts that it contained from the mass of unmeaning words in which Mr. Munder had artfully and lengthily involved them; and was finally pronounced, after all the pains that had been taken to render it intelligible, to be the most mysterious and bewildering document that mortal pen had ever produced.

The first practical suggestion, after the letter had been laid aside in despair, emanated from Rosamond. She proposed that her husband and herself (the baby included, as a matter of course) should start at once for Porthgenna, to question the servants minutely about the proceedings of Mrs. Jazeph and the foreign stranger who had accompanied her, and to examine the premises on the north side of the house, with a view to discovering a clew to the locality of the Myrtle Room, while events were still fresh in the memories of witnesses.

The plan thus advocated, however excellent in itself, was opposed by Mr. Orridge on medical grounds. Mrs. Frankland had caught cold by exposing herself too carelessly to the air, on first leaving her room, and the doctor refused to grant her permission to travel for at least a week to come, if not for a longer period.

The next proposal came from Mr. Frankland. He declared it to be perfectly clear to his mind that the only chance of penetrating the mystery of the Myrtle Room rested entirely on the discovery of some means of communicating with Mrs. Jazeph. He suggested that they should not trouble themselves to think of anything unconnected with the accomplishment of this purpose; and he proposed that the servant then in attendance on him at West Winston—a man who had been in his employment for many years, and whose zeal, activity, and intelligence could be thoroughly depended—on should be sent to Porthgenna forthwith, to start the necessary inquiries, and to examine the premises carefully on the north side of the house.

This advice was immediately acted on. At an hour's notice the servant started for Cornwall, thoroughly instructed as to what he was to do, and well supplied with money, in case he found it necessary to employ many persons in making the proposed inquiries. In due course of time he sent a report of his proceedings to his master. It proved to be of a most discouraging nature.

All trace of Mrs. Jazeph and her companion had been lost at the post-town of Porthgenna. Investigations had been made in every direction, but no reliable information had been obtained. People in totally different parts of the country declared readily enough that they had seen two persons answering to the description of the lady in the dark dress and the old foreigner; but when they were called upon to state the direction in which the two strangers were travelling, the answers received turned out to be of the most puzzling and contradictory kind.

No pains had been spared, no necessary expenditure of money had been grudged; but, so far, no results of the slightest value had been obtained. Whether the lady and the foreigner had gone east, west, north, or south, was more than Mr. Frankland's servant, at the present stage of the proceedings, could take it on himself to say.

The report of the examination of the north rooms was not more satisfactory. Here, again, nothing of any importance could be discovered. The servant had ascertained that there were twenty-two rooms on the uninhabited side of the house—six on the ground-floor opening into the deserted garden, eight on the first floor, and eight above that, on the second story. He had examined all the doors carefully from top to bottom, and had come to the conclusion that none of them had been opened.

The evidence afforded by the lady's own actions led to nothing. She had, if the testimony of the servant could be trusted, dropped the keys on the floor of the hall. She was found, as the housekeeper and the steward asserted, lying, in a fainting condition, at the top of the landing of the first flight of stairs. The door opposite to her, in this position, showed no more traces of having been recently opened than any of the other doors of the other twenty-one rooms. Whether the room to which she wished to gain access was one of the eight on the first floor, or whether she had fainted on her way up to the higher range of eight rooms on the second floor, it was impossible to determine.

The only conclusions that could be fairly drawn from the events that had taken place in the house were two in number. First, it might be taken for granted that the lady had been disturbed before she had been able to use the keys to gain admission to the Myrtle Room. Secondly, it might be assumed, from the position in which she was found on the stairs, and from the evidence relating to the dropping of the keys, that the Myrtle Room was not on the ground-floor, but was one of the sixteen rooms situated on the first and second stories. Beyond this the writer of the report had nothing further to mention, except that he had ventured to decide on waiting at Porthgenna, in the event of his master having any further instructions to communicate.

What was to be done next? That was necessarily the first question suggested by the servant's announcement of the unsuccessful result of his inquiries at Porthgenna. How it was to be answered was not very easy to discover. Mrs. Frankland had nothing to suggest, Mr. Frankland had nothing to suggest, the doctor had nothing to suggest.

The more industriously they all three hunted through their minds for a new idea, the less chance there seemed to be of their succeeding in finding one. At last, Rosamond proposed, in despair, that they should seek the advice of some fourth person who could be depended on; and asked her husband's permission to write a confidential statement of their difficulties to the vicar of Long Beckley. Doctor Chennery was their oldest friend and adviser; he had known them both as children; he was well acquainted with the history of their families; he felt a fatherly interest in their fortunes; and he possessed that invaluable quality of plain, clear-headed commonsense which marked him out as the very man who would be most likely, as well as most willing, to help them.

Mr. Frankland readily agreed to his wife's suggestion; and Rosamond wrote immediately to Doctor Chennery, informing him of everything that had happened since Mrs. Jazeph's first introduction to her, and asking him for his opinion on the course of proceeding which it would be best for her husband and herself to adopt in the difficulty in which they were now placed. By return of post an answer was received, which amply justified Rosamond's reliance on her old friend. Doctor Chennery not only sympathized heartily with the eager curiosity which Mrs. Jazeph's language and conduct had excited in the mind of his correspondent, but he had also a plan of his own to propose for ascertaining the position of the Myrtle Room.

The vicar prefaced his suggestion by expressing a strong opinion against instituting any further search after Mrs. Jazeph. Judging by the circumstances, as they were related to him, he considered that it would be the merest waste of time to attempt to find her out. Accordingly he passed from that part of the subject at once, and devoted himself to the consideration of the more important question—How Mr. and Mrs. Frankland were to proceed in the endeavour to discover for themselves the mystery of the Myrtle Room?

On this point Doctor Chennery entertained a conviction of the strongest kind, and he warned Rosamond beforehand that she must expect to be very much surprised when he came to the statement of it. Taking it for granted that she and her husband could not hope to find out where the room was, unless they were assisted by someone better acquainted than themselves with the old local arrangements of the interior of Porthgenna Tower, the vicar declared it to be his opinion that there was only one individual living who could afford them the information they wanted, and that this person was no other than Rosamond's own cross-grained relative, Andrew Treverton.

This startling opinion Doctor Chennery supported by two reasons. In the first place, Andrew was the only surviving member of the elder generation who had lived at Porthgenna Tower in the by-gone days when all traditions connected with the north rooms were still fresh in the memories of the inhabitants of the house. The people who lived in it now were strangers, who had been placed in their situations by Mr. Frankland's father; and the servants employed in former days by Captain Treverton were dead or dispersed. The one available person, therefore, whose recollections were likely to be of any service to Mr. and Mrs. Frankland, was indisputably the brother of the old owner of Porthgenna Tower.

In the second place, there was the chance, even if Andrew Treverton's memory was not to be trusted, that he might possess written or printed information relating to the locality of the Myrtle Room. By his father's will—which had been made when Andrew was a young man just going to college, and which had not been altered at the period of his departure from England, or at any after-time—he had inherited the choice old collection of books in the library at Porthgenna.

Supposing that he still preserved these heirlooms, it was highly probable that there might exist among them some plan, or some description of the house as it was in the olden time, which would supply all the information that was wanted. Here, then, was another valid reason for believing that if a clew to the position of the Myrtle Room existed anywhere, Andrew Treverton was the man to lay his hand on it.

Assuming it, therefore, to be proved that the surly old misanthrope was the only person who could be profitably applied to for the requisite information, the next question was, How to communicate with him? The vicar understood perfectly that after Andrew's inexcusably heartless conduct toward her father and mother, it was quite impossible for Rosamond to address any direct application to him.

The obstacle, however, might be surmounted by making

the necessary communication proceed from Doctor Chennery. Heartily as the vicar disliked Andrew Treverton personally, and strongly as he disapproved of the old misanthrope's principles, he was willing to set aside his own antipathies and objections to serve the interests of his young friends; and he expressed his perfect readiness to write and recall himself to Andrew's recollection, and to ask, as if it was a matter of antiquarian curiosity, for information on the subject of the north side of Porthgenna Tower—including, of course, a special request to be made acquainted with the names by which the rooms had been individually known in former days.

In making this offer, the vicar frankly acknowledged that he thought the chances were very much against his receiving any answer at all to his application, no matter how carefully he might word it, with a view to humouring Andrew's churlish peculiarities. However, considering that, in the present posture of affairs, a forlorn hope was better than no hope at all, he thought it was at least worthwhile to make the attempt on the plan which he had just suggested.

If Mr. and Mrs. Frankland could devise any better means of opening communications with Andrew Treverton, or if they had discovered any new method of their own for obtaining the information of which they stood in need, Doctor Chennery was perfectly ready to set aside his own opinions and to defer to theirs.

A very brief consideration of the vicar's friendly letter convinced Rosamond and her husband that they had no choice but gratefully to accept the offer which it contained. The chances were certainly against the success of the proposed application; but were they more unfavourable than the chances against the success of any unaided investigations at Porthgenna? There was, at least, a faint hope of Doctor Chennery's request for information producing some results; but there seemed no hope at all of penetrating a mystery connected with one room only, by dint of wandering, in perfect ignorance of what to search for, through two ranges of rooms which reached the number of sixteen. Influenced by these considerations, Rosamond wrote back to the vicar to thank him for his kindness, and to beg that he would communicate with Andrew Treverton, as he had proposed, without a moment's delay.

Doctor Chennery immediately occupied himself in the composition of the important letter, taking care to make the application on purely antiquarian grounds, and accounting for his assumed curiosity on the subject of the interior of Porthgenna Tower by referring to his former knowledge of the Treverton family, and to his natural interest in the old house with which their name and fortunes had been so closely connected.

After appealing to Andrew's early recollections for the information that he wanted, he ventured a step further, and alluded to the library of old books, mentioning his own idea that there might be found among them some plan or verbal description of the house, which might prove to be of the greatest service, in the event of Mr. Treverton's memory not having preserved all particulars in connection with the names and positions of the north rooms.

In conclusion, he took the liberty of mentioning that the loan of any document of the kind to which he had alluded, or the permission to have extracts made from it, would be thankfully acknowledged as a great favour conferred; and he added, in a postscript, that, in order to save Mr. Treverton all trouble, a messenger would call for any answer he might be disposed to give the day after the delivery of the letter. Having completed the application in these terms, the vicar inclosed it under cover to his man of business in London, with directions that it was to be delivered by a trustworthy person, and that the messenger was to call again the next morning to know if there was any answer.

Three days after this letter had been dispatched to its destination—at which time no tidings of any sort had been received from Doctor Chennery—Rosamond at last obtained her medical attendant's permission to travel. Taking leave of Mr. Orridge, with many promises to let him know what progress they made toward discovering the Myrtle Room, Mr. and Mrs. Frankland turned their backs on West Winston, and for the third time started on the journey to Porthgenna Tower.

Chapter 2

The Beginning of the End

It was baking-day in the establishment of Mr. Andrew Treverton when the messenger intrusted with Doctor Chennery's letter found his way to the garden door of the cottage at Bayswater. After he had rung three times, he heard a gruff voice, on the other side of the wall, roaring at him to let the bell alone, and asking who he was, and what the devil he wanted.

"A letter for Mr. Treverton," said the messenger, nervously backing away from the door while he spoke.

"Chuck it over the wall, then, and be off with you!" answered the gruff voice.

The messenger obeyed both injunctions. He was a meek, modest, elderly man; and when Nature mixed up the ingredients of his disposition, the capability of resenting injuries was not among them.

The man with the gruff voice—or, to put it in plainer terms, the man Shrowl—picked up the letter, weighed it in his hand, looked at the address on it with an expression of contemptuous curiosity in his bull-terrier eyes, put it in his waistcoat pocket, and walked around lazily to the kitchen entrance of the cottage.

In the apartment which would probably have been called the pantry, if the house had belonged to civilized tenants, a hand-mill had been set up; and, at the moment when Shrowl made his way to this room, Mr. Treverton was engaged in asserting his independence of all the millers in England by grinding his own corn. He paused irritably in turning the handle of the mill when his servant appeared at the door.

"What do you come here for?" he asked. "When the flour's ready, I'll call for you. Don't let's look at each other oftener than we can help! I never set eyes on you, Shrowl, but I ask myself whether, in the whole range of creation, there is any animal as ugly as man? I saw a cat this morning on the garden wall, and there wasn't a single point in which you would bear comparison with him. The cat's eyes were clear—yours are muddy. The cat's nose was straight—yours is crooked. The cat's whiskers were clean—yours are dirty. The cat's coat fitted him—yours hangs about you like a sack. I tell you again, Shrowl, the species to which you (and I) belong is the ugliest on the whole face of creation. Don't let us revolt each other by keeping in company any longer. Go away, you last, worst, infirmest freak of Nature—go away!"

Shrowl listened to this complimentary address with an aspect of surly serenity. When it had come to an end, he took the letter from his waistcoat pocket, without condescending to make any reply. He was, by this time, too thoroughly conscious of his own power over his master to attach the smallest importance to anything Mr. Treverton might say to him.

"Now you've done your talking, suppose you take a look at that," said Shrowl, dropping the letter carelessly on a deal table by his master's side. "It isn't often that people trouble themselves to send letters to you—is it? I wonder whether your niece has took a fancy to write to you? It was put in the papers the other day that she'd got a son and heir.

"Open the letter, and see if it's an invitation to the christening. The company would be sure to want your smiling face at the table to make 'em jolly. Just let me take a grind at the mill, while you go out and get a silver mug. The son and heir expects a mug, you know, and his nurse expects half a guinea, and his mamma expects all your fortune. What a pleasure to make the three innocent creeturs happy! It's shocking to see you pulling wry faces, like that, over the letter. Lord! lord! where can all your natural affection have gone to?—"

"If I only knew where to lay my hand on a gag, I'd cram it into your infernal mouth!" cried Mr. Treverton. "'How dare you talk to me about my niece? You wretch! you know I hate her for her mother's sake. What do you mean by harping perpetually on my fortune? Sooner than leave it to the play-actress's child, I'd even leave it to you; and sooner than leave it to you, I would take every farthing of it out in a boat, and bury it forever at the bottom of the sea!"

Venting his dissatisfaction in these strong terms, Mr. Treverton snatched up Doctor Chennery's letter, and tore it open in a humour which by no means promised favourably for the success of the vicar's application.

He read the letter with an ominous scowl on his face, which grew darker and darker as he got nearer and nearer to the end. "When he came to the signature his humour changed and he laughed sardonically. "Faithfully yours, Robert Chennery," he repeated to himself. "Yes! faithfully mine, if I humour your whim. And what if I don't, parson?" He paused, and looked at the letter again, the scowl reappearing on his face as he did so. "There's a lie of some kind lurking about under these lines of fair writing," he muttered suspiciously. "I am not one of his congregation: the law gives him no privilege of imposing on me. What does he mean by making the attempt?" He stopped again, reflected a little, looked up suddenly at Shrowl, and said to him.

"Have you lighted the oven fire yet?"

"No, I haven't," answered Shrowl.

Mr. Treverton examined the letter for the third time—hesitated—then slowly tore it in half, and tossed the two pieces over contemptuously to his servant.

"Light the fire at once," he said. "And, if you want paper, there it is for you. Stop!" he added, after Shrowl had picked up the torn letter. "If anybody comes here tomorrow morning to ask for an answer, tell them I gave you the letter to light the fire with, and say that's the answer." With those words Mr. Treverton returned to the mill, and began to grind at it again, with a grin of malicious satisfaction on his haggard face.

Shrowl withdrew into the kitchen, closed the door, and, placing the torn pieces of the letter together on the dresser, applied himself, with the coolest deliberation, to the business of reading it. When he had gone slowly and carefully through it, from the address at the beginning to the name at the end, he scratched reflectively for a little while at his ragged beard, then folded the letter up carefully and put it in his pocket.

"I'll have another look at it later in the day," he thought to himself, tearing off a piece of an old newspaper to light the fire with. "It strikes me, just at present, that there may be better things done with this letter than burning it."

Resolutely abstaining from taking the letter out of his pocket again until all the duties of the household for that day had been duly performed, Shrowl lit the fire, occupied the morning in making and baking the bread, and patiently took his turn afterward at digging in the kitchen garden. It was four o'clock in the afternoon before he felt himself at liberty to think of his private affairs, and to venture on retiring into solitude with the object of secretly looking over the letter once more.

A second perusal of Doctor Chennery's unlucky application to Mr. Treverton helped to confirm Shrowl in his resolution not to destroy the letter. With great pains and perseverance, and much incidental scratching at his beard, he contrived to make himself master of three distinct points in it, which stood out, in his estimation, as possessing prominent and serious importance.

The first point which he contrived to establish clearly in his mind was that the person who signed the name of Robert Chennery was desirous of examining a plan, or printed account, of the north side of the interior of a certain old house in Cornwall, called Porthgenna Tower. The second point appeared to resolve itself into this, that Robert Chennery believed some such plan or printed account might be found among the collection of books belonging to Mr. Treverton. The third point was that this same Robert Chennery would receive the loan of the plan or printed account as one of the greatest favours that could be conferred on him.

Meditating on the latter fact, with an eye exclusively fixed on the contemplation of his own interests, Shrowl arrived at the conclusion that it might be well worth his while, in a pecuniary point of view, to try if he could not privately place himself in a position to oblige Robert Chennery by searching in secret among his master's books. "It might be worth a five- pound note to me, if I managed it well," thought Shrowl, putting the letter back in his pocket again, and ascending the stairs thoughtfully to the lumber-rooms at the top of the house.

These rooms were two in number, were entirely unfurnished, and were littered all over with the rare collection of books which had once adorned the library at Porthgenna Tower. Covered with dust, and scattered in all directions and positions over the floor, lay hundreds and hundreds of volumes, cast out of their packing-cases as coals are cast out of their sacks into a cellar.

Ancient books, which students would have treasured as price-less, lay in chaotic equality of neglect side by side with modern publications whose chief merit was the beauty of the binding by which they were inclosed. Into this wilderness of scattered volumes Shrowl now wandered, fortified by the supreme self-possession of ignorance, to search resolutely for one particular book, with no other light to direct him than the faint glimmer of the two guiding words—Porthgenna Tower.

Having got them firmly fixed in his mind, his next object was to search until he found them printed on the first page of any one of the hundreds of volumes that lay around him. This was, for the time being, emphatically his business in life, and there he now stood, in the largest of the two attics, doggedly prepared to do it.

He cleared away space enough with his feet to enable him to sit down comfortably on the floor, and then began to look over all the books that lay within arm's-length of him. Odd volumes of rare editions of the classics, odd volumes of the English histo-rians, odd volumes of plays by the Elizabethan dramatists, books of travel, books of sermons, books of jests, books of natural his-tory, books of sport, turned up in quaint and rapid succession; but no book containing on the title-page the words *Porthgenna Tower* rewarded the searching industry of Shrowl for the first ten minutes after he had sat himself down on the floor.

Before removing to another position, and contending with a

fresh accumulation of literary lumber, he paused and considered a little with himself, whether there might not be some easier and more orderly method than any he had yet devised of working his way through the scattered mass of volumes which yet remained to be examined.

The result of his reflections was that it would be less confusing to him if he searched through the books in all parts of the room indifferently, regulating his selection of them solely by their various sizes; disposing of all the largest to begin with; then, after stowing them away together, proceeding to the next largest, and so going on until he came down at last to the pocket volumes.

Accordingly, he cleared away another morsel of vacant space near the wall, and then, trampling over the books as coolly as if they were so many clods of earth on a plowed field, picked out the largest of all the volumes that lay on the floor.

It was an atlas; Shrowl turned over the maps, reflected, shook his head, and removed the volume to the vacant space which he had cleared close to the wall.

The next largest book was a magnificently bound collection of engraved portraits of distinguished characters. Shrowl saluted the distinguished characters with a grunt of Gothic disapprobation, and carried them off to keep the atlas company against the wall.

The third largest book lay under several others. It projected a little at one end, and it was bound in scarlet morocco. In another position, or bound in a quieter colour, it would probably have escaped notice. Shrowl drew it out with some difficulty, opened it with a portentous frown of distrust, looked at the title-page—and suddenly slapped his thigh with a great oath of exultation. There were the very two words of which he was in search, staring him in the face, as it were, with all the emphasis of the largest capital letters.

He took a step toward the door to make sure that his master was not moving in the house; then checked himself and turned back. "What do I care," thought Shrowl, "whether he sees me or not? If it comes to a tussle betwixt us which is to have his own way, I know who's master and who's servant in the. house by this time." Composing himself with that reflection, he turned to the first leaf of the book, with the intention of looking it over carefully, page by page, from beginning to end.

The first leaf was a blank. The second leaf had an inscription written at the top of it, in faded ink, which contained these words and initials: "Rare. Only six copies printed. J. A. T." Below, on the middle of the leaf, was the printed dedication:

"To John Arthur Treverton, Esquire, Lord of the Manor of Porthgenna, One of his Majesty's Justices of the Peace, F.R.S., etc., etc., etc., this work, in which an attempt is made to describe the ancient and honoured Mansion of his Ancestors—"

There were many more lines, filled to bursting with all the largest and most obsequious words to be found in the dictionary; but Shrowl wisely abstained from giving himself the trouble of reading them, and turned over at once to the title-page.

There were the all-important words:

"The History and Antiquities of Porthgenna Tower. From the period of its first erection to the present time; comprising interesting genealogical particulars relating to the Treverton family; with an inquiry into the Origin of Gothic Architecture, and a few thoughts on the Theory of Fortification after the period of the Norman Conquest. By the Reverend Job Dark, D.D.,. Rector of Porthgenna. The whole adorned with Portraits, Views, and Plans, executed in the highest style of art. Not published. Printed by Spaldock & Grimes, Truro, 1734."

That was the title-page. The next leaf contained an engraved view of Porthgenna Tower from the West. Then came several pages devoted to the Origin of Gothic Architecture. Then more pages, explaining the Norman Theory of Fortification. These were succeeded by another engraving—Porthgenna Tower from the East. After that followed more reading, under the title of *The Treverton Family;* and then came the third engraving—Porthgenna Tower from the North. Shrowl paused there, and looked with interest at the leaf opposite the print.

It only announced more reading still, about the Erection of the Mansion; and this was succeeded by engravings from family portraits in the gallery at Porthgenna. Placing his left thumb between the leaves to mark the place, Shrowl impatiently turned to the end of the book, to see what he could find there. The last leaf contained a plan of the stables; the leaf before that presented a plan of the north garden; and on the next leaf, turning backward, was the very thing described in Robert Chennery's letter—a plan of the interior arrangement of the north side of the house!

Shrowl's first impulse on making this discovery was to carry the book away to the safest hiding-place he could find for it, preparatory to secretly offering it for sale when the messenger called the next morning for an answer to the letter. A little reflection, however, convinced him that a proceeding of this sort bore a dangerously close resemblance to the act of thieving, and might get him into trouble if the person with whom he desired to deal asked him any preliminary questions touching his right to the volume which he wanted to dispose of. The only alternative that remained was to make the best copy he could of the Plan, and to traffic with that, as a document which the most scrupulous person in the world need not hesitate to purchase.

Resolving, after some consideration, to undergo the trouble of making the copy rather than run the risk of purloining the book, Shrowl descended to the kitchen, took, from one of the drawers of the dresser an old stump of a pen, a bottle of ink, and a crumpled half-sheet of dirty letter-paper, and returned to the garret to copy the Plan as he best might. It was of the simplest kind, and it occupied but a small portion of the page; yet it presented to his eyes a hopelessly involved and intricate appearance when he now examined it for the second time.

The rooms were represented by rows of small squares, with names neatly printed inside them; and the positions of doors, staircases, and passages were indicated by parallel lines of various lengths and breadths. After much cogitation, frowning, and pulling at his beard, it occurred to Shrowl that the easiest method of copying the Plan would be to cover it with the letter-paper—which, though hardly half the size of the page, was large enough to spread over the engraving on it and then to trace the lines which he saw through the paper as carefully as he could with his pen and ink. He puffed and snorted and grumbled, and got red in the face over his task; but he accomplished it—at last bating certain drawbacks in the shape of blots and smears—in a sufficiently creditable manner; then stopped to let the ink dry and to draw his breath freely, before he attempted to do anything more.

The next obstacle to be overcome consisted in the difficulty of copying the names of the rooms, which were printed inside the squares. Fortunately for Shrowl, who was one of the clumsiest of mankind in the use of the pen, none of the names were very long. As it was, he found the greatest difficulty in writing them in sufficiently small characters to fit into the squares.

One name in particular—that of the Myrtle Room—presented combinations of letters, in the word "Myrtle," which tried his patience and his fingers sorely when he attempted to reproduce them. Indeed, the result, in this case, when he had done his best, was so illegible, even to his eyes, that he wrote the word over again in larger characters at the top of the page, and connected it by a wavering line with the square which represented the Myrtle Room. The same accident happened to him in two other instances, and was remedied in the same way.

With the rest of the names, however, he succeeded better; and, when he had finally completed the business of transcription by writing the title, *Plan of the North Side*, his copy presented, on the whole, a more respectable appearance than might have been anticipated. After satisfying himself of its accuracy by a careful comparison of it with the original, he folded it up along with Doctor Chennery's letter, and deposited it in his pocket with a hoarse gasp of relief and a grim smile of satisfaction.

The next morning the garden door of the cottage presented itself to the public eye in the totally new aspect of standing hospitably ajar; and one of the bare posts had the advantage of being embellished by the figure of Shrowl, who leaned against it easily, with his legs crossed, his hands in his pockets, and his pipe in his mouth, looking out for the return of the messenger who had delivered Doctor Chennery's letter the day before.

CHAPTER 3
APPROACHING THE PRECIPICE

Travelling from London to Porthgenna, Mr. and Mrs. Frankland had stopped, on the ninth of May, at the West Winston station. On the eleventh of June they left it again to continue their journey to Cornwall. On the thirteenth, after resting two nights upon the road, they arrived toward the evening at Porthgenna Tower.

There had been storm and rain all the morning; it had lulled toward the afternoon, and at the hour when they reached the house the wind had dropped, a thick white fog hid the sea from view, and sudden showers fell drearily from time to time over the sodden land. Not even a solitary idler from the village was hanging about the west terrace as the carriage containing Mr. and Mrs. Frankland, the baby, and the two servants drove up to the house.

No one was waiting with the door open to receive the travellers; for all hope of their arriving on that day had been given up, and the ceaseless thundering of the surf, as the stormy sea surged in on the beach beneath, drowned the roll of the carriage-wheels over the terrace road. The driver was obliged to leave his seat and ring at the bell for admittance. A minute or more elapsed before the door was opened.

With the rain falling sullen and steady on the roof of the carriage, with the raw dampness of the atmosphere penetrating through all coverings and defences, with the booming of the surf sounding threateningly near in the dense obscurity of the fog, the young couple waited for admission to their own home, as strangers might have waited who had called at an ill-chosen time.

When the door was opened at last, the master and mistress,

whom the servants would have welcomed with the proper con-gratulations on any other occasion, were now received with the proper apologies instead. Mr. Munder, Mrs. Pentreath, Betsey, and Mr. Frankland's man all crowded together in the hall, and all begged pardon confusedly for not having been ready at the door when the carriage drove up. The appearance of the baby changed the conventional excuses of the housekeeper and the maid into conventional expressions of admiration; but the men remained grave and gloomy, and spoke of the miserable weather apologetically, as if the rain and the fog had been of their own making.

The reason for their persistency in dwelling on this one dreary topic came out while Mr. and Mrs. Frankland were be-ing conducted up the west staircase. The storm of the morning had been fatal to three of the Porthgenna fishermen, who had been lost with their boat at sea, and whose deaths had thrown the whole village into mourning. The servants had done noth-ing but talk of the catastrophe ever since the intelligence of it had reached them early in the afternoon; find Mr. Munder now thought it his duty to explain that the absence of the villagers, on the occasion of the arrival of his master and mistress, was en-tirely attributable to the effect produced among the little com-munity by the wreck of the fishing-boat.

Under any less lamentable circumstances the west terrace would have been crowded, and the appearance of the carriage would have been welcomed with cheers.

"Lenny, I almost wish we had waited a little longer before we came here," whispered Rosamond, nervously pressing her husband's arm. "It is very dreary and disheartening to return to my first home on such a day as this. That story of the poor fishermen is a sad story, love, to welcome me back to the place of my birth. Let us send the first thing tomorrow morning, and see what we can do for the poor helpless women and children. I shall not feel easy in my mind, after hearing that story, till we have done something to comfort them."

"I trust you will approve of the repairs, ma'am," said the

housekeeper, pointing to the staircase which led to the second story.

"The repairs?" said Rosamond, absently. "Repairs! I never hear the word now without thinking of the north rooms, and of the plans we devised for getting my poor dear father to live in them. Mrs. Pentreath, I have a host of questions to ask you and Mr. Munder about all the extraordinary things that happened when the mysterious lady and the incomprehensible foreigner came here. But tell me first—this is the west front, I suppose?-how far are we from the north rooms? I mean, how long would it take us to get to them, if we wanted to go now to that part of the house?"

"Oh, dear me, ma'am, not five, minutes!" answered Mrs. Pentreath.

"Not five minutes!" repeated Rosamond, whispering to her husband again. "Do you hear that, Lenny? In five minutes we might be in the Myrtle Room!"

"Yet," said Mr. Frankland, smiling, "in our present state of ignorance, we are just as far from it as if we were at West Winston still."

"I can't think that, Lenny. It may be only my fancy, but now we are on the spot I feel as if we had driven the mystery into its last hiding-place. We are actually in the house that holds the Secret; and nothing will persuade me that we are not half-way already toward finding it out. But don't let us stop on this cold landing. Which way are we to go next?"

"This way, ma'am," said Mr. Munder, seizing the first opportunity of placing himself in a prominent position. "There is a fire in the drawing-room. Will you allow me the honour of leading and conducting you, sir, to the apartment in question?" he added, officiously stretching out his hand to Mr. Frankland.

"Certainly not!" interposed Rosamond, sharply. She had noticed with her usual quickness of observation that Mr. Munder wanted the delicacy of feeling which ought to have restrained him from staring curiously at his blind master in her presence, and she was unfavourably disposed toward him in consequence.

"Wherever the apartment in question may happen to be," she continued, with satirical emphasis, "I will lead Mr. Frankland to it, if you please. If you want to make yourself useful, you had better go on before us and open the door."

Outwardly crestfallen, but inwardly indignant, Mr. Munder led the way to the drawing-room. The fire burned brightly, the old-fashioned furniture displayed itself to the most picturesque advantage, the paper on the walls looked comfortably mellow, the carpet, faded as it was, felt soft and warm under foot. Rosamond led her husband to an easy-chair by the fireside, and began to feel at home for the first time.

"This looks really comfortable," she said. "When we have shut out that dreary white fog, and the candles are lit, and the tea is on the table, we shall have nothing in the world to complain of. You enjoy this nice warm atmosphere, don't you, Lenny? There is a piano in the room, my dear; I can play to you in the evening at Porthgenna just as I used in London. Nurse, sit down and make yourself and the baby as comfortable as you can.

"Before we take our bonnets off, I must go away with Mrs. Pentreath and see about the bedrooms. What is your name, you very rosy, good-natured-looking girl? Betsey, is it? Well, then, Betsey, suppose you go down and get the tea; and we shall like you all the better if you can contrive to bring us some cold meat with it." Giving her orders in those good-humoured terms, and not noticing that her husband looked a little uneasy while she was talking so familiarly to a servant, Rosamond left the room in company with Mrs. Pentreath.

When she returned her face and manner were altered; she looked and spoke seriously and quietly.

"I hope I have arranged everything for the best, Lenny," she said. "The airiest and largest room, Mrs. Pentreath tells me, is the room in which my mother died. But I thought we had better not make use of that: I felt as if it chilled and saddened me only to look at it. Further on, along the passage, there is a room that was my nursery. I almost fancied, when Mrs. Pentreath told me she had heard I used to sleep there, that I remembered the pretty little arched doorway leading into the second room—the night-nursery it used to be called in former days.

"I have ordered the fire to be lighted there, and the beds to be made. There is a third room on the right hand, which communicates with the day-nursery. I think we might manage to establish ourselves very comfortably in the three rooms—if you felt no objection—though they are not so large or so grandly furnished as the company bedrooms. I will change the arrangement, if you like—but the house looks rather lonesome and dreary, just at first and my heart warms to the old nursery—and I think we might at least try it, to begin with, don't you, Lenny?"

Mr. Frankland was quite of his wife's opinion, and was ready to accede to any domestic arrangements that she might think fit to make. While he was assuring her of this the tea came up, and the sight of it helped to restore Rosamond to her usual spirits. When the meal was over, she occupied herself in seeing the baby comfortably established for the night, in the room on the right hand which communicated with the day-nursery. That maternal duty performed, she came back to her husband in the drawing-room; and the conversation between them turned—as it almost always turned now when they were alone—on the two perplexing subjects of Mrs. Jazeph and the Myrtle Room.

"I wish it was not night," said Rosamond. "I should like to begin exploring at once. Mind, Lenny, you must be with me in all my investigations. I lend you my eyes, and you give me your advice. You must never lose patience, and never tell me that you can be of no use.

"How I do wish we were starting on our voyage of discovery at this very moment! But we may make inquiries, at any rate," she continued, ringing the bell. "Let us have the housekeeper and the steward up, and try if we can't make them tell us something more than they told us in their letter."

The bell was answered by Betsey. Rosamond desired that Mr. Munder and Mrs. Pentreath might be sent upstairs. Betsey having heard Mrs. Frankland express her intention of questioning the housekeeper and the steward, guessed why they were wanted, and smiled mysteriously.

"Did you see anything of those strange visitors who behaved so oddly?" asked Rosamond, detecting the smile. "Yes, I am sure you did. Tell us what you saw. We want to hear everything that happened—everything, down to the smallest trifle."

Appealed to in these direct terms, Betsey contrived, with much circumlocution and confusion, to relate what her own personal experience had been of the proceedings of Mrs. Jazeph and her foreign companion. When she had done, Rosamond stopped her on her way to the door by asking this question:

"You say the lady was found lying in a fainting-fit at the top of the stairs. Have you any notion, Betsey, why she fainted?"

The servant hesitated.

"Come! come!" said Rosamond. "You have some notion, I can see. Tell us what it is."

"I'm afraid you will be angry with me, ma'am," said Betsey, expressing embarrassment by drawing lines slowly with her forefinger on a table at her side.

"Nonsense! I shall only be angry with you if you won't speak. Why do you think the lady fainted?"

Betsey drew a very long line with her embarrassed forefinger, wiped it afterward on her apron, and answered:

"I think she fainted, if you please, ma'am, because she see the ghost."

"The ghost! What! is there a ghost in the house? Lenny, here is a romance that we never expected. What sort of ghost is it? Let us have the whole story."

The whole story, as Betsey told it, was not of a nature to afford her hearers any extraordinary information, or to keep them very long in suspense. The ghost was a lady who had been at a remote period the wife of one of the owners of Porthgenna Tower, and who had been guilty of deceiving her husband in some way unknown. She had been condemned in consequence to walk about the north rooms as long as ever the walls of them held together.

She had long, curling, light-brown hair, and very white teeth, and a dimple in each cheek, and was altogether "awful beautiful" to look at. Her approach was heralded to any mortal creature who was unfortunate enough to fall in her way by the blowing of a cold wind, and nobody who had once felt that wind had the slightest chance of ever feeling warm again. That was all Betsey knew about the ghost; and it was in her opinion enough to freeze a person's blood only to think of it.

Rosamond smiled, then looked grave again. "I wish you could have told us a little more," she said. "But, as you cannot, we must try Mrs. Pentreath and Mr. Munder next. Send them up here, if you please, Betsey, as soon as you get downstairs."

The examination of the housekeeper and the steward led to no result whatever. Nothing more than they had already communicated in their letter to Mrs. Frankland could be extracted from either of them. Mr. Munder's dominant idea was that the foreigner had entered the doors of Porthgenna Tower with felonious ideas on the subject of the family plate.

Mrs. Pentreath concurred in that opinion, and mentioned, in connection with it, her own private impression that the lady in the quiet dress was an unfortunate person who had escaped from a madhouse.

As to giving a word of advice, or suggesting a plan for solving the mystery, neither the housekeeper nor the steward appeared to think that the rendering of any assistance of that sort lay at all within their province. They took their own practical view of the suspicious conduct of the two strangers, and no mortal power could persuade them to look an inch beyond it.

"Oh, the stupidity, the provoking, impenetrable, pretentious stupidity of respectable English servants!" exclaimed Rosamond, when she and her husband were alone again. "No help, Lenny, to be hoped for from either of those two people. We have nothing to trust to now but the examination of the house tomorrow; and that resource may fail us, like all the rest. What can Doctor Chennery be about? Why did we not hear from him before we left West Winston?"

"Patience, Rosamond, patience. We shall see what the post

brings tomorrow."

"Pray don't talk about patience, dear! My stock of that virtue was never a very large one, and it was all exhausted ten days ago, at least. Oh, the weeks and weeks I have been vainly asking myself—Why should Mrs. Jazeph warn me against going into the Myrtle Room? Is she afraid of my discovering a crime? or afraid of my tumbling through the floor? What did she want to do in the room, when she made that attempt to get into it? Why, in the name of wonder, should she know something about this house that I never knew, that my father never knew, that nobody else—"

"Rosamond!" cried Mr. Frankland, suddenly changing colour, and starting in his chair—"I think I can guess who Mrs. Jazeph is!"

"Good gracious, Lenny! What do you mean?"

"Something in those last words of yours started the idea in my mind the instant you spoke. Do you remember, when we were staying at St. Swithin's-on-Sea, and talking about the chances for and against our prevailing on your father to live with us here—do you remember, Rosamond, telling me at that time of certain unpleasant associations which he had with the house, and mentioning among them the mysterious disappearance of a servant on the morning of your mother's death?"

Rosamond turned pale at the question. "How came we never to think of that before?" she said.

"You told me," pursued Mr. Frankland, "that this servant left a strange letter behind her, in which she confessed that your mother had charged her with the duty of telling a secret to your father—a secret that she was afraid to divulge, and that she was afraid of being questioned about. I am right, am I not, in stating those two reasons as the reasons she gave for her disappearance?"

"Quite right."

"And your father never heard of her again?"

"Never!"

"It is a bold guess to make, Rosamond, but the impression

is strong on my mind that, on the day when Mrs. Jazeph came into your room at West Winston, you and that servant met, and she knew it!"

"And the Secret, dear—the Secret she was afraid to tell my father?"

"Must be in some way connected with the Myrtle Room."

Rosamond said nothing in answer. She rose from her chair, and began to walk agitatedly up and down the room. Hearing the rustle of her dress, Leonard called her to him, and, taking her hand, laid his fingers on her pulse, and then lifted them for a moment to her cheek.

"I wish I had waited until tomorrow morning before I told you my idea about Mrs. Jazeph," he said. "I have agitated you to no purpose whatever, and have spoiled your chance of a good night's rest."

"No, no! nothing of the kind. Oh, Lenny, how this guess of yours adds to the interest—the fearful, breathless interest—we have in tracing that woman, and in finding out the Myrtle Room. Do you think—?"

"I have done with thinking for the night, my dear; and you must have done with it too. We have said more than enough about Mrs. Jazeph already. Change the subject, and I will talk of anything else you please."

"It is not so easy to change the subject," said Rosamond, pouting, and moving away to walk up and down the room again.

"Then let us change the place, and make it easier that way. I know you think me the most provokingly obstinate man in the world, but there is reason in my obstinacy, and you will acknowledge as much when you awake tomorrow morning refreshed by a good night's rest. Come, let us give our anxieties a holiday. Take me into one of the other rooms, and let me try if I can guess what it is like by touching the furniture."

The reference to his blindness which the last words contained brought Rosamond to his side in a moment. "You always know best," she said, putting her arm round his neck and kissing him. "I was looking cross, love, a minute ago, but the clouds are all gone now. We will change the scene, and explore some other room, as you propose."

She paused, her eyes suddenly sparkled, her colour rose, and she smiled to herself as if some new fancy had that instant crossed her mind.

"Lenny, I will take you where you shall touch a very remarkable piece of furniture indeed," she resumed, leading him to the door while she spoke. "We will see if you can tell me at once what it is like. You must not be impatient, mind; and you must promise to touch nothing till you feel me guiding your hand."

She drew him after her along the passage, opened the door of the room in which the baby had been put to bed, made a sign to the nurse to be silent, and, leading Leonard up to the cot, guided his hand down gently, so as to let the tips of his fingers touch the child's cheek.

"There, sir!" she cried, her face beaming with happiness as she saw the sudden flush of surprise and pleasure which changed her husband's natural quiet, subdued expression in an instant. "What do you say to that piece of furniture? Is it a chair, or a table? Or is it the most precious thing in all the house, in all Cornwall, in all England, in all the world? Kiss it, and see what it is—a bust of a baby by a sculptor, or a living cherub by your wife!" She turned, laughing, to the nurse—"Hannah, you look so serious that I am sure you must be hungry. Have you had your supper yet?" The woman smiled, and answered that she had arranged to go downstairs, as soon as one of the servants could relieve her in taking care of the child. "Go at once," said Rosamond. "I will stop here and look after the baby. Get your supper and come back again in half an hour."

When the nurse had left the room, Rosamond placed a chair for Leonard by the side of the cot, and seated herself on a low stool at his knees. Her variable disposition seemed to change again when she did this; her face grew thoughtful, her eyes softened, as they turned, now on her husband, now on the bed in which the child was sleeping by his side. After a minute or two of silence, she took one of his hands, placed it on his knee, and laid her cheek gently down on it.

"Lenny," she said, rather sadly, "I wonder whether we are any of us capable of feeling perfect happiness in this world?"

"What makes you ask that question, my dear?"

"I fancy that I could feel perfect happiness, and yet—"

"And yet what?"

"And yet it seems as if, with all my blessings, that blessing was never likely to be granted to me. I should be perfectly happy now but for one little thing. I suppose you can't guess what that thing is?"

"I would rather you told me, Rosamond."

"Ever since our child was born, love, I have had a little aching at the heart—especially when we are all three together, as we are now—a little sorrow that I can't quite put away from me on your account."

"On my account! Lift up your head, Rosamond, and come nearer to me. I feel something on my hand which tells me that you are crying."

She rose directly and laid her face close to his. "My own love," she said, clasping her arms fast round him. "My own heart's darling, you have never seen our child."

"Yes, Rosamond, I see him with your eyes."

"Oh, Lenny! I tell you everything I can—I do my best to lighten the cruel, cruel darkness which shuts you out from that lovely little face lying so close to you! But can I tell you how he looks when he first begins to take notice? can I tell you all the thousand pretty things he will do when he first tries to talk? God has been very merciful to us—but, oh, how much more heavily the sense of your affliction weighs on me now when I am more to you than your wife—now when I am the mother of your child!"

"And yet that affliction ought to weigh lightly on your spirits, Rosamond, for you have made it weigh lightly on mine."

"Have I? Really and truly, have I? It is something noble to live for, Lenny, if I can live for that! It is some comfort to hear you say, as you said just now, that you see with my eyes. They shall always serve you—oh, always! always!—as faithfully as if they were your own. The veriest trifle of a visible thing that I look at with any interest, you shall as good as look at too.

"I might have had my own little harmless secrets, dear, with another husband; but with you to have even so much as a thought in secret seems like taking the basest, the cruellest advantage of your blindness. I do love you so, Lenny.! I am so much fonder of you now than I was when we were first married—I never thought I should be, but I am. You are so much handsomer to me, so much cleverer to me, so much more precious to me in every way. But I am always telling you that, am I not? Do you get tired of hearing me? No? Are you sure of that? Very, very, very sure?"

She stopped, and looked at him earnestly, with a smile on her lips, and the tears still glistening in her eyes. Just then the child stirred a little in his cot and drew her attention away. She arranged the bedclothes over him, watched him in silence for a little while, then sat down again on the stool at Leonard's feet. "Baby has turned his face quite round toward you now," she said. "Shall I tell you exactly how he looks, and what his bed is like, and how the room is furnished?"

Without waiting for an answer, she began to describe the child's appearance and position with the marvellous minuteness of a woman's observation. While she proceeded, her elastic spirits recovered themselves, and its naturally bright happy expression reappeared on her face. By the time the nurse returned to her post, Rosamond was talking with all her accustomed vivacity, and amusing her husband with all her accustomed success.

When they went back to the drawing-room, she opened the piano and sat down to play. "I must give you your usual evening concert, Lenny," she said, "or I shall be talking again on the forbidden subject of the Myrtle Room."

She played some of Mr. Frankland's favourite airs, with a certain union of feeling and fancifulness in her execution of the music, which seemed to blend the charm of her own disposition with the charm of the melodies which sprang into life under her touch. After playing through the airs she could remember most easily, she ended with the *Last Waltz* of Weber. It was Leonard's favourite, and it was always reserved on that account to grace the close of the evening's performance.

She lingered longer than usual over the last plaintive notes of the waltz; then suddenly left the piano, and hastened across the room to the fireplace.

"Surely it has turned much colder within the last minute or two," she said, kneeling down on the rug and holding her face and hands over the fire.

"Has it?" returned Leonard. "I don't feel any change."

"Perhaps I have caught cold," said Rosamond. "Or perhaps," she added, laughing rather uneasily, "the wind that goes before the ghostly lady of the north rooms has been blowing over me. I certainly felt something like a sudden chill, Lenny, while I was playing the last notes of Weber."

"Nonsense, Rosamond. You are overfatigued and overexcited. Tell your maid to make you some hot wine and water, and lose no time in getting to bed."

Rosamond cowered closer over the fire. "It's lucky I am not superstitious," she said, "or I might fancy that I was predestined to see the ghost."

CHAPTER 4
STANDING ON THE BRINK

The first night at Porthgenna passed without the slightest noise or interruption of any kind. No ghost, or dream of a ghost, disturbed the soundness of Rosamond's slumbers. She awoke in her usual spirits and her usual health, and was out in the west garden before breakfast.

The sky was cloudy, and the wind veered about capriciously to all the points of the compass. In the course of her walk Rosamond met with the gardener, and asked him what he thought about the weather. The man replied that it might rain again before noon, but that, unless he was very much mistaken, it was going to turn to heat in the course of the next four-and-twenty hours.

"Pray, did you ever hear of a room on the north side of our old house called the Myrtle Room?" inquired Rosamond. She had resolved, on rising that morning, not to lose a chance of making the all-important discovery for want of asking questions of everybody in the neighbourhood; and she began with the gardener accordingly.

"I never heard tell of it, ma'am," said the man. "But it's a likely name enough, considering how the myrtles do grow in these parts."

"Are there any myrtles growing at the north side of the house?" asked Rosamond, struck with the idea of tracing the mysterious room by searching for it outside the building instead of inside. "I mean close to the walls," she added, seeing the man look puzzled; " under the windows, you know?"

"I never see anything under the windows in my time but weeds and rubbish," replied the gardener.

Just then the breakfast-bell rang. Rosamond returned to the house, determined to explore the north garden, and if she found any relic of a bed of myrtles to mark the window above it, and to have the room which that window lighted opened immediately. She confided this new scheme to her husband. He complimented her on her ingenuity, but confessed that he had no great hope of any discoveries being made out of doors, after what the gardener had said about the weeds and rubbish.

As soon as breakfast was over, Rosamond rang the bell to order the gardener to be in attendance, and to say that the keys of the north rooms would be wanted. The summons was answered by Mr. Frankland's servant, who brought up with him the morning's supply of letters, which the postman had just delivered. Rosamond turned them over eagerly, pounced on one with an exclamation of delight, and said to her husband—"The Long Beckley postmark! News from the vicar, at last!"

She opened the letter and ran her eye over it—then suddenly dropped it in her lap with her face all in a glow. "Lenny!" she exclaimed, "there is news here that is positively enough to turn one's head. I declare the vicar's letter has quite taken away my breath!"

"Read it," said Mr. Frankland; "pray read it at once."

Rosamond complied with the request in a very faltering, unsteady voice. Doctor Chennery began his letter by announcing that his application to Andrew Treverton had remained unanswered; but he added that it had, nevertheless, produced results which no one could possibly have anticipated. For information on the subject of those results, he referred Mr. and Mrs. Frankland to a copy subjoined of a communication marked private, which he had received from his man of business in London.

The communication contained a detailed report of an interview which had taken place between Mr. Treverton's servant and the messenger who had called for an answer to Doctor Chennery's letter. Shrowl, it appeared, had opened the interview by delivering his master's message, had then produced the vicar's torn letter and the copy of the Plan, and had announced his readiness to part with the latter for the consideration of a five-pound note.

The messenger had explained that he had no power to treat for the document, and had advised Mr. Treverton's servant to wait on Doctor Chennery's agent. After some hesitation, Shrowl had decided to do this, on pretence of going out on an errand—had seen the agent—had been questioned about how he became possessed of the copy—and, finding that there would be no chance of disposing of it unless he answered all inquiries, had related the circumstances under which the copy had been made.

After hearing his statement, the agent had engaged to apply immediately for instructions to Doctor Chennery; and had written accordingly, mentioning in a postscript that he had seen the transcribed Plan, and had ascertained that it really exhibited the positions of doors, staircases, and rooms, with the names attached to them.

Resuming his own letter, Doctor Chennery proceeded to say that he must now leave it entirely to Mr. and Mrs. Frankland to

decide what course they ought to adopt. He had already com-
promised himself a little in his own estimation, by assuming a
character which really did not belong to him, when he made his
application to Andrew Treverton; and he felt he could personally
venture no further in the affair, either by expressing an opinion
or giving any advice, now that it had assumed such a totally new
aspect. He felt quite sure that his young friends would arrive at
the wise and the right decision, after they had maturely considered the matter in all its bearings.

In that conviction, he had instructed his man of business not
to stir in the affair until he had heard from Mr. Frankland, and
to be guided entirely by any directions which that gentleman
might give.

"Directions!" exclaimed Rosamond, crumpling up the letter
in a high state of excitement as soon as she had read to the end
of it. "All the directions we have to give may be written in a
minute and read in a second! What in the world does the vicar
mean by talking about mature consideration? Of course," cried
Rosamond, looking, womanlike, straight on to the purpose she
had in view, without wasting a thought on the means by which
it was to be achieved—"Of course we give the man his five-
pound note, and get the Plan by return of post!"

Mr. Frankland shook his head gravely. "Quite impossible," he
said. "If you think for a moment, my dear, you will surely see
that it is out of the question to traffic with a servant for information that has been surreptitiously obtained from his master's
library."

"Oh, dear! dear! don't say that!" pleaded Rosamond, looking
quite aghast at the view her husband took of the matter. "What
harm are we doing, if we give the man his five pounds? He has
only made a copy of the Plan; he has not stolen anything."

"He has stolen information, according to my idea of it," said
Leonard.

"Well, but if he has," persisted Rosamond, "what harm does
it do to his master? In my opinion his master deserves to have
the information stolen, for not having had the common polite-

ness to send it to the vicar. We must have the Plan—oh, Lenny, don't shake your head, please!—we must have it, you know we must! What is the use of being scrupulous with an old wretch (I must call him so, though he is my uncle) who won't conform to the commonest usages of society? You can't deal with him—and I am sure the vicar would say so, if he was here—as you would with civilized people, or people in their senses, which every-body says he is not. What use is the Plan of the north rooms to him? And, besides, if it is of any use, he has got the original; so his information is not stolen, after all, because he has got it the whole time—has he not, dear?"

"Rosamond! Rosamond!" said Leonard, smiling at his wife's transparent sophistries, "you are trying to reason like a Jesuit."

"I don't care who I reason like, love, as long as I get the Plan."

Mr. Frankland still shook his head. Finding her arguments of no avail, Rosamond wisely resorted to the immemorial weapon of her sex—Persuasion; using it at such close quarters and to such good purposes that she finally won her husband's reluctant consent to a species of compromise, which granted her leave to give directions for purchasing the copied Plan on one condition.

This condition was that they should send back the Plan to Mr. Treverton as soon as it had served their purpose; making a full acknowledgment to him of the manner in which it had been obtained, and pleading in justification of the proceeding his own want of courtesy in withholding information, of no consequence in itself, which anyone else in his place would have communicated as a matter of course.

Rosamond tried hard to obtain the withdrawal or modifi-cation of this condition; but her husband's sensitive pride was not to be touched, on that point, with impunity, even by her light hand. "I have done too much violence already to my own convictions," he said, "and I will now do no more. If we are to degrade ourselves by dealing with this servant, let us at least prevent him from claiming us as his accomplices. Write in my name, Rosamond, to Doctor Chennery's man of business, and say that we are willing to purchase the transcribed Plan on the condition that I have stated—which condition he will of course place before the servant in the plainest possible terms."

"And suppose the servant refuses to risk losing his place, which he must do if he accepts your condition?" said Rosamond, going rather reluctantly to the writing-table.

"Let us not worry ourselves, my dear, by supposing anything. Let us wait and hear what happens, and act accordingly. When you are ready to write, tell me, and I will dictate your letter on this occasion. I wish to make the vicar's man of business understand that we act as we do, knowing, in the first place, that Mr. Andrew Treverton cannot be dealt with according to the established usages of society; and knowing, in the second place, that the information which his servant offers to us is contained in an extract from a printed book, and is in no way, directly or indirectly, connected with Mr. Treverton's private affairs. Now that you have made me consent to this compromise, Rosamond, I must justify it as completely as possible to others as well as to myself."

Seeing that his resolution was firmly settled, Rosamond had tact enough to abstain from saying anything more. The letter was written exactly as Leonard dictated it. When it had been placed in the postbag, and when the other letters of the morning had been read and answered, Mr. Frankland, reminded his wife of the intention she had expressed at breakfast-time of visiting the north garden, and requested that she would take him there with her.

He candidly acknowledged that, since he had been made acquainted with Doctor Chennery's letter, he would give five times the sum demanded by Shrowl for the copy of the Plan if the Myrtle Room could be discovered, without assistance from any one, before the letter to the vicar's man of business was put into the post. Nothing would give him so much pleasure, he said, as to be able to throw it into the fire, and to send a plain refusal to treat for the Plan in its place.

They went into the north garden, and there Rosamond's own eyes convinced her that she had not the slightest chance of discovering any vestige of a myrtle-bed near any one of the windows. From the garden they returned to the house, and had the door opened that led into the north hall.

They were shown the place on the pavement where the keys had been found, and the place at the top of the first flight of stairs where Mrs. Jazeph had been discovered when the alarm was given. At Mr. Frankland's suggestion, the door of the room which immediately fronted this spot was opened. It presented a dreary spectacle of dust and dirt and dimness.

Some old pictures were piled against one of the walls, some tattered chairs were heaped together in the middle of the floor, some broken china lay on the mantelpiece, and a rotten cabinet, cracked through from top to bottom, stood in one corner. These few relics of the furnishing and fitting-up of the room were all carefully examined, but nothing of the smallest importance—nothing tending in the most remote degree to clear up the mystery of the Myrtle Room—was discovered.

"Shall we have the other doors opened?" inquired Rosamond when they came out on the landing again.

"I think it will be useless," replied her husband. "Our only hope of finding out the mystery of the Myrtle Room—if it is as deeply hidden from us as I believe it to be—is by searching for it in that room, and no other. The search, to be effectual, must extend, if we find it necessary, to the pulling up of the floor and wainscots—perhaps even to the dismantling of the walls.

"We may do that with one room when we know where it is, but we cannot, by any process short of pulling the whole side of the house down, do it with the sixteen rooms, through which our present ignorance condemns us to wander without guide or clew. It is hopeless enough to be looking for we know not what; but let us discover, if we can, where the four walls are within which that unpromising search must begin and end. Surely the floor of the landing must be dusty? Are there no footmarks on it, after Mrs. Jazeph's visit, that might lead us to the right door?"

This suggestion led to a search for footsteps on the dusty floor of the landing, but nothing of the sort could be found. Matting had been laid down over the floor at some former period, and the surface, torn, ragged, and rotten with age, was too uneven in every part to allow the dust to lie smoothly on it. Here and there, where there was a hole through to the boards of the landing, Mr. Frankland's servant thought he detected marks in the dust which might have been produced by the toe or the heel of a shoe; but these faint and doubtful indications lay yards and yards apart from each other, and to draw any conclusion of the slightest importance from them was simply and plainly impossible.

After spending more than an hour in examining the north side of the house, Rosamond was obliged to confess that the servants were right when they predicted, on first opening the door in the hall, that she would discover nothing.

"The letter must go, Lenny," she said, when they returned to the breakfast-room.

"There is no help for it," answered her husband. "Send away the postbag, and let us say no more about it."

The letter was dispatched by that day's post. In the remote position of Porthgenna, and in the unfinished state of the railroad at that time, two days would elapse before an answer from London could be reasonably hoped for. Feeling that it would be better for Rosamond if this period of suspense was passed out of the house, Mr. Frankland proposed to fill up the time by a little excursion along the coast to some places famous for their scenery, which would be likely to interest his wife, and which she might occupy herself pleasantly in describing on the spot for the benefit of her husband. This suggestion was immediately acted on. The young couple left Porthgenna, and only returned on the evening of the second day.

On the morning of the third day the longed-for letter from the vicar's man of business lay on the table when Leonard and Rosamond entered the breakfast-room. Shrowl had decided to accept Mr. Frankland's condition—first, because he held that any man must be out of his senses who refused a five-pound note when it was offered to him; secondly, because he believed that his master was too absolutely dependent on him to turn him away for any cause whatever; thirdly, because, if Mr. Treverton did part with him, he was not sufficiently attached to his place to care at all about losing it. Accordingly the bargain had been struck in five minutes—and there was the copy of the Plan, inclosed with the letter of explanation to attest the fact!

"Rosamond spread the all-important document out on the table with trembling hands, looked it over eagerly for a few moments, and laid her finger on the square that represented the position of the Myrtle Room.

"Here it is!" she cried. "Oh, Lenny, how my heart beats! One, two, three, four—the fourth door on the first-floor landing is the door of the Myrtle Room!"

She would have called at once for the keys of the north rooms; but her husband insisted on her waiting until she had composed herself a little, and until she had taken some breakfast. In spite of all he could say, the meal was hurried over so rapidly that in ten minutes more his wife's arm was in his, and she was leading him to the staircase.

The gardener's prognostication about the weather had been verified: it had turned to heat—heavy, misty, vaporous, dull heat. One white quivering fog-cloud spread thinly over -all the heaven, rolled down seaward on the horizon line, and dulled the sharp edges of the distant moorland view. The sunlight shone pale and trembling; the lightest, highest leaves of flowers at open windows were still; the domestic animals lay about sleepily in dark corners.

Chance household noises sounded heavy and loud in the languid, airless stillness which the heat seemed to hold over the earth. Down in the servants' hall, the usual bustle of morning work was suspended. When Rosamond looked in, on her way to the housekeeper's room to get the keys, the women were fanning themselves, and the men were sitting with their coats off. They were all talking peevishly about the heat, and all agreeing that such a day as that, in the month of June, they had never known and never heard of before.

Rosamond took the keys, declined the housekeeper's offer to accompany her, and leading her husband along the passages, unlocked the door of the north hall.

"How unnaturally cool it is here!" she said, as they entered the deserted place.

At the foot of the stairs she stopped, and took a firmer hold of her husband's arm.

"Is anything the matter?" asked Leonard.

"Is the change to the damp coolness of this place affecting you in any way?"

"No, no," she answered hastily. "I am far too excited to feel either heat or damp, as I might feel them at other times. But, Lenny, supposing your guess about Mrs. Jazeph is right?—"

"Yes?"

"And supposing we discover the Secret of the Myrtle Room, might it not turn out to be something concerning my father or my mother which we ought not to know? I thought of that when Mrs. Pentreath offered to accompany us, and it determined me to come here alone with you."

"It is just likely that the Secret might be something we ought to know," replied Mr. Frankland. after a moment's thought. "In any case, my idea about Mrs. Jazeph is, after all, only a guess in the dark. However, Rosamond, if you feel any hesitation—"

"No! come what may of it, Lenny, we can't go back now. Give me your hand again. "We have traced the mystery thus far together, and together we will find it out."

She ascended the staircase, leading him after her, as she spoke. On the landing she looked again at the Plan, and satisfied herself that the first impression she had derived from it, of the position of the Myrtle Room, was correct. She counted the doors on to the fourth, and looked out from the bunch the key numbered "4," and put it in the lock.

Before she turned it she paused, and looked round at her husband.

He was standing by her side, with his patient face turned expectantly toward the door. She put her right hand on the key, turned it slowly in the lock, drew him closer to her with her left hand, and paused again.

"I don't know what has come to me," she whispered faintly. "I feel as if I was afraid to push open the door."

"Your hand is cold, Rosamond. Wait a little—lock the door again—put it off till another day."

He felt his wife's fingers close tighter and tighter on his hand while he said those words. Then there was an instant—one memorable, breathless instant, never to be forgotten afterward-of utter silence. Then he heard the sharp, cracking sound of the opening door, and felt himself drawn forward suddenly into a changed atmosphere, and knew that Rosamond and he were in the Myrtle Room.

Chapter 5
The Myrtle Room

A broad, square window, with small panes and dark sashes; dreary yellow light, glimmering through the dirt of half a century crusted on the glass; purer rays striking across the dimness through the fissures of three broken panes; dust floating upward, pouring downward, rolling smoothly round and round in the still atmosphere; lofty, bare, faded red walls; chairs in confusion, tables placed awry; a tall black bookcase, with an open door half dropping from its hinges; a pedestal, with a broken bust lying in fragments at its feet; a ceiling darkened by stains, a floor whitened by dust—such was the aspect of the Myrtle Room when Rosamond first entered it, leading her husband by the hand.

After passing the doorway, she slowly advanced a few steps, and then stopped, waiting with every sense on the watch, with every faculty strung up to the highest pitch of expectation-waiting in the ominous stillness, in the forlorn solitude, for the vague Something which the room might contain, which might rise visibly before her, which might sound audibly behind her, which might touch her on a sudden from above, from below, from either side. A minute or more she breathlessly waited; and nothing appeared, nothing sounded, nothing touched her. The silence and the solitude had their secret to keep, and kept it.

She looked round at her husband. His face, so quiet and composed at other times, expressed doubt and uneasiness now. His disengaged hand was outstretched, and moving backward and forward and up and down, in the vain attempt to touch something which might enable him to guess at the position in which he was placed. His look and action, as he stood in that new and strange sphere, the mute appeal which he made so sadly and so unconsciously to his wife's loving help, restored Rosamond's self-possession by recalling her heart to the dearest of all its interests, to the holiest of all its cares.

Her eyes, fixed so distrustfully but the moment before on the dreary spectacle of neglect and ruin which spread around them, turned fondly to her husband's face, radiant with the unfathomable brightness of pity and love. She bent quickly across him, caught his outstretched arm, and pressed it to his side.

"Don't do that, darling," she said, gently; "I don't like to see it. It looks as if you had forgotten that I was with you—as if you were left alone and helpless. What need have you of your sense of touch, when you have got me? Did you hear me open the door, Lenny? Do you know that we are in the Myrtle Boom?"

"What did you see, Rosamond, when you opened the door? What do you see now?" He asked those questions rapidly and eagerly, in a whisper.

"Nothing but dust and dirt and desolation. The loneliest moor in Cornwall is not so lonely looking as this room; but there is nothing to alarm us, nothing (except one's own fancy) that suggests an idea of danger of any kind."

" What made you so long before you spoke to me, Rosamond?"

"I was frightened, love, on first entering the room—not at what I saw, but at my own fanciful ideas of what I might see. I was child enough to be afraid of something starting out of the walls, or of something rising through the floor; in short, of I hardly know what. I have got over those fears, Lenny, but a certain distrust of the room still clings to me. Do you feel it?"

"I feel something like it," he replied uneasily. "I feel as if the night that is always before my eyes was darker to me in this place than in any other. Where are we standing now?"

"Just inside the door."

"Does the floor look safe to walk on?" He tried it suspiciously with his foot as he put the question.

"Quite safe," replied Rosamond. "It would never support the furniture that is on it if it was so rotten as to be dangerous. Come across the room with me, and try it." With these words she led him slowly to the window.

"The air seems as if it was nearer to me," he said, bending his face forward toward the lowest of the broken panes. "What is before us now?"

She told him, describing minutely the size and appearance of the window. He turned from it carelessly, as if that part of the room had no interest for him. Rosamond still lingered near the window, to try if she could feel a breath of the outer atmosphere. There was a momentary silence, which was broken by her husband.

"What are you doing now?" he asked anxiously.

"I am looking out at one of the broken panes of glass, and trying to get some air," answered Rosamond. "The shadow of the house is below me, resting on the lonely garden; but there is no coolness breathing up from it. I see the tall weeds rising straight and still, and the tangled wildflowers interlacing themselves heavily. There is a tree near me, and the leaves look as if they were all struck motionless. Away to the left, there is a peep of white sea and tawny sand quivering in the yellow heat. There are no clouds; there is no blue sky. The mist quenches the brightness of the sunlight, and lets nothing but the fire of it through. There is something threatening in the sky, and: the earth seems to know it!"

"But the room! the room!" said, Leonard, drawing her aside from the window. "Never mind the view; tell me what the room is like—exactly what it is like. I shall not feel easy about you, Rosamond, if you don't describe everything to me just as it is."

"My darling! You know you can depend on my describing everything. I am only doubting where to begin, and how to make sure of seeing for you what you are likely to think most worth looking at. Here is an old ottoman against the wall—the wall where the window is, I will take off my apron and dust the seat for you; and then you can sit down and listen comfortably while I tell you before we think of anything else, what the room is like, to begin with. First of all, I suppose, I must make you understand how large it is?"

"Yes, that is the first thing. Try if you can compare it with any room that I was familiar with before I lost my sight."

Rosamond looked backward and forward, from wall to wall then went to the fire-place, and walked slowly down the length of the room, counting her steps. Pacing over the dusty floor with a dainty regularity and a childish satisfaction in looking down at the gay pink rosettes on her morning shoes; holding up her crisp, bright muslin dress out of the dirt, and showing the fanciful embroidery of her petticoat, and the glossy stockings that fitted her little feet and ankles like a second skin, she moved through the dreariness, the desolation, the dingy ruin of the scene. around her, the most charming living contrast to its dead gloom that youth, health, and beauty could present.

Arrived at the bottom of the room, she reflected a little, and said to her husband—

"Do you remember the blue drawing-room, Lenny, in your father's house at Long Beckley? I think this room is quite as large, if not larger."

"What are the walls like?" asked Leonard, placing his hand on the wall behind him while he spoke. "They are covered with paper, are they not?"

"Yes; with faded red paper, except on one side, where strips have been torn off and thrown on the floor. There is wainscoting round the walls. It is cracked in many places, and has ragged holes in it, which seem to have been made by the rats and mice."

"Are there any pictures on the walls?"

"No. There is an empty frame over the fireplace. And opposite—I mean just above where I am standing now there is a small mirror, cracked in the centre, with broken branches for candlesticks projecting on either side of it. Above that, again, there is a stag's head and antlers; some of the face has dropped away, and a perfect maze of cobwebs is stretched between the horns. On the other walls there are large nails, with more cobwebs hanging down from them heavy with dirt—but no pictures anywhere. Now you know everything about the walls. What is the next thing? The floor?"

"I think, Rosamond, my feet have told me already what the floor is like?"

"They may have told you that it is bare, dear; but I can tell you more than that. It slopes down from every side toward the middle of the room. It is covered thick with dust, which is swept about, I suppose, by the wind blowing through the broken panes into strange, wavy, feathery shapes that quite hide the floor beneath. Lenny! suppose these boards should be made to take up anywhere! If we discover nothing today, we will have them swept tomorrow. In the meantime, I must go on telling you about the room, must I not? You know already what the size of it is, what the window is like, what the walls are like, what the floor is like. Is there anything else before we come to the furniture. Oh, yes! the ceiling—for that completes the shell of the room.

"I can't see much of it, it is so high. There are great cracks and stains from one end to the other, and the plaster has come away in patches in some places. The centre ornament seems to be made of alternate rows of small plaster cabbages and large plaster lozenges. Two bits of chain hang down from the middle, which, I suppose, once held a chandelier. The cornice is so dingy that I can hardly tell what pattern it represents. It is very broad and heavy, and it looks in some places as if it had once been coloured, and that is all I can say about it. Do you feel as if you thoroughly understood the whole room now, Lenny?"

"Thoroughly, my love; I have the same clear picture of it in my mind which you always give me of everything you see. You need waste no more time on me. We may now devote ourselves to the purpose for which we came here."

At those last words, the smile which had been dawning on Rosamond's face when her husband addressed her, vanished from it in a moment. She stole close to his side, and, bending down over him, with her arm on his shoulder, said, in low, whispering tones—

"When we had the other room opened, opposite the landing, we began by examining the furniture. We thought—if you remember that the mystery of the Myrtle Room might be connected with hidden valuables that had been stolen, or hidden papers that ought to have been destroyed, or hidden stains and traces of some crime, which even a chair or a table might betray. Shall we examine the furniture here?"

"Is there much of it, Rosamond?"

"More than there was in the other room," she answered.

"More than you can examine in one morning?"

"No; I think not."

"Then begin with the furniture, if you have no better plan to propose. I am but a helpless adviser at such a crisis as this. I must leave the responsibilities of decision, after all, to rest on your shoulders. Yours are the eyes that look and the hands that search; and if the secret of Mrs. Jazeph's reason for warning you against entering this room is to be found by seeking in the room, you will find it—"

"And you will know it, Lenny, as soon as it is found. I won't hear you talk, love, as if there was any difference between us, or any superiority in my position over yours. Now, let me see. What shall I begin with? The tall bookcase opposite the window? or the dingy old writing-table, in the recess behind the fireplace? Those are the two largest pieces of furniture that I can see in the room."

"Begin with the bookcase, my dear, as you seem to have noticed that first."

Rosamond advanced a few steps toward the bookcase—then stopped, and looked aside suddenly to the lower end of the room.

"Lenny! I forgot one thing, when I was telling you about the walls," she said. "There are two doors in the room besides the door we came in at. They are both in the wall to the right, as I stand now with my back to the window. Each is at the same distance from the corner, and each is of the same size and appearance.

Don't you think we ought to open them and see where they lead to?"

"Certainly. But are the keys in the locks?"

Rosamond approached more closely to the doors, and answered in the affirmative.

"Open them, then," said Leonard. "Stop! not by yourself. Take me with you. I don't like the idea of sitting here, and leaving you to open those doors by yourself."

Rosamond retraced her steps to the place where he was 'sitting, and then led him with her to the door that was furthest from the window. "Suppose there should be some dreadful sight behind it!" she said, trembling a little, as she stretched out her hand toward the key.

"Try to suppose (what is much more probable) that it only leads into another room," suggested Leonard.

Rosamond threw the door wide open, suddenly. Her husband was right. It merely led into the next room.

They passed on to the second door. "Can this one serve the same purpose as the other?" said Rosamond, slowly and distrustfully turning the key.

She opened it as she had opened the first door, put her head inside it for an instant, drew back, shuddering, and closed it again violently, with a faint exclamation of disgust.

"Don't be alarmed, Lenny," she said, leading him away abruptly. "The door only opens on a large, empty cupboard. But there are quantities of horrible, crawling brown creatures about the wall inside. I have shut them in again in their darkness and their secrecy; and now I am going to take you back to your seat, before we find out, next, what the bookcase contains."

The door of the upper part of the bookcase, hanging open and half dropping from its hinges, showed the emptiness of the shelves on one side at a glance. The corresponding door, when Rosamond pulled it open, disclosed exactly the same spectacle of barrenness on the other side. Over every shelf there spread the same dreary accumulation of dust and dirt, without a vestige of a book, without even a stray scrap of paper lying anywhere in a corner to attract the eye, from top to bottom.

The lower portion of the bookcase was divided into three cupboards. In the door of one of the three, the rusty key remained in the lock. Rosamond turned it with some difficulty, and looked into the cupboard. At the back of it were scattered a pack of playing-cards, brown with dirt. A morsel of torn, tangled muslin lay among them, which, when Rosamond spread it out, proved to be the remains of a clergyman's band.

In one corner she found a broken corkscrew and the winch of a fishing-rod; in another, some stumps of tobacco-pipes, a few old medicine bottles and a dog's-eared peddler's song-book. These were all the objects that the cupboard contained. After Rosamond had scrupulously described each one of them to her husband, just as she found it, she went on to the second cupboard. On trying the door, it turned out not to be locked. On looking inside, she discovered nothing but some pieces of blackened cotton wool, and the remains of a jeweller's packing-case.

The third door was locked, but the rusty key from the first cupboard opened it. Inside, there was but one object—a small wooden box, banded round with a piece of tape, the two edges of which were fastened together by a seal. Rosamond's flagging interest rallied instantly at this discovery. She described the box to her husband, and asked if he thought she was justified in breaking the seal.

"Can you see anything written on the cover?" he inquired.

Rosamond carried the box to the window, blew the dust off the top of it, and read, on a parchment label nailed to the cover:

"Papers. John Arthur Treverton. 1760."

"I think you may take the responsibility of breaking the seal," said Leonard. "If those papers had been of any family importance, they could scarcely have been left forgotten in an old bookcase by your father and his executors."

Rosamond broke the seal, then looked up doubtfully at her husband before she opened the box. "It seems mere waste of time to look into this," she said. "How can a box that has not been opened since seventeen hundred and sixty help us to discover the mystery of Mrs. Jazeph and the Myrtle Room?"

"But do we know that it has not been opened since then?" said Leonard. "Might not the tape and seal have been put round it by anybody at some more recent period of time? You can judge best, because you can see if there is any inscription on the tape, or any signs to form an opinion by upon the seal."

"The seal is a blank, Lenny, except that it has a flower like a forget-me-not in the middle. I can see no mark of a pen on either side of the tape. Anybody in the world might have opened the box before me," she continued, forcing up the lid easily with her hands, "for the lock is no protection to it. The wood of the cover is so rotten that I have pulled the staple out, and left it sticking by itself in the lock below."

On examination, the box proved to be full of papers. At the top of the uppermost packet were written these words:

"Election expenses. I won by four votes. Price fifty pounds each. J. A. Treverton."

The next layer of papers had no inscription. Rosamond opened them, and read on the first leaf:

"Birthday Ode. Respectfully addressed to the Mæcenas of modern times in his poetic retirement at Porthgenna."

Below this production appeared a collection of old bills, old notes of invitation, old doctor's prescriptions, and old leaves of betting-books, tied together with a piece of whipcord. Last of all, there lay on the bottom of the box one thin leaf of paper, the visible side of which presented a perfect blank.

Rosamond took it up, turned it to look at the other side, and saw some faint ink-lines crossing each other in various directions, and having letters of the alphabet attached to them in certain places. She had made her husband acquainted with the contents of all the other papers, as a matter of course; and when she had described this last paper to him, he explained to her that the lines and letters represented a mathematical problem.

"The bookcase tells us nothing," said Rosamond, slowly putting the papers back in the box. "Shall we try the writing-table by the fireplace next?"

"What does it look like, Rosamond?"

"It has two rows of drawers down each side; and the whole top is made in an odd, old-fashioned way to slope upward, like a very large writing-desk."

"Does the top open?"

Rosamond went to the table, examined it narrowly, and then tried to raise the top. "It is made to open, for I see the keyhole," she said. "But it is locked. And all the drawers," she continued, trying them one after another, "are locked too."

"Is there no key in any of them?" asked Leonard.

"Not a sign of one. But the top feels so loose that I really think it might be forced open—as I forced the little box open just now—by a pair of stronger hands than I can boast of. Let me take you to the table, dear; it may give way to your strength, though it will not to mine."

She placed her husband's hands carefully under the ledge formed by the overhanging top of the table. He exerted his whole strength to force it up; but in this case the wood was sound, the lock held, and all his efforts were in vain.

"Must we send for a locksmith?" asked Rosamond, with a look of disappointment.

"If the table is of any value, we must," returned her husband. "If not, a screwdriver and a hammer will open both the top and the drawers in anybody's hands."

"In that case, Lenny, I wish we had brought them with us when we came into the room, for the only value of the table lies in the secrets that it may be hiding from us. I shall not feel satisfied until you and I know what there is inside of it,"

While saying these words, she took her husband's hand to lead him back to his seat. As they passed before the fireplace, he stepped upon the bare stone hearth; and, feeling some new substance under his feet, instinctively stretched out the hand that was free. It touched a marble tablet, with figures on it in *bass-relief*, which had been let into the middle of the chimney-piece. He stopped immediately, and asked what the object was that his fingers had accidentally touched.

"A piece of sculpture," said Rosamond. "I did not notice it before. It is not very large and not particularly attractive, according to my taste. So far as I can tell, it seems to be intended to represent—"

Leonard stopped her before she could say any more. "Let me try, for once, if I can't make a discovery for myself," he said, a little impatiently. "Let me try if my fingers won't tell me what this sculpture is meant to represent."

He passed his hands carefully over the *bass-relief* (Rosamond watching their slightest movement with silent interest, the while), considered a little, and said:

"Is there not a figure of a man sitting down, in the right-hand corner? And are there not rocks and trees, very stiffly done, high up, at the left-hand side?"

Rosamond looked at him tenderly, and smiled. "My poor dear!" she said. "Your man sitting down is, in reality, a miniature copy of the famous ancient statue of Niobe and her child; your rocks are marble imitations of clouds, and your stiffly done trees are arrows darting out from some invisible Jupiter or Apollo, or other heathen god. Ah, Lenny, Lenny! you can't trust your touch, love, as you can trust me!"

A momentary shade of vexation passed across his face; but it vanished the instant she took his hand again to lead him back to his seat. He drew her to him gently and kissed her cheek. "You are right, Rosamond," he said. "The one faithful friend to me in my blindness, who never fails, is my wife."

Seeing him look a little saddened, and feeling, with the quick intuition of a woman's affection, that he was thinking of the days when he had enjoyed the blessing of sight, Rosamond returned abruptly, as soon as she saw him seated once more on the ottoman, to the subject of the Myrtle Room.

"Where shall I look next, dear?" she said. "The bookcase we have examined. The writing-table we must wait to examine. "What else is there that has a cupboard or a drawer in it?" She looked round her in perplexity; then walked away toward the part of the room to which her attention had been last drawn-the part where the fireplace was situated.

"I thought I noticed something here, Lenny, when I passed just now with you," she said, approaching the second recess behind the mantelpiece, corresponding with the recess in which the writing-table stood.

She looked into the place closely, and detected in a corner, darkened by the shadow of the heavy projecting mantelpiece, a narrow, rickety little table, made of the commonest mahogany the frailest, poorest, least conspicuous piece of furniture in the whole room. She pushed it out contemptuously into the light with her foot. It ran on clumsy old-fashioned casters and creaked wearily as it moved.

"Lenny, I have found another table," said Rosamond. "A miserable, forlorn-looking little thing, lost in a corner. I have just pushed it into the light, and I have discovered one drawer in it." She paused and tried to open the drawer; but it resisted her. "Another lock!" she exclaimed, impatiently. "Even this wretched thing is closed against us!"

She pushed the table sharply away with her hand. It swayed on its frail legs, tottered, and fell over on the floor—fell as heavily as a table of twice its size—fell with a shock that rang through the room, and repeated itself again and again in the echoes of the lonesome north hall.

Rosamond ran to her husband, seeing him start from his seat in alarm, and told him what had happened. "You call it a little table," he replied, in astonishment. "It fell like one of the largest pieces of furniture in the room!"

"Surely there must have been something heavy in the drawer!" said Rosamond, approaching the table with her spirits still fluttered by the shock of its unnaturally heavy fall. After waiting for a few moments to give the dust which it had raised, and which still hung over it in thick lazy clouds, time to disperse, she stooped down and examined it. It was cracked across the top from end to end, and the lock had been broken away from its fastenings by the fall.

She set the table up again carefully, drew out the drawer, and, after a glance at its contents, turned to her husband. "I knew it," she said, "I knew there must be something heavy in the drawer. It is full of pieces of copper-ore, like those specimens of my father's, Lenny, from Porthgenna mine. Wait! I think I feel something else, as far away at the back here as my hand can reach."

She extricated from the lumps of ore at the back of the drawer a small circular picture-frame of black wood, about the size of an ordinary hand-glass. It came out with the front part downward, and with the area which its circle inclosed filled up by a thin piece of wood, of the sort which is used at the backs of small frames to keep drawings and engravings steady in them.

This piece of wood (only secured to the back of the frame by one nail) had been forced out of its place, probably by the overthrow of the table; and when Rosamond took the frame out of the drawer, she observed between it and the dislodged piece of wood the end of a morsel of paper, apparently folded many times over, so as to occupy the smallest possible space. She drew out the piece of paper, laid it aside on the table without unfolding it, replaced the piece of wood in its proper position, and then turned the frame round, to see if there was a picture in front.

There was a picture—a picture painted in oils, darkened, but not much faded, by age. It represented the head of a woman, and the figure as far as the bosom.

The instant Rosamond's eyes fell on it she shuddered, and hurriedly advanced toward her husband with the picture in her hand.

"Well, what have you found now?" he inquired, hearing her approach.

"A picture," she answered, faintly, stopping to look at it again.

Leonard's sensitive ear detected a change in her voice. ' ' Is there anything that alarms you in the picture?" he asked, half in jest, half in earnest.

"There is something that startles me—something that seems to have turned me cold for the moment, hot as the day is," said Rosamond. "Do you remember the description the servant-girl gave us, on the night we arrived here, of the ghost of the north rooms?"

"Yes, I remember it perfectly."

"Lenny! that description and this picture are exactly alike! Here is the curling, light-brown hair. Here is the dimple on each cheek. Here are the bright regular teeth. Here is that leering, wicked, fatal beauty which the girl tried to describe, and did describe, when she said it was awful!"

Leonard smiled. "That vivid fancy of yours, my dear, takes strange flights sometimes," he said, quietly.

"Fancy!" repeated Rosamond to herself. "How can it be fancy when I see the face? how can it be fancy when I feel-She stopped, shuddered again, and, returning hastily to the table, placed the picture on it, face downward. As she did so, the morsel of folded paper which she had removed from the back of the frame caught her eye.

"There may be some account of the picture in this," she said, and stretched out her hand to it.

It was getting on toward noon. The heat weighed heavier on the air, and the stillness of all things was more intense than ever, as she took up the paper from the table.

Fold by fold she opened it, and saw that there were written characters inside, traced in ink that had faded to a light, yellow hue. She smoothed it out carefully on the table—then took it up again and looked at the first line of the writing.

The first line contained only three words—words which told

her that the paper with the writing on it was not a description of the picture, but a letter—words which made her start and change colour the moment her eye fell upon them. Without attempting to read any further, she hastily turned over the leaf to find out the place where the writing ended.

It ended at the bottom of the third page; but there was a break in the lines, near the foot of the second page, and in that break there were two names signed. She looked at the uppermost of the two—started again—and turned back instantly to the first page.

Line by line, and word by word, she read through the writing; her natural complexion fading out gradually the while, and a dull, equal whiteness overspreading all her face in its stead. When she had come to the end of the third page, the hand in which she held the letter dropped to her side, and she turned her head slowly toward Leonard. In that position she stood-no tears moistening her eyes, no change passing over her features, no word escaping her lips, no movement varying the position of her limbs in that position she stood, with the fatal letter crumpled up in her cold fingers, looking steadfastly, speechlessly, breathlessly at her blind husband.

He was still sitting as she had seen him a few minutes before, with his legs crossed, his hands clasped together in front of them, and his head turned expectantly in the direction in which he had last heard the sound of his wife's voice. But in a few moments the intense stillness in the room forced itself upon his attention. He changed his position—listened for a little, turning his head uneasily from side to side, and then called to his wife.

"Rosamond!"

At the sound of his voice her lips moved, and her fingers closed faster on the paper that they held; but she neither stepped forward nor spoke.

"Rosamond!"

Her lips moved again—faint traces of expression began to pass shadow-like over the blank whiteness of her face—she advanced one step, hesitated, looked at the letter, and stopped.

Hearing no answer, he rose, surprised and uneasy. Moving his poor, helpless, wandering hands to and fro before him in the air, he walked forward a few paces, straight out from the wall against which he had been sitting. A chair, which his hands were not held low enough to touch, stood in his way; and, as he still advanced, he struck his knee sharply against it.

A cry burst from Rosamond's lips, as if the pain of the blow had passed, at the instant of its infliction, from her husband to herself. She was by his side in a moment. "You are not hurt, Lenny?" she said, faintly.

"No, no." He tried to press his hand on the place where he had struck himself, but she knelt down quickly, and put her own hand there instead, nestling her head against him, while she was on her knees, in a strangely hesitating timid way. He lightly laid the hand which she had intercepted on her shoulder. The moment it touched her, her eyes began to soften; the tears rose in them, and fell slowly one by one down her cheeks.

"I thought you had left me," he said. "There was such a silence that I fancied you had gone out of the room."

"Will you come out of it with me now?" Her strength seemed to fail her while she asked the question; her head drooped on her breast, and she let the letter fall on the floor at her side.

"Are you tired already, Rosamond? Your voice sounds as if you were."

"I want to leave the room," she said, still in the same low, faint, constrained tone, "Is your knee easier, dear? Can you walk now?"

"Certainly. There is nothing in the world the matter with my knee. If you are tired, Rosamond—as I know you are, though you may not confess it—the sooner we leave the room the better."

She appeared not to hear the last words he said. Her fingers were working feverishly about her neck and bosom; two bright red spots were beginning to barn in her pale cheeks; her eyes were fixed vacantly on the letter at her side; her hands wavered about it before she picked it up. For a few seconds she waited on her knees, looking at it intently, with her head turned away from her husband—then rose and walked to the fireplace.

Among the dust, ashes, and other rubbish at the back of the grate were scattered some old torn pieces of paper. They caught her eye and held it fixed on them. She looked and looked, slowly bending down nearer and nearer to the grate. For one moment she held the letter out over the rubbish in both hands—the next she drew back shuddering violently, and turned round so as to face her husband again.

At the sight of him a faint inarticulate exclamation, half sigh, half sob, burst from her. "Oh, no, no !" she whispered to herself, clasping her hands together fervently, and looking at him with fond, mournful eyes. "Never, never, Lenny—come of it what may!"

"Were you speaking to me, Rosamond?"

"Yes, love. I was saying—She paused, and, with trembling fingers, folded up the paper again, exactly in the form in which she had found it.

"Where are you?" he asked. "Your voice sounds away from me at the other end of the room again. Where are you?"

She ran to him, flushed and trembling and tearful, took him by the arm, and, without an instant of hesitation, without the faintest sign of irresolution in her face, placed the folded paper boldly in his hand. "Keep that, Lenny," she said, turning deadly pale, but still not losing her firmness. "Keep that, and ask me to read it to you as soon as we are out of the Myrtle Room."

"What is it?" he asked.

"The last thing I have found, love," she replied, looking at him earnestly, with a deep sigh of relief.

"Is it of any importance?"

Instead of answering, she suddenly caught him to her bosom, clung to him with all the fervour of her impulsive nature, and breathlessly and passionately covered his face with kisses.

"Gently! gently!" said Leonard, laughing. "You take away my breath."

She drew back, and stood looking at him in silence, with a

hand laid on each of his shoulders. "Oh, my angel!" she murmured, tenderly. "I would give all I have in the world if I could
only know how much you love me!"

"Surely," he returned, still laughing—"Surely, Rosamond,
you ought to know by this time!"

"I shall know soon." She spoke those words in tones so quiet
and low that they were barely audible. Interpreting the change
in her voice as a fresh indication of fatigue, Leonard invited her
to lead him away by holding out his hand. She took it in silence,
and guided him slowly to the door.

CHAPTER 6
THE TELLING OF THE SECRET

On their way back to the inhabited side of the house, Rosamond made no further reference to the subject of the folded
paper which she had placed in her husband's hands.

All her attention, while they were returning to the west front,
seemed to be absorbed in the one act of jealously watching every inch of ground that Leonard walked over, to make sure that
it was safe and smooth before she suffered him to set his foot on
it. Careful and considerate as she had always been, from the first
day of their married life, whenever she led him from one place
to another, she was now unduly, almost absurdly anxious to preserve him from the remotest possibility of an accident. Finding
that he was the nearest to the outside of the open landing when
they left the Myrtle Room, she insisted on changing places, so
that he might be nearest to the wall.

While they were descending the stairs, she stopped him in
the middle, to inquire if he felt any pain in the knee which he
had struck against the chair. At the last step she brought him to
a standstill again, while she moved away the torn and tangled
remains of an old mat, for fear one of his feet should catch in it.
Walking across the north hall, she entreated that he would take
her arm and lean heavily upon her, because she felt sure that his
knee was not quite free from stiffness yet.

Even at the short flight of stairs which connected the entrance to the hall with the passages leading to the west side of the house, she twice stopped him on the way down, to place his foot on the sound parts of the steps, which she represented as dangerously worn away in more places than one. He laughed good-humouredly at her excessive anxiety to save him from all danger of stumbling, and asked if there was any likelihood, with their numerous stoppages, of getting back to the west side of the house in time for lunch.

She was not ready, as usual, with her retort; his laugh found no pleasant echo in hers; she only answered that it was impossible to be too anxious about him; and then went on in silence till they reached the door of the housekeeper's room.

Leaving him for a moment outside, she went in to give the keys back again to Mrs. Pentreath.

"Dear me, ma'am!" exclaimed the housekeeper, "you look quite overcome by the heat of the day, and the close air of those old rooms. Can I get you a glass of water, or may I give you my bottle of salts?"

Rosamond declined both offers.

"May I be allowed to ask, ma'am, if anything has been found this time in the north rooms?" inquired Mrs. Pentreath, hanging up the bunch of keys.

"Only some old papers," replied Rosamond, turning away.

"I beg pardon again, ma'am," pursued the housekeeper; "but, in case any of the gentry of the neighbourhood should call to-day?"

"We are engaged. No matter who it may be? we are both engaged." Answering briefly in these terms, Rosamond left Mrs. Pentreath and rejoined her husband.

With the same excess of attention and care which she had shown on the way to the housekeeper's room, she now led him up the west staircase. The library door happening to stand open, they passed through it on their way to the drawing-room, which was the larger and cooler apartment of the two. Having guided Leonard to a seat, Rosamond returned to the library, and took from the table a tray containing a bottle of water and a tumbler, which she had noticed when she passed through.

"I may feel faint as well as frightened," she said quickly to herself, turning round with the tray in her hand to return to the drawing-room.

After she had put the water down on a table in a corner, she noiselessly locked the door leading into the library, then the door leading into the passage. Leonard, hearing her moving about, advised her to keep quiet on the sofa. She patted him gently on the cheek, and was about to make some suitable answer, when she accidentally beheld her face reflected in the looking-glass under which he was sitting. The sight of her own white cheeks and startled eyes suspended the words on her lips. She hastened away to the window, to catch any breath of air that might be wafted toward her from the sea.

The heat-mist still hid the horizon. Nearer, the oily, colourless surface of the water was just visible, heaving slowly, from time to time, in one vast monotonous wave that rolled itself out smoothly and endlessly till it was lost in the white obscurity of the mist. Close on the shore the noisy surf was hushed. No sound came from the beach except at long, wearily long intervals, when a quick thump, and a still splash, just audible 'and no more, announced the fall of one tiny, mimic wave upon the parching sand.

On the terrace in front of the house, the changeless hum of summer insects was all that told of life and movement. Not a human figure was to be seen anywhere on the shore; no sign of a sail loomed shadowy through the heat at sea; no breath of air waved the light tendrils of the creepers that twined up the house-wall, or refreshed the drooping flowers ranged in the windows. Rosamond turned away from the outer prospect, after a moment's weary contemplation of it. As she looked into the room again, her husband spoke to her.

"What precious thing lies hidden in this paper?" he asked, producing the letter and smiling as he opened it. "Surely there must be something besides writing—some inestimable powder, or some bank-note of fabulous value—wrapped up in all these folds?"

Rosamond's heart sank within her as he opened the letter and passed his finger over the writing inside, with a mock expression of anxiety, and a light jest about sharing all treasures discovered at Porthgenna with his wife.

"I will read it to you directly, Lenny," she said, dropping into the nearest seat, and languidly pushing her hair back from her temples. "But put it away for a few minutes now, and let us talk of anything else you like that does not remind us of the Myrtle Room. I am very capricious, am I not, to be so suddenly weary of the very subject that I have been fondest of talking about for so many weeks past? Tell me, love," she added, rising abruptly and going to the back of his chair; "do I get worse with my whims and fancies and faults?—or am I improved, since the time when we were first married?"

He tossed the letter aside carelessly on a table which was always placed by the arm of his chair, and shook his forefinger at her with a frown of comic reproof. "Oh, fie, Rosamond! are you trying to entrap me into paying you compliments?"

The light tone that he persisted in adopting seemed absolutely to terrify her. She shrank away from his chair, and sat down again at a little distance from him.

"I remember I used to offend you," she continued, quickly and confusedly. "No, no, not to offend—only to vex you a little—by talking too familiarly to the servants. You might almost have fancied, at first, if you had not known me so well, that it was a habit with me because I had once been a servant myself. Suppose I had been a servant—the servant who had helped to nurse you in your illnesses, the servant who led you about in your blindness more carefully than anyone else—would you have thought much, then, of the difference between us? would you—"

She stopped. The smile had vanished from Leonard's face, and he had turned a little away from her. "What is the use, Rosamond, of supposing events that never could have happened?" he asked rather impatiently.

She went to the side-table, poured out some of the water she had brought from the library, and drank it eagerly; then walked to the window and plucked a few of the flowers that were placed there. She threw some of them away again the next moment; but kept the rest in her hand, thoughtfully arranging them so as to contrast their colours with the best effect. When this was done, she put them into her bosom, looked down absently at them, took them out again, and, returning to her husband, placed the little nosegay in the buttonhole of his coat.

"Something to make you look gay and bright, love—as I always wish to see you," she said, seating herself in her favourite attitude at his feet, and looking up at him sadly, with her arms resting on his knees.

"What are you thinking about, Rosamond?" he asked, after an interval of silence.

"I was wondering, Lenny, whether any woman in the world could be as fond of you as I am. I feel almost afraid that there are others who would ask nothing better than to live and die for you, as well as me. There is something in your face, in your voice, in all your ways—something besides the interest of your sad, sad affliction—that would draw any woman's heart to you, I think. If I were to die—"

"If you were to die!" He started as he repeated the words after her, and, leaning forward, anxiously laid his hand upon her forehead. "You are thinking and talking very strangely this morning, Rosamond! Are you not well?"

She rose on her knees and looked closer at him, her face brightening a little, and a faint smile just playing round her lips. "I wonder if you will always be as anxious about me, and as fond of me, as you are now?" she whispered, kissing his hand as she removed it from her forehead. He leaned back again in the chair, and told her jestingly not to look too far into the future. The words, lightly as they were spoken, struck deep into her heart.

"There are times, Lenny," she said, "when all one's happiness in the present depends upon one's certainty of the future." She looked at the letter, which her husband had left open on a table near him, as she spoke; and, after a momentary struggle with herself, took it in her hand to read it. At the first word her voice failed her; the deadly paleness overspread her face again; she threw the letter back on the table, and walked away to the other end of the room.

"The future?" asked Leonard. "What future, Rosamond, can you possibly mean?"

"Suppose I meant our future at Porthgenna?" she said, moistening her dry lips with a few drops of water. "Shall we stay here as long as we thought we should, and be as happy as we have been everywhere else? You told me on the journey that I should find it dull, and that I should be driven to try all sorts of extraordinary occupations to amuse myself. You said you expected that I should begin with gardening and end by writing a novel. A novel!"

She approached her husband again, and watched his face eagerly while she went on. "Why not? More women write novels now than men. What is to prevent me from trying? The first great requisite, I suppose, is to have an idea of a story; and that I have got." She advanced a few steps further, reached the table on which the letter lay, and placed her hand on it, keeping her eyes still fixed intently on Leonard's face.

"And what is your idea, Rosamond?" he asked.

"This," she replied. "I mean to make the main interest of the story centre in two young married people. They shall be very fond of each other—as fond as we are, Lenny—and they shall be in our rank of life. After they have been happily married some time, and when they have got one child to make them love each other more dearly than ever, a terrible discovery shall fall upon them like a thunderbolt. The husband shall have chosen for his wife a young lady bearing as ancient a family name as—"

"As your name?" suggested Leonard.

"As the name of the Treverton family," she continued, after a pause, during which her hand had been restlessly moving the letter to and fro on the table. "The husband shall be well-born—as well-born as you, Lenny—and the terrible discovery shall be, that his wife has no right to the ancient name that she bore when he married her."

"I can't say, my love, that I approve of your idea. Your story will decoy the reader into feeling an interest in a woman who turns out to be an impostor."

"No!" cried Rosamond, warmly. "A true woman—a woman who never stooped to a deception—a woman full of faults and failings, but a teller of the truth at all hazards and all sacrifices. Hear me out, Lenny, before you judge." Hot tears rushed into her eyes; but she dashed them away passionately, and went on. "The wife shall grow up to womanhood, and shall marry, in total ignorance—mind that! in total ignorance of her real history. The sudden disclosure of the truth shall overwhelm her—she shall find herself struck by a calamity which she had no hand in bringing about.

"She shall be staggered in her very reason by the discovery; it shall burst upon her when she has no one but herself to depend on; she shall have the power of keeping it a secret from her husband with perfect impunity; she shall be tried, she shall be shaken in her mortal frailness, by one moment of fearful temptation; she shall conquer it, and, of her own free will, she shall tell her husband all that she knows herself. Now, Lenny, what do you call that woman? an impostor?"

"No: a victim."

"Who goes of her own accord to the sacrifice? and who is to be sacrificed?"

"I never said that."

"What would you do with her, Lenny, if you were writing the story? I mean, how would you make her husband behave to her? It is a, question in which a man's nature is concerned, and a woman is not competent to decide it. I am perplexed about how to end the story. How would you end it, love?" As she ceased, her voice sank sadly to its gentlest pleading tones. She came close to him, and twined her fingers in his hair fondly. "How would you end it, love?" she repeated, stooping down till her trembling lips just touched his forehead.

He moved uneasily in his chair, and replied—"I am not a writer of novels, Rosamond."

"But how would you act, Lenny, if you were that husband?"

"It is hard for me to say," he answered. "I have not your vivid imagination, my dear. I have no power of putting myself, at a moment's notice, into a position that is not my own, and of knowing how I should act in it."

"But suppose your wife was close to you—as close as I am now? Suppose she had just told you the dreadful secret, and was standing before you—as I am standing now—with the happiness of her whole life to come depending on one kind word from your lips? Oh, Lenny, you would not let her drop broken-hearted at your feet? You would know, let her birth be what it might, that she was still the same faithful creature who had cherished and served and trusted and worshiped you since her marriage-day, and who asked nothing in return but to lay her head on your bosom, and to hear you say that you loved her?

"You would know that she had nerved herself to tell the fatal secret, because, in her loyalty and love to her husband, she would rather die forsaken and despised, than live, deceiving him? You would know all this, and you would open your arms to the mother of your child, to the wife of your first love, though she was the lowliest of all lowly born women in the estimation of the world? Oh, you would, Lenny, I know you would!"

"Rosamond! how your hands tremble; how your voice alters! You are agitating yourself about this supposed story of yours, as if you were talking of real events."

"You would take her to your heart, Lenny? You would open your arms to her without an instant of unworthy doubt?"

"Hush! hush! I hope I should."

"Hope? only hope? Oh, think again, love, think again; and say you know you should!"

"Must I, Rosamond? Then I do say it."

She drew back as the words passed his lips, and took the letter from the table.

"You have not yet asked me, Lenny, to read the letter that I found in the Myrtle Room. I offer to read it now of my own accord."

She trembled a little as she spoke those few decisive words, but her utterance of them was clear and steady, as if her consciousness of being now irrevocably pledged to make the disclosure had strengthened her at last to dare all hazards and end all suspense.

Her husband turned toward the place from which the sound of her voice had reached him, with a mixed expression of perplexity and surprise in his face. "You pass so suddenly from one subject to another," he said, "that I hardly know how to follow you. What in the world, Rosamond, takes you, at one jump, from a romantic argument about a situation in a novel, to the plain, practical business of reading an old letter?"

"Perhaps there is a closer connection between the two than you suspect," she answered.

"A closer connection? What connection? I don't understand."

"The letter will explain."

"Why the letter? Why should you not explain?"

She stole one anxious look at his face, and saw that a sense of something serious to come was now overshadowing his mind for the first time.

"Rosamond!" he exclaimed, "there is some mystery—"

"There are no mysteries between us two," she interposed quickly. "There never have been any, love; there never shall be." She moved a little nearer to him to take her old favourite place on his knee, then checked herself and drew back again to the table. Warning tears in her eyes bade her distrust her own firmness, and read the letter where she could not feel the beating of his heart.

"Did I tell you," she resumed, after waiting an instant to compose herself, "where I found the folded piece of paper which I put into your hand in the Myrtle Room?"

"No," he replied, "I think not."

"I found it at the back of the frame of that picture—the pic-

302

ture of the ghostly woman with the wicked face. I opened it immediately, and saw that it was a letter. The address inside, the first line under it, and one of the two signatures which it contained, were in a handwriting that I knew."

" Whose!"

"The handwriting of the late Mrs. Treverton."

"Of your mother?"

"Of the late Mrs. Treverton."

"Gracious God, Rosamond! why do you speak of her in that way?"

"Let me read, and you will know. You have seen, with my eyes, what the Myrtle Room is like; you have seen, with my eyes, every object which the search through it brought to light; you must now see, with my eyes, what this letter contains. It is the Secret of the Myrtle Room."

She bent close over the faint, faded writing, and read these words:

To My Husband—

We have parted, Arthur, forever, and I have not had the courage to embitter our farewell by confessing that I have deceived you—cruelly and basely deceived you. But a few minutes since, you were weeping by my bedside and speaking of our child. My wronged, my beloved husband, the little daughter of your heart is not yours, is not mine. She is a love-child, whom I have imposed on you for mine. Her father was a miner at Porthgenna; her mother is my mind, Sarah Leeson.

Rosamond paused, but never raised her head from the letter. She heard her husband lay his hand suddenly on the table; she heard him start to his feet; she heard him draw his breath heavily in one quick gasp; she heard him whisper to himself the instant after—"A love-child!" With a fearful, painful distinctness she heard those three words. The tone in which he whispered them turned her cold. But she never moved, for there was more to read; and while more remained, if her life had depended on it, she could not have looked up.

In a moment more she went on, and read these lines next:

I have many heavy sins to answer for, but this one sin you must pardon, Arthur, for I committed it through fondness for you. That fondness told me a secret which you sought to hide from me. That fondness told me that your barren wife would never make your heart all her own until she had borne you a child; and your lips proved it true. Your first words, when you came back from sea, and when the infant was placed in your arms, were—'I have never loved you, Rosamond, as I love you now.' If you had not said that, I should never have kept my guilty secret.

I can add no more, for death is very near me. How the fraud was committed, and what my other motives were, I must leave you to discover from the mother of the child, who writes this under my dictation, and who is charged to give it to you when I am no more. You will be merciful to the poor little creature who bears my name. Be merciful also to her unhappy parent: she is only guilty of too blindly obeying me. If there is anything that mitigates the bitterness of my remorse, it is the remembrance that my act of deceit saved the most faithful and the most affectionate of women from shame that she had not deserved. Remember me forgivingly, Arthur—words may tell how I have sinned against you; no words can tell how I have loved you!

She had struggled on thus far, and had reached the last line on the second page of the letter, when she paused again, and then tried to read the first of the two signatures—"Rosamond Treverton." She faintly repeated two syllables of that familiar Christian name—the name that was on her husband's lips every hour of the day!—and strove to articulate the third, but her voice failed her. All the sacred household memories which that ruthless letter had profaned forever seemed to tear themselves away from her heart at the same moment. With a low, moaning cry she dropped her arms on the table, and laid her head down on them, and hid her face.

She heard nothing, she was conscious of nothing, until she felt a touch on her shoulder—a light touch from a hand that trembled. Every pulse in her body bounded in answer to it, and she looked up.

Her husband had guided himself near to her by the table. The tears were glistening in his dim, sightless eyes. As she rose and touched him, his arms opened, and closed fast around her.

"My own Rosamond!" he said, "come to me and be comforted!"

BOOK 6

CHAPTER 1
UNCLE JOSEPH

The day and the night had passed, and the new morning had come, before the husband and wife could trust themselves to speak calmly of the Secret, and to face resignedly the duties and the sacrifices which the discovery of it imposed on them.

Leonard's first question referred to those lines in the letter which Rosamond had informed him were in a handwriting that she knew. Finding that he was at a loss to understand what means she could have of forming an opinion on this point, she explained that, after Captain Treverton's death, many letters had naturally fallen into her possession which had been written by Mrs. Treverton to her husband.

They treated of ordinary domestic subjects, and she had read them often enough to become thoroughly acquainted with the peculiarities of Mrs. Treverton's handwriting. It was remarkably large, firm, and masculine in character; and the address, the line under it, and the uppermost of the two signatures in the letter which had been found in the Myrtle Room, exactly resembled it in every particular.

The next question related to the body of the letter. The writing of this, of the second signature ("Sarah Leeson"), and of the additional lines on the third page, also signed by Sarah Leeson, proclaimed itself in each case to be the production of the same person. While stating that fact to her husband, Rosamond did not forget to explain to him that, while reading the letter on the previous day, her strength and courage had failed her before she got to the end of it, She added that the postscript which she had thus omitted to read was of importance, because it mentioned the circumstances under which the Secret had been hidden; and begged that he would listen while she made him acquainted with its contents without any further delay.

Sitting as close to his side, now, as if they were enjoying their first honeymoon days over again, she read these last lines—the lines which her mother had written sixteen years before, on the morning when she fled from Porthgenna Tower:

> If this paper should ever be found (which I pray with my whole heart it never may be), I wish to say that I have come to the resolution of hiding it, because I dare not show the writing that it contains to my master, to whom it is addressed. In doing what I now propose to do, though I am acting against my mistress's last wishes, I am not breaking the solemn engagement which she obliged me to make before her on her deathbed. That engagement forbids me to destroy this letter, or to take it away with me if I leave the house. I shall do neither—my purpose is to conceal it in the place, of all others, where I think there is least chance of its ever being found again. Any hardship or misfortune which may follow as a consequence of this deceitful proceeding on my part will fall on myself. Others, I believe, in my conscience, will be the happier for the hiding of the dreadful Secret which this letter contains.

"There can be no doubt, now," said Leonard, when his wife had read to the end; "Mrs. Jazeph, Sarah Leeson, and the servant who disappeared from Porthgenna Tower, are one and the same person."

"Poor creature!" said Rosamond, sighing as she put down the letter. "We know now why she warned me so anxiously not to go into the Myrtle Boom. Who can say what she must have suffered when she came as a stranger to my bedside? Oh, what would I not give if I had been less hasty with her! It is dreadful to remember that I spoke to her as a servant whom I expected to obey me; it is worse still to feel that I cannot, even now, think of her as a child should think of a mother. How can I ever tell her that I know the Secret? how—" She paused, with a heart-sick consciousness of the slur that was cast on her birth; she paused, shrinking as she thought of the name that her husband had given to her, and of her own parentage, which the laws of society disdained to recognize.

"Why do you stop?" asked Leonard.

"I was afraid—" she began, and paused again.

"Afraid," he said, finishing the sentence for her, "that words of pity for that unhappy woman might wound my sensitive pride by reminding me of the circumstances of your birth? Rosamond! I should be unworthy of your matchless truthfulness toward me, if I, on my side, did not acknowledge that this discovery has wounded me as only a proud man can be wounded. My pride has been born and bred in me. My pride, even while I am now speaking to you, takes advantage of my first moments of composure, and deludes me into doubting, in face of all probability, whether the words you have read to me can, after all, be words of truth.

"But, strong as that inborn and inbred feeling is—hard as it may be for me to discipline and master it as I ought, and must and will—there is another feeling in my heart that is stronger yet." He felt for her hand, and took it in his; then added—"From the hour when you first devoted your life to your blind husband—from the hour when you won all his gratitude, as you had already won all his love, you took a place in his heart, Rosamond, from which nothing, not even such a shock as has now assailed us, can move you! High as I have always held the worth of rank in ray estimation, I have learned, even before the event of yesterday, to hold the worth of my wife, let her parentage be what it may, higher still."

"Oh, Lenny, Lenny, I can't hear you praise me, if you talk in the same breath as if I had made a sacrifice in marrying you! But for my blind husband I might never have deserved what you have just said of me. When I first read that fearful letter, I had one moment of vile, ungrateful doubt if your love for me would hold out against the discovery of the Secret. I had one moment of horrible temptation, that drew me away from you when I ought to have put the letter into your hand.

"It was the sight of you, waiting for me to speak again, so innocent of all knowledge of what happened close by you, that brought me back to my senses, and told me what I ought to do. It was the sight of my blind husband that made me conquer the temptation to destroy that letter in the first hour of discovering it. Oh, if I had been the hardest-hearted of women, could I have ever taken your hand again—could I kiss you, could I lie down by your side, and hear you fall asleep, night after night, feeling that I had abused your blind dependence on me to serve my own selfish interests? knowing that I had only succeeded in my deceit because your affliction made you incapable of suspecting deception?

"No, no; I can hardly believe that the basest of women could be guilty of such baseness as that; and I can claim nothing more for myself than the credit of having been true to my trust. You said yesterday, love, in the Myrtle Room, that the one faithful friend to you in your blindness, who never failed, was your wife. It is reward enough and consolation enough for me, now that the worst is over, to know that you can say so still."

"Yes, Rosamond, the worst is over; but we must not forget that there may be hard trials still to meet."

"Hard trials, love? To what trials do you refer?"

"Perhaps, Rosamond, I overrate the courage that the sacrifice demands; but, to me, at least, it will be a hard sacrifice of my own feelings to make strangers partakers in the knowledge that we now possess."

Rosamond looked at her husband in astonishment. "Why need we tell the Secret to any one?" she asked.

"Assuming that we can satisfy ourselves of the genuineness of that letter," he answered, "we shall have no choice but to tell it to strangers. You cannot forget the circumstances under which your father—under which Captain Treverton—"

"Call him my father," said Rosamond, sadly. "Remember how he loved me, and how I loved him, and say 'my father' still."

"I am afraid I must say 'Captain Treverton' now," returned Leonard, "or I shall hardly be able to explain simply and plainly what it is very necessary that you should know. Captain Treverton died without leaving a will. His only property was the purchase-money of this house and estate; and you inherited it, as his next of kin—"

Rosamond started back in her chair and clasped her hands in dismay. "Oh, Lenny," she said simply, "I have thought so much of you, since I found the letter, that I never remembered this!"

"It is time to remember it, my love. If you are not Captain Treverton's daughter, you have no right to one farthing of the fortune that you possess; and it must be restored at once to the person who is Captain Treverton's next of kin—or, in other words,' to his brother."

"To that man!" exclaimed Rosamond. "To that man who is a stranger to us, who holds our very name in contempt! Are we to be made poor that he may be made rich?—"

"We are to do what is honourable and just, at any sacrifice of our own interests and ourselves," said Leonard, firmly. "I believe, Rosamond, that my consent, as your husband, is necessary, according to the law, to effect this restitution. If Mr. Andrew Treverton was the bitterest enemy I had on earth, and if the restoring of this money utterly ruined us both in our worldly circumstances, I would give it back of my own accord to the last farthing—and so would you!"

The blood mantled in his cheeks as he spoke. Rosamond

looked at him admiringly in silence. "Who would have him less proud," she thought, fondly, "when his pride speaks in such words as those!"

"You understand now," continued Leonard, "that we have duties to perform which will oblige us to seek help from others, and which will therefore render it impossible to keep the Secret to ourselves? If we search all England for her, Sarah Leeson must be found. Our future actions depend upon her answers to our inquiries, upon her testimony to the genuineness of that letter. Although I am resolved beforehand to shield myself behind no technical quibbles and delays—although I want nothing but evidence that is morally conclusive, however legally imperfect it may be—it is still impossible to proceed without seeking advice immediately. The lawyer who always managed Captain Treverton's affairs, and who now manages ours, is the proper person to direct us in instituting a search, and to assist us, if necessary, in making the restitution."

"How quietly and firmly you speak of it, Lenny! Will not the abandoning of my fortune be a dreadful loss to us?"

"We must think of it as a gain to our consciences, Rosamond, and must alter our way of life resignedly to suit our altered means. But we need speak no more of that until we are assured of the necessity of restoring the money. My immediate anxiety, and your immediate anxiety, must turn now on the discovery of Sarah Leeson—no! on the discovery of your mother; I must learn to call her by that name, or I shall not learn to pity and forgive her."

Rosamond nestled closer to her husband's side. "Every word you say, love, does my heart good," she whispered, laying her head on his shoulder. "You will help me and strengthen me, when the time comes, to meet my mother as I ought? Oh, how pale and worn and weary she was when she stood by my bedside, and looked at me and my child! Will it be long before we find her? Is she far away from us, I wonder? or nearer, much nearer than we think?"

Before Leonard could answer, he was interrupted by a knock

at the door, and Rosamond was surprised by the appearance of the maid-servant. Betsey was flushed, excited, and out of breath; but she contrived to deliver intelligibly a brief message from Mr. Munder, the steward, requesting permission to speak to Mr. Frankland, or to Mrs. Frankland, on business of importance.

"What is it? What does he want?" asked Rosamond.

"I think, ma'am, he wants to know whether he had better send for the constable or not," answered Betsey.

"Send for the constable !" repeated Rosamond. "Are there thieves in the house in broad daylight?"

"Mr. Munder says he don't know but what it may be worse than thieves," replied Betsey. "It's the foreigner again, if you please, ma'am. He come up and rung at the door as bold as brass, and asked if he could see Mrs. Frankland."

"The foreigner!" exclaimed Rosamond, laying her hand eagerly on her husband's arm.

"Yes, ma'am," said Betsey. "Him as come here to go over the house along with the lady—"

Rosamond, with characteristic impulsiveness, started to her feet. "Let me go down!" she began.

"Wait," interposed Leonard, catching her by the hand. "There is not the least need for you to go downstairs.—Show the foreigner up here," he continued, addressing himself to Betsey, "and tell Mr. Munder that we will take the management of this business into our own hands."

Rosamond sat down again by her husband's side. "This is a very strange accident," she said, in a low, serious tone. "It must be something more than mere chance that puts the clew into our hands, at the moment when we least expected to find it."

The door opened for the second time, and there appeared, modestly, on the threshold, a little old man, with rosy cheeks and long white hair. A small leather case was slung by a strap at his side, and the stem of a pipe peeped out of the breast-pocket of his coat. He advanced one step into the room, stopped, raised both his hands, with his felt hat crumpled up in them, to his heart, and made five fantastic bows in quick succession—two to

Mrs. Frankland, two to her husband, and one to Mrs. Frankland again, as an act of separate and special homage to the lady.

Never had Rosamond seen a more complete embodiment in human form of perfect innocence and perfect harmlessness than the foreigner who was described in the housekeeper's letter as an audacious vagabond, and who was dreaded by Mr. Munder as something worse than a thief!

"Madam and good sir," said the old man, advancing a little nearer at Mrs. Frankland's invitation, "I ask your pardon for intruding myself, My name is Joseph Buschmann. I live in the town of Truro, where I work in cabinets and tea-caddies, and other shining woods. I am also, if you please, the same little foreign man who was scolded by the big *major-domo* when I came to see the house.

"All that I ask of your kindness is, that you will let me say for my errand here and for myself, and for another person who is very near to my love—one little word. I will be but few minutes, madam and good sir, and then I will go my ways again, with my best wishes and my best thanks."

"Pray consider, Mr. Buschmann, that our time is your time," said Leonard. "We have no engagement whatever which need oblige you to shorten your visit. I must tell you beforehand, in order to prevent any embarrassment on either side, that I have the misfortune to be blind. I can promise you, however, my best attention as far as listening goes. Rosamond, is Mr. Buschmann seated?"

Mr. Buschmann was still standing near the door, and was expressing sympathy by bowing to Mr. Frankland again, and crumpling his felt hat once more over his heart.

"Pray come nearer and sit down," said Rosamond. "And don't imagine for one moment that any opinion of the steward's has the least influence on us, or that we feel it at all necessary for you to apologize for what took place the last time you came to this house. We have an interest—a very great interest," she added, with her usual hearty frankness, "in hearing anything that you have to tell us. You are the person of all others whom we are, just at this time—" She stopped, feeling her foot touched by her husband's, and rightly interpreting the action as a warning not to speak too unrestrainedly to the visitor before he had explained his object in coming to the house.

Looking very much pleased, and a little surprised, also, when he heard Rosamond's last words, Uncle Joseph drew a chair near to the table by which Mr. and Mrs. Frankland were sitting, crumpled his felt hat up smaller than ever, and put it in one of his side pockets, drew from the other a little packet of letters, placed them on his knees as he sat down, patted them gently with both hands, and entered on his explanation in these terms:

"Madam and good sir," he began, " before I can say comfortably my little word, I must, with your leave, travel backward to the last time when I came to this house in company with my niece."

"Your niece!" exclaimed Rosamond and Leonard, both speaking together.

"My niece, Sarah," said Uncle Joseph, "the only child of my sister Agatha. It is for the love of Sarah, if you please, that I am here now. She is the one last morsel of my flesh and blood that is left to me in the world. The rest, they are all gone! My wife, my little Joseph, my brother Max, my sister Agatha and the husband she married, the good and noble Englishman, Leeson—they are all, all gone!"

"Leeson," said Rosamond, pressing her husband's hand significantly under the table. "Your niece's name is Sarah Leeson?"

Uncle Joseph sighed and shook his head. "One day," he said, "of all the days in the year the evil most for Sarah, she changed that name. Of the man she married—who is dead now, madam—it is little or nothing that I know but this: His name was Jazeph, and he used her ill, for which I think him the First Scoundrel! Yes," exclaimed Uncle Joseph, with the nearest approach to anger and bitterness which his nature was capable of making, and with an idea that he was using one of the strongest superlatives in the language—"Yes! if he was to come to life again at this very moment of time, I would say it of him to his face—Englishman Jazeph, you are the First Scoundrel!"

Rosamond pressed her husband's hand for the second time. If their own convictions had not already identified Mrs. Jazeph with Sarah Leeson, the old man's last words must have amply sufficed to assure them that both names had been borne by the same person.

"Well, then, I shall now travel backward to the time when I was herewith Sarah, my niece," resumed Uncle Joseph. "I must, if you please, speak the truth in this business, or, now that I am already backward where I want to be, I shall stick fast in my place, and get on no more for the rest of my life. Sir and good madam, will you have the great kindness to forgive me and Sarah, my niece, if I confess that it was not to see the house that we came here and rang at the bell, and gave deal of trouble, and wasted much breath of the big *major-domos* with the scolding that we got.

"It was only to do one curious little thing that we came together to this place—or, no, it was all about a secret of Sarah's, which is still as black and dark to me as the middle of the blackest and darkest night that ever was in the world—and as I nothing knew about it, except that there was no harm in it to anybody or anything, and that Sarah was determined to go, and that I could not let her go by herself; as also for the good reason that she told me she had the best right of anybody to take the letter and to hide it again, seeing that she was afraid of its being found if longer in that room she left it, which was she room where she had hidden it before—why, so it happened that I—no, that she—no, no, that I—*Ach Gott!*" cried Uncle Joseph, striking his forehead in despair, and relieving himself by an invocation in his own language. "I am lost in my own muddlement; and whereabouts the right place is, and how I am to get myself back into it, as I am a living sinner, is more than I know!"

"There is not the least need to go back on our account," said Rosamond, forgetting all caution and self-restraint in her anxiety to restore the old man's confidence and composure. "Pray don't try to repeat your explanations. We know already—"

"We will suppose," said Leonard, interposing abruptly before his wife could add another word, "that we know already everything you can desire to tell us in relation to your niece's secret, and to your motives for desiring to see the house."

"You will suppose that!" exclaimed Uncle Joseph, looking greatly relieved. "Ah! thank you, sir, and you, good madam, a thousand times for helping me out of my own muddlement with a 'Suppose.' I am all over confusion from my tops to my toes; but I can go on now, I think, and lose myself no more. So! Let us say it in this way: I and Sarah, my niece, are in the house—that is the first 'Suppose.' I and Sarah, my niece, are out of the house—that is the second 'Suppose' Good! now we go on once more.

"On my way back to my own home at Truro, I am frightened for Sarah, because of the faint she fell into on your stairs here, and because of a look in her face that it makes me heavy at my heart to see. Also, I am sorry for her sake, because she has not done that one curious little thing which she came into the house to do. I fret about these same matters, but I console myself too; and my comfort is that Sarah will stop with me in my house at Truro, and that I shall make her happy and well again, as soon as we are settled in our life together.

"Judge, then, sir, what a blow falls on me when I hear that she will not make her home where I make mine. Judge you, also, good madam, what my surprise must be, when I ask for her reason, and she tells me she must leave Uncle Joseph, because she is afraid of being found out by you." He stopped, and looked anxiously at Rosamond's face, saw it sadden and turn away from him after he had spoken his last words. "Are you sorry, madam, for Sarah, my niece? do you pity her?" he asked, with a little hesitation and trembling in his voice.

"I pity her with my whole heart," said Rosamond, warmly.

"And with my whole heart, for that pity I thank you!" rejoined Uncle Joseph. "Ah, madam, your kindness gives me the courage to go on, and to tell you that we parted from each other on the day of our getting back to Truro! When she came to see me this time, it was years and years, long and lonely and very many, since we two had met. I was afraid that many more would pass again and I tried to make her stop with me to the very last.

"But she had still the same fear—to drive her away the fear of being found and put to the question by you. So, with the tears in her eyes (and in mine), and the grief at her heart (and at mine), she went away to hide herself in the empty bigness of the great city, London, which swallows up all people and all things that pour into it, and which has now swallowed up Sarah, my niece, with the rest.

"'My child, you will write sometimes to Uncle Joseph,' I said, and she answered me: 'I will write often.' It is three weeks now since that time, and here, on my knee, are four letters she has written to me. I shall ask your leave to put them down open before you, because they will help me to get on further yet with what I must say, and because I see in your face, madam, that you are indeed sorry for Sarah, my niece, from your heart."

He untied the packet of letters, opened them, kissed them one by one, and put them down in a row on the table, smoothing them out carefully with his hand, and taking great pains to arrange them all in a perfectly straight line. A glance at the first of the little series showed Rosamond that the handwriting in it was the same as the handwriting in the body of the letter which had been found in the Myrtle Room.

"There is not much to read," said Uncle Joseph. "But if you will look through them first, madam, I can tell you after all the reason for showing them that I have."

The old man was right. There was very little to read in the letters, and they grew progressively shorter as they became more recent in date. All four were written in the formal, conventionally correct style of a person taking up the pen with a fear of making mistakes in spelling and grammar, and were equally destitute of any personal particulars relative to the writer; all four anxiously entreated that Uncle Joseph would not be uneasy, inquired after his health, and expressed gratitude and love for him as warmly as their timid restraints of style would permit; all four contained these two questions relating to Rosamond—First, had Mrs. Frankland arrived yet at Porthgenna Tower? Second, if she had arrived, what had Uncle Joseph heard about her?

And, finally, all four gave the same instructions for addressing an answer—"Please direct to me, 'S. J., Post-office, Smith Street, London'"—followed by the same apology, "Excuse my not giving my address, in case of accidents; for even in London I am still afraid of being followed and found out. I send every morning for letters; so I am sure to get your answer."

"I told you, madam," said the old man, when Rosamond raised her head from the letters, "that I was frightened and sorry for Sarah when she left me. Now see, if you please, why I got more frightened and more sorry yet, when I have all the four letters that she writes to me. They begin here, with the first, at my left hand; and they grow shorter, and shorter, and shorter, as they get nearer to my right, till the last is but eight little lines.

"Again, see, if you please. The writing of the first letter, here, at my left hand, is very fine—I mean it is very fine to me, because I love Sarah, and because I write very badly myself; but it is not so good in the second letter—it shakes a little, it blots a little, it crooks itself a little in the last lines. In the third it is worse—more shake, more blot, more crook. In the fourth, where there is least to do, there is still more shake, still more blot, still more crook, than in all the other three put together. I see this; I remember that she was weak and worn and weary when she left me, and I say to myself, 'She is ill, though she will not tell it, for the writing betrays her!'"

Rosamond looked down again at the letters, and followed the significant changes for the worse in the handwriting, line by line, as the old man pointed them out.

"I say to myself that," he continued; "I wait, and think a little; and I hear my own heart whisper to me, 'Go you, Uncle Joseph, to London, and, while there is yet time, bring her back to be cured and comforted and made happy in your own home!' After that I wait, and think a little again—not about leaving my business; I would leave it forever sooner than Sarah should come to harm—but about what I am to do to get her to come back.

"That thought makes me look at the letters again; the letters show me always the same questions about Mistress Frankland; I see it plainly as my own hand before me that I shall never get Sarah, my niece, back, unless I can make easy her mind about those questions of Mistress Frankland's that she dreads as if there was death to her in every one of them.

"I see it! it makes my pipe go out; it drives me up from my chair; it puts my hat on my head; it brings me here, where I have once intruded myself already, and where I have no right, I know, to intrude myself again; it makes me beg and pray now, of your compassion for my niece and of your goodness for me, that you will not deny me the means of bringing Sarah back. If I may only say to her, I have seen Mistress Frankland, and she has told me with her own lips that she will ask none of those questions that you fear so much—if I may only say that, Sarah will come back with me, and I shall thank you every day of my life for making me a happy man!"

The simple eloquence of his words, the innocent earnestness of his manner, touched Rosamond to the heart. "I will do anything, I will promise anything," she answered, eagerly, "to help you to bring her back! If she will only let me see her, I promise not to say one word that she would not wish me to say; I promise not to ask one question—no, not one—that it will pain her to answer. Oh, what comforting message can I send besides? what can I say—?" She stopped confusedly, feeling her husband's foot touching hers again.

"Ah, say no more! say no more!" cried Uncle Joseph, tying up his little packet of letters, with his eyes sparkling and his ruddy face all in a glow. "Enough said to bring Sarah back! enough said to make me grateful for all my life! Oh, I am so happy, so happy, so happy—my skin is too small to hold me!" He tossed up the packet of letters into the air, caught it, kissed it, and put it back again in his pocket, all in an instant.

"You are not going?" said Rosamond. "Surely you are not

going, yet?"

"It is my loss to go away from here, which I must put up with, because it is also my gain to get sooner to Sarah," replied Uncle Joseph. "For that reason only, I shall ask your pardon if I take my leave with my heart full of thanks, and go my ways home again."

"When do you propose to start for London, Mr. Buschmann?" inquired Leonard.

"Tomorrow, in the morning early, sir," replied Uncle Joseph. "I shall finish the work that I must do tonight, and shall leave the rest to Samuel (who is my very good friend, and my shopman too), and shall then go to Sarah by the first coach."

"May I ask for your niece's address in London, in case we wish to write to you?"

"She gives me no address, sir, but the post-office; for even at the great distance of London, the same fear that she had all the way from this house still sticks to her. But here is the place where I shall get my own bed," continued the old man, producing a small shop card. "It is the house of a countryman of my own, a fine baker of buns, sir, and a very good man indeed."

"Have you thought of any plan for finding out your niece's address?" inquired Rosamond, copying the direction on the card while she spoke.

"Ah, yes—for I am always quick at making my plans," said Uncle Joseph. "I shall present myself to the master of the post, and to him I shall say just this and no more—'Good-morning, sir. I am the man who writes the letters to S. J. She is my niece, if you please; and all that I want to know is—Where does she live?' There is something like a plan, I think? Aha!" He spread out both his hands interrogatively, and looked at Mrs. Frankland with a self-satisfied smile.

"I am afraid," said Rosamond, partly amused, partly touched by his simplicity, "that the people at the post-office are not at all likely to be trusted with the address. I think you would do better to take a letter with you, directed to 'S. J.'; to deliver it in the morning when letters are received from the country; to wait near the door, and then to follow the person who is sent by your niece (as she tells you herself) to ask for letters for S. J."

"You think that is better?" said Uncle Joseph, secretly convinced that his own idea was unquestionably the most ingenious of the two. "Good! The least little word that you say to me, madam, is a command that I follow with all my heart." He took the crumpled felt hat out of his pocket, and advanced to say farewell, when Mr. Frank- land spoke to him again.

"If you rind your niece well, and willing to travel," said Leonard, "you will bring her back to Truro at once? And you will let us know when you are both at home again?"

"At once, sir," said Uncle Joseph. "To both these questions, I say, At once."

"If a week from this time passes," continued Leonard, "and we hear nothing from you, we must conclude, then, either that some unforeseen obstacle stands in the way of your return, or that your fears on your niece's account have been but too well-founded, and that she is not able to travel?"

"Yes, sir; so let it be. But I hope you will hear from me before the week is out."

"Oh, so do I! most earnestly, most anxiously!" said Rosamond. "You remember my message?"

"I have got it here, every word of it," said Uncle Joseph, touching his heart. He raised the hand which Rosamond held out to him to his lips. "I shall try to thank you better when I have come back," he said. "For all your kindness to me and to my niece, God bless you both, and keep you happy, till we meet again." "With these words, he hastened to the door, waved his hand gaily, with the old crumpled hat in it, and went out.

"Dear, simple, warm-hearted old man!" said Rosamond, as the door closed. "I wanted to tell him everything, Lenny. Why did you stop me?"

"My love, it is that very simplicity which you admire, and which I admire, too, that makes me cautious. At the first sound of his voice I felt as warmly toward him as you do; but the more I heard him talk the more convinced I became that it would be rash to trust him, at first, for fear of his disclosing too abruptly to your mother that we know her secret.

"Our chance of winning her confidence and obtaining an interview with her depends, I can see, upon our own tact in dealing with her exaggerated suspicions and her nervous fears. That good old man, with the best and kindest intentions in the world, might ruin everything. He will have done all that we can hope for, and all that we can wish, if he only succeeds in bringing her back to Truro,"

"But if he fails?—if anything happens?—if she is really ill?"

"Let us wait till the week is over, Rosamond. It will be time enough then to decide what we shall do next."

CHAPTER 2
WAITING AND HOPING

The week of expectation passed, and no tidings from Uncle Joseph reached Porthgenna Tower.

On the eighth day Mr. Frankland sent a messenger to Truro, with orders to find out the cabinet-maker's shop kept by Mr. Buschmann, and to inquire of the person left in charge there whether he had received any news from his master. The messenger returned in the afternoon, and brought word that Mr. Buschmann had written one short note to his shopman since his departure, announcing that he had arrived safely toward nightfall in London; that he had met with a hospitable welcome from his countryman, the German baker; and that he had discovered his niece's address, but had been prevented from seeing her by an obstacle which he hoped would be removed at his next visit. Since the delivery of that note, no further communication had been received from him, and nothing therefore was known of the period at which he might be expected to return.

The one fragment of intelligence thus obtained was not of a nature to relieve the depression of spirits which the doubt and suspense of the past week had produced in Mrs. Frankland. Her husband endeavoured to combat the oppression of mind from which she was suffering, by reminding her that the ominous silence of Uncle Joseph might be just as probably occasioned by his niece's unwillingness as by her inability to return with him to Truro.

Remembering the obstacle at which the old man's letter hinted, and taking also into consideration her excessive sensitiveness and her unreasoning timidity, he declared it to be quite possible that Mrs. Frankland's message, instead of reassuring her, might only inspire her with fresh apprehensions, and might consequently strengthen her resolution to keep herself out of reach of all communications from Porthgenna Tower.

Rosamond listened patiently while this view of the case was placed before her, and acknowledged that the reasonableness of it was beyond dispute; but her readiness in admitting that her husband might be right and that she might be wrong was accompanied by no change for the better in the condition of her spirits.

The interpretation which the old man had placed upon the alteration for the worse in Mrs. Jazeph's handwriting had produced a vivid impression on her mind, which had been strengthened by her own recollection of her mother's pale, worn face when they met as strangers at West Winston. Reason, therefore, as convincingly as he might, Mr. Frankland was unable to shake his wife's conviction that the obstacle mentioned in Uncle Joseph's letter, and the silence which he had maintained since, were referable alike to the illness of his niece.

The return of the messenger from Truro suggested, besides this topic of discussion, another question of much greater importance. After having waited one day beyond the week that had been appointed, what was the proper course of action for Mr. and Mrs. Frankland now to adopt, in the absence of any information from London or from Truro to decide their future proceedings?

Leonard's first idea was to write immediately to Uncle Joseph, at the address which he had given on the occasion of his visit to Porthgenna Tower. When this project was communicated to Rosamond, she opposed it, on the ground that the necessary delay before the answer to the letter could arrive would involve a serious waste of time, when it might, for aught they knew to the contrary, be of the last importance to them not to risk the loss of a single day.

If illness prevented Mrs. Jazeph from travelling, it would be necessary to see her at once, because that illness might increase. If she were only suspicious of their motives, it was equally important to open personal communications with her before she could find an opportunity of raising some fresh obstacle, and of concealing herself again in some place of refuge which Uncle Joseph himself might not be able to trace.

The truth of these conclusions was obvious, but Leonard hesitated to adopt them, because they involved the necessity of a journey to London. If he went there without his wife, his blindness placed him at the mercy of strangers and servants, in conducting investigations of the most delicate and most private nature. If Rosamond accompanied him, it would be necessary to risk all kinds of delays and inconveniences by taking the child with them on a long and wearisome journey of more than two hundred and fifty miles.

Rosamond met both these difficulties with her usual directness and decision. The idea of her husband travelling anywhere, under any circumstances, in his helpless, dependent state, without having her to attend on him, she dismissed at once as too preposterous for consideration. The second objection, of subjecting the child to the chances and fatigues of a long journey, she met by proposing that they should travel to Exeter at their own time and in their own conveyance, and that they should afterward insure plenty of comfort and plenty of room by taking a carriage to themselves when they reached the railroad at Exeter.

After thus smoothing away the difficulties which seemed to set themselves in opposition to the journey, she again reverted to the absolute necessity of undertaking it. She reminded Leonard of the serious interest that they both had in immediately obtaining Mrs. Jazeph's testimony to the genuineness of the letter which had been found in the Myrtle Room, as well as in ascertaining all the details of the extraordinary fraud which had been practiced by Mrs. Treverton on her husband.

She pleaded also her own natural anxiety to make all the atonement in her power for the pain she must have unconsciously inflicted, in the bedroom at West Winston, on the person of all others whose failings and sorrows she was most bound to respect; and having thus stated the motives which urged her husband and herself to lose no time in communicating personally with Mrs. Jazeph, she again drew the inevitable conclusion that there was no alternative, in the position in which they were now placed, but to start forthwith on the journey to London.

A little further consideration satisfied Leonard that the emergency was of such a nature as to render all attempts to meet it by half-measures impossible. He felt that his own convictions agreed with his wife's; and he resolved accordingly to act at once, without further indecision or further delay. Before the evening was over, the servants at Porthgenna were amazed by receiving directions to pack the trunks for travelling, and to order horses at the post-town for an early hour the next morning.

On the first day of the journey, the travellers started as soon as the carriage was ready, rested on the road toward noon, and remained for the night at Liskeard. On the second day they arrived at Exeter, and slept there. On the third day they reached London by the railway, between six and seven o'clock in the evening.

When they were comfortably settled for the night at their hotel, and when an hour's rest and quiet had enabled them to recover a little after the fatigues of the journey, Rosamond wrote two notes under her husband's direction. The first was addressed to Mr. Buschmann: it simply informed him of their arrival, and of their earnest desire to see him at the hotel as early as possible the next morning, and it concluded by cautioning him to wait until he had seen them before he announced their presence in London to his niece.

The second note was addressed to the family solicitor, Mr. Nixon—the same gentleman who, more than a year since, had written, at Mrs. Frankland's request, the letter which informed Andrew Treverton of his brother's decease, and of the circumstances under which the Captain had died.

All that Rosamond now wrote, in her husband's name and her own, to ask of Mr. Nixon, was that he would endeavour to call at their hotel on his way to business the next morning, to give his opinion on a private matter of great importance, which had obliged them to undertake the journey from Porthgenna to London. This note, and the note to Uncle Joseph, were sent to their respective addresses by a messenger on the evening when they were written.

The first visitor who arrived the next morning was the solicitor—a clear-headed, fluent, polite old gentleman, who had known Captain Treverton and his father before him. He came to the hotel fully expecting to be consulted on some difficulties connected with the Porthgenna estate, which the local agent was perhaps unable to settle, and which might be of too confused and intricate a nature to be easily expressed in writing.

When he heard what the emergency really was, and when the letter that had been found in the Myrtle Room was placed in his hands, it is not too much to say that, for the first time in the course of a long life and a varied practice among all sorts and conditions of clients, sheer astonishment utterly paralysed Mr. Nixon's faculties, and bereft him for some moments of the power of uttering a single word.

When, however, Mr. Frankland proceeded from making the disclosure to announcing his resolution to give up the purchase-money of Porthgenna Tower, if the genuineness of the letter could be proved to his own satisfaction, the old lawyer recovered the use of his tongue immediately, and protested against his client's intention with the sincere warmth of a man who thoroughly understood the advantage of being rich, and who knew what it was to gain and to lose a fortune of forty thousand pounds.

Leonard listened with patient attention while Mr. Nixon argued from his professional point of view against regarding the letter, taken by itself, as a genuine document, and against accepting Mrs. Jazeph's evidence, taken with it, as decisive on the subject of Mrs. Frankland's real parentage. He expatiated on the improbability of Mrs. Treverton's alleged fraud upon her husband having been committed without other persons besides her maid and herself being in the secret.

He declared it to be in accordance with all received experience of human nature that one or more of those other persons must have spoken of the secret either from malice or from want of caution, and that the consequent exposure of the truth must, in the course of so long a period as twenty-two years, have come to the knowledge of some among the many people in the West of England, as well as in London, who knew the Treverton family personally or by reputation.

From this objection he passed to another, which admitted the possible genuineness of the letter as a written document; but which pleaded the probability of its having been produced under the influence of some mental delusion on Mrs. Treverton's part, which her maid might have had an interest in humouring at the time, though she might have hesitated, after her mistress's death, at risking the possible consequences of attempting to profit by the imposture.

Having stated this theory, as one which not only explained the writing of the letter, but the hiding of it also, Mr. Nixon further observed, in reference to Mrs. Jazeph, that any evidence she might give was of little or no value in a legal point of view, from the difficulty—or, he might say, the impossibility—of satisfactorily identifying the infant mentioned in the letter with the lady whom he had now the honour of addressing as Mrs. Frankland, and whom no unsubstantiated document in existence should induce him to believe to be any other than the daughter of his old friend and client, Captain Treverton.

Having heard the lawyer's objections to the end, Leonard admitted their ingenuity, but acknowledged at the same time that they had produced no alteration in his impression on the subject of the letter, or in his convictions as to the course of duty which he felt bound to follow. He would wait, he said, for Mrs. Jazeph's testimony before he acted decisively; but if that testimony were of such a nature, and were given in such a manner, as to satisfy him that his wife had no moral right to the fortune that she possessed, he would restore it at once to the person who had—Mr. Andrew Treverton.

Finding that no fresh arguments or suggestions could shake Mr. Frankland's resolution, and that no separate appeal to Rosamond had the slightest effect in stimulating her to use her influence for the purpose of inducing her husband to alter his determination; and feeling convinced, moreover, from all that he heard, that Mr. Frankland would, if he was opposed by many more objections, either employ another professional adviser, or risk committing some fatal legal error by acting for himself in the matter of restoring the money, Mr. Nixon at last consented, under protest, to give his client what help he needed in case it became necessary to hold communication with Andrew Treverton.

He listened with polite resignation to Leonard's brief statement of the questions that he intended to put to Mrs. Jazeph; and said, with the slightest possible dash of sarcasm, when it came to his turn, to speak, that they were excellent questions in a moral point of view, and would doubtless produce answers which would be full of interest of the most romantic kind. "But," he added, "as you have one child already, Mr. Frankland, and as you may, perhaps, if I may venture on suggesting such a thing, have more in the course of years; and as those children, when they grow up, may hear of the loss of their mother's fortune, and may wish to know why it was sacrificed, I should recommend-resting the matter on family grounds alone, and not going further to make a legal point of it also—that you procure from Mrs. Jazeph, besides the *viva voce* evidence you propose to extract (against the admissibility of which, in this case, I again protest), a written declaration, which you may leave behind you at your death, and which may justify you in the eyes of your children, in case the necessity for such justification should arise at some future period."

This advice was too plainly valuable to be neglected. At Leonard's request, Mr. Nixon drew out at once a form of declaration, affirming the genuineness of the letter addressed by the late Mrs. Treverton on her deathbed to her husband, since also deceased, and bearing witness to the truth of the statements therein contained, both as regarded the fraud practiced on Captain Treverton and the asserted parentage of the child.

Telling Mr. Frankland that he would do well to have Mrs. Jazeph's signature to this document attested by the names of two competent witnesses, Mr. Nixon handed the declaration to Rosamond to read aloud to her husband, and, finding that no objection was made to any part of it, and that he could be of no further use in the present early stage of the proceedings, rose to take his leave. Leonard engaged to communicate with him again in the course of the day, if necessary; and he retired, reiterating his protest to the last, and declaring that he had never met with such an extraordinary case and such a self-willed client before in the whole course of his practice.

Nearly an hour elapsed after the departure of the lawyer before any second visitor was announced. At the expiration of that time, the welcome sound of footsteps was heard approaching the door, and Uncle Joseph entered the room.

Rosamond's observation, stimulated by anxiety, detected a change in his look and manner the moment he appeared. His face was harassed and fatigued, and his gait, as he advanced into the room, had lost the briskness and activity which so quaintly distinguished it when she saw him, for the first time, at Porthgenna Tower. He tried to add to his first words of greeting an apology for being late; but Rosamond interrupted him, in her eagerness to ask the first important question.

"We know that you have discovered her address," she said, anxiously, "but we know nothing more. Is she as you feared to find her? Is she ill?"

The old man shook his head sadly. "When I showed you her letter," he said, "what did I tell you? She is so ill, madam, that not even the message your kindness gave to me will do her any good."

Those few simple words struck Rosamond's heart with a strange fear, which silenced her against her own will when she tried to speak again. Uncle Joseph understood the anxious look she fixed on him, and the quick sign she made toward the chair standing nearest to the sofa on which she and her husband were sitting. There he took his place, and there he confided to them all that he had to tell.

He had followed, he said, the advice which Rosamond had given to him at Porthgenna, by taking a letter addressed to "S. J." to the post-office the morning after his arrival in London. The messenger—a maid-servant—had called to inquire, as was anticipated, and had left the post-office with his letter in her hand. He had followed her to a lodging-house in a street near, had seen her let herself in at the door, and had then knocked and inquired for Mrs. Jazeph.

The door was answered by an old woman, who looked like the landlady; and the reply was that no one of that name lived there. He had then explained that he wished to see the person for whom letters were sent to the neighbouring post-office, addressed to "S. J."; but the old woman had answered, in the surliest way, that they had nothing to do with anonymous people or their friends in that house, and had closed the door in his face. Upon this he had gone back to his friend, the German baker, to get advice; and had been recommended to return, after allowing some little time to elapse, to ask if he could see the servant who waited on the lodgers, to describe his niece's appearance, and to put half a crown into the girl's hand to help her to understand what he wanted.

He had followed these directions, and had discovered that his niece was lying ill in the house, under the assumed name of "Mrs. James." A little persuasion (after the present of the half-crown) had induced the girl to go upstairs and announce his name. After that there were no more obstacles to be overcome, and he was conducted immediately to the room occupied by his niece.

He was inexpressibly shocked and startled when he saw her by the violent nervous agitation which she manifested as he approached her bedside. But he did not lose heart and hope until he had communicated Mrs. Frankland's message, and had found that it failed altogether in producing the reassuring effect on her spirits which he had trusted and believed that it would exercise. Instead of soothing, it seemed to excite and alarm her afresh.

Among a host of minute inquiries about Mrs. Frankland's looks, about her manner toward him, about the exact words she had spoken, all of which he was able to answer more or less to her satisfaction, she had addressed two questions to him, to which he was utterly unable to reply. The first of the questions was, whether Mrs. Frankland had said anything about the Secret? The second was, whether she had spoken any chance word to lead to the suspicion that she had found out the situation of the Myrtle Room?

The doctor in attendance had come in, the old man added, while he was still sitting by his niece's bedside, and still trying ineffectually to induce her to accept the friendly and reassuring language of Mrs. Frankland's message.

After making some inquiries and talking a little while on indifferent matters, the doctor had privately taken him aside; had informed him that the pain over the region of the heart and the difficulty in breathing, which were the symptoms of which his niece complained, were more serious in their nature than persons uninstructed in medical matters might be disposed to think; and had begged him to give her no more messages from anyone, unless he felt perfectly sure beforehand that they would have the effect of clearing her mind, at once and forever, from the secret anxieties that now harassed it—anxieties which he might rest assured were aggravating her malady day by day, and rendering all the medical help that could be given of little or no avail.

Upon this, after sitting longer with his niece, and after holding counsel with himself, he had resolved to write privately to Mrs. Frankland that evening, after getting back to his friend's house. The letter had taken him longer to compose than any one accustomed to writing would believe. At last, after delays in making a fair copy from many rough drafts, and delays in leaving his task to attend to his niece, he had completed a letter narrating what had happened since his arrival in London, in language which he hoped might be understood. Judging by comparison of dates, this letter must have crossed Mr. and Mrs. Frankland on the road.

It contained nothing more than he had just been relating with his own lips—except that it also communicated, as a proof that distance had not diminished the fear which tormented his niece's mind, the explanation she had given to him of her concealment of her name, and of her choice of an abode among strangers, when she had friends in London to whom she might have gone. That explanation it was perhaps needless to have lengthened the letter by repeating, for it only involved his saying over again, in substance, what he had already said in speaking of the motive which had forced Sarah to part from him at Truro.

With last words such as those, the sad and simple story of the old man came to an end. After waiting a little to recover her self-possession and to steady her voice, Rosamond touched her husband to draw his attention to herself, and whispered to him—

"I may say all, now, that I wished to say at Porthgenna?"

"All," he answered. "If you can trust yourself, Rosamond, it is fittest that he should hear it from your lips."

After the first natural burst of astonishment was over, the effect of the disclosure of the Secret on Uncle Joseph exhibited the most striking contrast that can be. imagined to the effect of it on Mr. Nixon. No shadow of doubt darkened the old man's face, not a word of objection dropped from his lips.

The one emotion excited in him was simple, unreflecting, unalloyed delight. He sprang to his feet with all his natural activity, his eyes sparkled again with all their natural brightness; one moment he clapped his hands like a child; the next he caught up his hat, and entreated Rosamond to let him lead her at once to his niece's bedside. "If you will only tell Sarah what you have just told me," he cried, hurrying across the room to open the door, "you will give her back her courage, you will raise her up from her bed, you will cure her before the day is out!"

A warning word from Mr. Frankland stopped him on a sudden, and brought him back, silent and attentive, to the chair that he had left the moment before.

"Think a little of what the doctor told you," said Leonard. "The sudden surprise which has made you so happy might do fatal mischief to your niece. Before we take the responsibility of speaking to her on a subject which is sure to agitate her violently, however careful we may be in introducing it, we ought first, I think, for safety's sake, to apply to the doctor for advice."

Rosamond warmly seconded her husband's suggestion, and, with her characteristic impatience of delay, proposed that they should find out the medical man immediately. Uncle Joseph announced—a little unwillingly, as it seemed—in answer to her inquiries, that he knew the place of the doctor's residence, and that he was generally to be found at home before one o'clock in the afternoon. It was then just half-past twelve; and Rosamond, with her husband's approval, rang the bell at once to send for a cab.

She was about to leave the room to put on her bonnet, after giving the necessary order, when the old man stopped her by asking, with some appearance of hesitation and confusion, if it was considered necessary that he should go to the doctor with Mr. and Mrs. Frankland; adding, before the question could be answered, that he would greatly prefer, if there was no objection to it on their parts, being left to wait at the hotel to receive any instructions they might wish to give him on their return. Leonard immediately complied with his request, without inquiring into his reasons for making it; but Rosamond's curiosity was aroused, and she asked why he preferred remaining by himself at the hotel to going with them to the doctor.

"I like him not," said the old man. "When he speaks about Sarah, he looks and talks as if he thought she would never get up from her bed again." Answering in those brief words, he walked away uneasily to the window, as if he desired to say no more.

The residence of the doctor was at some little distance, but Mr. and Mrs. Frankland arrived there before one o'clock, and found him at home. He was a young man, with a mild, grave face, and a quiet, subdued manner. Daily contact with suffering and sorrow had perhaps prematurely steadied and saddened his character. Merely introducing her husband and herself to him, as persons who were deeply interested in his patient at the lodging-house, Rosamond left it to Leonard to ask the first questions relating to the condition of her mother's health.

The doctor's answer was ominously prefaced by a few polite words, which were evidently intended to prepare his hearers for a less hopeful report than they might have come there expecting to receive. Carefully divesting the subject of all professional technicalities, he told them that his patient was undoubtedly affected with serious disease of the heart. The exact nature of this disease he candidly acknowledged to be a matter of doubt, which various medical men might decide in various ways.

According to the opinion which he had himself formed from the symptoms, he believed that the patient's malady was connected with the artery which conveys blood directly from the heart through the system. Having found her singularly unwilling to answer questions relating to the nature of her past life, he could only guess that the disease was of long standing; that it was originally produced by some great mental shock, followed by long-wearing anxiety (of which her face showed palpable traces); and that it had been seriously aggravated by the fatigue of a journey to London, which she acknowledged she had undertaken at a time when great nervous exhaustion rendered her totally unfit to travel.

Speaking according to this view of the case, it was his painful duty to tell her friends that any violent emotion would unquestionably put her life in danger. At the same time, if the mental uneasiness from which she was now suffering could be removed, and if she could be placed in a quiet, comfortable country home, among people who would be unremittingly careful in keeping her composed, and in suffering her to want for nothing, there was reason to hope that the progress of the disease might be arrested, and that her life might be spared for some years to come.

Rosamond's heart bounded at the picture of the future which her fancy drew from the suggestions that lay hidden in the doctor's last words. "She can command every advantage you have mentioned, and more, if more is required!" she interposed eagerly, before her husband could speak again. "Oh, sir, if rest among kind friends is all that her poor weary heart wants, thank God we can give it!"

"We can give it," said Leonard, continuing the sentence for his wife, "if the doctor will sanction our making a communication to his patient, which is of a nature to relieve her of all anxiety, but which, it is necessary to add, she is at present quite unprepared to receive."

"May I ask," said the doctor, "who is to be intrusted with the responsibility of making the communication you mention?"

"There are two persons who could be intrusted with it," answered Leonard. "One is the old man whom you have seen by your patient's bedside. The other is my wife."

"In that case," rejoined the doctor, looking at Rosamond, "there can be no doubt that this lady is the fittest person to undertake the duty." He paused, and reflected for a moment; then added—"May I inquire, however, before I venture on guiding your decision one way or the other, whether the lady is as familiarly known to my patient, and is on the same intimate terms with her, as the old man?"

"I am afraid I must answer No to both those questions," replied Leonard. "And I ought, perhaps, to tell you, at the same time, that your patient believes my wife to be now in Cornwall. Her first appearance in the sick-room would, I fear, cause great surprise to the sufferer, and possibly some little alarm as well."

"Under those circumstances," said the doctor, "the risk of trusting the old man, simple as he is, seems to be infinitely the least risk of the two—for the plain reason that his presence can cause her no surprise. However unskilfully he may break the news, he will have the great advantage over this lady of not appearing unexpectedly at the bedside. If the hazardous experiment must be tried—and I assume that 'it must, from what you have said—you have no choice, I think, but to trust it, with proper cautions and instructions, to the old man to carry out."

After arriving at that conclusion, there was no more to be said on either side The interview terminated, and Rosamond and her husband hastened back to give Uncle Joseph his instructions at the hotel.

As they approached the door of their sitting- room they were surprised by hearing the sound of music inside. On entering, they found the old man crouched upon a stool, listening to a shabby little musical box which was placed on a table close by him, and which was playing an air that Rosamond recognized immediately as the "*Batti, Batti*" of Mozart.

"I hope you will pardon me for making music to keep myself company while you were away," said Uncle Joseph, starting up in some little confusion, and touching the stop of the box. "This is, if you please, of all my friends and companions, the oldest that is left. The divine Mozart, the king of all the composers that ever lived, gave it with his own hand, madam, to my brother, when Max was a boy in the music school at Vienna. Since my niece left me in Cornwall, I have not had the heart to make Mozart sing to me out of this little bit of box until today.

"Now that you have made me happy about Sarah again, my ears ache once more for the tiny ting-ting that has always the same friendly sound to my heart, travel where I may. But enough so!" said the old man, placing the box in the leather case by his side, which Rosamond had noticed there when she first saw him at Porthgenna. "I shall put back my singing-bird into his cage, and shall ask, when that is done, if you will be pleased to tell me what it is that the doctor has said?"

Rosamond answered his request by relating the substance of the conversation which had passed between her husband and the doctor. She then, with many preparatory cautions, proceeded to instruct the old man how to disclose the discovery of the Secret to his niece. She told him that the circumstances in connection with it must be first stated, not as events that had really happened, but as events that might be supposed to have happened.

She put the words that he would have to speak into his mouth, choosing the fewest and the plainest that would answer the purpose; she showed him how he might glide almost imperceptibly from referring to the discovery as a thing that might be supposed, to referring to it as a thing that had really happened; and she impressed upon him, as most important of all, to keep perpetually before his niece's mind the fact that the discovery of the Secret had not awakened one bitter feeling or one resentful thought toward her, in the minds of either of the persons who had been so deeply interested in finding it out.

Uncle Joseph listened with unwavering attention until Rosamond had done; then rose from his seat, fixed his eyes intently on her face, and detected an expression of anxiety and doubt in it which he rightly interpreted as referring to himself.

"May I make you sure, before I go away, that I shall forget nothing?" he asked, very earnestly. "I have no head to invent, it is true; but I have something in me that can remember, and the more especially when it is for Sarah's sake. If you please, listen now, and hear if I can say to you over again all that you have said to me?"

Standing before Rosamond, with something in his look and manner strangely and touchingly suggestive of the long-past days of his childhood, and of the time when he had said his earliest lessons at his mother's knee, he now repeated, from first to last, the instructions that had been given to him, with a verbal exactness, with an easy readiness of memory, which, in a man of his age, was nothing less than astonishing. "Have I kept it all as I should?" he asked simply, when he had come to an end. "And may I go my ways now, and take my good news to Sarah's bedside?"

It was still necessary to detain him, while Rosamond and

her husband consulted together on the best and safest means of following up the avowal that the Secret was discovered by the announcement of their own presence in London.

After some consideration, Leonard asked his wife to produce the document which the lawyer had drawn out that morning, and to write a few lines, from his dictation, on the blank side of the paper, requesting Mrs. Jazeph to read the form of declaration, and to affix her signature to it, if she felt that it required her, in every particular, to affirm nothing that was not the exact truth. When this had been done, and when the leaf on which Mrs. Frankland had written had been folded outward, so that it might be the first page to catch the eye, Leonard directed that the paper should be given to the old man, and explained to him what he was to do with it, in these words:

"When you have broken the news about the Secret to your niece," he said, "and when you have allowed her full time to compose herself, if she asks questions about my wife and myself (as I believe she will), hand that paper to her for answer, and beg her to read it. Whether she is willing to sign it or not, she is sure to inquire how you came by it. Tell her in return that you have received it from Mrs. Frankland—using the word 'received,' so that she may believe at first that it was sent to you from Porthgenna by post. If you find that she signs the declaration, and that she is not much agitated after doing so, then tell her, in the same gradual way in which you tell the truth about the discovery of the Secret, that my wife gave the paper to you with her own hands, and that she is now in London—"

"Waiting and longing to see her," added Rosamond. "You, who forget nothing, will not, I am sure, forget to say that."

The little compliment to his powers of memory made Uncle Joseph colour with pleasure, as if he was a boy again. Promising to prove worthy of the trust reposed in him, and engaging to come back and relieve Mrs. Frankland of all suspense before the day was out, he took his leave, and went forth hopefully on his momentous errand.

Rosamond watched him from the window, threading his way

337

in and out among the throng of passengers on the pavement, until he was lost to view. How nimbly the light little figure sped away out of sight! How gaily the unclouded sunlight poured down on the cheerful bustle in the street! The whole being of the great city basked in the summer glory of the day; all its mighty pulses beat high, and all its myriad voices whispered of hope!

CHAPTER 3
THE STORY OF THE PAST

The afternoon wore away and the evening came, and still there were no signs of Uncle Joseph's return.

Toward seven o'clock Rosamond was summoned by the nurse, who reported that the child was awake and fretful. After soothing and quieting him, she took him back with her to the sitting-room, having first, with her usual consideration for the comfort of any servant whom she employed, sent the nurse downstairs, with a leisure hour at her own disposal, after the duties of the day. "I don't like to be away from you, Lenny, at this anxious time," she said, when she rejoined her husband; "so I have brought the child in here. He is not likely to be troublesome again, and the having him to take care of is really a relief to me in our present state of suspense."

The clock on the mantelpiece chimed the half hour past seven. The carriages in the street were following one another more and more rapidly, filled with people in full dress, on their way to dinner, or on their way to the opera. The hawkers were shouting proclamations of news in the neighbouring square, with the second editions of the evening papers under their arms.

People who had been serving behind the counter all day were standing at the shop door to get a breath of fresh air. Working men were trooping homeward, now singly, now together, in weary, shambling gangs. Idlers, who had come out after dinner, were lighting cigars at corners of streets, and looking about them, uncertain which way they should turn their steps next.

It was just that transitional period of the evening at which the street-life of the day is almost over, and the street-life of the night has not quite begun—just the time, also, at which Rosamond, after vainly trying to find relief from the weariness of waiting by looking out of window, was becoming more and more deeply absorbed in her own anxious thoughts—when her attention was abruptly recalled to events in the little world about her by the opening of the room door. She looked up immediately from the child lying asleep on her lap, and saw that Uncle Joseph had returned at last.

The old man came in silently, with the form of declaration which he had taken away with him, by Mr. Frankland's desire, open in his hand. As he approached nearer to the window, Rosamond noticed that his face looked as if it had grown strangely older during the few hours of his absence. He came close up to her, and still not saying a word, laid his trembling forefinger low down on the open paper, and held it before her so that she could look at the place thus indicated without rising from her chair.

His silence and the change in his face struck her with a sudden dread which made her hesitate before she spoke to him. "Have you told her all?" she asked, after a moment's delay, putting the question in low, whispering tones, and not heeding the paper.

"This answers that I have," he said, still pointing to the declaration. "See! here is the name, signed in the place that was left for it—signed by her own hand."

Rosamond glanced at the paper. There indeed was the signature, "S. Jazeph"; and underneath it were added, in faintly traced, lines of parenthesis, these explanatory words: "Formerly, Sarah Leeson."

"Why don't you speak?" exclaimed Rosamond, looking at him in growing alarm. "Why don't you tell us how she bore it?"

"Ah! don't ask me, don't ask me!" he answered, shrinking back from her hand, as she tried in her eagerness to lay it on his arm. "I forgot nothing. I said the words as you taught me to say them—I went the roundabout way to the truth with my tongue; but my face took the short cut, and got to the end first. Pray, of your goodness to mo, ask nothing about it! Be satisfied, if you please, with knowing that she is better and quieter and happier now. The bad is over and past, and the good is all to come. If I tell you how she looked, if I tell you what she said, if I tell you all that happened when first she knew the truth, the fright will catch me round the heart again, and all the sobbing and crying that I have swallowed down will rise once more and choke me. I must keep my head clear and my eyes dry—or how shall I say to you all the things that I have promised Sarah, as I love my own soul and hers, to tell, before I lay myself down to rest tonight?"

He stopped, took out a coarse little cotton pocket-handkerchief, with a flaring white pattern on a dull blue ground, and dried a few tears that had risen in his eyes while he was speaking. "My life has had so much happiness in it," he said, self-reproachfully, looking at Rosamond, "that my courage, when it is wanted for the time of trouble, is not easy to find. And yet, I am German! all my nation are philosophers!—why is it that I alone am as soft in my brains, and as weak in my heart, as the pretty little baby there, that is lying asleep in your lap?"

"Don't speak again; don't tell us anything till you feel more composed," said Rosamond. "We are relieved from, our worst suspense now that we know you have left her quieter and better. I will ask no more questions; at least," she added, after a pause, "I will only ask one." She stopped; and her eyes wandered inquiringly toward Leonard. He had hitherto been listening with silent interest to all that had passed; but he now interposed gently, and advised his wife to wait a little before she ventured on saying anything more.

"It is such an easy question to answer," pleaded Rosamond. "I only wanted to hear whether she has got my message—whether she knows that I am waiting and longing to see her, if she will but let me come?"

"Yes, yes," said the old man, nodding to Rosamond with an air of relief. "That question is easy; easier even than you think, for it brings me straight to the beginning of all that I have got to say."

He had been hitherto walking restlessly about the room; sitting down one moment, and getting up the next. He now placed a chair for himself midway between Rosamond—who was sitting, with the child, near the window—and her husband, who occupied the sofa at the lower end of the room. In this position, which enabled him to address himself alternately to Mr. and Mrs. Frankland without difficulty, he soon recovered composure enough to open his heart unreservedly to the interest of his subject.

"When the worst was over and past," he said, addressing Rosamond—"when she could listen and when I could speak, the first words of comfort that I said to her were the words of your message. Straight she looked at me, with doubting, fearing eyes. 'Was her husband there to hear her?' she says. 'Did he look angry? did he look sorry? did he change ever so little, when you got that message from her?' And I said: 'No; no change, no anger, no sorrow—nothing like it.' And she said again: 'Has it made between them no misery? has it nothing wrenched away of all the love and all the happiness that binds them the one to the other?'

"And once more I answered to that, 'No! no misery, no wrench. See now! I shall go my ways at once to the good wife, and fetch her here to answer for the good husband with her own tongue'. While I speak those words there flies out over all her face a look—no, not a look—a light, like a sun-flash. While I can count one, it lasts; before I can count two, it is gone; the face is all dark again; it is turned away from, me on the pillow, and I see the hand that is outside the bed begin to crumple up the sheet. 'I shall go my ways, then, and fetch the good wife,' I say again.

"And she says, 'No, not yet. I must not see her, I dare not see her till she knows——;' and there she stops, and the hand crumples up the sheet again, and softly, softly, I say to her: 'Knows what?' and she answers me, 'What I, her mother, cannot tell, her to her face, for shame.' And I say, 'So, so, my child! tell it not, then—tell it not at all.'

"She shakes her head at me, and wrings her two hands together, like this, on the bed-cover. 'I must tell it,' she says. 'I must rid my heart of all that has been gnawing, gnawing, gnawing at it, or how shall I feel the blessing that the seeing her will bring to me, if my conscience is only clear?' Then she stops a little, and lifts up her two hands, so, and cries out loud, 'Oh, will God's mercy show me no way of telling it that will spare me before my child!'

"And I say, 'Hush, then! there is a way. Tell it to Uncle Joseph, who is the same as father to you! Tell it to Uncle Joseph, whose little son died in your arms; whose tears your hand wiped away, in the grief time long ago. Tell it, my child, to me; and I shall take the risk, and the shame (if there is shame), of telling it again. I, with nothing to speak for me but my white hair; I, with nothing to help me but my heart that means no harm—I shall go to that good and true woman, with the burden of her mother's grief to lay before her; and, in my soul of souls I believe it, she will not turn away!'"

He paused, and looked at Rosamond. Her head was bent down over her child; her tears were dropping slowly, one by one, on the bosom of his little white dress. Waiting a moment to collect herself before she spoke, she held out her hand to the old man, and firmly and gratefully met the look he fixed on her. "Oh, go on, go on!" she said. "Let me prove to you that your generous confidence in me is not misplaced."

"I knew it was not, from the first, as surely as I know it now!" said Uncle Joseph. "And Sarah, when I had spoken to her, she knew it too. She was silent for a little; she cried for a little; she leaned over from the pillow and kissed me here, on my cheek, as I sat by the bedside; and then she looked back, back, back, in her mind, to the Long Ago, and very quietly, very slowly, with her eyes looking into my eyes, and her hand resting so in mine, she spoke the words to me that I must now speak again to you, who sit here today as her judge, before you go to her tomorrow as her child."

"Not as her judge!" said Rosamond. "I cannot, I must not

hear you say that."

"I speak her words, not mine," rejoined the old man, gravely. "Wait before you bid me change them for others—wait till you know the end."

He drew his chair a little nearer to Rosamond, paused for a minute or two to arrange his recollections, and to separate them one from the other; then resumed.

"As Sarah began with me," he said, "so I, for my part, must begin also—which means to say, that I go down now through the years that are past, to the time when my niece went out to her first service. You know that the sea-captain, the brave and good man Treverton, took for his wife an artist on the stage— what they call play-actress here? A grand, big woman, and a handsome; with a life and a spirit and a will in her that is not often seen; a woman of the sort who can say.

"We will do this thing, or that thing—and do it in the spite and face of all the scruples, all the obstacles, all the oppositions in the world. To this lady there comes for maid to wait upon her, Sarah, my niece—a young girl—then, pretty and kind and gentle, and very, very shy. Out of many others who want the place, and who are bolder and bigger and quicker girls, Mistress Treverton, nevertheless, picks Sarah.

"This is strange, but it is stranger yet that Sarah, on her part, when she comes out of her first fears and doubts, and pains of shyness about herself, gets to be fond with all her heart of that grand and handsome mistress, who has a life and a spirit and a will of the sort that is not often seen. This is strange to say, but it is also, as I know from Sarah's own lips, every word of it true."

"True beyond a doubt," said Leonard. "Most strong attachments are formed between people who are unlike each other."

"So the life they led in that ancient house of Porthgenna began happily for them all," continued the old man. "The love that the mistress had for her husband was so full in her heart that it overflowed in kindness to everybody who was about her, and to Sarah, her maid, before all the rest. She would have nobody but Sarah to read to her, to work for her, to dress her in the morning and the evening, and to undress her at night.

"She was as familiar as a sister might have been with Sarah, when they two were alone, in the long days of rain. It was the game of her idle time—the laugh that she liked most—to astonish the poor country maid, who had never so much as seen what a theatre's inside was like, by dressing in fine clothes, and painting her face, and speaking and doing all that she had done on the theatre-scene in the days that were before her marriage. The more she puzzled Sarah with these jokes and pranks of masquerade, the better she was always pleased.

"For a year this easy, happy life went on in the ancient house—happy for all the servants—happier still for the master and mistress, but for the want of one thing to make the whole complete, one little blessing that was always hoped for, and that never came—the same, if you please, as the blessing in the long white frock, with the plump, delicate face and the tiny arms, that I see before me now."

He paused, to point the allusion by nodding and smiling at the child in Rosamond's lap; then resumed.

"As the new year gets on," he said, "Sarah sees in the mistress a change. The good sea-captain is a man who loves children, and is fond of getting to the house all the little boys and girls of his friends round about. He plays with them, he kisses them, he makes them presents—he is the best friend the little boys and girls love ever had. The mistress, who should be their best friend, too, looks on and says nothing—looks on, red sometimes, and sometimes pale; goes away into her room where Sarah is at work for her, and walks about and finds fault; and one day lets the evil temper fly out of her at her tongue, and says:

"'Why have I got no child for my husband to be fond of? Why must he kiss and play always with the children of other women? They take his love away for something that is not mine. I hate those children and their mothers too!' It is her passion that speaks then, but it speaks what is near the truth for all that. She will not make friends with any of those mothers; the ladies she is familiar-fond with are the ladies who have no children, or the ladies whose families are all upgrown. You think that was wrong of the mistress?"

He put the question to Rosamond, who was toying thoughtfully with one of the baby's hands which was resting in hers. "I think Mrs. Treverton was very much to be pitied," she answered, gently lifting the child's hand to her lips.

"Then I, for my part, think so too," said Uncle Joseph. "To be pitied?—yes! To be more pitied some months after, when there is still no child and no hope of a child, and the good sea-captain says, one day, 'I rust here, I get old with much idleness; I want to be on the sea again. I shall ask for a ship.' And he asks for a ship, and they give it him; and he goes away on his cruises—with much kissing and fondness at parting from his wife but still he goes away.

"And when he is gone, the mistress comes in again where Sarah is at work for her on a fine new gown, and snatches it away, and casts it down on the floor, and throws after it all the fine jewels she has got on her table, and stamps and cries with the misery and the passion that is in her. 'I would give all those fine things, and go in rags for the rest of my life, to have a child!' she says. 'I am losing my husband's love: he would never have gone away from me if I had brought him a child!'

"Then she looks in the glass, and says between her teeth: 'Yes! yes! I am a fine woman, with a fine figure, and I would change places with the ugliest, crookedest wretch in all creation if I could only have a child!'

"And then she tells Sarah that the Captain's brother spoke the vilest of all vile words of her, when she was married, because she was an artist on the stage; and she says, 'If I have no child, who but he—the rascal-monster that I wish I could kill!—who but he will come to possess all that the Captain has got?' And then she cries again, and says, 'I am losing his love—ah, I know it, I know it!—I am losing his love!' Nothing that Sarah can say will alter her thoughts about that.

"And the months go on, and the sea-captain comes back, and still there is always the same secret grief growing and growing in the mistress's heart—growing and growing till it is now the third year since the marriage, and there is no hope yet of a child; and once more the sea-captain gets tired on the land, and goes off again for his cruises—long cruises, this time; away, away, away, at the other end of the world."

Here Uncle Joseph paused once more, apparently hesitating a little about how he should go on with the narrative. His mind seemed to be soon relieved of its doubts, but his face saddened, and his tones sank lower, when he addressed Rosamond again.

"I must, if you please, go away from the mistress now," he said, "and get back to Sarah, my niece, and say one word also of a mining man, with the Cornish name of Polwheal. This was a young man that worked well and got good wage, and kept a good character. He lived with his mother in the little village that is near the ancient house; and, seeing Sarah from time to time, took much fancy to her, and she to him.

"So the end came that the marriage-promise was between them given and taken; as it happened, about the time when the sea-captain was back after his first cruises, and just when he was thinking of going away in a ship again. Against the marriage-promise nor he nor the lady his wife had a word to object, for the miner, Polwheal, had good wage and kept a good character.

"Only the mistress said that the loss of Sarah would be sad to her—very sad; and Sarah answered that there was yet no hurry to part. So the weeks go on, and the sea-captain sails away again for his long cruises; and about the same time also the mistress finds out that Sarah frets, and looks not like herself, and that the miner, Polwheal, he lurks here and lurks there, round about the house; and she says to herself, 'So! so! Am I standing too much in the way of this marriage? For Sarah's sake, that shall not be!' And she calls for them both one evening, and talks to them kindly, and sends away to put up the banns next morning the young man Polwheal.

"That night, it is his turn to go down into the Porthgenna mine, and work after the hours of the day. With his heart all light, down into that dark he goes. When he rises to the world again, it is the dead body of him that is drawn up—the dead body, with all the young life, by the fall of a rock, crushed out in a moment. The news flies here; the news flies there.

"With no break, with no warning, with no comfort near, it comes on a sudden to Sarah, my niece. When to her sweetheart that evening she had said goodbye, she was a young, pretty girl; when, six little weeks after, she, from the sick-bed where the shock threw her, got up, all her youth was gone, all her hair was gray, and in her eyes the fright-look was fixed that has never left them since."

The simple words drew the picture of the miner's death, and of all that followed it, with a startling distinctness—with a fearful reality. Rosamond shuddered, and looked at her husband. "Oh, Lenny!" she murmured, "the first news of your blindness was a sore trial to me—but what was it to this!"

"Pity her!" said the old man. "Pity her for what she suffered then! Pity her for what came after, that was worse! Yet five, six, seven weeks pass, after the death of the mining man, and Sarah in the body suffers less, but in the mind suffers more. The mistress, who is kind and good to her as any sister could be, finds out, little by little, something in her face which is not the pain-look, nor the fright-look, nor the grief-look; something which the eyes can see, but which the tongue cannot put into words.

"She looks and thinks, looks and thinks, till there steals into her mind a doubt which makes her tremble at herself, which drives her straight forward into Sarah's room, which sets her eyes searching through and through Sarah to her inmost heart. 'There is something on your mind besides your grief for the dead and gone,' she says, and catches Sarah by both the arms before she can turn way, and looks her in the face, front to front, with curious eyes, that search and suspect steadily.

"'The miner man, Polwheal,' she says; 'my mind misgives me about the miner man, Polwheal. Sarah! I have been more friend to you than mistress. As your friend I ask you now—tell me all the truth?' The question waits; but no word of answer! only Sarah struggles to get away, and the mistress holds her tighter yet, and goes on and says, 'I know that the marriage-promise passed between you and miner Polwheal; I know that if ever there was truth in man, there was truth in him; I know that he went out from this place to put the banns up, for you and for him, in the church.

"'Have secrets from all the world besides, Sarah, but have none from me. Tell me, this minute—tell me the truth! Of all the lost creatures in this big, wide world, are you—?' Before she can say the words that are next to come, Sarah falls on her knees, and cries out suddenly to be let go away to hide and die, and be heard of no more. That was all the answer she gave. It was enough for the truth then; it is enough for the truth now."

He sighed bitterly, and ceased speaking for a little while. No voice broke the reverent silence that followed his last words. The one living sound that stirred in the stillness of the room was the light breathing of the child as he lay asleep in his mother's arms.

"That was all the answer," repeated the old man, "and the mistress who heard it says nothing for some time after, but still looks straight forward into Sarah's face, and grows paler and paler the longer she looks—paler and paler, till on a sudden she starts, and at one flash the red flies back into her face. 'No,' she says, whispering and looking at the door, 'once your friend, Sarah, always your friend. Stay in this house, keep your own counsel, do as I bid you, and leave the rest to me.' And with that she turns round quick on her heel, and falls to walking up and down the room—faster, faster, faster, till she is out of breath. Then she pulls the bell with an angry jerk, and calls out loud at the door—'The horses! I want to ride;' then turns upon Sarah 'My gown for riding in! Pluck up your heart, poor creature! On my life and honour, I will save you. My gown, my gown, then; I am mad for a gallop in the open air!'

"And she goes out, in a fever of the blood, and gallops, gallops, till the horse reeks again, and the groom man who rides after her wonders if she is mad. When she comes back, for all that ride in the air, she is not tired. The whole evening after, she is now walking about the room, and now striking loud tunes all mixed up together on the piano. At the bedtime, she cannot rest. Twice, three times in the night she frightens Sarah by coming in to see how she does, and by saying always those same words over again: 'Keep your own counsel, do as I bid you, and leave the rest to me.'

"'In the morning she lies late, sleeps, gets up very pale and quiet, and says to Sarah, 'No word more between us two of what happened yesterday—no word till the time comes when you fear the eyes of every stranger who looks at you. Then I shall speak again. Till that time let us be as we were before I put the question yesterday, and before you told the truth!'"

At this point he broke the thread of the narrative again, explaining as he did so that his memory was growing confused about a question of time, which he wished to state correctly in introducing the series of events that were next to be described.

"Ah, well! well!" he said, shaking his head, after vainly endeavouring to pursue the lost recollection. "For once, I must acknowledge that I forget. Whether it was two months, or whether it was three, after the mistress said those last words to Sarah, I know not—but at the end of the one time or of the other she one morning orders her carriage and goes away alone to Truro. In the evening she comes back with two large flat baskets.

"On the cover of the one there is a card, and written on it are the letters 'S. L.' On the cover of the other there is a card, and written on it are the letters 'R. T.' The baskets are taken into the mistress's room, and Sarah is called, and the mistress says to her, 'Open the basket with S. L. on it; for those are the letters of your name, and the things in it are yours.' Inside there is first a box, which holds a grand bonnet of black lace; then a fine dark shawl; then black silk of the best kind, enough to make a gown; then linen and stuff for the under garments, all of the finest sort.

"'Make up those things to fit yourself,' says the mistress. 'You are so much littler than I, that to make the things up new is less trouble than, from my fit to yours, to alter old gowns.' Sarah, to all this, says in astonishment, 'Why?' And the mistress answers, 'I will have no questions. Remember what I said—Keep your own counsel, and leave the rest to me!' So she goes out; and the next thing she does is to send for the doctor to see her.

"He asks what is the matter; gets for answer that Mistress Treverton feels strangely, and not like herself; also that she thinks the soft air of Cornwall makes her weak. The days pass, and the doctor comes and goes, and, say what he may, those two answers are always the only two that he can get. All this time Sarah is at work; and when she has done, the mistress says, 'Now for the other basket, with R. T. on it; for those are the letters of my name, and the things in it are mine.'

"Inside this, there is first a box which holds a common bonnet of black straw; then a coarse dark shawl; then a gown of good common black stuff; then linen, and other things for the under garments, that are only of the sort called second best. 'Make up all that rubbish,' says the mistress, 'to fit me. No questions! You have always done as I told you; do as I tell you now, or you are a lost woman.'

"When the rubbish is made up, she tries it on, and looks in the glass, and laughs in a way that is wild and desperate to hear. 'Do I make a fine, buxom, comely servant-woman?' she says. 'Ha! but I have acted that part times enough in my past days on the theatre-scene.' And then she takes off the clothes again, and bids Sarah pack them up at once in one trunk, and pack the things she has made for herself in another. 'The doctor orders me to go away out of this damp, soft Cornwall climate, to where the air is fresh and dry and cheerful-keen,' she says, and laughs again, till the room rings with it.

"At the same time Sarah begins to pack, and takes some knick-knack things off the table, and among them a brooch which has on it a likeness of the sea-captain's face. The mistress sees her, turns white in the cheeks, trembles all over, snatches the brooch away and locks it up in the cabinet in a great hurry, as if the look of it frightened her. 'I shall leave that behind me,' she says, and turns round on her heel, and goes quickly out of the room. You guess now what the thing was that Mistress Treverton had it in her mind to do?"

He addressed the question to Rosamond first, and then re-peated it to Leonard. They both answered in the affirmative, and entreated him to go on.

"You guess?" he said. "It is more than Sarah, at that time, could do. "What with the misery in her own mind, and the strange ways and strange words of her mistress, the wits that were in her were all confused. Nevertheless, what her mistress has said to her, that she has always done; and together alone those two from the house of Porthgenna drive away.

"Not a word says the mistress till they have got to the jour-ney's end for the first day, and are stopping at their inn among strangers for the night. Then at last she speaks out. 'Put you on, Sarah, the good linen and the good gown tomorrow,' she says, 'but keep the common bonnet and the common shawl till we get into the carriage again. I shall put on the coarse linen and the coarse gown, and keep the good bonnet and shawl. We shall pass so the people at the inn, on our way to the carriage, with-out very much risk of surprising them by our change of gown. When we are out on the road again, we can change bonnets and shawls in the carriage—and then, it is all done. You are the married lady, Mrs. Treverton, and I am your maid who waits on you, Sarah Leeson.'

"At that, the glimmering on Sarah's mind breaks in at last: she shakes with the fright it gives her, and all she can say is, 'Oh, mistress! for the love of Heaven, what is it you mean to do?' 'I mean,' the mistress answers, 'to save you, my faithful servant, from disgrace and ruin; to prevent every penny that the captain has got from going to that rascal-monster, his brother, who slan-dered me; and, last and most, I mean to keep my husband from going away to sea again, by making him love me as he has never loved me yet. Must I say more, you poor, afflicted, frightened creature—or is it enough so?'

"And all that Sarah can answer, is to cry bitter tears, and to say faintly 'No.' 'Do you doubt,' says the mistress, and grips her by the arm, and looks her close in the face with fierce eyes—'Do you doubt which is best, to cast yourself into the world forsaken and disgraced and ruined, or to save yourself from shame, and make a friend of me for the rest of your life? You weak, wavering, baby woman, if you cannot decide for yourself, I shall for you. As I will, so it shall be! Tomorrow, and the day after that, we go on and on, up to the north, where my good fool of a doctor says the air is cheerful-keen—up to the north, where nobody knows me or has heard my name. I, the maid, shall spread the report that you, the lady, are weak in your health. No strangers shall you see, but the doctor and the nurse, when the times to call them comes. Who they may be, I know not; but this I do know, that the one and the other will serve our purpose without the least suspicion of what it is; and that when we get back to Cornwall again, the secret between us two will to no third person have been trusted, and will remain a Dead Secret to the end of the world?'

"With all the strength of the strong will that is in her, at the hush of night and in a house of strangers, she speaks those words to the woman of all women the most frightened, and most afflicted, the most helpless, the most ashamed. What need to say the end?

"On that night Sarah first stooped her shoulders to the burden that has weighed heavier and heavier on them with every year, for all her afterlife."

"How many days did they travel toward the north?" asked Rosamond, eagerly. "Where did the journey end? In England or in Scotland?"

"In England," answered Uncle Joseph. "But the name of the place escapes my foreign tongue. It was a little town by the side of the sea—the great sea that washes between my country and yours.

"There they stopped, and there they waited till the time came to send for the doctor and the nurse. And as Mistress Treverton had said it should be, so, from the first to the last, it was. The doctor and the nurse, and the people of the house were all strangers; and to this day, if they still live, they believe that Sarah was the sea-captain's wife, and that Mistress Treverton was the maid who waited on her.

"Not till they were far back on their way home with the child did the two change gowns again, and return each to her proper place. The first friend at Porthgenna that the mistress sends for to show the child to, when she gets back, is the doctor who lives there. 'Did you think what was the matter with me, when you sent me away to change the air?' she says, and laughs.

"And the doctor, he laughs too, and says, 'Yes, surely! but I was too cunning to say what I thought in those early days, because, at such times, there is always fear of a mistake. And you found the fine dry air so good for you that you stopped?' he says. 'Well, that was right! right for yourself and right also for the child.'

"And the doctor laughs again and the mistress with him, and Sarah, who stands by and hears them, feels as if her heart would burst within her, with the horror, and the misery, and the shame of that deceit.

"When the doctor's back is turned, she goes down on her knees, and begs and prays with all her soul that the mistress will repent, and send her away with her child, to be heard of at Porthgenna no more. The mistress, with that tyrant will of hers, has but four words of answer to give—'It is too late!' Five weeks after, the sea-captain comes back, and the 'Too late' is a truth that no repentance can ever alter more.

"The mistress's cunning hand that has guided the deceit from the first, guides it always to the last—guides it so that the captain, for the love of her and of the child, goes back to the sea no more—guides it till the time when she lays her down on the bed to die, and leaves all the burden of the secret, and all the guilt of the confession, to Sarah—to Sarah, who, under the tyranny of that tyrant will, has lived in the house, for five long years, a stranger to her own child!"

"Five years!" murmured Rosamond, raising the baby gently in her arms, till his face touched hers. "Oh, me! five long years a stranger to the blood of her blood, to the heart of her heart!"

"And all the years after!" said the old man. "The lonesome

353

years and years among strangers, with no sight of the child that was growing up, with no heart to pour the story of her sorrow into the ear of any living creature, not even into mine! 'Better,' I said to her, when she could speak to me no more, and when her face was turned away again on the pillow—'a thousand times better, my child, if you had told the Secret!'

"'Could I tell it,' she said, 'to the master who trusted me? Could I tell it afterward to the child, whose birth was a reproach to me? Could she listen to the story of her mother's shame, told by her mother's lips? How will she listen to it now, Uncle Joseph, when she hears it from you? Remember the life she has led, and the high place she has held in the world. How can she forgive me? How can she ever look at me in kindness again?'"

"You never left her," cried Rosamond, interposing before he could say more—"surely, surely, you never left her with that thought in her heart!"

Uncle Joseph's head drooped on his breast. "What words of mine could change it?" he asked, sadly.

"Oh, Lenny, do you hear that? I must leave you, and leave the baby. I must go to her, or those last words about me will break my heart." The passionate tears burst from her eyes as she spoke; and she rose hastily from her seat, with the child in her arms.

"Not tonight," said Uncle Joseph. "She said to me at parting, 'I can bear no more tonight; give me till the morning to get as strong as I can.'"

"Oh, go back, then, yourself!" cried Rosamond. "Go, for God's sake, without wasting another moment, and make her think of me as she ought! Tell her how I listened to you, with my own child sleeping on my bosom all the time—tell her—oh, no, no! words are too cold for it!

"Come here, come close, Uncle Joseph (I shall always call you so now); come close to me and kiss my child—her grandchild!— Kiss him on this cheek, because it has lain nearest to my heart. And now, go back, kind and dear old man—go back to her bed-side, and say nothing but that I sent that kiss to her!"

CHAPTER 4
THE CLOSE OF DAY

The night, with its wakeful anxieties, wore away at last; and the morning light dawned hopefully, for it brought with it the promise of an end to Rosamond's suspense.

The first event of the day was the arrival of Mr. Nixon, who had received a note on the previous evening, written by Leonard's desire, to invite him to breakfast. Before the lawyer withdrew, he had settled with Mr. and Mrs. Frankland all the preliminary arrangements that were necessary to effect the restoration of the purchase-money of Porthgenna Tower, and had dispatched a messenger with a letter to Bayswater, announcing his intention of calling upon Andrew Treverton that afternoon, on private business of importance relating to the personal estate of his late brother.

Toward noon, Uncle Joseph arrived at the hotel to take Rosamond with him to the house where her mother lay ill.

He came in, talking, in the highest spirits, of the wonderful change for the better that had been wrought in his niece by the affectionate message which he had taken to her on the previous evening. He declared that it had made her look happier, stronger, younger, all in a moment; that it had given her the longest, quietest, sweetest night's sleep she had enjoyed for years and years past; and, last, best triumph of all, that its good influence had been acknowledged, not an hour since, by the doctor himself.

Rosamond listened thankfully, but it was with a wandering attention, with a mind ill at ease. When she had taken leave of her husband, and when she and Uncle Joseph were out in the street together, there was something in the prospect of the approaching interview between her mother and herself which, in spite of her efforts to resist the sensation, almost daunted her. If they could have come together, and have recognized each other without time to think what should be first said or done on either side, the meeting would have been nothing more than the natural result of the discovery of the Secret.

But, as it was, the waiting, the doubting, the mournful story of the past, which had filled up the emptiness of the last day of suspense, all had their depressing effect on Rosamond's impulsive disposition. Without a thought in her heart which was not tender, compassionate, and true toward her mother, she now felt, nevertheless, a vague sense of embarrassment, which increased to positive uneasiness the nearer she and the old man drew to their short journey's end.

As they stopped at last at the house door, she was shocked to find herself thinking beforehand of what first words it would be best to say, of what first things it would be best to do, as if she had been about to visit a total stranger, whose favourable opinion she wished to secure, and whose readiness to receive her cordially was a matter of doubt.

The first person whom they saw after the door was opened was the doctor. He advanced toward them from a little empty room at the end of the hall, and asked permission to speak with Mrs. Frankland for a few minutes. Leaving Rosamond to her interview with the doctor, Uncle Joseph gaily ascended the stairs to tell his niece of her arrival, with an activity which might well have been envied by many a man of half his years.

"Is she worse? Is there any danger in my seeing her?" asked Rosamond, as the doctor led her into the empty room.

"Quite the contrary," he replied. "She is much better this morning; and the improvement, I find, is mainly due to the composing and cheering influence on her mind of a message which she received from you last night. It is the discovery of this which makes me anxious to speak to you now on the subject of one particular symptom of her mental condition which surprised and alarmed me when I first discovered it, and which has perplexed me very much ever since.

"She is suffering—not to detain you, and to put the matter at once in the plainest terms—under a mental hallucination of a very extraordinary kind, which, so far as I have observed it, affects her, generally, toward the close of the day, when the light gets obscure. At such times, there is an expression in her eyes as if she fancied some person had walked suddenly into the room.

She looks and talks at perfect vacancy, as you or I might look or talk at someone who was really standing and listening to us.

"The old man, her uncle, tells me that he first observed this when she came to see him (in Cornwall, I think he said) a short time since. She was speaking to him then on private affairs of her own, when she suddenly stopped just as the evening was closing in, startled him by a question on the old superstitious subject of the reappearance of the dead, and then, looking away at a shadowed corner of the room, began to talk at it—exactly as I have seen her look and heard her talk upstairs.

"Whether she fancies that she is pursued by an apparition, or whether she imagines that some living person enters her room at certain times, is more than I can say; and the old man gives me no help in guessing at the truth. Can you throw any light on the matter?"

"I hear of it now for the first time," answered Rosamond, looking at the doctor in amazement and alarm,

"Perhaps," he rejoined, "she may be more communicative with you than she is with me. If you could manage to be by her bedside at dusk today or tomorrow, and if you think you are not likely to be frightened by it, I should very much wish you to see and hear her, when she is under the influence of her delusion. I have tried in vain to draw her attention away from it, at the time, or to get her to speak of it afterward.

"You have evidently considerable influence over her, and you might therefore succeed where I have failed. In her state of health, I attach great importance to clearing her mind of everything that clouds and oppresses it, and especially of such a serious hallucination as that which I have been describing. If you could succeed in combating it, you would be doing her the greatest service, and would be materially helping my efforts to improve her health. Do you mind trying the experiment?"

Rosamond promised to devote herself unreservedly to this service, or to any other which was for the patient's good. The doctor thanked her, and led the way back into the hall again. Uncle Joseph was descending the stairs as they came out of the room. "She is ready and longing to see you," he whispered in Rosamond's ear.

"I am sure I need not impress on you again the very serious necessity of keeping her composed," said the doctor, taking his leave. "It is, I assure you, no exaggeration to say that her life depends on it."

Rosamond bowed to him in silence, and in silence followed the old man up the stairs.

At the door of a back room on the second floor Uncle Joseph stopped.

"She is there," he whispered eagerly. "I leave you to go in by yourself, for it is best that you should be alone with her at first. I shall walk about the streets in the fine warm sunshine, and think of you both, and come back after a little. Go in; and the blessing and the mercy of God go with you!" He lifted her hand to his lips, and softly and quickly descended the stairs again.

Rosamond stood alone before the door. A momentary tremor shook her from head to foot as she stretched out her hand to knock at it. The same sweet voice that she had last heard in her bedroom at West Winston answered her now. As its tones fell on her ear, a thought of her child stole quietly into her heart and stilled its quick throbbing. She opened the door at once and went in.

Neither the look of the room inside, nor the view from the window; neither its characteristic ornaments, nor its prominent pieces of furniture; none of the objects in it or about it, which would have caught her quick observation at other times, struck it now. From the moment when she opened the door, she saw nothing but the pillows of the bed, the head resting on them, and the face turned toward hers. As she stepped across the threshold, that face changed; the eyelids drooped a little, and the pale cheeks were tinged suddenly with burning red.

Was her mother ashamed to look at her?

The bare doubt freed Rosamond in an instant from all the self-distrust, all the embarrassment, all the hesitation about choosing her words and directing her actions which had fettered her generous impulses up to this time. She ran to the bed, raised the worn, shrinking figure in her arms, and laid the poor weary head gently on her warm, young bosom. "I have come at last, mother, to take my turn at nursing you," she said. Her heart swelled as those simple words came from it—her eyes overflowed—she could say no more.

"Don't cry!" murmured the faint, sweet voice timidly. "I have no right to bring you here and make you sorry. Don't, don't cry"

"Oh, hush! hush! I shall do nothing but cry if you talk to me like that!" said Rosamond. "Let us forget that we have ever been parted—call me by my name—speak to me as I shall speak to my own child, it' God spares me to see him grow up. Say 'Rosamond,' and—oh, pray, pray—tell me to do something for you!" She tore asunder passionately the strings of her bonnet, and threw it from her on the nearest chair. "Look! here is your glass of lemonade on the table. Say 'Rosamond, bring me my lemonade!' say it familiarly, mother! say it as if you knew that I was bound to obey you!"

She repeated the words after her daughter, but still not in steady tones—repeated them with a sad, wondering smile, and with a lingering of the voice on the name of Rosamond, as if it was a luxury to her to utter it.

"You made me so happy with that message and with the kiss you sent me from your child," she said, when Rosamond had given her the lemonade and was seated quietly by the bedside again. "It was such a kind way of saying that you pardoned me! It gave me all the courage I wanted to speak to you as I am speaking now. Perhaps my illness has changed me—but I don't feel frightened and strange with you, as I thought I should, at our first meeting after you knew the Secret. I think I shall soon get well enough to see your child. Is he like what you were at his age?. If he is, he must be very, very—" She stopped. "I may think of that," she added, after waiting a little, "but I had better not talk of it, or I shall cry too; and I want to have done with sorrow now."

While she spoke those words, while her eyes were fixed with wistful eagerness on her daughter's face, the whole instinct of neatness was still mechanically at work in her weak, wasted fingers. Rosamond had tossed her gloves from her on the bed but the minute before; and already her mother had taken them up, and was smoothing them out carefully and folding them neatly together, all the while she spoke.

"Call me 'mother' again," she said, as Rosamond took the gloves from her and thanked her with a kiss for folding them up. "I have never heard you call me 'mother' till now—never, never till now, from the day when you were born!"

Rosamond checked the tears that were rising in her eyes again, and repeated the word.

"It is all the happiness I want, to lie here and look at you, and hear you say that! Is there any other woman in the world, my love, who has a face so beautiful and so kind as yours?" She paused and smiled faintly. "I can't look at those sweet rosy lips now," she said, "without thinking how many kisses they owe me!"

"If you had only let me pay the debt before!" said Rosamond, taking her mother's hand, as she was accustomed to take her child's, and placing it on her neck. "If you had only spoken the first time we met, when you came to nurse me! How sorrowfully I have thought of that since! Oh, mother, did I distress you much in my ignorance? Did it make you cry when you thought of me after that?"

"Distress me! All my distress, Rosamond, has been of my own making, not of yours. My kind, thoughtful love! you said, 'Don't be hard on her'—do you remember? When I was being sent away, deservedly sent away, dear, for frightening you, you said to your husband, 'Don't be hard on her!' Only five words but,—oh, what a comfort it was to me afterward to think that you had said them! I did want to kiss you so, Rosamond, when I was brushing your hair.

"I had such a hard fight of it to keep from crying out loud when I heard you, behind the bed-curtains, wishing your little child goodnight. My heart was in my mouth, choking me all that time. I took, your part afterward, when I went back to my mistress—I wouldn't hear her say a harsh word of you. I could have looked a hundred mistresses in the face then, and contradicted them all. Oh, no, no, no! you never distressed me. My worst grief at going away was years and years before I came to nurse you at West Winston. It was when I left my place at Porthgenna; when I stole into your nursery on that dreadful morning, and when I saw you with both your little arms round my master's neck.

"The doll you had taken to bed with you was in one of your hands, and your head was resting on the Captain's bosom, just as mine rests now—oh, so happily, Rosamond!—on yours. I heard the last words he was speaking to you—words you were too young to remember. 'Hush! Rosie, dear,' he said, 'don't cry any more for poor mamma. Think of poor papa, and try to comfort him!' There, my love—there was the bitterest distress and the hardest to bear! I, your own mother, standing like a spy, and hearing him say that to the child I dared not own!

"'Think of poor papa!' My own Rosamond! you know, now, what father I thought of when he said those words! How could I tell him the Secret? how could I give him the letter, with his wife dead that morning—with nobody but you to comfort him—with the awful truth crushing down upon my heart, at every word he spoke, as heavily as ever the rock crushed down upon the father you never saw!"

"Don't speak of it now!" said Rosamond. "Don't let us refer again to the past: I know all I ought to know, all I wish to know of it. We will talk of the future, mother, and of happier times to come. Let me tell you about my husband. If any words can praise him as he ought to be praised, and thank him as he ought to be thanked, I am sure mine ought—I am sure yours will! Let me tell you what he said and what he did when I read to him the letter that I found in the Myrtle Room. Yes, yes, do let me!"

Warned by a remembrance of the doctor's last injunctions; trembling in secret, as she felt under her hand the heavy, toilsome, irregular heaving of her mother's heart, as she saw the rapid changes of colour, from pale to red, and from red to pale again, that fluttered across her mother's face, she resolved to let no more words pass between them which were of a nature to recall painfully the sorrows and the suffering of the years that were gone.

After describing the interview between her husband and herself which ended in the disclosure of the Secret, she led her mother, with compassionate abruptness, to speak of the future, of the time when she would be able to travel again, of the happiness of returning together to Cornwall, of the little festival they might hold on arriving at Uncle Joseph's house in Truro, and of the time after that, when they might go on still further to Porthgenna, or perhaps to some other place where new scenes and new faces might help them to forget all sad associations which it was best to think of no more.

Rosamond was still speaking on these topics, her mother was still listening to her with growing interest in every word that she said, when Uncle Joseph returned. He brought in with him a basket of flowers and a basket of fruit, which he held up in triumph at the foot of his niece's bed.

"I have been walking about, my child, in the fine bright sunshine," he said, "and waiting to give your face plenty of time to look happy, so that I might see it again as I want to see it always, for the rest of my life. Aha, Sarah! it is I who have brought the right doctor to cure you!" he added gaily, looking at Rosamond. "She has made you better already. "Wait but a little while longer, and she shall get you up from your bed again, with your two cheeks as red, and your heart as light, and your tongue as fast to chatter as mine. See the fine flowers and the fruit I have bought that is nice to your eyes, and nice to your nose, and nicest of all to put into your mouth!

"It is festival-time with us today, and we must make the room bright, bright, bright, all over. And then, there is your dinner to come soon; I have seen it on the dish—a cherub among chicken-fowls! And, after that, there is your fine sound sleep, with

Mozart to sing the cradle song, and with me to sit for watch, and to go downstairs when you wake up again, and fetch your cup of tea. Ah, my child, my child, what a fine thing it is to have come at last to this festival-day!"

With a bright look at Rosamond, and with both his hands full of flowers, he turned away from his niece to begin decorating the room. Except when she thanked the old man for the presents he had brought, her attention had never wandered, all the while he had been speaking, from her daughter's face; and her first words, when he was silent again, were addressed to Rosamond alone.

"While I am happy with my child," she said, "I am keeping you from yours. I, of all persons, ought to be the last to part you from each other too long. Go back now, my love, to your husband and your child; and leave me to my grateful thoughts and my dreams of better times."

"If you please, answer yes to that, for your mother's sake," said Uncle Joseph, before Rosamond could reply. "The doctor says she must take her repose in the day as well as her repose in the night. And how shall I get her to close her eyes, so long as she has the temptation to keep them open upon you?"

Rosamond felt the truth of those last words, and consented to go back for a few hours to the hotel, on the understanding that she was to resume her place at the bedside in the evening. After making this arrangement, she waited long enough in the room to see the meal brought up which Uncle Joseph had announced, and to aid the old man in encouraging her mother to partake of it. When the tray had been removed, and when the pillows of the bed had been comfortably arranged by her own hands, she at last prevailed on herself to take leave.

Her mother's arms lingered round her neck; her mother's cheek nestled fondly against hers. "Go, my dear, go now, or I shall get too selfish to part with you even for a few hours," murmured the sweet voice, in the lowest, softest tones. "My own Rosamond! I have no words to bless you that are good enough; no words to thank you that will speak as gratefully for me as they ought! Happiness has been long in reaching me—but, oh, how mercifully it has come at last!"

Before she passed the door, Rosamond stopped and looked back into the room. The table, the mantelpiece, the little framed prints on the wall were bright with flowers; the musical box was just playing the first sweet notes of the air from Mozart; Uncle Joseph was seated already in his accustomed place by the bed, with the basket of fruit on his knees; the pale, worn face on the pillow was tenderly lighted up by a smile; peace and comfort and repose, all mingled together happily in the picture of the sick-room, all joined in leading Rosamond's thoughts to dwell quietly on the hope of a happier time.

Three hours passed. The last glory of the sun was lighting the long summer day to its rest in the western heaven, when Rosamond returned to her mother's bedside.

She entered the room softly. The one window in it looked toward the west, and on that side of the bed the chair was placed which Uncle Joseph had occupied when she left him, and in which she now found him still seated on her return. He raised his fingers to his lips, and looked toward the bed, as she opened the door. Her mother was asleep, with her hand resting in the hand of the old man.

As Rosamond noiselessly advanced, she saw that Uncle Joseph's eyes looked dim and weary. The constraint of the position that he occupied, which made it impossible for him to move without the risk of awakening his niece, seemed to be beginning to fatigue him. Rosamond removed her bonnet and shawl, and made a sign to him to rise and let her take his place.

"Yes, yes!" she whispered, seeing him reply by a shake of the head. "Let me take my turn, while you go out a little and enjoy the cool evening air. There is no fear of waking her; her hand is not clasping yours, but only resting in it—let me steal mine into its place gently, and we shall not disturb her."

She slipped her hand under her mother's while she spoke. Uncle Joseph smiled as he rose from his chair, and resigned his place to her. "You will have your way," he said; "you are too

364

quick and sharp for an old man like me."

"Has she been long asleep?" asked Rosamond.

"Nearly two hours," answered Uncle Joseph. "But it has not been the good sleep I wanted for her—a dreaming, talking, restless sleep. It is only ten little minutes since she has been so quiet as you see her now."

"Surely you let in too much light?" whispered Rosamond, looking round at the window, through which the glow of the evening sky poured warmly into the room.

"No, no!" he hastily rejoined. "Asleep or awake, she always wants the light. If I go away for a little while, as you tell me, and if it gets on to be dusk before I come back, light both those candles on the chimneypiece. I shall try to be here again before that; but if the time slips by too fast for me, and if it so happens that she wakes and talks strangely, and looks much away from you into that far corner of the room there, remember that the matches and the candles are together on the chimneypiece, and that the sooner you light them after the dim twilight-time, the better it will be." With those words he stole on tiptoe to the door and went out.

His parting directions recalled Rosamond to a remembrance of what had passed between the doctor and herself that morning. She looked round again anxiously to the window.

The sun was just sinking beyond the distant housetops; the close of day was not far off.

As she turned her head once more toward the bed, a momentary chill crept over her. She trembled a little, partly at the sensation itself, partly at the recollection it aroused of that other chill which had struck her in the solitude of the Myrtle Room.

Stirred by the mysterious sympathies of touch, her mother's hand at the same instant moved in hers, and over the sad peacefulness of the weary face there fluttered a momentary trouble—the flying shadow of a dream. The pale, parted lips opened, closed, quivered, opened again; the toiling breath came and went quickly and more quickly; the head moved uneasily on the pillow; the eyelids half unclosed themselves; low, faint, moaning sounds poured rapidly from the lips—changed ere long to half-articulated sentences—then merged softly into intelligible speech, and uttered these words:

"Swear that you will not destroy this paper! Swear that you will not take this paper away with you if you leave the house!"

The words that followed these were whispered so rapidly and so low that Rosamond's ear failed to catch them. They were followed by a short silence. Then the dreaming voice spoke again suddenly, and spoke louder.

"Where? where? where?" it said. "In the bookcase? In the table-drawer? Stop! stop! In the picture of the ghost—

The last words struck cold on Rosamond's heart. She drew back suddenly with a movement of alarm—checked herself the instant after, and bent down over the pillow again. But it was too late. Her hand had moved abruptly when she drew back, and her mother awoke with a start and a faint cry—with vacant, terror-stricken eyes and with the perspiration standing thick on her forehead.

"Mother!" cried Rosamond, raising her on the pillow. "I have come back. Don't you know me?"

"Mother?" she repeated, in mournful, questioning tones- "Mother?" At the second repetition of the word a bright flush of delight and surprise broke out on her face, and she clasped both arms suddenly round her daughter's neck. "Oh, my own Rosamond !" she said. "If I had ever been used to waking up and seeing your dear face look at me, I should have known you sooner, in spite of my dream! Did you wake me, my love? or did I wake myself?"

"I am afraid I awoke you, mother."

"Don't say 'afraid.' I would wake from the sweetest sleep that ever woman had to see your face and to hear you say 'mother' to me. You have delivered me, my love, from the terror of one of my dreadful dreams. Oh, Rosamond! I think I should live to be happy in your love, If I could only get Porthgenna Tower out of my mind—if I could only never remember again the bedchamber where my mistress died, and the room where I hid the letter "

"We will try and forget Porthgenna Tower now," said Rosamond. "Shall we talk about other places where I have lived, which you have never seen? Or shall I read to you, mother? Have you got any book here that you are fond of?"

She looked across the bed at the table on the other side. There was nothing on it but some bottles of medicine, a few of Uncle Joseph's flowers in a glass of water, and a little oblong workbox. She looked round at the chest of drawers behind her—there were no books placed on the top of it. Before she turned toward the bed again, her eyes wandered aside to the window. The sun was lost beyond the distant house-tops; the close of day was near at hand.

"If I could forget! Oh, me, if I could only forget!" said her mother, sighing wearily, and beating her hand on the coverlid of the bed.

"Are you well enough, dear, to amuse yourself with work?" asked Rosamond, pointing to the little oblong box on the table, and trying to lead the conversation to a harmless, everyday topic, by asking questions about it. "What work do you do? May I look at it?"

Her face lost its weary, suffering look, and brightened once more into a smile. "There is no work there," she said. "All the treasures I had in the world, till you came to see me, are shut up in that one little box. Open it, my love, and look inside."

Rosamond obeyed, placing the box on the bed where her mother could see it easily. The first object that she discovered inside was a little book, in dark, worn-binding. It was an old copy of Wesley's Hymns. Some withered blades of grass lay between its pages; and on one of its blank leaves was this inscription- "Sarah Leeson, her book. The gift of Hugh Polwheal."

"Look at it, my dear," said her mother. "I want you to know it again. When my time comes to leave you, Rosamond, lay it on my bosom with your own dear hands, and put a little morsel of your hair with it, and bury me in the grave in Porthgenna churchyard, where he has been waiting for me to come to him so many weary years.

"The other things in the box, Rosamond, belong to you; they are little stolen keepsakes that used to remind me of my child, when I was alone in the world. Perhaps, years and years hence, when your brown hair begins to grow gray like mine, you may like to show these poor trifles to your children when you talk about me. Don't mind telling them, Rosamond, how your mother sinned and how she suffered—you can always lot these little trifles speak for her at the end. The least of them will show that she always loved you."

She took out of the box a morsel of neatly folded white paper, which had been placed under the book of Wesley's Hymns, opened it, and showed her daughter a few faded laburnum leaves that lay inside. "I took these from your bed, Rosamond, when I came, as a stranger, to nurse you at West Winston. I tried to take a ribbon out of your trunk, love, after I had taken the flowers—a ribbon that I knew had been round your neck. But the doctor came near at the time, and frightened me."

She folded the paper up again, laid it aside on the table, and drew from the box next a small print which had been taken from the illustrations to a pocket-book. It represented a little girl, in gypsy-hat, sitting by the waterside, and weaving a daisy chain. As a design, it was worthless; as a print, it had not even the mechanical merit of being a good impression. Underneath it a line was written in faintly pencilled letters—"Rosamond when I last saw her."

"It was never pretty enough for you," she said. "But still there was something in it that helped me to remember what my own love was like when she was a little girl."

She put the engraving aside with the laburnum leaves, and took from the box a leaf of a copy-book, folded in two, out of which there dropped a tiny strip of paper, covered with small printed letters. She looked at the strip of paper first.

"The advertisement of your marriage, Rosamond," she said. "I used to be fond of reading it over and over again to myself when I was alone, and trying to fancy how you looked and what dress you wore. If I had only known when you were going to be married, I would have ventured into the church, my love, to look at you and at your husband.

"But that was not to be—and perhaps it was best so, for the seeing you in that stolen way might only have made my trials harder to bear afterward. I have had no other keepsake to remind me of you, Rosamond, except this leaf out of your first copy-book. The nursemaid at Porthgenna tore up the rest one day to light the fire, and I took this leaf when she was not looking. See! you had not got as far as words then—you could only do up-strokes and down-strokes. Oh me! how many times I have sat looking at this one leaf of paper, and trying to fancy that I saw your small child's hand travelling over it, with the pen held tight in the rosy little fingers. I think I have cried oftener, my darling, over that first copy of yours than over all my other keepsakes put together."

Rosamond turned aside her face toward the window to hide the tears which she could restrain no longer.

As she wiped them away, the first sight of the darkening sky warned her that the twilight dimness was coming soon. How dull and faint the glow in the west looked now! how near it was to the close of day!

When she turned toward the bed again, her mother was still looking at the leaf of the copy-book.

"That nursemaid who tore up all the rest of it to light the fire," she said, "was a kind friend to me in those early days at Porthgenna. She used sometimes to let me put you to bed, Rosamond; and never asked questions, or teased me, as the rest of them did. She risked the loss of her place by being so good to me. My mistress was afraid of my betraying myself and betraying her if I was much in the nursery, and she gave orders that I was not to go there, because it was not my place.

"None of the other women-servants were so often stopped from playing with you and kissing you, Rosamond, as I was. But the nursemaid—God bless and prosper her for it!—stood my friend. I often lifted you into your little cot, my love, and wished you goodnight, when my mistress thought I was at work in her room. You used to say you liked your nurse better than you liked me, but you never told me so fretfully; and you always put your laughing lips up to mine whenever I asked you for a kiss."

Rosamond laid her hand gently on the pillow by the side of her mother's. "Try to think less of the past, dear, and more of the future," she whispered, pleadingly; "try to think of the time when my child will help you to recall those old days without their sorrow—the time when you will teach him to put his lips up to yours, as I used to put mine."

"I will try, Rosamond—but my only thoughts of the future, for years and years past, have been thoughts of meeting you in heaven. If my sins are forgiven, how shall we meet there? Shall you be like my little child to me—the child I never saw again after she was five years old? I wonder if the mercy of God will recompense me for our long separation on earth?

"I wonder if you will first appear to me in the happy world with your child's face, and be what you should have been to me on earth, my little angel that I can carry in my arms? If we pray in heaven, shall I teach you your prayers there, as some comfort to me for never having taught them to you here?"

She paused, smiled sadly, and, closing her eyes, gave herself in silence to the dream-thoughts that were still floating in her mind. Thinking that she might sink to rest again if she was left undisturbed, Rosamond neither moved nor spoke. After watching the peaceful face for some time, she became conscious that the light was fading on it slowly. As that conviction impressed itself on her, she looked round at the window once more.

The western clouds wore their quiet twilight colours already: the close of day had come.

The moment she moved the chair she felt her mother's hand on her shoulder. When she turned again toward the bed, she saw her mother's eyes open and looking at her looking at her,—as she thought, with a change in their expression, a change to vacancy.

"Why do I talk of heaven?" she said, turning her face suddenly toward the darkening sky, and speaking in low, muttering tones. "How do I know I am fit to go there? And yet, Rosamond, I am not guilty of breaking my oath to my mistress. You can say for me that I never destroyed the letter, and that I never took it away with me when I left the house. I tried to get it out of the Myrtle Room; but I only wanted to hide it somewhere else. I never thought to take it away from the house: I never meant to break my oath."

"It will be dark soon, mother. Let me get up for one moment to light the candles."

Her hand crept softly upward, and clung fast round Rosamond's neck.

"I never swore to give him the letter," she said. "There was no crime in the hiding of it. You found it in a picture, Rosamond? They used to call it a picture of the Porthgenna ghost. Nobody knew how old it was, or when it came into the house. My mistress hated it, because the painted face had a strange likeness to hers. She told me, when first I lived at Porthgenna, to take it down from the wall and destroy it.

"I was afraid to do that; so I hid it away, before ever you were born, in the Myrtle Room. You found the letter at the back of the picture, Rosamond? And yet that was a likely place to hide it in. Nobody had ever found the picture. Why should anybody find the letter that was hid in it?"

"Let me get a light, mother! I am sure you would like to have a light!"

"No! no light now. Give the darkness time to gather down there in the corner of the room. Lift me up close to you, and let me whisper."

The clinging arm tightened its grasp as Rosamond raised her in the bed. The fading light from the window fell full on her face, and was reflected dimly in her vacant eyes.

"I am waiting for something that comes at dusk, before the candles are lighted," she whispered, in low, breathless tones. "My mistress!—down there!" And she pointed away to the furthest corner of the roam near the door.

"Mother! for God's sake, what is it! what has changed you so?"

"That's right! say 'mother.' If she does come, she can't stop when she hears you call me 'mother,' when she sees us together at last, loving and knowing each other in spite of her. Oh, my kind, tender, pitying child! if you can only deliver me from her, how long may I live yet!—how happy we may both be!"

"Don't talk so! don't look so! Tell me quietly—dear, dear mother, tell me quietly."

"Hush! hush! I am going to tell you. She threatened me on her deathbed, if I thwarted her—she said she would come to me from the other world. Rosamond! I have thwarted her and she has kept her promise—all my life since, she has kept her promise! Look! Down there!"

Her left arm was still clasped round Rosamond's neck. She stretched her right arm out toward the far corner of the room, and shook her hand slowly at the empty air.

"Look!" she said. "There she is as she always comes to me at the close of day—with the coarse, black dress on, that my guilty hands made for her—with the smile that there was on her face when she asked me if she looked like a servant. Mistress! mistress! Oh. rest at last! the Secret is ours no longer! Rest at last! my child is my own again! Rest, at last; and come between us no more!"

She ceased, panting for breath; and laid her hot, throbbing cheek against the cheek of her daughter. "Call me 'mother' again!" she whispered. "Say it loud; and send her away from me forever!"

Rosamond mastered the terror that shook her in every limb, and pronounced the word.

Her mother leaned forward a little, still gasping heavily for breath, and looked with straining eyes into the quiet twilight dimness at the lower end of the room.

"Gone!!!" she cried suddenly, with a scream of exultation. "Oh, merciful, merciful God! gone at last!"

The next instant she sprang up on her knees in the bed. For

one awful moment her eyes shone in the gray twilight with a radiant, unearthly beauty, as they fastened their last look of fondness on her daughter's face. "Oh, my love! my angel!" she murmured, "how happy we shall be together now!" As she said the words, she twined her arms round Rosamond's neck, and pressed her lips rapturously on the lips of her child.

The kiss lingered till her head sank forward gently on Rosamond's bosom—lingered, till the time of God's mercy came, and the weary heart rested at last.

CHAPTER 5
FORTY THOUSAND POUNDS

No popular saying is more commonly accepted than the maxim which asserts that Time is the great consoler; and, probably, no popular saying more imperfectly expresses the truth. The work that we must do, the responsibilities that we must undertake, the example that we must set to others—these are the great consolers, for these apply the first remedies to the malady of grief. Time possesses nothing but the negative virtue of helping it to wear itself out.

Who that has observed at all, has not perceived that those among us who soonest recover from the shock of a great grief for the dead are those who have the most duties to perform toward the living? "When the shadow of calamity rests on our houses, the question with us is not how much time will suffice to bring back the sunshine to us again, but how much occupation have we got to force us forward into the place where the sunshine is waiting for us to come? Time may claim many victories, but not the victory over grief. The great consolation for the loss of the dead who are gone is to be found in the great necessity of thinking of the living who remain.

The history of Rosamond's daily life, now that the darkness of a heavy affliction had fallen on it, was in itself the sufficient illustration of this truth. It was not the slow lapse of time that helped to raise her up again, but the necessity which would not wait for time—the necessity which made her remember what was due to the husband who sorrowed with her, to the child whose young life was linked to hers, and to the old man whose helpless grief found no support but in the comfort she could give, learned no lesson of resignation but from the example she could set.

From the first the responsibility of sustaining him had rested on her shoulders alone. Before the close of day had been counted out, by the first hour of the night, she had been torn from the bedside by the necessity of meeting him at the door, and preparing him to know that he was entering the chamber of death. To guide the dreadful truth gradually and gently, till it stood face to face with him, to support him under the shock of recognizing it, to help his mind to recover after the inevitable blow had struck it at last—these were the sacred duties which claimed all the devotion that Rosamond had to give, and which forbade her heart, for his sake, to dwell selfishly on its own grief.

He looked like a man whose faculties had been stunned past recovery. He would sit for hours with the musical box by his side, patting it absently from time to time, and whispering to himself, as he looked at it, but never attempting to set it playing. It was the one memorial left that reminded him of all the joys and sorrows, the simple family interests and affections of his past life.

When Rosamond first sat by his side and took his hand to comfort him, he looked backward and forward with forlorn eyes from her compassionate face to the musical box, and vacantly repeated to himself the same words over and over again: "They are all gone—my brother Max, my wife, my little Joseph, my sister Agatha, and Sarah, my niece! I and my little bit of box are left alone together in the world. Mozart can sing no more. He has sung to the last of them now!"

The second day there was no change in him. On the third, Rosamond placed the book of Hymns reverently on her mother's bosom, laid a lock of her own hair round it, and kissed the sad, peaceful face for the last time.

The old man was with her at that silent leave-taking, and followed her away when it was over. By the side of the coffin, and afterward, when she took him back with her to her husband, he was still sunk in the same apathy of grief which had overwhelmed him from the first. But when they began to speak of the removal of the remains the next day to Porthgenna churchyard, they noticed that his dim eyes brightened suddenly, and that his wandering attention followed every word they said.

After a while he rose from his chair, approached Rosamond, and looked anxiously in her face. "I think I could bear it better if you would let me go with her," he said. "We two should have gone back to Cornwall together, if she had lived. Will you let us still go back together now that she has died?"

Rosamond gently remonstrated, and tried to make him see that it was best to leave the remains to be removed under the charge of her husband's servant, whose fidelity could be depended on, and whose position made him the fittest person to be charged with cares and responsibilities which near relations were not capable of undertaking with sufficient composure. She told him that her husband intended to stop in London, to give her one day of rest and quiet, which she absolutely needed, and that they then proposed to return to Cornwall in time to be at Porthgenna before the funeral took place; and she begged earnestly that he would not think of separating his lot from theirs at a time of trouble and trial when they ought to be all three most closely united by the ties of mutual sympathy and mutual sorrow.

He listened silently and submissively while Rosamond was speaking, but he only repeated his simple petition when she had done. The one idea in his mind now was the idea of going back to Cornwall with all that was left on earth of his sister's child. Leonard and Rosamond both saw that it would be useless to oppose it, both felt that it would be cruelty to keep him with them, and kindness to let him go away.

After privately charging the servant to spare him all trouble and difficulty, to humour him by acceding to any wishes that he might express, and to give him all possible protection and help without obtruding either officiously on his attention, they left him free to follow the one purpose of his heart which still connected him with the interests and events of the passing day. "I shall thank you better soon," he said at leave-taking, "for letting me go away out of this din of London with all that is left to me of Sarah, my niece. I will dry up my tears as well as I can, and try to have more courage when we meet again."

On the next day, when they were alone, Rosamond and her husband sought refuge from the oppression of the present in speaking together of the future, and of the influence which the change in their fortunes ought to be allowed to exercise on their plans and projects for the time to come. After exhausting this topic, the conversation turned next on the subject of their friends, and on the necessity of communicating to some of the oldest of their associates the events which had followed the discovery in the Myrtle Room.

The first name on their lips while they were considering this question was the name of Doctor Chennery; and Rosamond, dreading the effect on her spirits of allowing her mind to remain unoccupied, volunteered to write to the vicar at once, referring briefly to what had happened since they had last communicated with him, and asking him to fulfil that year an engagement of long standing, which he had made with her husband and herself, to spend his autumn holiday with them at Porthgenna Tower.

Rosamond's heart yearned for a sight of her old friend; and she knew him well enough to be assured that a hint at the affliction which had befallen her, and at the hard trial which she had undergone, would be more than enough to bring them together the moment Doctor Chennery could make his arrangements for leaving home.

The writing of this letter suggested recollections which called to mind another friend, whose intimacy with Leonard and Rosamond was of recent date, but whose connection with the earlier among the train of circumstances which had led to the discovery of the Secret entitled him to a certain share in their confidence. This friend was Mr. Orridge, the doctor at

West Winston, who had accidentally been the means of bringing Rosamond's mother to her bedside.

To him she now wrote, acknowledging the promise which
she had made on leaving West Winston to communicate the result of their search for the Myrtle Room; and informing him
that it had terminated in the discovery of some very sad events,
of a family nature, which were now numbered with the events
of the past. More than this it was not necessary to say to a friend
who occupied such a position toward them as that held by Mr.
Orridge.

Rosamond had written the address of this second letter, and
was absently drawing lines on the blotting-paper with her pen,
when she was startled by hearing a contention of angry voices
in the passage outside. Almost before she had time to wonder
what the noise meant, the door was violently pushed open, and
a tall, shabbily dressed, elderly man, with a peevish haggard face,
and a ragged gray beard, stalked in, followed indignantly by the
head waiter of the hotel.

"I have three times told this person," began the waiter, with a
strong emphasis on the word "person," "that Mr. and Mrs. Frankland—"

"Were not at home," broke in the shabbily dressed man, finishing the sentence for the waiter. "Yes, you told me that; and I
told you that the gift of speech was only used by mankind for
the purpose of telling lies, and that consequently I didn't believe
you. You have told a lie. Here are Mr. and Mrs. Frankland both
at home. I come on business, and I mean to have five minutes'
talk with them. I sit down unasked, and I announce my own
name—Andrew Treverton."

With those words, he took his seat coolly on the nearest chair. Leonard's cheeks reddened with anger while he was
speaking, but Rosamond interposed before her husband could
say a word.

"It is useless, love, to be angry with him," she whispered. "The
quiet way is the best way with a man like that." She made a sign
to the waiter, which gave him permission to leave the room—

then turned to Mr. Treverton. "You have forced your presence on us, sir," she said quietly, "at a time when a very sad affliction makes us quite unfit for contentions of any kind. We are willing to show more consideration for your age than you have shown for our grief. If you have anything to say to my husband, he is ready to control himself and to hear you quietly, for my sake."

"And I shall be short with him and with you, for my own sake," rejoined Mr. Treverton. "No woman has ever yet had the chance of sharpening her tongue long on me, or ever shall. I have come here to say three things. First, your lawyer has told me all about the discovery in the Myrtle Room, and how you made it. Secondly, I have got your money. Thirdly, I mean to keep it. What do you think of that?"

"I think you need not give yourself the trouble of remaining in the room any longer, if your only object in coming here is to tell us what we know already," replied Leonard. "We know you have got the money; and we never doubted that you meant to keep it."

"You are quite sure of that, I suppose?" said Mr. Treverton. "Quite sure you have no lingering hope that any future twists and turns of the law will take the money out of my pocket again and put it back into yours? It is only fair to tell you that there is not the shadow of a chance of any such thing ever happening, or of my ever turning generous and rewarding you of my own accord for the sacrifice you have made. I have been to Doctors' Commons, I have taken out a grant of administration, I have got the money legally, I have lodged it safe at my banker's, and I have never had one kind feeling in my heart since I was born. That was my brother's character of me, and he knew more of my disposition, of course, than anyone else. Once again, I tell you both, not a farthing of all that large fortune will ever return to either of you."

"And once again I tell you," said Leonard, "that we have no desire to hear what we know already. It is a relief to my conscience and to my wife's to have resigned a fortune which we had no right to possess; and I speak for her as well as for myself when I tell you that your attempt to attach an interested motive to our renunciation of that money is an insult to us both which you ought to have been ashamed to offer."

"That is your opinion, is it?" said Mr. Treverton. "You, who have lost the money, speak to me, who have got it, in that manner, do you?—Pray, do you approve of your husband's treating a rich man who might make both your fortunes in that way?" he inquired, addressing himself sharply to Rosamond.

"Most assuredly I approve of it," she answered. "I never agreed with him more heartily in my life than I agree with him now."

"Oh!" said Mr. Treverton. "Then it seems you care no more for the loss of the money than he does?"

"He has told you already," said Rosamond, "that it is as great a relief to my conscience as to his, to have given it up."

Mr. Treverton carefully placed a thick stick which he carried with him upright between his knees, crossed his hands on the top of it, rested his chin on them, and, in that investigating position, stared steadily in Rosamond's face.

"I rather wish I had brought Shrowl here with me," he said to himself. "I should like him to have seen this. It staggers me, and I rather think it would have staggered him. Both these people," continued Mr. Treverton, looking perplexedly from Rosamond to Leonard, and from Leonard back again to Rosamond, "are, to all outward appearance, human beings. They walk on their hind legs, they express ideas readily by uttering articulate sounds, they have the usual allowance of features, and in respect of weight, height, and size, they appear to me to be mere average human creatures of the regular civilized sort. And yet, there they sit, taking the loss of a fortune of forty thousand pounds as easily as Croesus, King of Lydia, might have taken the loss of a half-penny!"

He rose, put on his hat, tucked the thick stick under his arm, and advanced a few steps toward Rosamond.

"I am going now," he said. "Would you like to shake hands?"

Rosamond turned her back on him contemptuously.

Mr. Treverton chuckled with an air of supreme satisfaction.

Meanwhile Leonard, who sat near the fireplace, and whose colour was rising angrily once more, had been feeling for the bell-rope, and had just succeeded in getting it into his hand as Mr. Treverton approached the door.

"Don't ring, Lenny," said Rosamond. "He is going of his own accord."

Mr. Treverton stepped out into the passage—then glanced back into the room with an expression of puzzled curiosity on his face, as if he was looking into a cage which contained two animals of a species that he had never heard of before. "I have seen some strange sights in my time," he said to himself. "I have had some queer experience of this trumpery little planet, and of the creatures who inhabit it—but I never was staggered yet by any human phenomenon as I am staggered now by those two." He shut the door without saying another word, and Rosamond heard him chuckle to himself again as he walked away along the passage.

Ten minutes afterward the waiter brought up a sealed letter addressed to Mrs. Frankland. It had been written, he said, in the coffee-room of the hotel by the "person" who had intruded himself into Mr. and Mrs. Frankland's presence. After giving it to the waiter to deliver, he had gone away in a hurry, swinging his thick stick complacently, and laughing to himself.

Rosamond opened the letter.

On one side of it was a crossed check, drawn in her name, for Forty Thousand Pounds.

On the other side were these lines of explanation:

Take your money back again. First, because you and your husband are the only two people I have ever met with who are not likely to be made rascals by being made rich. Secondly, because you have told the truth, when letting it out meant losing money, and keeping it in, saving a fortune. Thirdly, because you are not the child of the player-woman. Fourthly, because you can't help yourself—for I shall leave it to you at my death, if you won't have it now. Goodbye. Don't come and see me, don't write grateful letters to me, don't invite me into the country, don't praise my generosity, and, above all things, don't have anything more to do with Shrowl.

Andrew Treverton.

The first thing Rosamond did, when she and her husband had a little recovered from their astonishment, was to disobey the injunction which forbade her to address any grateful letters to Mr. Treverton. The messenger, who was sent with her note to Bayswater, returned without an answer, and reported that he had received directions from an invisible man, with a gruff voice, to throw it over the garden wall, and to go away immediately after, unless he wanted to have his head broken.

Mr. Nixon, to whom Leonard immediately sent word of what had happened, volunteered to go to Bayswater the same evening, and make an attempt to see Mr. Treverton on Mr. and Mrs. Frankland's behalf. He found Timon of London more approachable than he had anticipated. The misanthrope was, for once in his life, in a good humour. This extraordinary change in him had been produced by the sense of satisfaction which he experienced in having just turned Shrowl out of his situation, on the ground that his master was not fit company for him after having committed such an act of folly as giving Mrs. Frankland back her forty thousand pounds.

"I told him," said Mr. Treverton, chuckling over his recollection of the parting scene between his servant and himself—"I told him that I could not possibly expect to merit his continued approval after what I had done, and that I could not think of detaining him in his place under the circumstances. I begged him to view my conduct as leniently as he could, because the first cause that led to it was, after all, his copying the plan of Porthgenna, which guided Mrs. Frankland to the discovery in the Myrtle Room.

"I congratulated him on having got a reward of five pounds for being the means of restoring a fortune of forty thousand; and I bowed him out with a polite humility that half drove him mad. Shrowl and I have had a good many tussles in our time; he was always even with me till today, and now I've thrown him on his back at last!"

Although Mr. Treverton was willing to talk of the defeat and dismissal of Shrowl as long as the lawyer would listen to him, he was perfectly unmanageable on the subject of Mrs. Frankland, when Mr. Nixon tried to turn the conversation to that topic. He would hear no messages—he would give no promise of any sort for the future.

All that he could be prevailed on to say about himself and his own projects was that he intended to give up the house at Bayswater, and to travel again for the purpose of studying human nature, in different countries, on a plan that he had not tried yet—the plan of endeavouring to find out the good that there might be in people as well as the bad. He said the idea had been suggested to his mind by his anxiety to ascertain whether Mr. and Mrs. Frankland were perfectly exceptional human beings or not.

At present, he was disposed to think that they were, and that his travels were not likely to lead to anything at all remarkable in the shape of a satisfactory result. Mr. Nixon pleaded hard for something in the shape of a friendly message to take back, along with the news of his intended departure. The request produced nothing but a sardonic chuckle, followed by this parting speech, delivered to the lawyer at the garden gate.

"Tell those two superhuman people," said Timon of London, "that I may give up my travels in disgust when they least expect it; and that I may possibly come back to look at them again—I don't personally care about either of them—but I should like to get one satisfactory sensation more out of the lamentable spectacle of humanity before I die."

CHAPTER 6
THE DAWN OF A NEW LIFE

Four days afterward, Rosamond and Leonard and Uncle Joseph met together in the cemetery of the church of Porthgenna.

The earth to which we all return had closed over Her: the weary pilgrimage of Sarah Leeson had come to its quiet end at last. The miner's grave from which she had twice plucked in secret her few memorial fragments of grass had given her the home, in death, which, in life, she had never known. The roar of the surf was stilled to a low murmur before it reached the place of her rest; and the wind that swept joyously over the open moor paused a little when it met the old trees that watched over the graves, and wound onward softly through the myrtle hedge which held them all embraced alike in its circle of lustrous green.

Some hours had passed since the last words of the burial service had been read. The fresh turf was heaped already over the mound, and the old headstone with the miner's epitaph on it had been raised once more in its former place at the head of the grave. Rosamond was reading the inscription softly to her husband.

Uncle Joseph had walked a little apart from them while she was thus engaged, and had knelt down by himself at the foot of the mound. He was fondly smoothing and patting the newly laid turf—as he had often smoothed Sarah's hair in the long past days of her youth—as he had often patted her hand in the after-time, when her heart was weary and her hair was gray.

" Shall we add any new words to the old, worn letters as they stand now?" said Rosamond, when she had read the inscription to the end. "There is a blank space left on the stone. Shall we fill it, love, with the initials of my mother's name, and the date of her death? I feel something in my heart which seems to tell me to do that, and to do no more."

"So let it be, Rosamond," said her husband. "That short and simple inscription is the fittest and the best."

She looked away, as he gave that answer, to the foot of the grave, and left him for a moment to approach the old man. "Take my hand, Uncle Joseph," she said, and touched him gently on the shoulder. "Take my hand and let us go back together to the house."

He rose as she spoke and looked at her doubtfully. The musical box inclosed in its well-worn leather case lay on the grave near the place where he had been kneeling. Rosamond took it up from the grass and slung it in the old place at his side which it had always occupied when he was away from home. He sighed a little as he thanked her. "Mozart can sing no more," he said. "He has sung to the last of them now!"

"Don't say 'to the last,' yet," said Rosamond—"don't say 'to the last,' Uncle Joseph, while I am alive. Surely Mozart will sing to me, for my mother's sake?"

A smile—the first she had seen since the time of their grief—trembled faintly round his lips. "There is comfort in that," he said; "there is comfort for Uncle Joseph still, in hearing that."

"Take my hand," she repeated softly. "Come home with us now."

He looked down wistfully at the grave. "I will follow you," he said, "if you will go on before me to the gate."

Rosamond took her husband's arm, and guided him to the path that led out of the churchyard. As they passed from sight, Uncle Joseph knelt down once more at the foot of the grave, and pressed his lips on the fresh turf.

"Goodbye, my child," he whispered, and laid his cheek for a moment against the grass before he rose again.

At the gate, Rosamond was waiting for him. Her right hand was resting on her husband's arm; her left hand was held out for Uncle Joseph to take.

"How cool the breeze is!" said Leonard. "How pleasantly the sea sounds! Surely this is a fine summer day!"

"The calmest and loveliest of the year," said Rosamond. "The only clouds on the sky are clouds of shining white; the only shadows over the moor lie light as down on the heather. Oh, Lenny, it is such a different day from that day of dull oppression and misty heat when we found the letter in the Myrtle Room! Even the dark tower of our old house, yonder, looks its brightest and best, as if it waited to welcome us to the beginning of a new life. I will make it a happy life to you, and to Uncle Joseph, if I can—happy as the sunshine we are walking in now. You shall never repent, love, if I can help it, that you have married a wife who has no claim of her own to the honours of a family name."

"I can never repent my marriage, Rosamond, because I can never forget the lesson that my wife has taught me."

"What lesson, Lenny?"

"An old one, my dear, which some of us can never learn too often. The highest honours, Rosamond, are those which no accident can take away—the honours that are conferred by Love and Truth."

"Blow up with the Brig!"

A Sailor's Story

I have got an alarming confession to make. I am haunted by a ghost.

If you were to guess for a hundred years, you would never guess what my ghost is. I shall make you laugh to begin with—and afterward I shall make your flesh creep. My ghost is the ghost of a bedroom candlestick.

Yes, a bedroom candlestick and candle, or a flat candlestick and candle—put it which way you like—that is what haunts me. I wish it was something pleasanter and more out of the common way; a beautiful lady, or a mine of gold and silver, or a cellar of wine and a coach and horses, and such like. But, being what it is, I must take it for what it is, and make the best of it; and I shall thank you kindly if you will help me out by doing the same.

I am not a scholar myself, but I make bold to believe that the haunting of any man with anything under the sun begins with the frightening of him. At any rate, the haunting of me with a bedroom candlestick and candle began with the frightening of me with a bedroom candlestick and candle—the frightening of me half out of my life; and, for the time being, the frightening of me altogether out of my wits. That is not a very pleasant thing to confess before stating the particulars; but perhaps you will be the readier to believe that I am not a downright coward, because you find me bold enough to make a clean breast of it already, to my own great disadvantage so far.

Here are the particulars, as well as I can put them:

I was apprenticed to the sea when I was about as tall as my own walking-stick; and I made good enough use of my time to be fit for a mate's berth at the age of twenty-five years.

It was in the year eighteen hundred and eighteen, or nineteen, I am not quite certain which, that I reached the before-mentioned age of twenty-five. You will please to excuse my memory not being very good for dates, names, numbers, places, and such like. No fear, though, about the particulars I have undertaken to tell you of; I have got them all shipshape in my recollection; I can see them, at this moment, as clear as noonday in my own mind. But there is a mist over what went before, and, for the matter of that, a mist likewise over much that came after—and it's not very likely to lift at my time of life, is it?

Well, in eighteen hundred and eighteen, or nineteen, when there was peace in our part of the world—and not before it was wanted, you will say—there was fighting, of a certain scampering, scrambling kind, going on in that old battlefield which we seafaring men know by the name of the Spanish Main.

The possessions that belonged to the Spaniards in South America had broken into open mutiny and declared for themselves years before. There was plenty of bloodshed between the new Government and the old; but the new had got the best of it, for the most part, under one General Bolivar—a famous man in his time, though he seems to have dropped out of people's memories now.

Englishmen and Irishmen with a turn for fighting, and nothing particular to do at home, joined the general as volunteers; and some of our merchants here found it a good venture to send supplies across the ocean to the popular side. There was risk enough, of course, in doing this; but where one speculation of the kind succeeded, it made up for two, at the least, that failed. And that's the true principle of trade, wherever I have met with it, all the world over.

Among the Englishmen who were concerned in this Spanish-American business, I, your humble servant, happened in a small way to be one.

I was then mate of a brig belonging to a certain firm in the City, which drove a sort of general trade, mostly in queer out-of-the-way places, as far from home as possible; and which freighted the brig, in the year I am speaking of, with a cargo of gunpowder for General Bolivar and his volunteers. Nobody knew anything about our instructions, when we sailed, except the captain; and he didn't half seem to like them. I can't rightly say how many barrels of powder we had on board, or how much each barrel held I only know we had no other cargo. The name of the brig was the *Good Intent*—a queer name enough, you will tell me, for a vessel laden with gunpowder, and sent to help a revolution. And as far as this particular voyage was concerned, so it was. I mean that for a joke, and I hope you will encourage me by laughing at it.

The *Good Intent* was the craziest old tub of a vessel I ever went to sea in, and the worst found in all respects. She was two hundred and thirty, or two hundred and eighty tons burden, I forget which; and she had a crew of eight, all told—nothing like as many as we ought by rights to have had to work the brig. However, we were well and honestly paid our wages; and we had to set that against the chance of foundering at sea, and, on this occasion, likewise the chance of being blown up into the bargain.

In consideration of the nature of our cargo, we were harassed with new regulations, which we didn't at all like, relative to smoking our pipes and lighting our lanterns; and, as usual in such cases, the captain, who made the regulations, preached what he didn't practice. Not a man of us was allowed to have a bit of lighted candle in his hand when he went below—except the skipper; and he used his light, when he turned in, or when he looked over his charts on the cabin table, just as usual.

This light was a common kitchen candle or "dip," and it stood in an old battered flat candlestick, with all the japan worn and melted off, and all the tin showing through. It would have been more seaman-like and suitable in every respect if he had had a lamp or a lantern; but he stuck to his old candlestick; and that same old candlestick has ever afterward stuck to me. That's another joke, if you please, and a better one than the first, in my opinion.

Well (I said "well" before, but it's a word that helps a man on like), we sailed in the brig, and shaped our course, first, for the Virgin Islands, in the West Indies; and, after sighting them, we made for the Leeward Islands next, and then stood on due south, till the lookout at the mast-head hailed the deck and said he saw land. That land was the coast of South America. "We had had a wonderful voyage so far. We had lost none of our spars or sails, and not a man of us had been harassed to death at the pumps. It wasn't often the *Good Intent* made such a voyage as that, I can tell you.

I was sent aloft to make sure about the land, and I did make sure of it.

When I reported the same to the skipper, he went below, and had a look at his letter of instructions and the chart. When he came on deck again, he altered our course a trifle to the eastward—I forget the point on the compass, but that don't matter. What I do remember is, that it was dark before we closed in with the land. We kept the lead going, and hove the brig to in from four to five fathoms water, or it might be six—I can't say for certain.

I kept a sharp eye to the drift of the vessel, none of us knowing how the currents ran on that coast. We all wondered why the skipper didn't anchor; but he said No, he must first show a light at the foretopmast-head, and wait for an answering light on shore. We did wait, and nothing of the sort appeared. It was starlight and calm. What little wind there was came in puffs off the land. I suppose we waited, drifting a little to the westward, as I made it out, best part of an hour before anything happened—and then, instead of seeing the light on shore, we saw a boat coming toward us, rowed by two men only.

We hailed them, and they answered "Friends!" and hailed us by our name. They came on board. One of them was an Irishman, and the other was a coffee-coloured native pilot, who jabbered a little English.

The Irishman handed a note to our skipper, who showed it to me. It informed us that the part of the coast we were off was not oversafe for discharging our cargo, seeing that spies of the enemy (that is to say, of the old Government) had been taken and shot in the neighbourhood the day before. We might trust the brig to the native pilot; and he had his instructions to take us to another part of the coast.

The note was signed by the proper parties; so we let the Irishman go back alone in the boat, and allowed the pilot to exercise his lawful authority over the brig. Ho kept us stretching off from the land till noon the next day—his instructions, seemingly, ordering him to keep us well out of sight of the shore. We only altered our course in the afternoon, so as to close in with the land again a little before midnight.

This same pilot was about as ill-looking a vagabond as ever I saw; a skinny, cowardly, quarrelsome mongrel, who swore at the men in the vilest broken English, till they were every one of them ready to pitch him overboard. The skipper kept them quiet, and I kept them quiet; for the pilot being given us by our instructions, we were bound to make the best of him. Near nightfall, however, with the best will in the world to avoid it, I was unlucky enough to quarrel with him.

He wanted to go below with his pipe, and I stopped him, of course, because it was contrary to orders. Upon that he tried to hustle by me, and I put him away with my hand. I never meant to push him down; but somehow I did. He picked himself up as quick as lightning, and pulled out his knife. I snatched it out of his hand, slapped his murderous face for him, and threw his weapon overboard. He gave me one ugly look, and walked aft. I didn't think much of the look then, but I remembered it a little too well afterward.

We were close in with the land again, just as the wind failed us, between eleven and twelve that night, and dropped our anchor by the pilot's directions.

It was pitch-dark, and a dead, airless calm. The skipper was on deck, with two of our best men for watch. The rest were below, except the pilot, who coiled himself up, more like a snake than a man, on the forecastle. It was not my watch till four in the morning. But I didn't like the look of the night, or the pilot, or the state of things generally, and I shook myself down on deck to get my nap there, and be ready for anything at a moment's notice.

The last I remember was the skipper whispering to me that he didn't like the look of things either, and that he would go below and consult his instructions again. That is the last I remember, before the slow, heavy, regular roll of the old brig on the groundswell rocked me off to sleep.

I was awoke by a scuffle on the forecastle and a gag in my mouth. There was a man on my breast and a man on my legs, and I was bound hand and foot in half a minute.

The brig was in the hands of the Spaniards. They were swarming all over her. I heard six heavy splashes in the water, one after another. I saw the captain stabbed to the heart as he came running up the companion, and I heard a seventh splash in the water.

Except myself, every soul of us on board had been murdered and thrown into the sea. Why I was left, I couldn't think, till I saw the pilot stoop over me with a lantern and look, to make sure of who I was. There was a devilish grin on his face, and he nodded his head at me, as much as to say, You were the man who hustled me down and slapped my face, and I mean to play the game of cat and mouse with you in return for it!

I could neither move nor speak, but I could see the Spaniards take off the main hatch and rig the purchases for getting up the cargo. A quarter of an hour afterward I heard the sweeps of a schooner, or other small vessel, in the water. The strange craft was laid alongside of us, and the Spaniards set to work to discharge our cargo into her.

They all worked hard except the pilot; and he came from time to time, with his lantern, to have another look at me, and to grin and nod always in the same devilish way. I am old enough now not to be ashamed of confessing the truth, and I don't mind acknowledging that the pilot frightened me.

The fright, and the bonds, and the gag, and the not being able to stir hand or foot, had pretty nigh worn me out by the time the Spaniards gave over work. This was just as the dawn broke. They had shifted good part of our cargo on board their vessel, but nothing like all of it, and they were sharp enough to be off with what they had got before daylight.

I need hardly say that I had made up my mind by this time to the worst I could think of. The pilot, it was clear enough, was one of the spies of the enemy, who had wormed himself into the confidence of our consignees without being suspected. He, or more likely his employers, had got knowledge enough of us to suspect what our cargo was; we had been anchored for the night in the safest berth for them to surprise us in; and we had paid the penalty of having a small crew, and consequently an insufficient watch. All this was clear enough—but what did the pilot mean to do with me

On the word of a man, it makes my flesh creep now, only to tell you what he did with me.

After all the rest of them were out of the brig, except the pilot and two Spanish seamen, these last took me up, bound and gagged as I was, lowered me into the hold of the vessel, and laid me along on the floor, lashing me to it with ropes' ends, so that I could just turn from one side to the other, but could not roll myself fairly over, so as to change my place. They then left me. Both of them were the worse for liquor; but the devil of a pilot was sober—mind that!—as sober as I am at the present moment.

I lay in the dark for a little while, with my heart thumping as if it was going to jump out of me. I lay about five minutes or so when the pilot came down into the hold alone.

He had the captain's cursed flat candlestick and a carpenter's awl in one hand, and a long thin twist of cotton-yarn, well oiled, in the other. He put the candlestick, with a new "dip" candle lighted in it, down on the floor about two feet from my face, and close against the side of the vessel. The light was feeble enough; but it was sufficient to show a dozen barrels of gunpowder or more left all round me in the hold of the brig. I began to suspect what he was after the moment I noticed the barrels. The horrors laid hold of me from head to foot, and the sweat poured off my face like water.

I saw him go next to one of the barrels of powder standing against the side of the vessel in a line with the candle, and about three feet, or rather better, away from it. He bored a hole in the side of the barrel with his awl, and the horrid powder came trickling out, as black as hell, and dripped into the hollow of his hand, which he held to catch it. When he had got a good handful, he stopped up the hole by jamming one end of his oiled twist of cotton-yarn fast into it, and he then rubbed the powder into the whole length of the yarn till he had blackened every hairbreadth of it.

The next thing he did—as true as I sit here, as true as the heaven above us all—the next thing he did was to carry the free end of his long, lean, black, frightful slow-match to the lighted candle alongside my face. He tied it (the bloody-minded villain!) in several folds round the tallow dip, about a third of the distance down, measuring from the flame of the wick to the lip of the candlestick. He did that; he looked to see that my lashings were all safe; and then he put his face close to mine, and whispered in my ear, "Blow up with the brig!"

He was on deck again the moment after, and he and the two others shoved the hatch on over me. At the furthest end from where I lay they had not fitted it down quite true, and I saw a blink of daylight glimmering in when I looked in that direction. I heard the sweeps of the schooner fall into the water—splash! splash! fainter and fainter, as they swept the vessel out in the dead calm, to be ready for the wind in the offing. Fainter and fainter, splash, splash! for a quarter of an hour more.

While those sounds were in my ears, my eyes were fixed on the candle.

It had been freshly lighted. If left to itself, it would burn for between six and seven hours. The slow-match was twisted round it about a third of the way down, and therefore the flame would be about two hours reaching it.

There I lay, gagged, bound, lashed to the floor; seeing my own life burning down with the candle by my side—there I lay, alone on the sea, doomed to be blown to atoms, and to see that doom drawing on, nearer and nearer with every fresh second of time, through nigh on two hours to come; powerless to help myself, and speechless to call for help to others. The wonder to me is that I didn't cheat the flame, the slow-match, and the powder, and die of the horror of my situation before my first half-hour was out in the hold of the brig.

I can't exactly say how long I kept the command of my senses after I had ceased to hear the splash of the schooner's sweeps in the water. I can trace back everything I did and everything I thought, up to a certain point; but, once past that, I get all abroad, and lose myself in my memory now, much as I lost myself in my own feelings at the time.

The moment the hatch was covered over me, I began, as every other man would have begun in my place, with a frantic effort to free my hands. In the mad panic I was in, I cut my flesh with the lashings as if they had been knife-blades, but I never stirred them. There was less chance still of freeing my legs, or of tearing myself from the fastenings that held me to the floor. I gave in when I was all but suffocated for want of breath. The gag, you will please to remember, was a terrible enemy to me; I could only breathe freely through my nose and that is but a poor vent when a man is straining his strength as far as ever it will go.

I gave in and lay quiet, and got my breath again, my eyes glaring and straining at the candle all the time.

While I was staring at it, the notion struck me of trying to blow out the flame by pumping a long breath at it suddenly through my nostrils. It was too high above me, and too far away from me, to be reached in that fashion. I tried, and tried, and tried; and then I gave in again, and lay quiet again, always with my eyes glaring at the candle, and the candle glaring at me. The splash of the schooner's sweeps was very faint by this time. I could only just hear them in the morning stillness. Splash! splash!—fainter and fainter—splash! splash!

Without exactly feeling my mind going, I began to feel it getting queer as early as this. The snuff of the candle was growing taller and taller, and the length of tallow between the flame and the slow-match, which was the length of my life, was getting shorter and shorter. I calculated that I had rather less than an hour and a half to live.

An hour and a half! Was there a chance in that time of a boat pulling off to the brig from shore? Whether the land near which the vessel was anchored was in possession of our side, or in possession of the enemy's side, I made out that they must, sooner or later, send to hail the brig merely because she was a stranger in those parts. The question for me was, how soon? The sun had not risen yet, as I could tell by looking through the chink in the hatch.

There was no coast village near us, as we all knew, before the brig was seized, by seeing no lights on shore. There was no wind, as I could tell by listening, to bring any strange vessel near. If I had had six hours to live, there might have been a chance for me, reckoning from sunrise to noon. But with an hour and a half, which had dwindled to an hour and a quarter by this time—or, in other words, with the earliness of the morning, the uninhabited coast, and the dead calm all against me—there was not the ghost of a chance. As I felt that, I had another struggle-the last—with my bonds, and only cut myself the deeper for my pains. I gave in once more, and lay quiet, and listened for the splash of the sweeps.

Gone! Not a sound could I hear but the blowing of a fish now and then on the surface of the sea, and the creak of the brig's crazy old spars, as she rolled gently from side to side with the little swell there was on the quiet water.

An hour and a quarter. The wick grew terribly as the quarter slipped away, and the charred top of it began to thicken and spread out mushroom-shape. It would fall off soon. Would it fall off red-hot, and would the swing of the brig cant it over the side of the candle and let it down on the slow-match? If it would, I had about ten minutes to live instead of an hour.

This discovery set my mind for a minute on a new tack altogether. I began to ponder with myself what sort of a death blowing up might be. Painful! Well, it would be, surely, too sudden for that. Perhaps just one crash inside me, or outside me, or both; and nothing more! Perhaps not even a crash; that and death and the scattering of this living body of mine into millions of fiery sparks, might all happen in the same instant! I couldn't make it out; I couldn't settle how it would be. The minute of calmness in my mind left it before I had half done thinking; and I got all abroad again.

When I came back to my thoughts, or when they came back to me (I can't say which), the wick was awfully tall, the flame was burning with a smoke above it, the charred top was broad and red, and heavily spreading out to its fall.

My despair and horror at seeing it took me in a new way, which was good and right, at any rate, for my poor soul. I tried to pray—in my own heart, you will understand, for the gag put all lip-praying out of my power. I tried, but the candle seemed to burn it up in me. I struggled hard to force my eyes from the slow, murdering flame, and to look up through the chink in the hatch at the blessed daylight. I tried once, tried twice; and gave it up.

I next tried only to shut my eyes, and keep them shut— once—twice—and the second time I did it. "God bless old mother, and sister Lizzie; God keep them both, and forgive me." That was all I had time to say, in my own heart, before my eyes opened again, in spite of me, and the flame of the candle flew into them, flew all over me, and burned up the rest of my thoughts in an instant.

I couldn't hear the fish blowing now; I couldn't hear the creak of the spars; I couldn't think; I couldn't feel the sweat of my own death agony on my face—I could only look at the heavy, charred top of the wick. It swelled, tottered, bent over to one side, dropped—red-hot at the moment of its fall—black and harmless, even before the swing of the brig had canted it over into the bottom of the candlestick.

I caught myself laughing.

Yes! laughing at the safe fall of the bit of wick. But for the gag, I should have screamed with laughing. As it was, I shook with it inside me—shook till the blood was in my head, and I was all but suffocated for want of breath. I had just sense enough left to feel that my own horrid laughter at that awful moment was a sign of my brain going at last. I had just sense enough left to make another struggle before my mind broke loose like a frightened horse, and ran away with me.

One comforting look at the blink of daylight through the hatch was what I tried for once more. The fight to force my eyes from the candle and to get that one look at the daylight was the hardest I had had yet; and I lost the fight. The flame had hold of my eyes as fast as the lashings had hold of my hands. I couldn't look away from it. I couldn't even shut my eyes, when I tried that next, for the second time. There was the wick growing tall once more. There was the space of unburned candle between the light and the slow-match shortened to an inch or less.

How much life did that inch leave me? Three-quarters of an hour? Half an hour? Fifty minutes? Twenty minutes? Steady! an inch of tallow-candle would burn longer than twenty minutes. An inch of tallow! the notion of a man's body and soul being kept together by an inch of tallow!

Wonderful! Why, the greatest king that sits on a throne can't keep a man's body and soul together; and here's an inch of tallow that can do what the king can't! There's something to tell mother when I get home which will surprise her more than all the rest of my voyages put together. I laughed inwardly again at the thought of that, and shook and swelled and suffocated myself, till the light of the candle leaped in through my eyes, and licked up the laughter, and burned it out of me, and made me all empty and cold and quiet once more.

Mother and Lizzie. I don't know when they came back; but

they did come back—not, as it seemed to me into my mind this time, but right down bodily before me, in the hold of the brig.

Yes: sure enough, there was Lizzie, just as light-hearted as usual, laughing at me. Laughing? Well, why not? Who is to blame Lizzie for thinking I'm lying on my back, drunk in the cellar, with the beer-barrels all round me? Steady! she's crying now—spinning round and round in a fiery mist, wringing her hands, screeching out for help—fainter and fainter, like the splash of the schooner's sweeps. Gone—burned up in the fiery mist! Mist? fire? no; neither one nor the other.

It's mother makes the light—mother knitting, with ten flaming points at the ends of her fingers and thumbs, and slow-matches hanging in bunches all round her face instead of her own gray hair. Mother in her old armchair, and the pilot's long skinny hands hanging over the back of the chair, dripping with gunpowder.

No! no gunpowder, no chair, no mother—nothing but the pilot's face, shining red-hot, like a sun, in the fiery mist; turning upside down in the fiery mist; running backward and forward along the slow-match, in the fiery mist; spinning millions of miles in a minute, in the fiery mist—spinning itself smaller and smaller into one tiny point, and that point darting on a sudden straight into my head—and then, all fire and all mist—no hearing, no seeing, no thinking, no feeling—the brig, the sea, my own self, the whole world, all gone together!

After what I've just told you, I know nothing and remember nothing, till I woke up (as it seemed to me) in a comfortable bed, with two rough-and-ready men like myself sitting on each side of my pillow, and a gentleman standing watching me at the foot of the bed. It was about seven in the morning.

My sleep (or what seemed like my sleep to me) had lasted better than eight months—I was among my own countrymen in the island of Trinidad—the men at each side of my pillow were my keepers, turn and turnabout—and the gentleman standing at the foot of the bed was the doctor. What I said and did in those eight months, I never have known, and never shall. I woke out of it as if it had been one long sleep—that's all I know.

It was another two months or more before the doctor thought it safe to answer the questions I asked him.

The brig had been anchored, just as I had supposed, off a part of the coast which was lonely enough to make the Spaniards pretty sure of no interruption, so long as they managed their murderous work quietly under cover of night.

My life had not been saved from the shore, but from the sea. An American vessel, becalmed in the offing, had made out the brig as the sun rose; and the captain having his time on his hands in consequence of the calm, and seeing a vessel anchored where no vessel had any reason to be, had manned one of his boats and sent his mate with it, to look a little closer into the matter, and bring back a report of what he saw.

What he saw, when he and his men found the brig deserted and boarded her, was the gleam of candlelight through the chink in the hatchway. The flame was within about a thread's breadth of the slow-match when he lowered himself into the hold; and if he had not had the sense and coolness to cut the match in two with his knife before he touched the candle, he and his men might have been blown up along with the brig as well as me. The match caught, and turned into sputtering red fire, in the very act of putting the candle out; and if the communication with the powder-barrel had not been cut off, the Lord only knows what might have happened.

"What became of the Spanish schooner and the pilot, I have never heard from that day to this.

As for the brig, the Yankees took her, as they took me, to Trinidad, and claimed their salvage, and got it, I hope, for their own sakes. I was landed just in the same state as when they rescued me from the brig—that is to say, clean out of my senses. But please to remember, it was a long time ago; and, take my word for it, I was discharged cured, as I have told you. Bless your hearts, I'm all right now, as you may see. I'm a little shaken by telling the story, as is only natural—a little shaken, my good friends, that's all.

Mrs. Zant and the Ghost

1

The course of this narrative describes the return of a disem-
bodied spirit to earth, and leads the reader on new and strange
ground.

Not in the obscurity of midnight, but in the searching light
of day, did the supernatural influence assert itself. Neither revealed by a vision, nor announced by a voice, it reached mortal
knowledge through the sense which is least easily self-deceived:
the sense that feels.

The record of this event will of necessity produce conflicting
impressions. It will raise, in some minds, the doubt which reason
asserts; it will invigorate, in other minds, the hope which faith
justifies; and it will leave the terrible question of the destinies of
man, where centuries of vain investigation have left it—in the
dark.

Having only undertaken in the present narrative to lead the
way along a succession of events, the writer declines to follow modern examples by thrusting himself and his opinions on
the public view. He returns to the shadow from which he has
emerged, and leaves the opposing forces of incredulity and belief
to fight the old battle over again, on the old ground.

2

The events happened soon after the first thirty years of the
present century had come to an end.

On a fine morning, early in the month of April, a gentleman

of middle age (named Rayburn) took his little daughter Lucy out for a walk in the woodland pleasure-ground of Western London, called Kensington Gardens.

The few friends whom he possessed reported of Mr. Rayburn (not unkindly) that he was a reserved and solitary man. He might have been more accurately described as a widower devoted to his only surviving child. Although he was not more than forty years of age, the one pleasure which made life enjoyable to Lucy's father was offered by Lucy herself.

Playing with her ball, the child ran on to the southern limit of the Gardens, at that part of it which still remains nearest to the old Palace of Kensington. Observing close at hand one of those spacious covered seats, called in England "alcoves," Mr. Rayburn was reminded that he had the morning's newspaper in his pocket, and that he might do well to rest and read. At that early hour the place was a solitude.

"Go on playing, my dear," he said; "but take care to keep where I can see you."

Lucy tossed up her ball; and Lucy's father opened his newspaper. He had not been reading for more than ten minutes, when he felt a familiar little hand laid on his knee.

"Tired of playing?" he inquired—with his eyes still on the newspaper.

"I'm frightened, papa."

He looked up directly. The child's pale face startled him. He took her on his knee and kissed her.

"You oughtn't to be frightened, Lucy, when I am with you," he said, gently. "What is it?" He looked out of the alcove as he spoke, and saw a little dog among the trees. "Is it the dog?" he asked.

Lucy answered:

"It's not the dog—it's the lady."

The lady was not visible from the alcove.

"Has she said anything to you?" Mr. Rayburn inquired.

"No."

"What has she done to frighten you?"

The child put her arms round her father's neck.

"Whisper, papa," she said; "I'm afraid of her hearing us. I think she's mad."

"Why do you think so, Lucy?"

"She came near to me. I thought she was going to say something. She seemed to be ill."

"Well? And what then?"

"She looked at me."

There, Lucy found herself at a loss how to express what she had to say next—and took refuge in silence.

"Nothing very wonderful, so far," her father suggested.

"Yes, papa—but she didn't seem to see me when she looked."

"Well, and what happened then?"

"The lady was frightened—and that frightened me. I think," the child repeated positively, "she's mad."

It occurred to Mr. Rayburn that the lady might be blind. He rose at once to set the doubt at rest.

"Wait here," he said, "and I'll come back to you."

But Lucy clung to him with both hands; Lucy declared that she was afraid to be by herself. They left the alcove together.

The new point of view at once revealed the stranger, leaning against the trunk of a tree. She was dressed in the deep mourning of a widow. The pallor of her face, the glassy stare in her eyes, more than accounted for the child's terror—it excused the alarming conclusion at which she had arrived.

"Go nearer to her," Lucy whispered.

They advanced a few steps. It was now easy to see that the lady was young, and wasted by illness—but (arriving at a doubtful conclusion perhaps under the present circumstances) apparently possessed of rare personal attractions in happier days. As the father and daughter advanced a little, she discovered them. After some hesitation, she left the tree; approached with an evident intention of speaking; and suddenly paused. A change to astonishment and fear animated her vacant eyes. If it had not been plain before, it was now beyond all doubt that she was not a poor blind creature, deserted and helpless. At the same time, the expression of her face was not easy to understand. She could hardly have looked more amazed and bewildered, if the two strangers who were observing her had suddenly vanished from the place in which they stood.

Mr. Rayburn spoke to her with the utmost kindness of voice and manner.

"I am afraid you are not well," he said. "Is there anything that I can do—"

The next words were suspended on his lips. It was impossible to realize such a state of things; but the strange impression that she had already produced on him was now confirmed. If he could believe his senses, her face did certainly tell him that he was invisible and inaudible to the woman whom he had just addressed! She moved slowly away with a heavy sigh, like a person disappointed and distressed. Following her with his eyes, he saw the dog once more—a little smooth-coated terrier of the ordinary English breed. The dog showed none of the restless activity of his race. With his head down and his tail depressed, he crouched like a creature paralyzed by fear. His mistress roused him by a call. He followed her listlessly as she turned away.

After walking a few paces only, she suddenly stood still.

Mr. Rayburn heard her talking to herself.

"Did I feel it again?" she said, as if perplexed by some doubt that awed or grieved her. After a while her arms rose slowly, and opened with a gentle caressing action—an embrace strangely offered to the empty air! "No," she said to herself, sadly, after waiting a moment. "More perhaps when tomorrow comes—no more today." She looked up at the clear blue sky. "The beautiful sunlight! the merciful sunlight!" she murmured. "I should have died if it had happened in the dark."

Once more she called to the dog; and once more she walked slowly away.

"Is she going home, papa?' the child asked.

"We will try and find out," the father answered.

He was by this time convinced that the poor creature was

in no condition to be permitted to go out without someone to take care of her. From motives of humanity, he was resolved on making the attempt to communicate with her friends.

3

The lady left the Gardens by the nearest gate; stopping to lower her veil before she turned into the busy thoroughfare which leads to Kensington. Advancing a little way along the High Street, she entered a house of respectable appearance, with a card in one of the windows which announced that apartments were to let.

Mr. Rayburn waited a minute—then knocked at the door, and asked if he could see the mistress of the house. The servant showed him into a room on the ground floor, neatly but scantily furnished. One little white object varied the grim brown monotony of the empty table. It was a visiting-card.

With a child's unceremonious curiosity Lucy pounced on the card, and spelled the name, letter by letter: "Z, A, N, T," she repeated. "What does that mean?"

Her father looked at the card, as he took it away from her, and put it back on the table. The name was printed, and the address was added in pencil: "Mr. John Zant, Purley's Hotel."

The mistress made her appearance. Mr. Rayburn heartily wished himself out of the house again, the moment he saw her. The ways in which it is possible to cultivate the social virtues are more numerous and more varied than is generally supposed. This lady's way had apparently accustomed her to meet her fellow-creatures on the hard ground of justice without mercy. Something in her eyes, when she looked at Lucy, said: "I wonder whether that child gets punished when she deserves it?"

"Do you wish to see the rooms which I have to let?" she began.

Mr. Rayburn at once stated the object of his visit—as clearly, as civilly, and as concisely as a man could do it. He was conscious (he added) that he had been guilty perhaps of an act of intrusion.

The manner of the mistress of the house showed that she entirely agreed with him. He suggested, however, that his motive might excuse him. The mistress's manner changed, and asserted a difference of opinion.

"I only know the lady whom you mention," she said, "as a person of the highest respectability, in delicate health. She has taken my first-floor apartments, with excellent references; and she gives remarkably little trouble. I have no claim to interfere with her proceedings, and no reason to doubt that she is capable of taking care of herself."

Mr. Rayburn unwisely attempted to say a word in his own defence.

"Allow me to remind you—" he began.

"Of what, sir?"

"Of what I observed, when I happened to see the lady in Kensington Gardens."

"I am not responsible for what you observed in Kensington Gardens. If your time is of any value, pray don't let me detain you."

Dismissed in those terms, Mr. Rayburn took Lucy's hand and withdrew. He had just reached the door, when it was opened from the outer side. The Lady of Kensington Gardens stood before him. In the position which he and his daughter now occupied, their backs were toward the window. Would she remember having seen them for a moment in the Gardens?

"Excuse me for intruding on you," she said to the landlady. "Your servant tells me my brother-in-law called while I was out. He sometimes leaves a message on his card."

She looked for the message, and appeared to be disappointed: there was no writing on the card.

Mr. Rayburn lingered a little in the doorway on the chance of hearing something more. The landlady's vigilant eyes discovered him.

"Do you know this gentleman?" she said maliciously to her lodger.

"Not that I remember."

Replying in those words, the lady looked at Mr. Rayburn for the first time; and suddenly drew back from him.

"Yes," she said, correcting herself; "I think we met—"

Her embarrassment overpowered her; she could say no more.

Mr. Rayburn compassionately finished the sentence for her.

"We met accidentally in Kensington Gardens," he said.

She seemed to be incapable of appreciating the kindness of his motive. After hesitating a little she addressed a proposal to him, which seemed to show distrust of the landlady.

"Will you let me speak to you upstairs in my own rooms?" she asked.

Without waiting for a reply, she led the way to the stairs. Mr. Rayburn and Lucy followed. They were just beginning the ascent to the first floor, when the spiteful landlady left the lower room, and called to her lodger over their heads: "Take care what you say to this man, Mrs. Zant! He thinks you're mad."

Mrs. Zant turned round on the landing, and looked at him. Not a word fell from her lips. She suffered, she feared, in silence. Something in the sad submission of her face touched the springs of innocent pity in Lucy's heart. The child burst out crying.

That artless expression of sympathy drew Mrs. Zant down the few stairs which separated her from Lucy.

"May I kiss your dear little girl?" she said to Mr. Rayburn. The landlady, standing on the mat below, expressed her opinion of the value of caresses, as compared with a sounder method of treating young persons in tears: "If that child was mine," she remarked, "I would give her something to cry for."

In the meantime, Mrs. Zant led the way to her rooms.

The first words she spoke showed that the landlady had succeeded but too well in prejudicing her against Mr. Rayburn.

"Will you let me ask your child," she said to him, "why you think me mad?"

He met this strange request with a firm answer.

"You don't know yet what I really do think. Will you give me a minute's attention?"

"No," she said positively. "The child pities me, I want to speak to the child. What did you see me do in the Gardens, my dear, that surprised you?" Lucy turned uneasily to her father; Mrs. Zant persisted. "I first saw you by yourself, and then I saw you with your father," she went on. "When I came nearer to you, did I look very oddly—as if I didn't see you at all?"

Lucy hesitated again; and Mr. Rayburn interfered.

"You are confusing my little girl," he said. "Allow me to answer your questions—or excuse me if I leave you."

There was something in his look, or in his tone, that mastered her. She put her hand to her head.

"I don't think I'm fit for it," she answered vacantly. "My courage has been sorely tried already. If I can get a little rest and sleep, you may find me a different person. I am left a great deal by myself; and I have reasons for trying to compose my mind. Can I see you tomorrow? Or write to you? Where do you live?"

Mr. Rayburn laid his card on the table in silence. She had strongly excited his interest. He honestly desired to be of some service to this forlorn creature—abandoned so cruelly, as it seemed, to her own guidance. But he had no authority to exercise, no sort of claim to direct her actions, even if she consented to accept his advice. As a last resource he ventured on an allusion to the relative of whom she had spoken downstairs.

"When do you expect to see your brother-in-law again?" he said.

"I don't know," she answered. "I should like to see him—he is so kind to me."

She turned aside to take leave of Lucy.

"Goodbye, my little friend. If you live to grow up, I hope you will never be such a miserable woman as I am." She suddenly looked round at Mr. Rayburn. "Have you got a wife at home?" she asked.

"My wife is dead."

"And *you* have a child to comfort you! Please leave me; you harden my heart. Oh, sir, don't you understand? You make me envy you!"

Mr. Rayburn was silent when he and his daughter were out in the street again. Lucy, as became a dutiful child, was silent, too. But there are limits to human endurance—and Lucy's capacity for self-control gave way at last.

"Are you thinking of the lady, papa?" she said.

He only answered by nodding his head. His daughter had interrupted him at that critical moment in a man's reflections, when he is on the point of making up his mind. Before they were at home again Mr. Rayburn had arrived at a decision. Mrs. Zant's brother-in-law was evidently ignorant of any serious necessity for his interference—or he would have made arrangements for immediately repeating his visit. In this state of things, if any evil happened to Mrs. Zant, silence on Mr. Rayburn's part might be indirectly to blame for a serious misfortune. Arriving at that conclusion, he decided upon running the risk of being rudely received, for the second time, by another stranger.

Leaving Lucy under the care of her governess, he went at once to the address that had been written on the visiting-card left at the lodging-house, and sent in his name. A courteous message was returned. Mr. John Zant was at home, and would be happy to see him.

4

Mr. Rayburn was shown into one of the private sitting-rooms of the hotel.

He observed that the customary position of the furniture in a room had been, in some respects, altered. An armchair, a side-table, and a footstool had all been removed to one of the windows, and had been placed as close as possible to the light. On the table lay a large open roll of morocco leather, containing rows of elegant little instruments in steel and ivory. Waiting by the table, stood Mr. John Zant. He said "Good-morning" in a bass voice, so profound and so melodious that those two commonplace words assumed a new importance, coming from his lips.

His personal appearance was in harmony with his magnificent voice—he was a tall, finely-made man of dark complexion;

with big brilliant black eyes, and a noble curling beard, which hid the whole lower part of his face. Having bowed with a happy mingling of dignity and politeness, the conventional side of this gentleman's character suddenly vanished; and a crazy side, to all appearance, took its place. He dropped on his knees in front of the footstool. Had he forgotten to say his prayers that morning, and was he in such a hurry to remedy the fault that he had no time to spare for consulting appearances? The doubt had hardly suggested itself, before it was set at rest in a most unexpected manner. Mr. Zant looked at his visitor with a bland smile, and said:

"Please let me see your feet."

For the moment, Mr. Rayburn lost his presence of mind. He looked at the instruments on the side-table.

"Are you a corn-cutter?" was all he could say.

"Excuse me, sir," returned the polite operator, "the term you use is quite obsolete in our profession." He rose from his knees, and added modestly: "I am a Chiropodist."

"I beg your pardon."

"Don't mention it! You are not, I imagine, in want of my professional services. To what motive may I attribute the honour of your visit?"

By this time Mr. Rayburn had recovered himself.

"I have come here," he answered, "under circumstances which require apology as well as explanation."

Mr. Zant's highly polished manner betrayed signs of alarm; his suspicions pointed to a formidable conclusion—a conclusion that shook him to the innermost recesses of the pocket in which he kept his money.

"The numerous demands on me—" he began.

Mr. Rayburn smiled.

"Make your mind easy," he replied. "I don't want money. My object is to speak with you on the subject of a lady who is a relation of yours."

"My sister-in-law!" Mr. Zant exclaimed. "Pray take a seat."

Doubting if he had chosen a convenient time for his visit, Mr.

Rayburn hesitated.

"Am I likely to be in the way of persons who wish to consult you?" he asked.

"Certainly not. My morning hours of attendance on my clients are from eleven to one." The clock on the mantelpiece struck the quarter-past one as he spoke. "I hope you don't bring me bad news?" he said, very earnestly. "When I called on Mrs. Zant this morning, I heard that she had gone out for a walk. Is it indiscreet to ask how you became acquainted with her?"

Mr. Rayburn at once mentioned what he had seen and heard in Kensington Gardens; not forgetting to add a few words, which described his interview afterward with Mrs. Zant.

The lady's brother-in-law listened with an interest and sympathy, which offered the strongest possible contrast to the unprovoked rudeness of the mistress of the lodging-house. He declared that he could only do justice to his sense of obligation by following Mr. Rayburn's example, and expressing himself as frankly as if he had been speaking to an old friend.

"The sad story of my sister-in-law's life," he said, "will, I think, explain certain things which must have naturally perplexed you. My brother was introduced to her at the house of an Australian gentleman, on a visit to England. She was then employed as governess to his daughters. So sincere was the regard felt for her by the family that the parents had, at the entreaty of their children, asked her to accompany them when they returned to the Colony. The governess thankfully accepted the proposal."

"Had she no relations in England?" Mr. Rayburn asked.

"She was literally alone in the world, sir. When I tell you that she had been brought up in the Foundling Hospital, you will understand what I mean. Oh, there is no romance in my sister-in-law's story! She never has known, or will know, who her parents were or why they deserted her. The happiest moment in her life was the moment when she and my brother first met. It was an instance, on both sides, of love at first sight. Though not a rich man, my brother had earned a sufficient income in mercantile pursuits. His character spoke for itself. In a word, he altered all the poor girl's prospects, as we then hoped and believed, for the better. Her employers deferred their return to Australia, so that she might be married from their house. After a happy life of a few weeks only—"

His voice failed him; he paused, and turned his face from the light.

"Pardon me," he said; "I am not able, even yet, to speak composedly of my brother's death. Let me only say that the poor young wife was a widow, before the happy days of the honeymoon were over. That dreadful calamity struck her down. Before my brother had been committed to the grave, her life was in danger from brain-fever."

Those words placed in a new light Mr. Rayburn's first fear that her intellect might be deranged. Looking at him attentively, Mr. Zant seemed to understand what was passing in the mind of his guest.

"No!" he said. "If the opinions of the medical men are to be trusted, the result of the illness is injury to her physical strength—not injury to her mind. I have observed in her, no doubt, a certain waywardness of temper since her illness; but that is a trifle. As an example of what I mean, I may tell you that I invited her, on her recovery, to pay me a visit. My house is not in London—the air doesn't agree with me—my place of residence is at St. Sallins-on-Sea. I am not myself a married man; but my excellent housekeeper would have received Mrs. Zant with the utmost kindness. She was resolved—obstinately resolved, poor thing—to remain in London. It is needless to say that, in her melancholy position, I am attentive to her slightest wishes. I took a lodging for her; and, at her special request, I chose a house which was near Kensington Gardens.

"Is there any association with the Gardens which led Mrs. Zant to make that request?"

"Some association, I believe, with the memory of her husband. By the way, I wish to be sure of finding her at home, when I call tomorrow. Did you say (in the course of your interesting statement) that she intended—as you supposed—to return to

Kensington Gardens tomorrow? Or has my memory deceived me?"

"Your memory is perfectly accurate."

"Thank you. I confess I am not only distressed by what you have told me of Mrs. Zant—I am at a loss to know how to act for the best. My only idea, at present, is to try change of air and scene. What do you think yourself?"

"I think you are right."

Mr. Zant still hesitated.

"It would not be easy for me, just now," he said, "to leave my patients and take her abroad."

The obvious reply to this occurred to Mr. Rayburn. A man of larger worldly experience might have felt certain suspicions, and might have remained silent. Mr. Rayburn spoke.

"Why not renew your invitation and take her to your house at the seaside?" he said.

In the perplexed state of Mr. Zant's mind, this plain course of action had apparently failed to present itself. His gloomy face brightened directly.

"The very thing!" he said. "I will certainly take your advice. If the air of St. Sallins does nothing else, it will improve her health and help her to recover her good looks. Did she strike you as having been (in happier days) a pretty woman?"

This was a strangely familiar question to ask—almost an indelicate question, under the circumstances A certain furtive expression in Mr. Zant's fine dark eyes seemed to imply that it had been put with a purpose. Was it possible that he suspected Mr. Rayburn's interest in his sister-in-law to be inspired by any motive which was not perfectly unselfish and perfectly pure? To arrive at such a conclusion as this might be to judge hastily and cruelly of a man who was perhaps only guilty of a want of delicacy of feeling. Mr. Rayburn honestly did his best to assume the charitable point of view. At the same time, it is not to be denied that his words, when he answered, were carefully guarded, and that he rose to take his leave.

Mr. John Zant hospitably protested.

"Why are you in such a hurry? Must you really go? I shall have the honour of returning your visit tomorrow, when I have made arrangements to profit by that excellent suggestion of yours. Goodbye. God bless you."

He held out his hand: a hand with a smooth surface and a tawny colour, that fervently squeezed the fingers of a departing friend. "Is that man a scoundrel?" was Mr. Rayburn's first thought, after he had left the hotel. His moral sense set all hesitation at rest—and answered: "You're a fool if you doubt it."

5

Disturbed by presentiments, Mr. Rayburn returned to his house on foot, by way of trying what exercise would do toward composing his mind.

The experiment failed. He went upstairs and played with Lucy; he drank an extra glass of wine at dinner; he took the child and her governess to a circus in the evening; he ate a little supper, fortified by another glass of wine, before he went to bed—and still those vague forebodings of evil persisted in torturing him. Looking back through his past life, he asked himself if any woman (his late wife of course excepted!) had ever taken the predominant place in his thoughts which Mrs. Zant had assumed—without any discernible reason to account for it? If he had ventured to answer his own question, the reply would have been: Never!

All the next day he waited at home, in expectation of Mr. John Zant's promised visit, and waited in vain.

Toward evening the parlour-maid appeared at the family tea-table, and presented to her master an unusually large envelope sealed with black wax, and addressed in a strange handwriting. The absence of stamp and postmark showed that it had been left at the house by a messenger.

"Who brought this?" Mr. Rayburn asked.

"A lady, sir—in deep mourning."

"Did she leave any message?"

"No, sir."

Having drawn the inevitable conclusion, Mr. Rayburn shut himself up in his library. He was afraid of Lucy's curiosity and Lucy's questions, if he read Mrs. Zant's letter in his daughter's presence.

Looking at the open envelope after he had taken out the leaves of writing which it contained, he noticed these lines traced inside the cover:

My one excuse for troubling you, when I might have consulted my brother-in-law, will be found in the pages which I inclose. To speak plainly, you have been led to fear that I am not in my right senses. For this very reason, I now appeal to you. Your dreadful doubt of me, sir, is my doubt too. Read what I have written about myself—and then tell me, I entreat you, which I am: A person who has been the object of a supernatural revelation? or an unfortunate creature who is only fit for imprisonment in a mad-house?

Mr. Rayburn opened the manuscript. With steady attention, which soon quickened to breathless interest, he read what follows:

6
THE LADY'S MANUSCRIPT

Yesterday morning the sun shone in a clear blue sky—after a succession of cloudy days, counting from the first of the month.

The radiant light had its animating effect on my poor spirits. I had passed the night more peacefully than usual; undisturbed by the dream, so cruelly familiar to me, that my lost husband is still living—the dream from which I always wake in tears. Never, since the dark days of my sorrow, have I been so little troubled by the self-tormenting fancies and fears which beset miserable women, as when I left the house, and turned my steps toward Kensington Gardens—for the first time since my husband's death.

Attended by my only companion, the little dog who had been his favourite as well as mine, I went to the quiet corner of the Gardens which is nearest to Kensington.

On that soft grass, under the shade of those grand trees, we had loitered together in the days of our betrothal. It was his favourite walk; and he had taken me to see it in the early days of our acquaintance. There, he had first asked me to be his wife. There, we had felt the rapture of our first kiss. It was surely natural that I should wish to see once more a place sacred to such memories as these? I am only twenty-three years old; I have no child to comfort me, no companion of my own age, nothing to love but the dumb creature who is so faithfully fond of me.

I went to the tree under which we stood, when my dear one's eyes told his love before he could utter it in words. The sun of that vanished day shone on me again; it was the same noontide hour; the same solitude was around me. I had feared the first effect of the dreadful contrast between past and present. No! I was quiet and resigned. My thoughts, rising higher than earth, dwelt on the better life beyond the grave. Some tears came into my eyes. But I was not unhappy. My memory of all that happened may be trusted, even in trifles which relate only to myself—I was not unhappy.

The first object that I saw, when my eyes were clear again, was the dog. He crouched a few paces away from me, trembling pitiably, but uttering no cry. What had caused the fear that overpowered him?

I was soon to know.

I called to the dog; he remained immovable—conscious of some mysterious coming thing that held him spellbound. I tried to go to the poor creature, and fondle and comfort him.

At the first step forward that I took, something stopped me.

It was not to be seen, and not to be heard. It stopped me.

The still figure of the dog disappeared from my view: the lonely scene round me disappeared—excepting the light from heaven, the tree that sheltered me, and the grass in front of me. A sense of unutterable expectation kept my eyes riveted on the grass. Suddenly, I saw its myriad blades rise erect and shivering. The fear came to me of something passing over them with the invisible swiftness of the wind. The shivering advanced. It was all round me. It crept into the leaves of the tree over my head; they shuddered, without a sound to tell of their agitation; their pleasant natural rustling was struck dumb. The song of the birds had ceased. The cries of the water-fowl on the pond were heard no more. There was a dreadful silence.

But the lovely sunshine poured down on me, as brightly as ever.

In that dazzling light, in that fearful silence, I felt an Invisible Presence near me. It touched me gently.

At the touch, my heart throbbed with an overwhelming joy. Exquisite pleasure thrilled through every nerve in my body. I knew him! From the unseen world—himself unseen—he had returned to me. Oh, I knew him!

And yet, my helpless mortality longed for a sign that might give me assurance of the truth. The yearning in me shaped itself into words. I tried to utter the words. I would have said, if I could have spoken: "Oh, my angel, give me a token that it is You!" But I was like a person struck dumb—I could only think it.

The Invisible Presence read my thought. I felt my lips touched, as my husband's lips used to touch them when he kissed me. And that was my answer. A thought came to me again. I would have said, if I could have spoken: "Are you here to take me to the better world?"

I waited. Nothing that I could feel touched me.

I was conscious of thinking once more. I would have said, if I could have spoken: "Are you here to protect me?"

I felt myself held in a gentle embrace, as my husband's arms used to hold me when he pressed me to his breast. And that was my answer.

The touch that was like the touch of his lips, lingered and was lost; the clasp that was like the clasp of his arms, pressed me and fell away. The garden-scene resumed its natural aspect. I saw a human creature near, a lovely little girl looking at me.

At that moment, when I was my own lonely self again, the sight of the child soothed and attracted me. I advanced, intending to speak to her. To my horror I suddenly ceased to see her. She disappeared as if I had been stricken blind.

And yet I could see the landscape round me; I could see the heaven above me. A time passed—only a few minutes, as I thought—and the child became visible to me again; walking hand-in-hand with her father. I approached them; I was close enough to see that they were looking at me with pity and surprise. My impulse was to ask if they saw anything strange in my face or my manner. Before I could speak, the horrible wonder happened again. They vanished from my view.

Was the Invisible Presence still near? Was it passing between me and my fellow-mortals; forbidding communication, in that place and at that time?

It must have been so. When I turned away in my ignorance, with a heavy heart, the dreadful blankness which had twice shut out from me the beings of my own race, was not between me and my dog. The poor little creature filled me with pity; I called him to me. He moved at the sound of my voice, and followed me languidly; not quite awakened yet from the trance of terror that had possessed him.

Before I had retired by more than a few steps, I thought I was conscious of the Presence again. I held out my longing arms to it. I waited in the hope of a touch to tell me that I might return. Perhaps I was answered by indirect means? I only know that a resolution to return to the same place, at the same hour, came to me, and quieted my mind.

The morning of the next day was dull and cloudy; but the rain held off. I set forth again to the Gardens.

My dog ran on before me into the street—and stopped: waiting to see in which direction I might lead the way. When I turned toward the Gardens, he dropped behind me. In a little while I looked back. He was following me no longer; he stood irresolute. I called to him. He advanced a few steps—hesitated—and ran back to the house.

I went on by myself. Shall I confess my superstition? I thought the dog's desertion of me a bad omen.

Arrived at the tree, I placed myself under it. The minutes followed each other uneventfully. The cloudy sky darkened. The dull surface of the grass showed no shuddering consciousness of an unearthly creature passing over it.

I still waited, with an obstinacy which was fast becoming the obstinacy of despair. How long an interval elapsed, while I kept watch on the ground before me, I am not able to say. I only know that a change came.

Under the dull gray light I saw the grass move—but not as it had moved, on the day before. It shrivelled as if a flame had scorched it. No flame appeared. The brown underlying earth showed itself winding onward in a thin strip—which might have been a footpath traced in fire. It frightened me. I longed for the protection of the Invisible Presence. I prayed for a warning of it, if danger was near.

A touch answered me. It was as if a hand unseen had taken my hand—had raised it, little by little—had left it, pointing to the thin brown path that wound toward me under the shrivelled blades of grass.

I looked to the far end of the path.

The unseen hand closed on my hand with a warning pressure: the revelation of the coming danger was near me—I waited for it. I saw it.

The figure of a man appeared, advancing toward me along the thin brown path. I looked in his face as he came nearer. It showed me dimly the face of my husband's brother—John Zant.

The consciousness of myself as a living creature left me. I knew nothing; I felt nothing. I was dead.

When the torture of revival made me open my eyes, I found myself on the grass. Gentle hands raised my head, at the moment when I recovered my senses. Who had brought me to life again? Who was taking care of me?

I looked upward, and saw—bending over me—John Zant.

There, the manuscript ended.

Some lines had been added on the last page; but they had been so carefully erased as to be illegible. These words of explanation appeared below the cancelled sentences:

"I had begun to write the little that remains to be told, when it struck me that I might, unintentionally, be exercising an unfair influence on your opinion. Let me only remind you that I believe absolutely in the supernatural revelation which I have endeavoured to describe. Remember this—and decide for me what I dare not decide for myself."

There was no serious obstacle in the way of compliance with this request.

Judged from the point of view of the materialist, Mrs. Zant might no doubt be the victim of illusions (produced by a diseased state of the nervous system), which have been known to exist—as in the celebrated case of the book-seller, Nicolai, of Berlin—without being accompanied by derangement of the intellectual powers. But Mr. Rayburn was not asked to solve any such intricate problem as this. He had been merely instructed to read the manuscript, and to say what impression it had left on him of the mental condition of the writer; whose doubt of herself had been, in all probability, first suggested by remembrance of the illness from which she had suffered—brain-fever.

Under these circumstances, there could be little difficulty in forming an opinion. The memory which had recalled, and the judgment which had arranged, the succession of events related in the narrative, revealed a mind in full possession of its resources.

Having satisfied himself so far, Mr. Rayburn abstained from considering the more serious question suggested by what he had read.

At any time his habits of life and his ways of thinking would have rendered him unfit to weigh the arguments, which assert or deny supernatural revelation among the creatures of earth. But his mind was now so disturbed by the startling record of experience which he had just read, that he was only conscious of feeling certain impressions—without possessing the capacity to reflect on them. That his anxiety on Mrs. Zant's account had been increased, and that his doubts of Mr. John Zant had been encouraged, were the only practical results of the confidence placed in him of which he was thus far aware.

In the ordinary exigencies of life a man of hesitating disposition, his interest in Mrs. Zant's welfare, and his desire to discover what had passed between her brother-in-law and herself, after their meeting in the Gardens, urged him into instant action. In half an hour more, he had arrived at her lodgings. He was at once admitted.

8

Mrs. Zant was alone, in an imperfectly lighted room.

"I hope you will excuse the bad light," she said; "my head has been burning as if the fever had come back again. Oh, don't go away! After what I have suffered, you don't know how dreadful it is to be alone."

The tone of her voice told him that she had been crying. He at once tried the best means of setting the poor lady at ease, by telling her of the conclusion at which he had arrived, after reading her manuscript. The happy result showed itself instantly: her face brightened, her manner changed; she was eager to hear more.

"Have I produced any other impression on you?" she asked.

He understood the allusion. Expressing sincere respect for her own convictions, he told her honestly that he was not prepared to enter on the obscure and terrible question of supernatural interposition. Grateful for the tone in which he had answered her, she wisely and delicately changed the subject.

"I must speak to you of my brother-in-law," she said. "He has told me of your visit; and I am anxious to know what you think of him. Do you like Mr. John Zant?"

Mr. Rayburn hesitated.

The careworn look appeared again in her face. "If you had felt as kindly toward him as he feels toward you," she said, "I might have gone to St. Sallins with a lighter heart."

Mr. Rayburn thought of the supernatural appearances, described at the close of her narrative. "You believe in that terrible warning," he remonstrated; "and yet, you go to your brother-in-law's house!"

"I believe," she answered, "in the spirit of the man who loved me in the days of his earthly bondage. I am under *his* protection. What have I to do but to cast away my fears, and to wait in faith and hope? It might have helped my resolution if a friend had been near to encourage me."

She paused and smiled sadly. "I must remember," she resumed, "that your way of understanding my position is not my way. I ought to have told you that Mr. John Zant feels needless anxiety about my health. He declares that he will not lose sight of me until his mind is at ease. It is useless to attempt to alter his opinion. He says my nerves are shattered—and who that sees me can doubt it? He tells me that my only chance of getting better is to try change of air and perfect repose—how can I contradict him? He reminds me that I have no relation but himself, and no house open to me but his own—and God knows he is right!"

She said those last words in accents of melancholy resignation, which grieved the good man whose one merciful purpose was to serve and console her. He spoke impulsively with the freedom of an old friend.

"I want to know more of you and Mr. John Zant than I know now," he said. "My motive is a better one than mere curiosity. Do you believe that I feel a sincere interest in you?"

"With my whole heart."

That reply encouraged him to proceed with what he had to say. "When you recovered from your fainting-fit," he began, "Mr. John Zant asked questions, of course?"

"He asked what could possibly have happened, in such a quiet place as Kensington Gardens, to make me faint."

"And how did you answer?"

"Answer? I couldn't even look at him!"

"You said nothing?"

"Nothing. I don't know what he thought of me; he might have been surprised, or he might have been offended."

"Is he easily offended?" Mr. Rayburn asked.

"Not in my experience of him."

"Do you mean your experience of him before your illness?"

"Yes. Since my recovery, his engagements with country patients have kept him away from London. I have not seen him since he took these lodgings for me. But he is always considerate. He has written more than once to beg that I will not think him neglectful, and to tell me (what I knew already through my poor husband) that he has no money of his own, and must live by his profession."

"In your husband's lifetime, were the two brothers on good terms?"

"Always. The one complaint I ever heard my husband make of John Zant was that he didn't come to see us often enough, after our marriage. Is there some wickedness in him which we have never suspected? It may be—but *how* can it be? I have every reason to be grateful to the man against whom I have been supernaturally warned! His conduct to me has been always perfect. I can't tell you what I owe to his influence in quieting my mind, when a dreadful doubt arose about my husband's death."

"Do you mean doubt if he died a natural death?"

"Oh, no! no! He was dying of rapid consumption—but his sudden death took the doctors by surprise. One of them thought that he might have taken an overdose of his sleeping drops, by mistake. The other disputed this conclusion, or there might have been an inquest in the house. Oh, don't speak of it anymore! Let us talk of something else. Tell me when I shall see you again."

"I hardly know. When do you and your brother-in-law leave London?"

"Tomorrow." She looked at Mr. Rayburn with a piteous entreaty in her eyes; she said, timidly: "Do you ever go to the seaside, and take your dear little girl with you?"

The request, at which she had only dared to hint, touched on the idea which was at that moment in Mr. Rayburn's mind.

Interpreted by his strong prejudice against John Zant, what she had said of her brother-in-law filled him with forebodings of peril to herself; all the more powerful in their influence, for this reason—that he shrank from distinctly realizing them. If another person had been present at the interview, and had said to him afterward: "That man's reluctance to visit his sister-in-law, while her husband was living, is associated with a secret sense of guilt which her innocence cannot even imagine: he, and he alone, knows the cause of her husband's sudden death: his feigned anxiety about her health is adopted as the safest means of enticing her into his house"—if those formidable conclusions had been urged on Mr. Rayburn, he would have felt it his duty to reject them, as unjustifiable aspersions on an absent man. And yet, when he took leave that evening of Mrs. Zant, he had pledged himself to give Lucy a holiday at the seaside: and he had said, without blushing, that the child really deserved it, as a reward for general good conduct and attention to her lessons!

9

Three days later, the father and daughter arrived toward evening at St. Sallins-on-Sea. They found Mrs. Zant at the station.

The poor woman's joy, on seeing them, expressed itself like the joy of a child. "Oh, I am so glad! so glad!" was all she could say when they met. Lucy was half-smothered with kisses, and was made supremely happy by a present of the finest doll she had ever possessed. Mrs. Zant accompanied her friends to the rooms which had been secured at the hotel. She was able to speak confidentially to Mr. Rayburn, while Lucy was in the balcony hugging her doll, and looking at the sea.

The one event that had happened during Mrs. Zant's short residence at St. Sallins was the departure of her brother-in-law that morning, for London. He had been called away to operate on the feet of a wealthy patient who knew the value of his time: his housekeeper expected that he would return to dinner.

As to his conduct toward Mrs. Zant, he was not only as attentive as ever—he was almost oppressively affectionate in his language and manner. There was no service that a man could render which he had not eagerly offered to her. He declared that he already perceived an improvement in her health; he congratulated her on having decided to stay in his house; and (as a proof, perhaps, of his sincerity) he had repeatedly pressed her hand. "Have you any idea what all this means?" she said, simply.

Mr. Rayburn kept his idea to himself. He professed ignorance; and asked next what sort of person the housekeeper was.

Mrs. Zant shook her head ominously.

"Such a strange creature," she said, "and in the habit of taking such liberties that I begin to be afraid she is a little crazy."

"Is she an old woman?"

"No—only middle-aged. This morning, after her master had left the house, she actually asked me what I thought of my brother-in-law! I told her, as coldly as possible, that I thought he was very kind. She was quite insensible to the tone in which I had spoken; she went on from bad to worse. 'Do you call him the sort of man who would take the fancy of a young woman?' was her next question. She actually looked at me (I might have been wrong; and I hope I was) as if the 'young woman' she had in her mind was myself!

"I said: 'I don't think of such things, and I don't talk about them.' Still, she was not in the least discouraged; she made a personal remark next: 'Excuse me—but you do look wretchedly pale.' I thought she seemed to enjoy the defect in my complexion; I really believe it raised me in her estimation. 'We shall get on better in time,' she said; 'I am beginning to like you.' She walked out humming a tune. Don't you agree with me? Don't you think she's crazy?"

"I can hardly give an opinion until I have seen her. Does she look as if she might have been a pretty woman at one time of her life?"

"Not the sort of pretty woman whom I admire!"

Mr. Rayburn smiled. "I was thinking," he resumed, "that this person's odd conduct may perhaps be accounted for. She is probably jealous of any young lady who is invited to her master's house—and (till she noticed your complexion) she began by being jealous of you."

Innocently at a loss to understand how *she* could become an object of the housekeeper's jealousy, Mrs. Zant looked at Mr. Rayburn in astonishment. Before she could give expression to her feeling of surprise, there was an interruption—a welcome interruption. A waiter entered the room, and announced a visitor; described as "a gentleman."

Mrs. Zant at once rose to retire.

"Who is the gentleman?" Mr. Rayburn asked—detaining Mrs. Zant as he spoke.

A voice which they both recognized answered gaily, from the outer side of the door:

"A friend from London."

10

"Welcome to St. Sallins!" cried Mr. John Zant. "I knew that you were expected, my dear sir, and I took my chance at finding you at the hotel." He turned to his sister-in-law, and kissed her hand with an elaborate gallantry worthy of Sir Charles Grandison himself. "When I reached home, my dear, and heard that you had gone out, I guessed that your object was to receive our excellent friend. You have not felt lonely while I have been away? That's right! that's right!" he looked toward the balcony, and discovered Lucy at the open window, staring at the magnificent stranger. "Your little daughter, Mr. Rayburn? Dear child! Come and kiss me."

Lucy answered in one positive word: "No."

Mr. John Zant was not easily discouraged.

"Show me your doll, darling," he said. "Sit on my knee."

Lucy answered in two positive words—"I won't."

Her father approached the window to administer the necessary reproof. Mr. John Zant interfered in the cause of mercy with his best grace. He held up his hands in cordial entreaty. "Dear Mr. Rayburn! The fairies are sometimes shy; and *this* little fairy doesn't take to strangers at first sight. Dear child! All in good time. And what stay do you make at St. Sallins? May we hope that our poor attractions will tempt you to prolong your visit?"

He put his flattering little question with an ease of manner which was rather too plainly assumed; and he looked at Mr. Rayburn with a watchfulness which appeared to attach undue importance to the reply. When he said: "What stay do you make at St. Sallins?" did he really mean: "How soon do you leave us?" Inclining to adopt this conclusion, Mr. Rayburn answered cautiously that his stay at the seaside would depend on circumstances. Mr. John Zant looked at his sister-in-law, sitting silent in a corner with Lucy on her lap. "Exert your attractions," he said; "make the circumstances agreeable to our good friend. Will you dine with us today, my dear sir, and bring your little fairy with you?"

Lucy was far from receiving this complimentary allusion in the spirit in which it had been offered. "I'm not a fairy," she declared. "I'm a child."

"And a naughty child," her father added, with all the severity that he could assume.

"I can't help it, papa; the man with the big beard puts me out."

The man with the big beard was amused—amiably, paternally amused—by Lucy's plain speaking. He repeated his invitation to dinner; and he did his best to look disappointed when Mr. Rayburn made the necessary excuses.

"Another day," he said (without, however, fixing the day). "I think you will find my house comfortable. My housekeeper may perhaps be eccentric—but in all essentials a woman in a thousand. Do you feel the change from London already? Our air at St. Sallins is really worthy of its reputation. Invalids who come here are cured as if by magic. What do you think of Mrs. Zant? How does she look?"

Mr. Rayburn was evidently expected to say that she looked better. He said it. Mr. John Zant seemed to have anticipated a stronger expression of opinion.

"Surprisingly better!" he pronounced. "Infinitely better! We ought both to be grateful. Pray believe that we *are* grateful."

"If you mean grateful to me," Mr. Rayburn remarked, "I don't quite understand—"

"You don't quite understand? Is it possible that you have forgotten our conversation when I first had the honour of receiving you? Look at Mrs. Zant again."

Mr. Rayburn looked; and Mrs. Zant's brother-in-law explained himself.

"You notice the return of her colour, the healthy brightness of her eyes. (No, my dear, I am not paying you idle compliments; I am stating plain facts.) For that happy result, Mr. Rayburn, we are indebted to you."

"Surely not?"

"Surely yes! It was at your valuable suggestion that I thought of inviting my sister-in-law to visit me at St. Sallins. Ah, you remember it now. Forgive me if I look at my watch; the dinner hour is on my mind. Not, as your dear little daughter there seems to think, because I am greedy, but because I am always punctual, in justice to the cook. Shall we see you tomorrow? Call early, and you will find us at home."

He gave Mrs. Zant his arm, and bowed and smiled, and kissed his hand to Lucy, and left the room. Recalling their interview at the hotel in London, Mr. Rayburn now understood John Zant's object (on that occasion) in assuming the character of a helpless man in need of a sensible suggestion. If Mrs. Zant's residence under his roof became associated with evil consequences, he could declare that she would never have entered the house but for Mr. Rayburn's advice.

With the next day came the hateful necessity of returning this man's visit.

Mr. Rayburn was placed between two alternatives. In Mrs. Zant's interests he must remain, no matter at what sacrifice of his own inclinations, on good terms with her brother-in-law— or he must return to London, and leave the poor woman to her fate. His choice, it is needless to say, was never a matter of doubt. He called at the house, and did his innocent best—without in the least deceiving Mr. John Zant—to make himself agreeable during the short duration of his visit. Descending the stairs on his way out, accompanied by Mrs. Zant, he was surprised to see a middle-aged woman in the hall, who looked as if she was waiting there expressly to attract notice.

"The housekeeper," Mrs. Zant whispered. "She is impudent enough to try to make acquaintance with you."

This was exactly what the housekeeper was waiting in the hall to do.

"I hope you like our watering-place, sir," she began. "If I can be of service to you, pray command me. Any friend of this lady's has a claim on me—and you are an old friend, no doubt. I am only the housekeeper; but I presume to take a sincere interest in Mrs. Zant; and I am indeed glad to see you here. We none of us know—do we?—how soon we may want a friend. No offense, I hope? Thank you, sir. Good-morning."

There was nothing in the woman's eyes which indicated an unsettled mind; nothing in the appearance of her lips which suggested habits of intoxication. That her strange outburst of familiarity proceeded from some strong motive seemed to be more than probable. Putting together what Mrs. Zant had already told him, and what he had himself observed, Mr. Rayburn suspected that the motive might be found in the housekeeper's jealousy of her master.

11

Reflecting in the solitude of his own room, Mr. Rayburn felt that the one prudent course to take would be to persuade Mrs. Zant to leave St. Sallins. He tried to prepare her for this strong proceeding, when she came the next day to take Lucy out for a walk.

"If you still regret having forced yourself to accept your brother-in-law's invitation," was all he ventured to say, "don't forget that you are perfect mistress of your own actions. You have only to come to me at the hotel, and I will take you back to London by the next train."

She positively refused to entertain the idea.

"I should be a thankless creature, indeed," she said, "if I accepted your proposal. Do you think I am ungrateful enough to involve you in a personal quarrel with John Zant? No! If I find myself forced to leave the house, I will go away alone."

There was no moving her from this resolution. When she and Lucy had gone out together, Mr. Rayburn remained at the hotel, with a mind ill at ease. A man of readier mental resources might have felt at a loss how to act for the best, in the emergency that now confronted him. While he was still as far as ever from arriving at a decision, some person knocked at the door.

Had Mrs. Zant returned? He looked up as the door was opened, and saw to his astonishment—Mr. John Zant's housekeeper.

"Don't let me alarm you, sir," the woman said. "Mrs. Zant has been taken a little faint, at the door of our house. My master is attending to her."

"Where is the child?" Mr. Rayburn asked.

"I was bringing her back to you, sir, when we met a lady and her little girl at the door of the hotel. They were on their way to the beach—and Miss Lucy begged hard to be allowed to go with them. The lady said the two children were playfellows, and she was sure you would not object."

"The lady is quite right. Mrs. Zant's illness is not serious, I hope?"

"I think not, sir. But I should like to say something in her interests. May I? Thank you." She advanced a step nearer to him, and spoke her next words in a whisper. "Take Mrs. Zant away from this place, and lose no time in doing it."

Mr. Rayburn was on his guard. He merely asked: "Why?"

The housekeeper answered in a curiously indirect manner—partly in jest, as it seemed, and partly in earnest.

"When a man has lost his wife," she said, "there's some difference of opinion in Parliament, as I hear, whether he does right or wrong, if he marries his wife's sister. Wait a bit! I'm coming to the point. My master is one who has a long head on his shoulders; he sees consequences which escape the notice of people like me. In his way of thinking, if one man may marry his wife's sister, and no harm done, where's the objection if another man pays a compliment to the family, and marries his brother's widow? My master, if you please, is that other man. Take the widow away before she marries him."

This was beyond endurance.

"You insult Mrs. Zant," Mr. Rayburn answered, "if you suppose that such a thing is possible!"

"Oh! I insult her, do I? Listen to me. One of three things will happen. She will be entrapped into consenting to it—or frightened into consenting to it—or drugged into consenting to it—"

Mr. Rayburn was too indignant to let her go on.

"You are talking nonsense," he said. "There can be no marriage; the law forbids it."

"Are you one of the people who see no further than their noses?" she asked insolently. "Won't the law take his money? Is he obliged to mention that he is related to her by marriage, when he buys the license?" She paused; her humour changed; she stamped furiously on the floor. The true motive that animated her showed itself in her next words, and warned Mr. Rayburn to grant a more favourable hearing than he had accorded to her yet. "If you won't stop it," she burst out, "I will! If he marries anybody, he is bound to marry ME. Will you take her away? I ask you, for the last time—*will* you take her away?"

The tone in which she made that final appeal to him had its effect.

"I will go back with you to John Zant's house," he said, "and judge for myself."

She laid her hand on his arm:

"I must go first—or you may not be let in. Follow me in five minutes; and don't knock at the street door."

On the point of leaving him, she abruptly returned.

"We have forgotten something," she said. "Suppose my master refuses to see you. His temper might get the better of him; he might make it so unpleasant for you that you would be obliged to go."

"*My* temper might get the better of *me*," Mr. Rayburn replied; "and—if I thought it was in Mrs. Zant's interests—I might refuse to leave the house unless she accompanied me."

"That will never do, sir."

"Why not?"

"Because I should be the person to suffer."

"In what way?"

"In this way. If you picked a quarrel with my master, I should be blamed for it because I showed you upstairs. Besides, think of the lady. You might frighten her out of her senses, if it came to a struggle between you two men."

The language was exaggerated; but there was a force in this last objection which Mr. Rayburn was obliged to acknowledge.

"And, after all," the housekeeper continued, "he has more right over her than you have. He is related to her, and you are only her friend."

Mr. Rayburn declined to let himself be influenced by this consideration, "Mr. John Zant is only related to her by marriage," he said. "If she prefers trusting in me—come what may of it, I will be worthy of her confidence."

The housekeeper shook her head.

"That only means another quarrel," she answered. "The wise way, with a man like my master, is the peaceable way. We must manage to deceive him."

"I don't like deceit."

"In that case, sir, I'll wish you goodbye. We will leave Mrs. Zant to do the best she can for herself."

Mr. Rayburn was unreasonable. He positively refused to adopt this alternative.

"Will you hear what I have got to say?" the housekeeper asked.

"There can be no harm in that," he admitted. "Go on."

She took him at his word.

"When you called at our house," she began, "did you notice the doors in the passage, on the first floor? Very well. One of them is the door of the drawing-room, and the other is the door of the library. Do you remember the drawing-room, sir?"

"I thought it a large well-lighted room," Mr. Rayburn answered. "And I noticed a doorway in the wall, with a handsome curtain hanging over it."

"That's enough for our purpose," the housekeeper resumed. "On the other side of the curtain, if you had looked in, you would have found the library. Suppose my master is as polite as usual, and begs to be excused for not receiving you, because it is an inconvenient time. And suppose you are polite on your side and take yourself off by the drawing-room door. You will find me waiting downstairs, on the first landing. Do you see it now?"

"I can't say I do."

"You surprise me, sir. What is to prevent us from getting back softly into the library, by the door in the passage? And why shouldn't we use that second way into the library as a means of discovering what may be going on in the drawing-room? Safe behind the curtain, you will see him if he behaves uncivilly to Mrs. Zant, or you will hear her if she calls for help. In either case, you may be as rough and ready with my master as you find needful; it will be he who has frightened her, and not you. And who can blame the poor housekeeper because Mr. Rayburn did his duty, and protected a helpless woman? There is my plan, sir. Is it worth trying?"

He answered, sharply enough: "I don't like it."

The housekeeper opened the door again, and wished him good-by.

If Mr. Rayburn had felt no more than an ordinary interest in Mrs. Zant, he would have let the woman go. As it was, he stopped her; and, after some further protest (which proved to be useless), he ended in giving way.

"You promise to follow my directions?" she stipulated.

He gave the promise. She smiled, nodded, and left him. True to his instructions, Mr. Rayburn reckoned five minutes by his watch, before he followed her.

<h1 style="text-align:center">12</h1>

The housekeeper was waiting for him, with the street-door ajar.

"They are both in the drawing-room," she whispered, leading the way upstairs. "Step softly, and take him by surprise."

A table of oblong shape stood midway between the drawing-room walls. At the end of it which was nearest to the window, Mrs. Zant was pacing to and fro across the breadth of the room. At the opposite end of the table, John Zant was seated. Taken completely by surprise, he showed himself in his true character. He started to his feet, and protested with an oath against the intrusion which had been committed on him.

Heedless of his action and his language, Mr. Rayburn could look at nothing, could think of nothing, but Mrs. Zant. She was still walking slowly to and fro, unconscious of the words of sympathy which he addressed to her, insensible even as it seemed to the presence of other persons in the room.

John Zant's voice broke the silence. His temper was under control again: he had his reasons for still remaining on friendly terms with Mr. Rayburn.

"I am sorry I forgot myself just now," he said.

Mr. Rayburn's interest was concentrated on Mrs. Zant; he took no notice of the apology.

"When did this happen?" he asked.

"About a quarter of an hour ago. I was fortunately at home. Without speaking to me, without noticing me, she walked upstairs like a person in a dream."

Mr. Rayburn suddenly pointed to Mrs. Zant.

"Look at her!" he said. "There's a change!"

All restlessness in her movements had come to an end. She was standing at the further end of the table, which was nearest to the window, in the full flow of sunlight pouring at that moment over her face. Her eyes looked out straight before her—void of all expression. Her lips were a little parted: her head drooped slightly toward her shoulder, in an attitude which suggested listening for something or waiting for something. In the warm brilliant light, she stood before the two men, a living creature self-isolated in a stillness like the stillness of death.

John Zant was ready with the expression of his opinion.

"A nervous seizure," he said. "Something resembling cata-lepsy, as you see."

"Have you sent for a doctor?"

"A doctor is not wanted."

"I beg your pardon. It seems to me that medical help is ab-solutely necessary."

"Be so good as to remember," Mr. John Zant answered, "that the decision rests with me, as the lady's relative. I am sensible of the honour which your visit confers on me. But the time has been unhappily chosen. Forgive me if I suggest that you will do well to retire."

Mr. Rayburn had not forgotten the housekeeper's advice, or the promise which she had exacted from him. But the expression in John Zant's face was a serious trial to his self-control. He hesitated, and looked back at Mrs. Zant.

If he provoked a quarrel by remaining in the room, the one alternative would be the removal of her by force. Fear of the consequences to herself, if she was suddenly and roughly roused from her trance, was the one consideration which reconciled him to submission. He withdrew.

The housekeeper was waiting for him below, on the first landing. When the door of the drawing-room had been closed again, she signed to him to follow her, and returned up the stairs. After another struggle with himself, he obeyed.

They entered the library from the corridor—and placed themselves behind the closed curtain which hung over the doorway. It was easy so to arrange the edge of the drapery as to observe, without exciting suspicion, whatever was going on in the next room.

Mrs. Zant's brother-in-law was approaching her at the time when Mr. Rayburn saw him again.

In the instant afterward, she moved—before he had completely passed over the space between them. Her still figure began to tremble. She lifted her drooping head. For a moment there was a shrinking in her—as if she had been touched by something. She seemed to recognize the touch: she was still again.

John Zant watched the change. It suggested to him that she was beginning to recover her senses. He tried the experiment of speaking to her.

"My love, my sweet angel, come to the heart that adores you!"

He advanced again; he passed into the flood of sunlight pouring over her.

"Rouse yourself!" he said.

She still remained in the same position; apparently at his mercy, neither hearing him nor seeing him.

"Rouse yourself!" he repeated. "My darling, come to me!"

At the instant when he attempted to embrace her—at the instant when Mr. Rayburn rushed into the room—John Zant's arms, suddenly turning rigid, remained outstretched. With a shriek of horror, he struggled to draw them back—struggled, in the empty brightness of the sunshine, as if some invisible grip had seized him.

"What has got me?" the wretch screamed. "Who is holding my hands? Oh, the cold of it! the cold of it!"

His features became convulsed; his eyes turned upward until only the white eyeballs were visible. He fell prostrate with a crash that shook the room.

The housekeeper ran in. She knelt by her master's body. With one hand she loosened his cravat. With the other she pointed to the end of the table.

Mrs. Zant still kept her place; but there was another change. Little by little, her eyes recovered their natural living expression—then slowly closed. She tottered backward from the table, and lifted her hands wildly, as if to grasp at something which might support her. Mr. Rayburn hurried to her before she fell—lifted her in his arms—and carried her out of the room.

One of the servants met them in the hall. He sent her for a carriage. In a quarter of an hour more, Mrs. Zant was safe under his care at the hotel.

13

That night a note, written by the housekeeper, was delivered to Mrs. Zant.

"The doctors give little hope. The paralytic stroke is spreading upward to his face. If death spares him, he will live a helpless man. I shall take care of him to the last. As for you—forget him."

Mrs. Zant gave the note to Mr. Rayburn.

"Read it, and destroy it," she said. "It is written in ignorance of the terrible truth."

He obeyed—and looked at her in silence, waiting to hear more. She hid her face. The few words she had addressed to him, after a struggle with herself, fell slowly and reluctantly from her lips.

She said: "No mortal hand held the hands of John Zant. The guardian spirit was with me. The promised protection was with me. I know it. I wish to know no more."

Having spoken, she rose to retire. He opened the door for her, seeing that she needed rest in her own room.

Left by himself, he began to consider the prospect that was before him in the future. How was he to regard the woman who had just left him? As a poor creature weakened by disease, the victim of her own nervous delusion? or as the chosen object of a supernatural revelation—unparalleled by any similar revelation that he had heard of, or had found recorded in books? His first discovery of the place that she really held in his estimation dawned on his mind, when he felt himself recoiling from the conclusion which presented her to his pity, and yielding to the nobler conviction which felt with her faith, and raised her to a place apart among other women.

14

They left St. Sallins the next day.

Arrived at the end of the journey, Lucy held fast by Mrs. Zant's hand. Tears were rising in the child's eyes.

"Are we to bid her goodbye?" she said sadly to her father.

He seemed to be unwilling to trust himself to speak; he only said:

"My dear, ask her yourself."

But the result justified him. Lucy was happy again.

The Devil's Spectacles

1

MEMOIRS OF AN ARCTIC VOYAGER

'He says, sir, he thinks he's nigh to his latter end, and he would like, if convenient, to see you before he goes.'

'Do you mean before he dies?'

'That's about it, sir.'

I was in no humour (for reasons to be hereafter mentioned) for seeing anybody, under disastrous circumstances of any sort; but the person who had sent me word that he was 'nigh to his latter end' had special claims on my consideration.

He was an old sailor, who had first seen blue water under the protection of my father, then a post-captain in the navy. Born on our estate, and the only male survivor of our head game-keeper's family of seven children, he had received a good education through my father's kindness, and he ought to have got on well in the world; but he was one of those born vagabonds who set education at defiance. His term of service having expired, he disappeared for many years. During part of the time he was supposed to have been employed in the merchant navy.

At the end of that long interval he turned up one day at our country house, an invalided man, without a penny in his pocket. My good father, then nearing the end of his life, was invalided too. Whether he had a fellow-feeling for the helpless creature whom he had once befriended, or whether he only took counsel of his own generous nature, it is now needless to inquire. He appointed Septimus Notman to be lodge-keeper at the second of our two park gates, and he recommended Septimus to my personal care on his deathbed. 'I'm afraid he's an old scoundrel,' my father confessed; 'but somebody must look after him as long as he lasts, and if you don't take his part, Alfred, nobody else will.' After this Septimus kept his place at the gate while we were in the country.

When we returned to our London house the second gate was closed. The old sailor was lodged (by a strong exertion of my influence) in a room over a disused stable, which our coachman had proposed to turn into a hayloft. Everybody disliked Septimus Notman. He was said to be mad; to be a liar, a hypocrite, a vicious wretch, and a disagreeable brute. There were people who even reported that he had been a pirate during the time when we lost sight of him and who declared, when they were asked for their proof, that his crimes were written in his face.

He was not in the least affected by the opinions of his neighbours; he chewed his tobacco and drank his grog, and, in the words of the old song, 'He cared for nobody, no, not he!' Well had my poor father said that I didn't take his part nobody else would. And shall I tell you a secret? Though I strictly carried out my father's wishes, and though Septimus was disposed in his own rough way to be grateful to me, I didn't like him either.

So I went to the room over the stables (we were in London at the time) with dry eyes and I sat down by his bed and cut up a cake of tobacco for him, and said, 'Well, what's the matter?' as coolly as if he had sent me word that he thought he had caught a cold in the head.

'I'm called away.' Septimus answered, 'and before I go I've got a confession to make, and something useful to offer you. It's reported among the servants, Mr Alfred, that you're in trouble just now between two ladies. You may see your way clear in that matter, sir, if death spares me long enough to say a few last words.'

'Never mind me, Septimus. Has a doctor seen you?'

'The doctor knows no more about me than I know myself. The doctor be —!'

'Have you any last wishes I can attend to?'

'None, sir.'

'Shall I send for a clergyman?'

Septimus Notman looked at me as directly as he could—he was afflicted with a terrible squint. Otherwise he was a fine, stoutly-built man, with a ruddy face profusely encircled by white hair and whiskers, a hoarse, heavy voice, and the biggest hands I ever saw. He put one of these enormous hands under his pillow before he answered me.

'If you think,' he said, 'that a clergyman will come to a man who has got the Devil's Spectacles here, under his pillow, and who has only to put those Spectacles on to see through that clergyman's clothes, flesh, and what not, and read everything that's written in his secret mind as plain as print, fetch him, Master Alfred—fetch him!'

I thought the clergyman might not like this, and withdrew my suggestion accordingly. The least I could do, as a matter of common politeness, after giving up the clergyman, was to ask if I might look at the Devil's Spectacles.

'Hear how I came by them first!' said Septimus.

'Will it take long?' I inquired.

'It will take long, and it will make your flesh creep.'

I remembered my promise to my father, and placed myself and my flesh at the mercy of Septimus Notman. But he was not ready to begin yet.

'Do you see that white jug?' he said, pointing to the wash-stand.

'Yes. Do you want water?'

'I want grog. There's grog in the white jug. And there's a pewter mug on the chimney-piece. I must be strung up, Master Alfred—I must be strung up.'

The white jug contained at least half a gallon of rum and wa-ter, roughly calculated. I strung him up. In the case of any other dying person I might have hesitated. But a man who possessed the Devil's Spectacles was surely an exception to ordinary rules, and might finish his career and finish his grog at one and the same time.

'Now I'm ready,' he said, 'what do you think I was up to in the time when you all lost sight of me? The latter part of that time, I mean?'

'They say you were a pirate,' I replied.

'Worse than that. Guess again.'

'I tried to persuade myself that there might be such a human anomaly as a merciful pirate, and guessed once more.

'A murderer,' I suggested.

'Worse than that. Guess again.'

I declined to guess again. 'Tell me yourself what you have been,' I said.

He answered without the least appearance of discomposure, 'I've been a Cannibal.'

Perhaps it was weak of me—but I did certainly start to my feet and make for the door.

'Hear the circumstances,' said Septimus. 'You know the proverb, sir? Circumstances alter cases.'

There was no disputing the proverb. I sat down again. I was a young and tender man, which, in my present position, was certainly against me. But I had very little flesh on my bones and that was in my favour.

'It happened when I went out with the Arctic expedition,' Septimus proceeded. 'I've forgotten all my learning, and lost my memory for dates. The year escapes me, and the latitude and longitude escape me. But I can tell you the rest of it. We were an exploring party, you must know, with sledges. It was getting close to the end of the summer months in those parts, and we were higher than any of them have ever got since to the North Pole.

'We should have found our way there—don't you doubt it—but for three of our best men who fell sick of the scurvy. The second lieutenant, who was in command, called a halt, as the soldiers say. "With this loss of strength," says he, "it's my duty to take you back to the ships. We must let the North Pole be, and pray God that we may have no more invalided men to carry. I

441

give you half an hour's rest before we turn back."

'The carpenter was one of our sound men. He spoke next. He reported one of the two sledges not fit for service. "How long will you be making it fit?" says the lieutenant.

"'In a decent climate," says the carpenter, "I should say two or three hours, sir. Here, double that time, at least." You may say why not do without the sledge? I'll tell you why. On account of the sick men to be carried.

"'Be as quick about it as you can," says the lieutenant: "time means life in our predicament." Most of the men were glad enough to rest.

'Only two of us murmured at not going on. One was a boatswain's mate; t'other was me. "Do you think the North Pole's the other side of that rising ground there?" says the lieutenant.

'The boatswain's mate was young and self-conceited. "I should like to try, sir," he says, "if any other man has pluck enough to go along with me." He looked at me when he said that. I wasn't going to have my courage called in question publicly by a slip of a lad; and, moreover, I had a fancy to try for the North Pole, too. I volunteered to go along with him.

'Our notion, you will understand, was to take a compass and some grub with us; to try what we could find in a couple hours' march forward; and to get back in good time for our duty on the return journey.

'The lieutenant wouldn't hear of it. "I'm responsible for every man in my charge," says he. "You're a couple of fools. Stay where you are." We were a couple of fools. We watched our opportunity, while they were all unloading the broken-down sledge; and slipped off to try our luck, and get the reward for discovering the North Pole.'

There he stopped, and pointed to the grog. 'Dry-work, talking,' he said. 'Give us a drop more.'

I filled the pewter mug again. And again Septimus Notman emptied it.

'We set our course northwest by north,' he went on; 'and after a while (seeing the ground favoured us) we altered it again to due north. I can't tell you how long we walked (we neither of us had watches)—but this I'll swear to. Just as the last of the daylight was dying out, we got to the top of a hillock; and there we saw the glimmer of the open Polar Sea! No! Not the Sound that enters Kennedy's Channel, which has been mistaken for it, I know—but the real thing, the still and lonesome Polar Sea! What would you have done in our place? I'll tell you what we did. We sat down on some nice dry snow, and took out our biscuits and grog.

Freezing work, do you say? You'll find it in the books, if you don't believe me—the further north you get in those parts, the less cold there is, and the more open water you find. Ask Captain McClure what sort of a bed he slept upon, on the night of October thirtieth, 'fifty-one. Well, and what do you think we did when we had eaten and drunk? Lit our pipes. And what next? Fell fast asleep, after our long walk, on our nice dry snow.

And what sort of prospect met us when we woke? Darkness and drizzle and mist. I had the compass, and I tried to set our course on the way back. I could no more see the compass than if I had been blind. We had no means of striking a light, except my match-box. I had left it on the snow by my side when I fell asleep. Not a match would light. As for help of any sort, it was not to be thought of. We couldn't have been less than five miles distant from the place where we had left our messmates. So there we were, the boatswain's mate and me, alone in the desert, lost at the North Pole.'

I began to feel interested. 'You tried to get back, I suppose, dark as it was?' I said.

'We walked till we dropped,' Septimus answered; 'and then we yelled and shouted till we had no voices left; and then we hollowed out a hole in the snow, and waited for daylight.'

'What did you expect when daylight came?'

'I expected nothing, Master Alfred. The boatswain's mate (beginning to get a little light-headed, you know) expected the lieutenant to send in search of us, or wait till we returned. A likely thing for an officer in charge to do, with the lives of the sledging party depending on his getting them back to the ships, and only two men missing, who had broken orders and deserted their duty. A good riddance of bad rubbish—that's what he said of us when we were reported missing, I'll be bound.

'When the light came we tried to get back; and we did set our course cleverly enough. But, bless you, we had nothing left to eat or drink! When the light failed us again we were done up. We dropped on the snow, under the lee of a rock, and gave out. The boatswain's mate said his prayers, and I said Amen. Not the least use!

'On the contrary, as the night advanced it got colder and colder. We were both close together, to keep each other warm. I don't know how long it was, I only know it was still pitch dark, when I heard the boatswain's mate give a little flutter of a sigh, and no more. I opened his clothes, and put my hand on his heart. Dead, of cold and exhaustion, and no mistake. I shouldn't have been long after him but for my own presence of mind.'

'Your presence of mind? What did you do?'

'Stripped every rag of clothes off him, and put them all on myself. What are you shivering about? He couldn't feel it, could he? I tell you, he'd have been frozen stiff before the next day's light came—but for my presence of mind again. As well as my failing strength would let me, I buried him under the snow. Virtue, they say, Master Alfred, is its own reward. That good action proved to be the saving of my life.'

'What do you mean?'

'Didn't I tell you I buried him?'

'Well!'

'Well, in that freezing air, the burying of him kept him eatable. Don't you see?'

'You wretch!'

'Put yourself in my place, and don't call names. I held out till I was mad with hunger. And then I did open my knife with my teeth. And I did burrow down in the snow till I felt him —.'

I could hear no more of it. 'Get on to the end! I said. 'Why didn't you die at the North Pole?'

'Because somebody helped me to get away.'

'Who helped you?'

'The Devil.'

He showed his yellow old teeth in a horrible grin. I could draw but one conclusion—his mind was failing him before death. Anything that spared me his hideous confession of cannibalism was welcome. I asked how the supernatural rescue happened.

'More grog first,' he said. 'The horrors come on me when I think of it.' He was evidently sinking. Without the grog I doubt if he could have said much more.

'I can't tell you how many days passed,' he went on; 'I only know that the time was nigh when it was all dark and no light. The darker it got, the deeper I scooped the sort of cavern I'd made for myself under the snow. Whether it was night, or whether it was day I know no more than you do. On a sudden, in the awful silence and solitude, I heard a voice, high up, as it were, on the rock behind me. It was a cheering and a pleasant voice, and it said, "Well, Septimus Notman, is there much left of the boatswain's mate by this time? Did he eat short while he lasted?"

'I cried out in fright, "Who the devil—?" The voice stopped me before I could say the rest.

'"You've hit it," says the voice, "I am that person; and it's about time the Devil helped you out of this."

'"No," says I, "I'd rather perish by cold than fire any day."

'"Make your mind easy," says he, taking the point, "I don't want you in my place yet. I expect you to do a deal more in the way of degrading your humanity before you come to me, and I offer you a safe passage back to the nearest settlement. Friend Septimus, you're a man after my own heart."

'"As how, sir?" says I.

'"Because you're such a complete beast," says he. "A human being who elevates himself, and rises higher and higher to his immortal destiny, is a creature I hate. He gets above me, even in his earthly lifetime. But you have dropped—you dear good fellow—to the level of a famished wolf. You have gobbled up your dead companion; and if you ever had such a thing as a soul—ha,

Septimus!—it parted company with you at the first morsel you tasted of the Boatswain's mate. Do you think I'll leave such a prime specimen of the Animal Man as you are, deserted at the North Pole? No, no; I grant you a free pass by my railway; darkness and distance are no obstacles to Me. Are you ready?"

'You may not believe me; but I felt myself being lifted up, as it were, against my own will. "Give us a light," I says, "I can't travel in the dark."

'"Take my spectacles," says he, "they'll help you to see more than you bargain for. Look through them at your fellow mortals, and you'll see the inmost thoughts of their hearts as plain as I do, and, considering your nature, Septimus, that will drop you even below the level of a wolf."

'"Suppose I don't want to look," says I, "may I throw the spectacles away?"

'"They'll come back to you," says he.

'"May I smash them up?" "They'll put themselves together again."

'"What am I to do with them?"

'"Give them to another man. Now then! One, two, three—and away!"

'You may not believe me again; I lost my senses, Master Alfred. Hold me up; I'm losing them now. More grog—that's right—more grog. I came to myself at Upernavik, with the Devil's Spectacles in my pocket. Take them, sir. And read those two ladies' hearts. And act accordingly. Hush! I hear him speaking to me again. Behind my pillow. Just as he spoke on the rock. Most polite and cheering. Calling to me, as it were, "Come, Cannibal—come!" Like a song, isn't it? "Come, Cannibal—come!"'

He sang the last words faintly, and died with a smile on his face. Delirium or lies? With the Spectacles actually in my hands, I was inclined to think lies. They were of the old-fashioned sort, with big, circular glasses, and stout tortoise-shell frames; they smelt musty, but not sulphurous. I possess a sense of humour, I am happy to say. When they were thoroughly cleaned, I determined to try the Devil's Spectacles on the two ladies, and submit to the consequences, whatever they might be."

MEMOIRS OF MYSELF

Who were the two ladies?

They were both young and unmarried. As a matter of delicacy, I ask permission to mention them by their Christian names
only. Zilla, aged seventeen. Cecilia, aged two and twenty.

And what was my position between them?

I was the same age as Cecilia. She was my mother's companion and reader; handsome, well-born and poor. I had made her
a proposal, and had been accepted. There were no money difficulties in the way of our marriage, in spite of my sweetheart's
empty purse. I was an only child, and I had inherited, excepting
my mother's jointure, the whole of the large property that my
father left at his death.

In social rank Cecilia was more than my equal; we were
therefore not ill-matched from the worldly point of view. Nevertheless, there was an obstacle to our union, and a person interested in making the most of it. The obstacle was Zilla. The
person interested was my mother. Zilla was her niece—her elder
brother's daughter. The girl's parents had died in India, and she
had been sent to school in England, under the care of her uncle
and guardian. I had never seen her, and had hardly heard of her,
until there was a question of her spending the Christmas holidays (in the year when Septimus Notman died) at our house.

'Her uncle has no objection,' my mother said; 'and I shall be
more than glad to see her. A most interesting creature, as I hear.
So lovely, and so good, that they call her The Angel, at school.
I say nothing about her nice little fortune or the high military rank that her poor father possessed. You don't care for these
things. But, oh, Alfred, it would make me so happy if you fell in
love with Zilla and married her!'

Three days before, I had made my proposal to Cecilia, and
had been accepted—subject to my mother's approval. I thought
this a good opportunity of stating my case plainly; and I spoke

out. Never before had I seen my mother so outraged and disappointed—enraged with Cecilia; disappointed with me. 'A woman without a farthing of a dowry; a woman who was as old as I was; a woman who had taken advantage of her position in the house to mislead and delude me!' and so on.

Cecilia would certainly have been sent away if I had not declared that I should feel it my duty, in that event, to marry her immediately. My mother knew my temper, and refrained from giving Cecilia any cause of offence. Cecilia, on her side, showed what is called a proper pride; she declined to become my wife until my mother approved of her. She considered herself to be a martyr; and I considered myself to be an abominably treated man. Between us, I am afraid we made our good mother's life unendurable—she was obliged to be the first who gave way.

It was understood that we were to be married in the spring. It was also understood that Zilla was bitterly disappointed at having her holiday visit to us put off. 'She was so anxious to see you, poor child,' my mother said to me; 'but I really daren't ask her here under present circumstances. She is so fresh, so innocent, so infinitely superior in personal attractions to Cecilia, that I don't know what might happen if you saw her now. You are the soul of honour, Alfred; but you and Zilla had better remain strangers to each other—you might repent your rash engagement.' After this, it is needless to say that I was dying to see Zilla; while, at the same time, I never for an instant swerved from my fidelity to Cecilia.

Such was my position, on the memorable day when Septimus Notman died, leaving me possessor of the Devil's Spectacles.

3
THE TEST OF THE SPECTACLES

The first person whom I encountered on returning to the house was the butler. He met me in the hall, with a receipted account in his hand which I had sent him to pay. The amount was close on a hundred pounds, and I had paid it immediately. 'Is there no discount?' I asked, looking at the receipt.

'The parties expect cash, sir, and charge accordingly.'

He looked so respectable when he made this answer, he had served us for so many years, that I felt an irresistible temptation to try the Devil's Spectacles on the butler, before I ventured to look through them at the ladies of my family. Our honest old servant would be such an excellent test.

'I am afraid my sight is failing me,' I said.

With this exceedingly simple explanation I put on the spectacles and looked at the butler.

The hall whirled round with me; on my word of honour I tremble and turn cold while I write of it now. Septimus Notman had spoken the truth!

In an instant the butler's heart became hideously visible—a fat organ seen through the medium of the infernal glasses. The thought in him was plainly legible to me in these words: 'Does my master think I'm going to give him the five per cent off the bill? Beastly meanness, interfering with the butler's perquisites.'

I took off my spectacles and put them in my pocket.

'You are a thief,' I said to the butler. 'You have got the discount money on this bill—five pounds all but a shilling or two—in your pocket. Send in your accounts; you leave my service.'

'Tomorrow, sir, if you like!' answered the butler, indignantly. 'After serving your family for five-and-twenty years, to be called a thief for only taking my perquisites is an insult, Mr Alfred, that I have not deserved.' He put his handkerchief to his eyes and left me.

It was true that he had served us for a quarter of a century; it was also true that he had taken his perquisite and told a fib about it. But he had his compensating virtues. When I was a child he had given me many a ride on his knee and many a stolen drink of wine and water. His cellar-book had always been honestly kept; and his wife herself admitted that he was a model husband.

At other times I should have remembered this, I should have felt that I had been hasty, and have asked his pardon. At this time I failed to feel the slightest compassion for him, and never faltered for a moment in my resolution to send him away. What change had passed over me?

The library door opened, and an old schoolfellow and college friend of mine looked out. 'I thought I heard your voice in the hall,' he said; 'I have been waiting an hour for you.'

'Anything very important,' I asked, leading the way back to the library.

'Nothing of the least importance to you,' he replied, modestly.

I wanted no further explanation. More than once already I had lent him money, and, sooner or later, he had always repaid me. 'Another little loan?' I inquired, smiling pleasantly.

'I am really ashamed to ask you again, Alfred. But if you could lend me fifty pounds—just look at that letter?

He made some joke, suggested by the quaint appearance of the Spectacles. I was too closely occupied to appreciate his sense of humour. What had he just said to me? He had said. 'I am ashamed to ask you again.' And what had he thought while he was speaking? He had thought. 'When one has a milch cow at one's disposal, who but a fool would fail to take advantage of it?'

I handed him back the letter (from a lawyer, threatening 'proceedings') and I said, in my hardest tones, 'It's not convenient to oblige you this time.'

He stared at me like a man thunderstruck. 'Is this a joke, Alfred?' he asked.

'Do I look as if I was joking?'

He took up his hat. 'There is but one excuse for you,' he said. 'Your social position is too much for your weak brain—your money has got into your head. Good morning.'

I had been indebted to him for all sorts of kind services at school and college. He was an honourable man, and a faithful friend. If the galling sense of his own narrow means made him unjustly contemptuous towards rich people, it was a fault (in my case, an exasperating fault), no doubt. But who is perfect? And what are fifty pounds to me? This is what I should once have felt, before he could have found time enough to get to the door.

As things were, I let him go, and thought myself well rid of a mean hanger-on who only valued me for my money.

Being now free to visit the ladies, I rang the bell and asked if my mother was at home. She was in her *boudoir*. And where was Miss Cecilia? In the *boudoir*, too.

On entering the room I found visitors in the way, and put off the trial of the Spectacles until they had taken their leave. Just as they were going a thundering knock at the door announced more visitors. This time, fortunately, we escaped with no worse consequences than the delivery of cards. We actually had two minutes to ourselves. I seized the opportunity of reminding my mother that I was constitutionally inaccessible to the claims of Society, and that I thought we might as well have our house to ourselves for half an hour or so. 'Send word down stairs,' I said, 'that you are not at home.'

My mother—magnificent in her old lace, her admirably-dressed grey hair, and her finely falling robe of purple-silk—looked across the fireplace at Cecilia—tall, and lazy, and beautiful, with lovely brown eyes, luxuriant black hair, a warmly-pale complexion, and an amber-coloured dress—and said to me, 'You forget Cecilia. She likes Society.'

Cecilia looked at my mother with an air of languid surprise. 'What an extraordinary mistake! she answered. 'I hate Society.'

My mother smiled—rang the bell—and gave the order-Not at home. I produced my spectacles. There was an outcry at the hideous ugliness of them. I laid blame on 'my oculist,' and waited for what was to follow between the two ladies. My mother spoke. Consequently I looked at my mother.

[I present her words first, and her thoughts next, in parenthesis.]

'So you hate society, my dear? Surely you have changed your opinion lately?' ('She doesn't mind how she lies as long as she can curry favour with Alfred. False creature.')

[I report Cecilia's answer on the same plan.]

'Pardon me; I haven't in the least changed my opinion—I

was only afraid to express it. I hope I have not given offence by expressing it now.' ('She can't exist without gossip, and then she tries to lay it on me. Worldly old wretch!')

What I began to think of my mother, I am ashamed to record. What I thought of Cecilia may be stated in two words. I was more eager than ever to see 'The Angel of the school,' the good and lovely Zilla.

My mother stopped the further progress of my investigations. 'Take off those hideous Spectacles, Alfred, or leave us to our visitors. I don't say your sight may not be failing; I only say change your oculist.'

I took off the Spectacles, all the more willingly that I began to be really afraid of them. The talk between the ladies went on.

'Yours is a strange confession, my dear,' my mother said to Cecilia. 'May I ask what motive so young a lady can have for hating Society?'

'Only the motive of wanting to improve myself,' Cecilia answered. 'If I knew a little more of modern languages, and if I could be something better than a feeble amateur when I paint in water colours, you might think me worthier to be Alfred's wife. But Society is always in the way when I open my book or take up my brushes. In London I have no time to myself, and, I really can't disguise it, the frivolous life I lead is not to my taste.'

I thought this—(my Spectacles being in my pocket, remember)—very well and very prettily said. My mother looked at me. 'I quite agree with Cecilia,' I said, answering the look. 'We cannot count on having five minutes to ourselves in London from morning to night.' Another knock at the street door contributed its noisy support to my views as I spoke. 'We daren't even look out of the window,' I remarked, 'for fear Society may look up at the same moment, and see that we are at home.'

My mother smiled. 'You are certainly two remarkable young people,' she said, with an air of satirical indulgence—and paused for a moment, as if an idea had occurred to her which was more than usually worthy of consideration. If her eye had not been on me at the moment, I believe I should have taken my Spectacles out of my pocket.

'You are both so thoroughly agreed in disliking Society and despising London,' she resumed, 'that I feel it my duty, as a good mother, to make your lives a little more in harmony with your tastes, if I can. You complain, Alfred, that you can never count on having five minutes to yourself with Cecilia, Cecilia complains that she is perpetually interrupted in the laudable effort to improve her mind. I offer you both the whole day to yourselves, week after week, for the next three months. We will spend the winter at Long Fallas.'

Long Fallas was our country seat. There was no hunting; the shooting was let; the place was seven miles from Timbercombe town and station; and our nearest neighbour was a young Ritualistic clergyman, popularly reported in the village to be starving himself to death. I declined my mother's extraordinary proposal without a moment's hesitation. Cecilia, with the readiest and sweetest submission, accepted it.

This was our first open difference of opinion.

Even without the Spectacles I could see that my mother hailed it as a good sign. She had consented to our marriage in the spring, without in the least altering her opinion that the angelic Zilla was the right wife for me. 'Settle it between yourselves, my dears,' she said, and left her chair to look for her work. Cecilia rose immediately to save her the trouble.

The instant their backs were turned on me I put on the terrible glasses. Is there such a thing in anatomy as a back view of the heart? There is such a thing assuredly when you look through the Devil's Spectacles. My mother's private sentiments presented themselves to me, as follows: 'If they don't get thoroughly sick of each other in a winter at Long Fallas I give up all knowledge of human nature. He shall marry Zilla yet.'

Cecilia's motives asserted themselves with transparent simplicity in these words, 'His mother fully expects me to say "No." Horrible as the prospect is, I'll disappoint her by saying "Yes."'

'Horrible as the prospect is' was to my mind a very revolting expression, considering that I was personally included in the prospect. My mother's mischievous test of our affection for each other now presented itself to me in the light of a sensible proceeding.

In the solitude of Long Fallas, I should surely discover whether Cecilia was about to marry me for my money or for myself. I concealed my Spectacles, and said nothing at the time. But later, when my mother entered the drawing-room dressed to go out for dinner, I waylaid her, quite willing to go to Long Fallas. Cecilia came in dressed for dinner also. She had never looked so irresistibly lovely as when she was informed of my change of opinion. 'What a happy time we shall have,' she said, and smiled as if she really meant it?

They went away to their party. I was in the library when they returned. Hearing the carriage stop at the door I went out into the hall, and was suddenly checked on my way to the ladies by the sound of a man's voice: 'Many thanks; I am close at home now.'

My mother's voice followed: 'I will let you know if we go to the country, Sir John. You will ride over and see us?'

'With thee greatest pleasure. Goodnight, Miss Cecilia.' There was no mistaking the tone in which those last four words were spoken. Sir John's accent expressed indescribable tenderness. I retired again to the library.

My mother came in, followed by her charming companion.

'Here is a new complication,' she said. 'Cecilia doesn't want to go to Long Fallas.' I asked why.

Cecilia answered, without looking at me, 'Oh, I have changed my mind. She turned aside to relieve my mother of her fur cloak. I instantly consulted my Spectacles, and obtained my information in these mysterious terms: 'Sir John goes to Timbercombe.'

Very short, and yet suggestive of more than one interpretation. A little inquiry made the facts more clear. Sir John had been one of the guests at the dinner, and he and Cecilia had shaken hands like old friends. At my mother's request, he had been presented to her. He had produced such an excellent impression that she had taken him in her carriage part of his way home. She had also discovered that he was about to visit a relative living at Timbercombe (already mentioned, I think, as our nearest town).

Another momentary opportunity with the Spectacles completed my discoveries. Sir John had proposed marriage (unsuccessfully) to Cecilia, and being still persistently in love with her, only wanted a favourable opportunity to propose again. The excellent impression which he had produced on my mother was perfectly intelligible now.

In feeling reluctant to give her rejected lover that other opportunity, was Cecilia afraid of Sir John, or afraid of herself? My Spectacles informed me that she deliberately declined to face that question, even in her thoughts.

Under these circumstances, the test of a dreary winter residence at Long Fallas became, to my mind, more valuable than ever. Single-handed, Cecilia might successfully keep up appearances and deceive other people, though she might not deceive me.

But, in combination with Sir John, there was a chance that she might openly betray the true state of her feelings. If I was really the favoured man, she would, of course, be dearer to me than ever. If not (with more producible proof than the Devil's Spectacles to justify me), I need not hesitate to break off the engagement.

'Second thoughts are not always best, dear Cecilia,' I said. 'Do me a favour. Let us try Long Fallas, and if we find the place quite unendurable, let us return to London.'

Cecilia looked at me and hesitated—looked at my mother, and submitted to Long Fallas in the sweetest manner. The more they were secretly at variance, the better the two ladies appeared to understand each other.

We did not start for the country until three days afterward. The packing up was a serious matter to begin with, and my mother prolonged the delay by paying a visit to her niece at the school in the country. She kept the visit a secret from Cecilia, of course. But even when we were alone, and when I asked about Zilla, I was only favoured with a very brief reply.

She merely lifted her eyes to Heaven, and said, 'Perfectly charming!'

4
THE TEST OF LONG FALLAS

We had had a week of it. If we had told each other the truth we should have said, 'Let us go back to London.'

Thus far there had been no signs of Sir John. The Spectacles informed me that he had arrived at Timbercombe, and that Cecilia had written to him. But, strangely enough, they failed to disclose what she had said. Has she forgotten it already, or was there some defect, hitherto unsuspected, in my supernatural glasses?

Christmas Day was near at hand. The weather was, so far, almost invariably misty and wet. Cecilia began to yawn over her favourite intellectual resources. My mother waited with superhuman patience for events. As for myself, having literally nothing else to amuse me, I took to gratifying an improper curiosity in the outlying regions of the family circle. In plain English, I discovered a nice little needle-woman, who was employed at Long Fallas. Her name was Miss Peskey. When nobody was looking, I amused myself with Miss Peskey.

Let no person of strict principles be alarmed. It was an innocent flirtation, on my side; and the nice little needle-woman rigidly refused to give me the smallest encouragement. Quite a young girl, Miss Peskey had the self-possession of a mature woman. She allowed me time to see that she had a trim little figure, soft blue eyes, and glossy golden hair; and then, in the sweetest of voices, respectfully requested me to leave her to her work. If I tried to persuade her to let me stay a little longer, she rose meekly, and said 'I shall, most unwillingly, be compelled to place myself under the protection of the housekeeper.'

Once I attempted to take her hand. She put her handkerchief to her eyes and said, 'Is it manly, sir, to insult a defenceless girl?'

In one word, Miss Peskey foiled me at every point. For the first week I never even got the chance of looking at her through the Devil's Spectacles.

On the first day of the new week the weather cleared up wonderfully; spring seemed to have come to us in the middle of winter.

Cecilia and I went out riding. On our return, having nothing better to do, I accompanied the horses back to the stables, and naturally offended the groom, who thought I was 'watching him.' Returning toward the house, I passed the window of the ground-floor room, at the back of the building, devoted to the needlewoman.

A railed yard kept me at a respectful distance, but at the same time gave me a view of the interior of the room. Miss Peskey was not alone; my mother was with her. They were evidently talking, but not a word reached my ears. It mattered nothing. While I could see them through my Spectacles, their thoughts were visible to me before they found their way into words.

My mother was speaking—'Well, my dear, have you formed your opinion of him yet?'

Miss Peskey replied, 'Not quite yet.'

'You are wonderfully cautious in arriving at a conclusion. How much longer is this clever contrivance of yours to last?'

'Give me two days more, dear madam; I can't decide until Sir John helps me.'

'Is Sir John really coming here?'

'I think so.'

'And have you managed it?'

'If you will kindly excuse me, I would rather not answer just yet.'

The housekeeper entered the room, and called my mother away on some domestic business. As she walked to the door, I had time to read her thought before she went out—'Very extraordinary to find such resources of clever invention in such a young girl!'

Miss Peskey, left in maiden meditation with her work on

her lap, smiled to herself. I turned the glasses on her, and made a discovery that petrified me. To put it plainly, the charming needlewoman was deceiving us all (with the one exception of my mother) under an assumed name and vocation in life. Miss Peskey was no other than my cousin Zilla, 'the Angel of the school!'

Let me do my poor mother justice. She was guilty of the consenting to the deception, and of no more. The invention of the trick, and the entire responsibility of carrying it out, rested wholly and exclusively with Miss Zilla, aged seventeen.

I followed the train of thought which my mother's questions had set going in the mind of this young person. To justify my own conduct, I must report the result as briefly as I can. Have you heard of 'fasting' girls? have you heard of 'mesmeric' girls? have you heard of girls (in the newspapers) who have invented the most infamous charges against innocent men? Then don't accuse my Spectacles of seeing impossible sights!

My report of Miss Zilla's thoughts, as they succeeded each other, begins as follows:

First Thought: 'My small fortune is all very well; but I want to be mistress of a great establishment, and get away from school. Alfred, dear fellow, is reported to have fifteen thousand a year. Is his mother's companion to be allowed to catch this rich fish, without the least opposition? Not if I know it!'

Second Thought: 'How very simple old people are! His mother visits me, invites me to Long Fallas, and expects me to cut out Cecilia.
Men are such fools (the writing master has fallen in love with me) that she would only have to burst out crying, and keep him to herself. I have proposed a better way than fair fighting for Alfred, suggested by a play I read the other day. The old mother consents, with conditions. "I am sure you will do nothing, my dear, unbecoming to a young lady. Win him, as Miss Hardcastle won Mr Marlow in *She*

Stoops to Conquer, if you like; but do nothing to forfeit your self-respect." What astonishing simplicity! Where did she go to school when she was young?'

Third Thought: 'How amazingly lucky that Cecilia's maid is lazy, and that the needlewoman dines in the servants' hall! The maid had the prospect of getting up before six in the morning, to be ready to go in the chaise-car with the servant who does the household errands at Timbercombe—and for what? To take a note from her mistress to Sir John, and wait for an answer. The good little needlewoman hears this, smiles, and says, "I don't mind how early I get up; I'll take it for you, and bring back the answer."'

Fourth Thought: 'What a blessing it is to have blue eyes and golden hair! Sir John was quite struck with me. I thought at the time he would do instead of Alfred. Fortunately I have since asked the simple old mother about him. He is a poor baronet. Not to be thought of for an instant. "My Lady"—without a corresponding establishment! Too dreadful! But I didn't throw away my fascinations. I saw him wince when he read the letter. "No bad news, I hope, sir," I ventured to say.

He shook his head solemnly. "Your mistress" (he took me, of course, for Cecilia's maid) forbids me to call at Long Fallas." I thought to myself what a hypocrite Cecilia must be, and I said modestly to Sir John, to keep up appearances. Our private arrangement is that he is to ride over to Long Fallas tomorrow, and wait in the shrubbery at half-past two. If it rains or snows he is to try the next fine day. In either case the poor needlewoman will ask for a half holiday, and will induce Miss Cecilia to take a little walk in the right direction.

Sir John gave me two sovereigns and a kiss at parting. I accepted both tributes with the most becoming humility. He shall have his money's worth, though he is a poor baronet; he shall meet his young lady in the shrubbery. And I may catch the rich fish, after all!'

Fifth Thought: 'Bother this horrid work! It is all very well to be clever with one's needle, but how it disfigures one's forefinger! No matter, I must play my part while it lasts, or I shall be reported lazy by the most detestable woman I ever met with- the housekeeper at Long Fallas.'

She threaded her needle, and I put my Spectacles in my pocket.

I don't think I suspected it at the time; but I am now well aware that Septimus Notman's diabolical gift was exerting an influence over me. I was wickedly cool, under circumstances which would have roused my righteous indignation in the days before my Spectacles. Sir John and the Angel; my mother and her family interests; Cecilia and her unacknowledged lover- what a network of conspiracy and deception was wound about me! and what a perfectly fiendish pleasure I felt in planning to match them on their own ground!

The method of obtaining this object presented itself to me in the simplest form. I had only to take my mother for a walk in the near neighbourhood of the shrubbery—and the exposure would be complete! That night I studied the barometer with unutterable anxiety. The prospect of the weather was all that I could wish.

5

THE TRUTH IN THE SHRUBBERY

On the next day, the friendly sun shone, the balmy air invited everybody to go out. I made no further use of the Spectacles that morning: my purpose was to keep them in my pocket until the interview in the shrubbery was over. Shall I own the motive? It was simply fear—fear of making further discoveries, and of losing the masterly self-control on which the whole success of my project depended.

We lunched at one o'clock. Had Cecilia and Zilla come to a private understanding on the subject of the interview in the shrubbery? By way of ascertaining this, I asked Cecilia if she would like to go out riding in the afternoon. She declined the proposal—she wanted to finish a sketch. I was sufficiently answered.

'Cecilia complains that your manner has grown cold toward her lately,' mother said, when we were left together.

My mind was dwelling on Cecilia's letter to Sir John. Would any man have so easily adopted Zilla's suggestion not to take Cecilia on her word, unless there had been something to encourage him? I could only trust myself to answer my mother very briefly. 'Cecilia is changed towards me'—was all my reply.

My mother was evidently gratified by this prospect of a misunderstanding between us. 'Ah!' she said, 'if Cecilia only had Zilla's sweet temper.'

This was a little too much to endure—but I did endure it. 'Will you come out with me, mamma, for a walk in the grounds?' I asked.

My mother accepted the invitation so gladly, that I really think I should have felt ashamed of myself—if I had not had the contaminating Spectacles in my pocket.

We had just settled to start soon after two o'clock, when there was a timid knock at the door. The angelic needlewoman appeared to ask for her half holiday. My mother actually blushed! Old habits will cling to the members of the past generation. 'What is it?' she said, in low uncertain tones. 'Might I go to the village, ma'am, to buy some little things?'

'Certainly.'

The door closed again.

'Now for the shrubbery!' I thought. 'Make haste, mamma,' I said, 'the best of the day is going. And mind one thing—put on your thickest boots!'

On one side of the shrubbery were the gardens. The other side was bounded by a wooden fence. A footpath, running part of the way beside the fence, crossed the grass beyond, and made a short cut between the nearest park gate and the servants' offices. This was the safe place that I had chosen. We could hear perfectly—though the closely-planted evergreens might prevent the exercise of sight. I had recommended 'thick boots' because there was no help but to muffle the sound of our footsteps by walking on the wet grass. At its further end, the shrubbery joined the carriage road up to the house.

My mother's surprise at the place that I had chosen for our walk would have been expressed in words, as well as by looks, if I had not stopped her by a whispered warning. 'Keep perfectly quiet,' I said, 'and listen. I have a motive for bringing you here.'

The words had hardly passed my lips, before we heard the voices of Cecilia and the needlewoman in the shrubbery.

'Wait a minute,' said Cecilia; 'you must be a little more explicit, before I consent to go any farther. How came you to take my letter to Sir John, instead of my maid?'

'Only to oblige her, Miss. She was not very well, and she didn't fancy going all the way to Timbercombe. I can buy no good needles in the village, and I was glad of the opportunity of getting to the town.'

There was a pause. Cecilia was reflecting, as I supposed. My mother began to turn pale.

Cecilia resumed. 'There is nothing in Sir John's answer to my letter,' she said, ' that leads me to suppose he can be guilty of an act of rudeness. I have always believed him to be a gentleman. No gentleman would force his way into my presence, when I wrote expressly to ask him to spare me. Pray how did you know he was determined only to take his dismissal from my lips?'

'Gentlemen's feelings sometimes get the better of them, Miss. Sir John was very much distressed —'

Cecilia interrupted her. 'There was nothing in my letter to distress him,' she said.

'He was distressed, Miss; and he did say, "I cannot take my answer this way—I must and will see her." And then he asked me to get you to walk out today, and to say nothing so that he might take you by surprise. He is so madly in love with you, Miss, that he is all but beside himself. I am really afraid of what might happen, if you don't soften his disappointment to him in some way. How any lady can treat such a handsome gentleman so cruelly, passes my poor judgement!'

Cecilia instantly resented the familiarity implied in those last words. 'You are not called upon to exercise your judgement,' she said. 'You can go back to the house.'

'Hadn't I better see Sir John first, Miss?'

'Certainly not! You and Sir John have seen quite enough of each other already.'

There was another pause. My mother stood holding by my arm, pale and trembling. We could neither of us speak. My own mind was strangely agitated. Either Cecilia was a monster of deceit, or she had thus far spoken and acted as became a true and highly-bred woman.

The distant sound of horses' hoofs on the park road, told us both that the critical moment was at hand. In another minute, the sound ceased. Sir John had probably dismounted, and tied up his horse at the entrance of the shrubbery. After an interval, we heard Cecilia's voice again, farther away from us. We followed the voice. The interview which was to decide my future destiny in life had begun.

'No, Sir John; I must have my question answered first. Is there anything in my letter—was there anything in my conduct, when we met in London—which justifies this?'

'Love justifies everything, Cecilia!'

'You are not to call me Cecilia, if you please. Have you no plainer answer to give me?'

'Have you no mercy on a man, who cannot live without you? Is there really nothing in myself and my title to set against the perfectly obscure person, to whom you have so rashly engaged yourself? It would be an insult to suppose that his wealth has tempted you. What can be his merit in your eyes? His own friends can say no more in his favour than that he is a good-natured fool. I don't blame you; women often drift into engagements that they repent of afterwards. Do yourself justice! Be true to the nobility of character—and be the angel who makes our two lives happy, before it is too late!'

'Have you done, Sir John?'

There was a moment of silence. It was impossible to mistake her tone—Sir John's flow of eloquence came to a full stop.

'Before I answer you,' Cecilia proceeded, 'I have something to say first.

The girl who took my letter to you, was not my maid, as you may have supposed. She is a stranger to me; and I suspect her of being a false creature with some purpose of her own to serve. I find a difficulty in attributing to a person in your rank of life the mean deceit which answers my letter in terms that lead me to trust you, and then takes me by surprise in this way. My messenger (as I believe) is quite insolent enough to have suggested this course to you. Am I right? I expect a reply, Sir John, that is worthy in its entire truthfulness of you and your title. Am I right?'

'You are right, Miss Cecilia. Pray don't despise me. The temptation to plead with you once more —'

'I will speak to you, Sir John, as candidly as you have spoken to me. You are entirely wrong in supposing it possible for me to repent of my marriage engagement. The man, whose false friends have depreciated him in your estimation, is the only man I love, and the only man I will marry. And I beg you to understand, if he lost the whole of his fortune tomorrow, I would marry him the next day, if he asked me. Must I say more? or will you treat me with the delicacy of a gentleman, and take your leave?'

I don't remember whether he said anything or not, before he left her. I only know that they parted. Don't ask me to confess what I felt. Don't ask me to describe what my mother felt. Let the scene be changed, and the narrative be resumed at a later hour of the day.

6

THE END OF THE SPECTACLES

I asked myself a question, which I beg to repeat here. What did I owe to the Devil's Spectacles?

In the first place, I was indebted to my glasses for seeing all the faults, and none of the merits, in the persons about me. In the second place, I arrived at the discovery that, if we are to live usefully and happily with our fellow-creatures, we must take them at their best, and not at their worst. Having reached these conclusions, I trusted my own unassisted insight, and set myself to ascertain what the Devil had not helped me to discover in the two persons who were dearest to me—my mother and Cecilia.

I began with Cecilia, leaving my mother time to recover after the shock that had fallen on her.

It was impossible to acknowledge what I had seen through the Spectacles, or what I had heard at the shrubbery fence. In speaking to Cecilia, I could only attribute my coldness of manner to jealousy of the mere name of 'Sir John,' and ask to be pardoned for even a momentary distrust of the most constant and charming of women.

There was something, I suppose, in my contrite consciousness of having wronged her, that expressed itself in my looks and in my tones. We were sitting together on the sofa. For the first time since our engagement, she put her arm around my neck, and kissed me, without waiting to be kissed first.

I am not very demonstrative,' she said, softly; 'and I don't think, Alfred, you have ever known how fond I am of you. My dear, when Sir John and I met again at that dinner party, I was too faithful to you to even allow myself to think of him. Your poor mother irritated me by seeming to doubt whether I could trust myself within reach of Timbercombe, or I should never have consented to go to Long Fallas. You remember that she invited Sir John to ride over and see us. I wrote to him, informing him of my engagement to you, and telling him, in the plainest words, that if he did call at this house, nothing would induce me to see him. I had every reason to suppose that he would understand and respect my motives —'

She paused. The rich colour rose in her lovely face. I refused to let her distress herself by saying a word of what had happened in the shrubbery. Look back, if you have forgotten it, and see how completely the Spectacles failed to show me the higher and nobler motives that had animated her. The little superficial irritabilities and distrusts, they exhibited to perfection; but the true regard for each other, hidden below the surface in my mother and in my promised wife, was completely beyond them.

'Shall we go back to London, tomorrow?' I asked.

'Are you tired of being here with me, Alfred?'

'I am tired of waiting till the spring, my angel. I will live with you wherever you like, if you will only consent to hasten the transformation which makes you my wife. Will you consent?'

'If your mother asks me. Don't hurry her, Alfred.'

But I did hurry her. After what we had heard in the shrubbery I could look into my mother's heart (without assistance), and feel sure that the nobler part of her nature would justify my confidence in it. She was not only ready to 'ask Cecilia,' then and there—she was eager, poor soul, to confess hoe completely she had been mislaid by her natural interest in her brother's child.

Being firmly resolved to keep the secret of my discovery of her niece, I refused to hear her, as I had refused to hear Cecilia. Did I not know, without being told, what child's play it would be to Zilla to dazzle and delude my innocent mother? I merely asked if 'the needlewoman was still in the house.' The answer was thoroughly explicit: 'She is at the railway station by this time, and she will never enter any house of mine again.'

We returned to London the next morning.

I had a moment's private talk with the station-master at Timbercombe. Sir John had left his friends at the town, on the previous day. He and Zilla had met on the platform, waiting for the London train. She had followed him into the smoking-carriage. Just as the station-master was going to start the train, Sir John opened the door, with a strong expression of disgust, and took refuge in another carriage. She had tried the baronet as a last resource, and he had slipped through her fingers too.

What did it matter to Zilla? She had plenty of time before her, and she belonged to the order of persons who never fail to make the most of her advantages. The other day I saw the announcement of her marriage to a great ironmaster, a man worth millions of money, with establishments to correspond. Bravo, Zilla! No need to look for your nobler motives with the naked eye.

A few days before I became a married man I was a guest at the dinner table of a bachelor friend, and I met Sir John. It would have been ridiculous to leave the room; I merely charged my host to keep my name concealed. I sat next to the baronet, and he doesn't know, to this day, who his 'very agreeable neighbour' was.

Instead of spending our honeymoon abroad, Cecilia and I went back to Long Fallas. We found the place delightful, even in the winter time.

Did I take the Devil's Spectacles back with me?

No.

Did I throw them away or smash them into small morsels?

Neither. I remembered what Septimus Notman had told me. The one way of getting rid of them was to give them to some other man.

And to what other man did I give them?

I had not forgotten what my rival had said of me in the shrubbery. I gave the Devil's Spectacles to Sir John.

7
Between the Reader and the Editor

Are we to have no satisfactory explanation of the supernatural element in the story? How did it come into the Editor's hands? Was there neither name or address on the manuscript?

There was an address, if you must know. But I decline to mention it.

Suppose I guess that the address was at a lunatic asylum? What would you say to that?

I should say I suspected you of being a critic, and I should have the honour of wishing you good morning.

The Captain and the Nymph

1

"The Captain is still in the prime of life," the widow remarked. "He has given up his ship; he possesses a sufficient income, and he has nobody to live with him. I should like to know
why he doesn't marry."

"The Captain was excessively rude to Me," the widow's
younger sister added, on her side. "When we took leave of him
in London, I asked if there was any chance of his joining us at
Brighton this season. He turned his back on me as if I had mor-
tally offended him; and he made me this extraordinary answer:
'Miss! I hate the sight of the sea.' The man has been a sailor all
his life. What does he mean by saying that he hates the sight of
the sea?"

These questions were addressed to a third person present—
and the person was a man. He was entirely at the mercy of the
widow and the widow's sister. The other ladies of the family-
who might have taken him under their protection—had gone
to an evening concert. He was known to be the Captain's friend,
and to be well acquainted with events in the Captain's life.

As it happened, he had reasons for hesitating to revive associations connected with those events. But what polite alternative was left to him? He must either inflict disappointment, and,
worse still, aggravate curiosity—or he must resign himself to
circumstances, and tell the ladies why the Captain would never
marry, and why (sailor as he was) he hated the sight of the sea.
They were both young women and handsome women—and

the person to whom they had appealed (being a man) followed the example of submission the sex, first set in the garden of Eden. He enlightened the ladies, in the terms that follow:

2

The British merchantman, *Fortuna*, sailed from the port of Liverpool (at a date which it is not necessary to specify) with the morning tide. She was bound for certain islands in the Pacific Ocean, in search of a cargo of sandal-wood—a commodity which, in those days, found a ready and profitable market in the Chinese Empire.

A large discretion was reposed in the Captain by the owners, who knew him to be not only trustworthy, but a man of rare ability, carefully cultivated during the leisure hours of a seafaring life. Devoted heart and soul to his professional duties, he was a hard reader and an excellent linguist as well. Having had considerable experience among the inhabitants of the Pacific Islands, he had attentively studied their characters, and had mastered their language in more than one of its many dialects. Thanks to the valuable information thus obtained, the Captain was never at a loss to conciliate the islanders. He had more than once succeeded in finding a cargo under circumstances in which other captains had failed.

Possessing these merits, he had also his fair share of human defects. For instance, he was a little too conscious of his own good looks—of his bright chestnut hair and whiskers, of his beautiful blue eyes, of his fair white skin, which many a woman had looked at with the admiration that is akin to envy. His shapely hands were protected by gloves; a broad−brimmed hat sheltered his complexion in fine weather from the sun. He was nice in the choice of his perfumes; he never drank spirits, and the smell of tobacco was abhorrent to him.

New men among his officers and his crew, seeing him in his cabin, perfectly dressed, washed, and brushed until he was an object speckless to look upon—a merchant−captain soft of voice, careful in his choice of words, devoted to study in his leisure hours—were apt to conclude that they had trusted themselves at sea under a commander who was an anomalous mixture of a schoolmaster and a dandy.

But if the slightest infraction of discipline took place, or if the storm rose and the vessel proved to be in peril, it was soon discovered that the gloved hands held a rod of iron; that the soft voice could make itself heard through wind and sea from one end of the deck to the other; and that it issued orders which the greatest fool on board discovered to be orders that had saved the ship. Throughout his professional life, the general impression that this variously gifted man produced on the little world about him was always the same.

Some few liked him; everybody respected him; nobody understood him. The Captain accepted these results. He persisted in reading his books and protecting his complexion, with this result: his owners shook hands with him, and put up with his gloves.

The *Fortuna* touched at Rio for water, and for supplies of food which might prove useful in case of scurvy. In due time the ship rounded Cape Horn, favoured by the finest weather ever known in those latitudes by the oldest hand on board. The mate—one Mr. Duncalf—a boozing, wheezing, self-confident old sea-dog, with a flaming face and a vast vocabulary of oaths, swore that he didn't like it. "The foul weather's coming, my lads," said Mr. Duncalf.

"Mark my words, there'll be wind enough to take the curl out of the Captain's whiskers before we are many days older!"

For one uneventful week, the ship cruised in search of the islands to which the owners had directed her. At the end of that time the wind took the predicted liberties with the Captain's whiskers; and Mr. Duncalf stood revealed to an admiring crew in the character of a true prophet.

For three days and three nights the *Fortuna* ran before the storm, at the mercy of wind and sea. On the fourth morning the gale blew itself out, the sun appeared again toward noon, and the Captain was able to take an observation. The result informed him that he was in a part of the Pacific Ocean with which he was entirely unacquainted. Thereupon, the officers were called to a council in the cabin.

Mr. Duncalf, as became his rank, was consulted first. His opinion possessed the merit of brevity. "My lads, this ship's bewitched. Take my word for it, we shall wish ourselves back in our own latitudes before we are many days older." Which, being interpreted, meant that Mr. Duncalf was lost, like his superior officer, in a part of the ocean of which he knew nothing.

The remaining members of the council having no suggestions to offer, left the Captain to take his own way. He decided (the weather being fine again) to stand on under an easy press of sail for four-and-twenty hours more, and to see if anything came of it.

Soon after nightfall, something did come of it. The lookout forward hailed the quarter–deck with the dread cry, "Breakers ahead!" In less than a minute more, everybody heard the crash of the broken water. The *Fortuna* was put about, and came round slowly in the light wind. Thanks to the timely alarm and the fine weather, the safety of the vessel was easily provided for. They kept her under a short sail; and they waited for the morning.

The dawn showed them in the distance a glorious green island, not marked in the ship's charts—an island girt about by a coral-reef, and having in its midst a high-peaked mountain which looked, through the telescope, like a mountain of volcanic origin. Mr. Duncalf, taking his morning draught of rum and water, shook his groggy old head and said (and swore): "My lads, I don't like the look of that island." The Captain was of a different opinion.

He had one of the ship's boats put into the water; he armed himself and four of his crew who accompanied him; and away he went in the morning sunlight to visit the island.

Skirting round the coral reef, they found a natural breach, which proved to be broad enough and deep enough not only for the passage of the boat, but of the ship herself if needful. Crossing the broad inner belt of smooth water, they approached the

471

golden sands of the island, strewed with magnificent shells, and crowded by the dusky islanders—men, women, and children, all waiting in breathless astonishment to see the strangers land.

The Captain kept the boat off, and examined the islanders carefully. The innocent, simple people danced, and sang, and ran into the water, imploring their wonderful white visitors by gestures to come on shore. Not a creature among them carried arms of any sort; a hospitable curiosity animated the entire population.

The men cried out, in their smooth musical language, "Come and eat!" and the plump black-eyed women, all laughing together, added their own invitation, "Come and be kissed!" Was it in mortals to resist such temptations as these? The Captain led the way on shore, and the women surrounded him in an instant, and screamed for joy at the glorious spectacle of his whiskers, his complexion, and his gloves. So the mariners from the far north were welcomed to the newly-discovered island.

3

The morning wore on. Mr. Duncalf, in charge of the ship, cursing the island over his rum and water, as a "beastly green strip of a place, not laid down in any Christian chart," was kept waiting four mortal hours before the Captain returned to his command, and reported himself to his officers as follows:

He had found his knowledge of the Polynesian dialects sufficient to make himself in some degree understood by the natives of the new island. Under the guidance of the chief he had made a first journey of exploration, and had seen for himself that the place was a marvel of natural beauty and fertility. The one barren spot in it was the peak of the volcanic mountain, composed of crumbling rock; originally no doubt lava and ashes, which had cooled and consolidated with the lapse of time.

So far as he could see, the crater at the top was now an extinct crater. But, if he had understood rightly, the chief had spoken of earthquakes and eruptions at certain bygone periods, some of which lay within his own earliest recollections of the place.

Adverting next to considerations of practical utility, the Captain announced that he had seen sandal-wood enough on the island to load a dozen ships, and that the natives were willing to part with it for a few toys and trinkets generally distributed among them. To the mate's disgust, the *Fortuna* was taken inside the reef that day, and was anchored before sunset in a natural harbour. Twelve hours of recreation, beginning with the next morning, were granted to the men, under the wise restrictions in such cases established by the Captain. That interval over, the work of cutting the precious wood and loading the ship was to be unremittingly pursued.

Mr. Duncalf had the first watch after the *Fortuna* had been made snug. He took the boatswain aside (an ancient sea–dog like himself), and he said in a gruff whisper: "My lad, this here ain't the island laid down in our sailing orders. See if mischief don't come of disobeying orders before we are many days older."

Nothing in the shape of mischief happened that night. But at sunrise the next morning a suspicious circumstance occurred; and Mr. Duncalf whispered to the boatswain: "What did I tell you?" The Captain and the chief of the islanders held a private conference in the cabin, and the Captain, after first forbidding any communication with the shore until his return, suddenly left the ship, alone with the chief, in the chief's own canoe.

What did this strange disappearance mean? The Captain himself, when he took his seat in the canoe, would have been puzzled to answer that question. He asked, in the nearest approach that his knowledge could make to the language used in the island, whether he would be a long time or a short time absent from his ship.

The chief answered mysteriously (as the Captain understood him) in these words: "Long time or short time, your life depends on it, and the lives of your men."

Paddling his light little boat in silence over the smooth water inside the reef, the chief took his visitor ashore at a part of the island which was quite new to the Captain. The two crossed a ravine, and ascended an eminence beyond. There the chief stopped, and silently pointed out to sea.

The Captain looked in the direction indicated to him, and discovered a second and a smaller island, lying away to the southwest. Taking out his telescope from the case by which it was slung at his back, he narrowly examined the place. Two of the native canoes were lying off the shore of the new island; and the men in them appeared to be all kneeling or crouching in curiously chosen attitudes.

Shifting the range of his glass, he next beheld a white-robed figure, tall and solitary—the one inhabitant of the island whom he could discover. The man was standing on the highest point of a rocky cape. A fire was burning at his feet. Now he lifted his arms solemnly to the sky; now he dropped some invisible fuel into the fire, which made a blue smoke; and now he cast other invisible objects into the canoes floating beneath him, which the islanders reverently received with bodies that crouched in abject submission. Lowering his telescope, the Captain looked round at the chief for an explanation. The chief gave the explanation readily. His language was interpreted by the English stranger in these terms:

"Wonderful white man! the island you see yonder is a Holy Island. As such it is *Taboo*—an island sanctified and set apart. The honourable person whom you notice on the rock is an all-powerful favourite of the gods. He is by vocation a Sorcerer, and by rank a Priest. You now see him casting charms and blessings into the canoes of our fishermen, who kneel to him for fine weather and great plenty of fish. If any profane person, native or stranger, presumes to set foot on that island, my otherwise peaceful subjects will (in the performance of a religious duty) put that person to death. Mention this to your men. They will be fed by my male people, and fondled by my female people, so long as they keep clear of the Holy Isle. As they value their lives, let them respect this prohibition. Is it understood between us? Wonderful white man! my canoe is waiting for you. Let us go back."

Understanding enough of the chief's language (illustrated by his gestures) to receive in the right spirit the communication thus addressed to him, the Captain repeated the warning to the ship's company in the plainest possible English. The officers and men then took their holiday on shore, with the exception of Mr. Duncalf, who positively refused to leave the ship.

For twelve delightful hours they were fed by the male people, and fondled by the female people, and then they were mercilessly torn from the flesh-pots and the arms of their new friends, and set to work on the sandal-wood in good earnest. Mr. Duncalf superintended the loading, and waited for the mischief that was to come of disobeying the owners' orders with a confidence worthy of a better cause.

4

Strangely enough, chance once more declared itself in favour of the mate's point of view. The mischief did actually come; and the chosen instrument of it was a handsome young islander, who was one of the sons of the chief.

The Captain had taken a fancy to the sweet-tempered, intelligent lad. Pursuing his studies in the dialect of the island, at leisure hours, he had made the chief's son his tutor, and had instructed the youth in English by way of return. More than a month had passed in this intercourse, and the ship's lading was being rapidly completed—when, in an evil hour, the talk between the two turned on the subject of the Holy Island.

"Does nobody live on the island but the Priest?" the Captain asked.

The chief's son looked round him suspiciously. "Promise me you won't tell anybody!" he began very earnestly.

The Captain gave his promise.

"There is one other person on the island," the lad whispered; "a person to feast your eyes upon, if you could only see her! She is the Priest's daughter. Removed to the island in her infancy, she has never left it since. In that sacred solitude she has only looked on two human beings—her father and her mother. I once saw her from my canoe, taking care not to attract her notice, or to approach too near the holy soil. Oh, so young, dear master, and, oh, so beautiful!" The chief's son completed the description by kissing his own hands as an expression of rapture.

The Captain's fine blue eyes sparkled. He asked no more questions; but, later on that day, he took his telescope with him, and paid a secret visit to the eminence which overlooked the Holy Island. The next day, and the next, he privately returned to the same place. On the fourth day, fatal Destiny favoured him. He discovered the nymph of the island.

Standing alone upon the cape on which he had already seen her father, she was feeding some tame birds which looked like turtledoves. The glass showed the Captain her white robe, fluttering in the sea-breeze; her long black hair falling to her feet; her slim and supple young figure; her simple grace of attitude, as she turned this way and that, attending to the wants of her birds. Before her was the blue ocean; behind her rose the lustrous green of the island forest. He looked and looked until his eyes and arms ached. When she disappeared among the trees, followed by her favourite birds, the Captain shut up his telescope with a sigh, and said to himself: "I have seen an angel!"

From that hour he became an altered man; he was languid, silent, interested in nothing. General opinion, on board his ship, decided that he was going to be taken ill.

A week more elapsed, and the officers and crew began to talk of the voyage to their market in China. The Captain refused to fix a day for sailing. He even took offense at being asked to decide. Instead of sleeping in his cabin, he went ashore for the night.

Not many hours afterward (just before daybreak), Mr. Duncalf, snoring in his cabin on deck, was aroused by a hand laid on his shoulder. The swinging lamp, still alight, showed him the dusky face of the chief's son, convulsed with terror. By wild signs, by disconnected words in the little English which he had learned, the lad tried to make the mate understand him. Dense Mr. Duncalf, understanding nothing, hailed the second officer, on the opposite side of the deck. The second officer was young and intelligent; he rightly interpreted the terrible news that had come to the ship.

The Captain had broken his own rules. Watching his opportunity, under cover of the night, he had taken a canoe, and had secretly crossed the channel to the Holy Island. No one had been near him at the time but the chief's son.

The lad had vainly tried to induce him to abandon his desperate enterprise, and had vainly waited on the shore in the hope of hearing the sound of the paddle announcing his return. Beyond all reasonable doubt, the infatuated man had set foot on the shores of the tabooed island.

The one chance for his life was to conceal what he had done, until the ship could be got out of the harbour, and then (if no harm had come to him in the interval) to rescue him after nightfall. It was decided to spread the report that he had really been taken ill, and that he was confined to his cabin. The chief's son, whose heart the Captain's kindness had won, could be trusted to do this, and to keep the secret faithfully for his good friend's sake.

Toward noon, the next day, they attempted to take the ship to sea, and failed for want of wind. Hour by hour, the heat grew more oppressive. As the day declined, there were ominous appearances in the western heaven. The natives, who had given some trouble during the day by their anxiety to see the Captain, and by their curiosity to know the cause of the sudden preparations for the ship's departure, all went ashore together, looking suspiciously at the sky, and reappeared no more. Just at midnight, the ship (still in her snug berth inside the reef) suddenly trembled from her keel to her uppermost masts. Mr. Duncalf, surrounded by the startled crew, shook his knotty fist at the island as if he could see it in the dark. "My lads, what did I tell you? That was a shock of earthquake."

With the morning the threatening aspect of the weather unexpectedly disappeared. A faint hot breeze from the land, just enough to give the ship steerage-way, offered Mr. Duncalf a chance of getting to sea. Slowly the *Fortuna*, with the mate himself at the wheel, half sailed, half drifted into the open ocean. At a distance of barely two miles from the island the breeze was felt no more, and the vessel lay becalmed for the rest of the day.

At night the men waited their orders, expecting to be sent after their Captain in one of the boats. The intense darkness, the airless heat, and a second shock of earthquake (faintly felt in the ship at her present distance from the land) warned the mate to be cautious. "I smell mischief in the air," said Mr. Duncalf. "The Captain must wait till I am surer of the weather."

Still no change came with the new day. The dead calm continued, and the airless heat. As the day declined, another ominous appearance became visible. A thin line of smoke was discovered through the telescope, ascending from the topmost peak of the mountain on the main island. Was the volcano threatening an eruption?

The mate, for one, entertained no doubt of it. "By the Lord, the place is going to burst up!" said Mr. Duncalf.

"Come what may of it, we must find the Captain tonight!"

5

What was the Captain doing? and what chance had the crew of finding him that night?

He had committed himself to his desperate adventure, without forming any plan for the preservation of his own safety; without giving even a momentary consideration to the consequences which might follow the risk that he had run. The charming figure that he had seen haunted him night and day. The image of the innocent creature, secluded from humanity in her island solitude, was the one image that filled his mind. A man, passing a woman in the street, acts on the impulse to turn and follow her, and in that one thoughtless moment shapes the destiny of his future life. The Captain had acted on a similar impulse, when he took the first canoe he had found on the beach, and shaped his reckless course for the tabooed island.

Reaching the shore while it was still dark, he did one sensible thing—he hid the canoe so that it might not betray him when the daylight came. That done, he waited for the morning on the outskirts of the forest.

The trembling light of dawn revealed the mysterious solitude around him. Following the outer limits of the trees, first in one direction, then in another, and finding no trace of any living creature, he decided on penetrating to the interior of the island. He entered the forest.

An hour of walking brought him to rising ground. Continuing the ascent, he got clear of the trees, and stood on the grassy top of a broad cliff which overlooked the sea. An open hut was on the cliff. He cautiously looked in, and discovered that it was empty. The few household utensils left about, and the simple bed of leaves in a corner, were covered with fine sandy dust. Nightbirds flew blundering out of the inner cavities of the roof, and took refuge in the shadows of the forest below. It was plain that the hut had not been inhabited for some time past.

Standing at the open doorway and considering what he should do next, the Captain saw a bird flying toward him out of the forest. It was a turtledove, so tame that it fluttered close up to him. At the same moment the sound of sweet laughter became audible among the trees. His heart beat fast; he advanced a few steps and stopped. In a moment more the nymph of the island appeared, in her white robe, ascending the cliff in pursuit of her truant bird.

She saw the strange man, and suddenly stood still; struck motionless by the amazing discovery that had burst upon her. The Captain approached, smiling and holding out his hand. She never moved; she stood before him in helpless wonderment—her lovely black eyes fixed spellbound on his face; her dusky bosom palpitating above the fallen folds of her robe; her rich red lips parted in mute astonishment.

Feasting his eyes on her beauty in silence, the Captain after a while ventured to speak to her in the language of the main island. The sound of his voice, addressing her in the words that she understood, roused the lovely creature to action. She started, stepped close up to him, and dropped on her knees at his feet.

"My father worships invisible deities," she said, softly. "Are you a visible deity? Has my mother sent you?" She pointed as she spoke to the deserted hut behind them.

"You appear," she went on, "in the place where my mother died. Is it for her sake that you show yourself to her child? Beautiful deity, come to the Temple—come to my father!"

The Captain gently raised her from the ground. If her father saw him, he was a doomed man.

Infatuated as he was, he had sense enough left to announce himself plainly in his own character, as a mortal creature arriving from a distant land. The girl instantly drew back from him with a look of terror.

"He is not like my father," she said to herself; "he is not like me. Is he the lying demon of the prophecy? Is he the predestined destroyer of our island?"

The Captain's experience of the sex showed him the only sure way out of the awkward position in which he was now placed. He appealed to his personal appearance.

"Do I look like a demon?" he asked.

Her eyes met his eyes; a faint smile trembled on her lips. He ventured on asking what she meant by the predestined destruction of the island. She held up her hand solemnly, and repeated the prophecy.

The Holy Island was threatened with destruction by an evil being, who would one day appear on its shores. To avert the fatality the place had been sanctified and set apart, under the protection of the gods and their priest. Here was the reason for the taboo, and for the extraordinary rigor with which it was enforced. Listening to her with the deepest interest, the Captain took her hand and pressed it gently.

"Do I feel like a demon?" he whispered.

Her slim brown fingers closed frankly on his hand. "You feel soft and friendly," she said with the fearless candour of a child. "Squeeze me again. I like it!"

The next moment she snatched her hand away from him; the sense of his danger had suddenly forced itself on her mind. "If

480

my father sees you," she said, "he will light the signal fire at the Temple, and the people from the other island will come here and put you to death. Where is your canoe? No! It is daylight. My father may see you on the water." She considered a little, and, approaching him, laid her hands on his shoulders.

"Stay here till nightfall," she resumed. "My father never comes this way. The sight of the place where my mother died is horrible to him.

You are safe here. Promise to stay where you are till night-time."

The Captain gave his promise.

Freed from anxiety so far, the girl's mobile temperament recovered its native cheerfulness, its sweet gayety and spirit. She admired the beautiful stranger as she might have admired a new bird that had flown to her to be fondled with the rest. She patted his fair white skin, and wished she had a skin like it. She lifted the great glossy folds of her long black hair, and compared it with the Captain's bright curly locks, and longed to change colours with him from the bottom of her heart.

His dress was a wonder to her; his watch was a new revelation. She rested her head on his shoulder to listen delightedly to the ticking, as he held the watch to her ear. Her fragrant breath played on his face, her warm, supple figure rested against him softly. The Captain's arm stole round her waist, and the Captain's lips gently touched her cheek. She lifted her head with a look of pleased surprise. "Thank you," said the child of Nature, simply. "Kiss me again; I like it. May I kiss you?"

The tame turtledove perched on her shoulder as she gave the Captain her first kiss, and diverted her thoughts to the pets that she had left, in pursuit of the truant dove. "Come," she said, "and see my birds. I keep them on this side of the forest. There is no danger, so long as you don't show yourself on the other side. My name is Aimata. Aimata will take care of you. Oh, what a beautiful white neck you have!" She put her arm admiringly round his neck. The Captain's arm held her tenderly to him. Slowly the two descended the cliff, and were lost in the leafy solitudes of the forest. And the tame dove fluttered before them, a winged messenger of love, cooing to his mate.

6

The night had come, and the Captain had not left the island.

Aimata's resolution to send him away in the darkness was a forgotten resolution already. She had let him persuade her that he was in no danger, so long as he remained in the hut on the cliff; and she had promised, at parting, to return to him while the Priest was still sleeping, at the dawn of day.

He was alone in the hut. The thought of the innocent creature whom he loved was sorrowfully as well as tenderly present to his mind. He almost regretted his rash visit to the island. "I will take her with me to England," he said to himself. "What does a sailor care for the opinion of the world? Aimata shall be my wife."

The intense heat oppressed him. He stepped out on the cliff, toward midnight, in search of a breath of air.

At that moment, the first shock of earthquake (felt in the ship while she was inside the reef) shook the ground he stood on. He instantly thought of the volcano on the main island. Had he been mistaken in supposing the crater to be extinct? Was the shock that he had just felt a warning from the volcano, communicated through a submarine connection between the two islands? He waited and watched through the hours of darkness, with a vague sense of apprehension, which was not to be reasoned away. With the first light of daybreak he descended into the forest, and saw the lovely being whose safety was already precious to him as his own, hurrying to meet him through the trees.

She waved her hand distractedly as she approached him. "Go!" she cried; "go away in your canoe before our island is destroyed!"

He did his best to quiet her alarm. Was it the shock of earthquake that had frightened her? No: it was more than the shock of earthquake—it was something terrible which had followed the shock. There was a lake near the Temple, the waters of which were supposed to be heated by subterranean fires. The lake had risen with the earthquake, had bubbled furiously, and had then melted away into the earth and been lost.

Her father, viewing the portent with horror, had gone to the cape to watch the volcano on the main island, and to implore by prayers and sacrifices the protection of the gods. Hearing this, the Captain entreated Aimata to let him see the emptied lake, in the absence of the Priest. She hesitated; but his influence was all-powerful. He prevailed on her to turn back with him through the forest.

Reaching the furthest limit of the trees, they came out upon open rocky ground which sloped gently downward toward the centre of the island. Having crossed this space, they arrived at a natural amphitheatre of rock. On one side of it the Temple appeared, partly excavated, partly formed by a natural cavern. In one of the lateral branches of the cavern was the dwelling of the Priest and his daughter. The mouth of it looked out on the rocky basin of the lake. Stooping over the edge, the Captain discovered, far down in the empty depths, a light cloud of steam. Not a drop of water was visible, look where he might.

Aimata pointed to the abyss, and hid her face on his bosom. "My father says," she whispered, "that it is your doing."

The Captain started. "Does your father know that I am on the island?"

She looked up at him with a quick glance of reproach. "Do you think I would tell him, and put your life in peril?" she asked. "My father felt the destroyer of the island in the earthquake; my father saw the coming destruction in the disappearance of the lake."

Her eyes rested on him with a loving languor. "Are you indeed the demon of the prophecy?" she said, winding his hair round her finger. "I am not afraid of you, if you are. I am a creature bewitched; I love the demon."

She kissed him passionately. "I don't care if I die," she whispered between the kisses, "if I only die with you!"

The Captain made no attempt to reason with her. He took the wiser way—he appealed to her feelings.

"You will come and live with me happily in my own country," he said. "My ship is waiting for us. I will take you home with me, and you shall be my wife."

She clapped her hands for joy. Then she thought of her father, and drew back from him in tears.

The Captain understood her. "Let us leave this dreary place," he suggested. "We will talk about it in the cool glades of the forest, where you first said you loved me."

She gave him her hand. "Where I first said I loved you!" she repeated, smiling tenderly as she looked at him. They left the lake together.

7

The darkness had fallen again; and the ship was still becalmed at sea.

Mr. Duncalf came on deck after his supper. The thin line of smoke, seen rising from the peak of the mountain that evening, was now succeeded by ominous flashes of fire from the same quarter, intermittently visible. The faint hot breeze from the land was felt once more. "There's just an air of wind," Mr. Duncalf remarked. "I'll try for the Captain while I have the chance."

One of the boats was lowered into the water—under command of the second mate, who had already taken the bearings of the tabooed island by daylight. Four of the men were to go with him, and they were all to be well armed. Mr. Duncalf addressed his final instructions to the officer in the boat.

"You will keep a lookout, sir, with a lantern in the bows. If the natives annoy you, you know what to do. Always shoot natives. When you get anigh the island, you will fire a gun and sing out for the Captain."

"Quite needless," interposed a voice from the sea. "The Captain is here!"

Without taking the slightest notice of the astonishment that he had caused, the commander of the *Fortuna* paddled his canoe to the side of the ship. Instead of ascending to the deck, he stepped into the boat, waiting alongside.

"Lend me your pistols," he said quietly to the second officer, "and oblige me by taking your men back to their duties on board." He looked up at Mr. Duncalf and gave some further directions. "If there is any change in the weather, keep the ship standing off and on, at a safe distance from the land, and throw up a rocket from time to time to show your position. Expect me on board again by sunrise."

"What!" cried the mate. "Do you mean to say you are going back to the island—in that boat—all by yourself?"

"I am going back to the island," answered the Captain, as quietly as ever; "in this boat—all by myself." He pushed off from the ship, and hoisted the sail as he spoke.

"You're deserting your duty!" the old sea-dog shouted, with one of his loudest oaths.

"Attend to my directions," the Captain shouted back, as he drifted away into the darkness.

Mr. Duncalf—violently agitated for the first time in his life—took leave of his superior officer, with a singular mixture of solemnity and politeness, in these words:

"The Lord have mercy on your soul! I wish you good-evening."

8

Alone in the boat, the Captain looked with a misgiving mind at the flashing of the volcano on the main island.

If events had favoured him, he would have removed Aimata to the shelter of the ship on the day when he saw the emptied basin on the lake. But the smoke of the Priest's sacrifice had been discovered by the chief; and he had dispatched two canoes with instructions to make inquiries. One of the canoes had returned; the other was kept in waiting off the cape, to place a means of communicating with the main island at the disposal of the Priest.

The second shock of earthquake had naturally increased the alarm of the chief. He had sent messages to the Priest, entreating him to leave the island, and other messages to Aimata suggesting that she should exert her influence over her father, if he hesitated. The Priest refused to leave the Temple. He trusted in his gods and his sacrifices—he believed they might avert the fatality that threatened his sanctuary.

Yielding to the holy man, the chief sent re-enforcements of canoes to take their turn at keeping watch off the headland. Assisted by torches, the islanders were on the alert (in superstitious terror of the demon of the prophecy) by night as well as by day. The Captain had no alternative but to keep in hiding, and to watch his opportunity of approaching the place in which he had concealed his canoe.

It was only after Aimata had left him as usual, to return to her father at the close of evening, that the chances declared themselves in his favour. The fire-flashes from the mountain, visible when the night came, had struck terror into the hearts of the men on the watch. They thought of their wives, their children, and their possessions on the main island, and they one and all deserted their Priest. The Captain seized the opportunity of communicating with the ship, and of exchanging a frail canoe which he was ill able to manage, for a swift-sailing boat capable of keeping the sea in the event of stormy weather.

As he now neared the land, certain small sparks of red, moving on the distant water, informed him that the canoes of the sentinels had been ordered back to their duty.

Carefully avoiding the lights, he reached his own side of the island without accident, and, guided by the boat's lantern, anchored under the cliff. He climbed the rocks, advanced to the door of the hut, and was met, to his delight and astonishment, by Aimata on the threshold.

"I dreamed that some dreadful misfortune had parted us forever," she said; "and I came here to see if my dream was true. You have taught me what it is to be miserable; I never felt my heart ache till I looked into the hut and found that you had gone. Now I have seen you, I am satisfied. No! You must not go back with me. My father may be out looking for me. It is you that are in danger, not I. I know the forest as well by dark as by daylight."

The Captain detained her when she tried to leave him.

"Now you *are* here," he said, "why should I not place you at once in safety? I have been to the ship; I have brought back one of the boats. The darkness will befriend us—let us embark while we can."

She shrank away as he took her hand. "You forget my father!" she said.

"Your father is in no danger, my love. The canoes are waiting for him at the cape; I saw the lights as I passed."

With that reply he drew her out of the hut and led her toward the sea. Not a breath of the breeze was now to be felt. The dead calm had returned—and the boat was too large to be easily managed by one man alone at the oars.

"The breeze may come again," he said. "Wait here, my angel, for the chance."

As he spoke, the deep silence of the forest below them was broken by a sound. A harsh wailing voice was heard, calling:

"Aimata! Aimata!"

"My father!" she whispered; "he has missed me. If he comes here you are lost."

She kissed him with passionate fervour; she held him to her for a moment with all her strength.

"Expect me at daybreak," she said, and disappeared down the landward slope of the cliff.

He listened, anxious for her safety. The voices of the father and daughter just reached him from among the trees.

The Priest spoke in no angry tones; she had apparently found an acceptable excuse for her absence. Little by little, the failing sound of their voices told him that they were on their way back together to the Temple. The silence fell again. Not a ripple broke on the beach. Not a leaf rustled in the forest. Nothing moved but the reflected flashes of the volcano on the main island over the black sky. It was an airless and an awful calm.

He went into the hut, and laid down on his bed of leaves-not to sleep, but to rest. All his energies might be required to meet the coming events of the morning. After the voyage to and from the ship, and the long watching that had preceded it, strong as he was he stood in need of repose.

For some little time he kept awake, thinking. Insensibly the oppression of the intense heat, aided in its influence by his own fatigue, treacherously closed his eyes. In spite of himself, the weary man fell into a deep sleep.

He was awakened by a roar like the explosion of a park of artillery. The volcano on the main island had burst into a state of eruption. Smoky flame-light overspread the sky, and flashed through the open doorway of the hut. He sprang from his bed—and found himself up to his knees in water.

Had the sea overflowed the land?

He waded out of the hut, and the water rose to his middle. He looked round him by the lurid light of the eruption.

The one visible object within the range of view was the sea, stained by reflections from the blood-red sky, swirling and rippling strangely in the dead calm. In a moment more, he became conscious that the earth on which he stood was sinking under his feet. The water rose to his neck; the last vestige of the roof of the hut disappeared.

He looked round again, and the truth burst on him. The island was sinking—slowly, slowly sinking into volcanic depths, below even the depth of the sea! The highest object was the hut, and that had dropped inch by inch under water before his own eyes. Thrown up to the surface by occult volcanic influences, the island had sunk back, under the same influences, to the obscurity from which it had emerged!

A black shadowy object, turning in a wide circle, came slowly near him as the all-destroying ocean washed its bitter waters into his mouth. The buoyant boat, rising as the sea rose, had dragged its anchor, and was floating round in the vortex made by the slowly sinking island. With a last desperate hope that Aimata might have been saved as *he* had been saved, he swam to the boat, seized the heavy oars with the strength of a giant, and made for the place (so far as he could guess at it now) where the lake and the Temple had once been.

He looked round and round him; he strained his eyes in the vain attempt to penetrate below the surface of the seething dimpling sea. Had the panicstricken watchers in the canoes saved themselves, without an effort to preserve the father and daughter? Or had they both been suffocated before they could make an attempt to escape?

He called to her in his misery, as if she could hear him out of the fathomless depths: "Aimata! Aimata!" The roar of the distant eruption answered him. The mounting fires lit the solitary sea far and near over the sinking island.

The boat turned slowly and more slowly in the lessening vortex. Never again would those gentle eyes look at him with unutterable love! Never again would those fresh lips touch his lips with their fervent kiss! Alone, amid the savage forces of Nature in conflict, the miserable mortal lifted his hands in frantic supplication—and the burning sky glared down on him in its pitiless grandeur, and struck him to his knees in the boat. His reason sank with his sinking limbs. In the merciful frenzy that succeeded the shock, he saw afar off, in her white robe, an angel poised on the waters, beckoning him to follow her to the brighter and the better world. He loosened the sail, he seized the oars; and the faster he pursued it, the faster the mocking vision fled from him over the empty and endless sea.

9

The boat was discovered, on the next morning, from the ship.

All that the devotion of the officers of the *Fortuna* could do for their unhappy commander was done on the homeward voyage. Restored to his own country, and to skilled medical help, the Captain's mind by slow degrees recovered its balance. He has taken his place in society again—he lives and moves and manages his affairs like the rest of us. But his heart is dead to all new emotions; nothing remains in it but the sacred remembrance of his lost love. He neither courts nor avoids the society of women. Their sympathy finds him grateful, but their attractions seem to be lost on him; they pass from his mind as they pass from his eyes—they stir nothing in him but the memory of Aimata.

"Now you know, ladies, why the Captain will never marry, and why (sailor as he is) he hates the sight of the sea."

The Angler's Story of
the Lady of Glenwith Grange

I have known Miss Welwyn long enough to be able to bear personal testimony to the truth of many of the particulars which I am now about to relate. I knew her father, and her younger sister Rosamond; and I was acquainted with the Frenchman who became Rosamond's husband. These are the persons of whom it will be principally necessary for me to speak. They are the only prominent characters in my story.

Miss Welwyn's father died some years since. I remember him very well—though he never excited in me, or in any one else that I ever heard of, the slightest feeling of interest. When I have said that he inherited a very large fortune, amassed during his father's time, by speculations of a very daring, very fortunate, but not always very honourable kind, and that he bought this old house with the notion of raising his social position, by making himself a member of our landed aristocracy in these parts, I have told you as much about him, I suspect, as you would care to hear. He was a thoroughly commonplace man, with no great virtues and no great vices in him. He had a little heart, a feeble mind, an amiable temper, a tall figure, and a handsome face. More than this need not, and cannot, be said on the subject of Mr. Welwyn's character.

I must have seen the late Mrs. Welwyn very often as a child; but I cannot say that I remember anything more of her than that she was tall and handsome, and very generous and sweet-tempered toward me when I was in her company. She was her husband's superior in birth, as in everything else; was a great reader of books in all languages; and possessed such admirable talents as a musician, that her wonderful playing on the organ is remembered and talked of to this day among the old people in our country houses about here. All her friends, as I have heard, were disappointed when she married Mr. Welwyn, rich as he was; and were afterward astonished to find her preserving the appearance, at least, of being perfectly happy with a husband who, neither in mind nor heart, was worthy of her.

It was generally supposed (and I have no doubt correctly) that she found her great happiness and her great consolation in her little girl Ida—now the lady from whom we have just parted. The child took after her mother from the first—inheriting her mother's fondness for books, her mother's love of music, her mother's quick sensibilities, and, more than all, her mother's quiet firmness, patience, and loving kindness of disposition.

From Ida's earliest years, Mrs. Welwyn undertook the whole superintendence of her education. The two were hardly ever apart, within doors or without. Neighbours and friends said that the little girl was being brought up too fancifully, and was not enough among other children, was sadly neglected as to all reasonable and practical teaching, and was perilously encouraged in those dreamy and imaginative tendencies of which she had naturally more than her due share. There was, perhaps, some truth in this; and there might have been still more, if Ida had possessed an ordinary character, or had been reserved for an ordinary destiny. But she was a strange child from the first, and a strange future was in store for her.

Little Ida reached her eleventh year without either brother or sister to be her playfellow and companion at home. Immediately after that period, however, her sister Rosamond was born. Though Mr. Welwyn's own desire was to have had a son, there were, nevertheless, great rejoicings yonder in the old house on the birth of this second daughter. But they were all turned, only a few months afterward, to the bitterest grief and despair: the Grange lost its mistress. While Rosamond was still an infant in arms, her mother died.

Mrs. Welwyn had been afflicted with some disorder after the birth of her second child, the name of which I am not learned enough in medical science to be able to remember. I only know that she recovered from it, to all appearance, in an unexpectedly short time; that she suffered a fatal relapse, and that she died a lingering and a painful death. Mr. Welwyn (who, in after years, had a habit of vaingloriously describing his marriage as "a love-match on both sides") was really fond of his wife in his own frivolous, feeble way, and suffered as acutely as such a man could suffer, during the latter days of her illness, and at the terrible time when the doctors, one and all, confessed that her life was a thing to be despaired of.

He burst into irrepressible passions of tears, and was always obliged to leave the sick-room whenever Mrs. Welwyn spoke of her approaching end. The last solemn words of the dying woman, the tenderest messages that she could give, the dearest parting wishes that she could express, the most earnest commands that she could leave behind her, the gentlest reasons for consolation that she could suggest to the survivors among those who loved her, were not poured into her husband's ear, but into her child's.

From the first period of her illness, Ida had persisted in remaining in the sick-room, rarely speaking, never showing outwardly any signs of terror or grief, except when she was removed from it; and then bursting into hysterical passions of weeping, which no expostulations, no arguments, no commands—nothing, in short, but bringing her back to the bedside—ever availed to calm. Her mother had been her playfellow, her companion her dearest and most familiar friend; and there seemed something in the remembrance of this which, instead of overwhelming the child with despair, strengthened her to watch faithfully and bravely by her dying parent to the very last.

When the parting moment was over, and when Mr. Welwyn, unable to bear the shock of being present in the house of death at the time of his wife's funeral, left home and went to stay with one of his relations in a distant part of England, Ida, whom it had been his wish to take away with him, petitioned earnestly to be left behind. "I promised mamma before she died that I would be as good to my little sister Rosamond as she had been to me," said the child, simply; "and she told me in return that I might wait here and see her laid in her grave."

There happened to be an aunt of Mrs. Welwyn, and an old servant of the family, in the house at this time, who understood Ida much better than her father did, and they persuaded him not to take her away. I have heard my mother say that the effect of the child's appearance at the funeral on her, and on all who went to see it, was something that she could never think of without the tears coming into her eyes, and could never forget to the last day of her life.

It must have been very shortly after this period that I saw Ida for the first time.

I remember accompanying my mother on a visit to the old house we have just left, in the summer, when I was at home for the holidays. It was a lovely, sunshiny morning. There was nobody indoors, and we walked out into the garden. As we approached that lawn yonder, on the other side of the shrubbery, I saw, first, a young woman in mourning (apparently a servant) sitting reading; then a little girl, dressed all in black, moving toward us slowly over the bright turf, and holding up before her a baby, whom she was trying to teach to walk.

She looked, to my ideas, so very young to be engaged in such an occupation as this, and her gloomy black frock appeared to be such an unnaturally grave garment for a mere child of her age, and looked so doubly dismal by contrast with the brilliant sunny lawn on which she stood, that I quite started when I first saw her, and eagerly asked my mother who she was. The answer informed me of the sad family story, which I have been just relating to you. Mrs. Welwyn had then been buried about three months; and Ida, in her childish way, was trying, as she had promised, to supply her mother's place to her infant sister Rosamond.

I only mention this simple incident, because it is necessary, before I proceed to the eventful part of my narrative, that you should know exactly in what relation the sisters stood toward one another from the first. Of all the last parting words that Mrs. Welwyn had spoken to her child, none had been oftener repeated, none more solemnly urged, than those which had commended the little Rosamond to Ida's love and care. To other persons, the full, the all-trusting dependence which the dying mother was known to have placed in a child hardly eleven years old, seemed merely a proof of that helpless desire to cling even to the feeblest consolations, which the approach of death so often brings with it.

But the event showed that the trust so strangely placed had not been ventured vainly when it was committed to young and tender hands. The whole future existence of the child was one noble proof that she had been worthy of her mother's dying confidence, when it was first reposed in her. In that simple incident which I have just mentioned the new life of the two motherless sisters was all foreshadowed.

Time passed. I left school—went to college—travelled in Germany, and stayed there some time to learn the language. At every interval when I came home, and asked about the Welwyns, the answer was, in substance, almost always the same. Mr. Welwyn was giving his regular dinners, performing his regular duties as a county magistrate, enjoying his regular recreations as an a amateur farmer and an eager sportsman. His two daughters were never separate. Ida was the same strange, quiet, retiring girl, that she had always been; and was still (as the phrase went) "spoiling" Rosamond in every way in which it was possible for an elder sister to spoil a younger by too much kindness.

I myself went to the Grange occasionally, when I was in this neighbourhood, in holiday and vacation time; and was able to test the correctness of the picture of life there which had been drawn for me. I remember the two sisters, when Rosamond was four or five years old; and when Ida seemed to me, even then, to be more like the child's mother than her sister. She bore with her little caprices as sisters do not bear with one another.

She was so patient at lesson-time, so anxious to conceal any weariness that might overcome her in play hours, so proud when Rosamond's beauty was noticed, so grateful for Rosamond's kisses when the child thought of bestowing them, so quick to notice all that Rosamond did, and to attend to all that Rosamond said, even when visitors were in the room, that she seemed, to my boyish observation, altogether different from other elder sisters in other family circles into which I was then received.

I remember then, again, when Rosamond was just growing to womanhood, and was in high spirits at the prospect of spending a season in London, and being presented at court. She was very beautiful at that time—much handsomer than Ida. Her "accomplishments" were talked of far and near in our country circles. Few, if any, of the people, however, who applauded her playing and singing, who admired her water-colour drawings, who were delighted at her fluency when she spoke French, and amazed at her ready comprehension when she read German, knew how little of all this elegant mental cultivation and nimble manual dexterity she owed to her governess and masters, and how much to her elder sister.

It was Ida who really found out the means of stimulating her when she was idle; Ida who helped her through all her worst difficulties; Ida who gently conquered her defects of memory over her books, her inaccuracies of ear at the piano, her errors of taste when she took the brush and pencil in hand. It was Ida alone who worked these marvels, and whose all-sufficient reward for her hardest exertions was a chance word of kindness from her sister's lips.

Rosamond was not unaffectionate, and not ungrateful; but she inherited much of her father's commonness and frivolity of character. She became so accustomed to owe everything to her sister—to resign all her most trifling difficulties to Ida's ever-ready care—to have all her tastes consulted by Ida's ever-watchful kindness—that she never appreciated, as it deserved, the deep, devoted love of which she was the object. When Ida refused two good offers of marriage, Rosamond was as much astonished as the veriest strangers, who wondered why the elder Miss Welwyn seemed bent on remaining single all her life.

When the journey to London, to which I have already alluded, took place, Ida accompanied her father and sister. If she had consulted her own tastes, she would have remained in the country; but Rosamond declared that she should feel quite lost and helpless twenty times a day, in town, without her sister. It was in the nature of Ida to sacrifice herself to any one whom she loved, on the smallest occasions as well as the greatest.

Her affection was as intuitively ready to sanctify Rosamond's slightest caprices as to excuse Rosamond's most thoughtless faults. So she went to London cheerfully, to witness with pride all the little triumphs won by her sister's beauty; to hear, and never tire of hearing, all that admiring friends could say in her sister's praise.

At the end of the season Mr. Welwyn and his daughters returned for a short time to the country; then left home again to spend the latter part of the autumn and the beginning of the winter in Paris.

They took with them excellent letters of introduction, and saw a great deal of the best society in Paris, foreign as well as English. At one of the first of the evening parties which they attended, the general topic of conversation was the conduct of a certain French nobleman, the Baron Franval, who had returned to his native country after a long absence, and who was spoken of in terms of high eulogy by the majority of the guests present. The history of who Franval was, and of what he had done, was readily communicated to Mr. Welwyn and his daughters, and was briefly this:

The baron inherited little from his ancestors besides his high rank and his ancient pedigree. On the death of his parents, he and his two unmarried sisters (their only surviving children) found the small territorial property of the Franvals, in Normandy, barely productive enough to afford a comfortable subsistence for the three. The baron, then a young man of three-and-twenty endeavoured to obtain such military or civil employment as might become his rank; but, although the Bourbons were at that time restored to the throne of France, his efforts were ineffectual.

Either his interest at court was bad, or secret enemies were at work to oppose his advancement. He failed to obtain even the slightest favour; and, irritated by undeserved neglect, resolved to leave France, and seek occupation for his energies in foreign countries, where his rank would be no bar to his bettering his fortunes, if he pleased, by engaging in commercial pursuits.

An opportunity of the kind that he wanted unexpectedly offered itself. He left his sisters in care of an old male relative of the family at the *château* in Normandy, and sailed, in the first instance, to the West Indies; afterward extending his wanderings to the continent of South America, and there engaging in mining transactions on a very large scale.

After fifteen years of absence (during the latter part of which time false reports of his death had reached Normandy), he had just returned to France, having realized a handsome independence, with which he proposed to widen the limits of his ancestral property, and to give his sisters (who were still, like himself, unmarried) all the luxuries and advantages that affluence could bestow. The baron's independent spirit and generous devotion to the honour of his family and the happiness of his surviving relatives were themes of general admiration in most of the social circles of Paris. He was expected to arrive in the capital every day; and it was naturally enough predicted that his reception in society there could not fail to be of the most flattering and most brilliant kind.

The Welwyns listened to this story with some little interest; Rosamond, who was very romantic, being especially attracted by it, and openly avowing to her father and sister, when they got back to their hotel, that she felt as ardent a curiosity as anybody to see the adventurous and generous baron. The desire was soon gratified. Franval came to Paris, as had been anticipated—was introduced to the Welwyns—met them constantly in society-made no favourable impression on Ida, but won the good opinion of Rosamond from the first; and was regarded with such high approval by their father, that when he mentioned his intentions of visiting England in the spring of the new year, he was cordially invited to spend the hunting season at Glenwith Grange.

I came back from Germany about the same time that the Welwyns returned from Paris, and at once set myself to improve my neighbourly intimacy with the family. I was very fond of Ida; more fond, perhaps, than my vanity will now allow me to—; but that is of no consequence. It is much more to the purpose to tell you that I heard the whole of the baron's story enthusiastically related by Mr. Welwyn and Rosamond; that he came to the Grange at the appointed time; that I was introduced to him; and that he produced as unfavourable an impression upon me as he had already produced upon Ida.

It was whimsical enough; but I really could not tell why I disliked him, though I could account very easily, according to my own notions, for his winning the favour and approval of Rosamond and her father. He was certainly a handsome man as far as features went; he had a winning gentleness and graceful respect in his manner when he spoke to women; and he sang remarkably well, with one of the sweetest tenor voices I ever heard. These qualities alone were quite sufficient to attract any girl of Rosamond's disposition; and I certainly never wondered why he was a favourite of hers.

Then, as to her father, the baron was not only fitted to win his sympathy and regard in the field, by proving himself an ardent sportsman and an excellent rider; but was also, in virtue of some of his minor personal peculiarities, just the man to gain the friendship of his host. Mr. Welwyn was as ridiculously prejudiced as most weak-headed Englishmen are, on the subject of foreigners in general. In spite of his visit to Paris, the vulgar notion of a Frenchman continued to be *his* notion, both while he was in France and when he returned from it.

Now, the baron was as unlike the traditional "Mounseer" of English songs, plays, and satires, as a man could well be; and it was on account of this very dissimilarity that Mr. Welwyn first took a violent fancy to him, and then invited him to his house. Franval spoke English remarkably well; wore neither beard, moustache, nor whiskers; kept his hair cut almost unbecomingly short; dressed in the extreme of plainness and modest good taste; talked little in general society; uttered his words, when he did speak, with singular calmness and deliberation; and, to crown all, had the greater part of his acquired property invested in English securities. In Mr. Welwyn's estimation, such a man as this was a perfect miracle of a Frenchman, and he admired and encouraged him accordingly.

I have said that I disliked him, yet could not assign a reason for my dislike; and I can only repeat it now. He was remarkably polite to me; we often rode together in hunting, and sat near each other at the Grange table; but I could never become familiar with him. He always gave me the idea of a man who had some mental reservation in saying the most trifling thing. There was a constant restraint, hardly perceptible to most people, but plainly visible, nevertheless, to me, which seemed to accompany his lightest words, and to hang about his most familiar manner.

This, however, was no just reason for my secretly disliking and distrusting him as I did. Ida said as much to me, I remember, when I confessed to her what my feelings toward him were, and tried (but vainly) to induce her to be equally candid with me in return. She seemed to shrink from the tacit condemnation of Rosamond's opinion which such a confidence on her part would have implied.

And yet she watched the growth of that opinion—or, in other words, the growth of her sister's liking for the baron—with an apprehension and sorrow which she tried fruitlessly to conceal. Even her father began to notice that her spirits were not so good as usual, and to suspect the cause of her melancholy. I remember he jested, with all the dense insensibility of a stupid man, about Ida having invariably been jealous, from a child, if Rosamond looked kindly upon anybody except her elder sister.

The spring began to get far advanced toward summer. Franval paid a visit to London; came back in the middle of the season to Glenwith Grange; wrote to put off his departure for France; and at last (not at all to the surprise of anybody who was intimate with the Welwyns) proposed to Rosamond, and was accepted. He was candour and generosity itself when the preliminaries of the marriage-settlement were under discussion. He quite over-powered Mr. Welwyn and the lawyers with references, papers, and statements of the distribution and extent of his property, which were found to be perfectly correct. His sisters were written to, and returned the most cordial answers; saying that the state of their health would not allow them to come to England for the marriage; but adding a warm invitation to Normandy for the bride and her family. Nothing, in short, could be more straightforward and satisfactory than the baron's behaviour, and the testimonies to his worth and integrity which the news of the approaching marriage produced from his relatives and his friends.

The only joyless face at the Grange now was Ida's. At any time it would have been a hard trial to her to resign that first and foremost place which she had held since childhood in her sister's heart, as she knew she must resign it when Rosamond married. But, secretly disliking and distrusting Franval as she did, the thought that he was soon to become the husband of her beloved sister filled her with a vague sense of terror which she could not explain to herself; which it was imperatively necessary that she should conceal; and which, on those very accounts, became a daily and hourly torment to her that was almost more than she could bear.

One consolation alone supported her: Rosamond and she were not to be separated. She knew that the baron secretly disliked her as much as she disliked him; she knew that she must bid farewell to the brighter and happier part of her life on the day when she went to live under the same roof with her sister's husband; but, true to the promise made years and years ago by her dying mother's bed—true to the affection which was the ruling and beautiful feeling of her whole existence—she never hesitated about indulging Rosamond's wish, when the girl, in her bright, light-hearted way, said that she could never get on comfortably in the marriage state unless she had Ida to live with her and help her just the same as ever. The baron was too polite a man even to *look* dissatisfied when he heard of the proposed arrangement; and it was therefore settled from the beginning that Ida was always to live with her sister.

The marriage took place in the summer, and the bride and bridegroom went to spend their honeymoon in Cumberland. On their return to Glenwith Grange, a visit to the baron's sisters, in Normandy, was talked of; but the execution of this project was suddenly and disastrously suspended by the death of Mr. Welwyn, from an attack of pleurisy.

In consequence of this calamity, the projected journey was of course deferred; and when autumn and the shooting season came, the baron was unwilling to leave the well-stocked preserves of the Grange. He seemed, indeed, to grow less and less inclined, as time advanced, for the trip to Normandy; and wrote excuse after excuse to his sisters, when letters arrived from them urging him to pay the promised visit.

In the winter-time, he said he would not allow his wife to risk a long journey. In the spring, his health was pronounced to be delicate. In the genial summer-time, the accomplishment of the proposed visit would be impossible, for at that period the baroness expected to become a mother. Such were the apologies which Franval seemed almost glad to be able to send to his sisters in France.

The marriage was, in the strictest sense of the term, a happy one. The baron, though he never altogether lost the strange restraint and reserve of his manner, was, in his quiet, peculiar way, the fondest and kindest of husbands. He went to town occasionally on business, but always seemed glad to return to the baroness; he never varied in the politeness of his bearing toward his wife's sister; he behaved with the most courteous hospitality toward all the friends of the Welwyns; in short, he thoroughly justified the good opinion which Rosamond and her father had formed of him when they first met at Paris.

And yet no experience of his character thoroughly reassured Ida. Months passed on quietly and pleasantly; and still that secret sadness, that indefinable, unreasonable apprehension on Rosamond's account, hung heavily on her sister's heart.

At the beginning of the first summer months, a little domestic inconvenience happened, which showed the baroness, for the first time, that her husband's temper could be seriously ruffled-and that by the veriest trifle. He was in the habit of taking in two French provincial newspapers—one published at Bordeaux and the other at Havre.

He always opened these journals the moment they came, looked at one particular column of each with the deepest attention, for a few minutes, then carelessly threw them aside into his waste-paper basket. His wife and her sister were at first rather surprised at the manner in which he read his two papers; but they thought no more of it when he explained that he only took them in to consult them about French commercial intelligence, which might be, occasionally, of importance to him.

These papers were published weekly. On the occasion to which I have just referred, the Bordeaux paper came on the proper day, as usual; but the Havre paper never made its appearance. This trifling circumstance seemed to make the baron seriously uneasy. He wrote off directly to the country post-office and to the newspaper agent in London.

His wife, astonished to see his tranquillity so completely overthrown by so slight a cause, tried to restore his good humour by jesting with him about the missing newspaper. He replied by the first angry and unfeeling words that she had heard issue from his lips. She was then within about six weeks of her confinement, and very unfit to bear harsh answers from anybody—least of all from her husband.

On the second day no answer came. On the afternoon of the third, the baron rode off to the post town to make inquiries.

About an hour after he had gone, a strange gentleman came to the Grange and asked to see the baroness. On being informed that she was not well enough to receive visitors, he sent up a message that his business was of great importance and that he would wait downstairs for a second answer.

On receiving this message, Rosamond turned, as usual, to her elder sister for advice. Ida went downstairs immediately to see the stranger. What I am now about to tell you of the extraordinary interview which took place between them, and of the shocking events that followed it, I have heard from Miss Welwyn's own lips.

She felt unaccountably nervous when she entered the room. The stranger bowed very politely, and asked, in a foreign accent, if she were the Baroness Franval. She set him right on this point, and told him she attended to all matters of business for the baroness; adding that, if his errand at all concerned her sister's husband, the baron was not then at home.

The stranger answered that he was aware of it when he called, and that the unpleasant business on which he came could not be confided to the baron—at least, in the first instance.

She asked why. He said he was there to explain; and expressed himself as feeling greatly relieved at having to open his business to her, because she would, doubtless, be best able to prepare her sister for the bad news that he was, unfortunately, obliged to bring. The sudden faintness which overcame her, as he spoke those words, prevented her from addressing him in return. He poured out some water for her from a bottle which happened to be standing on the table, and asked if he might depend on her fortitude.

She tried to say "Yes"; but the violent throbbing of her heart seemed to choke her. He took a foreign newspaper from his pocket, saying that he was a secret agent of the French police—that the paper was the Havre *Journal*, for the past week, and that it had been expressly kept from reaching the baron, as usual, through his (the agent's) interference. He then opened the newspaper, and begged that she would nerve herself sufficiently (for her sister's sake) to read certain lines, which would give her some hint of the business that brought him there. He pointed to the passage as he spoke. It was among the "Shipping Entries," and was thus expressed:

"Arrived, the *Berenice*, from San Francisco, with a valuable cargo of hides. She brings one passenger, the Baron Franval, of *Château* Franval, in Normandy."

As Miss Welwyn read the entry, her heart, which had been throbbing violently but the moment before, seemed suddenly to cease from all action, and she began to shiver, though it was a warm June evening. The agent held the tumbler to her lips, and made her drink a little of the water, entreating her very earnestly to take courage and listen to him. He then sat down, and referred again to the entry, every word he uttered seeming to burn itself in forever (as she expressed it) on her memory and her heart.

He said: "It has been ascertained beyond the possibility of doubt that there is no mistake about the name in the lines you have just read. And it is as certain as that we are here, that there is only *one* Baron Franval now alive. The question, therefore, is, whether the passenger by the *Berenice* is the true baron, or—I beg you most earnestly to bear with me and to compose yourself—or the husband of your sister. The person who arrived last week at Harve was scouted as an impostor by the ladies at the *château*, the moment he presented himself there as the brother, returning to them after sixteen years of absence. The authorities were communicated with, and I and my assistants were instantly sent for from Paris.

"We wasted no time in questioning the supposed impostor. He either was, or affected to be, in a perfect frenzy of grief and indignation. We just ascertained, from competent witnesses, that he bore an extraordinary resemblance to the real baron, and that he was perfectly familiar with places and persons in and about the *château*; we just ascertained that, and then proceeded to confer with the local authorities, and to examine their private entries of suspected persons in their jurisdiction, ranging back over a past period of twenty years or more.

"One of the entries thus consulted contained these particulars: 'Hector Auguste Monbrun, son of a respectable proprietor in Normandy. Well educated; gentleman-like manners. On bad terms with his family. Character: bold, cunning, unscrupulous, self-possessed. Is a clever mimic. May be easily recognized by his striking likeness to the Baron Franval. Imprisoned at twenty for theft and assault.' "

Miss Welwyn saw the agent look up at her after he had read this extract from the police-book, to ascertain if she was still able to listen to him. He asked, with some appearance of alarm, as their eyes met, if she would like some more water. She was just able to make a sign in the negative. He took a second extract from his pocket-book, and went on.

He said: "The next entry under the same name was dated four years later, and ran thus:—

"'H. A. Monbrun, condemned to the galleys for life, for assassination, and other crimes not officially necessary to be here specified. Escaped from custody at Toulon. Is known, since the expiration of his first term of imprisonment, to have allowed his beard to grow, and to have worn his hair long, with the intention of rendering it impossible for those acquainted with him in his native province to recognize him, as heretofore, by his likeness to the Baron Franval.'

"There were more particulars added, not important enough for extract. We immediately examined the supposed impostor; for, if he was Monbrun, we knew that we should find on his shoulder the two letters of the convict brand, 'T. F.,' standing for *Travaux Forcés*. After the minutest examination with the mechanical and chemical tests used on such occasions, not the slightest trace of the brand was to be found.

"The moment this astounding discovery was made, I started to lay an embargo on the forthcoming numbers of the Havre *Journal* for that week, which were about to be sent to the English agent in London. I arrived at Havre on Saturday (the morning of publication), in time to execute my design. I waited there long enough to communicate by telegraph with my superiors in Paris, then hastened to this place. What my errand here is, you may—"

He might have gone on speaking for some moments longer; but Miss Welwyn heard no more.

Her first sensation of returning consciousness was the feeling that water was being sprinkled on her face. Then she saw that all the windows in the room had been set wide open, to give her air; and that she and the agent were still alone. At first she felt bewildered, and hardly knew who he was; but he soon recalled to her mind the horrible realities that had brought him there, by apologizing for not having summoned assistance when she fainted. He said it was of the last importance, in Franval's absence, that no one in the house should imagine that anything unusual was taking place in it.

Then, after giving her an interval of a minute or two to collect what little strength she had left, he added that he would not increase her sufferings by saying anything more, just then, on the shocking subject of the investigation which it was his duty to make—that he would leave her to recover herself, and to consider what was the best course to be taken with the baroness in the present terrible emergency—and that he would privately return to the house between eight and nine o'clock that evening, ready to act as Miss Welwyn wished, and to afford her and her sister any aid and protection of which they might stand in need. With these words he bowed, and noiselessly quitted the room.

For the first few awful minutes after she was left alone, Miss Welwyn sat helpless and speechless; utterly numbed in heart, and mind, and body—then a sort of instinct (she was incapable of thinking) seemed to urge her to conceal the fearful news from her sister as long as possible. She ran upstairs to Rosamond's sitting-room, and called through the door (for she dared not trust herself in her sister's presence) that the visitor had come on some troublesome business from their late father's lawyers, and that she was going to shut herself up, and write some long letters in connection with that business.

After she had got into her own room, she was never sensible of how time was passing—never conscious of any feeling within her, except a baseless, helpless hope that the French police might yet be proved to have made some terrible mistake—until she heard a violent shower of rain come on a little after sunset. The noise of the rain, and the freshness it brought with it in the air, seemed to awaken her as if from a painful and a fearful sleep.

The power of reflection returned to her; her heart heaved and bounded with an overwhelming terror, as the thought of Rosamond came back vividly to it; her memory recurred despairingly to the long-past day of her mother's death, and to the farewell promise she had made by her mother's bedside. She burst into an hysterical passion of weeping that seemed to be tearing her to pieces. In the midst of it she heard the clatter of a horse's hoofs in the courtyard, and knew that Rosamond's husband had come back.

Dipping her handkerchief in cold water, and passing it over her eyes as she left the room, she instantly hastened to her sister.

Fortunately the daylight was fading in the old-fashioned chamber that Rosamond occupied. Before they could say two words to each other, Franval was in the room. He seemed violently irritated; said that he had waited for the arrival of the mail—that the missing newspaper had not come by it—that he had got wet through—that he felt a shivering fit coming on—and that he believed he had caught a violent cold.

His wife anxiously suggested some simple remedies. He roughly interrupted her, saying there was but one remedy, the remedy of going to bed; and so left them without another word. She just put her handkerchief to her eyes, and said softly to her sister, "How he is changed!" then spoke no more. They sat silent for half an hour or longer.

After that, Rosamond went affectionately and forgivingly to

see how her husband was. She returned, saying that he was in bed, and in a deep, heavy sleep; and predicting hopefully that he would wake up quite well the next morning. In a few minutes more the clock stuck nine; and Ida heard the servant's step ascending the stairs. She suspected what his errand was, and went out to meet him. Her presentiment had not deceived her; the police agent had arrived, and was waiting for her downstairs.

He asked her if she had said anything to her sister, or had thought of any plan of action, the moment she entered the room; and, on receiving a reply in the negative, inquired, further, if "the baron" had come home yet. She answered that he had; that he was ill and tired, and vexed, and that he had gone to bed. The agent asked in an eager whisper if she knew that he was asleep, and alone in bed? and, when he received her reply, said that he must go up into the bedroom directly.

She began to feel the faintness coming over her again, and with it sensations of loathing and terror that she could neither express to others nor define to herself. He said that if she hesitated to let him avail himself of this unexpected opportunity, her scruples might lead to fatal results He reminded her that if "the baron" were really the convict Monbrun, the claims of society and of justice demanded that he should be discovered by the first available means; and that if he were not—if some inconceivable mistake had really been committed—then such a plan for getting immediately at the truth as was now proposed would insure the delivery of an innocent man from suspicion; and at the same time spare him the knowledge that he had ever been suspected. This last argument had its effect on Miss Welwyn. The baseless, helpless hope that the French authorities might yet be proved to be in error, which she had already felt in her own room, returned to her now. She suffered the agent to lead her upstairs.

He took the candle from her hand when she pointed to the door; opened it softly; and, leaving it ajar, went into the room.

She looked through the gap with a feverish, horror-struck curiosity. Franval was lying on his side in a profound sleep, with his back turned toward the door. The agent softly placed the candle upon a small reading-table between the door and the bedside, softly drew down the bedclothes a little away from the sleeper's back, then took a pair of scissors from the toilet-table, and very gently and slowly began to cut away, first the loose folds, then the intervening strips of linen, from the part of Franval's night-gown that was over his shoulders. When the upper part of his back had been bared in this way, the agent took the candle and held it near the flesh. Miss Welwyn heard him ejaculate some word under his breath, then saw him looking round to where she was standing, and beckoning to her to come in.

Mechanically she obeyed; mechanically she looked down where his finger was pointing. It was the convict Monbrun—there, just visible under the bright light of the candle, were the fatal letters "T. F." branded on the villain's shoulder!

Though she could neither move nor speak, the horror of this discovery did not deprive her of her consciousness. She saw the agent softly draw up the bedclothes again into their proper position, replace the scissors on the toilet-table, and take from it a bottle of smelling-salts. She felt him removing her from the bedroom, and helping her quickly downstairs, giving her the salts to smell to by the way.

When they were alone again, he said, with the first appearance of agitation that he had yet exhibited, "Now, madam, for God's sake, collect all your courage, and be guided by me. You and your sister had better leave the house immediately. Have you any relatives in the neighbourhood with whom you could take refuge?" They had none.

"What is the name of the nearest town where you could get good accommodation for the night?" Harleybrook (he wrote the name down on his tablets). "How far off is it?" Twelve miles. "You had better have the carriage out at once, to go there with as little delay as possible, leaving me to pass the night here. I will communicate with you tomorrow at the principal hotel. Can you compose yourself sufficiently to be able to tell the head servant, if I ring for him, that he is to obey my orders till further notice?"

The servant was summoned, and received his instructions, the agent going out with him to see that the carriage was got ready quietly and quickly. Miss Welwyn went upstairs to her sister.

How the fearful news was first broken to Rosamond, I cannot relate to you. Miss Welwyn has never confided to me, has never confided to anybody, what happened at the interview between her sister and herself that night. I can tell you nothing of the shock they both suffered, except that the younger and the weaker died under it; that the elder and the stronger has never recovered from it, and never will.

They went away the same night, with one attendant, to Harleybrook, as the agent had advised. Before daybreak Rosamond was seized with the pains of premature labour. She died three days after, unconscious of the horror of her situation, wandering in her mind about past times, and singing old tunes that Ida had taught her as she lay in her sister's arms.

The child was born alive, and lives still. You saw her at the window as we came in at the back way to the Grange. I surprised you, I dare say, by asking you not to speak of her to Miss Welwyn. Perhaps you noticed something vacant in the little girl's expression. I am sorry to say that her mind is more vacant still. If "idiot" did not sound like a mocking word, however tenderly and pityingly one may wish to utter it, I should tell you that the poor thing had been an idiot from her birth.

You will, doubtless, want to hear now what happened at Glenwith Grange after Miss Welwyn and her sister had left it. I have seen the letter which the police agent sent the next morning to Harleybrook; and, speaking from my recollection of that, I shall be able to relate all you can desire to know.

First, as to the past history of the scoundrel Monbrun, I need only tell you that he was identical with an escaped convict, who, for a long term of years, had successfully eluded the vigilance of the authorities all over Europe, and in America as well. In conjunction with two accomplices, he had succeeded in possessing himself of large sums of money by the most criminal means. He also acted secretly as the "banker" of his convict brethren, whose dishonest gains were all confided to his hands for safe-keeping.

He would have been certainly captured, on venturing back to France, along with his two associates, but for the daring imposture in which he took refuge; and which, if the true Baron Franval had really died abroad, as was reported, would, in all probability, never have been found out.

Besides his extraordinary likeness to the baron, he had every other requisite for carrying on his deception successfully. Though his parents were not wealthy, he had received a good education. He was so notorious for his gentleman-like manners among the villainous associates of his crimes and excesses, that they nicknamed him "the Prince."

All his early life had been passed in the neighbourhood of the Château Franval. He knew what were the circumstances which had induced the baron to leave it. He had been in the country to which the baron had emigrated. He was able to refer familiarly to persons and localities, at home and abroad, with which the baron was sure to be acquainted.

And, lastly, he had an expatriation of fifteen years to plead for him as his all-sufficient excuse, if he made any slight mistakes before the baron's sisters, in his assumed character of their long-absent brother. It will be, of course, hardly necessary for me to tell you, in relation to this part of the subject, that the true Franval was immediately and honourably reinstated in the family rights of which the impostor had succeeded for a time in depriving him.

According to Monbrun's own account, he had married poor Rosamond purely for love; and the probabilities certainly are, that the pretty, innocent English girl had really struck the villain's fancy for the time; and that the easy, quiet life he was leading at the Grange pleased him, by contrast with his perilous and vagabond existence of former days. What might have happened if he had had time enough to grow wearied of his ill-fated wife and his English home, it is now useless to inquire. What really did happen on the morning when he awoke after the flight of Ida and her sister can be briefly told.

As soon as his eyes opened they rested on the police agent, sitting quietly by the bedside, with a loaded pistol in his hand. Monbrun knew immediately that he was discovered; but he never for an instant lost the self-possession for which he was famous. He said he wished to have five minutes allowed him to deliberate quietly in bed, whether he should resist the French authorities on English ground, and so gain time by obliging the one Government to apply specially to have him delivered up by the other—or whether he should accept the terms officially offered to him by the agent, if he quietly allowed himself to be captured.

He chose the latter course—it was suspected, because he wished to communicate personally with some of his convict associates in France, whose fraudulent gains were in his keeping, and because he felt boastfully confident of being able to escape again, whenever he pleased. Be his secret motives, however, what they might, he allowed the agent to conduct him peaceably from the Grange; first writing a farewell letter to poor Rosamond, full of heartless French sentiment and glib sophistries about Fate and Society. His own fate was not long in overtaking him. He attempted to escape again, as it had been expected he would, and was shot by the sentinel on duty at the time. I remember hearing that the bullet entered his head and killed him on the spot.

My story is done. It is ten years now since Rosamond was buried in the churchyard yonder; and it is ten years also since Miss Welwyn returned to be the lonely inhabitant of Glenwith Grange. She now lives but in the remembrances that it calls up before her of her happier existence of former days. There is hardly an object in the old house which does not tenderly and solemnly remind her of the mother, whose last wishes she lived to obey; of the sister, whose happiness was once her dearest earthly care.

Those prints that you noticed on the library walls Rosamond used to copy in the past time, when her pencil was often guided by Ida's hand. Those music-books that you were looking over, she and her mother have played from together through many a long and quiet summer's evening. She has no ties now to bind her to the present but the poor child whose affliction it is her constant effort to lighten, and the little peasant population around her, whose humble cares and wants and sorrows she is always ready to relieve.

Far and near her modest charities have penetrated among us; and far and near she is heartily beloved and blessed in many a labourer's household. There is no poor man's hearth, not in this village only, but for miles away from it as well, at which you would not be received with the welcome given to an old friend, if you only told the cottagers that you knew the Lady of Glenwith Grange!

The Nun's Story of Gabriel's Marriage

CHAPTER 1

One night, during the period of the first French Revolution, the family of François Sarzeau, a fisherman of Brittany, were all waking and watching at a late hour in their cottage on the peninsula of Quiberon. François had gone out in his boat that evening, as usual, to fish. Shortly after his departure, the wind had risen, the clouds had gathered; and the storm, which had been threatening at intervals throughout the whole day, burst forth furiously about nine o'clock.

It was now eleven; and the raging of the wind over the barren, heathy peninsula still seemed to increase with each fresh blast that tore its way out upon the open sea; the crashing of the waves on the beach was awful to hear; the dreary blackness of the sky terrible to behold. The longer they listened to the storm, the oftener they looked out at it, the fainter grew the hopes which the fisherman's family still strove to cherish for the safety of François Sarzeau and of his younger son who had gone with him in the boat.

There was something impressive in the simplicity of the scene that was now passing within the cottage.

On one side of the great, rugged, black fireplace crouched two little girls; the younger half asleep, with her head in her sister's lap. These were the daughters of the fisherman; and opposite to them sat their eldest brother, Gabriel. His right arm had been badly wounded in a recent encounter at the national game of the *Soule*, a sport resembling our English football; but played on both sides in such savage earnest by the people of Brittany as to end always in bloodshed, often in mutilation, sometimes even in loss of life.

On the same bench with Gabriel sat his betrothed wife—a girl of eighteen—clothed in the plain, almost monastic black-and-white costume of her native district. She was the daughter of a small farmer living at some little distance from the coast. Between the groups formed on either side of the fireplace, the vacant space was occupied by the foot of a truckle-bed. In this bed lay a very old man, the father of François Sarzeau. His haggard face was covered with deep wrinkles; his long white hair flowed over the coarse lump of sacking which served him for a pillow, and his light gray eyes wandered incessantly, with a strange expression of terror and suspicion, from person to person, and from object to object, in all parts of the room.

Whenever the wind and sea whistled and roared at their loudest, he muttered to himself and tossed his hands fretfully on his wretched coverlet. On these occasions his eyes always fixed themselves intently on a little delf image of the Virgin placed in a niche over the fireplace. Every time they saw him look in this direction Gabriel and the young girls shuddered and crossed themselves; and even the child, who still kept awake, imitated their example.

There was one bond of feeling at least between the old man and his grandchildren, which connected his age and their youth unnaturally and closely together. This feeling was reverence for the superstitions which had been handed down to them by their ancestors from centuries and centuries back, as far even as the age of the Druids. The spirit warnings of disaster and death which the old man heard in the wailing of the wind, in the crashing of the waves, in the dreary, monotonous rattling of the casement, the young man and his affianced wife and the little child who cowered by the fireside heard too.

All differences in sex, in temperament, in years, superstition was strong enough to strike down to its own dread level, in the fisherman's cottage, on that stormy night.

Besides the benches by the fireside and the bed, the only piece of furniture in the room was a coarse wooden table, with a loaf of black bread, a knife, and a pitcher of cider placed on it. Old nets, coils of rope, tattered sails, hung, about the walls and over the wooden partition which separated the room into two compartments. Wisps of straw and ears of barley drooped down through the rotten rafters and gaping boards that made the floor of the granary above.

These different objects, and the persons in the cottage, who composed the only surviving members of the fisherman's family, were strangely and wildly lit up by the blaze of the fire and by the still brighter glare of a resin torch stuck into a block of wood in the chimney-corner. The red and yellow light played full on the weird face of the old man as he lay opposite to it, and glanced fitfully on the figures of the young girl, Gabriel, and the two children; the great, gloomy shadows rose and fell, and grew and lessened in bulk about the walls like visions of darkness, animated by a supernatural spectre-life, while the dense obscurity outside spreading before the curtainless window seemed as a wall of solid darkness that had closed in forever around the fisherman's house. The night scene within the cottage was almost as wild and as dreary to look upon as the night scene without.

For a long time the different persons in the room sat together without speaking, even without looking at each other. At last the girl turned and whispered something into Gabriel's ear.

"Perrine, what were you saying to Gabriel?" asked the child opposite, seizing the first opportunity of breaking the desolate silence—doubly desolate at her age—which was preserved by all around her.

"I was telling him," answered Perrine, simply, "that it was time to change the bandages on his arm; and I also said to him, what I have often said before, that he must never play at that terrible game of the *Soule* again."

The old man had been looking intently at Perrine and his

grandchild as they spoke. His harsh, hollow voice mingled with the last soft tones of the young girl, repeating over and over again the same terrible words, "Drowned! drowned! Son and grandson, both drowned! both drowned!"

"Hush, grandfather," said Gabriel, "we must not lose all hope for them yet. God and the Blessed Virgin protect them!" He looked at the little delf image, and crossed himself; the others imitated him, except the old man. He still tossed his hands over the coverlet, and still repeated, "Drowned! drowned!"

"Oh, that accursed *Soule!*" groaned the young man. "But for this wound I should have been with my father. The poor boy's life might at least have been saved; for we should then have left him here."

"Silence!" exclaimed the harsh voice from the bed. "The wail of dying men rises louder than the loud sea; the devil's psalm-singing roars higher than the roaring wind! Be silent, and listen! François drowned! Pierre drowned! Hark! Hark!"

A terrific blast of wind burst over the house as he spoke, shaking it to its centre, overpowering all other sounds, even to the deafening crash of the waves. The slumbering child awoke, and uttered a scream of fear. Perrine, who had been kneeling before her lover binding the fresh bandages on his wounded arm, paused in her occupation, trembling from head to foot. Gabriel looked toward the window; his experience told him what must be the hurricane fury of that blast of wind out at sea, and he sighed bitterly as he murmured to himself, "God help them both—man's help will be as nothing to them now!"

"Gabriel!" cried the voice from the bed in altered tones-very faint and trembling.

He did not hear or did not attend to the old man. He was trying to soothe and encourage the young girl at his feet.

"Don't be frightened, love," he said, kissing her very gently and tenderly on the forehead. You are as safe here as anywhere. Was I not right in saying that it would be madness to attempt taking you back to the farmhouse this evening? You can sleep in that room, Perrine, when you are tired—you can sleep with the two girls."

"Gabriel! brother Gabriel!" cried one of the children. "Oh, look at grandfather!"

Gabriel ran to the bedside. The old man had raised himself into a sitting position; his eyes were dilated, his whole face was rigid with terror, his hands were stretched out convulsively toward his grandson. "The White Women!" he screamed. "The White Women; the grave-diggers of the drowned are out on the sea!"

The children, with cries of terror, flung themselves into Perrine's arms; even Gabriel uttered an exclamation of horror, and started back from the bedside.

Still the old man reiterated, "The White Women! The White Women! Open the door, Gabriel! look-out westward, where the ebb-tide has left the sand dry. You'll see them bright as lightning in the darkness, mighty as the angels in stature, sweeping like the wind over the sea, in their long white garments, with their white hair trailing far behind them!

"Open the door, Gabriel! You'll see them stop and hover over the place where your father and your brother have been drowned; you'll see them come on till they reach the sand, you'll see them dig in it with their naked feet and beckon awfully to the raging sea to give up its dead. Open the door, Gabriel—or, though it should be the death of me, I will get up and open it myself!"

Gabriel's face whitened even to his lips, but he made a sign that he would obey. It required the exertion of his whole strength to keep the door open against the wind while he looked out.

"Do you see them, grandson Gabriel? Speak the truth, and tell me if you see them," cried the old man.

"I see nothing but darkness—pitch darkness," answered Gabriel, letting the door close again.

"Ah! woe! woe!" groaned his grandfather, sinking back exhausted on the pillow. "Darkness to *you;* but bright as lightning to the eyes that are allowed to see them. Drowned! drowned! Pray for their souls, Gabriel—*I* see the White Women even where

I lie, and dare not pray for them. Son and grandson drowned! both drowned!"

The young man went back to Perrine and the children.

"Grandfather is very ill tonight," he whispered. "You had better all go into the bedroom, and leave me alone to watch by him."

They rose as he spoke, crossed themselves before the image of the Virgin, kissed him one by one, and, without uttering a word, softly entered the little room on the other side of the partition. Gabriel looked at his grandfather, and saw that he lay quiet now, with his eyes closed as if he were already dropping asleep. The young man then heaped some fresh logs on the fire, and sat down by it to watch till morning.

Very dreary was the moaning of the night storm; but it was not more dreary than the thoughts which now occupied him in his solitude—thoughts darkened and distorted by the terrible superstitions of his country and his race. Ever since the period of his mother's death he had been oppressed by the conviction that some curse hung over the family.

At first they had been prosperous, they had got money, a little legacy had been left them. But this good fortune had availed only for a time; disaster on disaster strangely and suddenly succeeded. Losses, misfortunes, poverty, want itself had overwhelmed them; his father's temper had become so soured, that the oldest friends of François Sarzeau declared he was changed beyond recognition. And now, all this past misfortune—the steady, withering, household blight of many years—had ended in the last, worst misery of all—in death.

The fate of his father and his brother admitted no longer of a doubt; he knew it, as he listened to the storm, as he reflected on his grandfather's words, as he called to mind his own experience of the perils of the sea. And this double bereavement had fallen on him just as the time was approaching for his marriage with Perrine; just when misfortune was most ominous of evil, just when it was hardest to bear!

Forebodings, which he dared not realize, began now to mingle with the bitterness of his grief, whenever his thoughts wandered from the present to the future; and as he sat by the lonely fireside, murmuring from time to time the Church prayer for the repose of the dead, he almost involuntarily mingled with it another prayer, expressed only in his own simple words, for the safety of the living—for the young girl whose love was his sole earthly treasure; for the motherless children who must now look for protection to him alone.

He had sat by the hearth a long, long time, absorbed in his thoughts, not once looking round toward the bed, when he was startled by hearing the sound of his grandfather's voice once more.

"Gabriel," whispered the old man, trembling and shrinking as he spoke, "Gabriel, do you hear a dripping of water—now slow, now quick again—on the floor at the foot of my bed?"

"I hear nothing, grandfather, but the crackling of the fire, and the roaring of the storm outside."

"Drip, drip, drip! Faster and faster; plainer and plainer. Take the torch, Gabriel; look down on the floor—look with all your eyes. Is the place wet there? Is it the rain from heaven that is dropping through the roof?"

Gabriel took the torch with trembling fingers and knelt down on the floor to examine it closely. He started back from the place, as he saw that it was quite dry—the torch dropped upon the hearth—he fell on his knees before the statue of the Virgin and hid his face.

"Is the floor wet? Answer me, I command you—is the floor wet?" asked the old man, quickly and breathlessly.

Gabriel rose, went back to the bedside, and whispered to him that no drop of rain had fallen inside the cottage. As he spoke the words, he saw a change pass over his grandfather's face—the sharp features seemed to wither up on a sudden; the eager expression to grow vacant and death-like in an instant. The voice, too, altered; it was harsh and querulous no more; its tones became strangely soft, slow, and solemn, when the old man spoke again.

"I hear it still," he said, "drip! drip! faster and plainer than ever. That ghostly dropping of water is the last and the surest of the fatal signs which have told of your father's and your brother's deaths tonight, and I know from the place where I hear it—the foot of the bed I lie on—that it is a warning to me of my own approaching end. I am called where my son and my grandson have gone before me; my weary time in this world is over at last. Don't let Perrine and the children come in here, if they should awake—they are too young to look at death."

Gabriel's blood curdled when he heard these words—when he touched his grandfather's hand, and felt the chill that it struck to his own—when he listened to the raging wind, and knew that all help was miles and miles away from the cottage. Still, in spite of the storm, the darkness, and the distance, he thought not for a moment of neglecting the duty that had been taught him from his childhood—the duty of summoning the priest to the bedside of the dying. "I must call Perrine," he said, "to watch by you while I am away."

"Stop!" cried the old man. "Stop, Gabriel; I implore, I command you not to leave me!"

"The priest, grandfather—your confession—"

"It must be made to you. In this darkness and this hurricane no man can keep the path across the heath. Gabriel, I am dying—I should be dead before you got back. Gabriel, for the love of the Blessed Virgin, stop here with me till I die—my time is short—I have a terrible secret that I must tell to somebody before I draw my last breath! Your ear to my mouth—quick! quick!"

As he spoke the last words, a slight noise was audible on the other side of the partition, the door half opened, and Perrine appeared at it, looking affrightedly into the room. The vigilant eyes of the old man—suspicious even in death—caught sight of her directly.

"Go back!" he exclaimed faintly, before she could utter a word; "go back—push her back, Gabriel, and nail down the latch in the door, if she won't shut it of herself!"

"Dear Perrine! go in again," implored Gabriel. "Go in, and keep the children from disturbing us. You will only make him worse—you can be of no use here!"

She obeyed without speaking, and shut the door again.

While the old man clutched him by the arm, and repeated, "Quick! quick! your ear close to my mouth," Gabriel heard her say to the children (who were both awake), "Let us pray for grandfather." And as he knelt down by the bedside, there stole on his ear the sweet, childish tones of his little sisters, and the soft, subdued voice of the young girl who was teaching them the prayer, mingling divinely with the solemn wailing of wind and sea, rising in a still and awful purity over the hoarse, gasping whispers of the dying man.

"I took an oath not to tell it, Gabriel—lean down closer! I'm weak, and they mustn't hear a word in that room—I took an oath not to tell it; but death is a warrant to all men for breaking such an oath as that. Listen; don't lose a word I'm saying! Don't look away into the room: the stain of blood-guilt has defiled it forever! Hush! hush! hush! Let me speak.

"Now your father's dead, I can't carry the horrid secret with me into the grave. Just remember, Gabriel—try if you can't re-member the time before I was bedridden, ten years ago and more—it was about six weeks, you know, before your mother's death; you can remember it by that. You and all the children were in that room with your mother; you were asleep, I think; it was night, not very late—only nine o'clock.

"Your father and I were standing at the door, looking out at the heath in the moonlight. He was so poor at that time, he had been obliged to sell his own boat, and none of the neighbours would take him out fishing with them—your father wasn't liked by any of the neighbours. Well; we saw a stranger coming toward us; a very young man, with a knapsack on his back. He looked like a gentleman, though he was but poorly dressed. He came up, and told us he was dead tired, and didn't think he could reach the town that night and asked if we would give him shelter till morning.

"And your father said yes, if he would make no noise, because the wife was ill, and the children were asleep. So he said all he wanted was to go to sleep himself before the fire. We had nothing to give him but black bread. He had better food with him than that, and undid his knapsack to get at it, and—and—Gabriel! I'm sinking—drink! something to drink—I'm parched with thirst."

Silent and deadly pale, Gabriel poured some of the cider from the pitcher on the table into a drinking-cup, and gave it to the old man. Slight as the stimulant was, its effect on him was almost instantaneous. His dull eyes brightened a little, and he went on in the same whispering tones as before:

"He pulled the food out of his knapsack rather in a hurry, so that some of the other small things in it fell on the floor. Among these was a pocketbook, which your father picked up and gave him back; and he put it in his coat-pocket—there was a tear in one of the sides of the book, and through the hole some bank-notes bulged out. I saw them, and so did your father (don't move away, Gabriel; keep close, there's nothing in me to shrink from).

"Well, he shared his food, like an honest fellow, with us; and then put his hand in his pocket, and gave me four or five *livres*, and then lay down before the fire to go to sleep. As he shut his eyes, your father looked at me in a way I didn't like. He'd been behaving very bitterly and desperately toward us for some time past, being soured about poverty, and your mother's illness, and the constant crying out of you children for more to eat.

"So when he told me to go and buy some wood, some bread, and some wine with money I had got, I didn't like, somehow, to leave him alone with the stranger; and so made excuses, saying (which was true) that it was too late to buy things in the village that night. But he told me in a rage to go and do as he bid me, and knock the people up if the shop was shut.

"So I went out, being dreadfully afraid of your father—as indeed we all were at that time—but I couldn't make up my mind to go far from the house; I was afraid of something happening, though I didn't dare to think what. I don't know how it was, but I stole back in about ten minutes on tiptoe to the cottage; I looked in at the window, and saw—O God! forgive him! O God! forgive me!—I saw—I—more to drink, Gabriel! I can't speak again—more to drink!"

The voices in the next room had ceased; but in the minute of silence which now ensued, Gabriel heard his sisters kissing Perrine, and wishing her goodnight. They were all three trying to go asleep again.

"Gabriel, pray yourself, and teach your children after you to pray, that your father may find forgiveness where he is now gone. I saw him as plainly as I now see you, kneeling with his knife in one hand over the sleeping man. He was taking the little book with the notes in it out of the stranger's pocket. He got the book into his possession, and held it quite still in his hand for an instant, thinking. I believe—oh no! no! I'm sure—he was repenting; I'm sure he was going to put the book back; but just at that moment the stranger moved, and raised one of his arms, as if he was waking up.

"Then the temptation of the devil grew too strong for your father—I saw him lift the hand with the knife in it—but saw nothing more. I couldn't look in at the window—I couldn't move away—I couldn't cry out; I stood with my back turned toward the house, shivering all over, though it was a warm summer-time, and hearing no cries, no noises at all, from the room behind me. I was too frightened to know how long it was before the opening of the cottage door made me turn round; but when I did, I saw your father standing before me in the yellow moonlight, carrying in his arms the bleeding body of the poor lad who had shared his food with us and slept on our hearth. Hush! hush! Don't groan and sob in that way! Stifle it with the bedclothes. Hush! you'll wake them in the next room!"

"Gabriel—Gabriel!" exclaimed a voice from behind the partition. "What has happened? Gabriel! let me come out and be with you!"

"No! no!" cried the old man, collecting the last remains of his strength in the attempt to speak above the wind, which was just then howling at the loudest; "stay where you are—don't speak, don't come out—I command you! Gabriel" (his voice dropped to a faint whisper), "raise me up in bed—you must hear the whole of it now; raise me; I'm choking so that I can hardly speak. Keep close and listen—I can't say much more. Where was I?—Ah, your father! He threatened to kill me if I didn't swear to keep it secret; and in terror of my life I swore.

"He made me help him to carry the body—we took it all across the heath—oh! horrible, horrible, under the bright moon—(lift me higher, Gabriel). You know the great stones yonder, set up by the heathens; you know the hollow place under the stones they call 'The Merchant's Table'; we had plenty of room to lay him in that, and hide him so; and then we ran back to the cottage. I never dared to go near the place afterward; no, nor your father either! (Higher, Gabriel! I'm choking again.) We burned the pocket-book and the knapsack—never knew his name—we kept the money to spend. (You're not lifting me; you're not listening close enough!)

"Your father said it was a legacy, when you and your mother asked about the money. (You hurt me, you shake me to pieces, Gabriel, when you sob like that.) It brought a curse on us, the money; the curse has drowned your father and your brother; the curse is killing me; but I've confessed—tell the priest I confessed before I died. Stop her; stop Perrine! I hear her getting up. Take his bones away from the Merchant's Table, and bury them for the love of God! and tell the priest (lift me higher, lift me till I am on my knees)—if your father was alive, he'd murder me; but tell the priest—because of my guilty soul—to pray, and—remember the Merchant's Table—to bury, and to pray—to pray always for—"

As long as Perrine heard faintly the whispering of the old man, though no word that he said reached her ear, she shrank from opening the door in the partition. But, when the whispering sounds, which terrified her she knew not how or why, first faltered, then ceased altogether; when she heard the sobs that followed them; and when her heart told her who was weeping in the next room—then, she began to be influenced by a new feeling which was stronger than the strongest fear, and she opened the door without hesitation, almost without trembling.

The coverlet was drawn up over the old man; Gabriel was kneeling by the bedside, with his face hidden. When she spoke to him, he neither answered nor looked at her. After a while the sobs that shook him ceased; but still he never moved, except once when she touched him, and then he shuddered—shuddered under *her* hand! She called in his little sisters, and they spoke to him, and still he uttered no word in reply. They wept. One by one, often and often, they entreated him with loving words; but the stupor of grief which held him speechless and motionless was beyond the power of human tears, stronger even than the strength of human love.

It was near daybreak, and the storm was lulling, but still no change occurred at the bedside. Once or twice, as Perrine knelt near Gabriel, still vainly endeavouring to arouse him to a sense of her presence, she thought she heard the old man breathing feebly, and stretched out her hand toward the coverlet; but she could not summon courage to touch him or to look at him.

This was the first time she had ever been present at a death-bed; the stillness in the room, the stupor of despair that had seized on Gabriel, so horrified her, that she was almost as helpless as the two children by her side. It was not till the dawn looked in at the cottage window   so coldly, so drearily, and yet so reassuringly—that she began to recover her self-possession at all. Then she knew that her best resource would be to summon assistance immediately from the nearest house.

While she was trying to persuade the two children to remain alone in the cottage with Gabriel during her temporary absence, she was startled by the sound of footsteps outside the door. It opened, and a man appeared on the threshold, standing still there for a moment in the dim, uncertain light.

She looked closer—looked intently at him. It was François Sarzeau himself

CHAPTER 2

The fisherman was dripping with wet; but his face, always pale and inflexible, seemed to be but little altered in expression by the perils through which he must have passed during the night. Young Pierre lay almost insensible in his arms. In the astonishment and fright of the first moment, Perrine screamed as she recognized him.

"There, there, there!" he said, peevishly, advancing straight to the hearth with his burden; "don't make a noise. You never expected to see us alive again, I dare say. We gave ourselves up as lost, and only escaped after all by a miracle."

He laid the boy down where he could get the full warmth of the fire; and then, turning round, took a wicker-covered bottle from his pocket, and said, "If it hadn't been for the brandy—" He stopped suddenly—started—put down the bottle on the bench near him—and advanced quickly to the bedside.

Perrine looked after him as he went; and saw Gabriel, who had risen when the door was opened, moving back from the bed as François approached. The young man's face seemed to have been suddenly struck to stone—its blank, ghastly whiteness was awful to look at. He moved slowly backward and backward till he came to the cottage wall—then stood quite still, staring on his father with wild, vacant eyes, moving his hands to and fro before him, muttering, but never pronouncing one audible word.

François did not appear to notice his son; he had the coverlet of the bed in his hand.

"Anything the matter here?" he asked, as he drew it down.

Still Gabriel could not speak. Perrine saw it, and answered for him.

"Gabriel is afraid that his poor grandfather is dead," she whispered, nervously.

"Dead!" There was no sorrow in the tone as he echoed the word. "Was he very bad in the night before his death happened? Did he wander in his mind? He has been rather lightheaded lately."

"He was very restless, and spoke of the ghostly warnings that we all know of; he said he saw and heard many things which told him from the other world that you and Pierre—Gabriel!" she screamed, suddenly interrupting herself, "look at him! Look at his face! Your grandfather is not dead!"

At this moment, François was raising his father's head to look closely at him. A faint spasm had indeed passed over the deathly face; the lips quivered, the jaw dropped. François shuddered as he looked, and moved away hastily from the bed. At the same instant Gabriel started from the wall; his expression altered, his pale cheeks flushed suddenly, as he snatched up the wicker-cased bottle, and poured all the little brandy that was left in it down his grandfather's throat.

The effect was nearly instantaneous; the sinking vital forces rallied desperately. The old man's eyes opened again, wandered round the room, then fixed themselves intently on François as he stood near the fire. Trying and terrible as his position was at that moment, Gabriel still retained self-possession enough to whisper a few words in Perrine's ear. "Go back again into the bedroom, and take the children with you," he said. "We may have something to speak about which you had better not hear."

"Son Gabriel, your grandfather is trembling all over," said François. "If he is dying at all, he is dying of cold; help me to lift him, bed and all, to the hearth."

"No, no! don't let him touch me!" gasped the old man. "Don't let him look at me in that way! Don't let him come near me, Gabriel! Is it his ghost? or is it himself?"

As Gabriel answered he heard a knocking at the door. His father opened it, and disclosed to view some people from the neighbouring fishing village, who had come—more out of curiosity than sympathy—to inquire whether François and the boy Pierre had survived the night. Without asking anyone to enter, the fisherman surlily and shortly answered the various questions addressed to him, standing in his own doorway.

While he was thus engaged, Gabriel heard his grandfather muttering vacantly to himself, "Last night—how about last night, grandson? What was I talking about last night? Did I say your father was drowned? Very foolish to say he was drowned, and then see him come back alive again! But it wasn't that—I'm so weak in my head, I can't remember. What was it, Gabriel? Something too horrible to speak of? Is that what you're whispering and trembling about? I said nothing horrible.

"A crime! Bloodshed! I know nothing of any crime or bloodshed here—I must have been frightened out of my wits to talk in that way! The Merchant's Table? Only a big heap of old stones! What with the storm, and thinking I was going to die, and being afraid about your father, I must have been light-headed. Don't give another thought to that nonsense, Gabriel! I'm better now. We shall all live to laugh at poor grandfather for talking nonsense about crime and bloodshed in his sleep. Ah, poor old man—last night—light-headed—fancies and nonsense of an old man—why don't you laugh at it? I'm laughing—so light-headed, so light—"

He stopped suddenly. A low cry, partly of terror and partly of pain, escaped him; the look of pining anxiety and imbecile cunning which had distorted his face while he had been speaking, faded from it forever. He shivered a little, breathed heavily once or twice, then became quite still.

Had he died with a falsehood on his lips?

Gabriel looked round and saw that the cottage door was closed, and that his father was standing against it. How long he had occupied that position, how many of the old man's last words he had heard, it was impossible to conjecture, but there was a lowering suspicion in his harsh face as he now looked away from the corpse to his son, which made Gabriel shudder; and the first question that he asked, on once more approaching the bedside, was expressed in tones which, quiet as they were, had a fearful meaning in them.

"What did your grandfather talk about last night?" he asked.

Gabriel did not answer. All that he had heard, all that he had seen, all the misery and horror that might yet be to come, had stunned his mind. The unspeakable dangers of his present position were too tremendous to be realized. He could only feel them vaguely in the weary torpor that oppressed his heart; while in every other direction the use of his faculties, physical and mental, seemed to have suddenly and totally abandoned him.

"Is your tongue wounded, son Gabriel, as well as your arm?" his father went on, with a bitter laugh. "I come back to you, saved by a miracle; and you never speak to me. Would you rather I had died than the old man there? He can't hear you now—why shouldn't you tell me what nonsense he was talking last night? You won't? I say you shall!" (He crossed the room and put his back to the door.)

"Before either of us leave this place, you shall confess it! You know that my duty to the Church bids me to go at once and tell the priest of your grandfather's death. If I leave that duty unfulfilled, remember it is through your fault! *You* keep me here—for here I stop till I'm obeyed. Do you hear that, idiot? Speak! Speak instantly, or you shall repeat it to the day of your death! I ask again—what did your grandfather say to you when he was wandering in his mind last night?"

"He spoke of a crime committed by another, and guiltily kept secret by him," answered Gabriel, slowly and sternly. "And this morning he denied his own words with his last living breath. But last night, if he spoke the truth—"

"The truth!" echoed François. "What truth?"

He stopped, his eyes fell, then turned toward the corpse. For a few minutes he stood steadily contemplating it; breathing quickly, and drawing his hand several times across his forehead. Then he faced his son once more. In that short interval he had become in outward appearance a changed man; expression, voice, and manner, all were altered.

"Heaven forgive me!" he went on, "but I could almost laugh at myself, at this solemn moment, for having spoken and acted just now so much like a fool! Denied his words, did he? Poor old man! they say sense often comes back to light-headed people just before death; and he is a proof of it. The fact is, Gabriel, my own wits must have been a little shaken—and no wonder—by what I went through last night, and what I have come home to this morning.

"As if you, or anybody, could ever really give serious credit to the wandering speeches of a dying old man! (Where is Perrine? Why did you send her away?) I don't wonder at your still looking a little startled, and feeling low in your mind, and all that— for you've had a trying night of it, trying in every way. He must have been a good deal shaken in his wits last night, between fears about himself and fears about me. (To think of my being angry with you, Gabriel, for being a little alarmed—very naturally— by an old man's queer fancies!)

"Come out, Perrine—come out of the bedroom whenever you are tired of it: you must learn sooner or later to look at death calmly. Shake hands, Gabriel; and let us make it up, and say no more about what has passed. You won't? Still angry with me for what I said to you just now? Ah! you'll think better about it by the time I return. Come out, Perrine; we've no secrets here."

"Where are you going to?" asked Gabriel, as he saw his father hastily open the door.

"To tell the priest that one of his congregation is dead, and to have the death registered," answered François. "These are *my* duties, and must be performed before I take any rest."

He went out hurriedly as he said these words. Gabriel almost trembled at himself when he found that he breathed more freely, that he felt less horribly oppressed both in mind and body, the moment his father's back was turned. Fearful as thought was now, it was still a change for the better to be capable of thinking at all.

Was the behaviour of his father compatible with innocence? Could the old man's confused denial of his own words in the morning, and in the presence of his son, be set for one instant against the circumstantial confession that he had made during the night alone with his grandson? These were the terrible questions which Gabriel now asked himself, and which he shrank involuntarily from answering. And yet that doubt, the solution of which would, one way or the other, irrevocably affect the whole future of his life, must sooner or later be solved at any hazard!

Was there any way of setting it at rest? Yes, one way—to go instantly, while his father was absent, and examine the hollow place under the Merchant's Table. If his grandfather's confession had really been made while he was in possession of his senses, this place (which Gabriel knew to be covered in from wind and weather) had never been visited since the commission of the crime by the perpetrator, or by his unwilling accomplice; though time had destroyed all besides, the hair and the bones of the victim would still be left to bear witness to the truth—if truth had indeed been spoken.

As this conviction grew on him, the young man's cheek paled; and he stopped irresolute half-way between the hearth and the door. Then he looked down doubtfully at the corpse on the bed; and then there came upon him suddenly a revulsion of feeling. A wild, feverish impatience to know the worst without another instant of delay possessed him. Only telling Perrine that he should be back soon, and that she must watch by the dead in his absence, he left the cottage at once, without waiting to hear her reply, even without looking back as he closed the door behind him.

There were two tracks to the Merchant's Table. One, the longer of the two, by the coast cliffs; the other across the heath. But this latter path was also, for some little distance, the path which led to the village and the church. He was afraid of at-tracting his father's attention here, so he took the direction of the coast. At one spot the track trended inland, winding round some of the many Druid monuments scattered over the country. This place was on high ground, and commanded a view, at no great distance, of the path leading to the village, just where it branched off from the heathy ridge which ran in the direction of the Merchant's Table. Here Gabriel descried the figure of a man standing with his back toward the coast.

This figure was too far off to be identified with absolute certainty, but it looked like, and might well be, François Sarzeau. Whoever he was, the man was evidently uncertain which way he should proceed. When he moved forward, it was first to advance several paces toward the Merchant's Table; then he went back again toward the distant cottages and the church. Twice he hesitated thus; the second time pausing long before he appeared finally to take the way that led to the village.

Leaving the post of observation among the stones, at which he had instinctively halted for some minutes past, Gabriel now proceeded on his own path. Could this man really be his father? And if it were so, why did François Sarzeau only determine to go to the village where his business lay, after having twice vainly attempted to persevere in taking the exactly opposite direction of the Merchant's Table? Did he really desire to go there? Had he heard the name mentioned, when the old man referred to it in his dying words? And had he failed to summon courage enough to make all safe by removing—? This last question was too horrible to be pursued; Gabriel stifled it affrightedly in his own heart as he went on.

He reached the great Druid monument without meeting a living soul on his way. The sun was rising, and the mighty storm-clouds of the night were parting asunder wildly over the whole eastward horizon. The waves still leaped and foamed gloriously: but the gale had sunk to a keen, fresh breeze.

As Gabriel looked up, and saw how brightly the promise of a lovely day was written in the heavens, he trembled as he thought of the search which he was now about to make. The sight of the fair, fresh sunrise jarred horribly with the suspicions of committed murder that were rankling foully in his heart. But he knew that his errand must be performed, and he nerved himself to go through with it; for he dared not return to the cottage until the mystery had been cleared up at once and forever.

The Merchant's Table was formed by two huge stones resting horizontally on three others. In the troubled times of more than half a century ago, regular tourists were unknown among the Druid monuments of Brittany; and the entrance to the hollow place under the stones—since often visited by strangers—was at this time nearly choked up by brambles and weeds. Gabriel's first look at this tangled nook of briers convinced him that the place had not been entered perhaps for years, by any living being. Without allowing himself to hesitate (for he felt that the slightest delay might be fatal to his resolution), he passed as gently as possible through the brambles, and knelt down at the low, dusky, irregular entrance of the hollow place under the stones.

His heart throbbed violently, his breath almost failed him; but he forced himself to crawl a few feet into the cavity, and then groped with his hand on the ground about him.

He touched something! Something which it made his flesh creep to handle; something which he would fain have dropped, but which he grasped tight in spite of himself. He drew back into the outer air and sunshine. Was it a human bone? No! he had been the dupe of his own morbid terror—he had only taken up a fragment of dried wood!

Feeling shame at such self-deception as this, he was about to throw the wood from him before he re-entered the place, when another idea occurred to him.

Though it was dimly lighted through one or two chinks in the stones, the far part of the interior of the cavity was still too dusky to admit of perfect examination by the eye, even on a bright sunshiny morning. Observing this, he took out the tinder-box and matches, which, like the other inhabitants of the district, he always carried about with him for the purpose of lighting his pipe, determining to use the piece of wood as a torch which might illuminate the darkest corner of the place when he next entered it. Fortunately the wood had remained so long and had been preserved so dry in its sheltered position, that it caught fire almost as easily as a piece of paper. The moment it was fairly aflame Gabriel went into the cavity, penetrating at once—this time—to its furthest extremity.

He remained among the stones long enough for the wood to burn down nearly to his hand. When he came out, and flung the burning fragment from him, his face was flushed deeply, his eyes sparkled. He leaped carelessly on to the heath, over the bushes through which he had threaded his way so warily but a few minutes before, exclaiming, "I may marry Perrine with a clear conscience now; I am the son of as honest a man as there is in Brittany!"

He had closely examined the cavity in every corner, and not the slightest sign that any dead body had ever been laid there was visible in the hollow place under the Merchant's Table.

CHAPTER 3

"I may marry Perrine with a clear conscience now!"

There are some parts of the world where it would be drawing no natural picture of human nature to represent a son as believing conscientiously that an offense against life and the laws of hospitality, secretly committed by his father, rendered him, though innocent of all participation in it, unworthy to fulfil his engagement with his affianced wife.

Among the simple inhabitants of Gabriel's province, however, such acuteness of conscientious sensibility as this was no extraordinary exception to all general rules. Ignorant and superstitious as they might be, the people of Brittany practiced the duties of hospitality as devoutly as they practiced the duties of the national religion. The presence of the stranger-guest, rich or poor, was a sacred presence at their hearths. His safety was their especial charge, his property their especial responsibility. They might be half starved, but they were ready to share the last crust with him, nevertheless, as they would share it with their own children.

Any outrage on the virtue of hospitality, thus born and bred in the people, was viewed by them with universal disgust, and punished with universal execration. This ignominy was uppermost in Gabriel's thoughts by the side of his grandfather's bed; the dread of this worst dishonour, which there was no wiping out, held him speechless before Perrine, shamed and horrified him so that he felt unworthy to look her in the face; and when the result of his search at the Merchant's Table proved the absence there of all evidence of the crime spoken of by the old man, the blessed relief, the absorbing triumph of that discovery, was expressed entirely in the one thought which had prompted his first joyful words: He could marry Perrine with a clear conscience, for he was the son of an honest man!

When he returned to the cottage, François had not come back. Perrine was astonished at the change in Gabriel's manner; even Pierre and the children remarked it. Rest and warmth had by this time so far recovered the younger brother, that he was able to give some account of the perilous adventures of the night at sea. They were still listening to the boy's narrative when François at last returned. It was now Gabriel who held out his hand, and made the first advances toward reconciliation.

To his utter amazement, his father recoiled from him. The variable temper of François had evidently changed completely during his absence at the village. A settled scowl of distrust darkened his face as he looked at his son.

"I never shake hands with people who have once doubted me," he exclaimed, loudly and irritably; "for I always doubt them forever after. You are a bad son! You have suspected your father of some infamy that you dare not openly charge him with, on no other testimony than the rambling nonsense of a half-witted, dying old man. Don't speak to me! I won't hear you! An innocent man and a spy are bad company.

"Go and denounce me, you Judas in disguise! I don't care for your secret or for you. What's that girl Perrine doing here still? Why hasn't she gone home long ago? The priest's coming; we don't want strangers in the house of death. Take her back to the farmhouse, and stop there with her, if you like; nobody wants you here!"

There was something in the manner and look of the speaker as he uttered these words, so strange, so sinister, so indescribably suggestive of his meaning much more than he said, that Gabriel felt his heart sink within him instantly; and almost at the same moment this fearful question forced itself irresistibly on his mind: might not his father have followed him to the Merchant's Table?

Even if he had been desired to speak, he could not have spoken now, while that question and the suspicion that it brought with it were utterly destroying all the reassuring hopes and convictions of the morning. The mental suffering produced by the sudden change from pleasure to pain in all his thoughts, reacted on him physically. He felt as if he were stifling in the air of the cottage, in the presence of his father; and when Perrine hurried on her walking attire, and with a face which alternately flushed and turned pale with every moment, approached the door, he went out with her as hastily as if he had been flying from his home. Never had the fresh air and the free daylight felt like heavenly and guardian influences to him until now!

He could comfort Perrine under his father's harshness, he could assure her of his own affection, which no earthly influence could change, while they walked together toward the farmhouse; but he could do no more. He durst not confide to her the subject that was uppermost in his mind; of all human beings she was the last to whom he could reveal the terrible secret that was festering at his heart.

As soon as they got within sight of the farmhouse, Gabriel stopped; and, promising to see her again soon, took leave of Perrine with assumed ease in his manner and with real despair in his heart. Whatever the poor girl might think of it, he felt, at that moment, that he had not courage to face her father, and hear him talk happily and pleasantly, as his custom was, of Perrine's approaching marriage.

Left to himself, Gabriel wandered hither and thither over the open heath, neither knowing nor caring in what direction he turned his steps. The doubts about his father's innocence which had been dissipated by his visit to the Merchant's Table, that father's own language and manner had now revived—had even confirmed, though he dared not yet acknowledge so much to himself.

It was terrible enough to be obliged to admit that the result of his morning's search was, after all, not conclusive—that the mystery was, in very truth, not yet cleared up. The violence of his father's last words of distrust; the extraordinary and indescribable changes in his father's manner while uttering them—what did these things mean? Guilt or innocence? Again, was it any longer reasonable to doubt the deathbed confession made by his grandfather?

Was it not, on the contrary, far more probable that the old man's denial in the morning of his own words at night had been made under the influence of a panic terror, when his moral consciousness was bewildered, and his intellectual faculties were sinking? The longer Gabriel thought of these questions, the less competent—possibly also the less willing—he felt to answer them. Should he seek advice from others wiser than he? No; not while the thousandth part of a chance remained that his father was innocent.

This thought was still in his mind, when he found himself once more in sight of his home. He was still hesitating near the door, when he saw it opened cautiously. His brother Pierre looked out, and then came running toward him. "Come in, Gabriel; oh, do come in!" said the boy, earnestly. "We are afraid to be alone with father. He's been beating us for talking of you."

Gabriel went in. His father looked up from the hearth where he was sitting, muttered the word "Spy!" and made a gesture of contempt but did not address a word directly to his son. The hours passed on in silence; afternoon waned into evening, and evening into night; and still he never spoke to any of his children. Soon after it was dark, he went out, and took his net with him, saying that it was better to be alone on the sea than in the house with a spy.

When he returned the next morning there was no change in him. Days passed—weeks, months, even elapsed, and still, though his manner insensibly became what it used to be toward his other children, it never altered toward his eldest son At the rare periods when they now met, except when absolutely obliged to speak, he preserved total silence in his intercourse with Gabriel. He would never take Gabriel out with him in the boat; he would never sit alone with Gabriel in the house; he would never eat a meal with Gabriel; he would never let the other children talk to him about Gabriel; and he would never hear a word in expostulation, a word in reference to anything his dead father had said or done on the night of the storm, from Gabriel himself.

The young man pined and changed, so that even Perrine hardly knew him again, under this cruel system of domestic excommunication; under the wearing influence of the one unchanging doubt which never left him; and, more than all, under the incessant reproaches of his own conscience, aroused by the sense that he was evading a responsibility which it was his solemn, his immediate duty to undertake. But no sting of conscience, no ill treatment at home, and no self-reproaches for failing in his duty of confession as a good Catholic, were powerful enough in their influence over Gabriel to make him disclose the secret, under the oppression of which his very life was wasting away.

He knew that if he once revealed it, whether his father was ultimately proved to be guilty or innocent, there would remain a slur and a suspicion on the family, and on Perrine besides, from her approaching connection with it, which in their time and in their generation could never be removed. The reproach of the world is terrible even in the crowded city, where many of the dwellers in our abiding-place are strangers to us—but it is far more terrible in the country, where none near us are strangers, where all talk of us and know of us, where nothing intervenes between us and the tyranny of the evil tongue. Gabriel had not courage to face this, and dare the fearful chance of life-long ignominy—no, not even to serve the sacred interests of justice, of atonement, and of truth.

Chapter 4

While Gabriel still remained prostrated under the affliction that was wasting his energies of body and mind, Brittany was visited by a great public calamity, in which all private misfortunes were overwhelmed for a while.

It was now the time when the ever-gathering storm of the

French Revolution had risen to its hurricane climax. Those chiefs of the new republic were in power whose last, worst madness it was to decree the extinction of religion and the overthrow of everything that outwardly symbolized it throughout the whole of the country that they governed. Already this decree had been executed to the letter in and around Paris; and now the soldiers of the Republic were on their way to Brittany, headed by commanders whose commission was to root out the Christian religion in the last and the surest of the strongholds still left to it in France.

These men began their work in a spirit worthy of the worst of their superiors who had sent them to do it. They gutted churches, they demolished chapels, they overthrew road-side crosses wherever they found them. The terrible guillotine devoured human lives in the villages of Brittany as it had devoured them in the streets of Paris; the musket and the sword, in highway and byway, wreaked havoc on the people—even on women and children kneeling in the act of prayer; the priests were tracked night and day from one hiding-place, where they still offered up worship, to another, and were killed as soon as overtaken—every atrocity was committed in every district; but the Christian religion still spread wider than the widest bloodshed; still sprang up with ever-renewed vitality from under the very feet of the men whose vain fury was powerless to trample it down.

Everywhere the people remained true to their Faith; everywhere the priests stood firm by them in their sorest need. The executioners of the Republic had been sent to make Brittany a country of apostates; they did their worst, and left it a country of martyrs.

One evening, while this frightful persecution was still raging, Gabriel happened to be detained unusually late at the cottage of Perrine's father. He had lately spent much of his time at the farm house; it was his only refuge now from that place of suffering, of silence, and of secret shame, which he had once called home! Just as he had taken leave of Perrine for the night, and was about to open the farmhouse door, her father stopped him, and pointed to a chair in the chimney-corner.

"Leave us alone, my dear," said the old man to his daughter; "I want to speak to Gabriel. You can go to your mother in the next room."

The words which Père Bonan—as he was called by the neighbours—had now to say in private were destined to lead to very unexpected events. After referring to the alteration which had appeared of late in Gabriel's manner, the old man began by asking him, sorrowfully but not suspiciously, whether he still preserved his old affection for Perrine.

On receiving an eager answer in the affirmative, Père Bonan then referred to the persecution still raging through the country, and to the consequent possibility that he, like others of his countrymen, might yet be called to suffer, and perhaps to die, for the cause of his religion. If this last act of self-sacrifice were required of him, Perrine would be left unprotected, unless her affianced husband performed his promise to her, and assumed, without delay, the position of her lawful guardian. "Let me know that you will do this," concluded the old man; "I shall be resigned to all that may be required of me, if I can only know that I shall not die leaving Perrine unprotected." Gabriel gave the promise—gave it with his whole heart. As he took leave of Père Bonan, the old man said to him:

"Come here tomorrow; I shall know more then than I know now—I shall be able to fix with certainty the day for the fulfilment of your engagement with Perrine."

Why did Gabriel hesitate at the farmhouse door, looking back on Père Bonan as though he would fain say something, and yet not speaking a word? Why, after he had gone out and had walked onward several paces, did he suddenly stop, return quickly to the farmhouse, stand irresolute before the gate, and then retrace his steps, sighing heavily as he went, but never pausing again on his homeward way?

Because the torment of his horrible secret had grown harder to bear than ever, since he had given the promise that had been required of him. Because, while a strong impulse moved him frankly to lay bare his hidden dread and doubt to the father whose beloved daughter was soon to be his wife, there was a yet stronger passive influence which paralyzed on his lips the terrible confession that he knew not whether he was the son of an honest man, or the son of an assassin, and a robber.

Made desperate by his situation, he determined, while he hastened homeward, to risk the worst, and ask that fatal question of his father in plain words. But this supreme trial for parent and child was not to be. When he entered the cottage, François was absent. He had told the younger children that he should not be home again before noon on the next day.

Early in the morning Gabriel repaired to the farmhouse, as he had been bidden. Influenced, by his love for Perrine, blindly confiding in the faint hope (which, in despite of heart and conscience, he still forced himself to cherish) that his father might be innocent, he now preserved the appearance at least of perfect calmness. "If I tell my secret to Perrine's father, I risk disturbing in him that confidence in the future safety of his child for which I am his present and only warrant."

Something like this thought was in Gabriel's mind, as he took the hand of Père Bonan, and waited anxiously to hear what was required of him on that day.

"We have a short respite from danger, Gabriel," said the old man. "News has come to me that the spoilers of our churches and the murderers of our congregations have been stopped on their way hitherward by tidings which have reached them from another district. This interval of peace and safety will be a short one—we must take advantage of it while it is yet ours. My name is among the names on the list of the denounced. If the soldiers of the Republic find me here—but we will say nothing more of this; it is of Perrine and of you that I must now speak.

"On this very evening your marriage may be solemnized with all the wonted rites of our holy religion, and the blessing may be pronounced over you by the lips of a priest. This evening, therefore, Gabriel, you must become the husband and the protector of Perrine. Listen to me attentively, and I will tell you how."

This was the substance of what Gabriel now heard from Père Bonan:

Not very long before the persecutions broke out in Brittany, a priest, known generally by the name of Father Paul, was appointed to a curacy in one of the northern districts of the province. He fulfilled all the duties of his station in such a manner as to win the confidence and affection of every member of his congregation, and was often spoken of with respect, even in parts of the country distant from the scene of his labours.

It was not, however, until the troubles broke out, and the destruction and bloodshed began, that he became renowned far and wide, from one end of Brittany to another. From the date of the very first persecutions the name of Father Paul was a rallying-cry of the hunted peasantry; he was their great encouragement under oppression, their example in danger, their last and only consoler in the hour of death. Wherever havoc and ruin raged most fiercely, wherever the pursuit was hottest and the slaughter most cruel, there the intrepid priest was sure to be seen pursuing his sacred duties in defiance of every peril.

His hairbreadth escapes from death; his extraordinary reappearances in parts of the country where no one ever expected to see him again, were regarded by the poorer classes with superstitious awe. Wherever Father Paul appeared, with his black dress, his calm face, and the ivory crucifix which he always carried in his hand, the people reverenced him as more than mortal; and grew at last to believe, that, single-handed, he would successfully defend his religion against the armies of the Republic.

But their simple confidence in his powers of resistance was soon destined to be shaken. Fresh re-enforcements arrived in Brittany, and overran the whole province from one end to the other. One morning, after celebrating service in a dismantled church, and after narrowly escaping with his life from those who pursued him, the priest disappeared. Secret inquiries were made after him in all directions; but he was heard of no more.

Many weary days had passed, and the dispirited peasantry

had already mourned him as dead, when some fishermen on the northern coast observed a ship of light burden in the offing, making signals to the shore. They put off to her in their boats; and on reaching the deck saw standing before them the well-remembered figure of Father Paul.

The priest had returned to his congregations, and had founded the new altar that they were to worship at on the deck of the ship! Razed from the face of the earth, their church had not been destroyed—for Father Paul and the priests who acted with him had given that church a refuge on the sea. Henceforth, their children could still be baptized, their sons and daughters could still be married, the burial of their dead could still be solemnized, under the sanction of the old religion for which, not vainly, they had suffered so patiently and so long.

Throughout the remaining time of trouble the services were uninterrupted on board the ship. A code of signals was established by which those on shore were always enabled to direct their brethren at sea toward such parts of the coast as happened to be uninfested by the enemies of their worship. On the morning of Gabriel's visit to the farmhouse these signals had shaped the course of the ship toward the extremity of the peninsula of Quiberon. The people of the district were all prepared to expect the appearance of the vessel sometime in the evening, and had their boats ready at a moment's notice to put off, and attend the service. At the conclusion of this service Père Bonan had arranged that the marriage of his daughter and Gabriel was to take place.

They waited for evening at the farmhouse. A little before sunset the ship was signalled as in sight; and then Père Bonan and his wife, followed by Gabriel and Perrine, set forth over the heath to the beach. With the solitary exception of François Sarzeau, the whole population of the neighbourhood was already assembled there, Gabriel's brother and sisters being among the number.

It was the calmest evening that had been known for months. There was not a cloud in the lustrous sky—not a ripple on the still surface of the sea. The smallest children were suffered by their mothers to stray down on the beach as they pleased; for the waves of the great ocean slept as tenderly and noiselessly on their sandy bed as if they had been changed into the waters of an inland lake.

Slow, almost imperceptible, was the approach of the ship—there was hardly a breath of wind to carry her on—she was just drifting gently with the landward set of the tide at that hour, while her sails hung idly against the masts. Long after the sun had gone down, the congregation still waited and watched on the beach. The moon and stars were arrayed in their glory of the night before the ship dropped anchor. Then the muffled tolling of a bell came solemnly across the quiet waters; and then, from every creek along the shore, as far as the eye could reach, the black forms of the fishermen's boats shot out swift and stealthy into the shining sea.

By the time the boats had arrived alongside of the ship, the lamp had been kindled before the altar, and its flame was gleaming red and dull in the radiant moonlight. Two of the priests on board were clothed in their robes of office, and were waiting in their appointed places to begin the service. But there was a third, dressed only in the ordinary attire of his calling, who mingled with the congregation, and spoke a few words to each of the persons composing it, as, one by one, they mounted the sides of the ship.

Those who had never seen him before knew by the famous ivory crucifix in his hand that the priest who received them was Father Paul. Gabriel looked at this man, whom he now beheld for the first time, with a mixture of astonishment and awe; for he saw that the renowned chief of the Christians of Brittany was, to all appearance, but little older than himself.

The expression on the pale, calm face of the priest was so gentle and kind, that children just able to walk tottered up to him, and held familiarly by the skirts of his black gown, whenever his clear blue eyes rested on theirs, while he beckoned them to his side. No one would ever have guessed from the countenance of Father Paul what deadly perils he had confronted, but for the scar of a sabre-wound, as yet hardly healed, which ran across his forehead.

That wound had been dealt while he was kneeling before the altar in the last church in Brittany which had escaped spoliation. He would have died where he knelt, but for the peasants who were praying with him, and who, unarmed as they were, threw themselves like tigers on the soldiery, and at awful sacrifice of their own lives saved the life of their priest. There was not a man now on board the ship who would have hesitated, had the occasion called for it again, to have rescued him in the same way.

The service began. Since the days when the primitive Christians worshiped amid the caverns of the earth, can any service be imagined nobler in itself, or sublimer in the circumstances surrounding it, than that which was now offered up? Here was no artificial pomp, no gaudy profusion of ornament, no attendant grandeur of man's creation.

All around this church spread the hushed and awful majesty of the tranquil sea. The roof of this cathedral was the immeasurable heaven, the pure moon its one great light, the countless glories of the stars its only adornment. Here were no hired singers or rich priest-princes; no curious sight-seers, or careless lovers of sweet sounds. This congregation and they who had gathered it together, were all poor alike, all persecuted alike, all worshiping alike, to the overthrow of their worldly interests, and at the imminent peril of their lives.

How brightly and tenderly the moonlight shone upon the altar and the people before it! how solemnly and divinely the deep harmonies, as they chanted the penitential Psalms, mingled with the hoarse singing of the freshening night breeze in the rigging of the ship! how sweetly the still rushing murmur of many voices, as they uttered the responses together, now died away, and now rose again softly into the mysterious night!

Of all the members of the congregation—young or old—there was but one over whom that impressive service exercised no influence of consolation or of peace; that one was Gabriel.

Often, throughout the day, his reproaching conscience had spoken within him again and again.

Often when he joined the little assembly on the beach, he turned away his face in secret shame and apprehension from Perrine and her father. Vainly, after gaining the deck of the ship, did he try to meet the eye of Father Paul as frankly, as readily, and as affectionately as others met it. The burden of concealment seemed too heavy to be borne in the presence of the priest—and yet, torment as it was, he still bore it!

But when he knelt with the rest of the congregation and saw Perrine kneeling by his side—when he felt the calmness of the solemn night and the still sea filling his heart—when the sounds of the first prayers spoke with a dread spiritual language of their own to his soul—then the remembrance of the confession which he had neglected, and the terror of receiving unprepared the sacrament which he knew would be offered to him—grew too vivid to be endured; the sense that he merited no longer, though once worthy of it, the confidence in his perfect truth and candour placed in him by the woman with whom he was soon to stand before the altar, overwhelmed him with shame: the mere act of kneeling among that congregation, the passive accomplice by his silence and secrecy, for aught he knew to the contrary, of a crime which it was his bounden duty to denounce, appalled him as if he had already committed sacrilege that could never be forgiven.

Tears flowed down his cheeks, though he strove to repress them: sobs burst from him, though he tried to stifle them. He knew that others besides Perrine were looking at him in astonishment and alarm; but he could neither control himself, nor move to leave his place, nor raise his eyes even—until suddenly he felt a hand laid on his shoulder. That touch, slight as it was, ran through him instantly He looked up, and saw Father Paul standing by his side.

Beckoning him to follow, and signing to the congregation not to suspend their devotions, he led Gabriel out of the assembly—then paused for a moment, reflecting—then beckoning him again, took him into the cabin of the ship, and closed the door carefully.

"You have something on your mind," he said, simply and quietly, taking the young man by the hand. "I may be able to relieve you, if you tell me what it is."

As Gabriel heard these gentle words, and saw, by the light of a lamp which burned before a cross fixed against the wall, the sad kindness of expression with which the priest was regarding him, the oppression that had lain so long on his heart seemed to leave it in an instant. The haunting fear of ever divulging his fatal suspicions and his fatal secret had vanished, as it were, at the touch of Father Paul's hand. For the first time he now repeated to another ear—the sounds of prayer and praise rising grandly the while from the congregation above—his grandfather's death-bed confession, word for word almost, as he had heard it in the cottage on the night of the storm.

Once, and once only, did Father Paul interrupt the narrative, which in whispers was addressed to him. Gabriel had hardly repeated the first two or three sentences of his grandfather's confession, when the priest, in quick, altered tones, abruptly asked him his name and place of abode.

As the question was answered, Father Paul's calm face became suddenly agitated; but the next moment, resolutely resuming his self-possession, he bowed his head as a sign that Gabriel was to continue; clasped his trembling hands, and raising them as if in silent prayer, fixed his eyes intently on the cross. He never looked away from it while the terrible narrative proceeded. But when Gabriel described his search at the Merchant's Table; and, referring to his father's behaviour since that time, appealed to the priest to know whether he might even yet, in defiance of appearances, be still filially justified in doubting whether the crime had been really perpetrated—then Father Paul moved near to him once more, and spoke again.

"Compose yourself, and look at me," he said, with his former sad kindness of voice and manner. "I can end your doubts forever. Gabriel, your father was guilty in intention and in act; but the victim of his crime still lives. I can prove it."

Gabriel's heart beat wildly; a deadly coldness crept over him as he saw Father Paul loosen the fastening of his cassock round the throat.

At that instant the chanting of the congregation above ceased; and then the sudden and awful stillness was deepened rather than interrupted by the faint sound of one voice praying. Slowly and with trembling fingers the priest removed the band round his neck—paused a little—sighed heavily—and pointed to a scar which was now plainly visible on one side of his throat. He said something at the same time; but the bell above tolled while he spoke.

It was the signal of the elevation of the Host. Gabriel felt an arm passed round him, guiding him to his knees, and sustaining him from sinking to the floor. For one moment longer he was conscious that the bell had stopped, that there was dead silence, that Father Paul was kneeling by him beneath the cross, with bowed head—then all objects around vanished; and he saw and knew nothing more.

When he recovered his senses, he was still in the cabin; the man whose life his father had attempted was bending over him, and sprinkling water on his face; and the clear voices of the women and children of the congregation were joining the voices of the men in singing the *Agnus Dei*.

"Look up at me without fear, Gabriel," said the priest. "I desire not to avenge injuries: I visit not the sins of the father on the child. Look up, and listen! I have strange things to speak of; and I have a sacred mission to fulfil before the morning, in which you must be my guide."

Gabriel attempted to kneel and kiss his hand but Father Paul stopped him, and said, pointing to the cross: "Kneel to that—not to me; not to your fellow-mortal, and your friend—for I will be your friend, Gabriel; believing that God's mercy has ordered it so. And now listen to me," he proceeded, with a brotherly tenderness in his manner which went to Gabriel's heart. "The service is nearly ended. What I have to tell you must be told at once; the errand on which you will guide me must be performed before tomorrow dawns. Sit here near me, and attend to what I now say!"

Gabriel obeyed; Father Paul then proceeded thus:

"I believe the confession made to you by your grandfather to have been true in every particular. On the evening to which he referred you, I approached your cottage, as he said, for the purpose of asking shelter for the night. At that period I had been studying hard to qualify myself for the holy calling which I now pursue; and, on the completion of my studies, had indulged in the recreation of a tour on foot through Brittany, by way of innocently and agreeably occupying the leisure time then at my disposal, before I entered the priesthood.

"When I accosted your father I had lost my way, had been walking for many hours, and was glad of any rest that I could get for the night. It is unnecessary to pain you now, by reference to the events which followed my entrance under your father's roof. I remember nothing that happened from the time when I lay down to sleep before the fire, until the time when I recovered my senses at the place which you call the Merchant's Table.

"My first sensation was that of being moved into the cold air; when I opened my eyes I saw the great Druid stones rising close above me, and two men on either side of me rifling my pockets. They found nothing valuable there, and were about to leave me where I lay, when I gathered strength enough to appeal to their mercy through their cupidity. Money was not scarce with me then, and I was able to offer them a rich reward (which they ultimately received as I had promised) if they would take me to any place where I could get shelter and medical help.

"I supposed they inferred by my language and accent—perhaps also by the linen I wore, which they examined closely-that I belonged to the higher ranks of the community, in spite of the plainness of my outer garments; and might, therefore, be in a position to make good my promise to them. I heard one say to the other, 'Let us risk it'; and then they took me in their arms, carried me down to a boat on the beach, and rowed to a vessel in the offing. The next day they disembarked me at Paimboeuf, where I got the assistance which I so much needed. I learned, through the confidence they were obliged to place in me in order to give me the means of sending them their promised reward, that these men were smugglers, and that they were in the habit of using the cavity in which I had been laid as a place of concealment for goods, and for letters of advice to their accomplices. This accounted for their finding me. As to my wound, I was informed by the surgeon who attended me that it had missed being inflicted in a mortal part by less than a quarter of an inch, and that, as it was, nothing but the action of the night air in coagulating the blood over the place, had, in the first instance, saved my life. To be brief, I recovered after a long illness, returned to Paris, and was called to the priesthood. The will of my superiors obliged me to perform the first duties of my vocation in the great city; but my own wish was to be appointed to a cure of souls in your province, Gabriel. Can you imagine why?"

The answer to this question was in Gabriel's heart; but he was still too deeply awed and affected by what he had heard to give it utterance.

"I must tell you, then, what my motive was," said Father Paul. "You must know first that I uniformly abstained from disclosing to any one where and by whom my life had been attempted. I kept this a secret from the men who rescued me—from the surgeon—from my own friends even. My reason for such a proceeding was, I would fain believe, a Christian reason. I hope I had always felt a sincere and humble desire to prove myself, by the help of God, worthy of the sacred vocation to which I was destined.

"But my miraculous escape from death made an impression on my mind, which gave me another and an infinitely higher view of this vocation—the view which I have since striven, and shall always strive for the future, to maintain. As I lay, during the first days of my recovery, examining my own heart, and considering in what manner it would be my duty to act toward your father when I was restored to health, a thought came into my mind which calmed, comforted, and resolved all my doubts. I said within myself, 'In a few months more I shall be called to be one of the chosen ministers of God.

"If I am worthy of my vocation, my first desire toward this man who has attempted to take my life should be, not to know that human justice has overtaken him, but to know that he has truly and religiously repented and made atonement for his guilt. To such repentance and atonement let it be my duty to call him; if he reject that appeal, and be hardened only the more against me because I have forgiven him my injuries, then it will be time enough to denounce him for his crimes to his fellow-men. Surely it must be well for me, here and hereafter, if I begin my career in the holy priesthood by helping to save from hell the soul of the man who, of all others, has most cruelly wronged me.

"It was for this reason, Gabriel—it was because I desired to go straightway to your father's cottage, and reclaim him after he had believed me to be dead—that I kept the secret and entreated of my superiors that I might be sent to Brittany. But this, as I have said, was not to be at first, and when my desire was granted, my place was assigned me in a far district. The persecution under which we still suffer broke out; the designs of my life were changed; my own will became no longer mine to guide me.

"But, through sorrow and suffering, and danger and blood-shed, I am now led, after many days, to the execution of that first purpose which I formed on entering the priesthood. Gabriel, when the service is over, and the congregation are dispersed, you must guide me to the door of your father's cottage."

He held up his hand, in sign of silence, as Gabriel was about to answer. Just then the officiating priests above were pronouncing the final benediction. When it was over, Father Paul opened the cabin door. As he ascended the steps, followed by Gabriel, Père Bonan met them. The old man looked doubtfully and searchingly on his future son-in-law, as he respectfully whispered a few words in the ear of the priest.

Father Paul listened attentively, answered in a whisper, and then turned to Gabriel, first begging the few people near them to withdraw a little.

"I have been asked whether there is any impediment to your marriage," he said, "and have answered that there is none. What you have said to me has been said in confession, and is a secret between us two. Remember that; and forget not, at the same time, the service which I shall require of you tonight, after the marriage-ceremony is over. Where is Perrine Bonan?" he added, aloud, looking round him. Perrine came forward. Father Paul took her hand and placed it in Gabriel's. "Lead her to the altar steps," he said, "and wait there for me."

It was more than an hour later; the boats had left the ship's side; the congregation had dispersed over the face of the country—but still the vessel remained at anchor. Those who were left in her watched the land more anxiously than usual; for they knew that Father Paul had risked meeting the soldiers of the Republic by trusting himself on shore.

A boat was awaiting his return on the beach; half of the crew, armed, being posted as scouts in various directions on the high land of the heath. They would have followed and guarded the priest to the place of his destination; but he forbade it; and, leaving them abruptly, walked swiftly onward with one young man only for his companion.

Gabriel had committed his brother and his sisters to the charge of Perrine. They were to go to the farmhouse that night with his newly-married wife and her father and mother. Father Paul had desired that this might be done. When Gabriel and he were left alone to follow the path which led to the fisherman's cottage, the priest never spoke while they walked on—never looked aside either to the right or the left—always held his ivory crucifix clasped to his breast. They arrived at the door.

"Knock," whispered Father Paul to Gabriel, "and then wait here with me."

The door was opened. On a lovely moonlight night François Sarzeau had stood on that threshold, years since, with a bleeding body in his arms. On a lovely moonlight night he now stood there again, confronting the very man whose life he had attempted, and knowing him not.

Father Paul advanced a few paces, so that the moonlight fell fuller on his features, and removed his hat.

François Sarzeau looked, started, moved one step back, then stood motionless and perfectly silent, while all traces of expression of any kind suddenly vanished from his face. Then the calm, clear tones of the priest stole gently on the dead silence. "I bring a message of peace and forgiveness from a guest of former years," he said; and pointed, as he spoke, to the place where he had been wounded in the neck.

For one moment, Gabriel saw his father trembling violently from head to foot—then his limbs steadied again—stiffened suddenly, as if struck by catalepsy. His lips parted, but without quivering; his eyes glared, but without moving in the orbits. The lovely moonlight itself looked ghastly and horrible, shining on the supernatural panic deformity of that face! Gabriel turned away his head in terror. He heard the voice of Father Paul saying to him: "Wait here till I come back."

Then there was an instant of silence again—then a low groaning sound that seemed to articulate the name of God; a sound unlike his father's voice, unlike any human voice he had ever heard—and then the noise of a closing door. He looked up, and saw that he was standing alone before the cottage.

Once, after an interval, he approached the window.

He just saw through it the hand of the priest holding on high the ivory crucifix; but stopped not to see more, for he heard such words, such sounds, as drove him back to his former place. There he stayed, until the noise of something falling heavily within the cottage struck on his ear. Again he advanced toward the door; heard Father Paul praying; listened for several minutes; then heard a moaning voice, now joining itself to the voice of the priest, now choked in sobs and bitter wailing.

Once more he went back out of hearing, and stirred not again from his place. He waited a long and a weary time there-so long that one of the scouts on the lookout came toward him, evidently suspicious of the delay in the priest's return. He waved the man back, and then looked again toward the door. At last he saw it open—saw Father Paul approach him, leading François Sarzeau by the hand.

The fisherman never raised his downcast eyes to his son's face; tears trickled silently over his cheeks; he followed the hand that led him, as a little child might have followed it, listened anxiously and humbly at the priest's side to every word that he spoke.

"Gabriel," said Father Paul, in a voice which trembled a little for the first time that night—"Gabriel, it has pleased God to grant the perfect fulfilment of the purpose which brought me to this place; I tell you this, as all that you need—as all, I believe, that you would wish—to know of what has passed while you have been left waiting for me here. Such words as I have now to speak to you are spoken by your father's earnest desire.

"It is his own wish that I should communicate to you his confession of having secretly followed you to the Merchant's Table, and of having discovered (as you discovered) that no evidence of his guilt remained there. This admission, he thinks, will be enough to account for his conduct toward yourself from that time to this. I have next to tell you (also at your father's desire) that he has promised in my presence, and now promises again in yours, sincerity of repentance in this manner:

"When the persecution of our religion has ceased—as cease it will, and that speedily, be assured of it—he solemnly pledges himself henceforth to devote his life, his strength and what worldly possessions he may have, or may acquire, to the task of re-erecting and restoring the roadside crosses which have been sacrilegiously overthrown and destroyed in his native province, and to doing good, go where he may. I have now said all that is required of me, and may bid you farewell—bearing with me the happy remembrance that I have left a father and son reconciled and restored to each other. May God bless and prosper you, and those dear to you, Gabriel! May God accept your father's repentance, and bless him also throughout his future life!"

He took their hands, pressed them long and warmly, then turned and walked quickly down the path which led to the beach. Gabriel dared not trust himself yet to speak; but he raised his arm, and put it gently round his father's neck. The two stood together so, looking out dimly through the tears that filled their eyes to the sea. They saw the boat put off in the bright track of the moonlight, and reach the vessel's side; they watched the spreading of the sails, and followed the slow course of the ship till she disappeared past a distant headland from sight.

After that, they went into the cottage together. They knew it not then, but they had seen the last, in this world, of Father Paul.

CHAPTER 5

The events foretold by the good priest happened sooner even than he had anticipated. A new government ruled the destinies of France, and the persecution ceased in Brittany.

Among other propositions which were then submitted to the Parliament, was one advocating the restoration of the road-side crosses throughout the province. It was found, however, on inquiry, that these crosses were to be counted by thousands, and that the mere cost of wood required to re-erect them necessitated an expenditure of money which the bankrupt nation could ill afford to spare.

While this project was under discussion, and before it was finally rejected, one man had undertaken the task which the Government shrank from attempting. When Gabriel left the cottage, taking his brother and sisters to live with his wife and himself at the farmhouse, François Sarzeau left it also, to perform in highway and byway his promise to Father Paul. For months and months he laboured without intermission at his task; still, always doing good, and rendering help and kindness and true charity to any whom he could serve. He walked many a weary mile, toiled through many a hard day's work, humbled himself even to beg of others, to get wood enough to restore a single cross.

No one ever heard him complain, ever saw him impatient, ever detected him in faltering at his task. The shelter in an out-house, the crust of bread and drink of water, which he could always get from the peasantry, seemed to suffice him. Among the people who watched his perseverance, a belief began to gain ground that his life would be miraculously prolonged until he had completed his undertaking from one end of Brittany to the other. But this was not to be.

He was seen one cold autumn evening, silently and stead-ily at work as usual, setting up a new cross on the site of one which had been shattered to splinters in the troubled times. In the morning he was found lying dead beneath the sacred sym-bol which his own hands had completed and erected in its place during the night. They buried him where he lay; and the priest who consecrated the ground allowed Gabriel to engrave his fa-ther's epitaph in the wood of the cross. It was simply the ini-tial letters of the dead man's name, followed by this inscription: "Pray for the repose of his soul: he died penitent, and the doer of good works."

Once, and once only, did Gabriel hear anything of Father Paul. The good priest showed, by writing to the farmhouse, that he had not forgotten the family so largely indebted to him for their happiness. The letter was dated "Rome." Father Paul said that such services as he had been permitted to render to the Church in Brittany had obtained for him a new and a far more glorious trust than any he had yet held. He had been recalled from his curacy, and appointed to be at the head of a mission which was shortly to be dispatched to convert the inhabitants of a savage and far distant land to the Christian faith.

He now wrote, as his brethren with him were writing, to take leave of all friends forever in this world, before setting out—for it was well known to the chosen persons intrusted with the new mission that they could only hope to advance its object by cheerfully risking their own lives for the sake of their religion. He gave his blessing to François Sarzeau, to Gabriel, and to his family; and bade them affectionately farewell for the last time.

There was a postscript to the letter, which was addressed to Perrine, and which she often read afterward with tearful eyes. The writer begged that, if she should have any children, she would show her friendly and Christian remembrance of him by teaching them to pray (as he hoped she herself would pray) that a blessing might attend Father Paul's labours in the distant land.

The priest's loving petition was never forgotten. When Perrine taught its first prayer to her first child, the little creature was instructed to end the few simple words pronounced at its mother's knees, with, "God bless Father Paul."

In those words the nun concluded her narrative. After it was ended, she pointed to the old wooden cross, and said to me:

"That was one of the many that he made. It was found, a few years since, to have suffered so much from exposure to the weather that it was unfit to remain any longer in its old place. A priest in Brittany gave it to one of the nuns in this convent. Do you wonder now that the Mother Superior always calls it a Relic?"

"No," I answered. "And I should have small respect indeed for the religious convictions of anyone who could hear the story of that wooden cross, and not feel that the Mother Superior's name for it is the very best that could have been chosen."

The Last Stage Coachman

The last stage coachman! It falls upon the ear of everyone but a shareholder in railways, with a boding, melancholy sound. In spite of our natural reverence for the wonders of science, our hearts grow heavy at the thought of never again beholding the sweet-smelling nosegay, the unimpeachable top boots, and fair white breeches; once so prominent as the uniform of the fraternity. With all respect for expeditious and business-like travelling, we experience a feeling nearly akin to disgust, at being marshalled to our places by a bell and a fellow with a badge on his shoulder; instead of hearing the cheery summons 'Now then, gentlemen,' and being regaled by a short and instructive conversation with a ruddy-faced personage in a dustless olive green coat and prismatic belcher handkerchief.

What did we want with smoke? Had we not the coachman's cigar, if we were desirous of observing its shapes and appearances? Who would be so unreasonable as to languish for steam, when he could inhale it on a cool, autumnal morning, naturally concocted from the backs of four blood horses? Who!—Alas! We may propose questions and find out answers to the end of the chapter, and yet fail in reforming the perverted taste of the present generation; we know that the attempt is useless, and we give up in sorrowful and philosophic resignation, and proceed undaunted by the probable sneers of railway directors, to the recital of—

A Vision
Methought I walked forth one autumn evening to observe

the arrival of a stage coach. I wandered on, yet nothing of the kind met my eye. I tried many an old public road—they were now grass-grown and miry, or desecrated by the abominable presence of a 'station.' I wended my way towards a famous roadside inn: it was desolate and silent, or in other words, 'To Let.' I looked for 'the commercial room:' not a pot of beer adorned the mouldering tables, and not a pipe lay scattered over the wild and beautiful seclusions of its once numerous 'boxes.' It was deserted and useless; the voice of the traveller rung no longer round its walls, and the merry horn of the guard startled no more the sleepy few, who once congregated round its hospitable door. The chill fireplace and broad, antiquated mantel-piece presented but one bill—the starting time of an adjacent railroad; surmounted by a representation of those engines of destruction, in dull, frowsy lithograph.

I turned to the yard. Where was the ostler with his unbraced breeches and his upturned shirt sleeves? Where was the stable boy with his wisp of straw and his sieve of oats? Where were the coquettish mares and the tall blood horses? Where was the manger and the stable door?—All gone—all disappeared: the buildings dilapidated and tottering—of what use is a stable to a stoker? The ostler and stable boy had passed away—what fellowship have either with a boiler?

The inn yard was no more! The very dunghill in its farthest corner was choked by dust and old bricks, and the cock, the pride of the country round, clamoured no longer on the ruined and unsightly wall. I thought it was possible that he had satisfied long since the cravings of a railway committee; and I sat down on a ruined water-tub to give way to the melancholy reflections called up by the sight before me.

I know not how long I meditated. There was no officious waiter to ask me, 'What I would please to order?' No chambermaid to simper out 'This way, Sir,'—not even a stray cat to claim acquaintance with the calves of my legs, or a horse's hoof to tread upon my toe. There was nothing to disturb my miserable reverie, and I anathematised railways without distinction or exception.

The distant sound of slow and stealthy footsteps at last attracted my attention. I looked to the far end of the yard. Heavens above! A stage coachman was pacing its worn and weedy pavement.

There was no mistaking him—he wore the low-crowned, broad-brimmed, whitey-brown, well-brushed hat; the voluminous checked neckcloth; the ample-skirted coat; the striped waistcoat; the white cords; and last, not least, the immortal boots. But alas! The calf that had once filled them out, had disappeared; they clanked heavily on the pavement, instead of creaking tightly and noisily wherever he went. His waistcoat, evidently once filled almost to bursting, hung in loose, uncomfortable folds about his emaciated waist: large wrinkles marred the former beauty of the fit of his coat: and his face was all lines and furrows, instead of smiles and jollity. The spirit of the fraternity had passed away from him—he was the stage coachman only in dress.

He walked backwards and forwards for some time without turning his head one way or the other, except now and then to peer into the deserted stable, or to glance mournfully at the whip held in his hand: at last the sound of the arrival of a train struck upon his ear!

He drew himself up to his full height, slowly and solemnly shook his clenched fist in the direction of the sound, and looked—Oh that look! it spoke annihilation to the mightiest engine upon the rail, it scoffed at steam, and flashed furious derision at the largest terminus that ever was erected; it was an awfully comprehensive look—the concentrated essence of the fierce and deadly enmity of all the stage coachmen in England to steam conveyance.

To my utter astonishment, not, it must be owned, unmixed with fear, he suddenly turned his eyes towards my place of shelter, and walked up to me.

'That's the rail,' said he, between his set teeth.

'It is,' said I, considerably embarrassed.

'Damn it!' returned the excited Stage Coachman.

There was something inexpressibly awful about this execration; and I confess I felt a strong internal conviction that the next day's paper would teem with horrible railway accidents in every column.

'I did my utmost to hoppose 'em,' said the Stage Coachman, in softened accents. 'I wos the last that guv' in, I kep' a losing day after day, and yet I worked on; I wos determined to do my dooty, and I drove a coach the last day with an old hooman and a carpet bag inside, and three little boys and seven whopping empty portmanteaus outside. I wos determined my last kick to have some passengers to show to the rail, so I took my wife and children 'cos nobody else wouldn't go, and then we guv' in. Hows'ever, the last time as I wos on the road I didn't go and show 'em an empty coach—we wasn't full, but we wasn't empty; we wos game to the last!'

A grim smile of triumph lit up the features of the deposed Coachman as he gave vent to this assertion. He took hold of me by the button-hole, and led the way into the house.

'This landlord wos an austerious sort of a man,' said he; 'he used to hobserve, that he only wished a Railway Committee would dine at his house, he'd pison 'em all, and emigrate; and he'd ha' done it, too!'

I did not venture to doubt this, so the Stage Coachman continued.

'I've smoked my pipe by the hour together in that fireplace; I've read *The Times* advertisements and Perlice Reports in that box till I fell asleep; I've walked up and down this here room a saying all sorts of things about the rail, and a busting for happiness. Outside this wery door I've bin a drownded in thankys from ladies for never lettin' nobody step through their bandboxes. The chambermaids used to smile, and the dogs used to bark, wherever I came.—But it's all hover now—the poor feller as kep' this place takes tickets at a Station, and the chambermaids makes scalding hot tea behind a mahuggany counter for people as has no time to drink it in!'

As the Stage Coachman uttered these words, a contemptuous sneer puckered in his sallow cheek. He led me back into the yard; the ruined appearance of which, looked doubly mournful, under the faint rays of moonlight that every here and there stole through the dilapidated walls of the stable. An owl had taken up his abode, where the chief ostler's bedroom had once rejoiced in the grotesque majesty of huge portraits of every winner of every 'Derby,' since the first days of Epsom. The bird of night flew heavily off at our approach, and my companion pointed gloomily up to the fragments of mouldy, worm-eaten wood, the last relics of the stable loft.

'He wos a great friend of mine, was that h'ostler,' said the Coachman, 'but he's left this railway-bothered world—he wos finished by the train.'

At my earnest entreaty to hear further, he continued,

'When this h'old place wos guv'up and ruinated; the h'ostler as 'ud never look at the rail before, went down to have a sight of it, and as he wos a leaning his elbows on the wall, and a wishing as how he had the stabling of all the steam h'ingines (he'd ha' done 'em justice!) wot should he see, but one of his osses as wos thrown out of employ by the rail, a walking along jist where the train wos coming.

'Bill jumped down, and as he wos a leading of him h'off, up comes the train, and went over his leg and cut the 'os in two—"Tom," says he to me when we picked him up; "I'm a going eleven mile an hour, to the last stage as is left for me to do. I've always done my dooty with the osses; I've bin and done it now—bury that ere poor os and me out of the noise of the rail." We got the surgeons to him, but he never spoke no more, Poor Bill! Poor Bill!'

This last recollection seemed too much for the Stage Coachman, he wrung my hand, and walked abruptly to the farthest corner of the yard.

I took care not to interrupt him, and watched him carefully from a distance.

At first, the one expression of his countenance was melancholy; but by degrees, other thoughts came crowding from his mind, and mantled on his woe-be-gone visage. Poor fellow, I could see that he was again in imagination the beloved of the ladies and the adored of the chambermaids: a faint reflection of the affable, yet majestic demeanour, required by his calling, flitted occasionally over his pinched, attenuated features: and brightened the cold, melancholy expression of his countenance.

As I still looked, it grew darker and darker, yet the face of the Stage Coachman was never for an instant hidden from me. The same artificial expression of pleasure characterised its lineaments as before. Suddenly I heard a strange, unnatural noise in the air—now it seemed like the distant trampling of horses; and now again, like the rumbling of a heavily laden coach along a public road.

A faint, sickly light, spread itself over that part of the Heavens whence the sounds proceeded; and after an interval, a fully equipped Stage Coach appeared in the clouds, with a railway director strapped fast to each wheel, and a stoker between the teeth of each of the four horses.

In place of luggage, fragments of broken steam carriages, and red carpet bags filled with other mementos of railway accidents, occupied the roof. Chance passengers appeared to be the only tenants of the outside places. In front sat Julius Cæsar and Mrs Hannah Moore; and behind, Sir Joseph Banks and Mrs Brownrigge. Of all the 'insides,' I could, I grieve to say, see nothing.

On the box was a little man with fuzzy hair and large iron grey whiskers; clothed in a coat of engineers' skin, with gloves of the hide of railway police. He pulled up opposite my friend, and bowing profoundly motioned to him to the box seat.

A gleam of unutterable joy irradiated the Stage Coachman's countenance, as he stepped lightly into his place, seized the reins, and with one hearty 'good night,' addressed to an imaginary inn-full of people, started the horses.

Off they drove! My friend in the plenitude of his satisfaction cracking the whip every instant as he drove the phantom coach into the air. And amidst the shrieks of the railway directors at the wheel, the groans of James Watt, the bugle of the guard, and the tremendous cursing of the invisible 'insides,' fast and furiously disappeared from my eyes.